THE BATMAN ADVENTURES

VOLUME 3

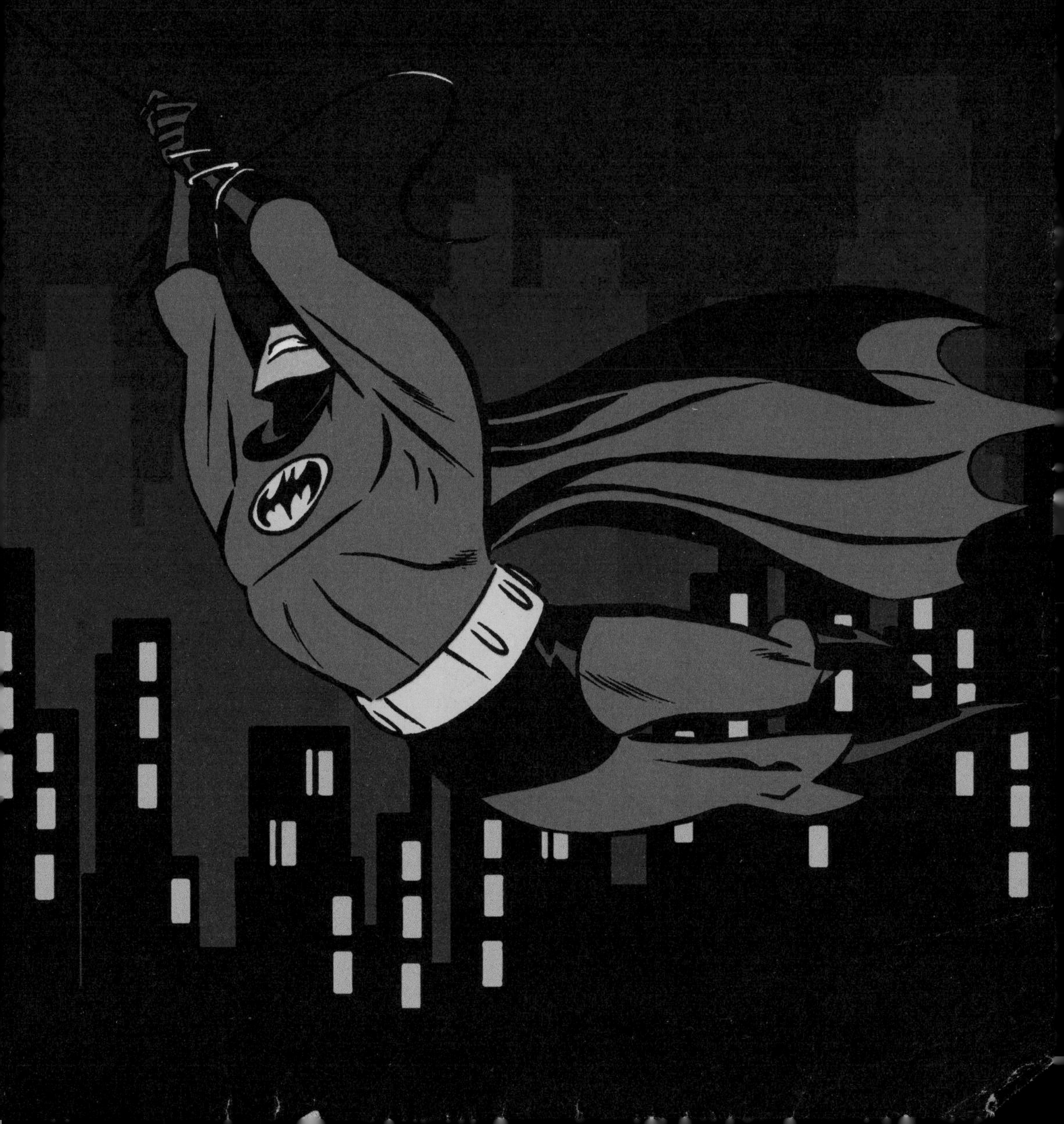

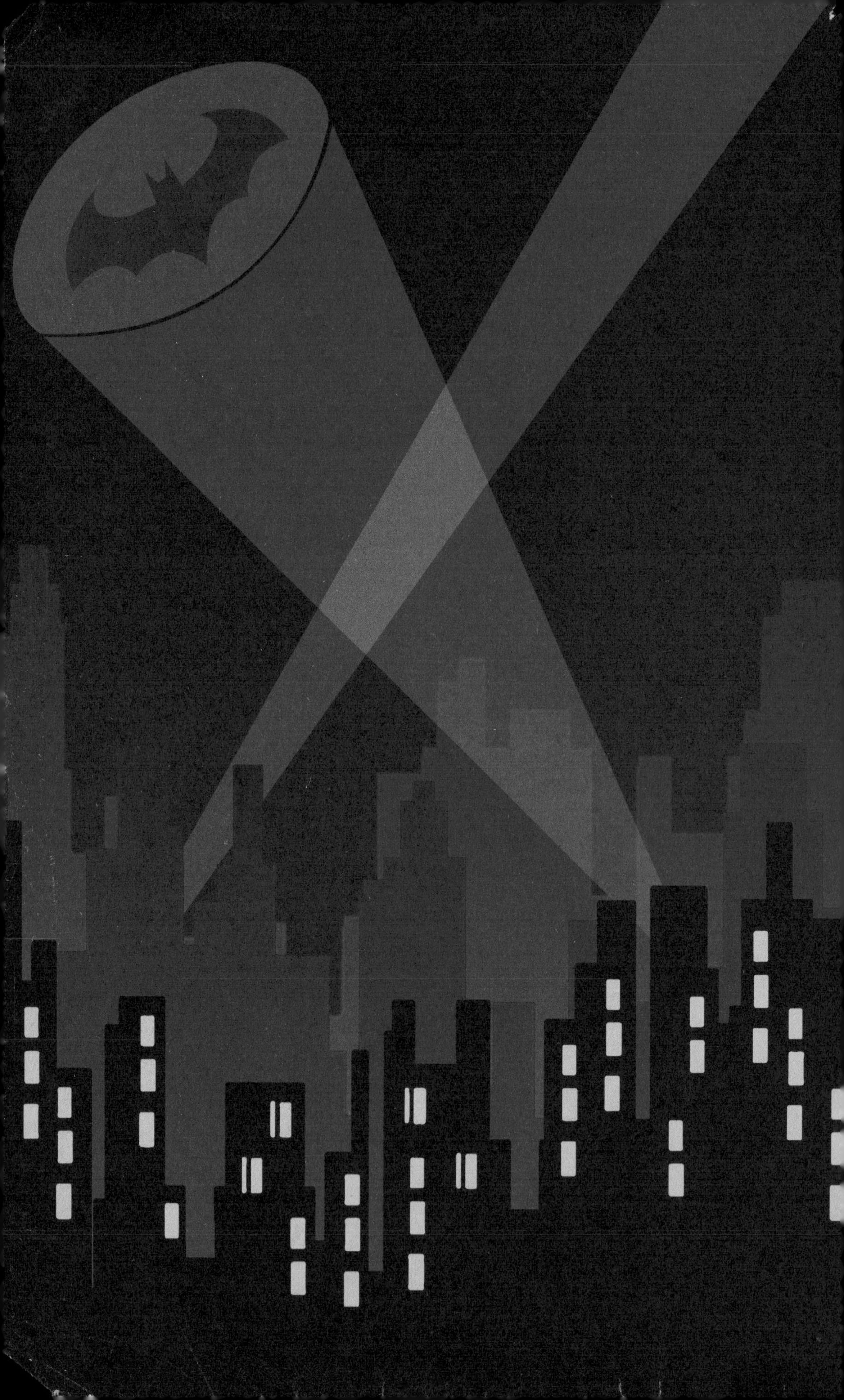

THE BATMAN ADVENTURES

VOLUME 3

PAUL DINI
KELLEY PUCKETT
MICHAEL REAVES
writers

BRUCE TIMM
MATT WAGNER
KLAUS JANSON
JOHN BYRNE
DAN DECARLO
MIKE PAROBECK
RICK BURCHETT
artists

RICK TAYLOR
BRUCE TIMM
colorists

STARKINGS/COMICRAFT
letterer

BRUCE TIMM
collection cover artist

BATMAN created by BOB KANE

SUPERMAN created by
JERRY SIEGEL and JOE SHUSTER
By special arrangement with the
JERRY SIEGEL FAMILY

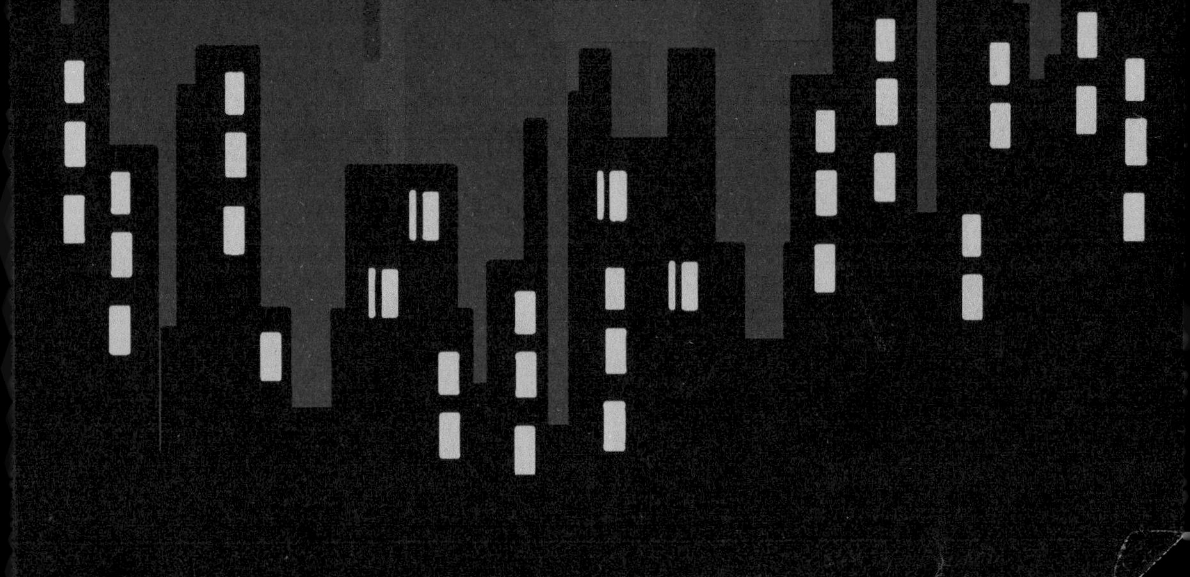

Scott Peterson	Editor – Original Series
Darren Vincenzo	Assistant Editor – Original Series
Jeb Woodard	Group Editor – Collected Editions
Sarabeth Kett	Publication Design
Bob Harras	Senior VP – Editor-in-Chief, DC Comics
Diane Nelson	President
Dan DiDio and Jim Lee	Co-Publishers
Geoff Johns	Chief Creative Officer
Amit Desai	Senior VP – Marketing & Global Franchise Management
Nairi Gardiner	Senior VP – Finance
Sam Ades	VP – Digital Marketing
Bobbie Chase	VP – Talent Development
Mark Chiarello	Senior VP – Art, Design & Collected Editions
John Cunningham	VP – Content Strategy
Anne DePies	VP – Strategy Planning & Reporting
Don Falletti	VP – Manufacturing Operations
Lawrence Ganem	VP – Editorial Administration & Talent Relations
Alison Gill	Senior VP – Manufacturing & Operations
Hank Kanalz	Senior VP – Editorial Strategy & Administration
Jay Kogan	VP – Legal Affairs
Derek Maddalena	Senior VP – Sales & Business Development
Jack Mahan	VP – Business Affairs
Dan Miron	VP – Sales Planning & Trade Development
Nick Napolitano	VP – Manufacturing Administration
Carol Roeder	VP – Marketing
Eddie Scannell	VP – Mass Account & Digital Sales
Courtney Simmons	Senior VP – Publicity & Communications
Jim (Ski) Sokolowski	VP – Comic Book Specialty & Newsstand Sales
Sandy Yi	Senior VP – Global Franchise Management

THE BATMAN ADVENTURES VOLUME 3

Published by DC Comics. Compilation Copyright © 2015 DC Comics. All Rights Reserved.

Originally published in single magazine form in THE BATMAN ADVENTURES 21-27, THE BATMAN ADVENTURES ANNUAL 1. Copyright © 1994 DC Comics. All Rights Reserved. All characters, their distinctive likenesses and related elements featured in this publication are trademarks of DC Comics. The stories, characters and incidents featured in this publication are entirely fictional. DC Comics does not read or accept unsolicited ideas, stories or artwork.

DC Comics, 4000 Warner Blvd., Burbank, CA 91522
A Warner Bros. Entertainment Company.
Printed by RR Donnelley, Salem, VA, USA. 9/25/15 First Printing.
ISBN: 978-1-4012-5872-6

Library of Congress Cataloging-in-Publication Data is Available.

PEFC Certified

Printed on paper from
sustainably managed
forests and controlled
sources

PEFC/29-31-75   www.pefc.org

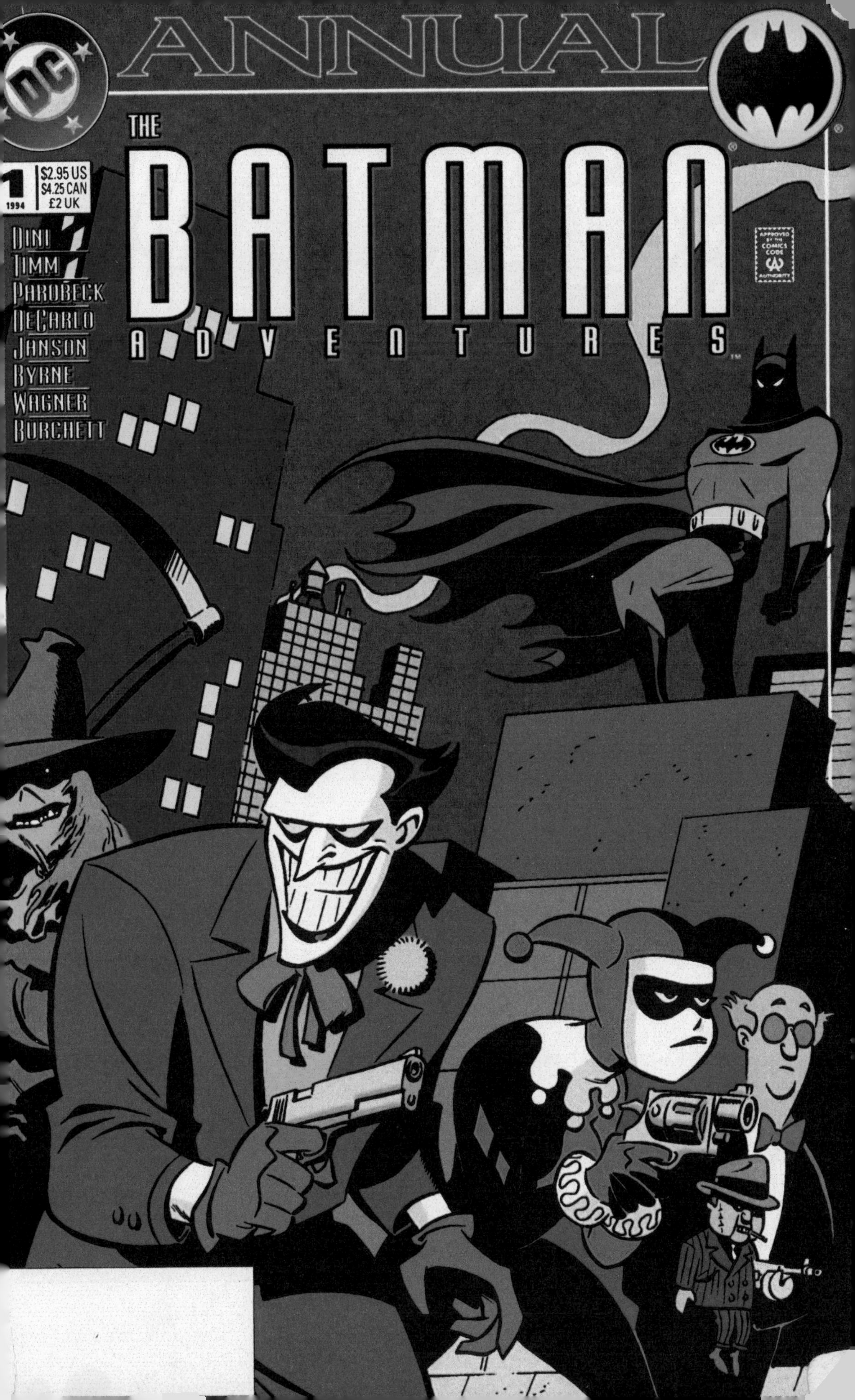
ANNUAL
DC
THE BATMAN ADVENTURES
1
1994
$2.95 US
$4.25 CAN
£2 UK
DINI
TIMM
PAROBECK
DECARLO
JANSON
BYRNE
WAGNER
BURCHETT

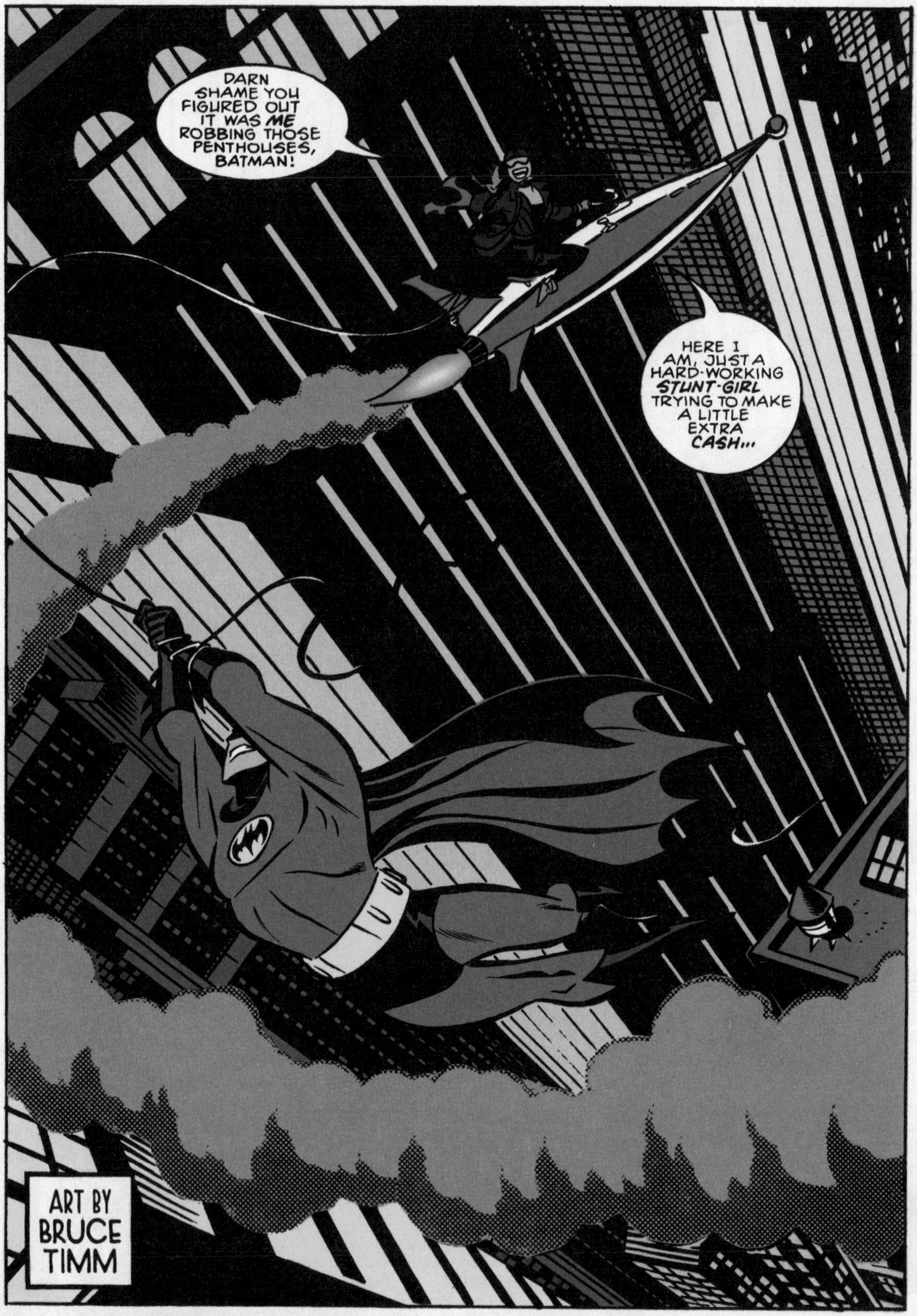
DARN SHAME YOU FIGURED OUT IT WAS ME ROBBING THOSE PENTHOUSES, BATMAN!
HERE I AM, JUST A HARD-WORKING STUNT-GIRL TRYING TO MAKE A LITTLE EXTRA CASH...
ART BY BRUCE TIMM

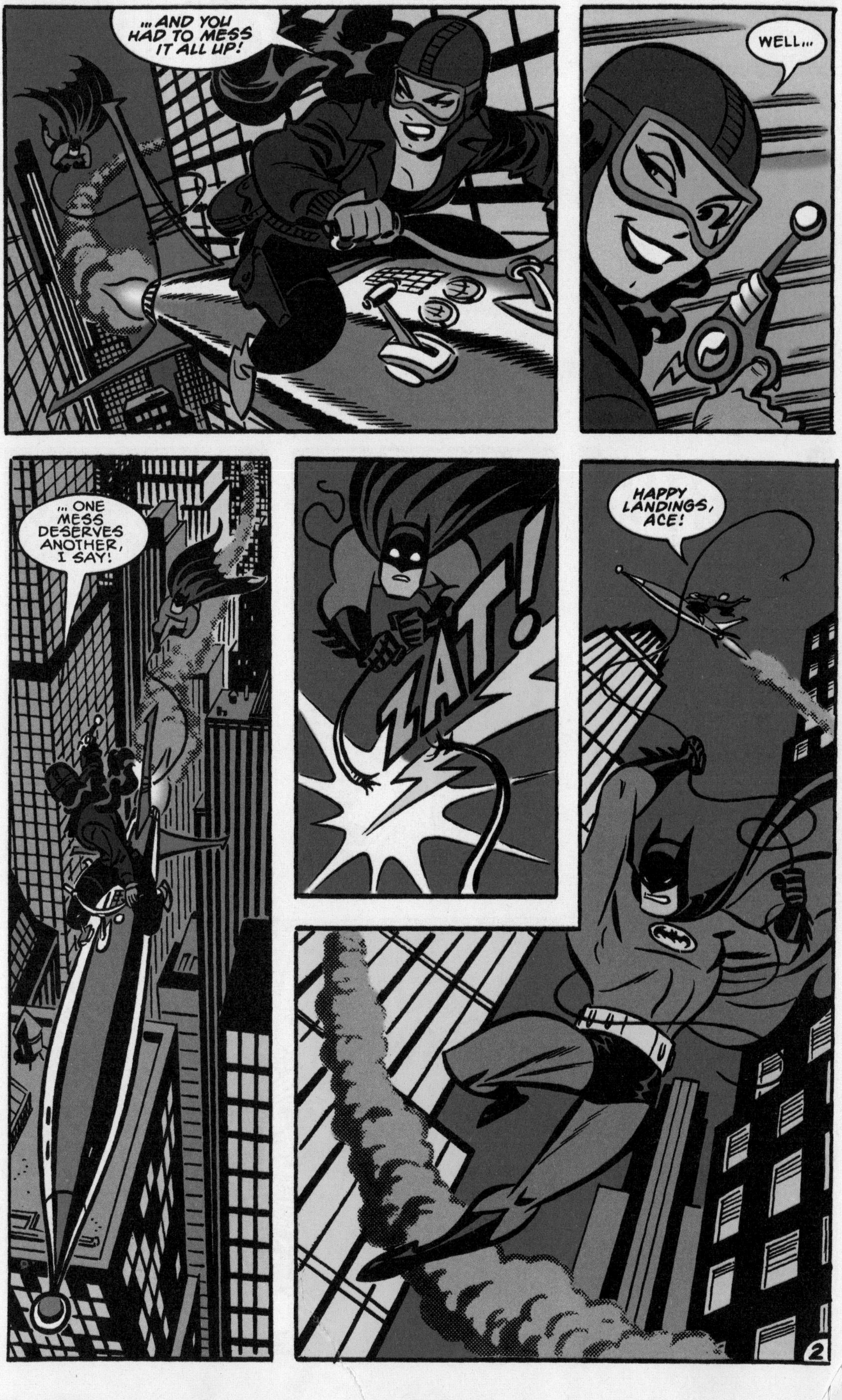
...AND YOU HAD TO MESS IT ALL UP!
WELL...
...ONE MESS DESERVES ANOTHER, I SAY!
ZAT!
HAPPY LANDINGS, ACE!

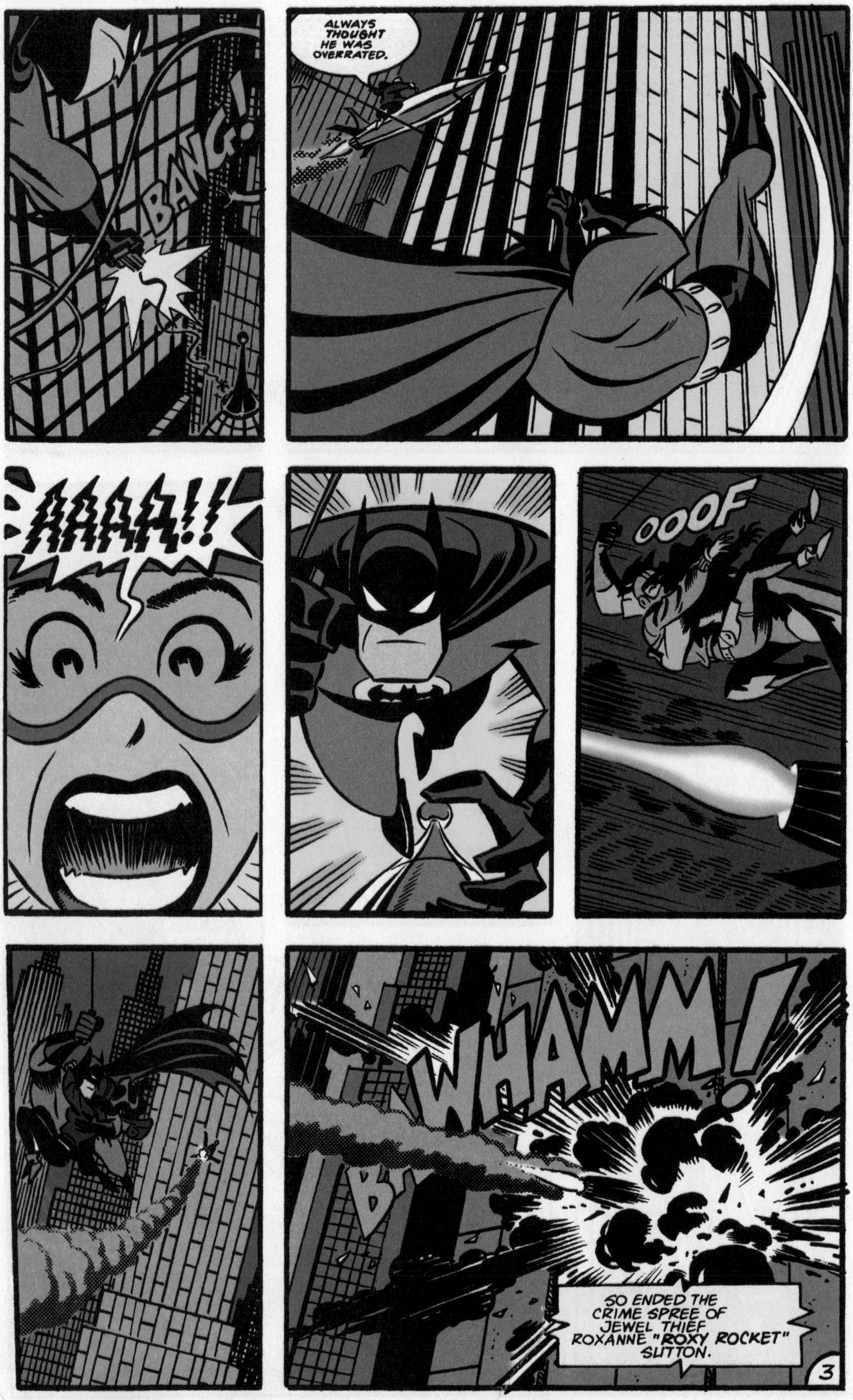
BANG!
ALWAYS THOUGHT HE WAS OVERRATED.
AAAA!!
OOOF
WHAMM!
SO ENDED THE CRIME SPREE OF JEWEL THIEF ROXANNE "ROXY ROCKET" SUTTON.

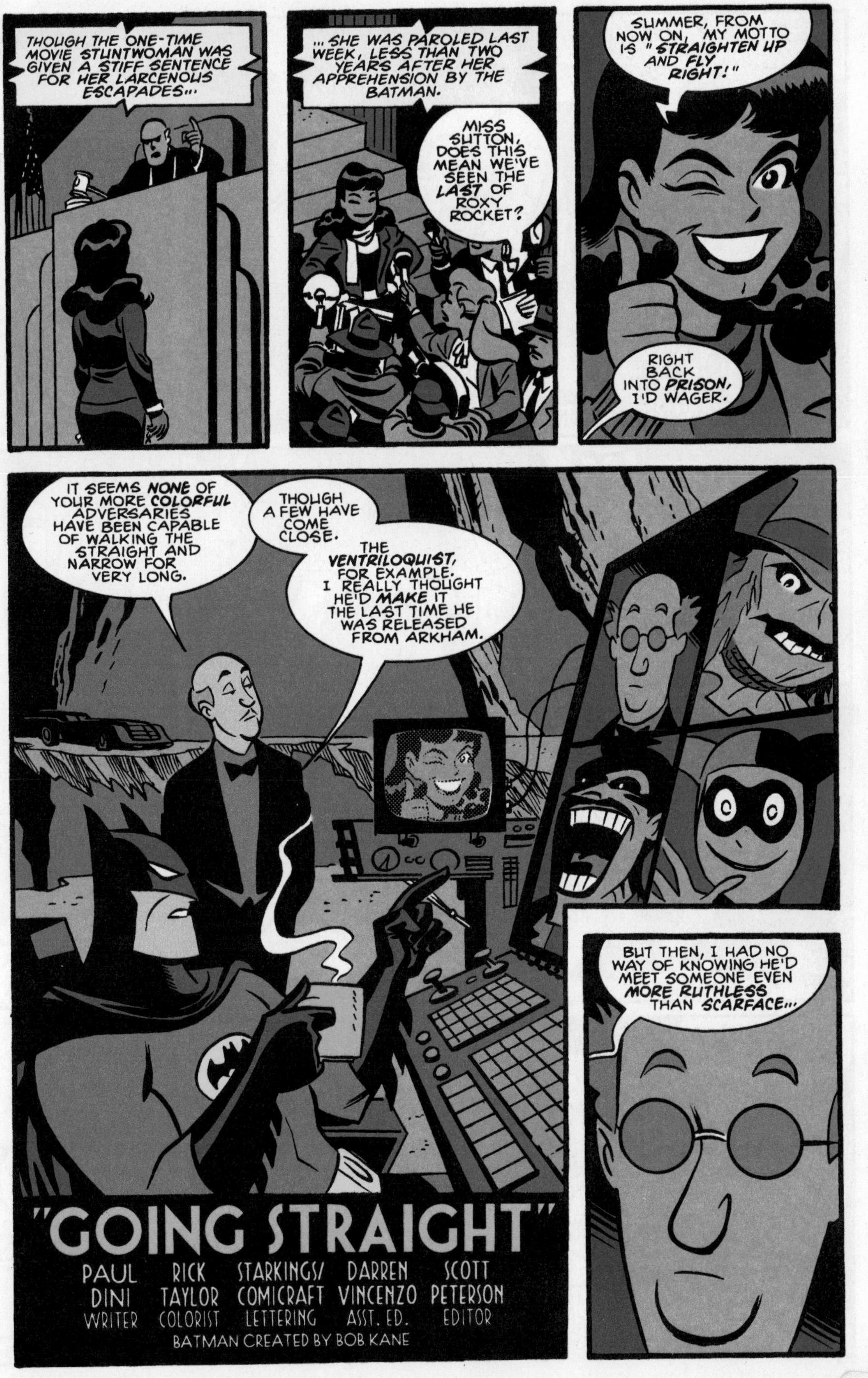
THOUGH THE ONE-TIME MOVIE STUNTWOMAN WAS GIVEN A STIFF SENTENCE FOR HER LARCENOUS ESCAPADES...
...SHE WAS PAROLED LAST WEEK, LESS THAN TWO YEARS AFTER HER APPREHENSION BY THE BATMAN.
MISS SUTTON, DOES THIS MEAN WE'VE SEEN THE LAST OF ROXY ROCKET?
SUMMER, FROM NOW ON, MY MOTTO IS "STRAIGHTEN UP AND FLY RIGHT!"
RIGHT BACK INTO PRISON, I'D WAGER.
IT SEEMS NONE OF YOUR MORE COLORFUL ADVERSARIES HAVE BEEN CAPABLE OF WALKING THE STRAIGHT AND NARROW FOR VERY LONG.
THOUGH A FEW HAVE COME CLOSE.
THE VENTRILOQUIST, FOR EXAMPLE. I REALLY THOUGHT HE'D MAKE IT THE LAST TIME HE WAS RELEASED FROM ARKHAM.
BUT THEN, I HAD NO WAY OF KNOWING HE'D MEET SOMEONE EVEN MORE RUTHLESS THAN SCARFACE...
"GOING STRAIGHT"
PAUL DINI WRITER
RICK TAYLOR COLORIST
STARKINGS/ COMICRAFT LETTERING
DARREN VINCENZO ASST. ED.
SCOTT PETERSON EDITOR
BATMAN CREATED BY BOB KANE

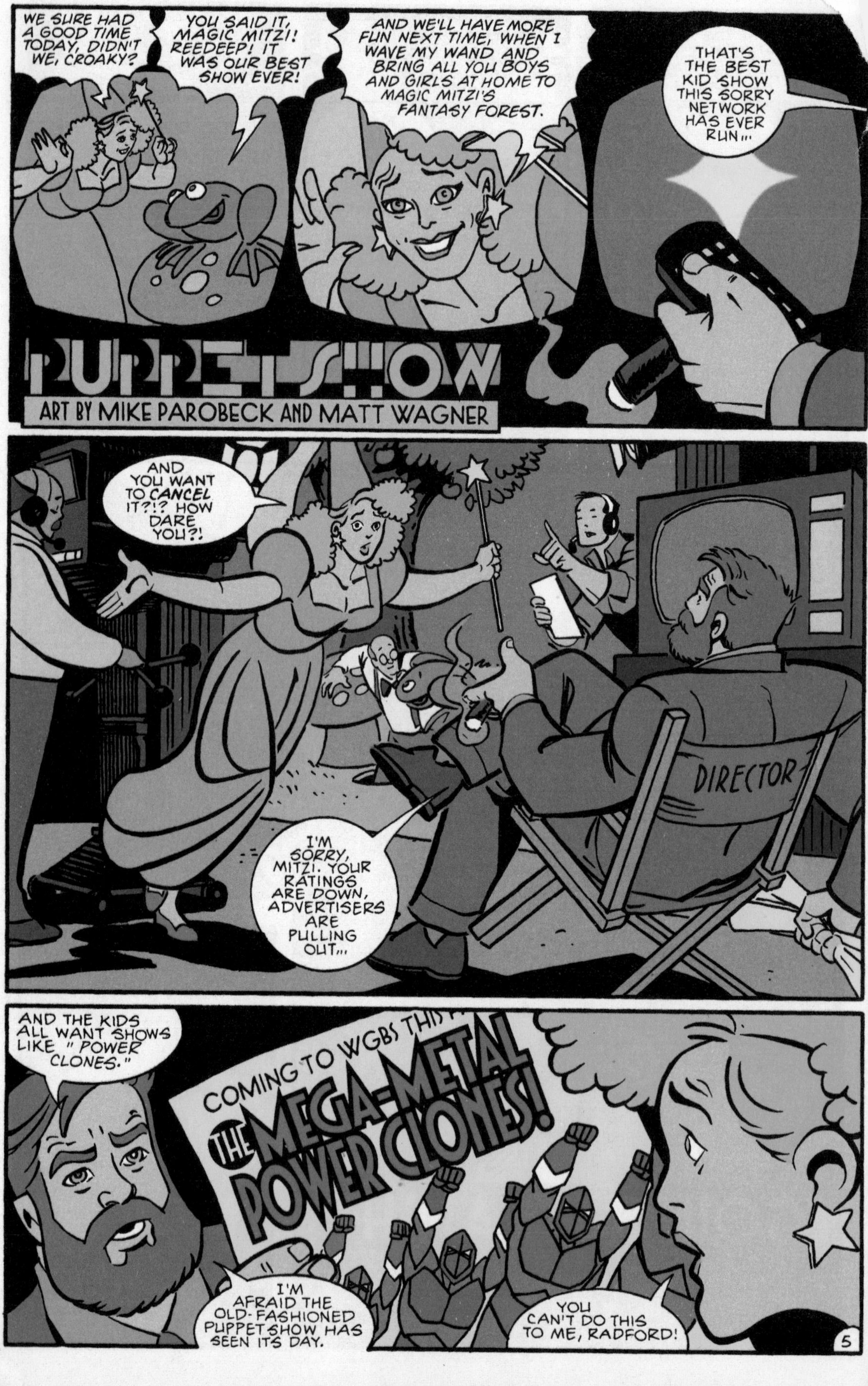
WE SURE HAD A GOOD TIME TODAY, DIDN'T WE, CROAKY?
YOU SAID IT, MAGIC MITZI! REEDEEP! IT WAS OUR BEST SHOW EVER!
AND WE'LL HAVE MORE FUN NEXT TIME, WHEN I WAVE MY WAND AND BRING ALL YOU BOYS AND GIRLS AT HOME TO MAGIC MITZI'S FANTASY FOREST.
THAT'S THE BEST KID SHOW THIS SORRY NETWORK HAS EVER RUN...
PUPPETSHOW
ART BY MIKE PAROBECK AND MATT WAGNER
AND YOU WANT TO CANCEL IT?!? HOW DARE YOU?!
DIRECTOR
I'M SORRY, MITZI. YOUR RATINGS ARE DOWN, ADVERTISERS ARE PULLING OUT...
AND THE KIDS ALL WANT SHOWS LIKE "POWER CLONES."
COMING TO WGBS THIS
THE MEGA-METAL POWER CLONES!
I'M AFRAID THE OLD-FASHIONED PUPPET SHOW HAS SEEN ITS DAY.
YOU CAN'T DO THIS TO ME, RADFORD!

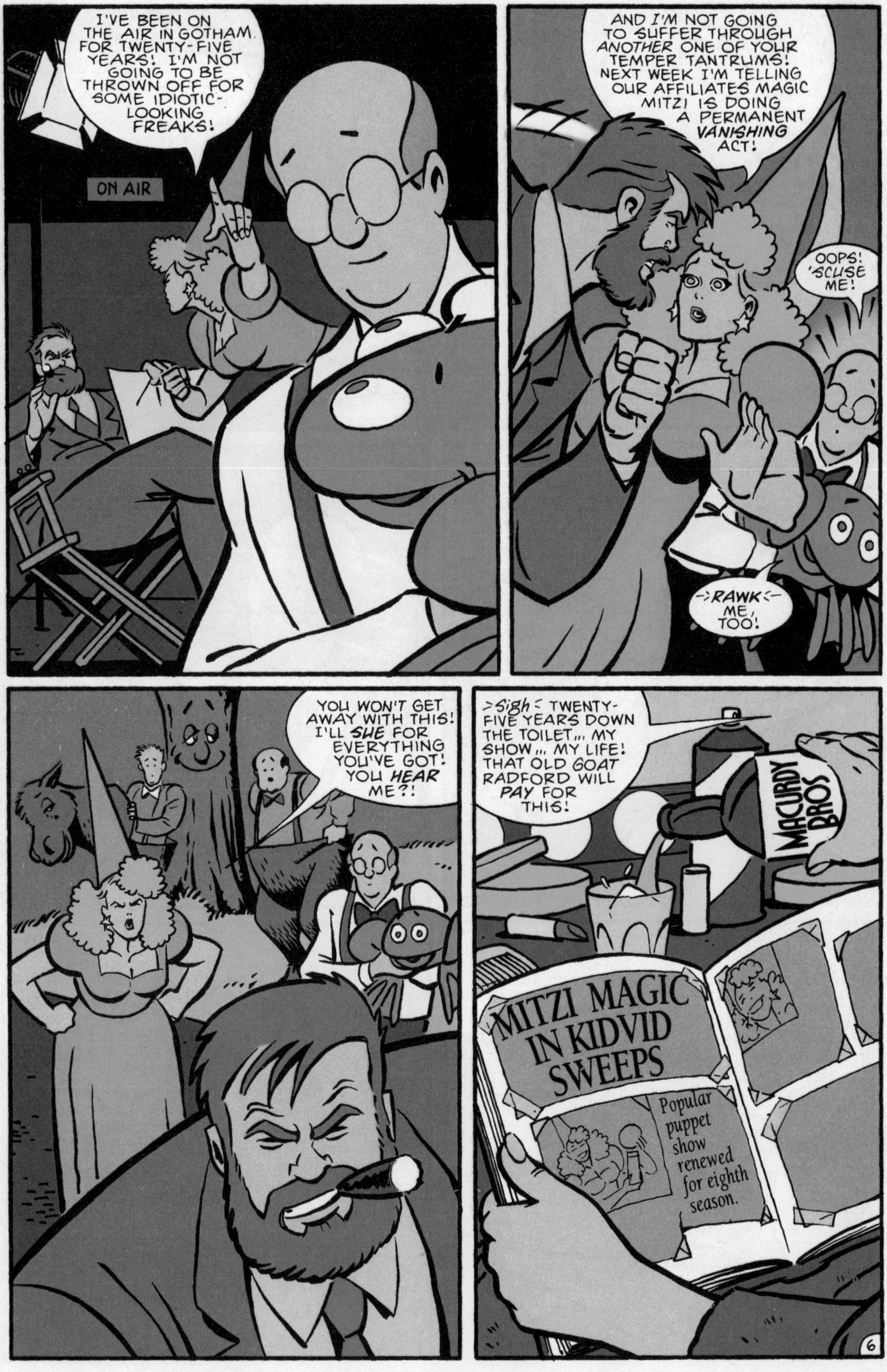
I'VE BEEN ON THE AIR IN GOTHAM FOR TWENTY-FIVE YEARS! I'M NOT GOING TO BE THROWN OFF FOR SOME IDIOTIC-LOOKING FREAKS!
ON AIR
AND I'M NOT GOING TO SUFFER THROUGH ANOTHER ONE OF YOUR TEMPER TANTRUMS! NEXT WEEK I'M TELLING OUR AFFILIATES MAGIC MITZI IS DOING A PERMANENT VANISHING ACT!
OOPS! 'SCUSE ME!
RAWK ME, TOO!
YOU WON'T GET AWAY WITH THIS! I'LL SUE FOR EVERYTHING YOU'VE GOT! YOU HEAR ME?!
Sigh TWENTY-FIVE YEARS DOWN THE TOILET... MY SHOW... MY LIFE! THAT OLD GOAT RADFORD WILL PAY FOR THIS!
MACURDY BROS
MITZI MAGIC IN KIDVID SWEEPS
Popular puppet show renewed for eighth season.

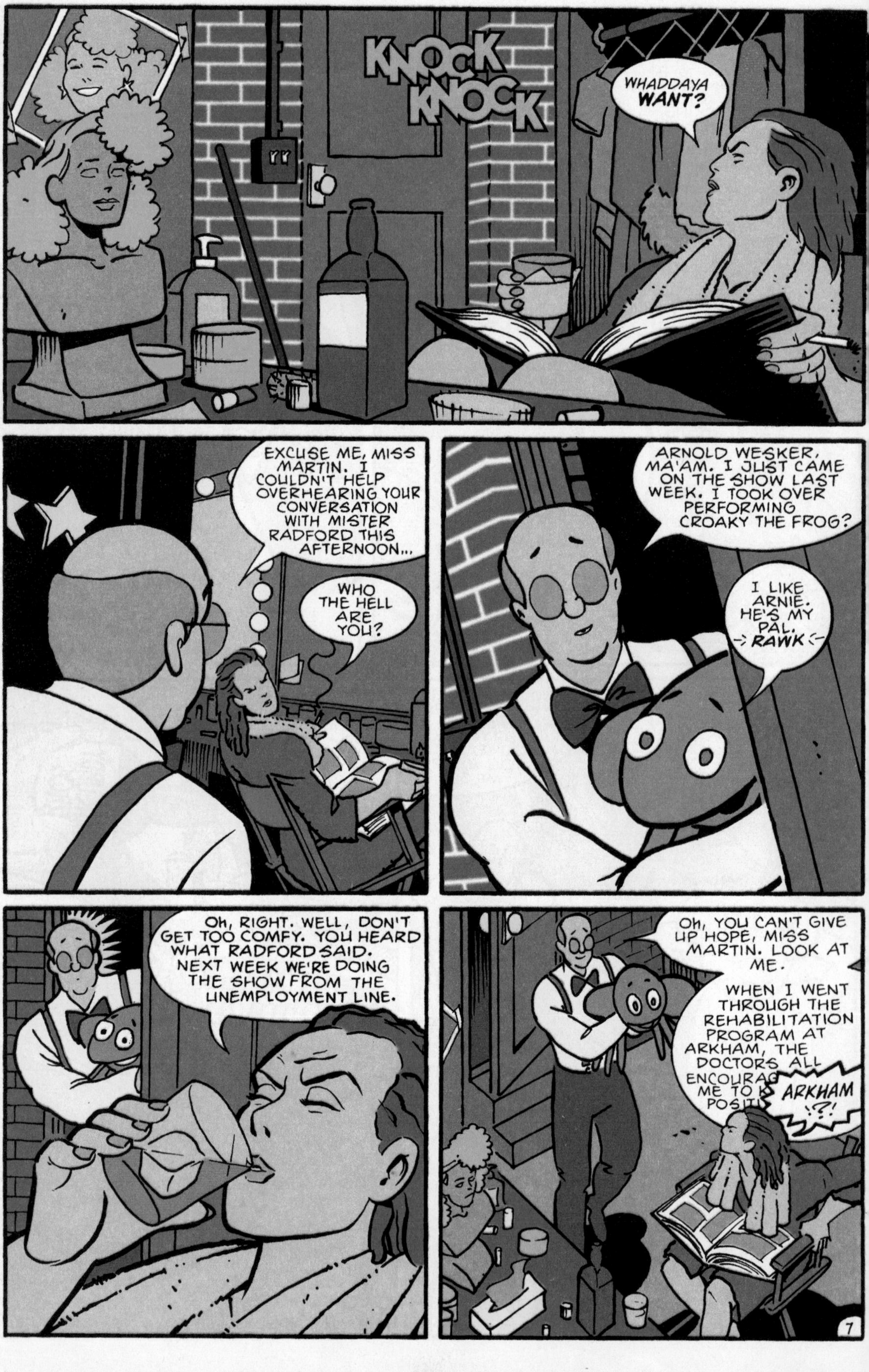
KNOCK KNOCK
WHADDAYA WANT?
EXCUSE ME, MISS MARTIN. I COULDN'T HELP OVERHEARING YOUR CONVERSATION WITH MISTER RADFORD THIS AFTERNOON...
WHO THE HELL ARE YOU?
ARNOLD WESKER, MA'AM. I JUST CAME ON THE SHOW LAST WEEK. I TOOK OVER PERFORMING CROAKY THE FROG?
I LIKE ARNIE. HE'S MY PAL. RAWK
OH, RIGHT. WELL, DON'T GET TOO COMFY. YOU HEARD WHAT RADFORD SAID. NEXT WEEK WE'RE DOING THE SHOW FROM THE UNEMPLOYMENT LINE.
OH, YOU CAN'T GIVE UP HOPE, MISS MARTIN. LOOK AT ME.
WHEN I WENT THROUGH THE REHABILITATION PROGRAM AT ARKHAM, THE DOCTORS ALL
ARKHAM!?!

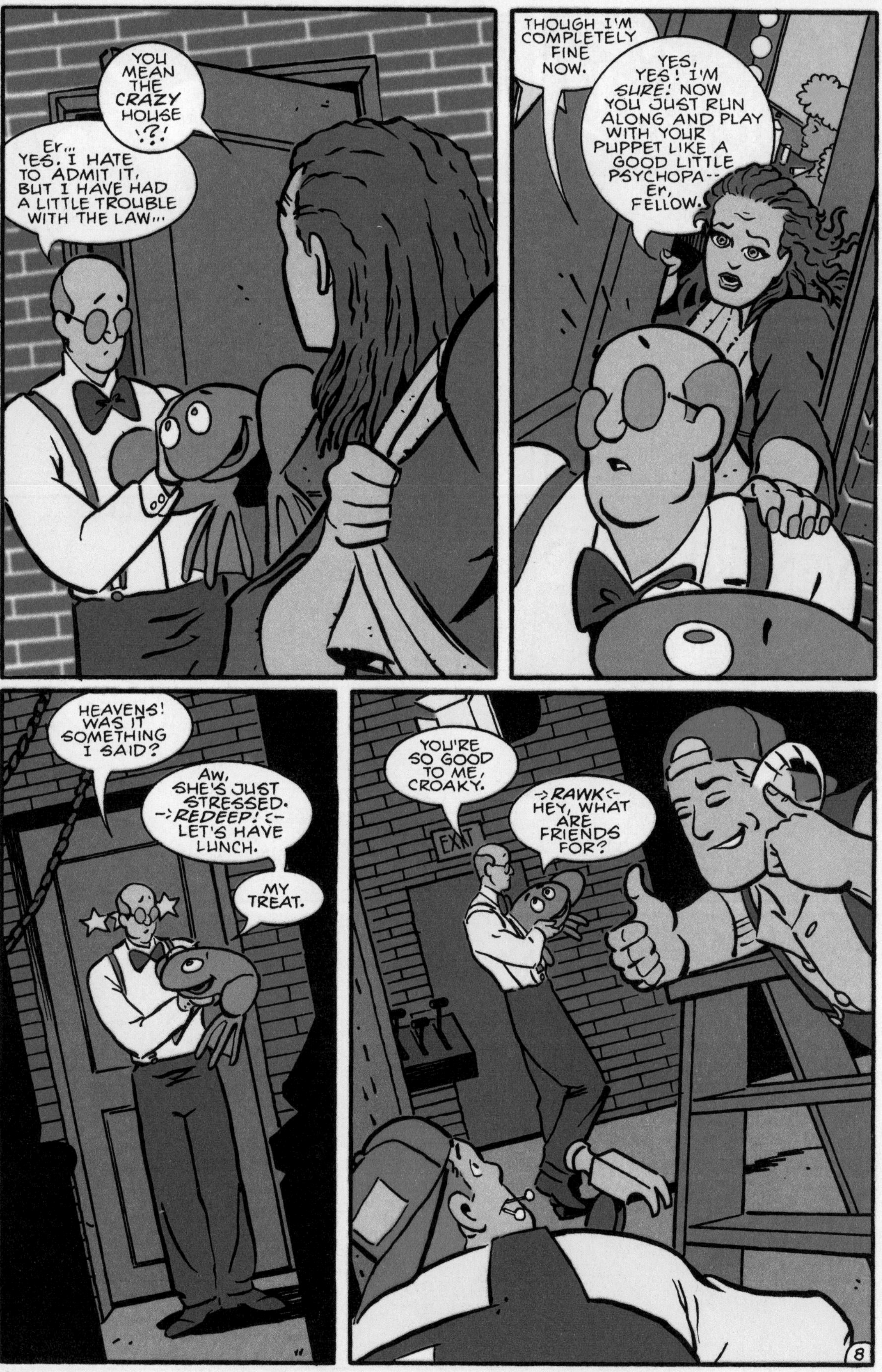
YOU MEAN THE CRAZY HOUSE !?!
Er... YES. I HATE TO ADMIT IT, BUT I HAVE HAD A LITTLE TROUBLE WITH THE LAW...
THOUGH I'M COMPLETELY FINE NOW.
YES, YES! I'M SURE! NOW YOU JUST RUN ALONG AND PLAY WITH YOUR PUPPET LIKE A GOOD LITTLE PSYCHOPA-- Er, FELLOW.
HEAVENS! WAS IT SOMETHING I SAID?
AW, SHE'S JUST STRESSED. ->REDEEP!<- LET'S HAVE LUNCH.
MY TREAT.
YOU'RE SO GOOD TO ME, CROAKY.
->RAWK<- HEY, WHAT ARE FRIENDS FOR?
EXIT
8

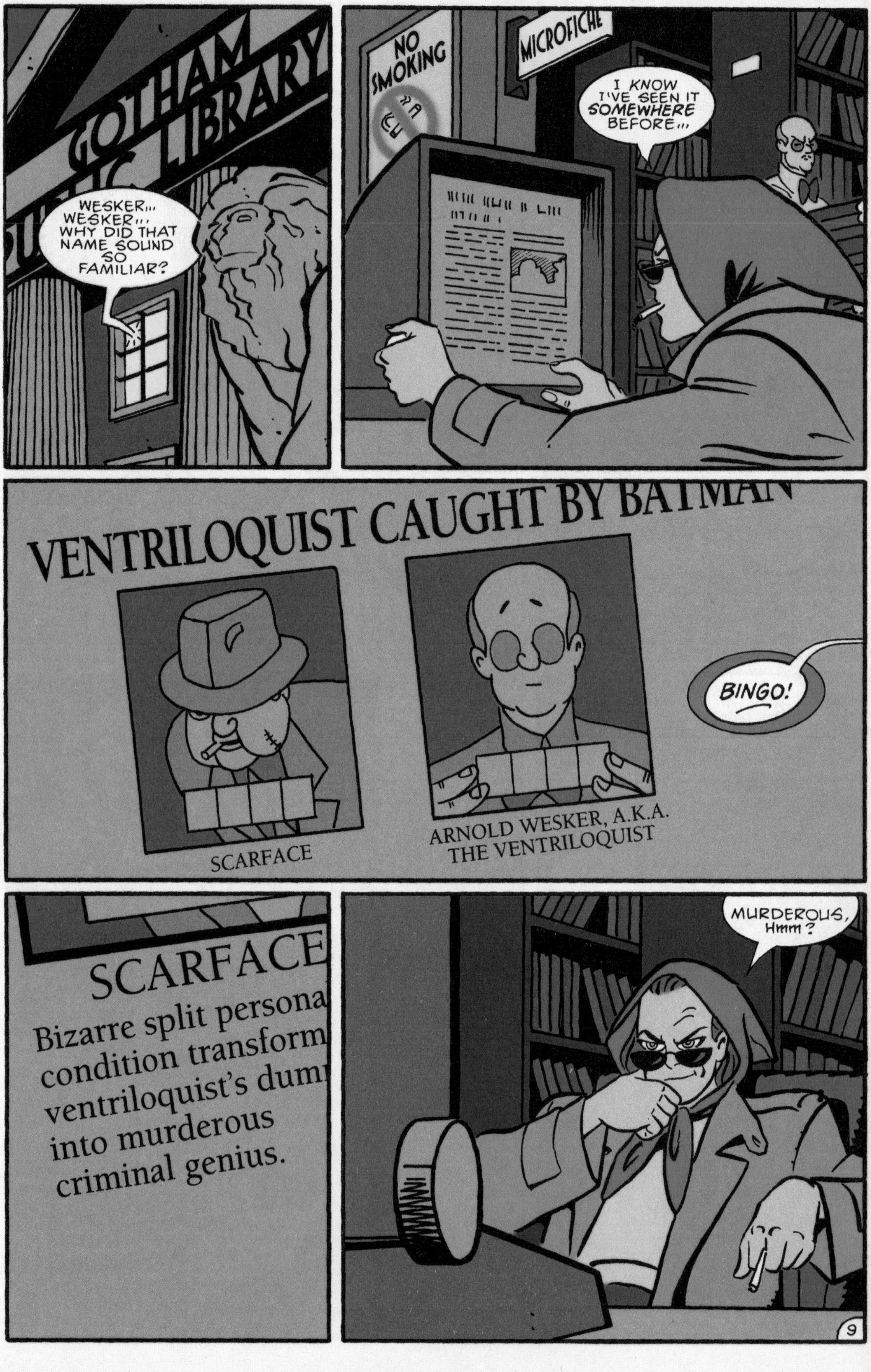
GOTHAM PUBLIC LIBRARY
WESKER... WESKER... WHY DID THAT NAME SOUND SO FAMILIAR?
NO SMOKING
MICROFICHE
I KNOW I'VE SEEN IT SOMEWHERE BEFORE...
VENTRILOQUIST CAUGHT BY BATMAN
SCARFACE
ARNOLD WESKER, A.K.A. THE VENTRILOQUIST
BINGO!
SCARFACE
Bizarre split persona
condition transform
ventriloquist's dum
into murderous
criminal genius.
MURDEROUS, Hmm?
9

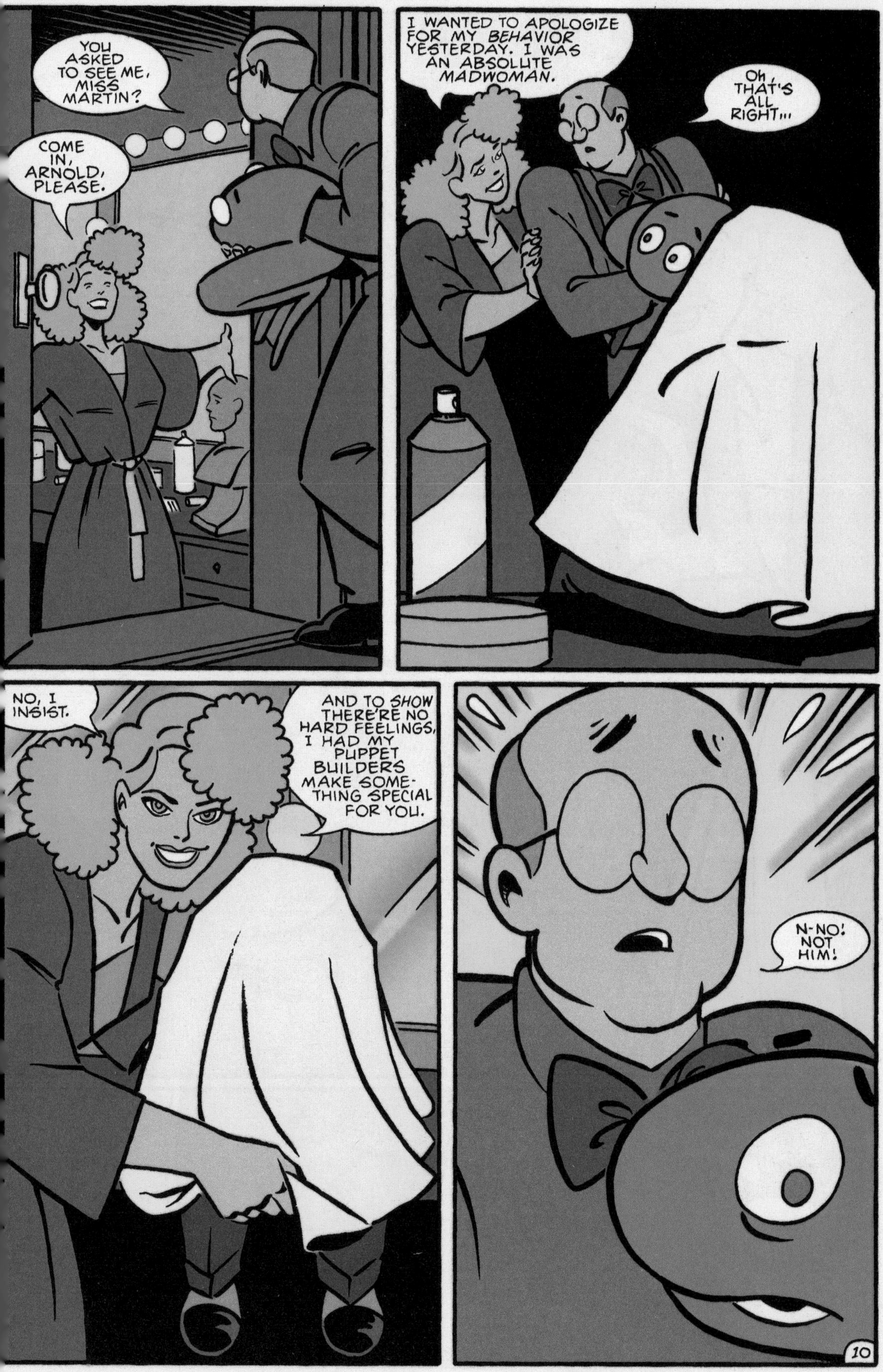
YOU ASKED TO SEE ME, MISS MARTIN?
COME IN, ARNOLD, PLEASE.
I WANTED TO APOLOGIZE FOR MY BEHAVIOR YESTERDAY. I WAS AN ABSOLUTE MADWOMAN.
Oh, THAT'S ALL RIGHT...
NO, I INSIST.
AND TO SHOW THERE'RE NO HARD FEELINGS, I HAD MY PUPPET BUILDERS MAKE SOME-THING SPECIAL FOR YOU.
N-NO! NOT HIM!

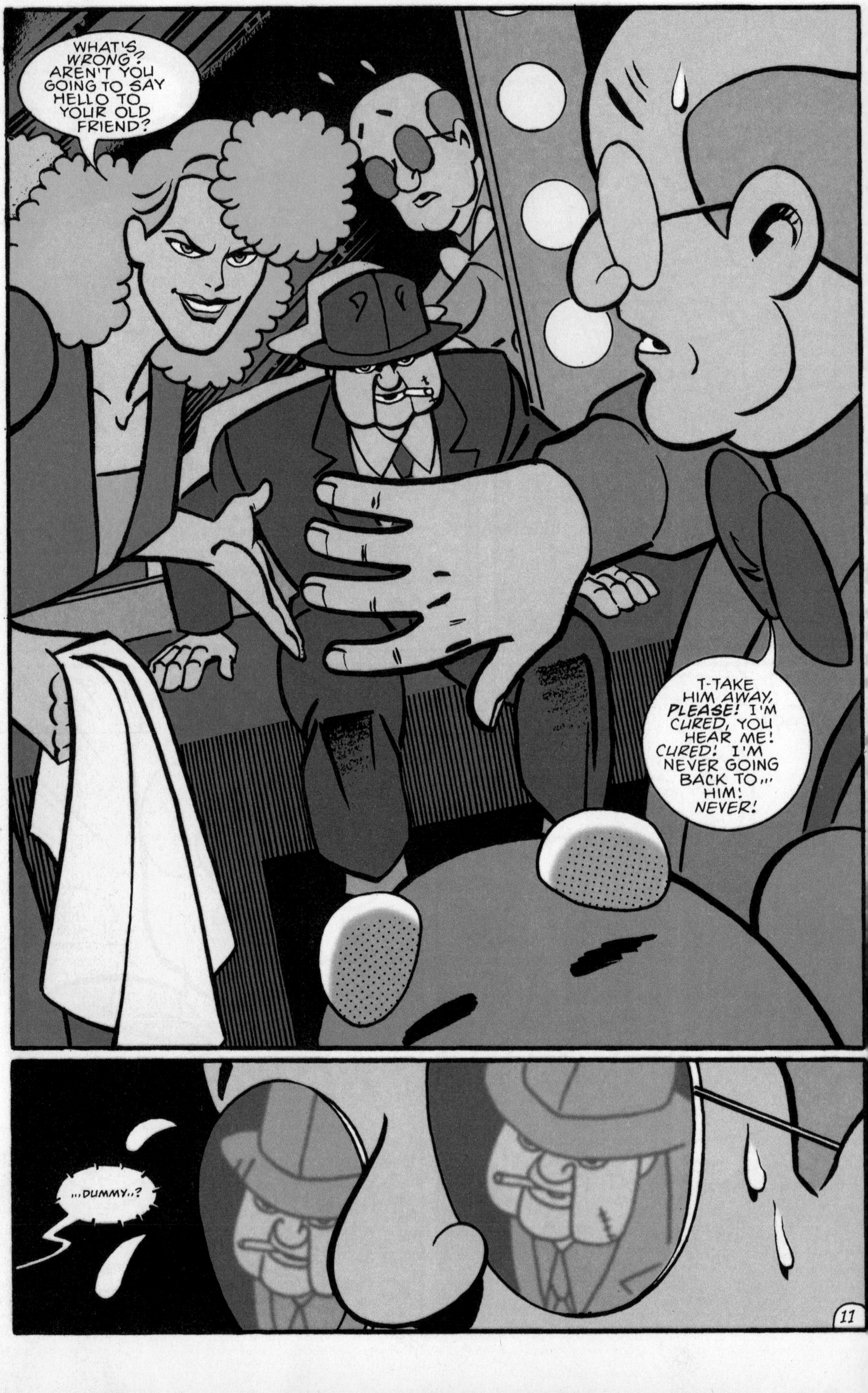
WHAT'S WRONG? AREN'T YOU GOING TO SAY HELLO TO YOUR OLD FRIEND?
T-TAKE HIM AWAY, PLEASE! I'M CURED, YOU HEAR ME! CURED! I'M NEVER GOING BACK TO... HIM! NEVER!
...DUMMY..?

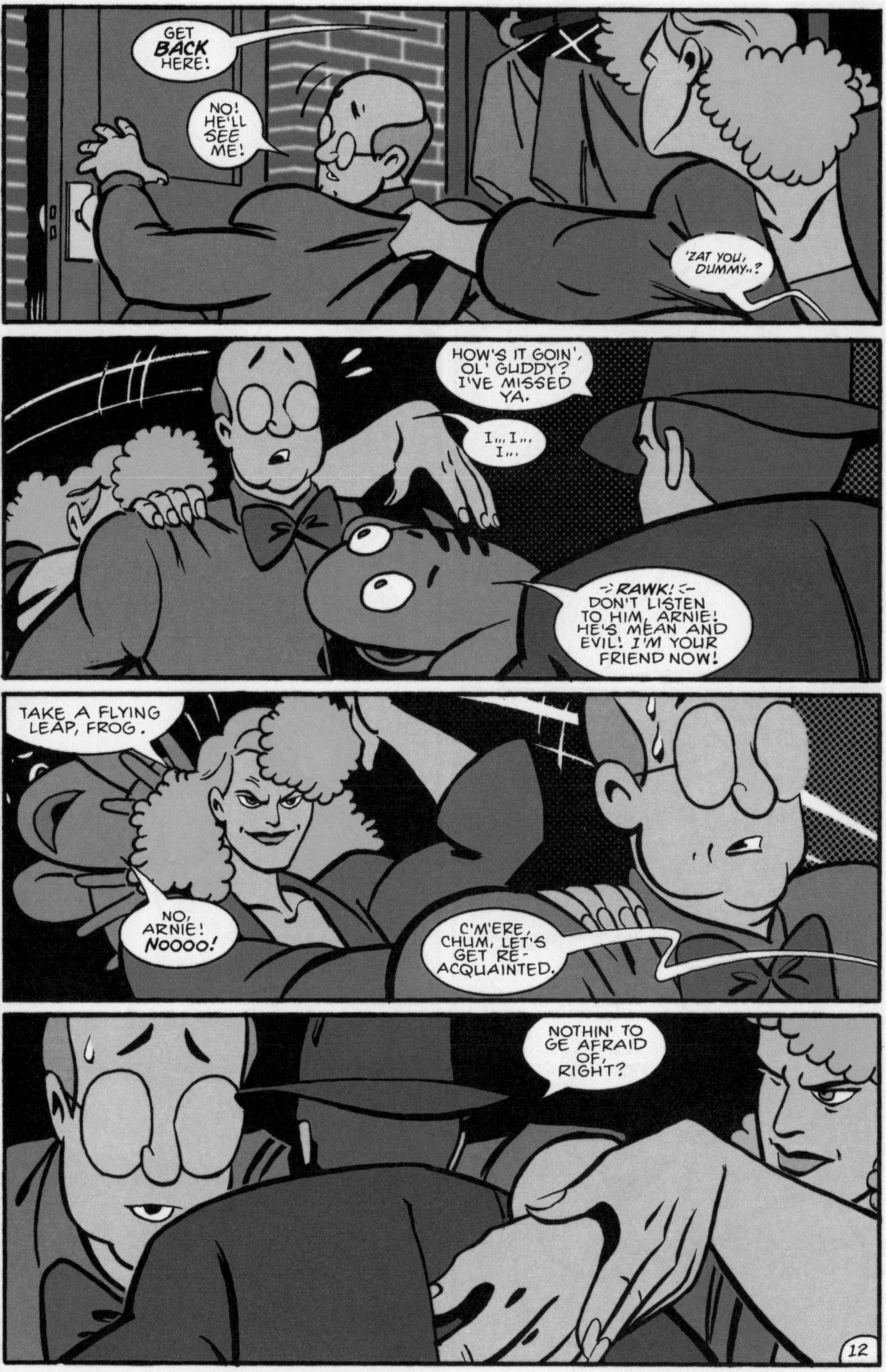
GET BACK HERE!
NO! HE'LL SEE ME!
'ZAT YOU, DUMMY..?
HOW'S IT GOIN', OL' GUDDY? I'VE MISSED YA.
I.., I.., I..
RAWK! DON'T LISTEN TO HIM, ARNIE! HE'S MEAN AND EVIL! I'M YOUR FRIEND NOW!
TAKE A FLYING LEAP, FROG.
NO, ARNIE! NOOOO!
C'M'ERE, CHUM, LET'S GET RE-ACQUAINTED.
NOTHIN' TO GE AFRAID OF, RIGHT?

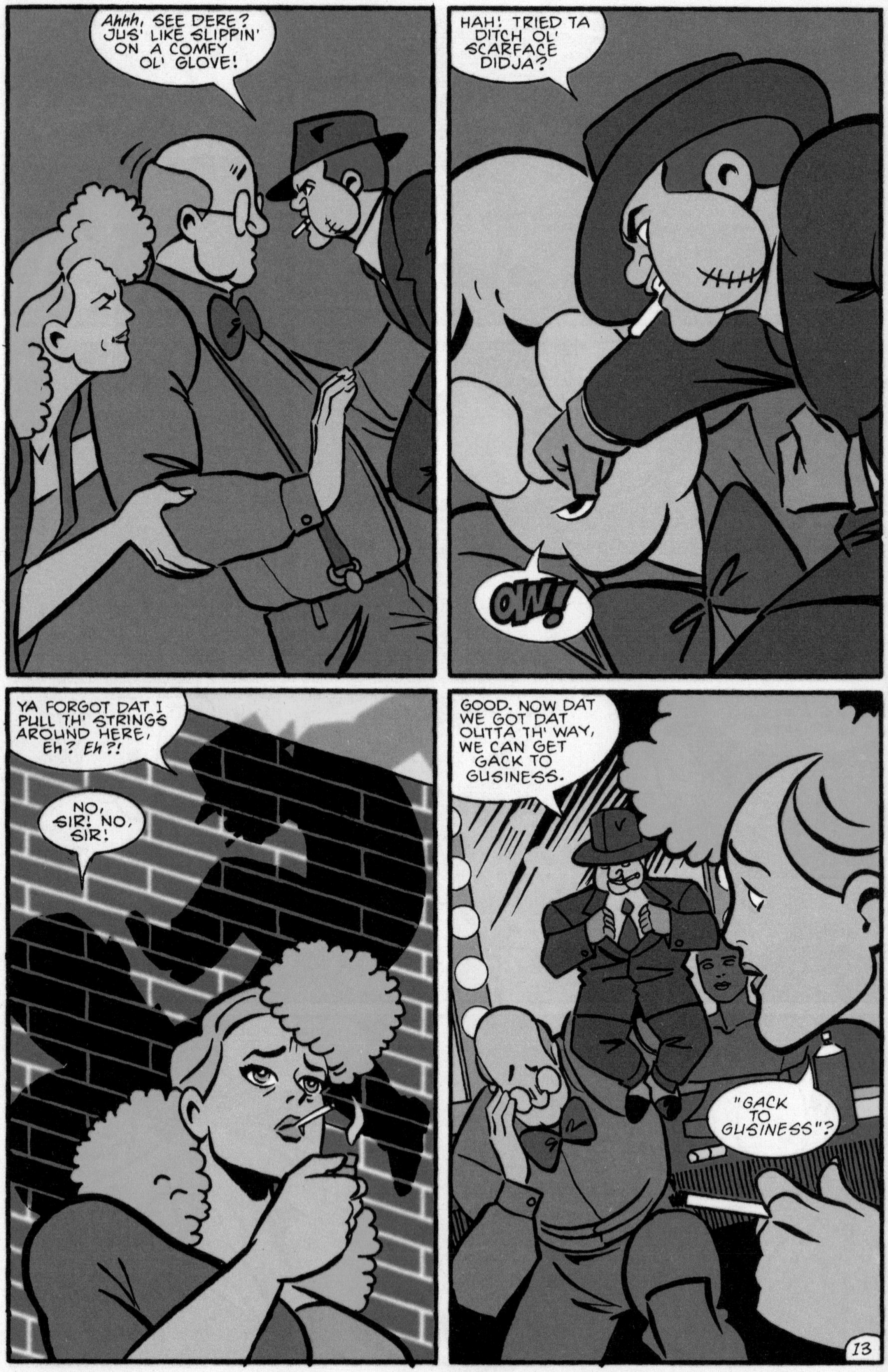

Ahhh, SEE DERE? JUS' LIKE SLIPPIN' ON A COMFY OL' GLOVE!
HAH! TRIED TA DITCH OL' SCARFACE DIDJA?
OW!
YA FORGOT DAT I PULL TH' STRINGS AROUND HERE, Eh? Eh?!
NO, SIR! NO, SIR!
GOOD. NOW DAT WE GOT DAT OUTTA TH' WAY, WE CAN GET GACK TO GUSINESS.
"GACK TO GUSINESS"?

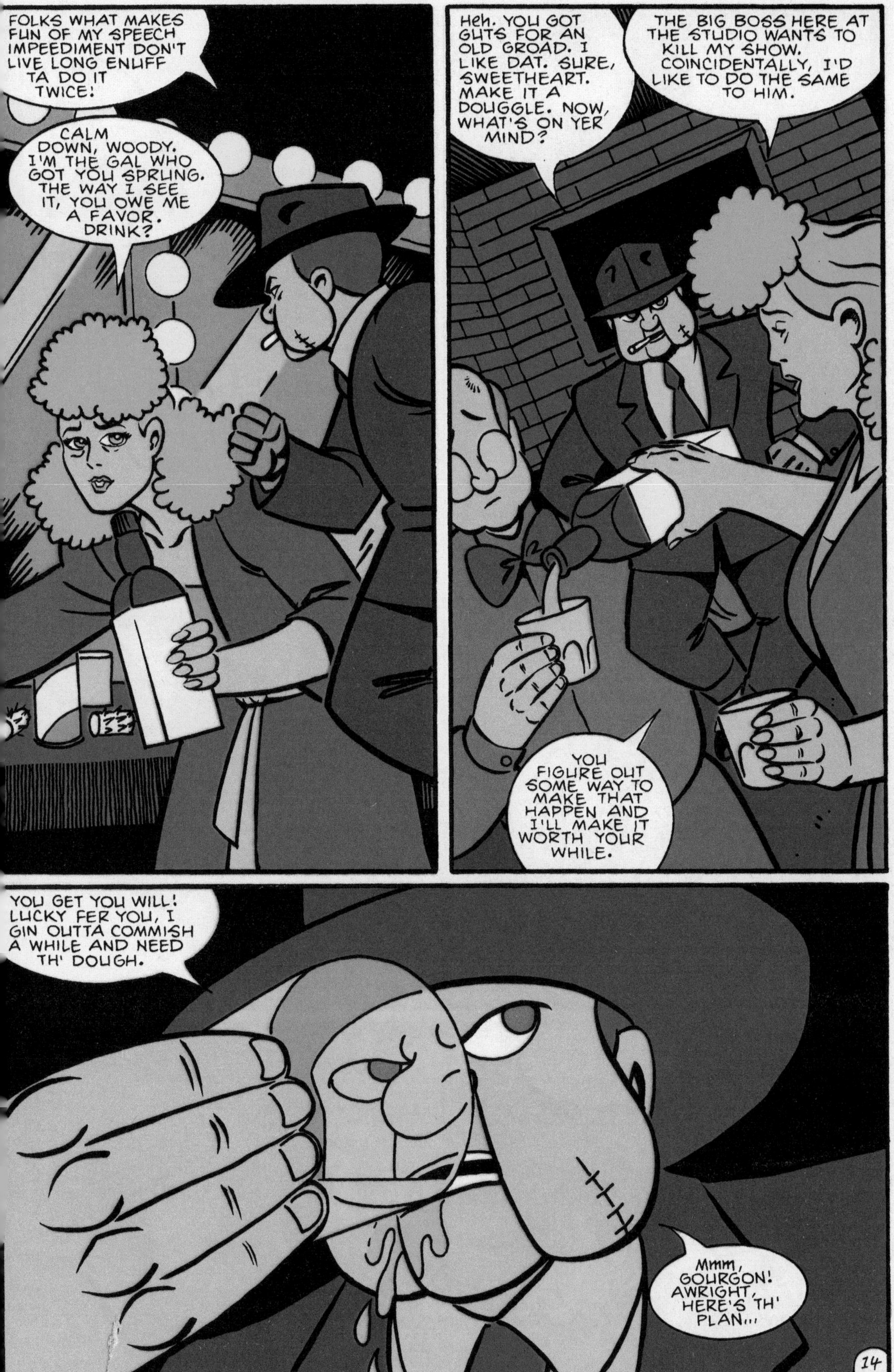
FOLKS WHAT MAKES FUN OF MY SPEECH IMPEEDIMENT DON'T LIVE LONG ENUFF TA DO IT TWICE!
CALM DOWN, WOODY. I'M THE GAL WHO GOT YOU SPRUNG. THE WAY I SEE IT, YOU OWE ME A FAVOR. DRINK?
Heh. YOU GOT GUTS FOR AN OLD GROAD. I LIKE DAT. SURE, SWEETHEART. MAKE IT A DOUGGLE. NOW, WHAT'S ON YER MIND?
THE BIG BOSS HERE AT THE STUDIO WANTS TO KILL MY SHOW. COINCIDENTALLY, I'D LIKE TO DO THE SAME TO HIM.
YOU FIGURE OUT SOME WAY TO MAKE THAT HAPPEN AND I'LL MAKE IT WORTH YOUR WHILE.
YOU GET YOU WILL! LUCKY FER YOU, I GIN OUTTA COMMISH A WHILE AND NEED TH' DOUGH.
Mmm, GOURGON! AWRIGHT, HERE'S TH' PLAN...
14

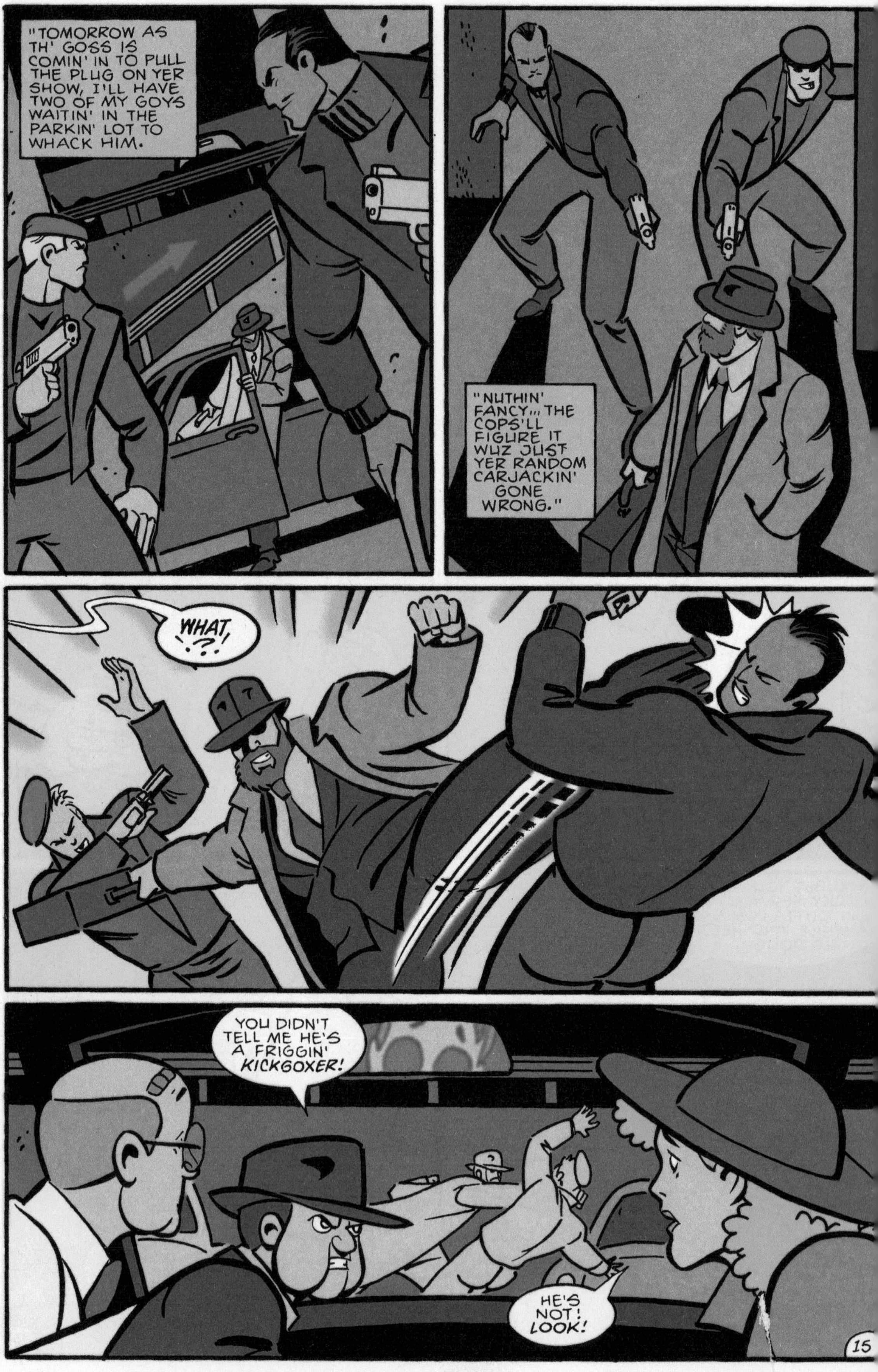
"TOMORROW AS TH' GOSS IS COMIN' IN TO PULL THE PLUG ON YER SHOW, I'LL HAVE TWO OF MY GOYS WAITIN' IN THE PARKIN' LOT TO WHACK HIM.
"NUTHIN' FANCY... THE COPS'LL FIGURE IT WUZ JUST YER RANDOM CARJACKIN' GONE WRONG."
WHAT, ?!
YOU DIDN'T TELL ME HE'S A FRIGGIN' KICKGOXER!
HE'S NOT! LOOK!

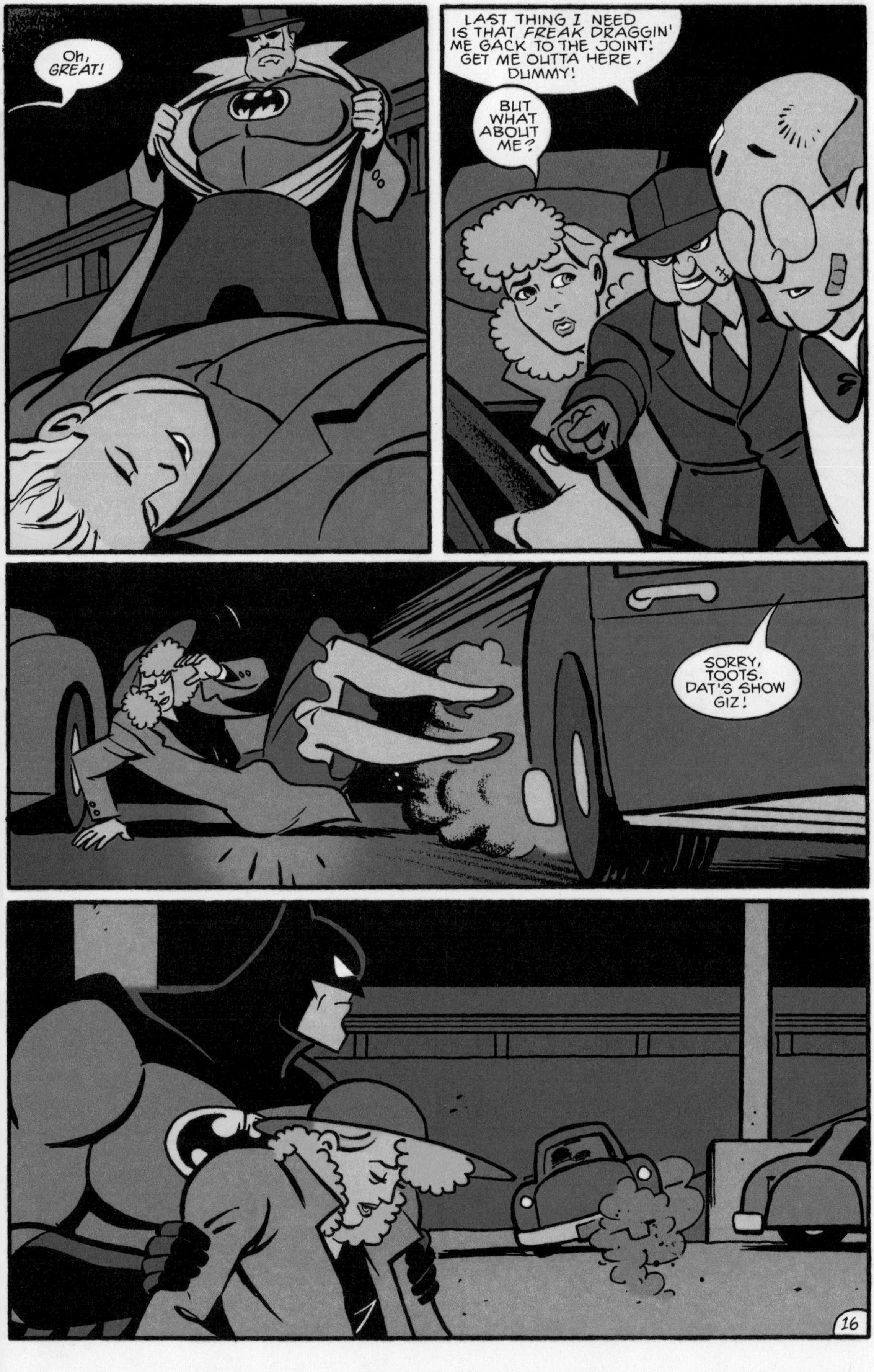
Oh, GREAT!
LAST THING I NEED IS THAT FREAK DRAGGIN' ME GACK TO THE JOINT! GET ME OUTTA HERE, DUMMY!
BUT WHAT ABOUT ME?
SORRY, TOOTS. DAT'S SHOW GIZ!

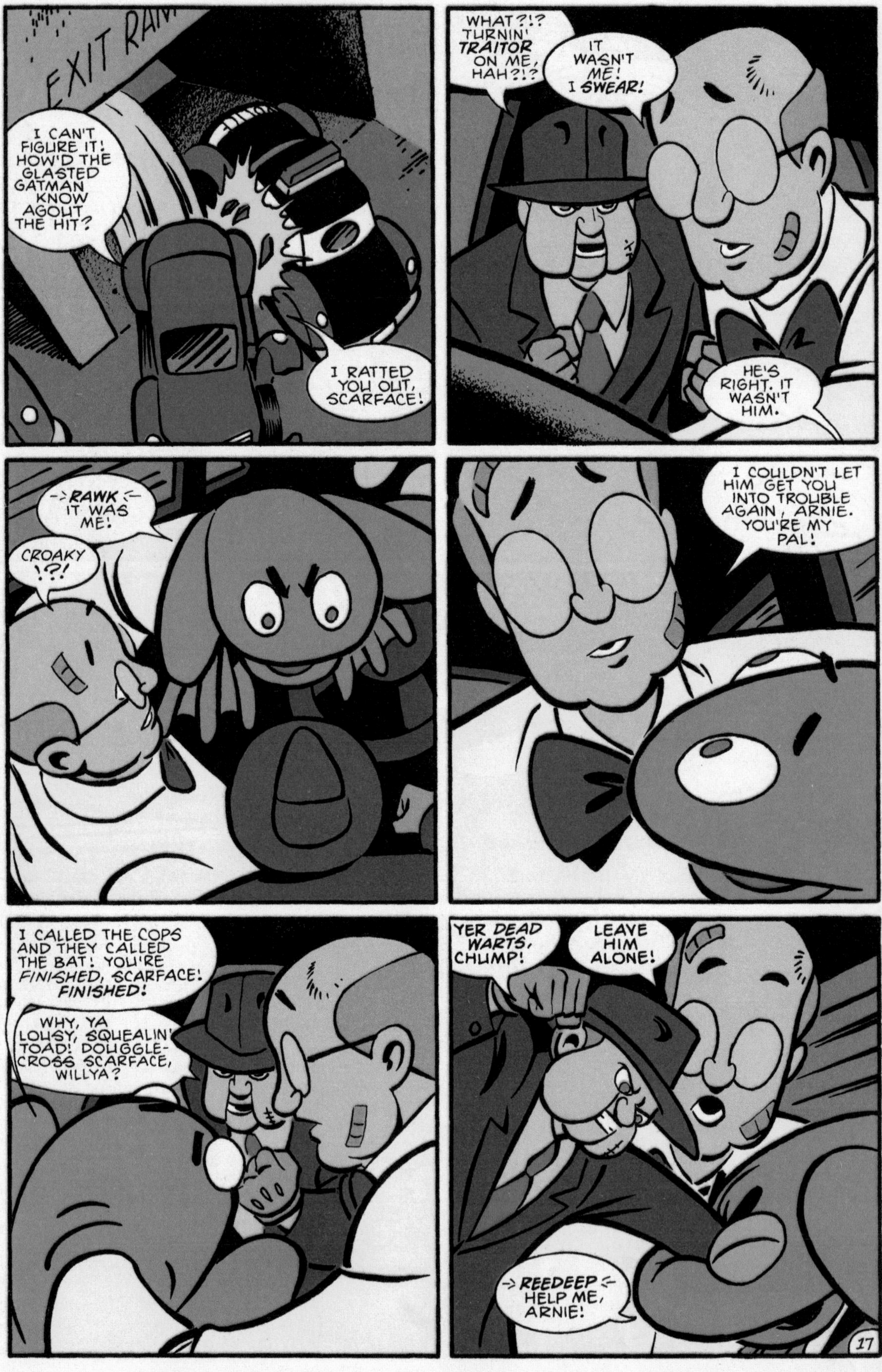
EXIT RAM
I CAN'T FIGURE IT! HOW'D THE GLASTED GATMAN KNOW AGOUT THE HIT?
I RATTED YOU OUT, SCARFACE!
WHAT?!? TURNIN' TRAITOR ON ME, HAH?!?
IT WASN'T ME! I SWEAR!
HE'S RIGHT. IT WASN'T HIM.
-> RAWK <- IT WAS ME!
CROAKY !?!
I COULDN'T LET HIM GET YOU INTO TROUBLE AGAIN, ARNIE. YOU'RE MY PAL!
I CALLED THE COPS AND THEY CALLED THE BAT! YOU'RE FINISHED, SCARFACE! FINISHED!
WHY, YA LOUSY, SQUEALIN' TOAD! DOUGGLE-CROSS SCARFACE, WILLYA?
YER DEAD WARTS, CHUMP!
LEAVE HIM ALONE!
-> REEDEEP <- HELP ME, ARNIE!

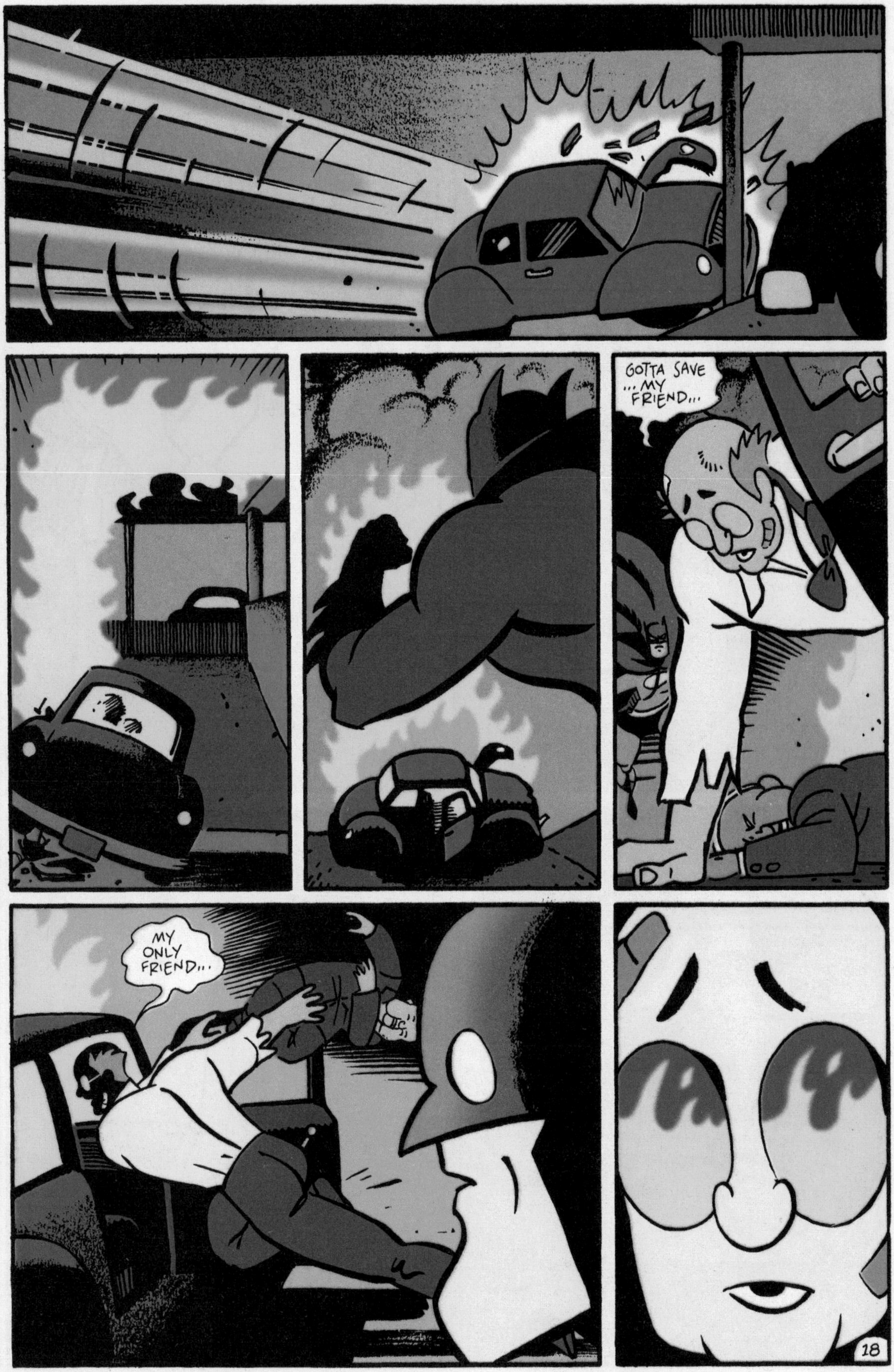
GOTTA SAVE ...MY FRIEND...
MY ONLY FRIEND...

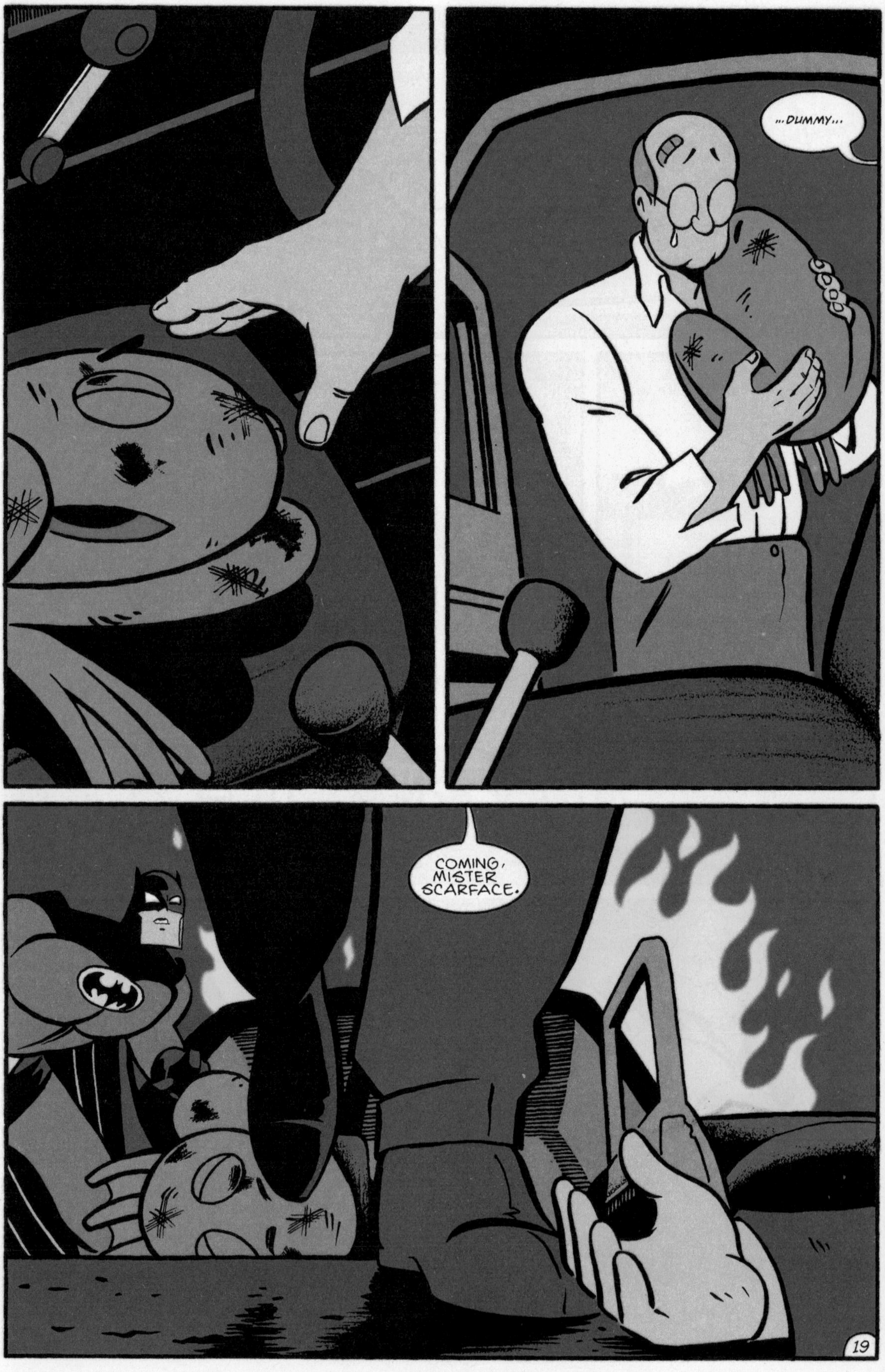
...DUMMY...
COMING, MISTER SCARFACE.

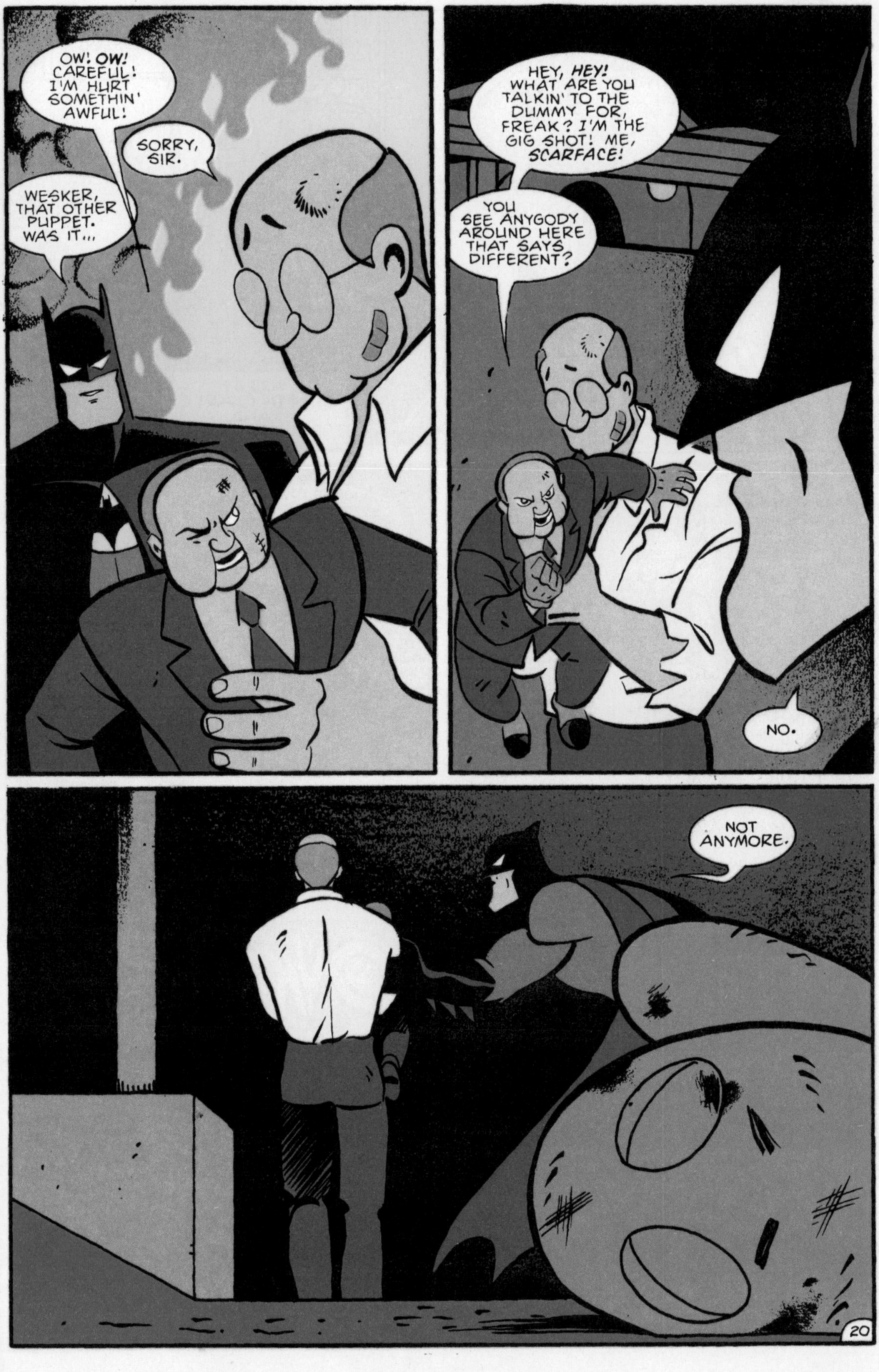

OW! OW! CAREFUL! I'M HURT SOMETHIN' AWFUL!
SORRY, SIR.
WESKER, THAT OTHER PUPPET. WAS IT...
HEY, HEY! WHAT ARE YOU TALKIN' TO THE DUMMY FOR, FREAK? I'M THE GIG SHOT! ME, SCARFACE!
YOU SEE ANYGODY AROUND HERE THAT SAYS DIFFERENT?
NO.
NOT ANYMORE.

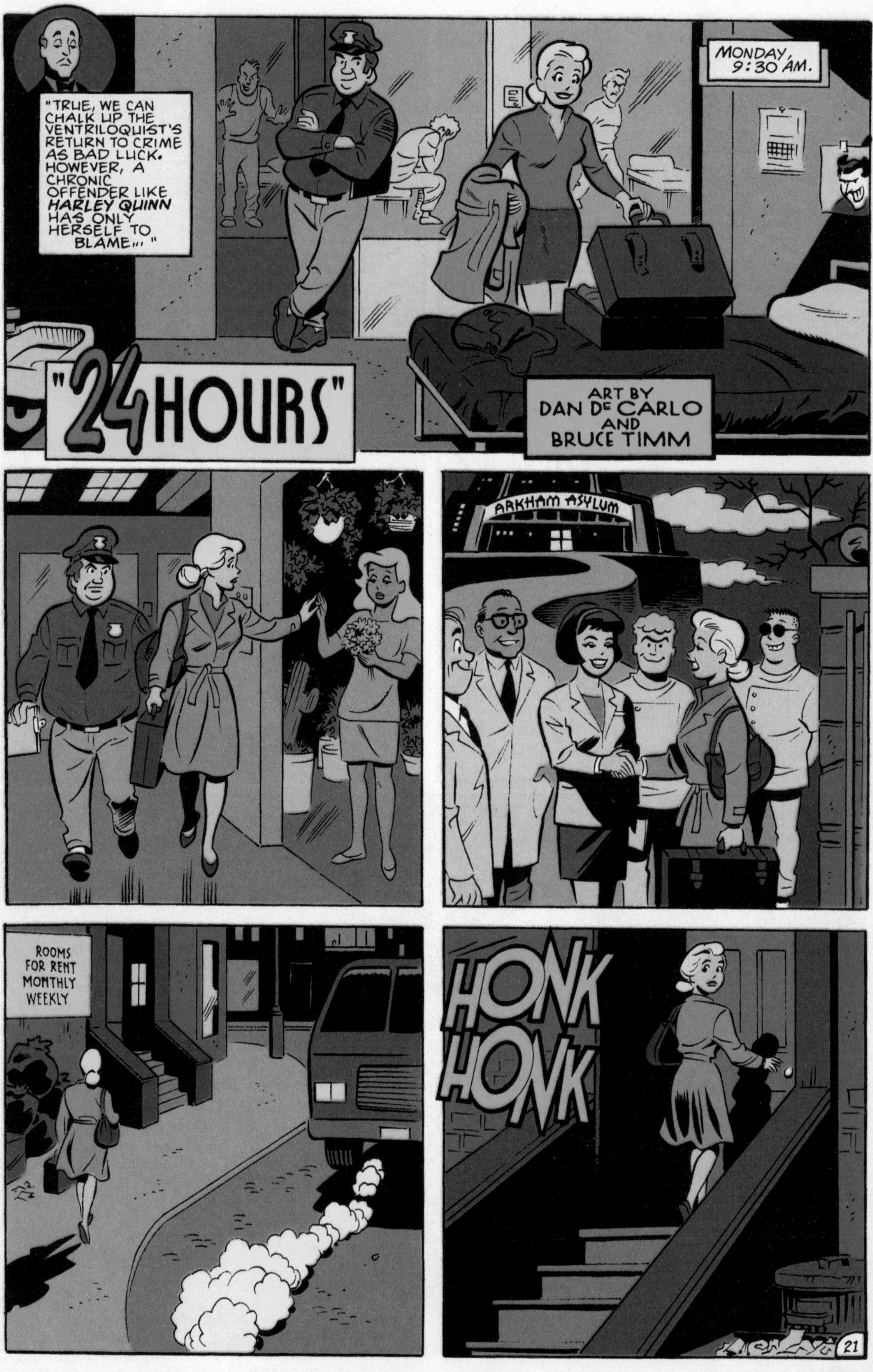
"TRUE, WE CAN CHALK UP THE VENTRILOQUIST'S RETURN TO CRIME AS BAD LUCK. HOWEVER, A CHRONIC OFFENDER LIKE HARLEY QUINN HAS ONLY HERSELF TO BLAME..."
MONDAY, 9:30 AM.
"24 HOURS"
ART BY DAN DeCARLO AND BRUCE TIMM
ARKHAM ASYLUM
ROOMS FOR RENT MONTHLY WEEKLY
HONK HONK

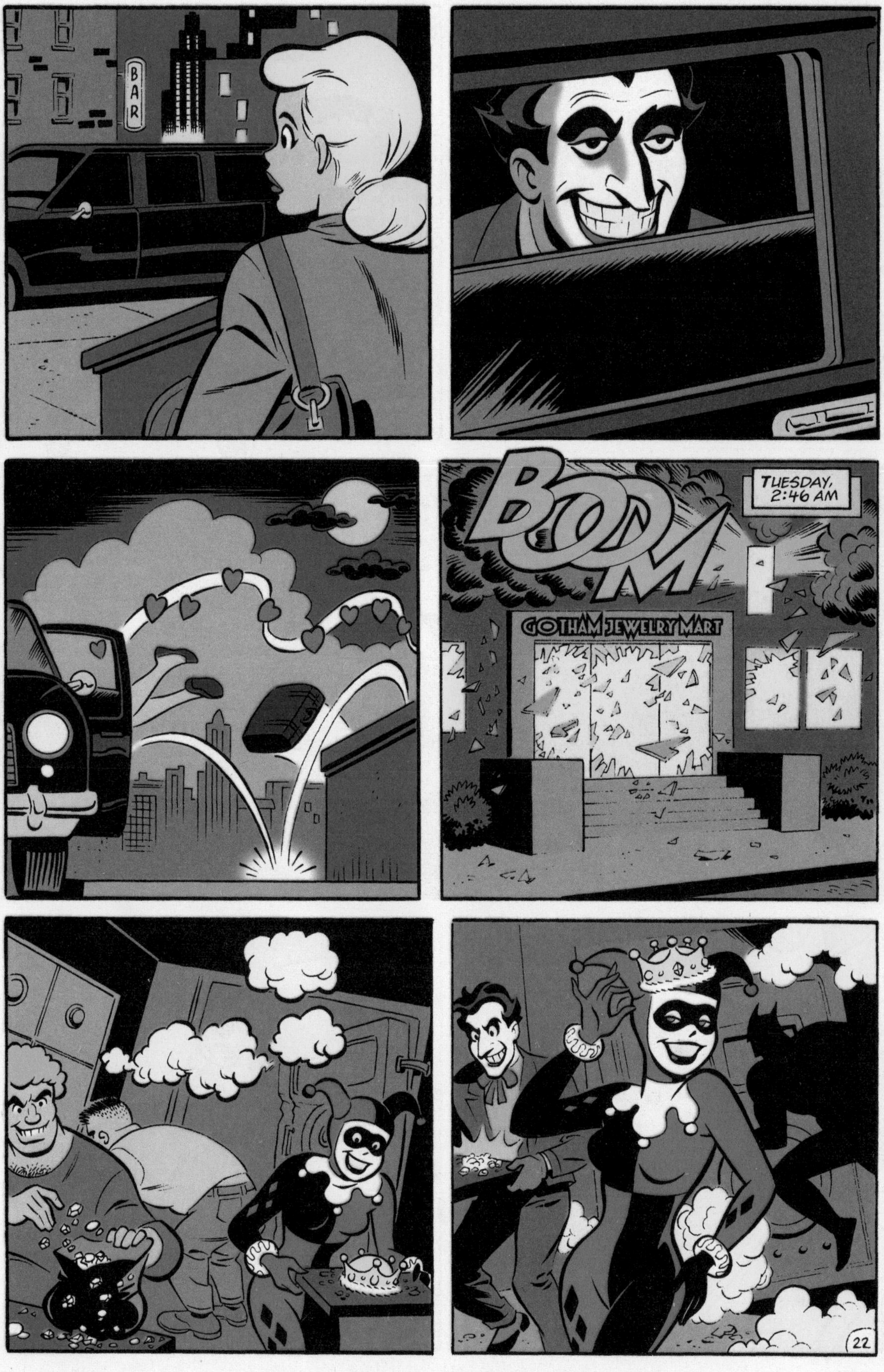
BAR
BOOM
TUESDAY, 2:46 AM
GOTHAM JEWELRY MART

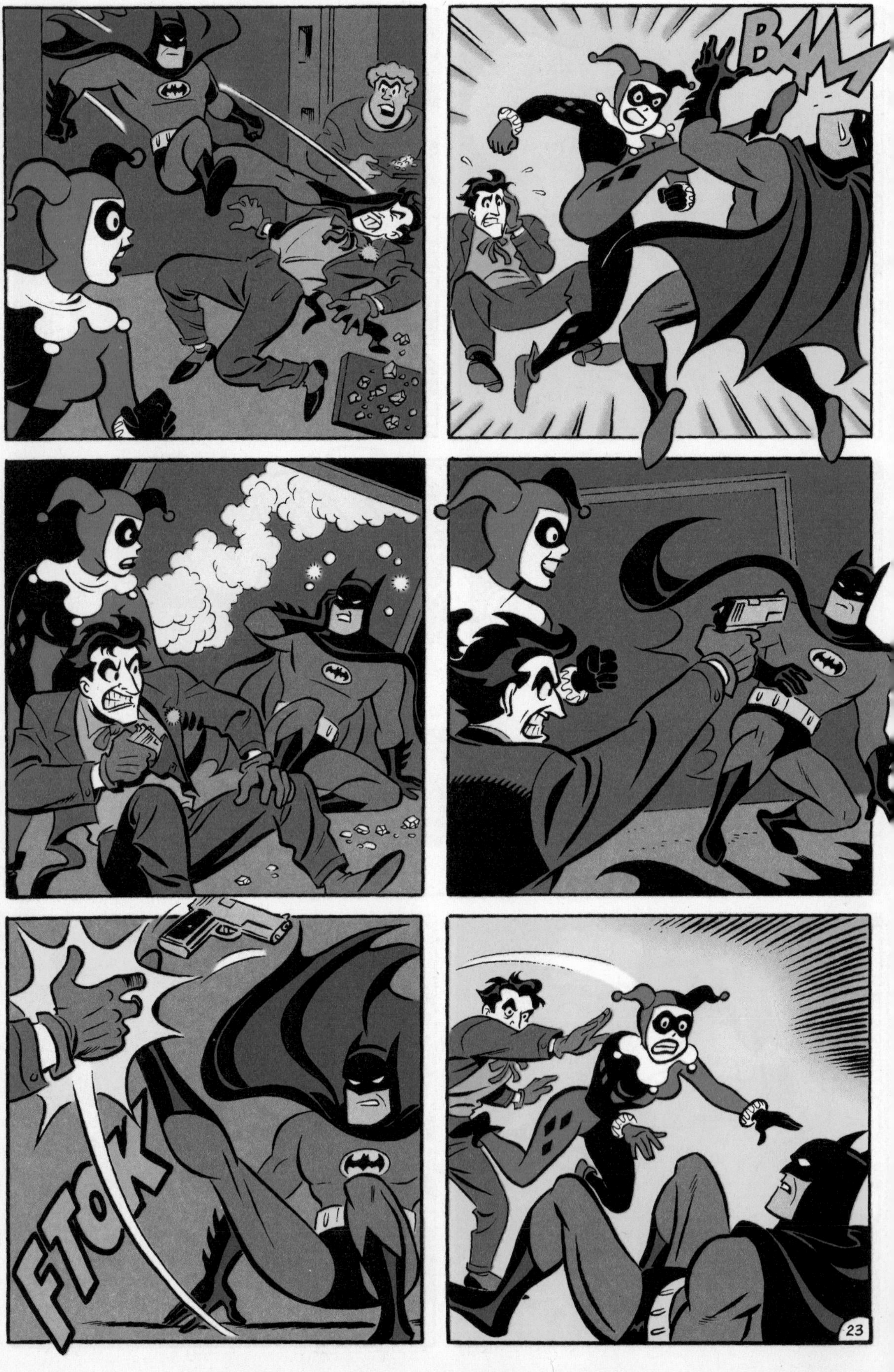
BAM
FTOK

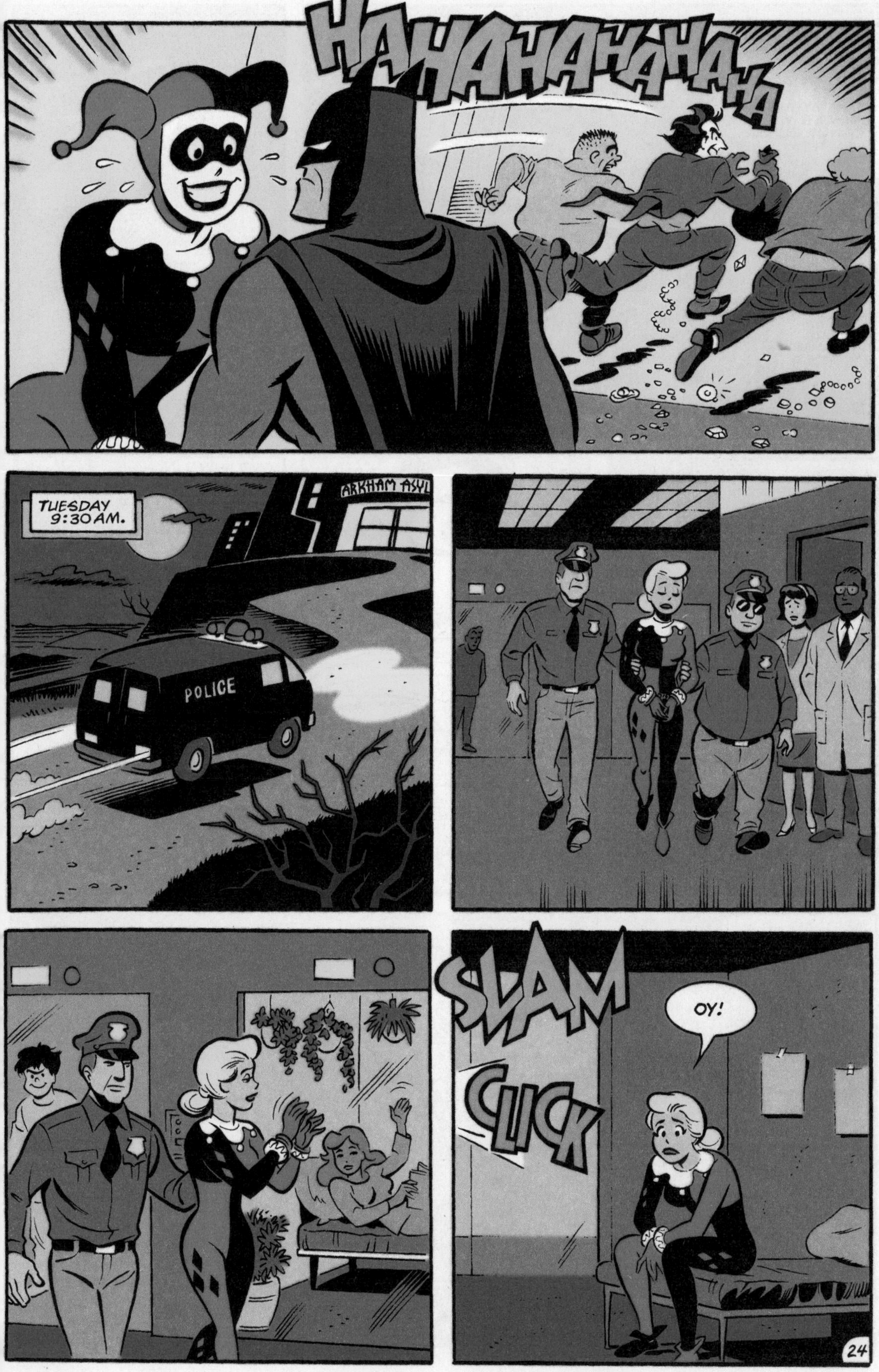
HAHAHAHAHAHAHAHA
TUESDAY 9:30 AM.
ARKHAM ASYL
POLICE
SLAM
CLICK
OY!

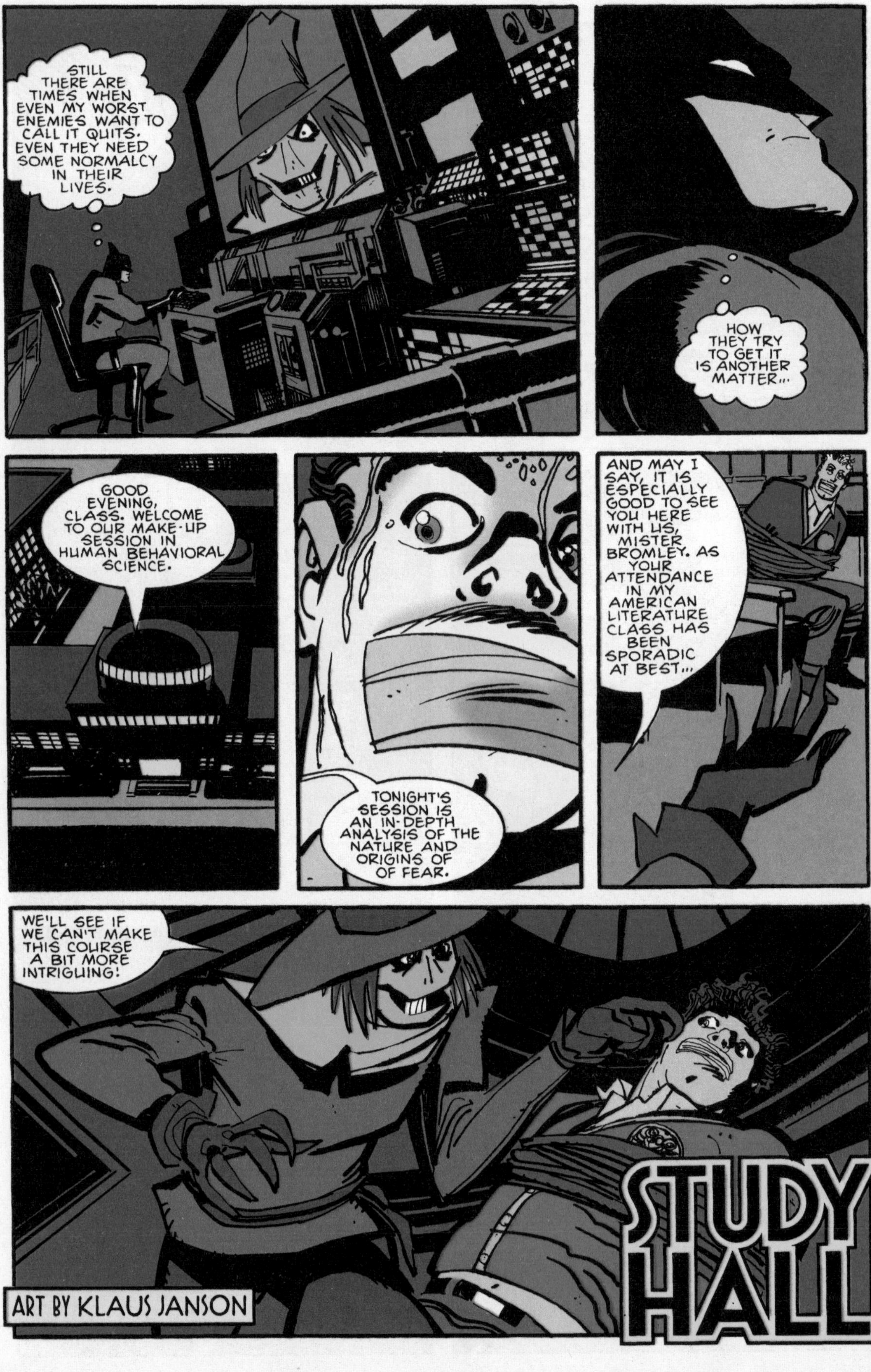
STILL THERE ARE TIMES WHEN EVEN MY WORST ENEMIES WANT TO CALL IT QUITS. EVEN THEY NEED SOME NORMALCY IN THEIR LIVES.
HOW THEY TRY TO GET IT IS ANOTHER MATTER...
GOOD EVENING, CLASS. WELCOME TO OUR MAKE-UP SESSION IN HUMAN BEHAVIORAL SCIENCE.
TONIGHT'S SESSION IS AN IN-DEPTH ANALYSIS OF THE NATURE AND ORIGINS OF OF FEAR.
AND MAY I SAY, IT IS ESPECIALLY GOOD TO SEE YOU HERE WITH US, MISTER BROMLEY. AS YOUR ATTENDANCE IN MY AMERICAN LITERATURE CLASS HAS BEEN SPORADIC AT BEST...
WE'LL SEE IF WE CAN'T MAKE THIS COURSE A BIT MORE INTRIGUING!
STUDY HALL
ART BY KLAUS JANSON

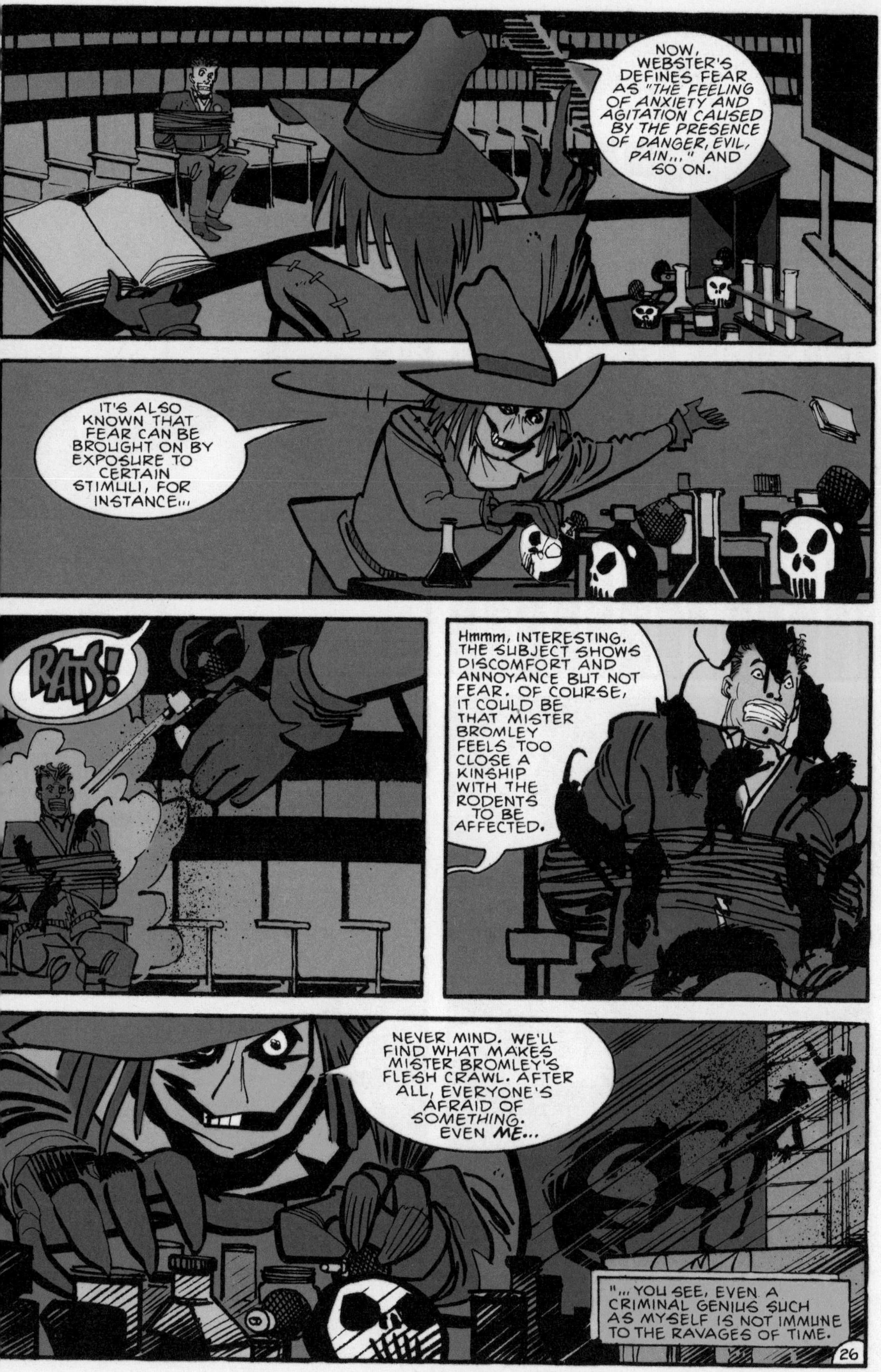
NOW, WEBSTER'S DEFINES FEAR AS "THE FEELING OF ANXIETY AND AGITATION CAUSED BY THE PRESENCE OF DANGER, EVIL, PAIN..." AND SO ON.
IT'S ALSO KNOWN THAT FEAR CAN BE BROUGHT ON BY EXPOSURE TO CERTAIN STIMULI, FOR INSTANCE...
RATS!
Hmmm, INTERESTING. THE SUBJECT SHOWS DISCOMFORT AND ANNOYANCE BUT NOT FEAR. OF COURSE, IT COULD BE THAT MISTER BROMLEY FEELS TOO CLOSE A KINSHIP WITH THE RODENTS TO BE AFFECTED.
NEVER MIND. WE'LL FIND WHAT MAKES MISTER BROMLEY'S FLESH CRAWL. AFTER ALL, EVERYONE'S AFRAID OF SOMETHING. EVEN ME...
"...YOU SEE, EVEN A CRIMINAL GENIUS SUCH AS MYSELF IS NOT IMMUNE TO THE RAVAGES OF TIME.
26

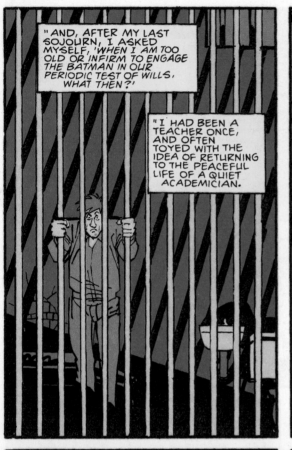

"AND, AFTER MY LAST SOJOURN, I ASKED MYSELF, 'WHEN I AM TOO OLD OR INFIRM TO ENGAGE THE BATMAN IN OUR PERIODIC TEST OF WILLS, WHAT THEN?'

"I HAD BEEN A TEACHER ONCE, AND OFTEN TOYED WITH THE IDEA OF RETURNING TO THE PEACEFUL LIFE OF A QUIET ACADEMICIAN.

"SO, AFTER WRITING A NEW SET OF RELEASE PAPERS, I SET OUT TO MAKE THAT DREAM HAPPEN.

"NATURALLY, IT WAS CHILD'S PLAY FOR ONE OF MY INTELLECT TO FORGE THE DOCUMENTS NECESSARY TO SECURE A POSITION AT THIS SMALL UPSTATE COLLEGE, AND THUS I BEGAN A NEW LIFE AS IRVING DIEDRICH, ENGLISH PROFESSOR.

"ON THE WHOLE, MY PUPILS WERE A DREARY LOT, A DEPRESSINGLY TYPICAL ASSORTMENT OF BRAIN-DEAD QUARTERBACKS AND PREENING CO-EDS.

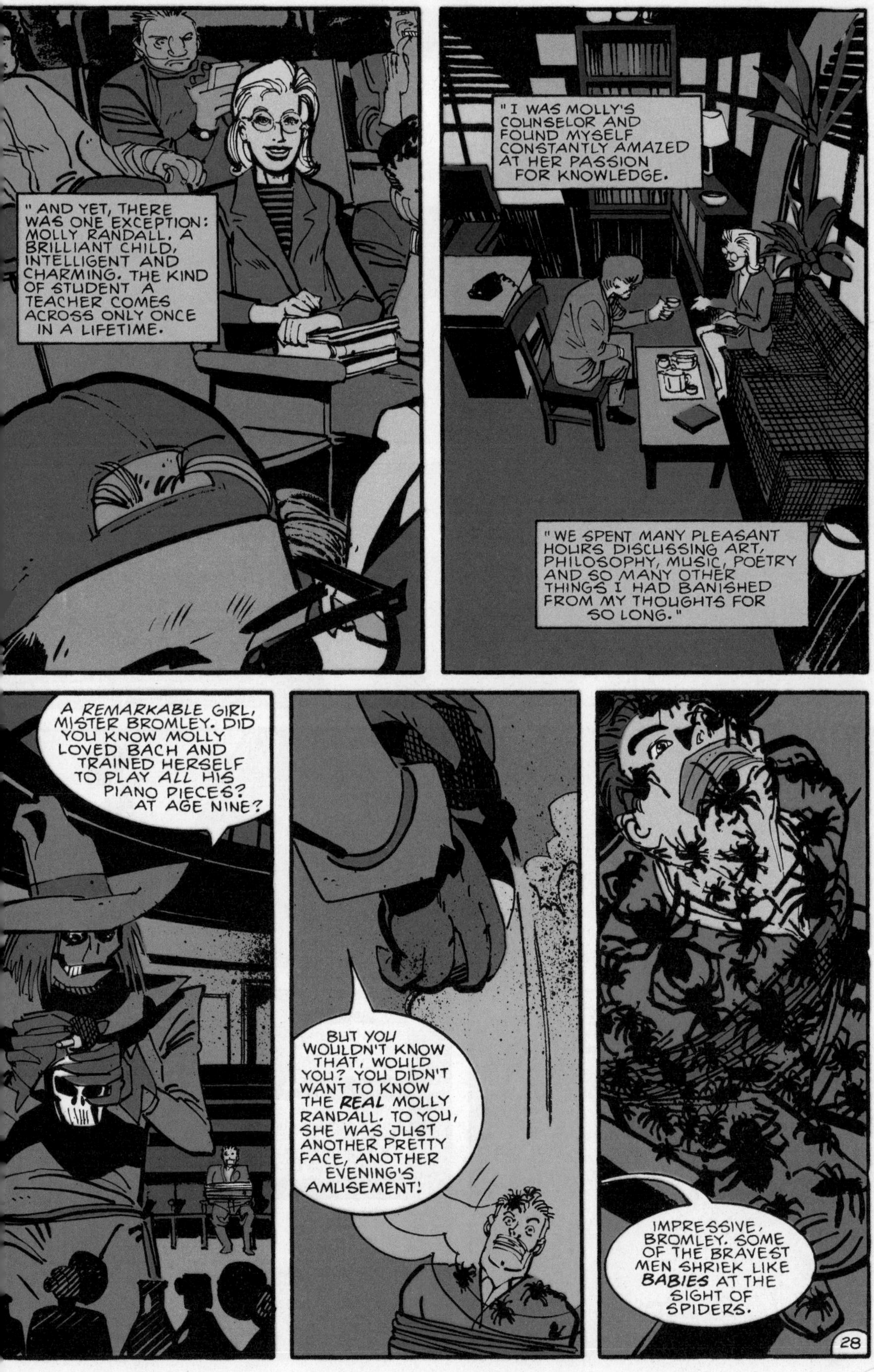
"AND YET, THERE WAS ONE EXCEPTION: MOLLY RANDALL. A BRILLIANT CHILD, INTELLIGENT AND CHARMING. THE KIND OF STUDENT A TEACHER COMES ACROSS ONLY ONCE IN A LIFETIME.
"I WAS MOLLY'S COUNSELOR AND FOUND MYSELF CONSTANTLY AMAZED AT HER PASSION FOR KNOWLEDGE.
"WE SPENT MANY PLEASANT HOURS DISCUSSING ART, PHILOSOPHY, MUSIC, POETRY AND SO MANY OTHER THINGS I HAD BANISHED FROM MY THOUGHTS FOR SO LONG."
A *REMARKABLE* GIRL, MISTER BROMLEY. DID YOU KNOW MOLLY LOVED BACH AND TRAINED HERSELF TO PLAY *ALL* HIS PIANO PIECES? AT AGE NINE?
BUT YOU WOULDN'T KNOW THAT, WOULD YOU? YOU DIDN'T WANT TO KNOW THE ***REAL*** MOLLY RANDALL. TO YOU, SHE WAS JUST ANOTHER PRETTY FACE, ANOTHER EVENING'S AMUSEMENT!
IMPRESSIVE, BROMLEY. SOME OF THE BRAVEST MEN SHRIEK LIKE ***BABIES*** AT THE SIGHT OF SPIDERS.

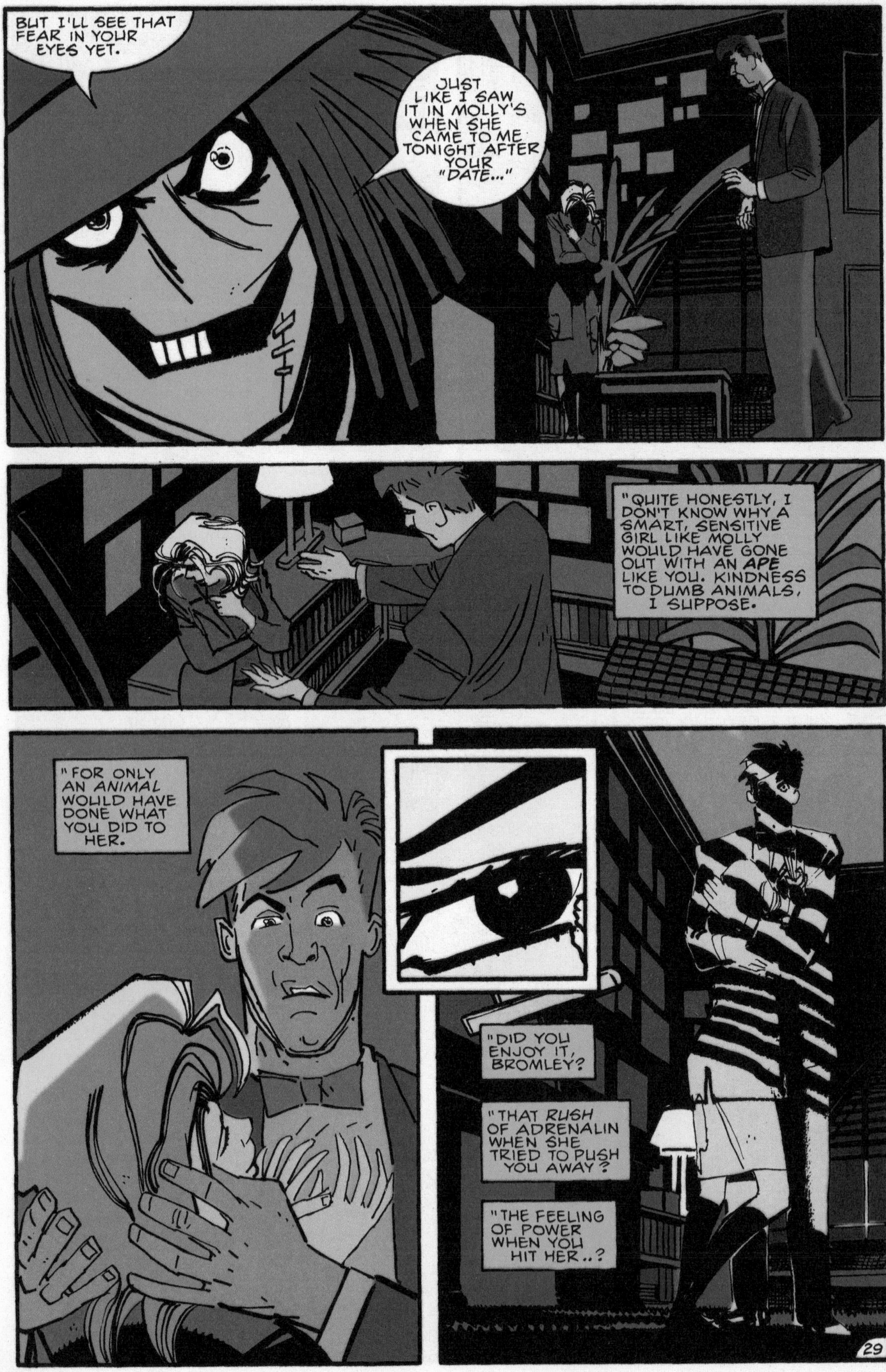

BUT I'LL SEE THAT FEAR IN YOUR EYES YET.
JUST LIKE I SAW IT IN MOLLY'S WHEN SHE CAME TO ME TONIGHT AFTER YOUR "DATE..."
"QUITE HONESTLY, I DON'T KNOW WHY A SMART, SENSITIVE GIRL LIKE MOLLY WOULD HAVE GONE OUT WITH AN APE LIKE YOU. KINDNESS TO DUMB ANIMALS, I SUPPOSE.
"FOR ONLY AN ANIMAL WOULD HAVE DONE WHAT YOU DID TO HER.
"DID YOU ENJOY IT, BROMLEY?
"THAT RUSH OF ADRENALIN WHEN SHE TRIED TO PUSH YOU AWAY?
"THE FEELING OF POWER WHEN YOU HIT HER..?

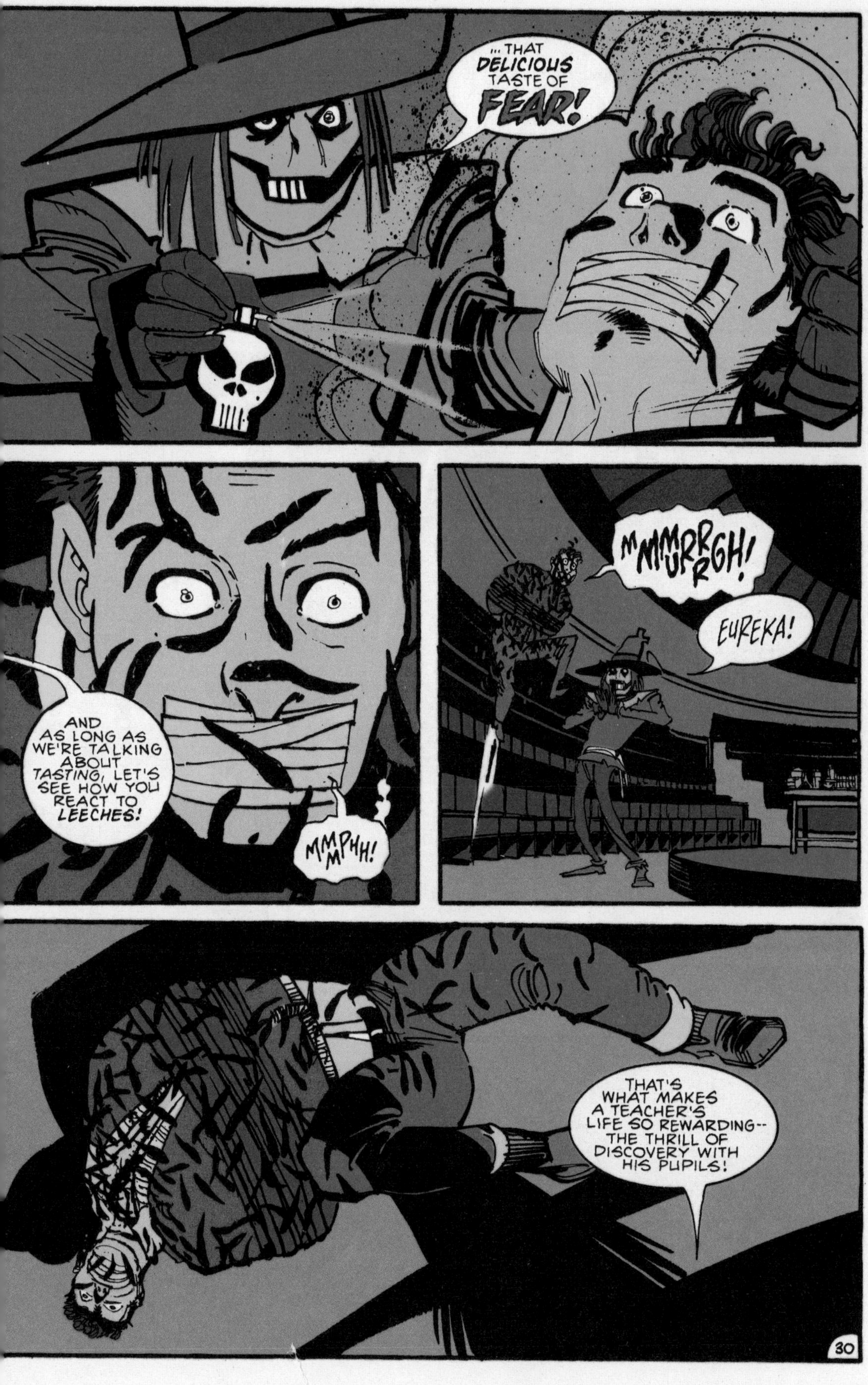

...THAT DELICIOUS TASTE OF FEAR!
AND AS LONG AS WE'RE TALKING ABOUT TASTING, LET'S SEE HOW YOU REACT TO LEECHES!
MMMPHH!
MMMURRRGH!
EUREKA!
THAT'S WHAT MAKES A TEACHER'S LIFE SO REWARDING-- THE THRILL OF DISCOVERY WITH HIS PUPILS!

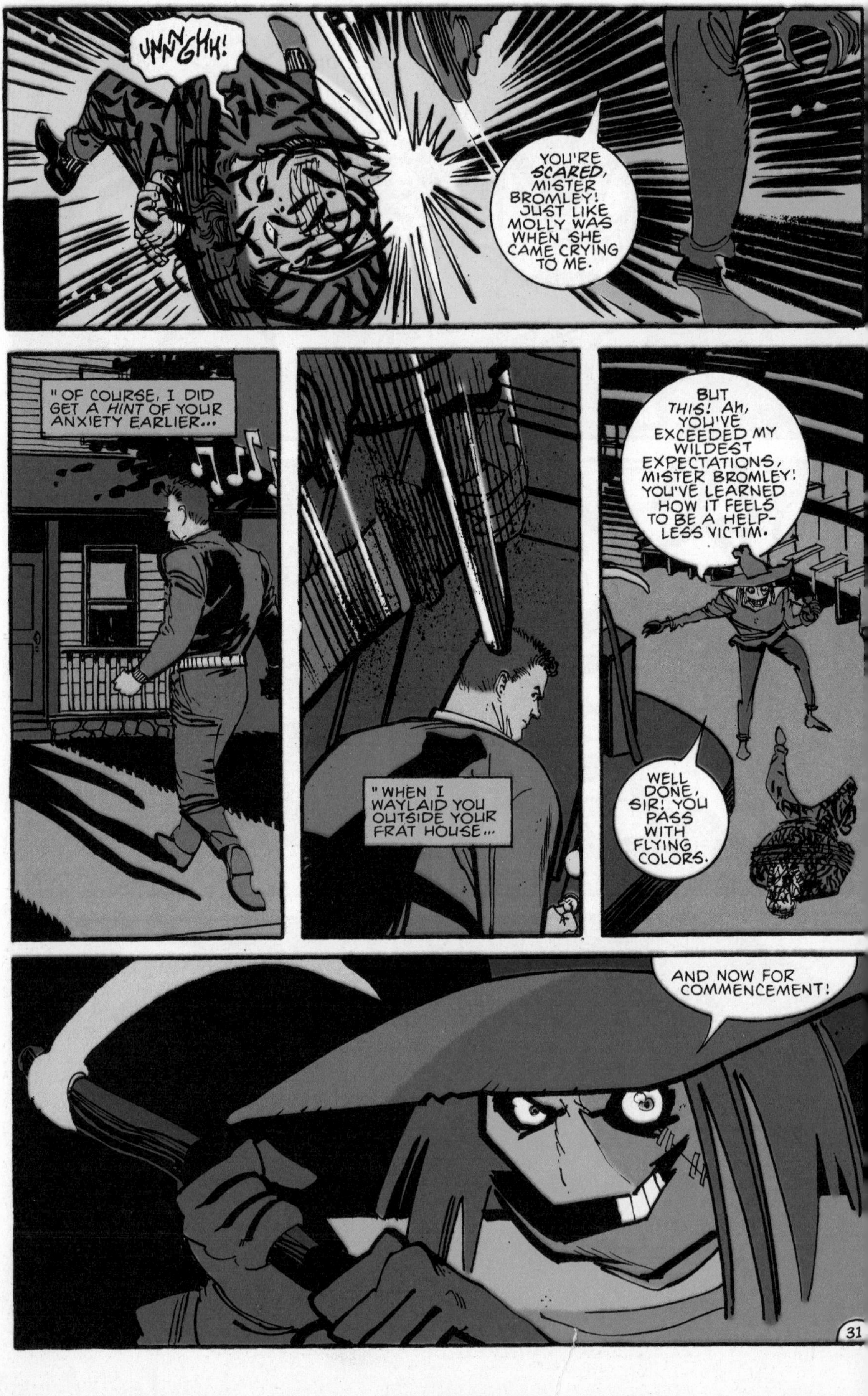

UNNNGHK!
YOU'RE SCARED, MISTER BROMLEY! JUST LIKE MOLLY WAS WHEN SHE CAME CRYING TO ME.
"OF COURSE, I DID GET A HINT OF YOUR ANXIETY EARLIER...
"WHEN I WAYLAID YOU OUTSIDE YOUR FRAT HOUSE...
BUT THIS! AH, YOU'VE EXCEEDED MY WILDEST EXPECTATIONS, MISTER BROMLEY! YOU'VE LEARNED HOW IT FEELS TO BE A HELPLESS VICTIM.
WELL DONE, SIR! YOU PASS WITH FLYING COLORS.
AND NOW FOR COMMENCEMENT!

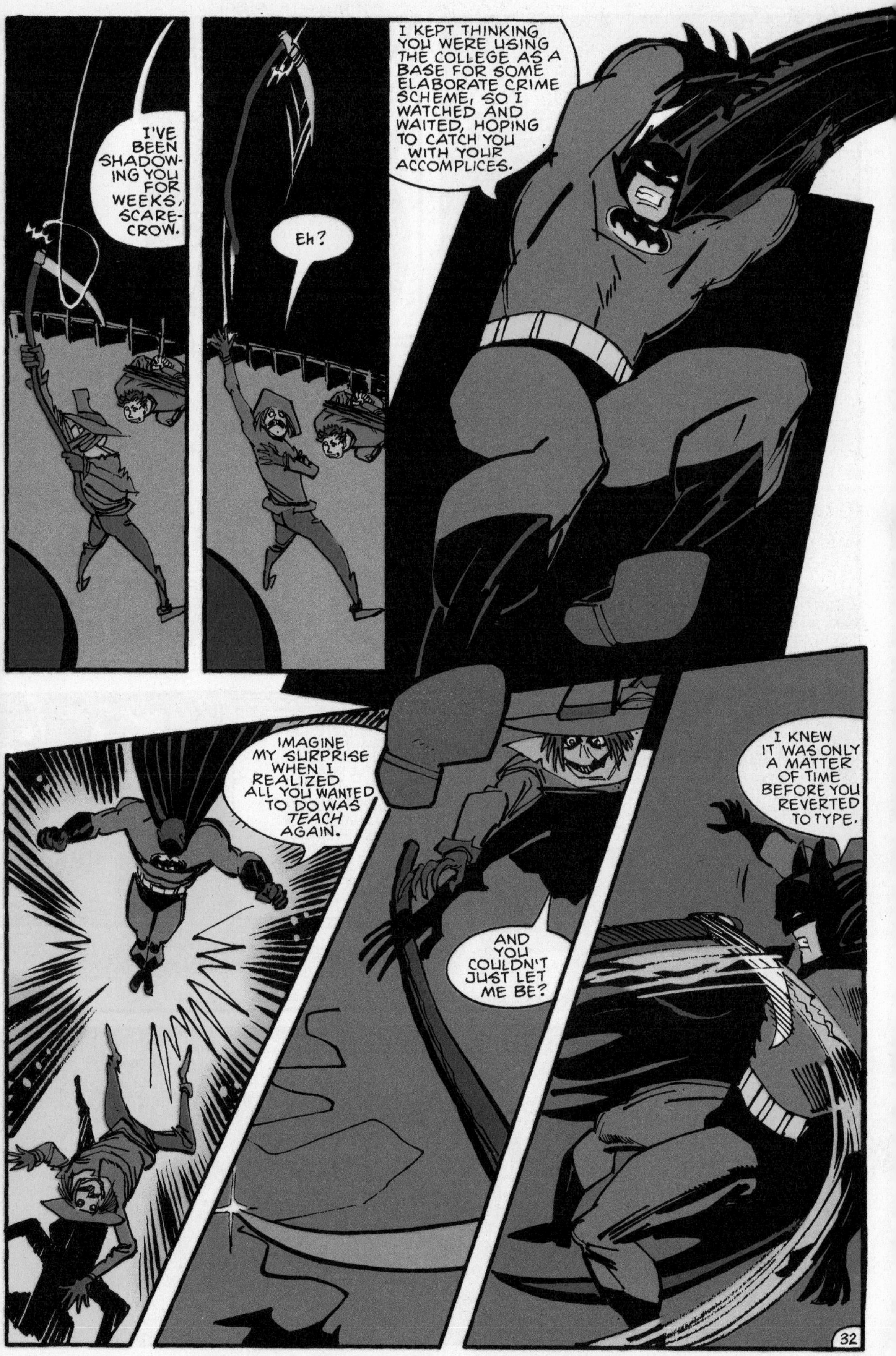
I'VE BEEN SHADOWING YOU FOR WEEKS, SCARECROW.
Eh?
I KEPT THINKING YOU WERE USING THE COLLEGE AS A BASE FOR SOME ELABORATE CRIME SCHEME, SO I WATCHED AND WAITED, HOPING TO CATCH YOU WITH YOUR ACCOMPLICES.
IMAGINE MY SURPRISE WHEN I REALIZED ALL YOU WANTED TO DO WAS *TEACH* AGAIN.
AND YOU COULDN'T JUST LET ME BE?
I KNEW IT WAS ONLY A MATTER OF TIME BEFORE YOU REVERTED TO TYPE.

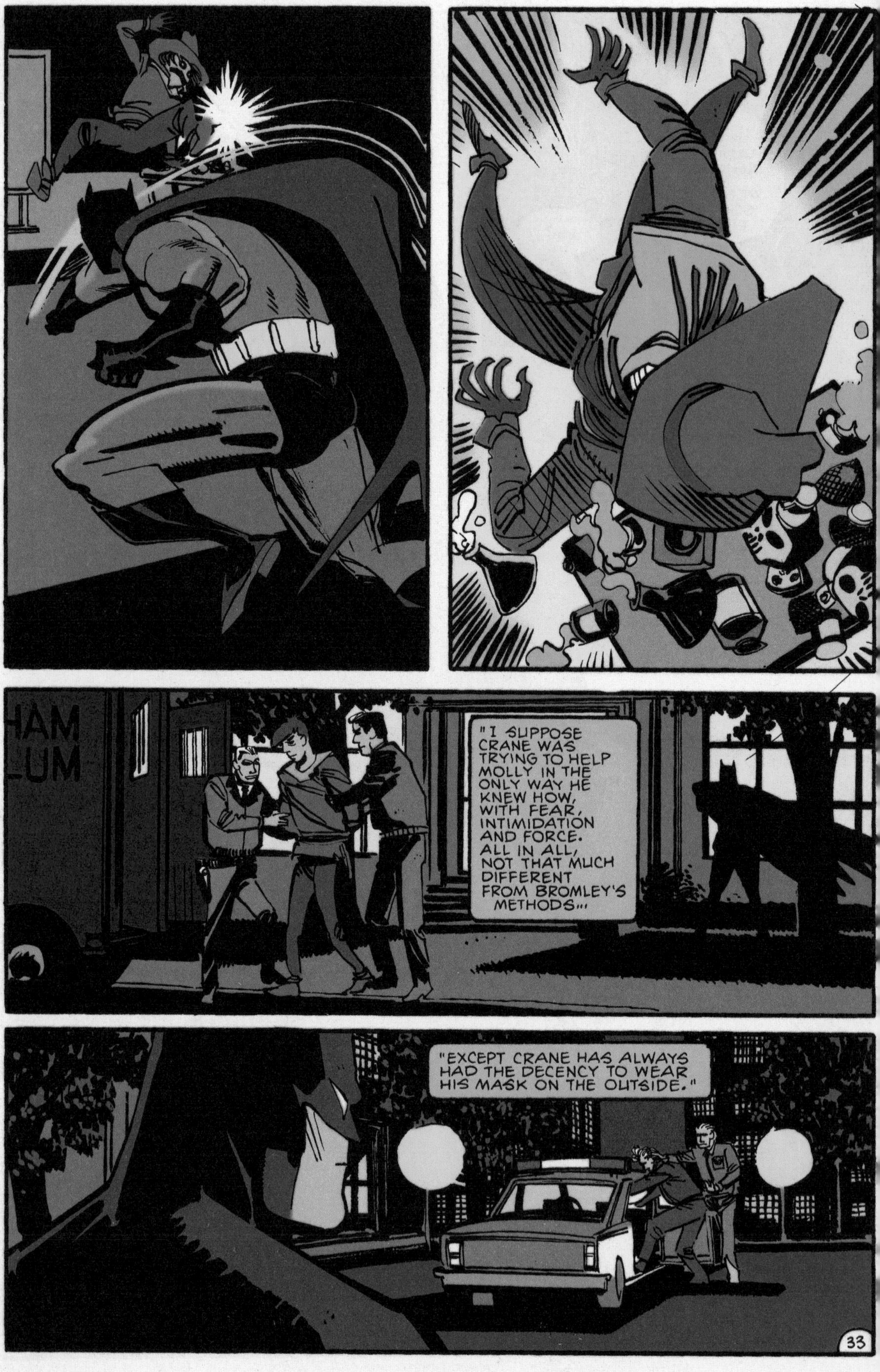
HAM
LUM
"I SUPPOSE CRANE WAS TRYING TO HELP MOLLY IN THE ONLY WAY HE KNEW HOW, WITH FEAR, INTIMIDATION AND FORCE. ALL IN ALL, NOT THAT MUCH DIFFERENT FROM BROMLEY'S METHODS...
"EXCEPT CRANE HAS ALWAYS HAD THE DECENCY TO WEAR HIS MASK ON THE OUTSIDE."

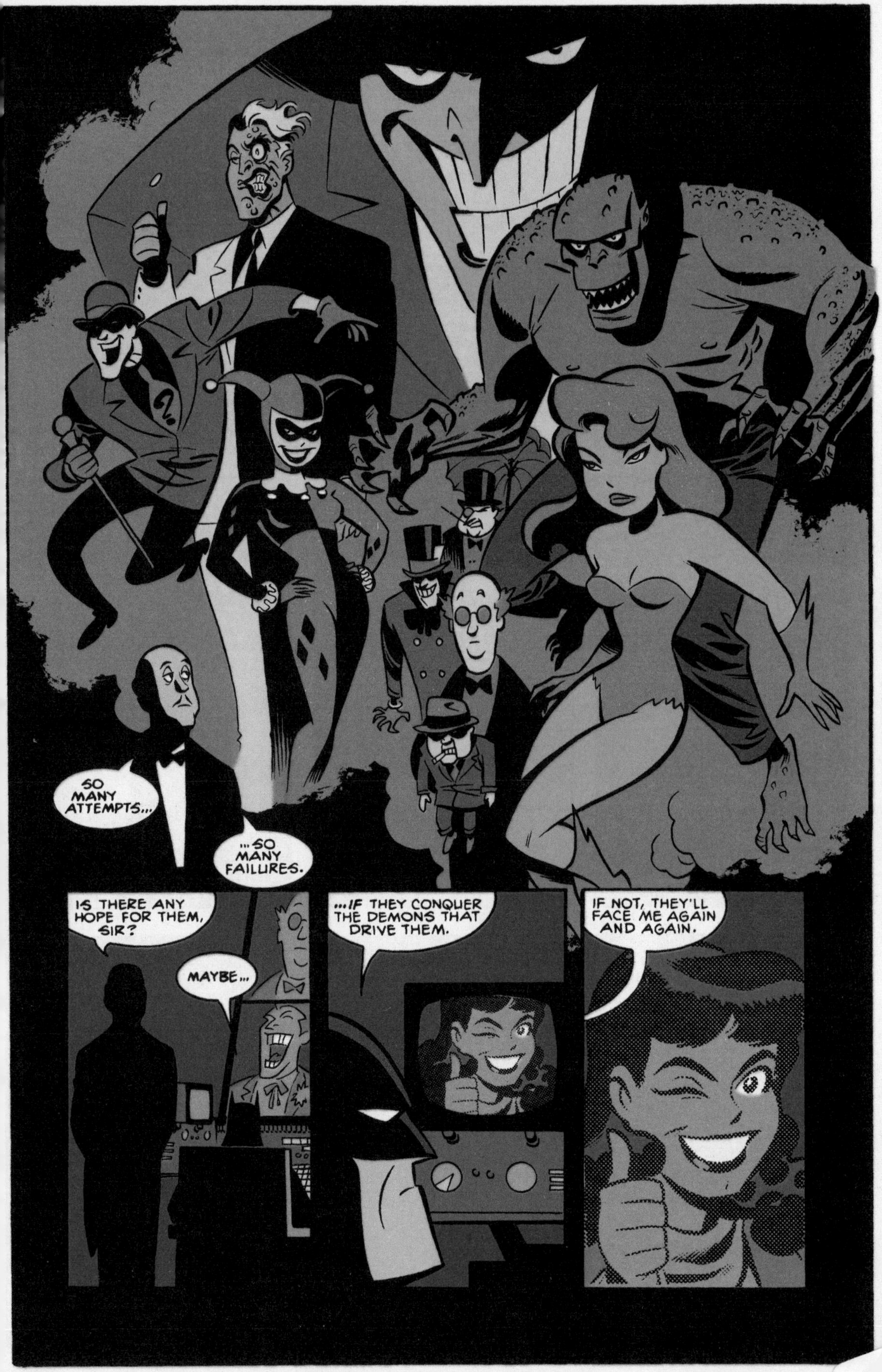
SO MANY ATTEMPTS...
...SO MANY FAILURES.
IS THERE ANY HOPE FOR THEM, SIR?
MAYBE...
...IF THEY CONQUER THE DEMONS THAT DRIVE THEM.
IF NOT, THEY'LL FACE ME AGAIN AND AGAIN.

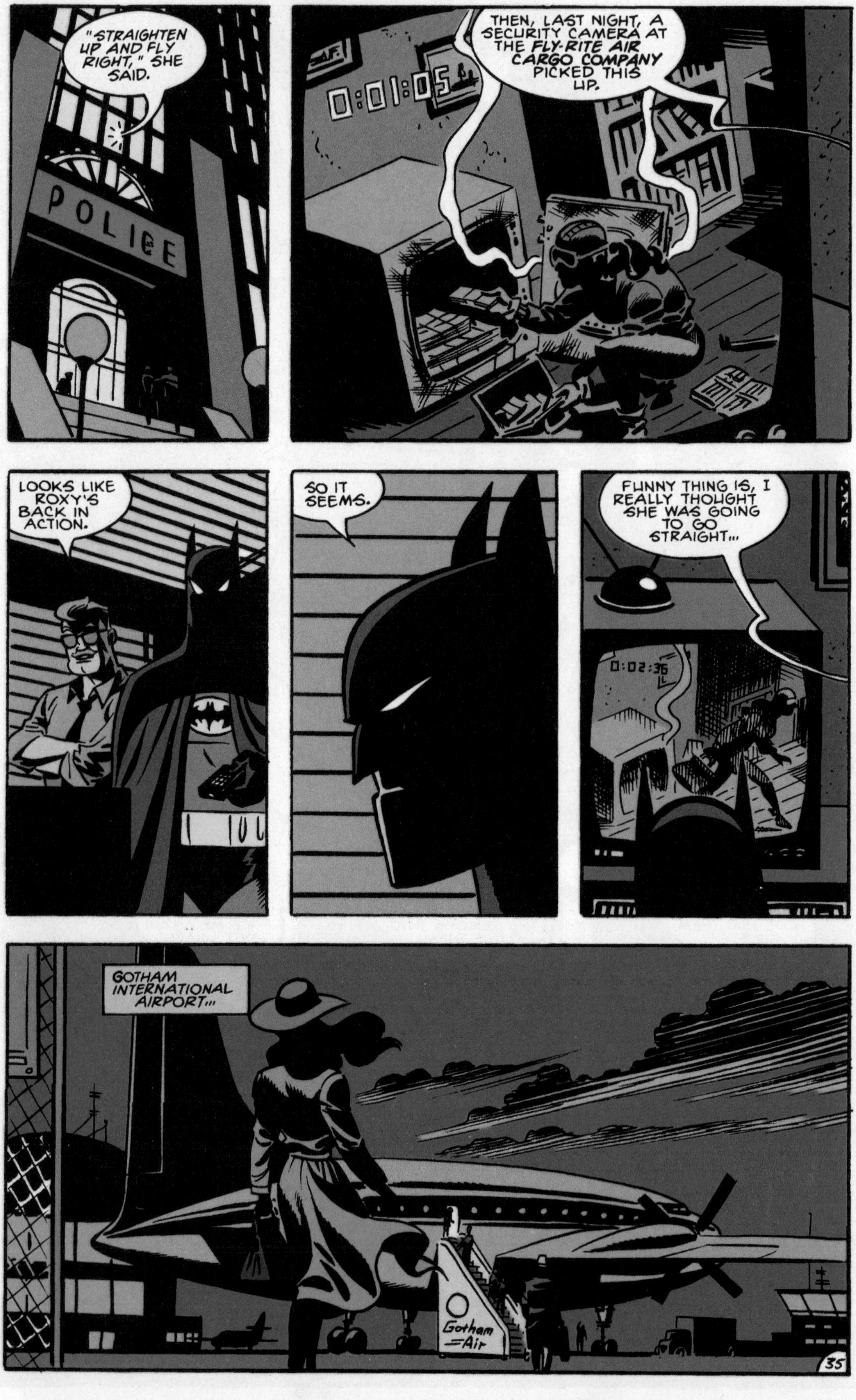
"STRAIGHTEN UP AND FLY RIGHT," SHE SAID.
POLICE
THEN, LAST NIGHT, A SECURITY CAMERA AT THE FLY-RITE AIR CARGO COMPANY PICKED THIS UP.
0:01:05
LOOKS LIKE ROXY'S BACK IN ACTION.
SO IT SEEMS.
FUNNY THING IS, I REALLY THOUGHT SHE WAS GOING TO GO STRAIGHT...
0:02:36
GOTHAM INTERNATIONAL AIRPORT...
Gotham Air

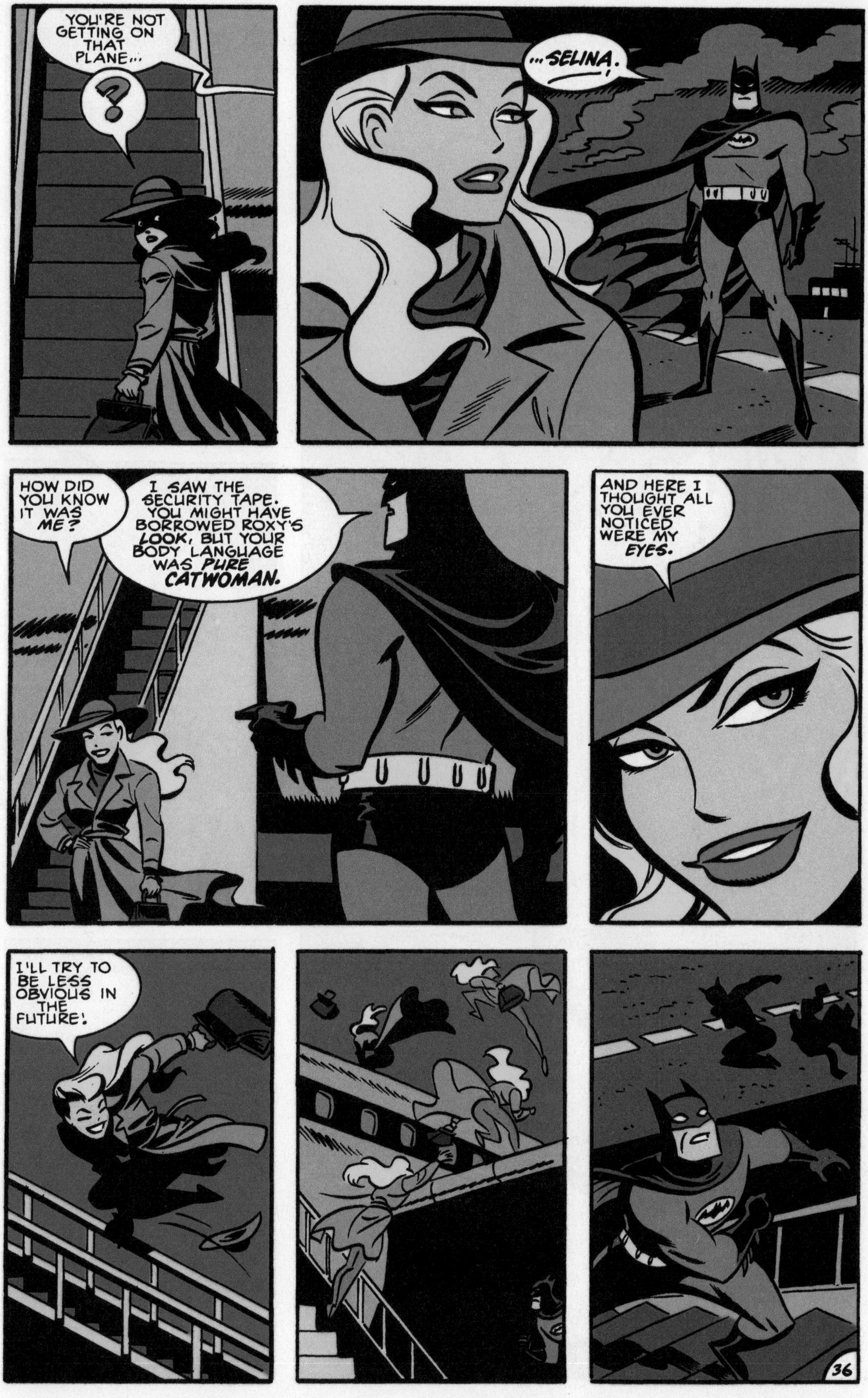
YOU'RE NOT GETTING ON THAT PLANE...
?
...SELINA.
HOW DID YOU KNOW IT WAS ME?
I SAW THE SECURITY TAPE. YOU MIGHT HAVE BORROWED ROXY'S LOOK, BUT YOUR BODY LANGUAGE WAS PURE CATWOMAN.
AND HERE I THOUGHT ALL YOU EVER NOTICED WERE MY EYES.
I'LL TRY TO BE LESS OBVIOUS IN THE FUTURE!

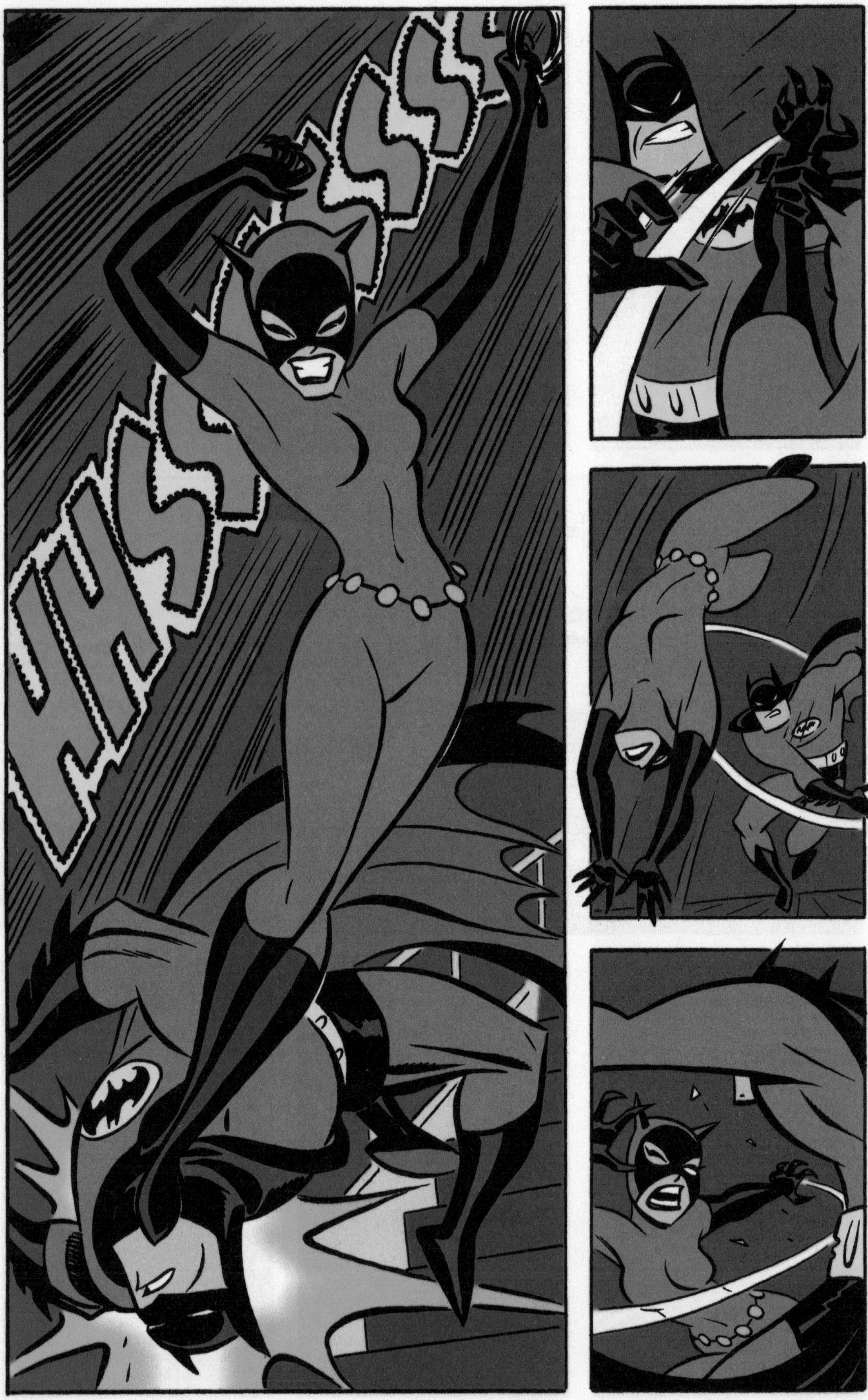
HISSSSSS

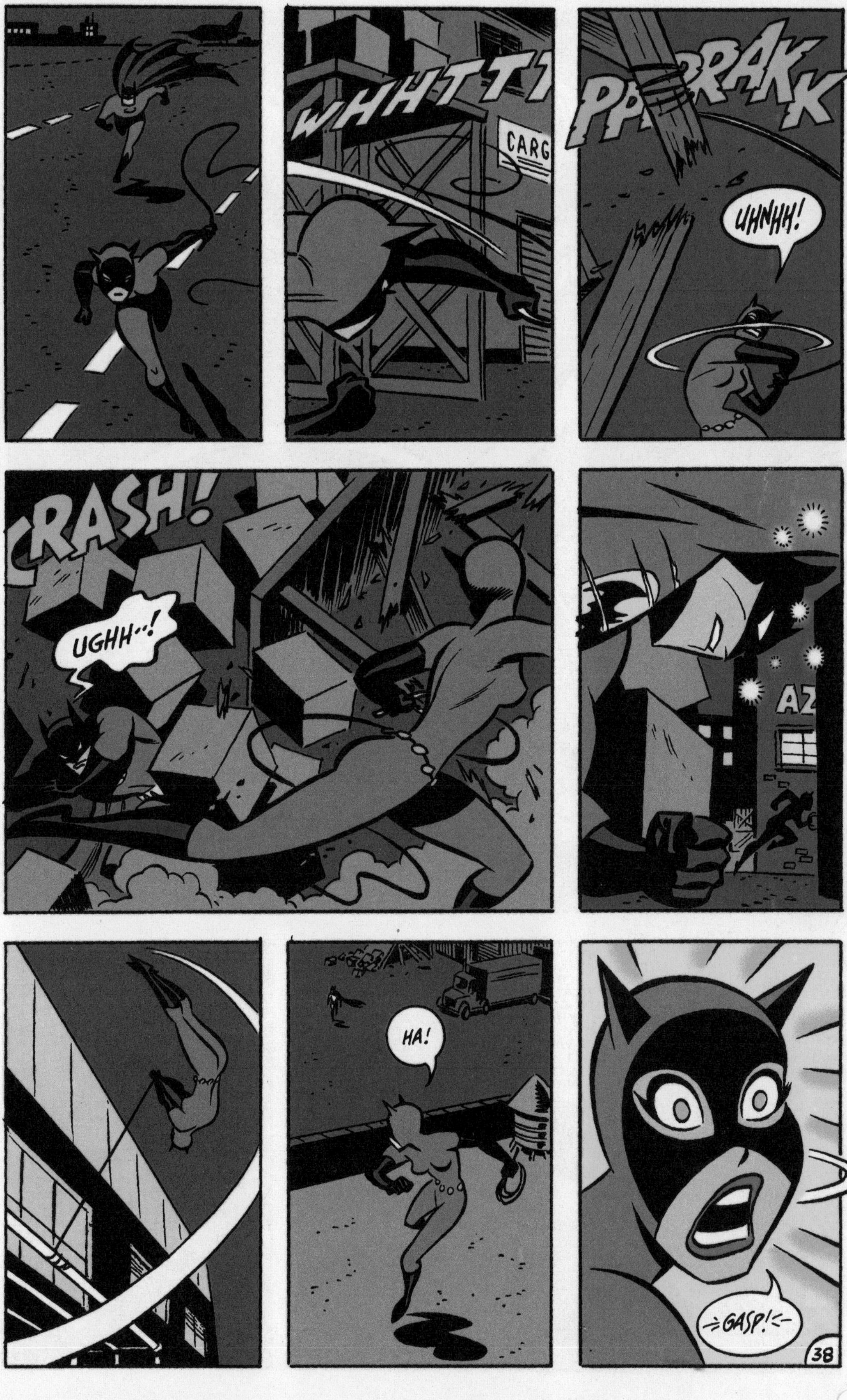
WHHTTT
PPBRAKK
CARG
UHNHH!
CRASH!
UGHH--!
AZ
HA!
GASP!
38

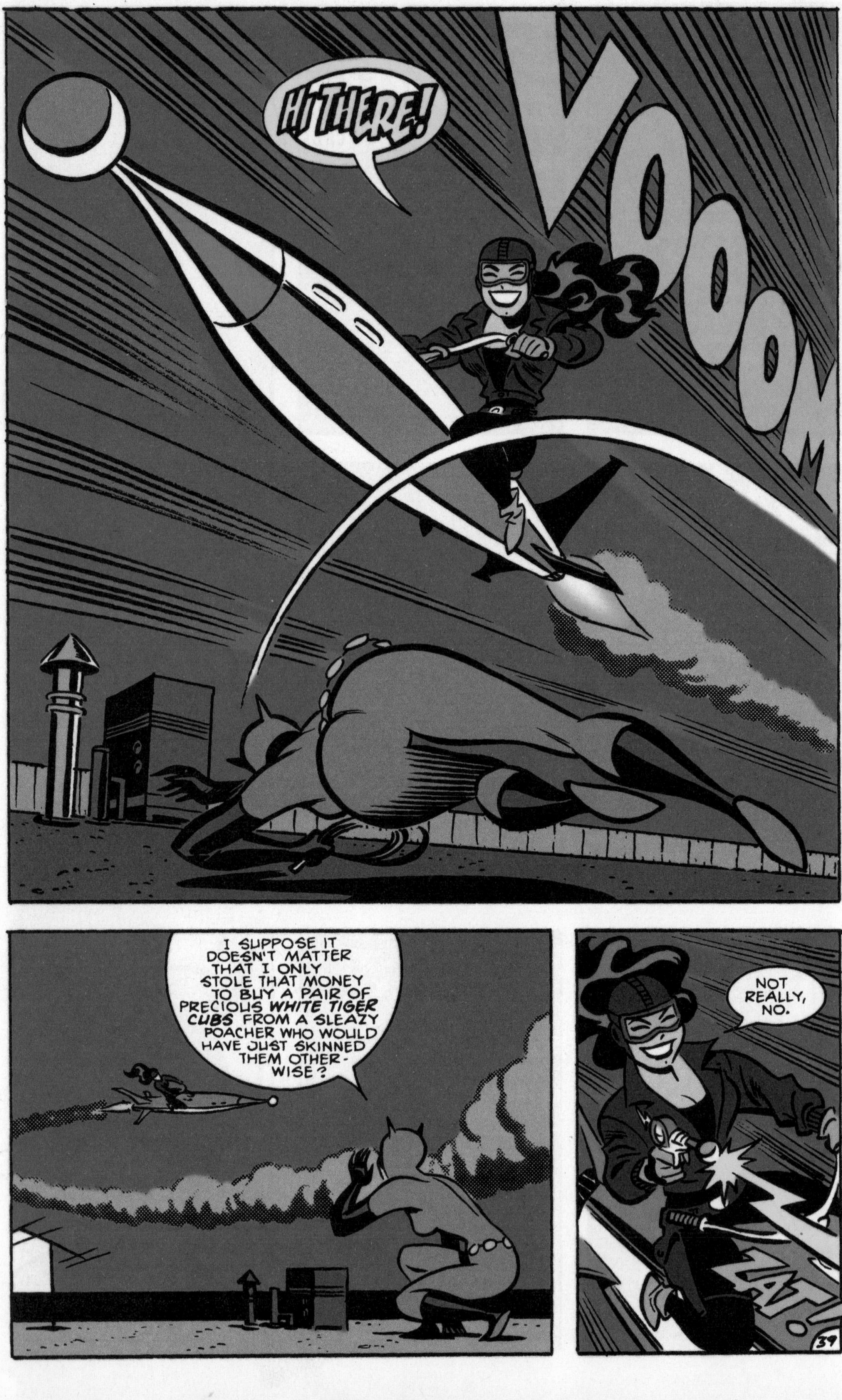
HI THERE!
VOOOOM
I SUPPOSE IT DOESN'T MATTER THAT I ONLY STOLE THAT MONEY TO BUY A PAIR OF PRECIOUS WHITE TIGER CUBS FROM A SLEAZY POACHER WHO WOULD HAVE JUST SKINNED THEM OTHER-WISE?
NOT REALLY, NO.
ZZAT!

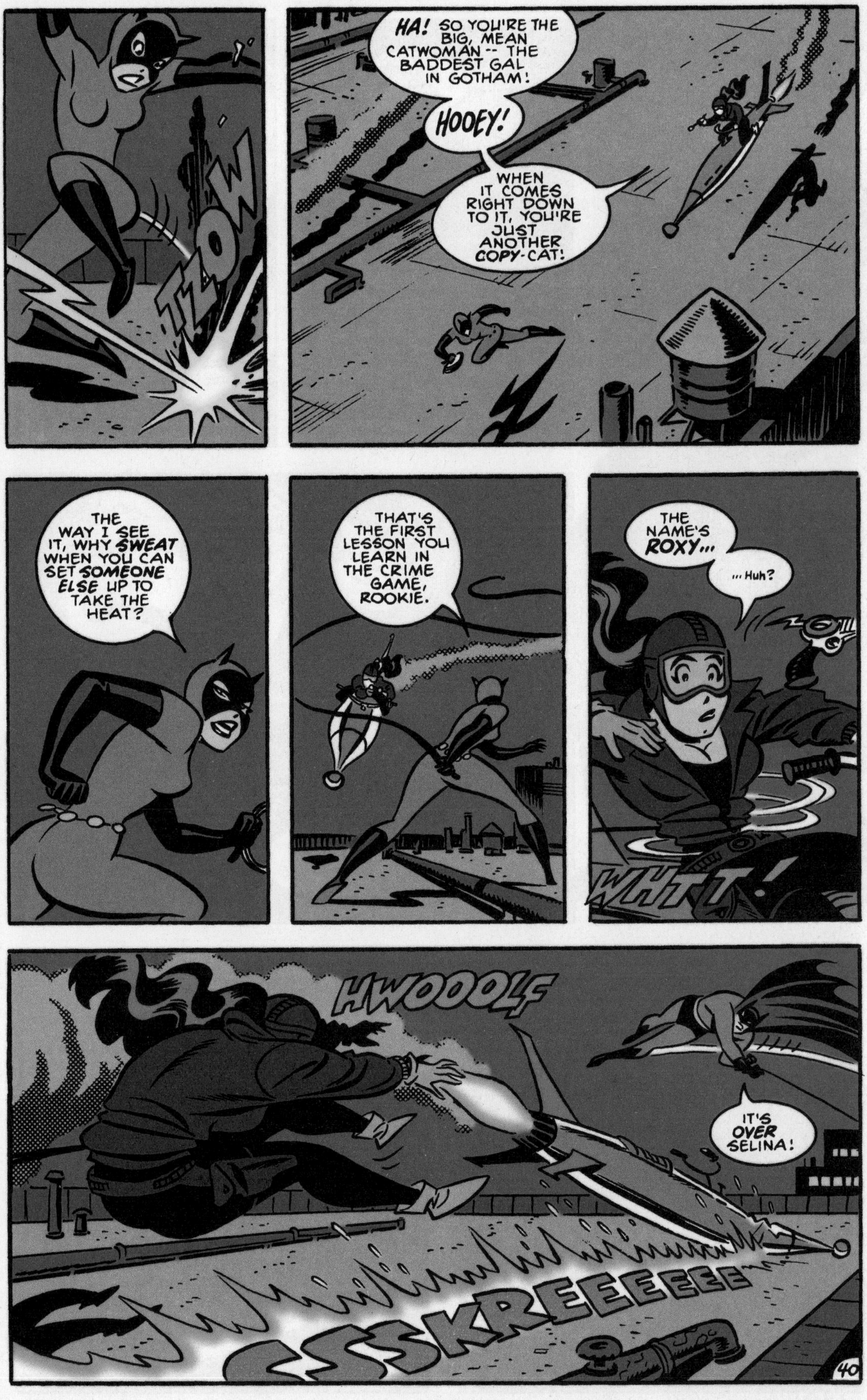
TZOW
HA! SO YOU'RE THE BIG, MEAN CATWOMAN -- THE BADDEST GAL IN GOTHAM!
HOOEY!
WHEN IT COMES RIGHT DOWN TO IT, YOU'RE JUST ANOTHER COPY-CAT!
THE WAY I SEE IT, WHY SWEAT WHEN YOU CAN SET SOMEONE ELSE UP TO TAKE THE HEAT?
THAT'S THE FIRST LESSON YOU LEARN IN THE CRIME GAME, ROOKIE.
THE NAME'S ROXY...
...Huh?
WHTT!
HWOOOLF
IT'S OVER SELINA!
CSSKREEEEEE
40

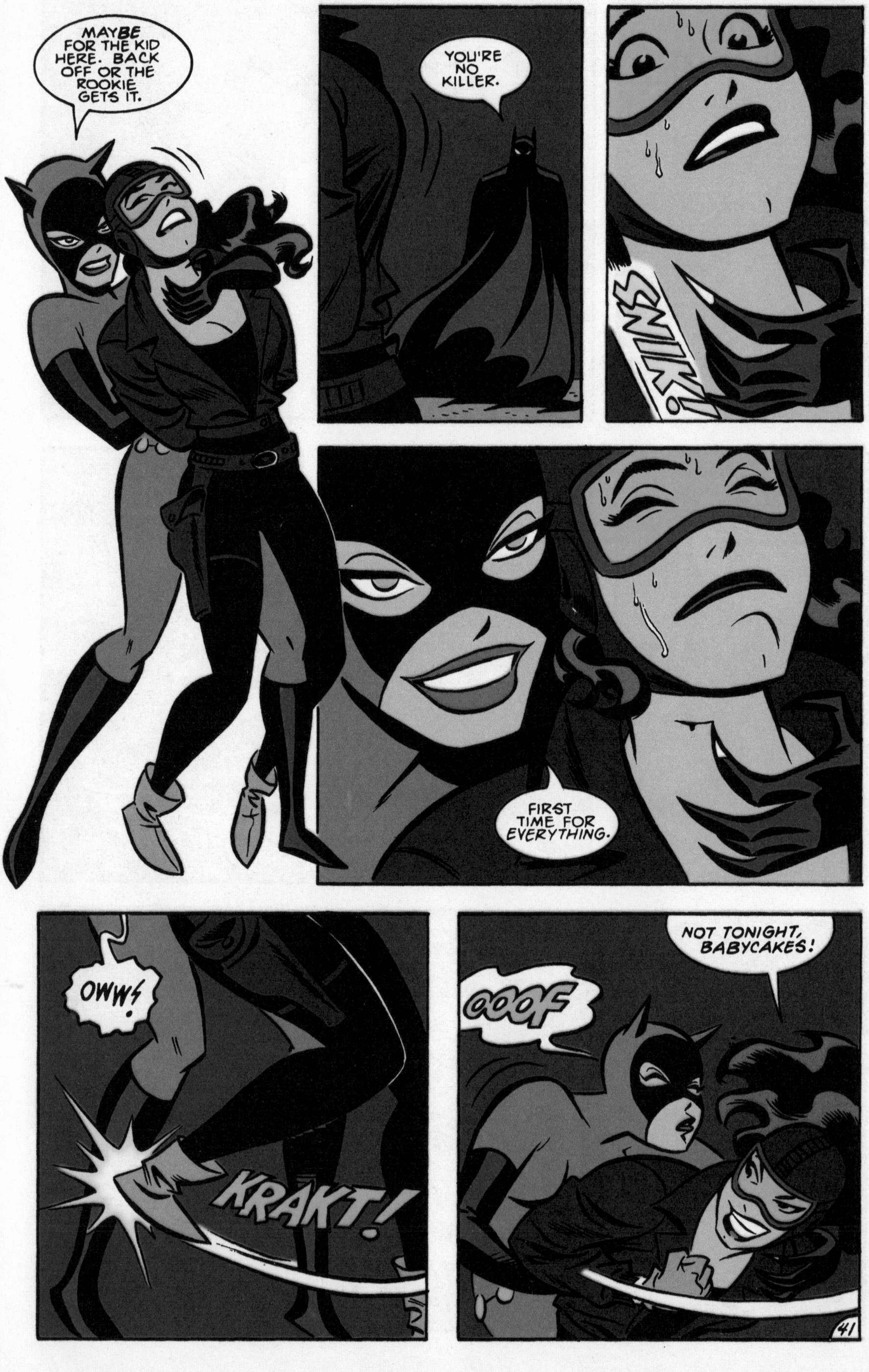
MAYBE FOR THE KID HERE. BACK OFF OR THE ROOKIE GETS IT.
YOU'RE NO KILLER.
SNIK!
FIRST TIME FOR EVERYTHING.
OWW!
KRAKT!
OOOF
NOT TONIGHT, BABYCAKES!
41

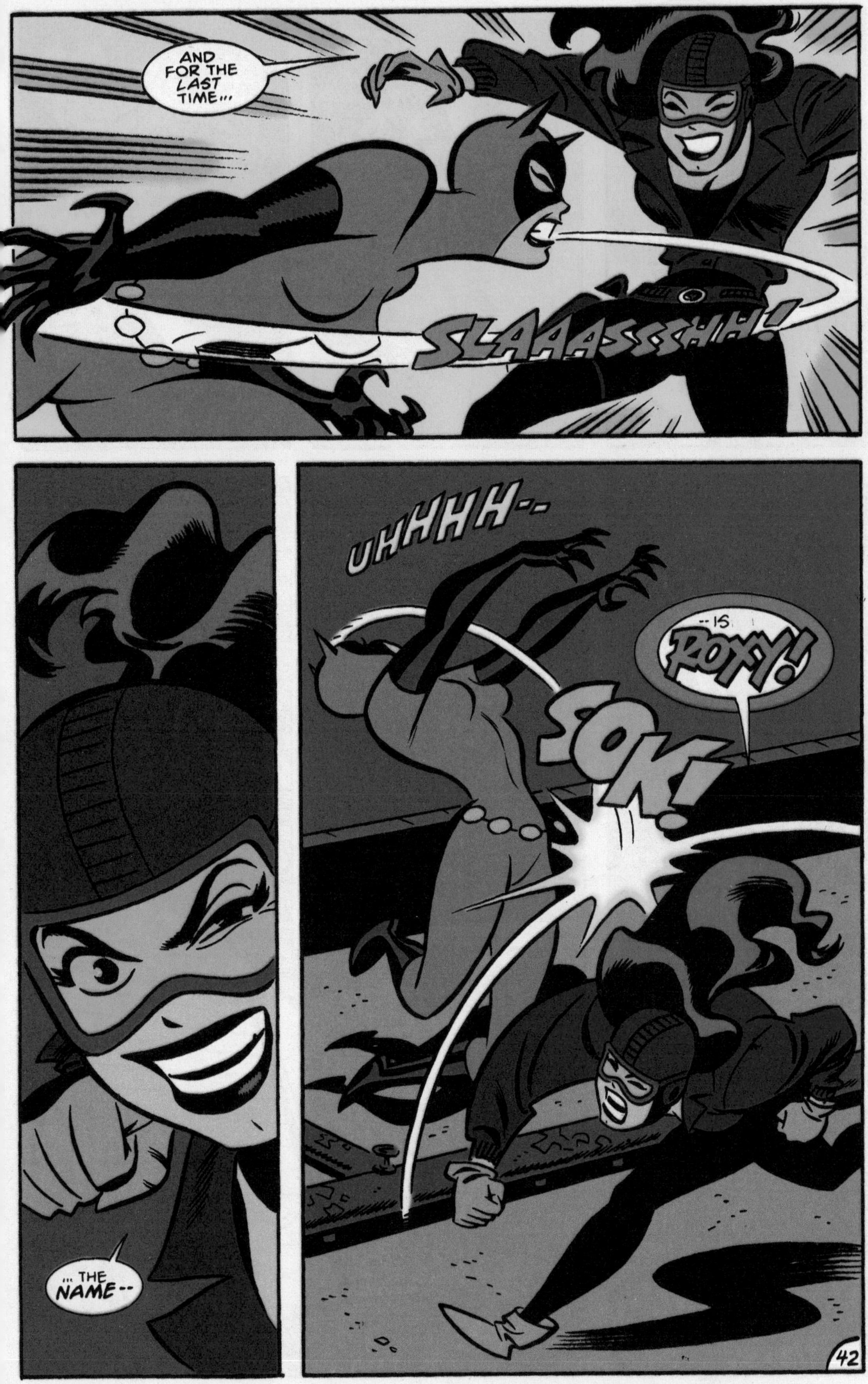
AND FOR THE LAST TIME...
SLAAASSSHH!
... THE NAME--
UHHHH--
--IS ROXY!
SOK!
42

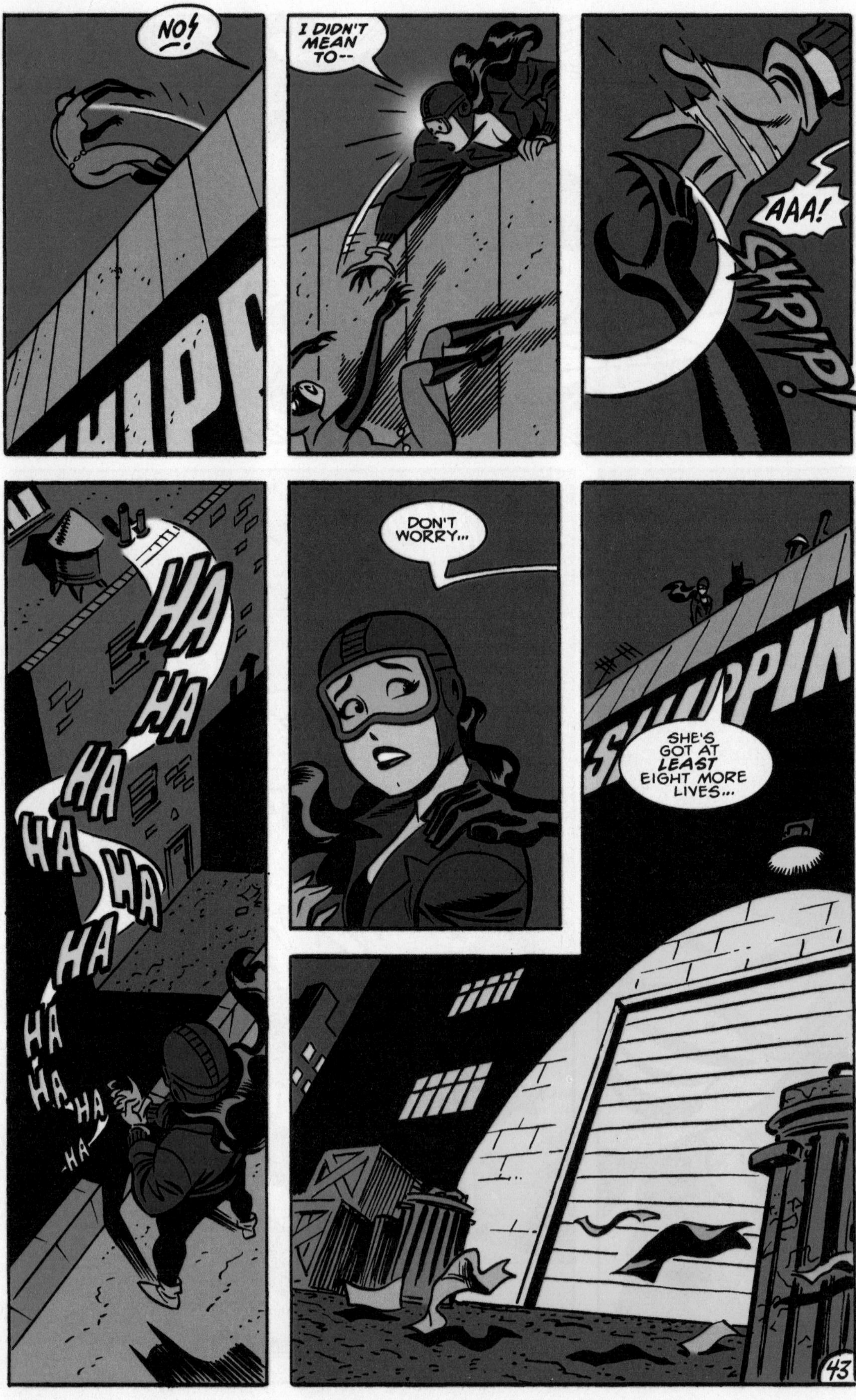
NO!
I DIDN'T MEAN TO--
AAA!
SHRIP!
HA HA HA HA HA HA HA HA HA HA HA
DON'T WORRY...
SHE'S GOT AT LEAST EIGHT MORE LIVES...

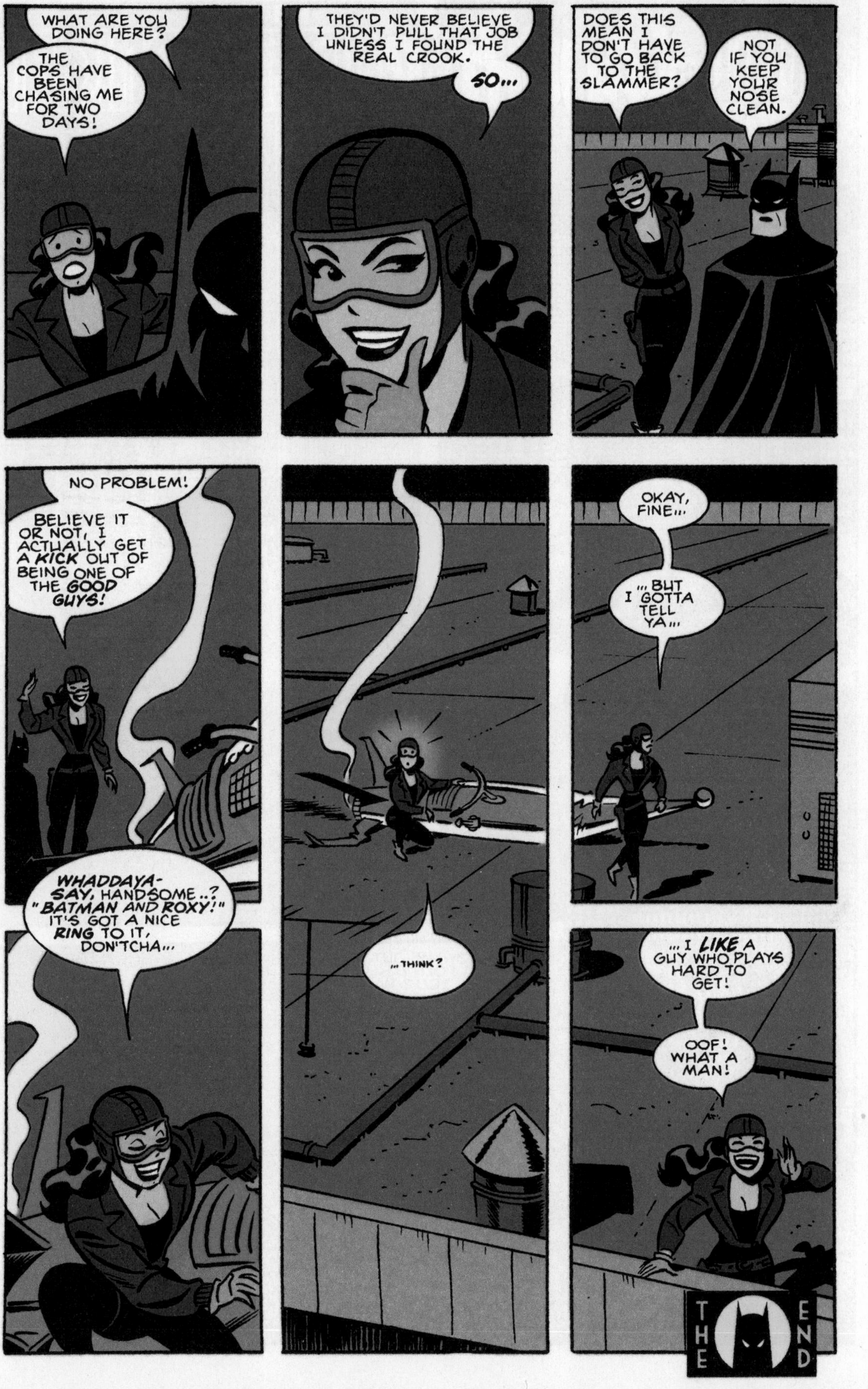
WHAT ARE YOU DOING HERE?
THE COPS HAVE BEEN CHASING ME FOR TWO DAYS!
THEY'D NEVER BELIEVE I DIDN'T PULL THAT JOB UNLESS I FOUND THE REAL CROOK.
SO...
DOES THIS MEAN I DON'T HAVE TO GO BACK TO THE SLAMMER?
NOT IF YOU KEEP YOUR NOSE CLEAN.
NO PROBLEM!
BELIEVE IT OR NOT, I ACTUALLY GET A KICK OUT OF BEING ONE OF THE GOOD GUYS!
WHADDAYA-SAY, HANDSOME..? "BATMAN AND ROXY!" IT'S GOT A NICE RING TO IT, DON'TCHA...
...THINK?
OKAY, FINE...
...BUT I GOTTA TELL YA...
...I LIKE A GUY WHO PLAYS HARD TO GET!
OOF! WHAT A MAN!
THE END

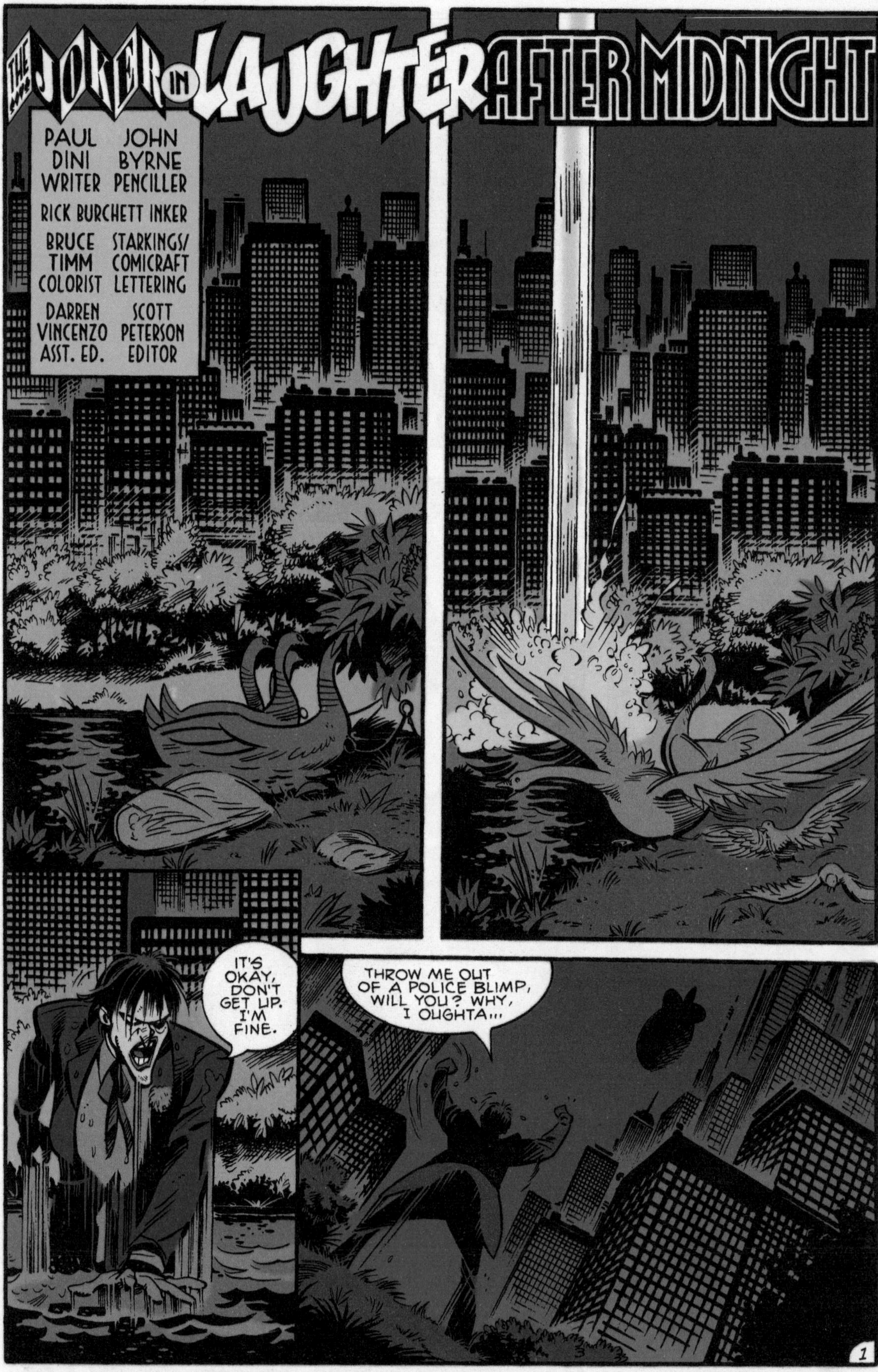

THE JOKER IN LAUGHTER AFTER MIDNIGHT
PAUL DINI WRITER
JOHN BYRNE PENCILLER
RICK BURCHETT INKER
BRUCE TIMM COLORIST
STARKINGS/ COMICRAFT LETTERING
DARREN VINCENZO ASST. ED.
SCOTT PETERSON EDITOR
IT'S OKAY, DON'T GET UP. I'M FINE.
THROW ME OUT OF A POLICE BLIMP, WILL YOU? WHY, I OUGHTA...

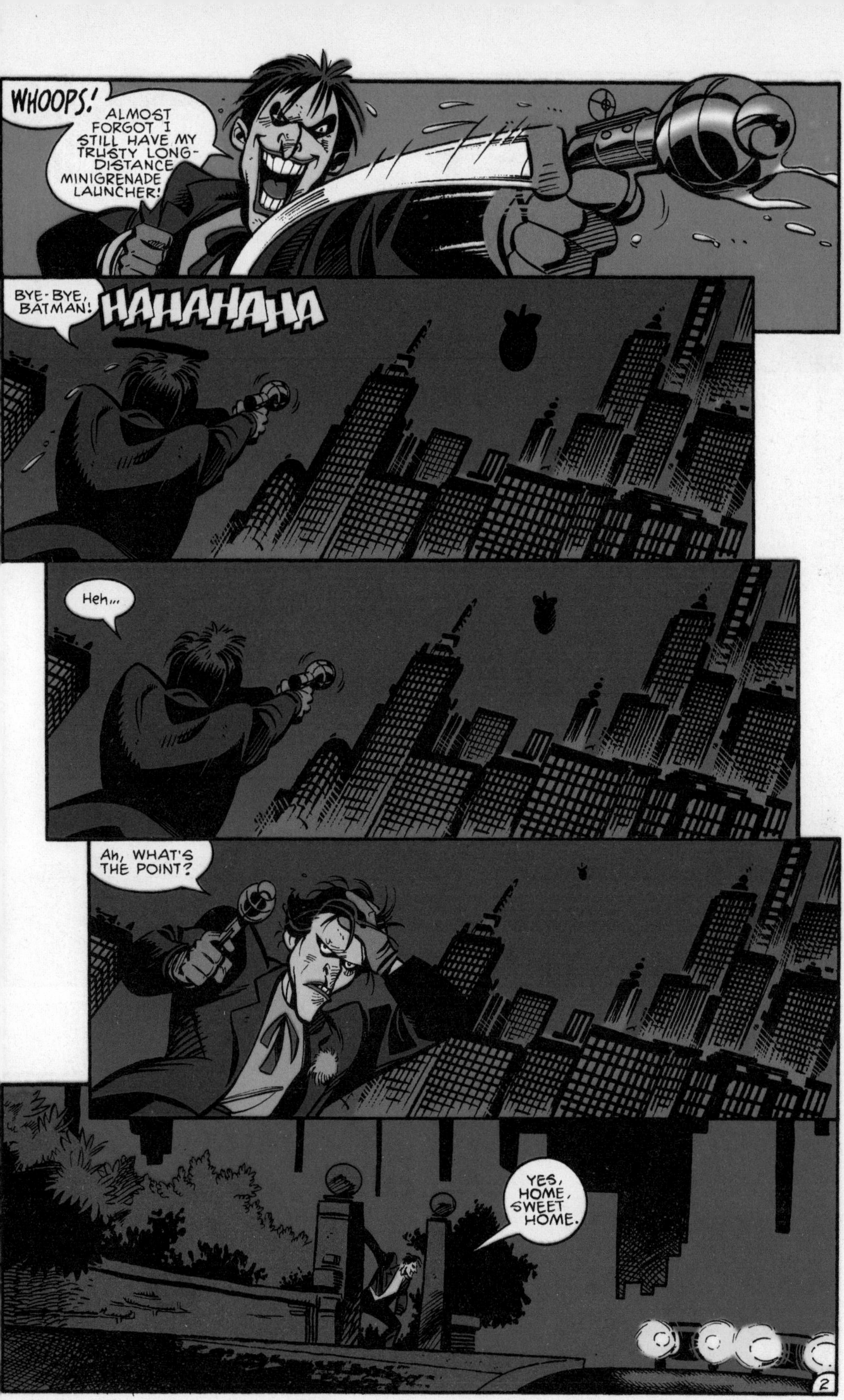

WHOOPS! ALMOST FORGOT I STILL HAVE MY TRUSTY LONG-DISTANCE MINIGRENADE LAUNCHER!
BYE-BYE, BATMAN!
HAHAHAHA
Heh...
Ah, WHAT'S THE POINT?
YES, HOME, SWEET HOME.

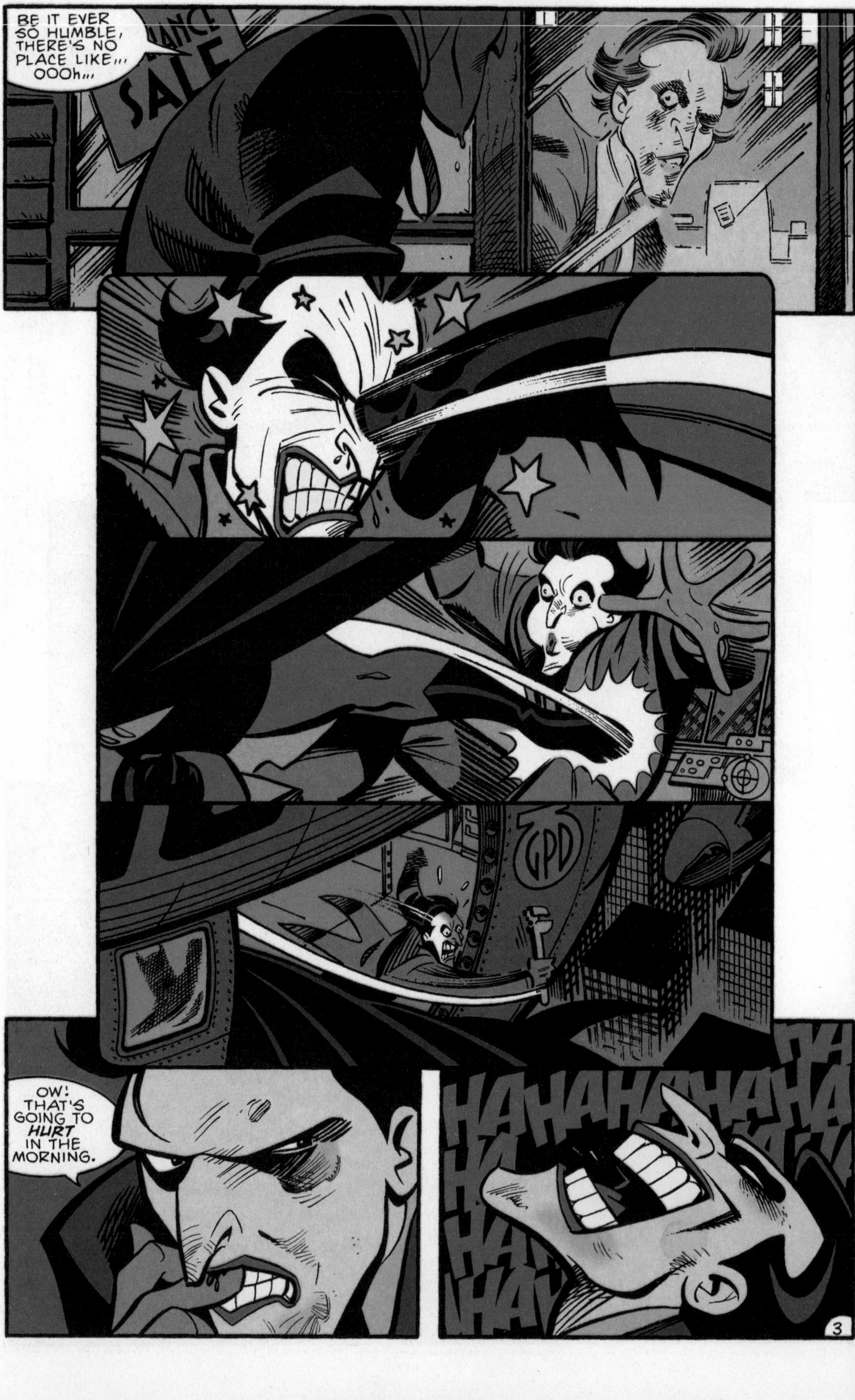
BE IT EVER SO HUMBLE, THERE'S NO PLACE LIKE... OOOh...
SALE
GPD
OW! THAT'S GOING TO HURT IN THE MORNING.
HAHAHAHAHAHA

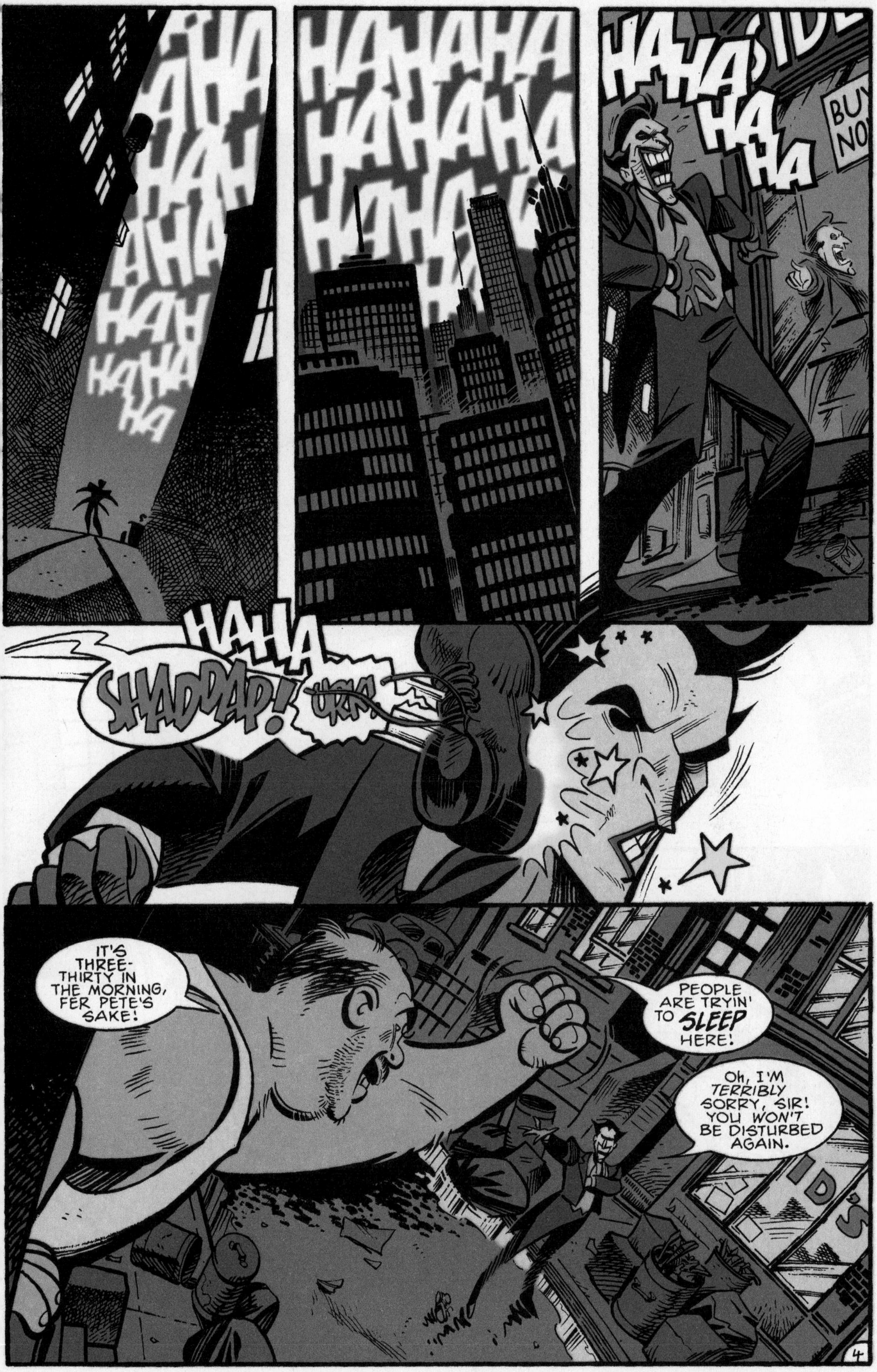

HAHA HAHA HAHA HAHA HAHA HAHA HA
HAHAHAHA HAHAHAHA
HAHAHA HA HA
BUY NO
HAHA
SHADDAP!
URK
IT'S THREE-THIRTY IN THE MORNING, FER PETE'S SAKE!
PEOPLE ARE TRYIN' TO SLEEP HERE!
Oh, I'M TERRIBLY SORRY, SIR! YOU WON'T BE DISTURBED AGAIN.

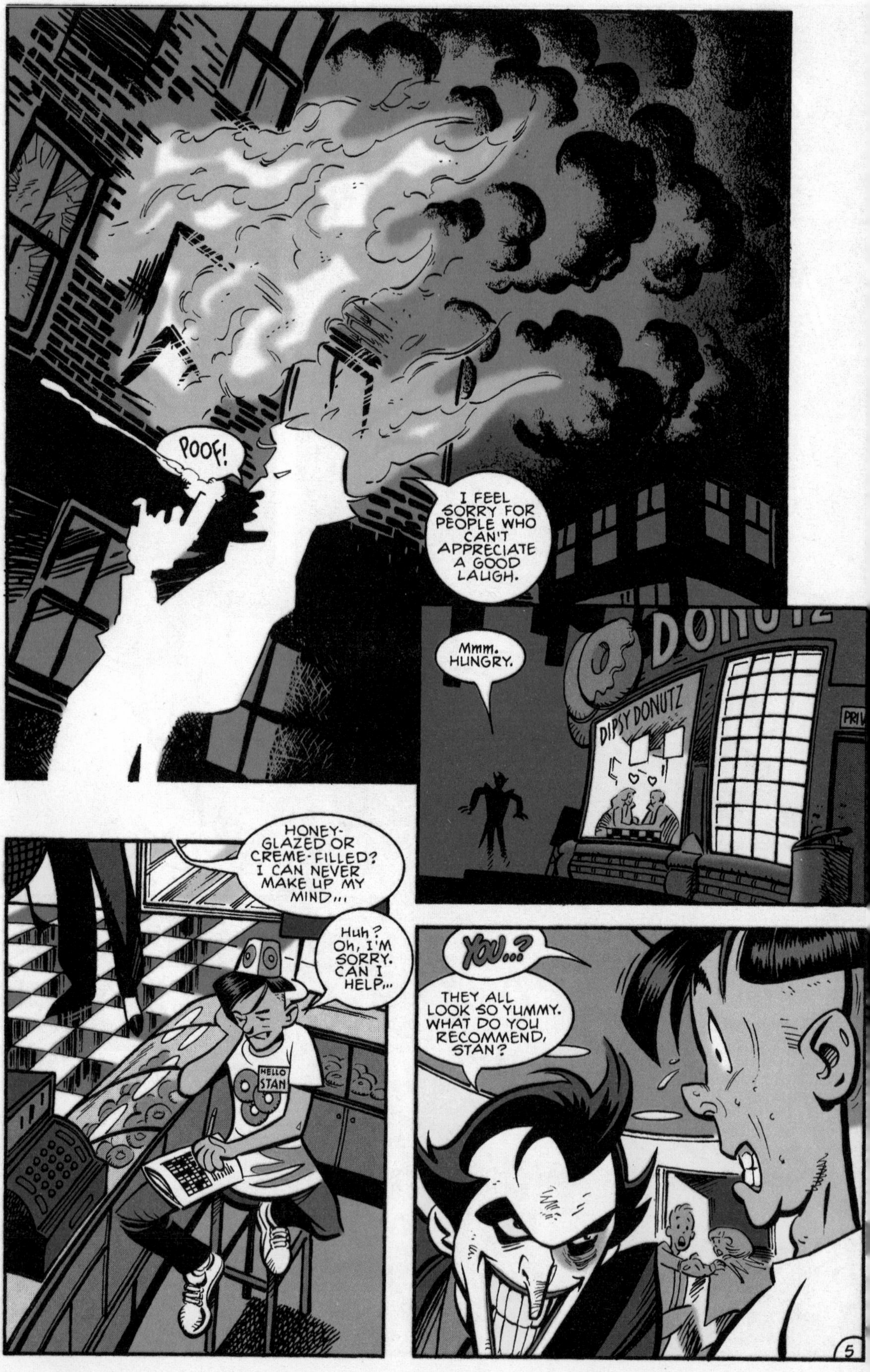
POOF!
I FEEL SORRY FOR PEOPLE WHO CAN'T APPRECIATE A GOOD LAUGH.
Mmm. HUNGRY.
DONUTZ
DIPSY DONUTZ
PRIV
HONEY-GLAZED OR CREME-FILLED? I CAN NEVER MAKE UP MY MIND...
Huh? Oh, I'M SORRY. CAN I HELP...
HELLO STAN
YOU..?
THEY ALL LOOK SO YUMMY. WHAT DO YOU RECOMMEND, STAN?

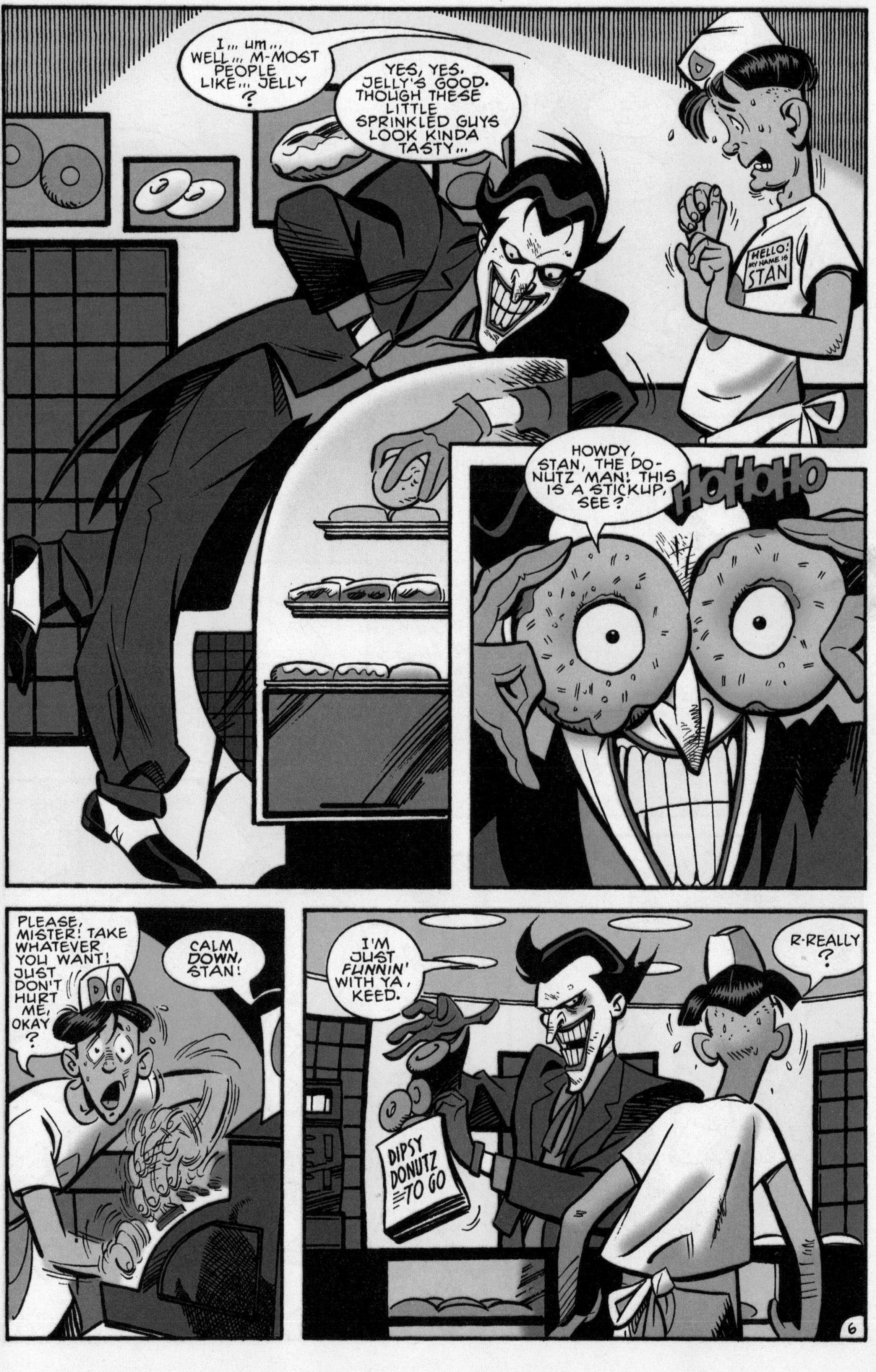

I... um... WELL... M-MOST PEOPLE LIKE... JELLY ?
YES, YES. JELLY'S GOOD. THOUGH THESE LITTLE SPRINKLED GUYS LOOK KINDA TASTY...
HELLO! MY NAME IS STAN
HOWDY, STAN, THE DO-NUTZ MAN! THIS IS A STICKUP, SEE?
HOHOHO
PLEASE, MISTER! TAKE WHATEVER YOU WANT! JUST DON'T HURT ME, OKAY ?
CALM DOWN, STAN!
I'M JUST FUNNIN' WITH YA, KEED.
R-REALLY ?
DIPSY DONUTZ TO GO

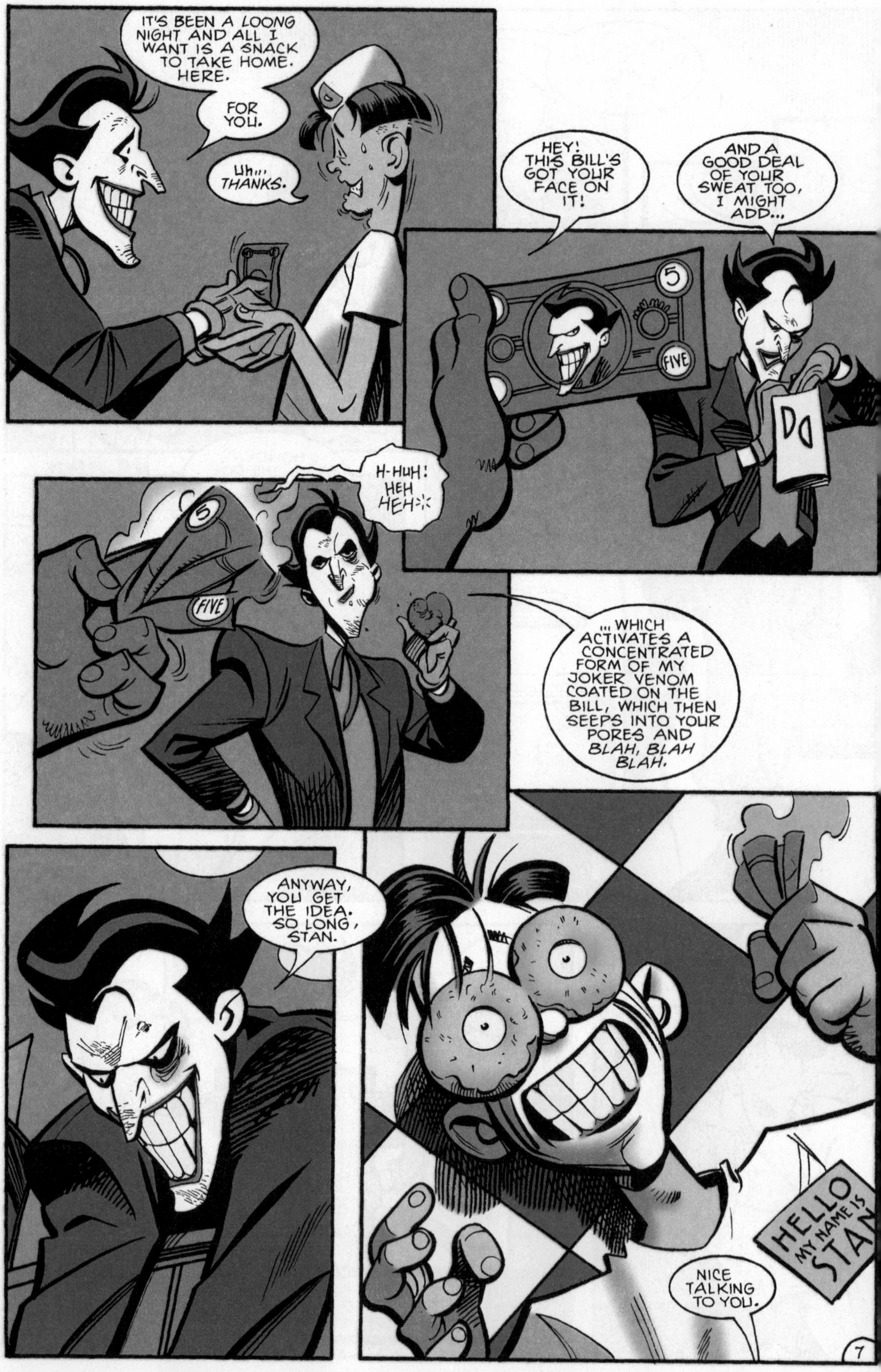
IT'S BEEN A LOONG NIGHT AND ALL I WANT IS A SNACK TO TAKE HOME. HERE.
FOR YOU.
Uh... THANKS.
HEY! THIS BILL'S GOT YOUR FACE ON IT!
AND A GOOD DEAL OF YOUR SWEAT TOO, I MIGHT ADD...
5
FIVE
DD
H-HUH! HEH HEH
...WHICH ACTIVATES A CONCENTRATED FORM OF MY JOKER VENOM COATED ON THE BILL, WHICH THEN SEEPS INTO YOUR PORES AND BLAH, BLAH BLAH.
ANYWAY, YOU GET THE IDEA. SO LONG, STAN.
HELLO MY NAME IS STAN
NICE TALKING TO YOU.

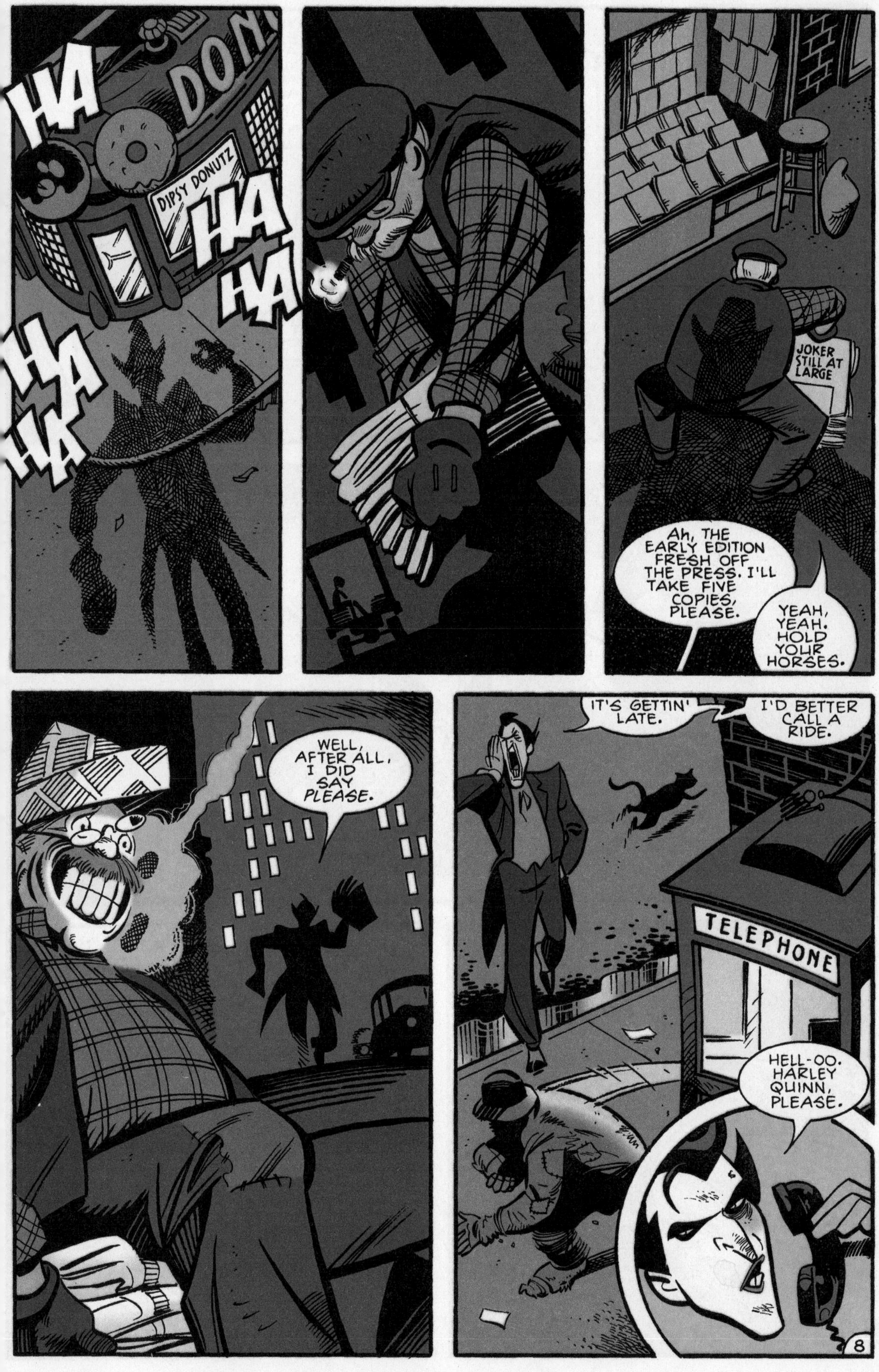
HA
DON
DIPSY DONUTZ
HA
HA
HA
HA
HA
JOKER STILL AT LARGE
Ah, THE EARLY EDITION FRESH OFF THE PRESS. I'LL TAKE FIVE COPIES, PLEASE.
YEAH, YEAH. HOLD YOUR HORSES.
WELL, AFTER ALL, I DID SAY PLEASE.
IT'S GETTIN' LATE.
I'D BETTER CALL A RIDE.
TELEPHONE
HELL-OO. HARLEY QUINN, PLEASE.
8

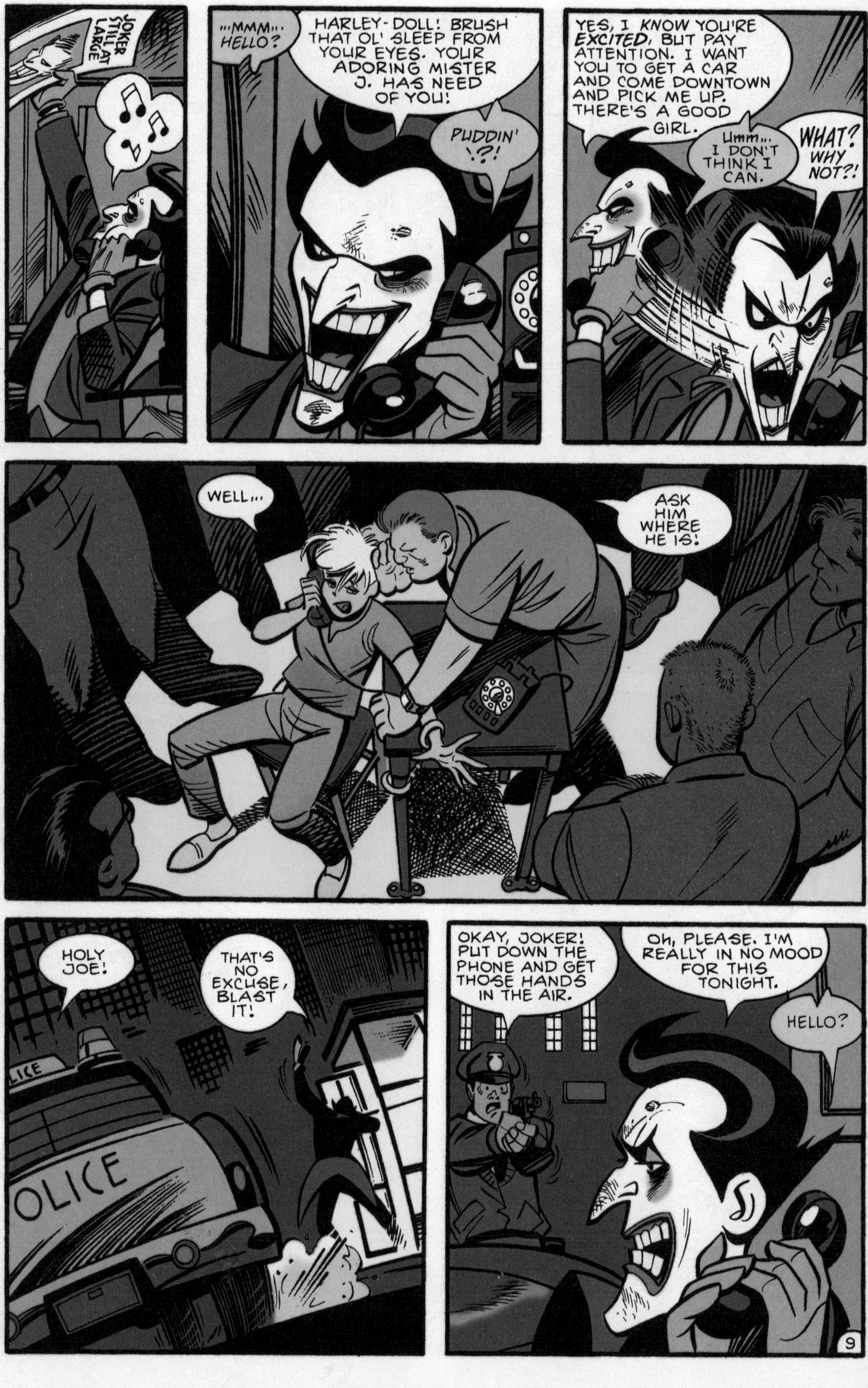
JOKER STILL AT LARGE
...MMM... HELLO?
HARLEY-DOLL! BRUSH THAT OL' SLEEP FROM YOUR EYES. YOUR ADORING MISTER J. HAS NEED OF YOU!
PUDDIN' !?!
YES, I KNOW YOU'RE EXCITED, BUT PAY ATTENTION. I WANT YOU TO GET A CAR AND COME DOWNTOWN AND PICK ME UP. THERE'S A GOOD GIRL.
Umm... I DON'T THINK I CAN.
WHAT? WHY NOT?!
WELL...
ASK HIM WHERE HE IS!
HOLY JOE!
THAT'S NO EXCUSE, BLAST IT!
OLICE
OKAY, JOKER! PUT DOWN THE PHONE AND GET THOSE HANDS IN THE AIR.
Oh, PLEASE. I'M REALLY IN NO MOOD FOR THIS TONIGHT.
HELLO?

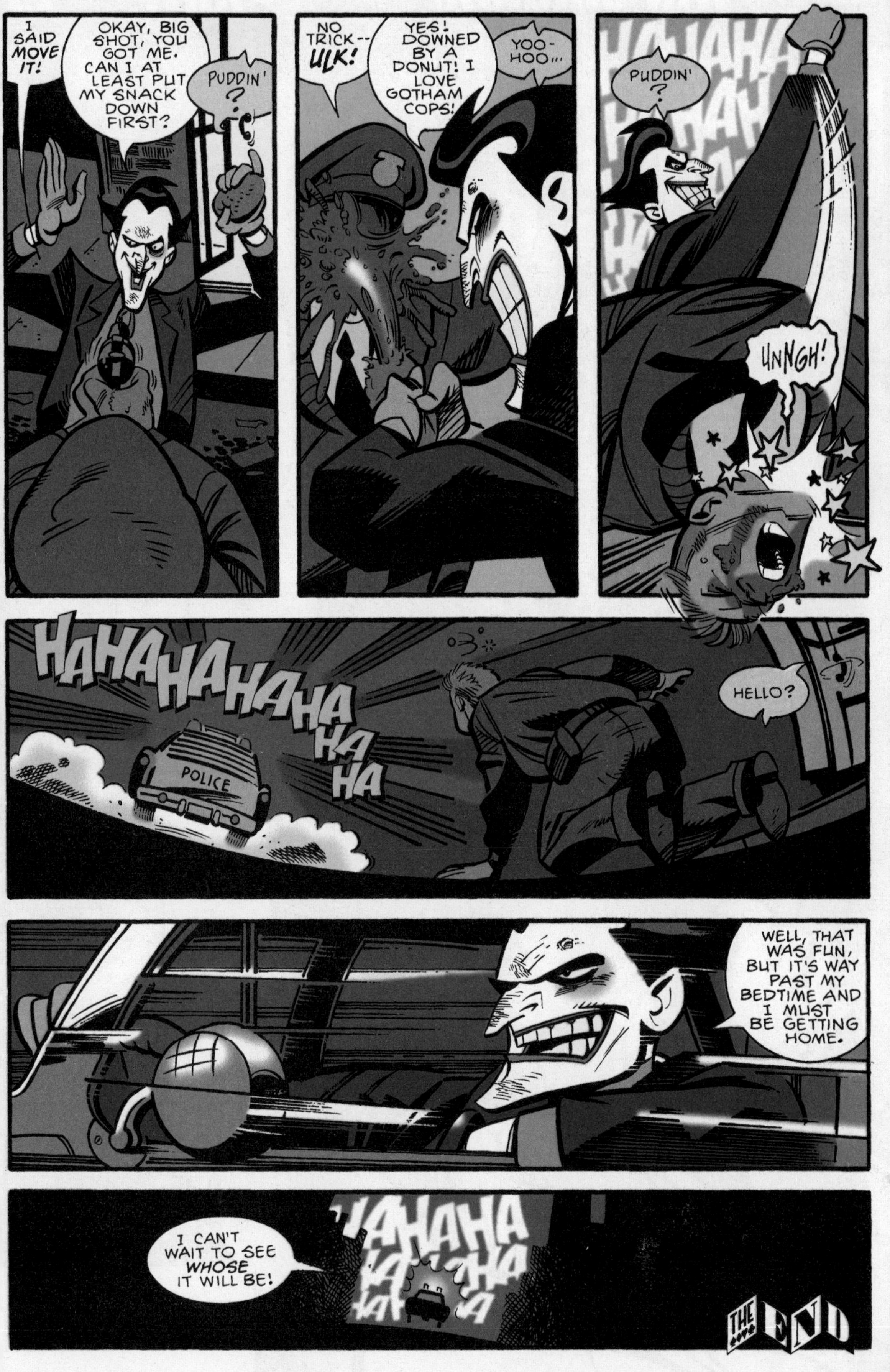
I SAID MOVE IT!
OKAY, BIG SHOT, YOU GOT ME. CAN I AT LEAST PUT MY SNACK DOWN FIRST?
PUDDIN' ?
NO TRICK-- ULK!
YES! DOWNED BY A DONUT! I LOVE GOTHAM COPS!
YOO-HOO...
HAHAHAHAHA
PUDDIN' ?
UNNGH!
HAHAHAHAHAHAHAHA
POLICE
HELLO?
WELL, THAT WAS FUN, BUT IT'S WAY PAST MY BEDTIME AND I MUST BE GETTING HOME.
I CAN'T WAIT TO SEE WHOSE IT WILL BE!
HAHAHA HA HA HA HA HA
THE END

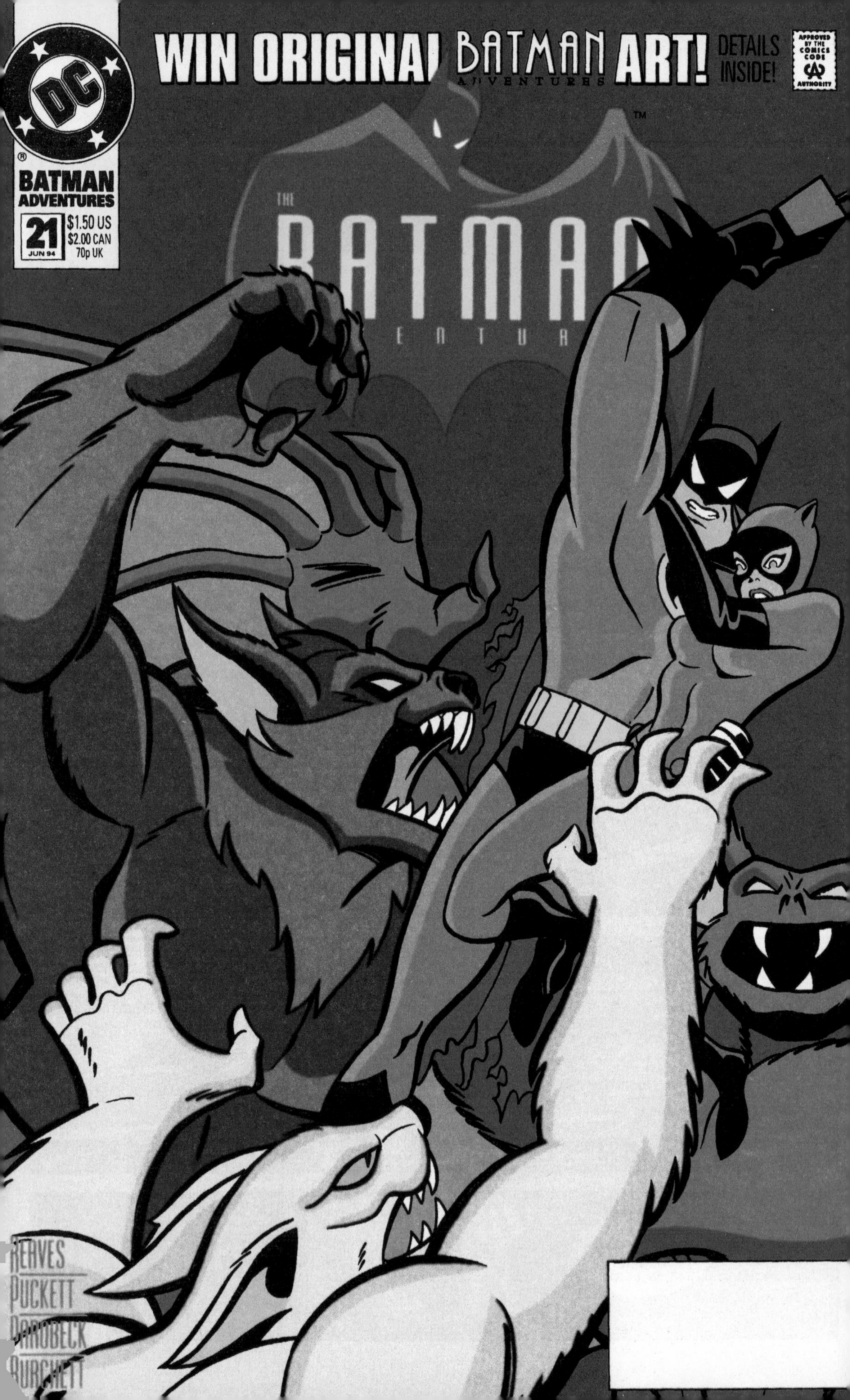
WIN ORIGINAL BATMAN ADVENTURES ART!
DETAILS INSIDE!
APPROVED BY THE COMICS CODE AUTHORITY
DC
BATMAN ADVENTURES
21
JUN 94
$1.50 US
$2.00 CAN
70p UK
THE
REAVES
PUCKETT

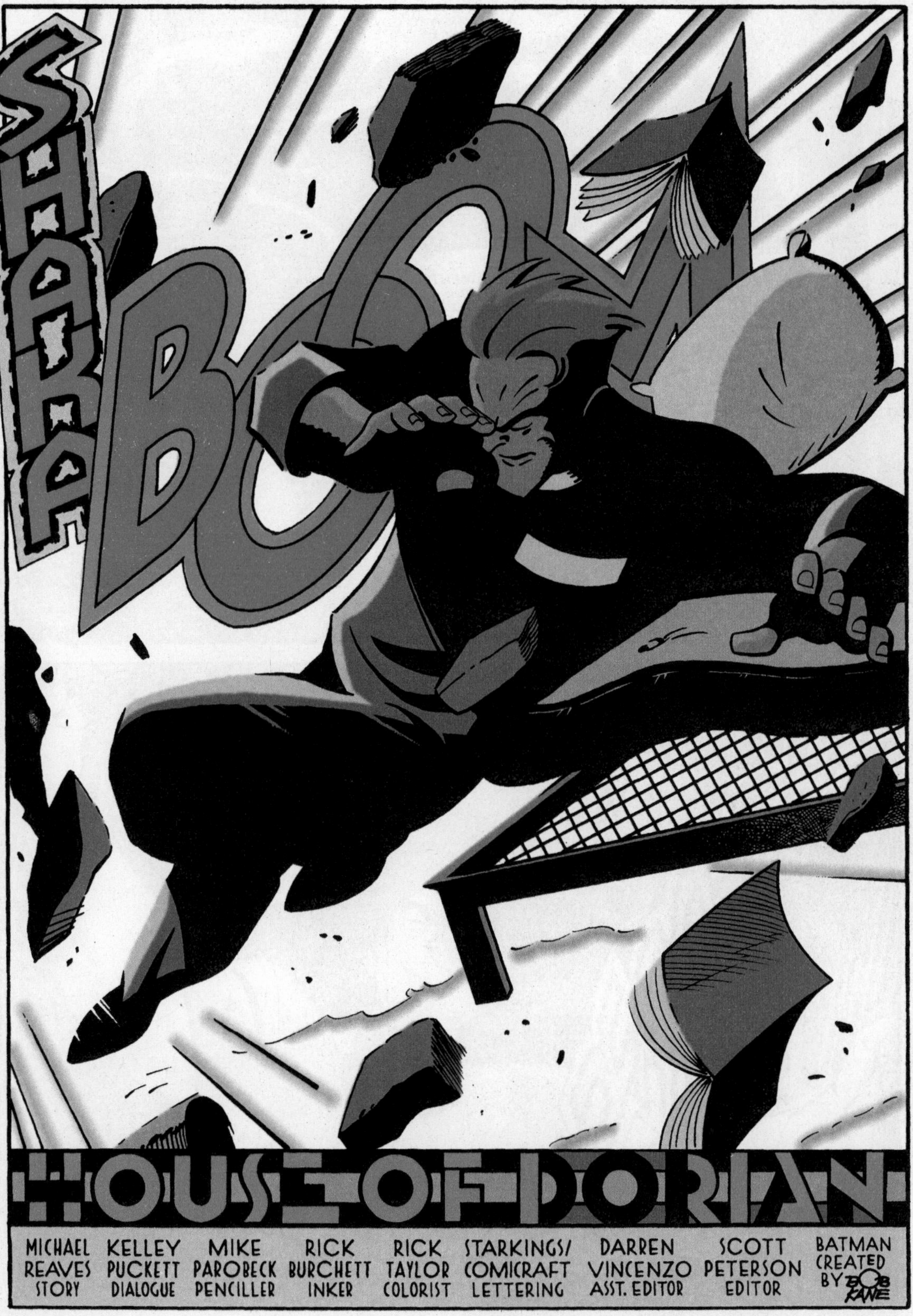
SHAKA
BOOM
HOUSE OF DORIAN
MICHAEL REAVES STORY
KELLEY PUCKETT DIALOGUE
MIKE PAROBECK PENCILLER
RICK BURCHETT INKER
RICK TAYLOR COLORIST
STARKINGS/ COMICRAFT LETTERING
DARREN VINCENZO ASST. EDITOR
SCOTT PETERSON EDITOR
BATMAN CREATED BY BOB KANE

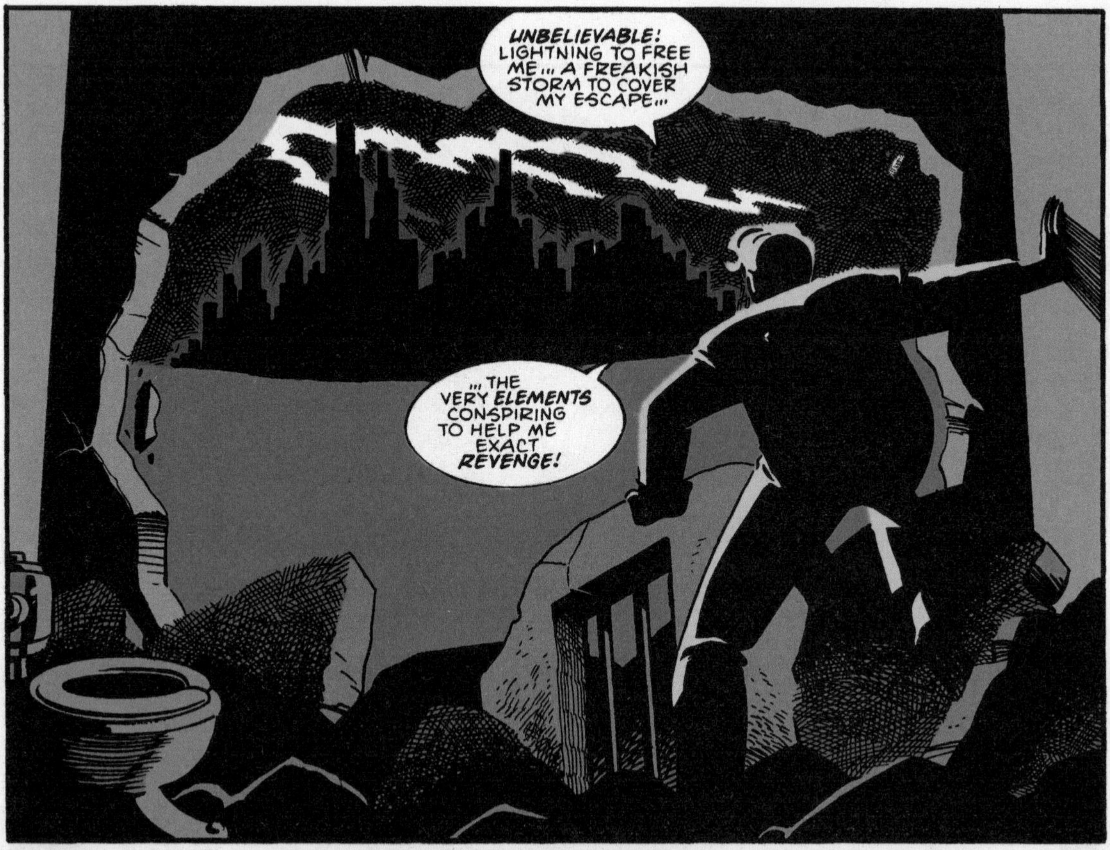
UNBELIEVABLE! LIGHTNING TO FREE ME... A FREAKISH STORM TO COVER MY ESCAPE...
...THE VERY ELEMENTS CONSPIRING TO HELP ME EXACT REVENGE!

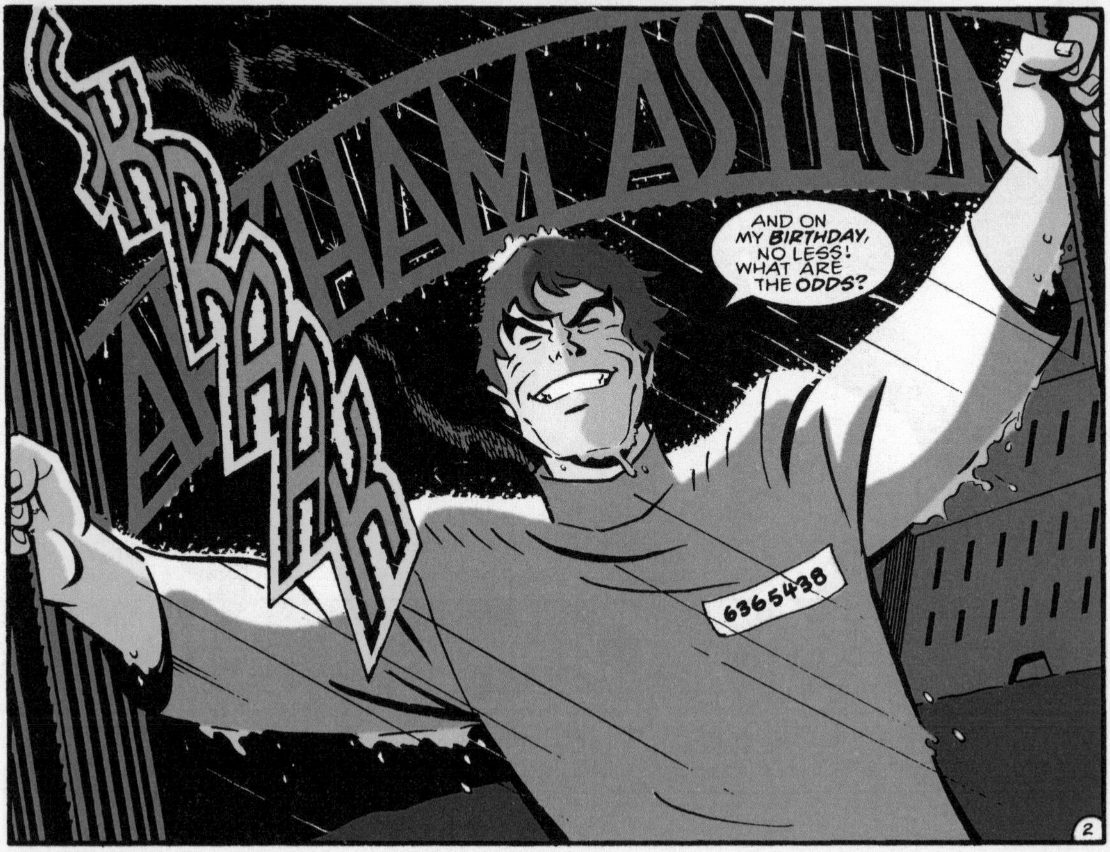
KRAAAK
ARKHAM ASYLUM
AND ON MY BIRTHDAY, NO LESS! WHAT ARE THE ODDS?
6365438

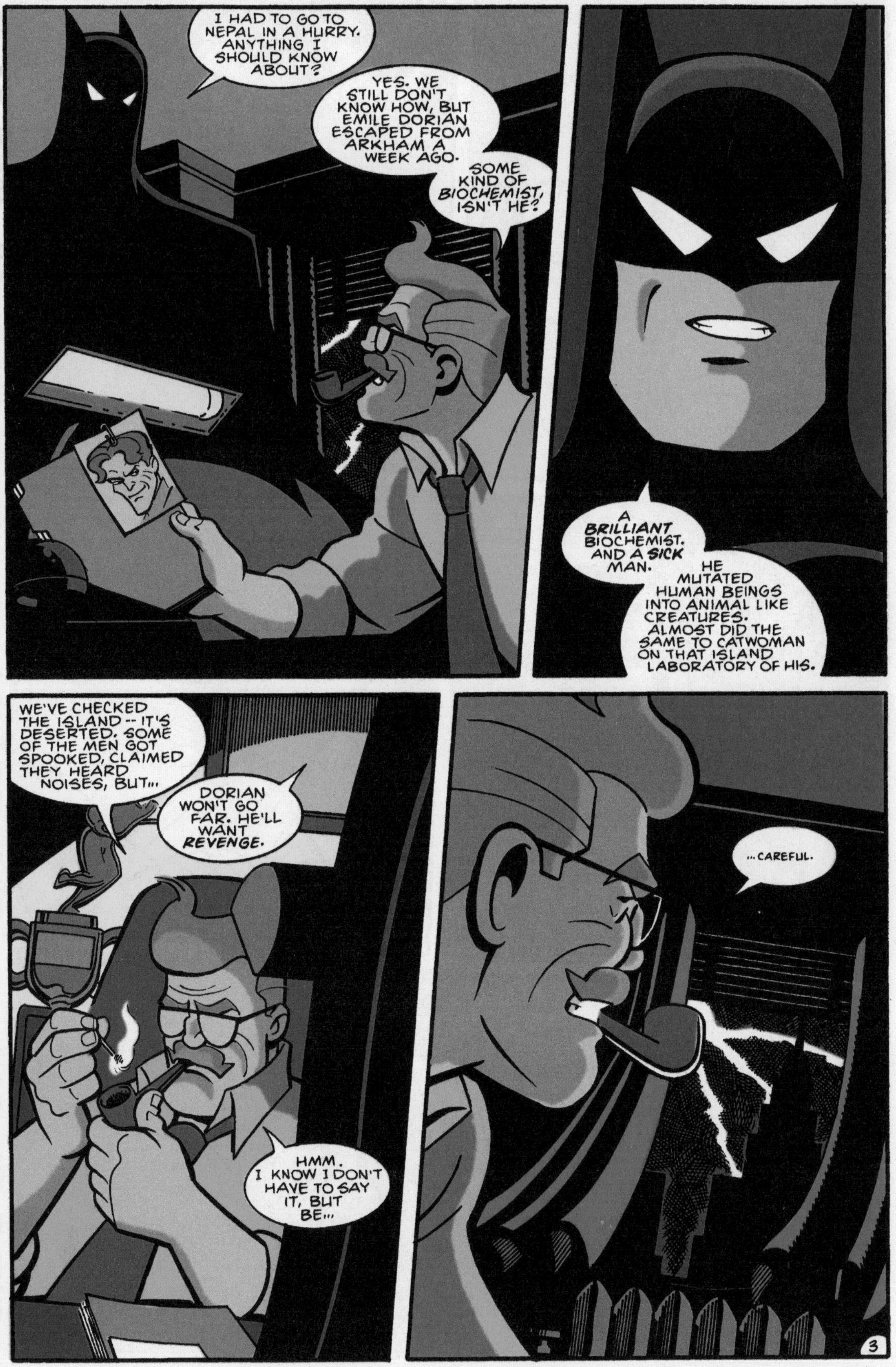
I HAD TO GO TO NEPAL IN A HURRY. ANYTHING I SHOULD KNOW ABOUT?
YES. WE STILL DON'T KNOW HOW, BUT EMILE DORIAN ESCAPED FROM ARKHAM A WEEK AGO.
SOME KIND OF BIOCHEMIST, ISN'T HE?
A BRILLIANT BIOCHEMIST. AND A SICK MAN.
HE MUTATED HUMAN BEINGS INTO ANIMAL LIKE CREATURES. ALMOST DID THE SAME TO CATWOMAN ON THAT ISLAND LABORATORY OF HIS.
WE'VE CHECKED THE ISLAND -- IT'S DESERTED. SOME OF THE MEN GOT SPOOKED, CLAIMED THEY HEARD NOISES, BUT...
DORIAN WON'T GO FAR. HE'LL WANT REVENGE.
HMM. I KNOW I DON'T HAVE TO SAY IT, BUT BE...
...CAREFUL.
3

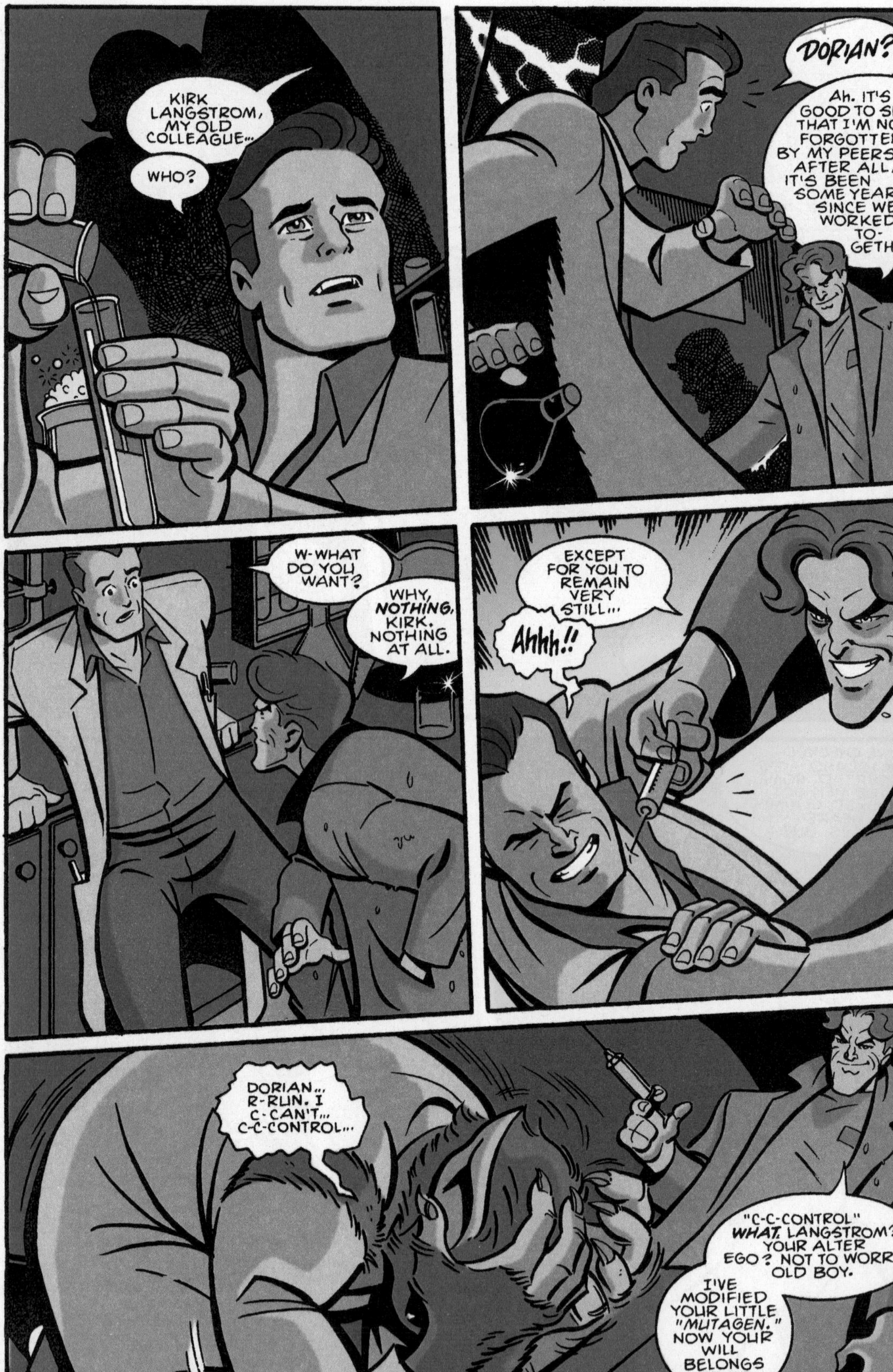

KIRK LANGSTROM, MY OLD COLLEAGUE...
WHO?
DORIAN?
Ah. IT'S GOOD TO SEE THAT I'M NOT FORGOTTEN BY MY PEERS. AFTER ALL, IT'S BEEN SOME YEARS SINCE WE WORKED TO-GETHER.
W-WHAT DO YOU WANT?
WHY, NOTHING, KIRK. NOTHING AT ALL.
EXCEPT FOR YOU TO REMAIN VERY STILL...
Ahhh!!
DORIAN... R-RUN. I C-CAN'T... C-C-CONTROL...
"C-C-CONTROL" WHAT, LANGSTROM? YOUR ALTER EGO? NOT TO WORRY, OLD BOY.
I'VE MODIFIED YOUR LITTLE "MUTAGEN." NOW YOUR WILL BELONGS TO ME.
4

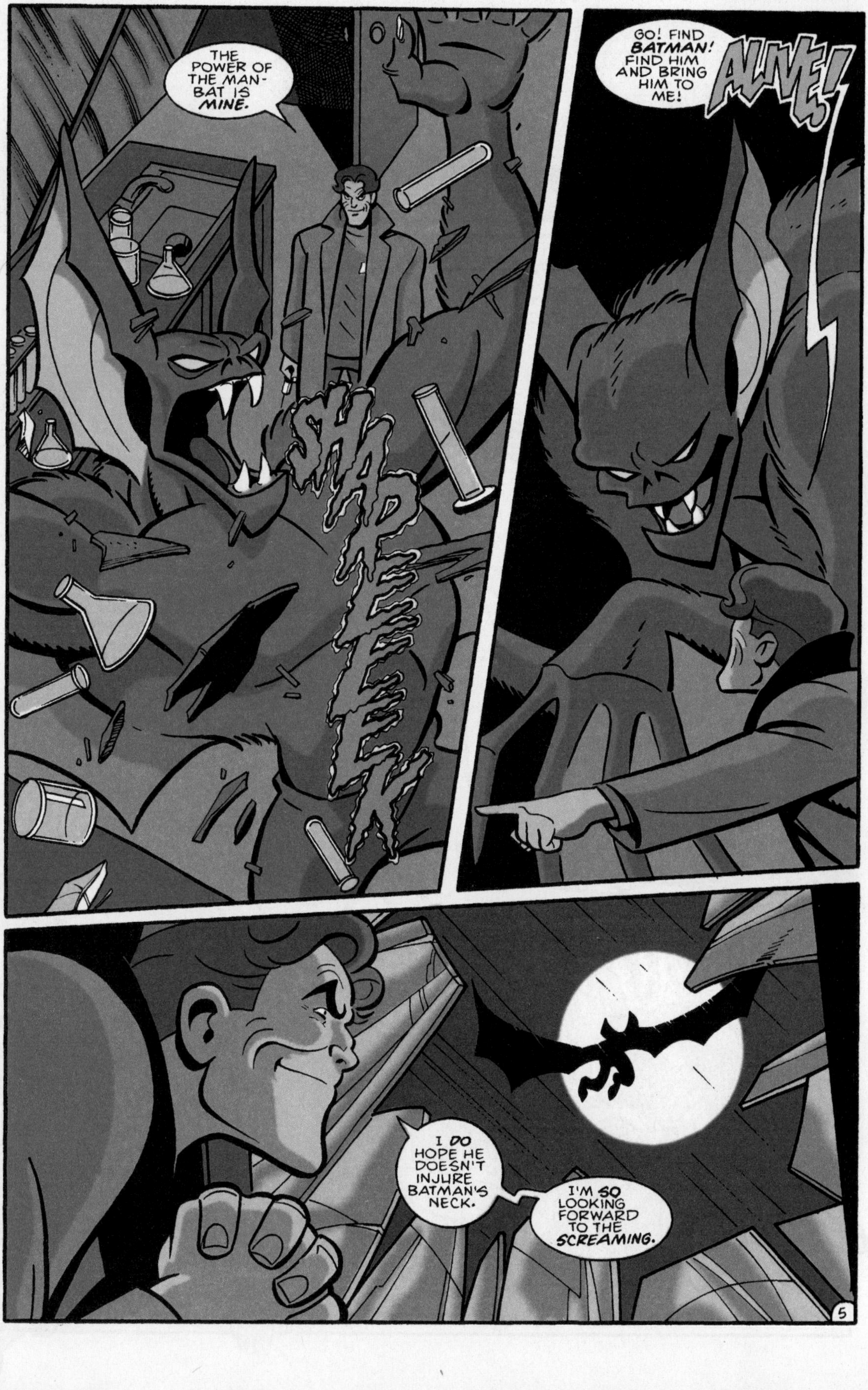
THE POWER OF THE MAN-BAT IS MINE.
SHA-REEEK
GO! FIND BATMAN! FIND HIM AND BRING HIM TO ME!
ALIVE!
I DO HOPE HE DOESN'T INJURE BATMAN'S NECK.
I'M SO LOOKING FORWARD TO THE SCREAMING.

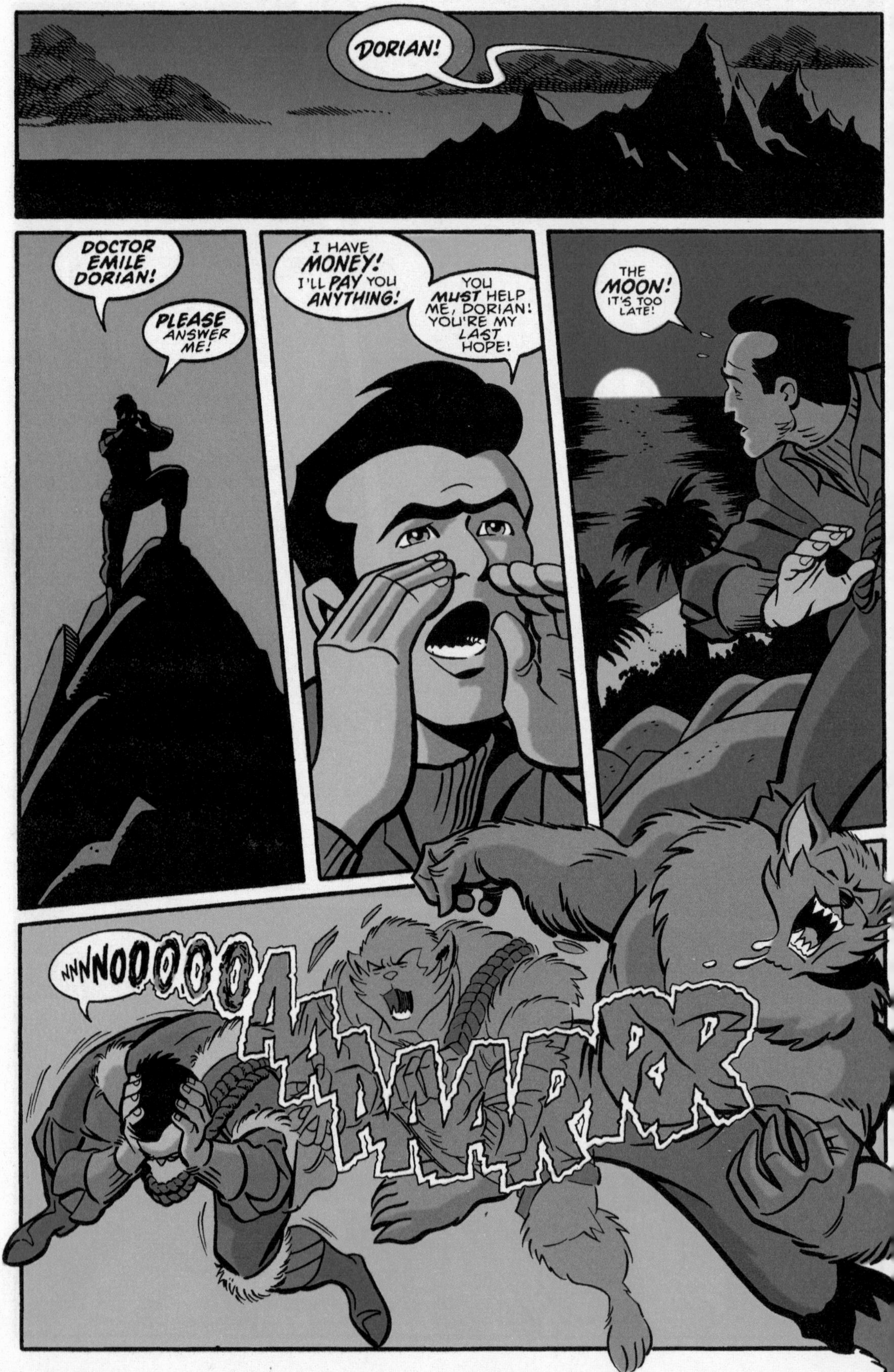
DORIAN!
DOCTOR EMILE DORIAN!
PLEASE ANSWER ME!
I HAVE MONEY! I'LL PAY YOU ANYTHING!
YOU MUST HELP ME, DORIAN! YOU'RE MY LAST HOPE!
THE MOON! IT'S TOO LATE!
NNNNOOOOO
AAAWWRRR

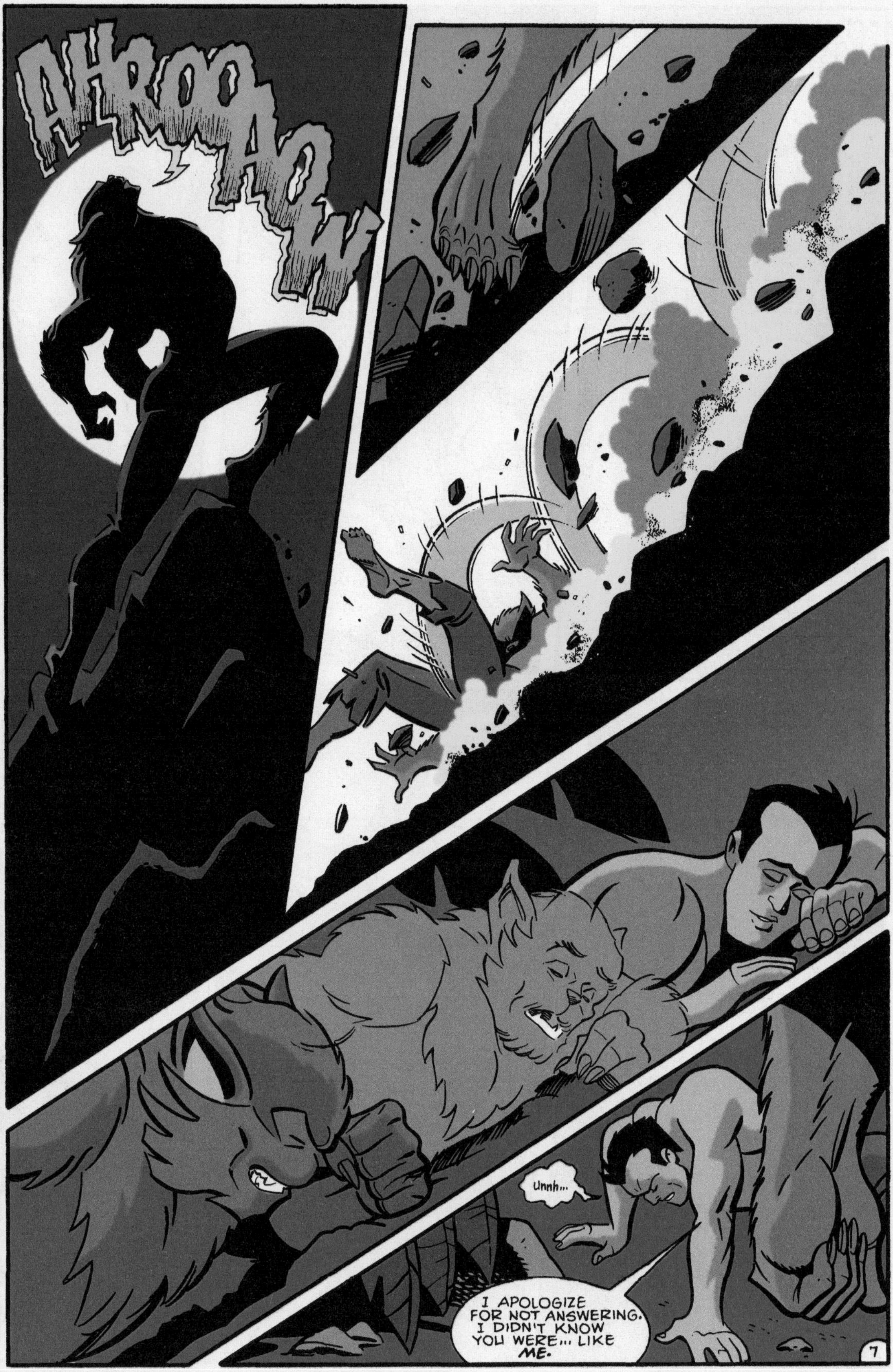
AHROOAOW
Unnh...
I APOLOGIZE FOR NOT ANSWERING. I DIDN'T KNOW YOU WERE... LIKE ME.
7

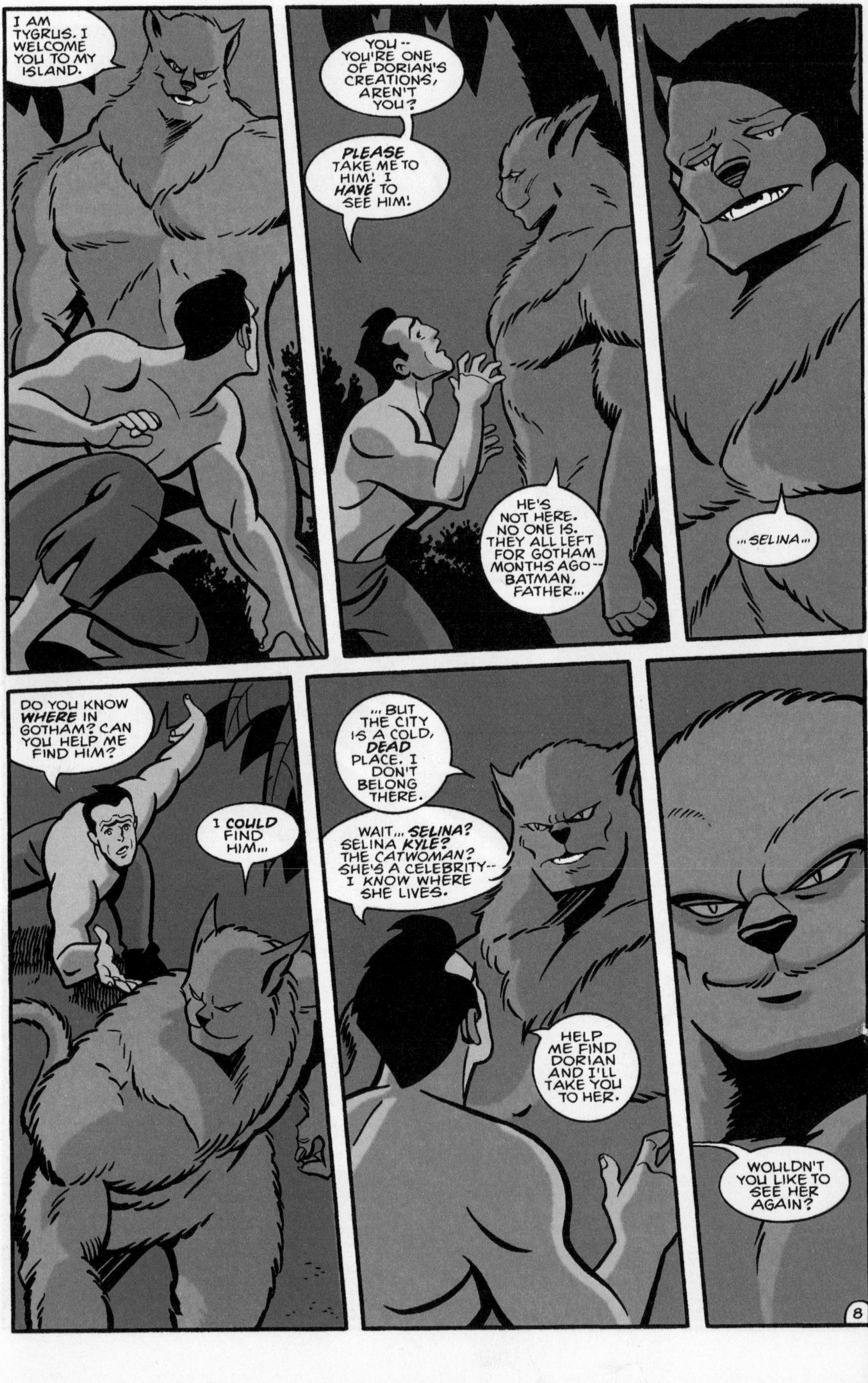
I AM TYGRUS. I WELCOME YOU TO MY ISLAND.
YOU -- YOU'RE ONE OF DORIAN'S CREATIONS, AREN'T YOU?
PLEASE TAKE ME TO HIM! I HAVE TO SEE HIM!
HE'S NOT HERE. NO ONE IS. THEY ALL LEFT FOR GOTHAM MONTHS AGO-- BATMAN, FATHER...
...SELINA...
DO YOU KNOW WHERE IN GOTHAM? CAN YOU HELP ME FIND HIM?
I COULD FIND HIM...
...BUT THE CITY IS A COLD, DEAD PLACE. I DON'T BELONG THERE.
WAIT... SELINA? SELINA KYLE? THE CATWOMAN? SHE'S A CELEBRITY-- I KNOW WHERE SHE LIVES.
HELP ME FIND DORIAN AND I'LL TAKE YOU TO HER.
WOULDN'T YOU LIKE TO SEE HER AGAIN?

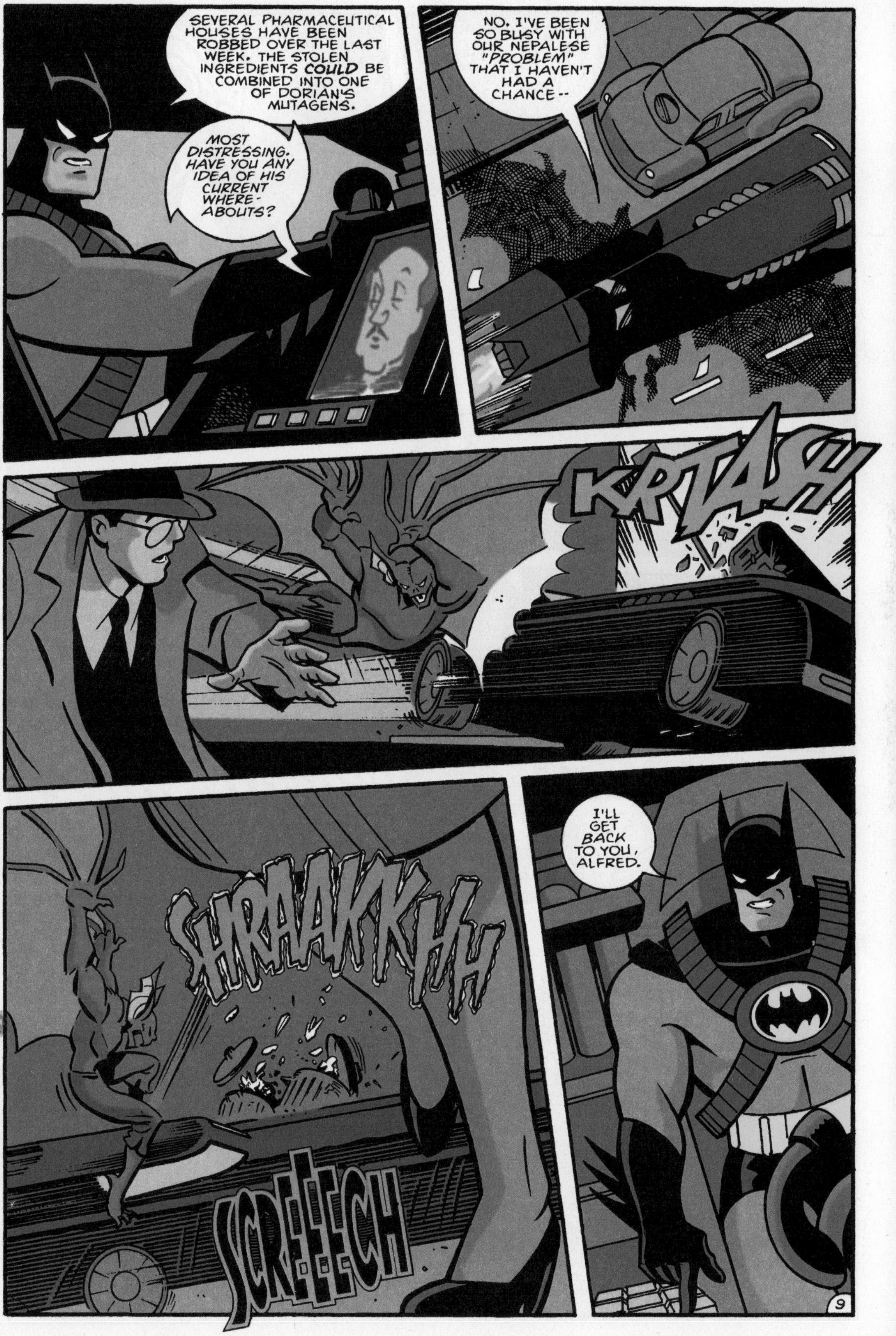
SEVERAL PHARMACEUTICAL HOUSES HAVE BEEN ROBBED OVER THE LAST WEEK. THE STOLEN INGREDIENTS COULD BE COMBINED INTO ONE OF DORIAN'S MUTAGENS.
MOST DISTRESSING. HAVE YOU ANY IDEA OF HIS CURRENT WHERE-ABOUTS?
NO. I'VE BEEN SO BUSY WITH OUR NEPALESE "PROBLEM" THAT I HAVEN'T HAD A CHANCE --
KRTASH
SHRAAKKHH
SCREEECH
I'LL GET BACK TO YOU, ALFRED.

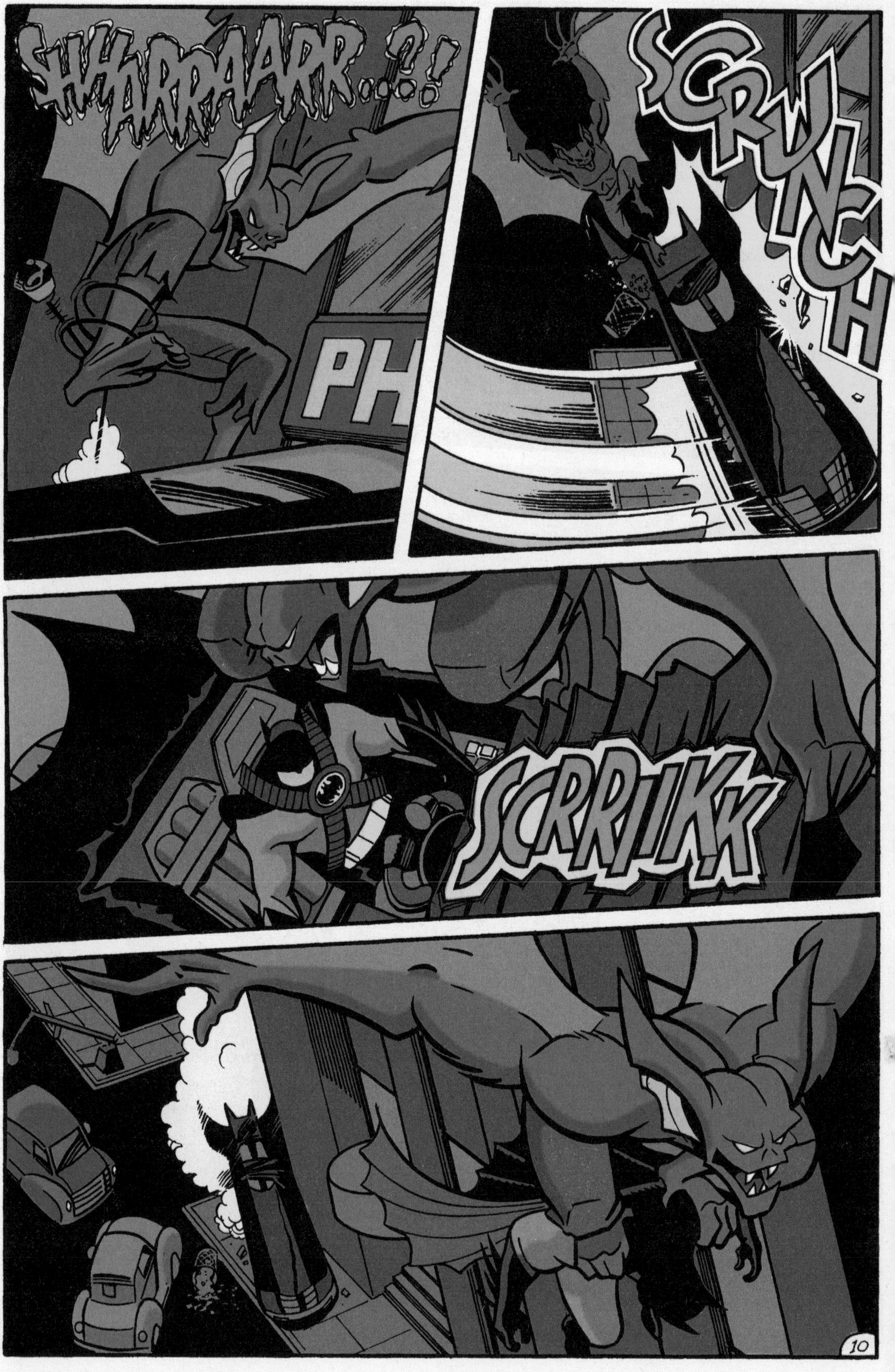
SHHARRAARR..?!
PH
SCRUNCH
SCRRIIKK
10

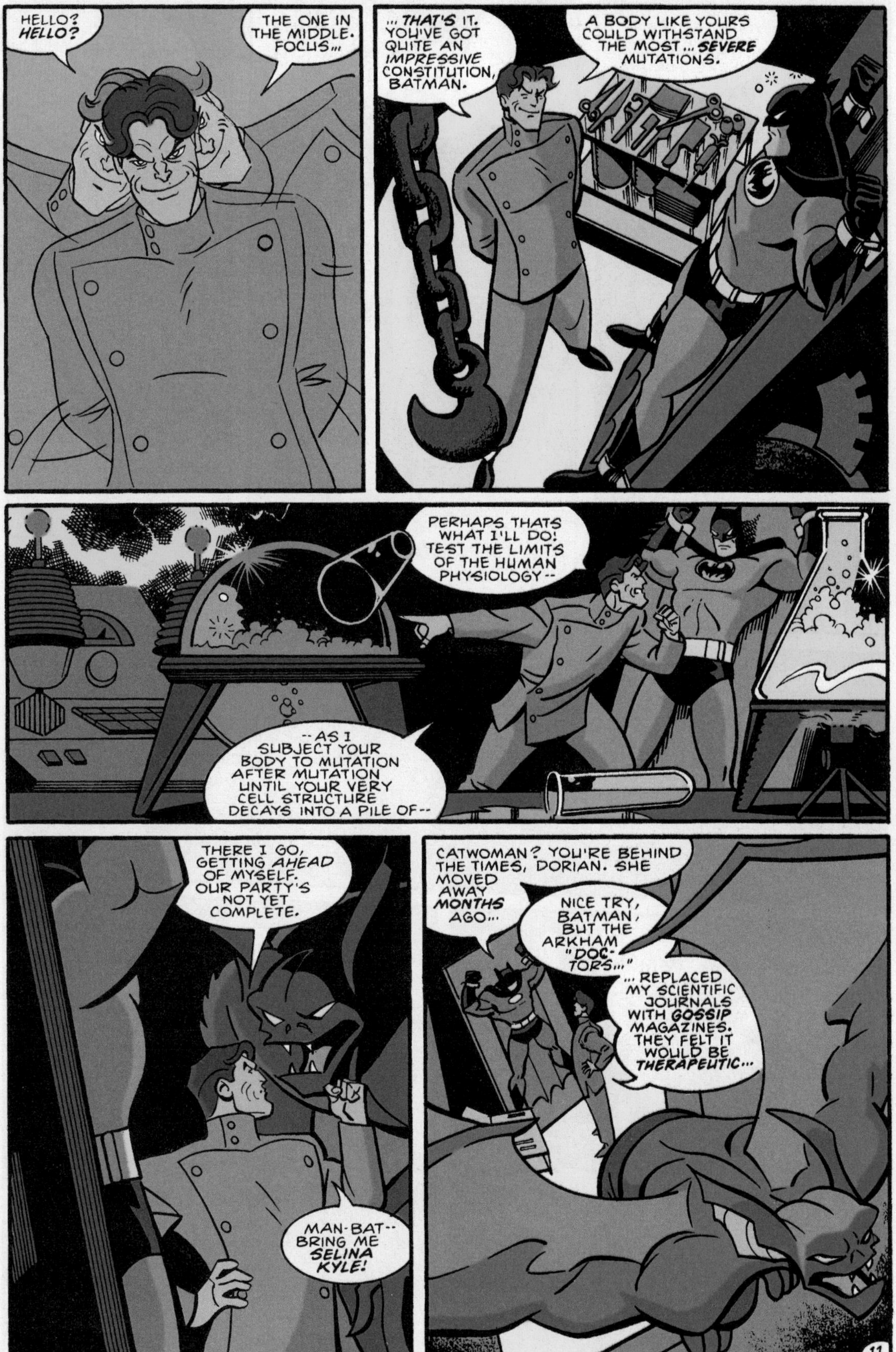
HELLO? HELLO?
THE ONE IN THE MIDDLE. FOCUS...
...THAT'S IT. YOU'VE GOT QUITE AN IMPRESSIVE CONSTITUTION, BATMAN.
A BODY LIKE YOURS COULD WITHSTAND THE MOST... SEVERE MUTATIONS.
PERHAPS THATS WHAT I'LL DO! TEST THE LIMITS OF THE HUMAN PHYSIOLOGY--
--AS I SUBJECT YOUR BODY TO MUTATION AFTER MUTATION UNTIL YOUR VERY CELL STRUCTURE DECAYS INTO A PILE OF--
THERE I GO, GETTING AHEAD OF MYSELF. OUR PARTY'S NOT YET COMPLETE.
MAN-BAT-- BRING ME SELINA KYLE!
CATWOMAN? YOU'RE BEHIND THE TIMES, DORIAN. SHE MOVED AWAY MONTHS AGO...
NICE TRY, BATMAN, BUT THE ARKHAM "DOC-TORS..."
...REPLACED MY SCIENTIFIC JOURNALS WITH GOSSIP MAGAZINES. THEY FELT IT WOULD BE THERAPEUTIC...
11

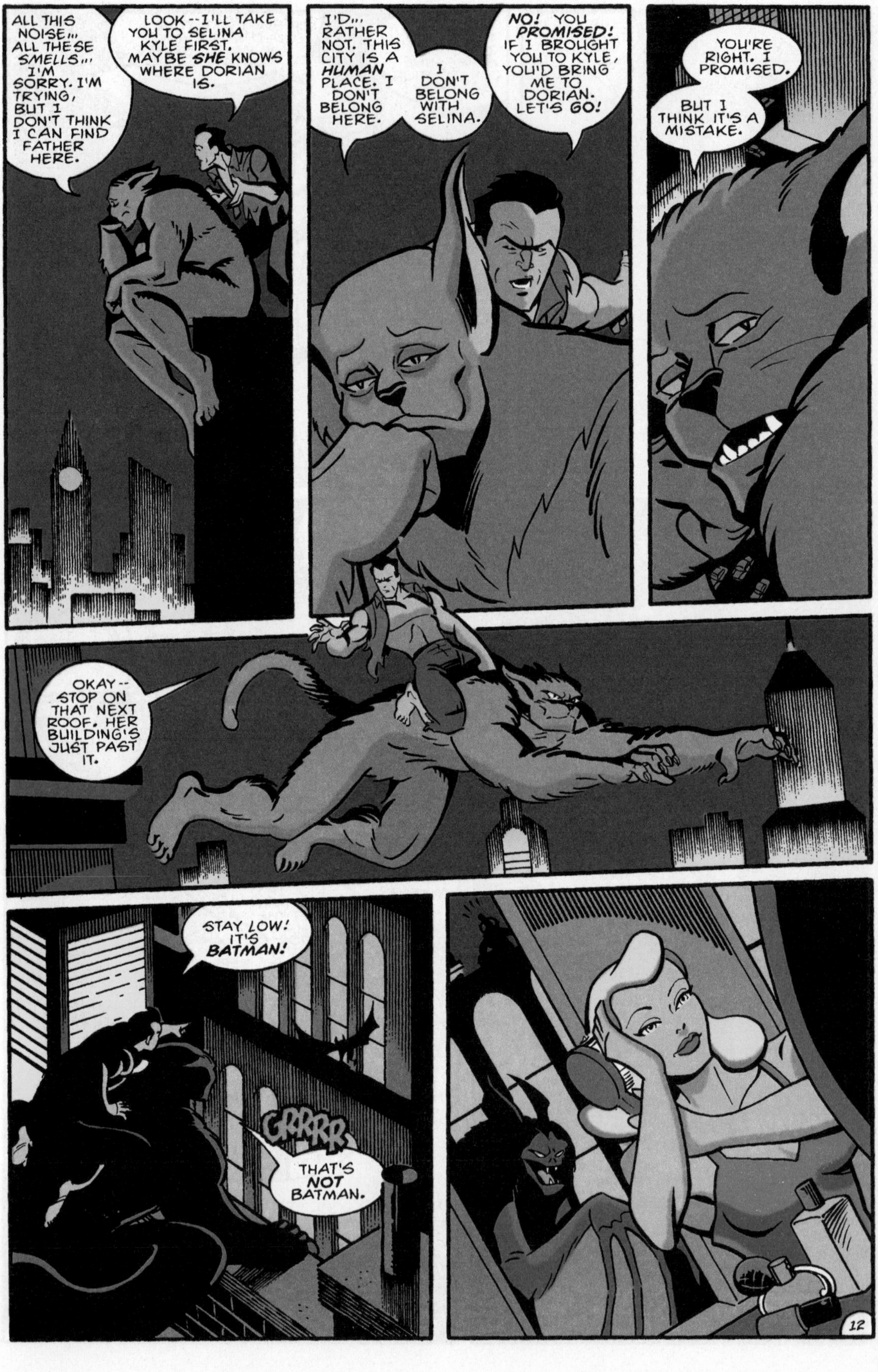
ALL THIS NOISE... ALL THESE SMELLS... I'M SORRY. I'M TRYING, BUT I DON'T THINK I CAN FIND FATHER HERE.
LOOK--I'LL TAKE YOU TO SELINA KYLE FIRST. MAYBE SHE KNOWS WHERE DORIAN IS.
I'D... RATHER NOT. THIS CITY IS A HUMAN PLACE. I DON'T BELONG HERE.
I DON'T BELONG WITH SELINA.
NO! YOU PROMISED! IF I BROUGHT YOU TO KYLE, YOU'D BRING ME TO DORIAN. LET'S GO!
YOU'RE RIGHT. I PROMISED.
BUT I THINK IT'S A MISTAKE.
OKAY-- STOP ON THAT NEXT ROOF. HER BUILDING'S JUST PAST IT.
STAY LOW! IT'S BATMAN!
GRRRR
THAT'S NOT BATMAN.

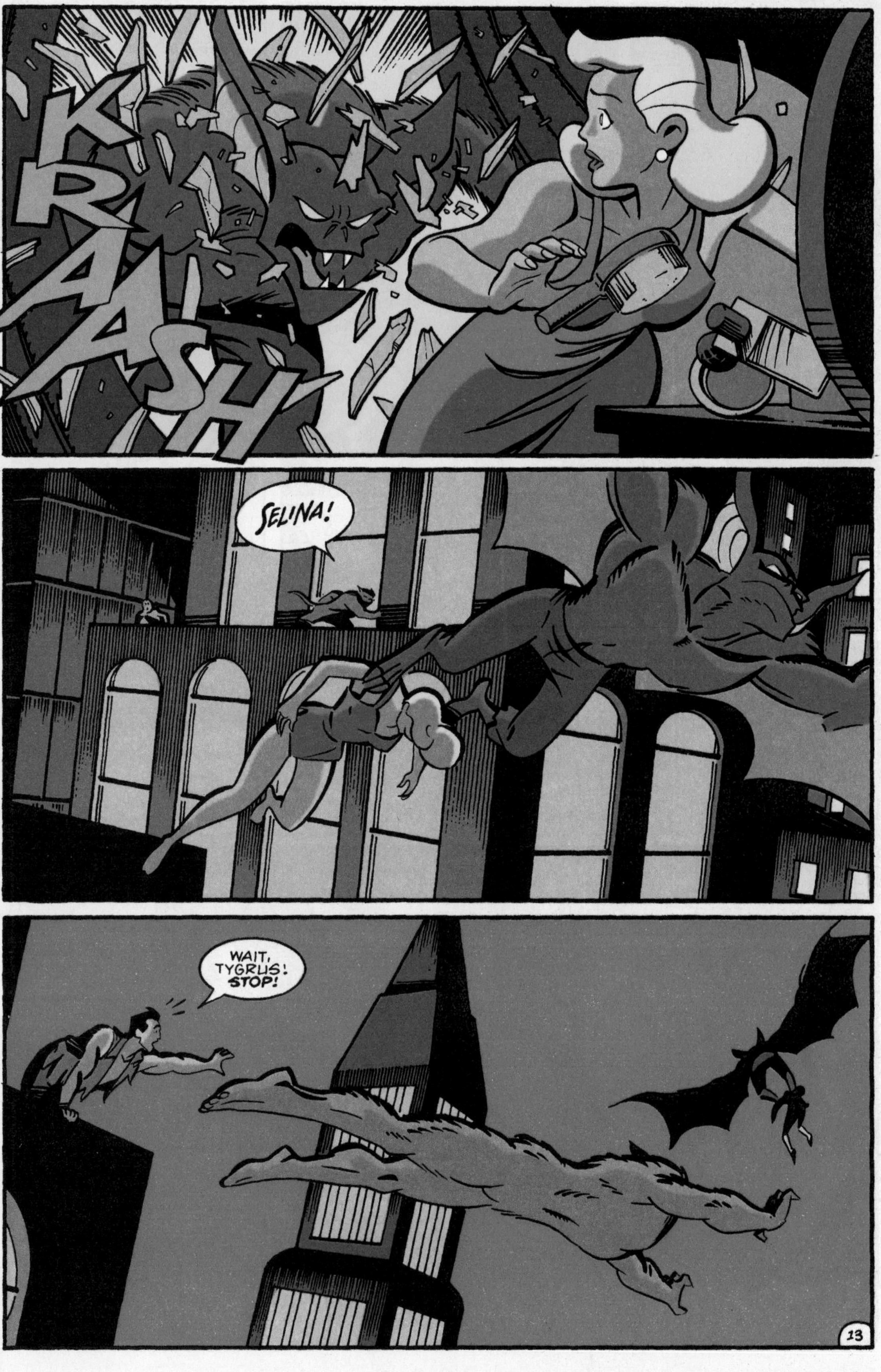
KRAASH
SELINA!
WAIT, TYGRUS! STOP!

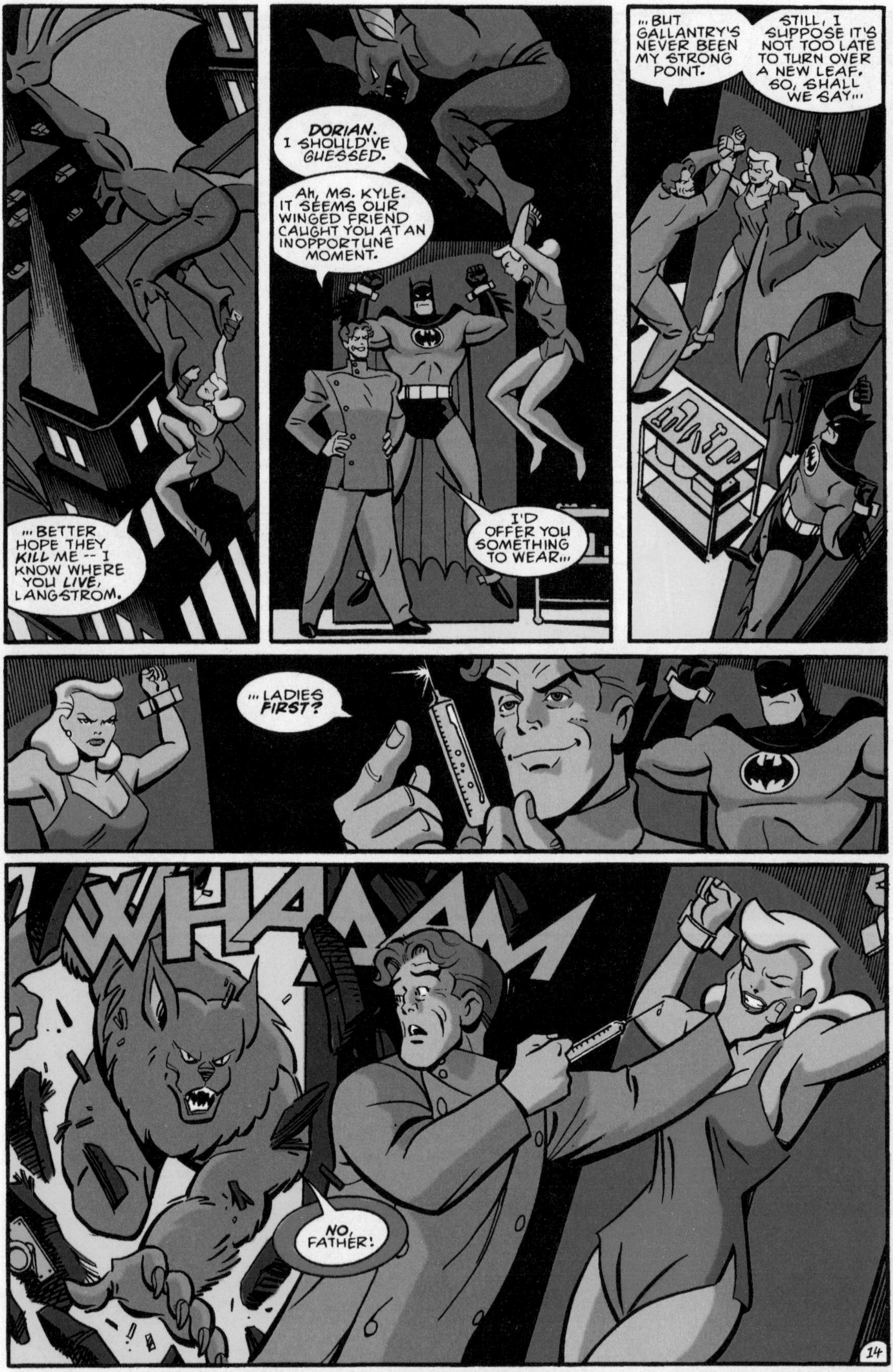
...BETTER HOPE THEY KILL ME -- I KNOW WHERE YOU LIVE, LANGSTROM.
DORIAN. I SHOULD'VE GUESSED.
Ah, MS. KYLE. IT SEEMS OUR WINGED FRIEND CAUGHT YOU AT AN INOPPORTUNE MOMENT.
I'D OFFER YOU SOMETHING TO WEAR...
...BUT GALLANTRY'S NEVER BEEN MY STRONG POINT.
STILL, I SUPPOSE IT'S NOT TOO LATE TO TURN OVER A NEW LEAF. SO, SHALL WE SAY...
...LADIES FIRST?
WHAAM
NO, FATHER!
14

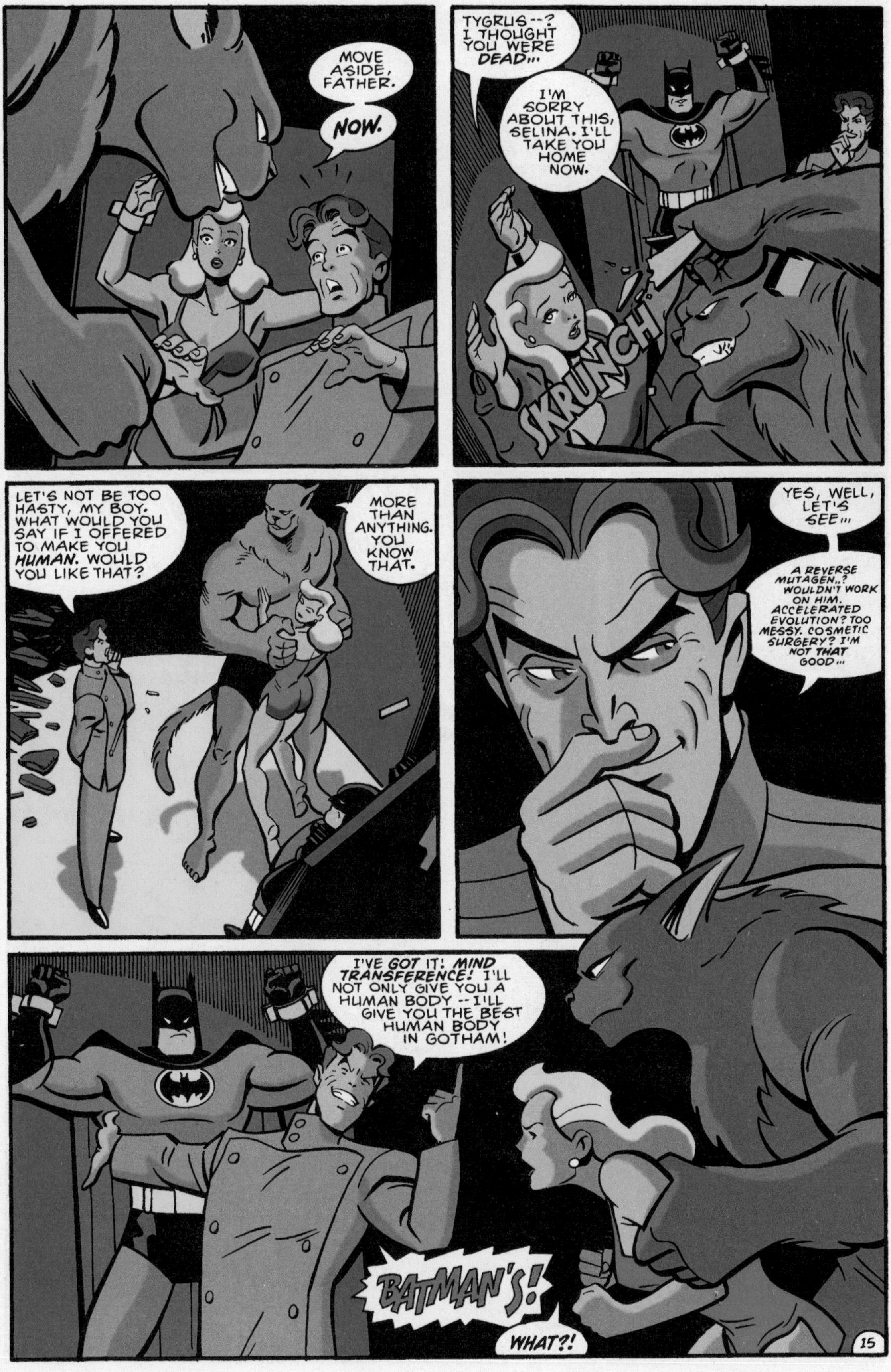
MOVE ASIDE, FATHER.
NOW.
TYGRUS--? I THOUGHT YOU WERE DEAD...
I'M SORRY ABOUT THIS, SELINA. I'LL TAKE YOU HOME NOW.
SKRUNCH
LET'S NOT BE TOO HASTY, MY BOY. WHAT WOULD YOU SAY IF I OFFERED TO MAKE YOU HUMAN. WOULD YOU LIKE THAT?
MORE THAN ANYTHING. YOU KNOW THAT.
YES, WELL, LET'S SEE...
A REVERSE MUTAGEN..? WOULDN'T WORK ON HIM. ACCELERATED EVOLUTION? TOO MESSY. COSMETIC SURGERY? I'M NOT THAT GOOD...
I'VE GOT IT: MIND TRANSFERENCE! I'LL NOT ONLY GIVE YOU A HUMAN BODY --I'LL GIVE YOU THE BEST HUMAN BODY IN GOTHAM!
BATMAN'S!
WHAT?!

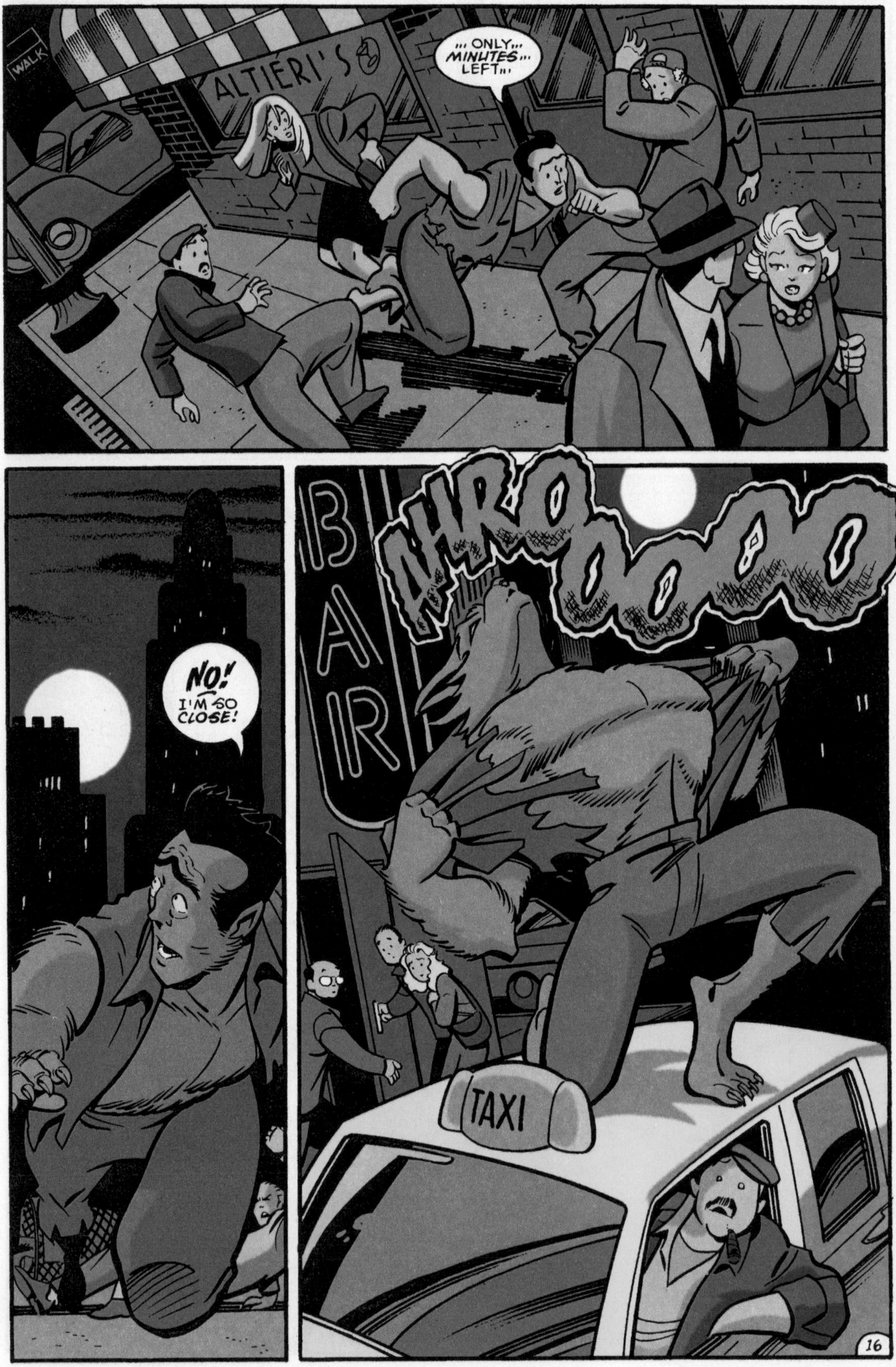
WALK
ALTIERI'S
... ONLY... MINUTES... LEFT...
NO! I'M SO CLOSE!
BAR
AHROOOOO
TAXI

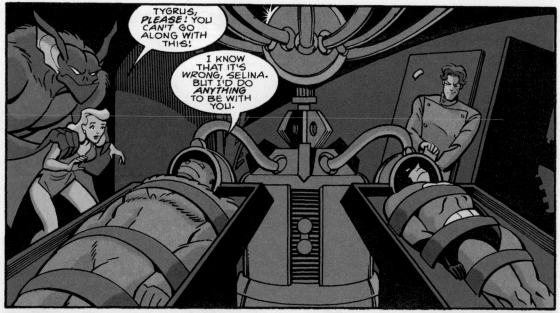

TYGRUS, *PLEASE!* YOU CAN'T GO ALONG WITH THIS!

I KNOW THAT IT'S *WRONG,* SELINA. BUT I'D DO *ANYTHING* TO BE WITH YOU.

BUT THIS IS *CRAZY!* I COULDN'T LOVE ANYONE WHO DID SOMETHING LIKE THIS!

PERHAPS. BUT I *KNOW* YOU COULDN'T LOVE SOMEONE WHO *LOOKS* LIKE THIS.

I'M KICKING MYSELF, BATMAN. MIND TRANSFERENCE SHOULD HAVE OCCURRED TO ME EARLIER. I WAS ONLY PLANNING ON A FEW *DAYS* OF TORTURE...

... BUT IN *TYGRUS'* BODY, YOU'LL LAST FOR *WEEKS.* SHALL WE BEGIN"?

17

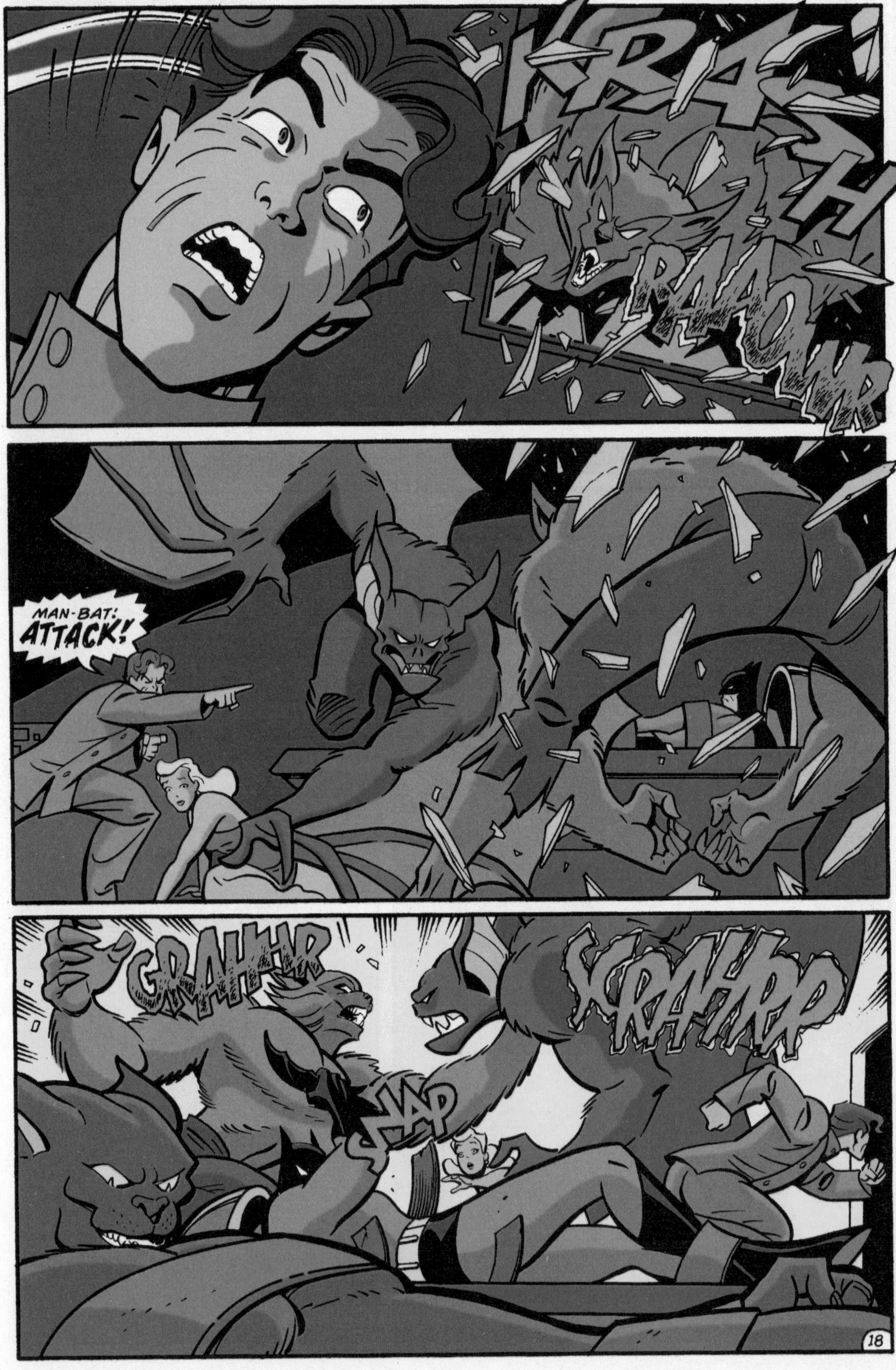
KRASH
RAAOWR
MAN-BAT: ATTACK!
GRAHHR
SCRAHRR
SNAP

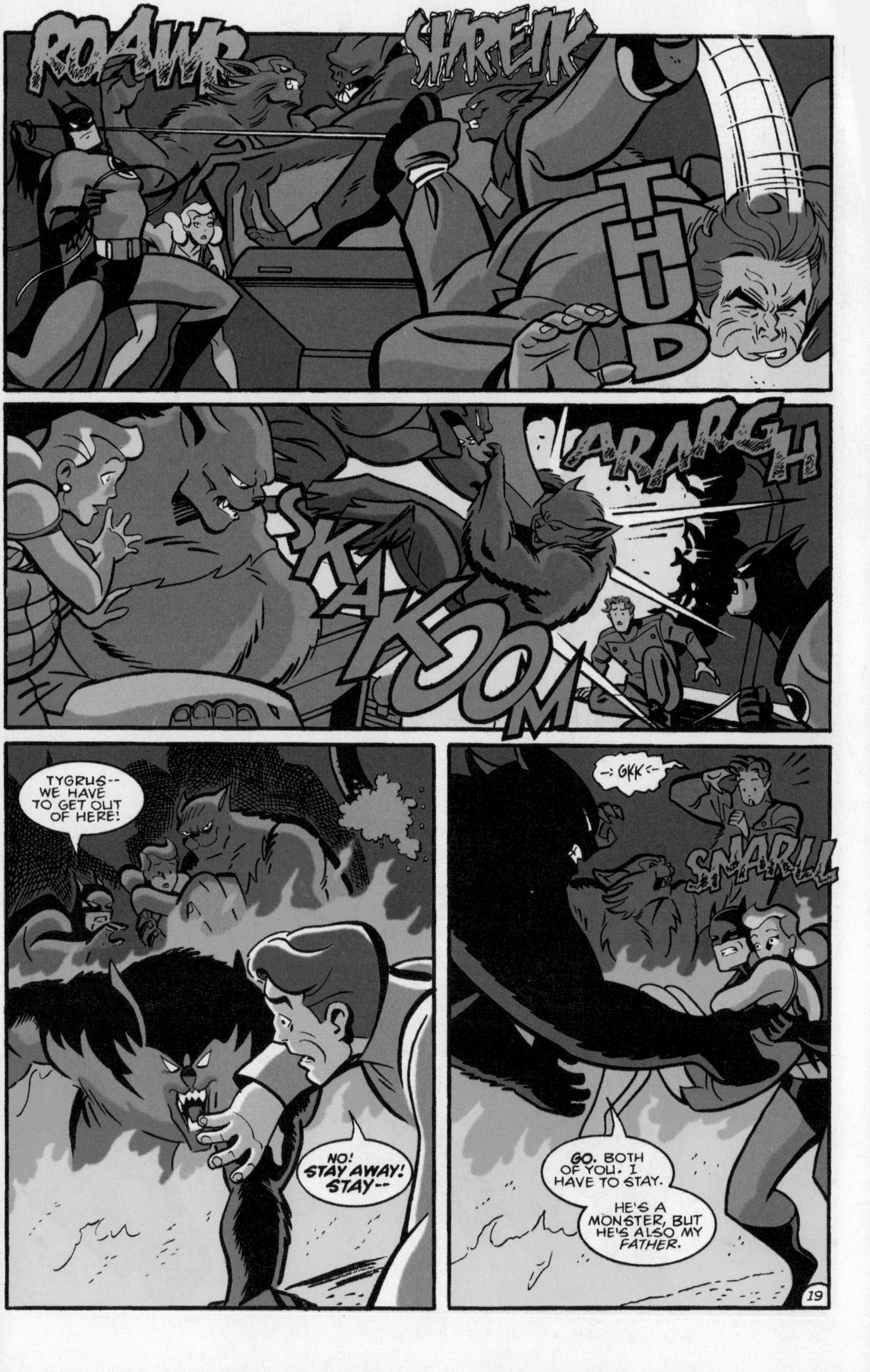
ROAWR
SHREIK
THUD
ARARGH
SKAKOOOM
TYGRUS-- WE HAVE TO GET OUT OF HERE!
NO! STAY AWAY! STAY--
-GKK-
SNARLL
GO. BOTH OF YOU. I HAVE TO STAY.
HE'S A MONSTER, BUT HE'S ALSO MY FATHER.

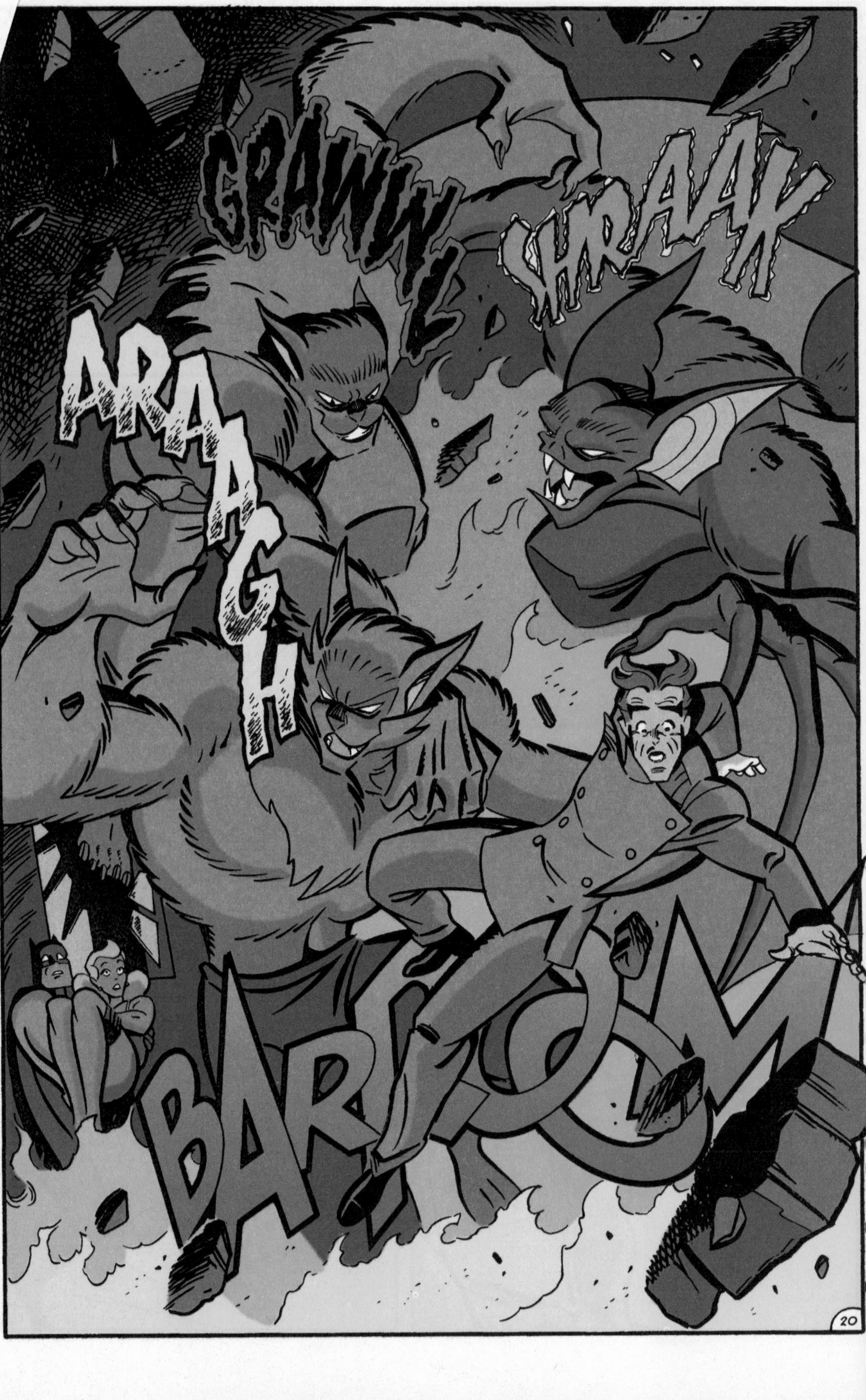
GRAWWL
SHRAAK
ARAAGH
BARHOOM

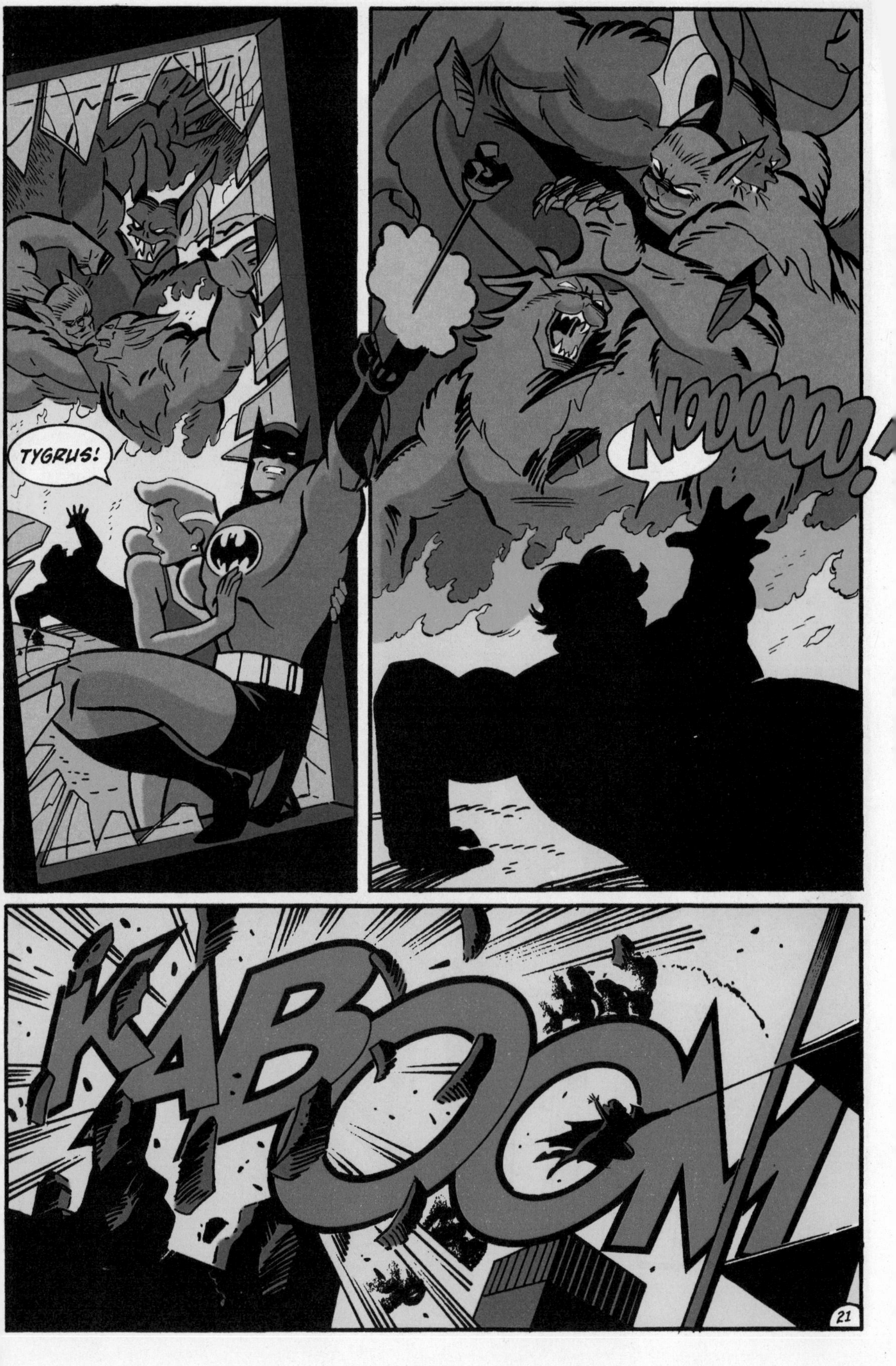
TYGRUS!
NOOOOOO!
KABOOM!

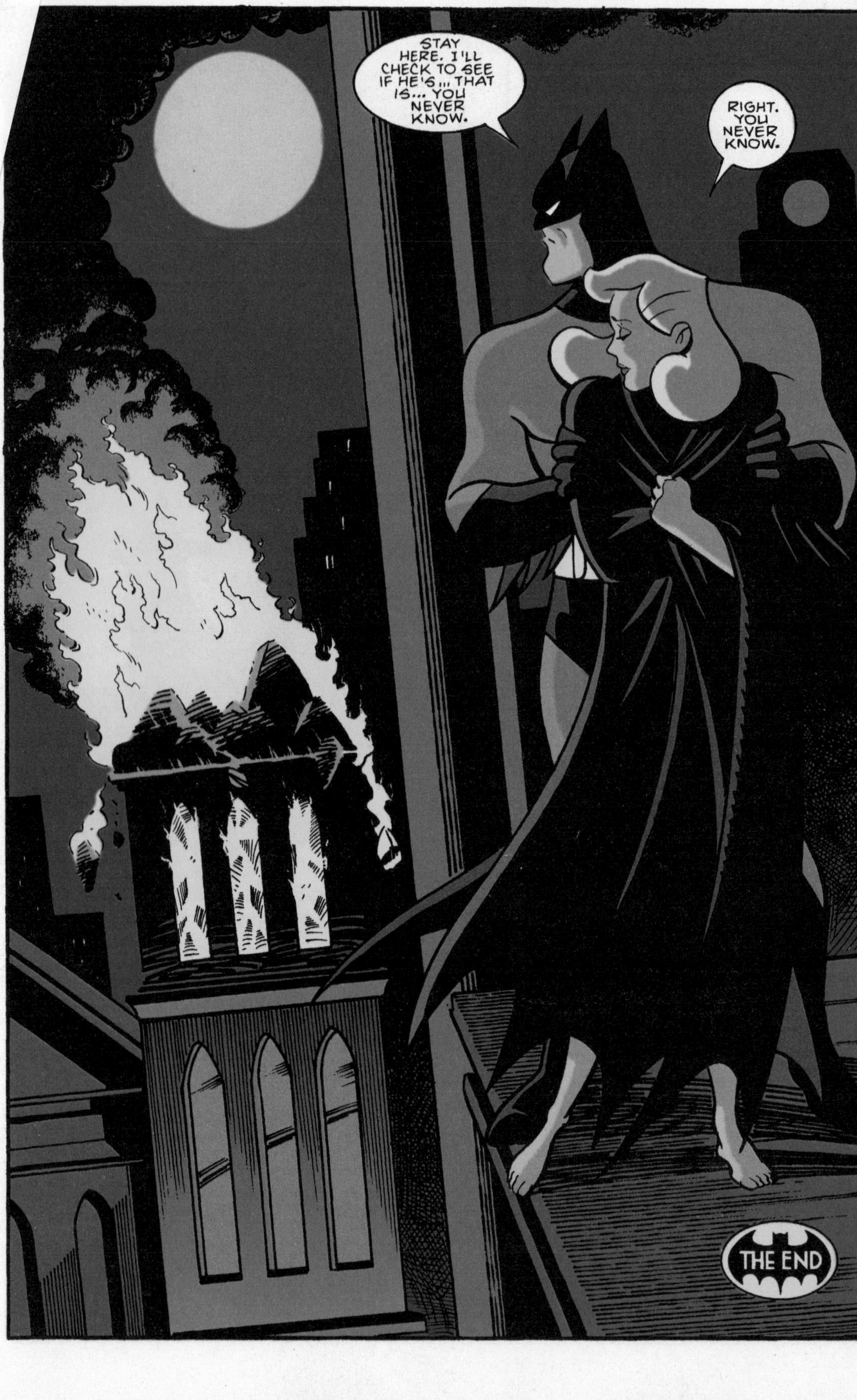
STAY HERE. I'LL CHECK TO SEE IF HE'S... THAT IS... YOU NEVER KNOW.
RIGHT. YOU NEVER KNOW.
THE END

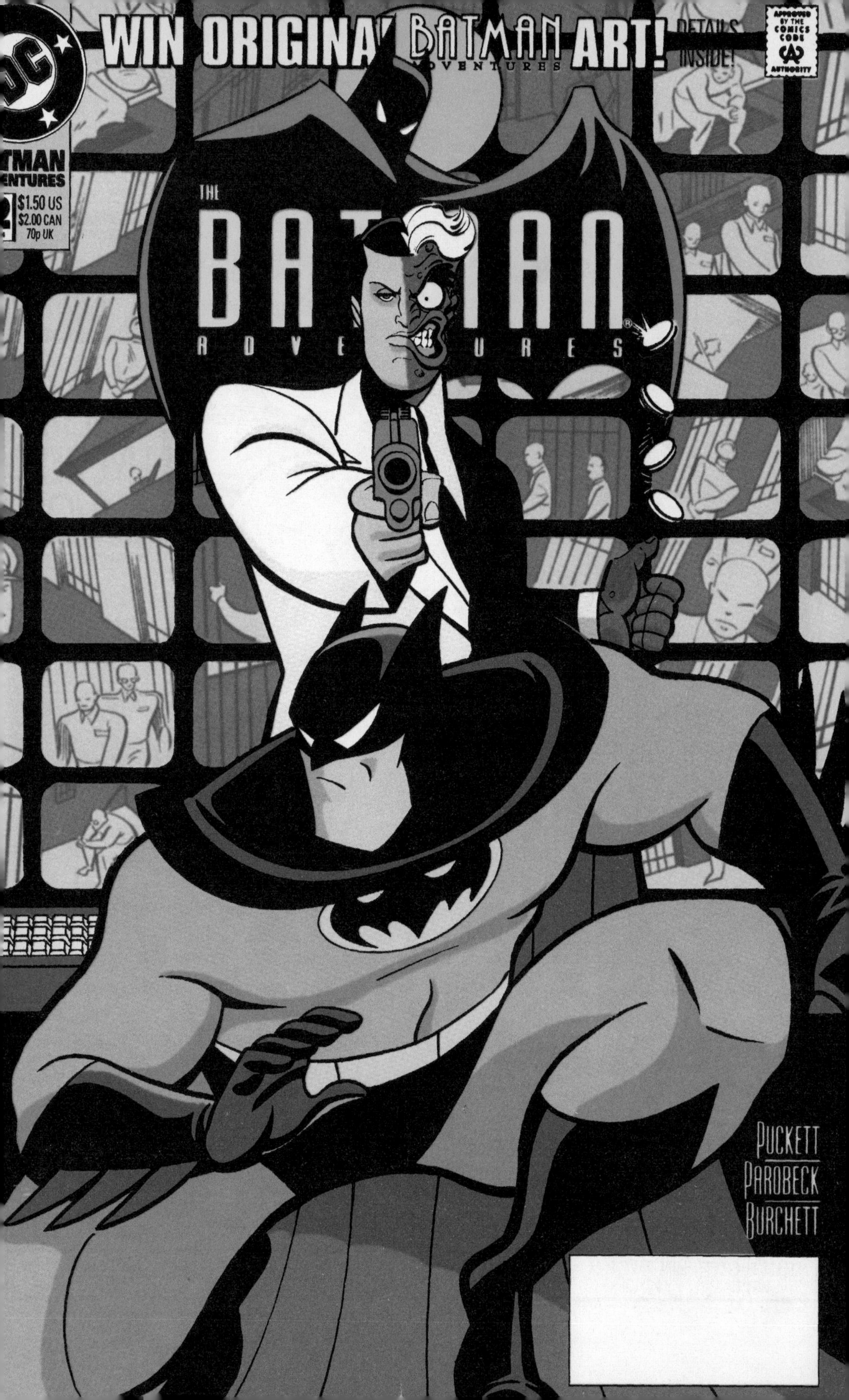
WIN ORIGINAL BATMAN ADVENTURES ART! DETAILS INSIDE!
APPROVED BY THE COMICS CODE AUTHORITY
DC
BATMAN ADVENTURES
2
$1.50 US
$2.00 CAN
70p UK
THE BATMAN ADVENTURES
PUCKETT
PAROBECK
BURCHETT

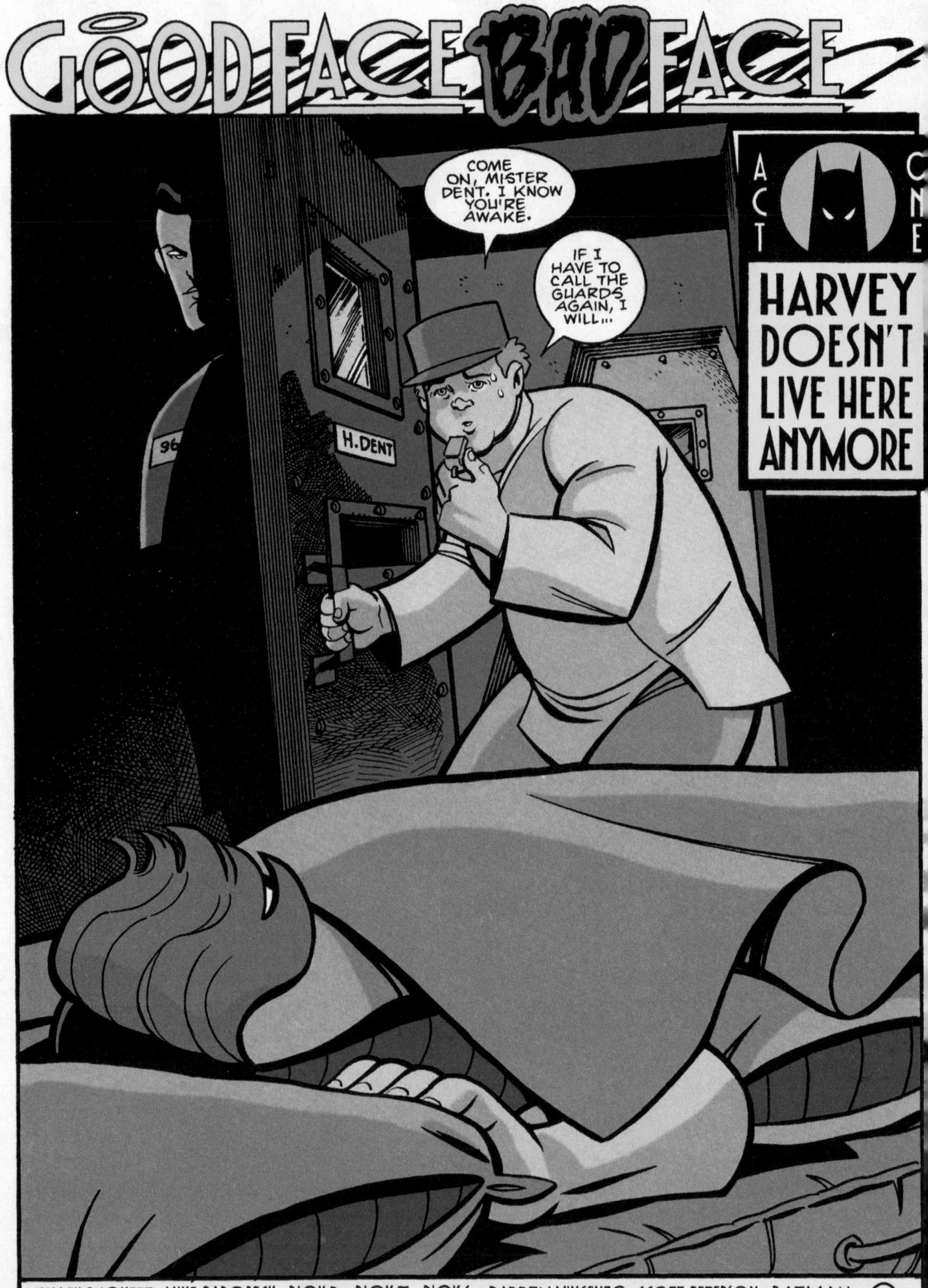
GOOD FACE BAD FACE
ACT ONE
HARVEY DOESN'T LIVE HERE ANYMORE
COME ON, MISTER DENT. I KNOW YOU'RE AWAKE.
IF I HAVE TO CALL THE GUARDS AGAIN, I WILL...
H. DENT
96
KELLEY PUCKETT WRITER
MIKE PAROBECK PENCILS
RICK B. INKS
RICK T. COLORS
RICK S. LETTERS
DARREN VINCENZO ASST. EDITOR
SCOTT PETERSON EDITOR
BATMAN CREATED BY BOB KANE

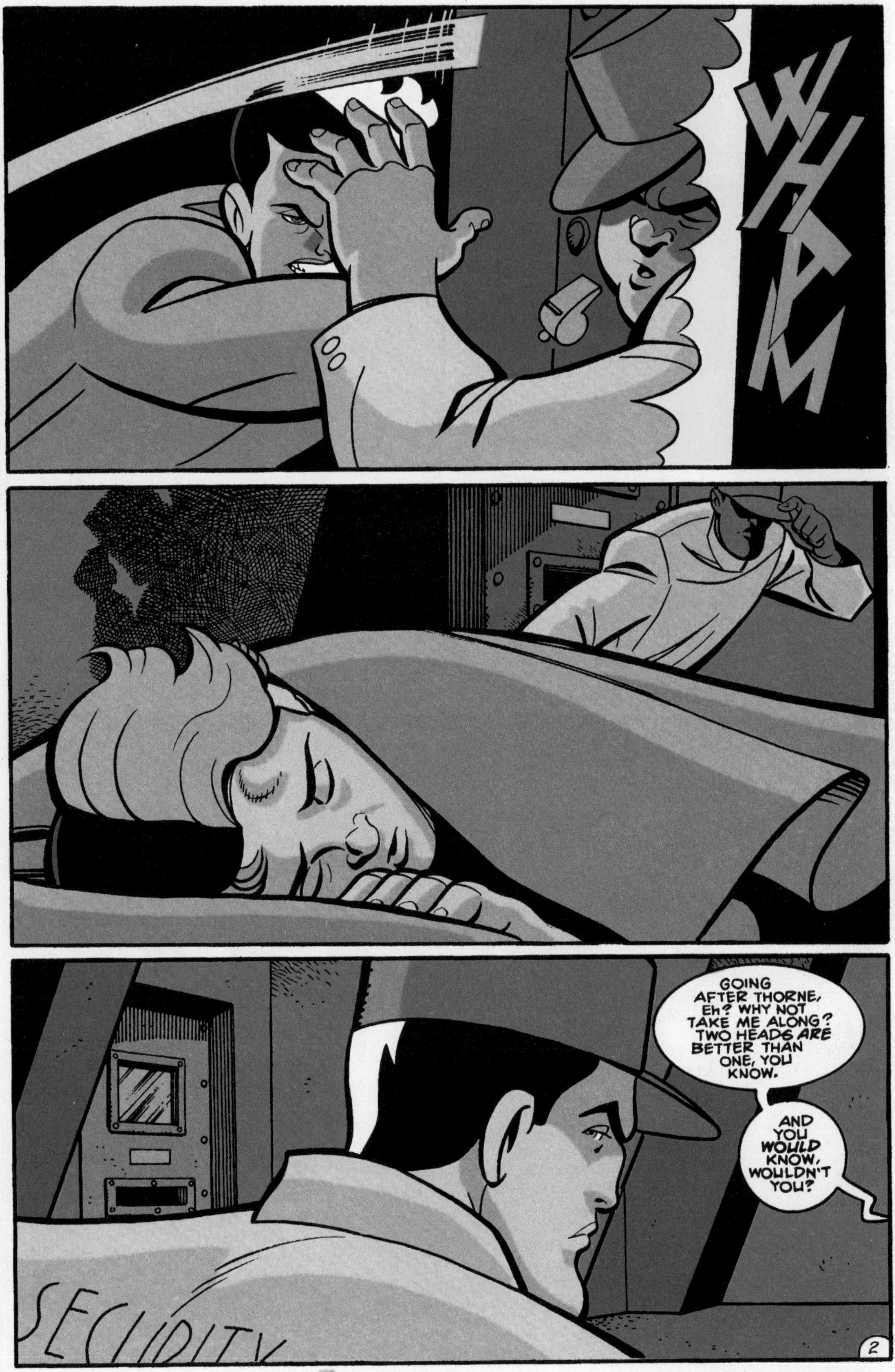
WHAM
GOING AFTER THORNE, Eh? WHY NOT TAKE ME ALONG? TWO HEADS ARE BETTER THAN ONE, YOU KNOW.
AND YOU WOULD KNOW, WOULDN'T YOU?

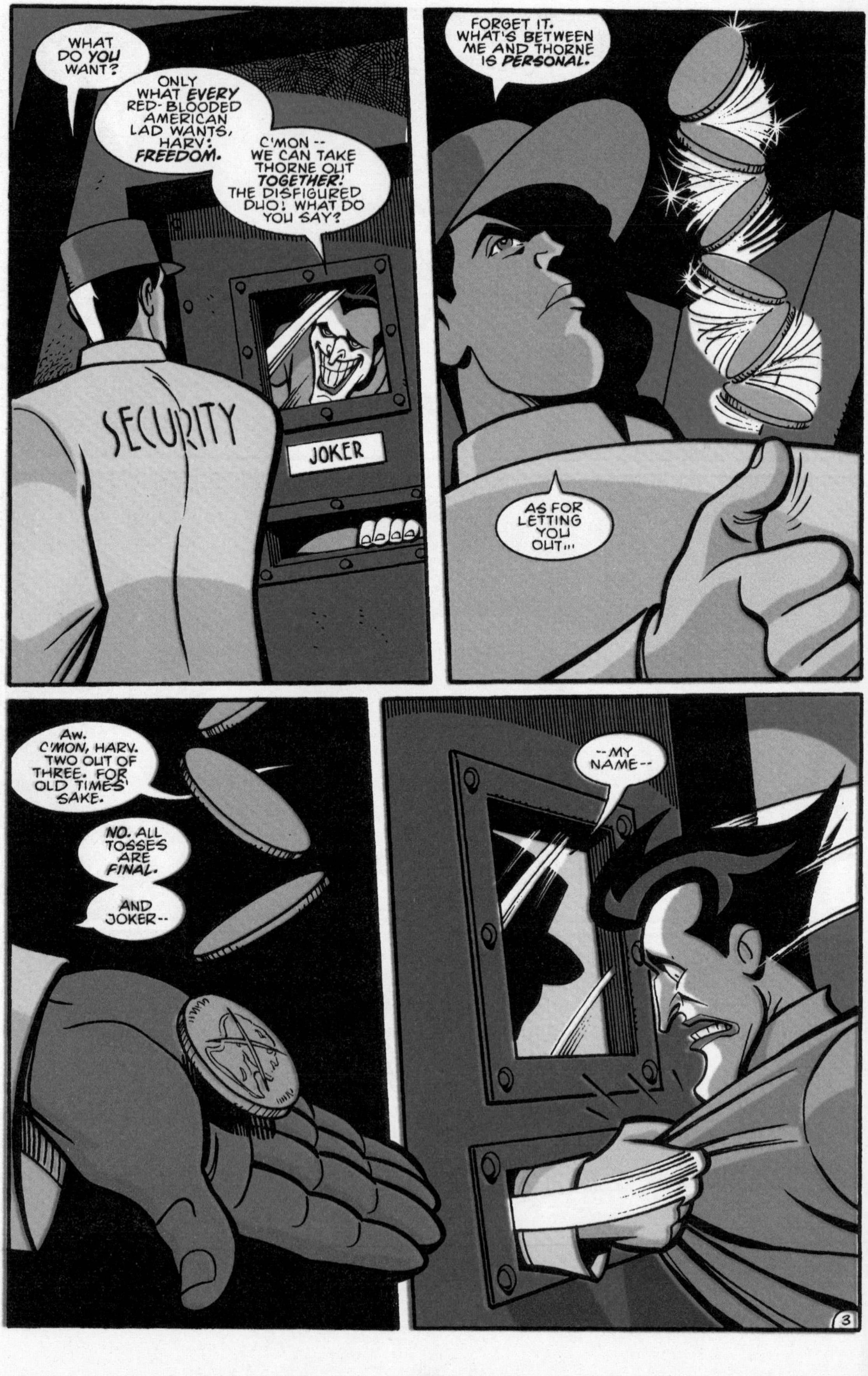
WHAT DO YOU WANT?
ONLY WHAT EVERY RED-BLOODED AMERICAN LAD WANTS, HARV: FREEDOM.
C'MON -- WE CAN TAKE THORNE OUT TOGETHER: THE DISFIGURED DUO! WHAT DO YOU SAY?
SECURITY
JOKER
FORGET IT. WHAT'S BETWEEN ME AND THORNE IS PERSONAL.
AS FOR LETTING YOU OUT...
AW. C'MON, HARV. TWO OUT OF THREE. FOR OLD TIMES' SAKE.
NO. ALL TOSSES ARE FINAL.
AND JOKER--
--MY NAME--

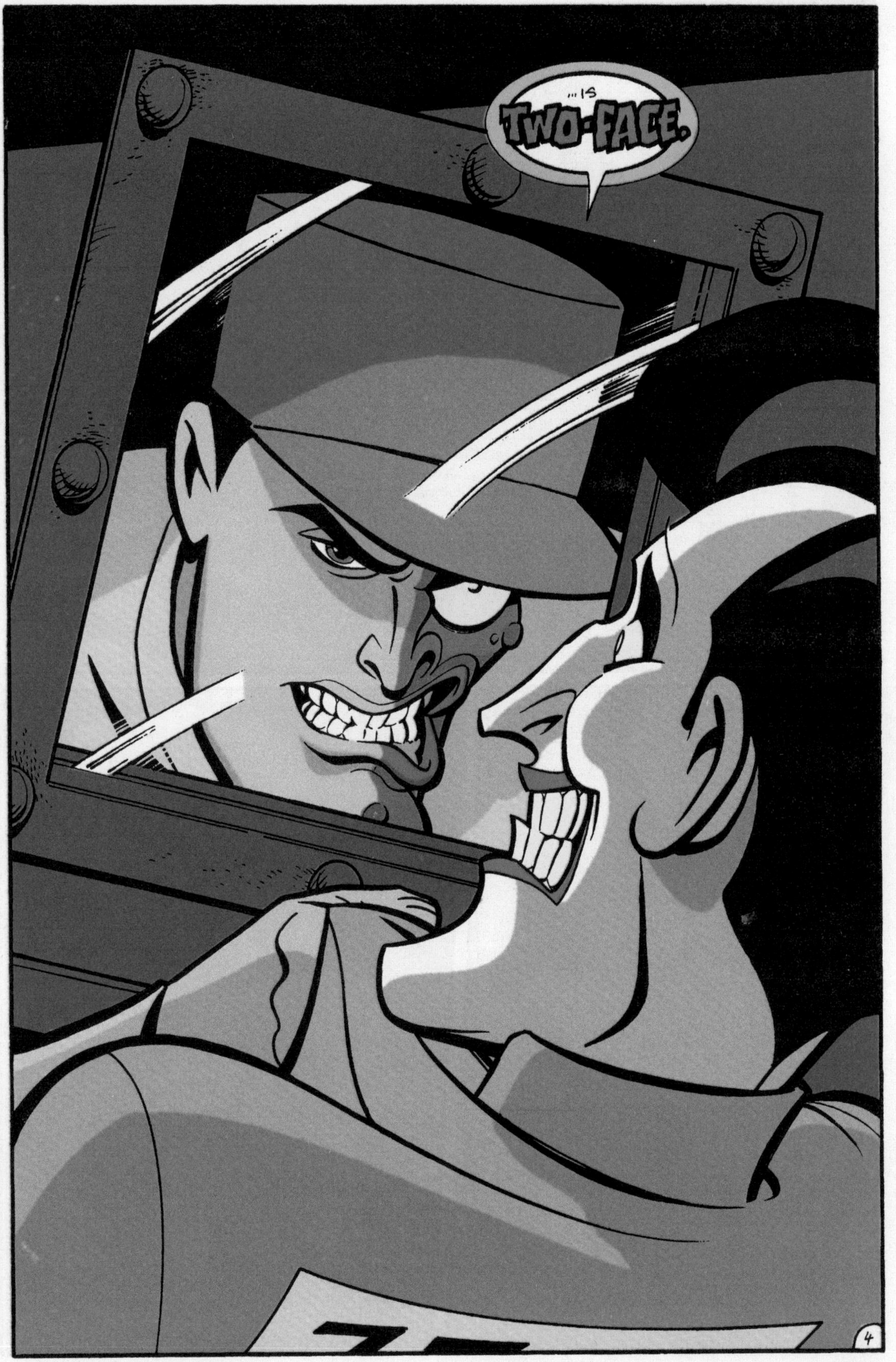
...IS TWO-FACE.

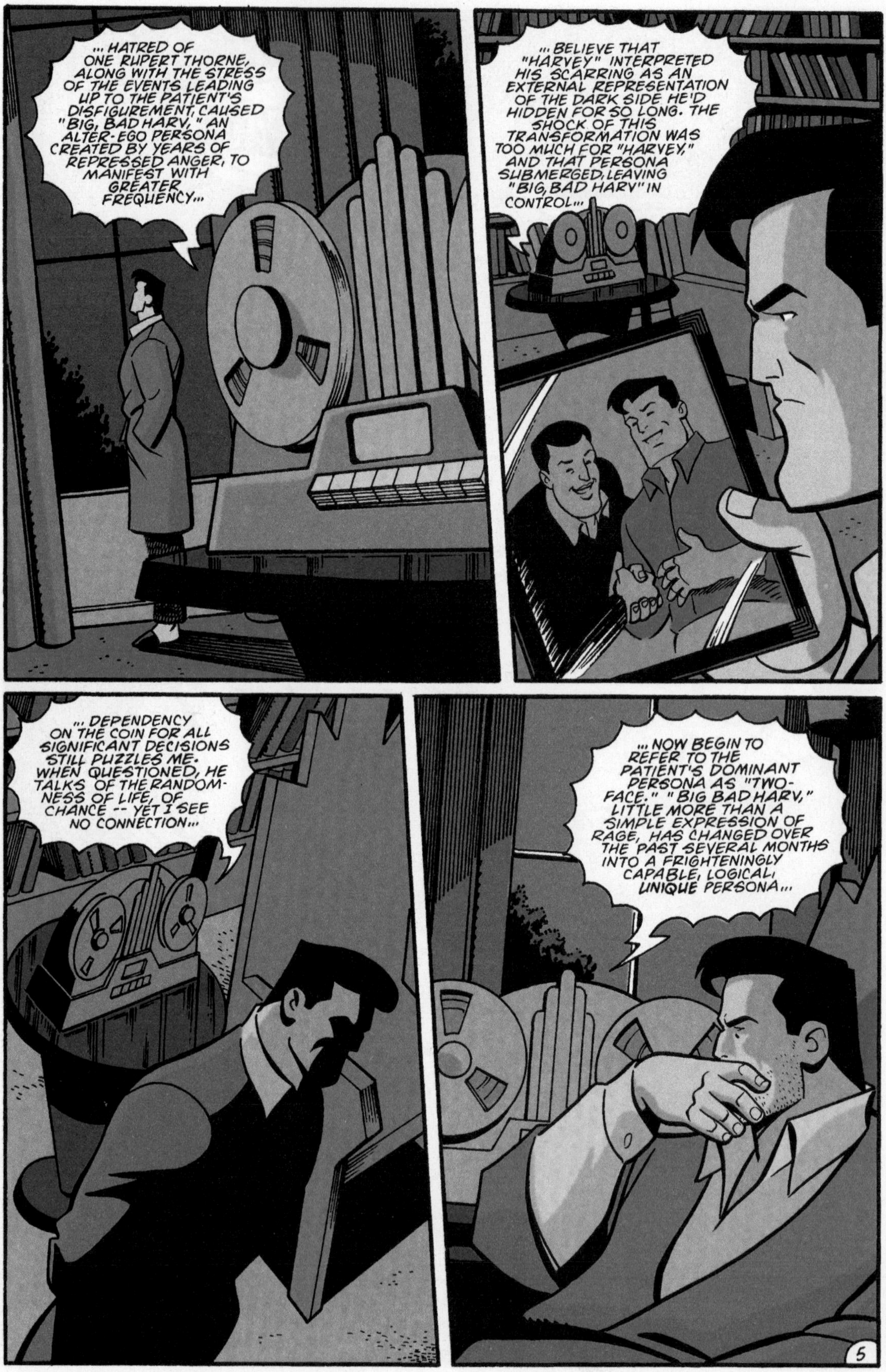
...HATRED OF ONE RUPERT THORNE, ALONG WITH THE STRESS OF THE EVENTS LEADING UP TO THE PATIENT'S DISFIGUREMENT, CAUSED "BIG, BAD HARV," AN ALTER-EGO PERSONA CREATED BY YEARS OF REPRESSED ANGER, TO MANIFEST WITH GREATER FREQUENCY...
...BELIEVE THAT "HARVEY" INTERPRETED HIS SCARRING AS AN EXTERNAL REPRESENTATION OF THE DARK SIDE HE'D HIDDEN FOR SO LONG. THE SHOCK OF THIS TRANSFORMATION WAS TOO MUCH FOR "HARVEY," AND THAT PERSONA SUBMERGED, LEAVING "BIG, BAD HARV" IN CONTROL...
...DEPENDENCY ON THE COIN FOR ALL SIGNIFICANT DECISIONS STILL PUZZLES ME. WHEN QUESTIONED, HE TALKS OF THE RANDOMNESS OF LIFE, OF CHANCE -- YET I SEE NO CONNECTION...
...NOW BEGIN TO REFER TO THE PATIENT'S DOMINANT PERSONA AS "TWO-FACE." "BIG BAD HARV," LITTLE MORE THAN A SIMPLE EXPRESSION OF RAGE, HAS CHANGED OVER THE PAST SEVERAL MONTHS INTO A FRIGHTENINGLY CAPABLE, LOGICAL, UNIQUE PERSONA...
5

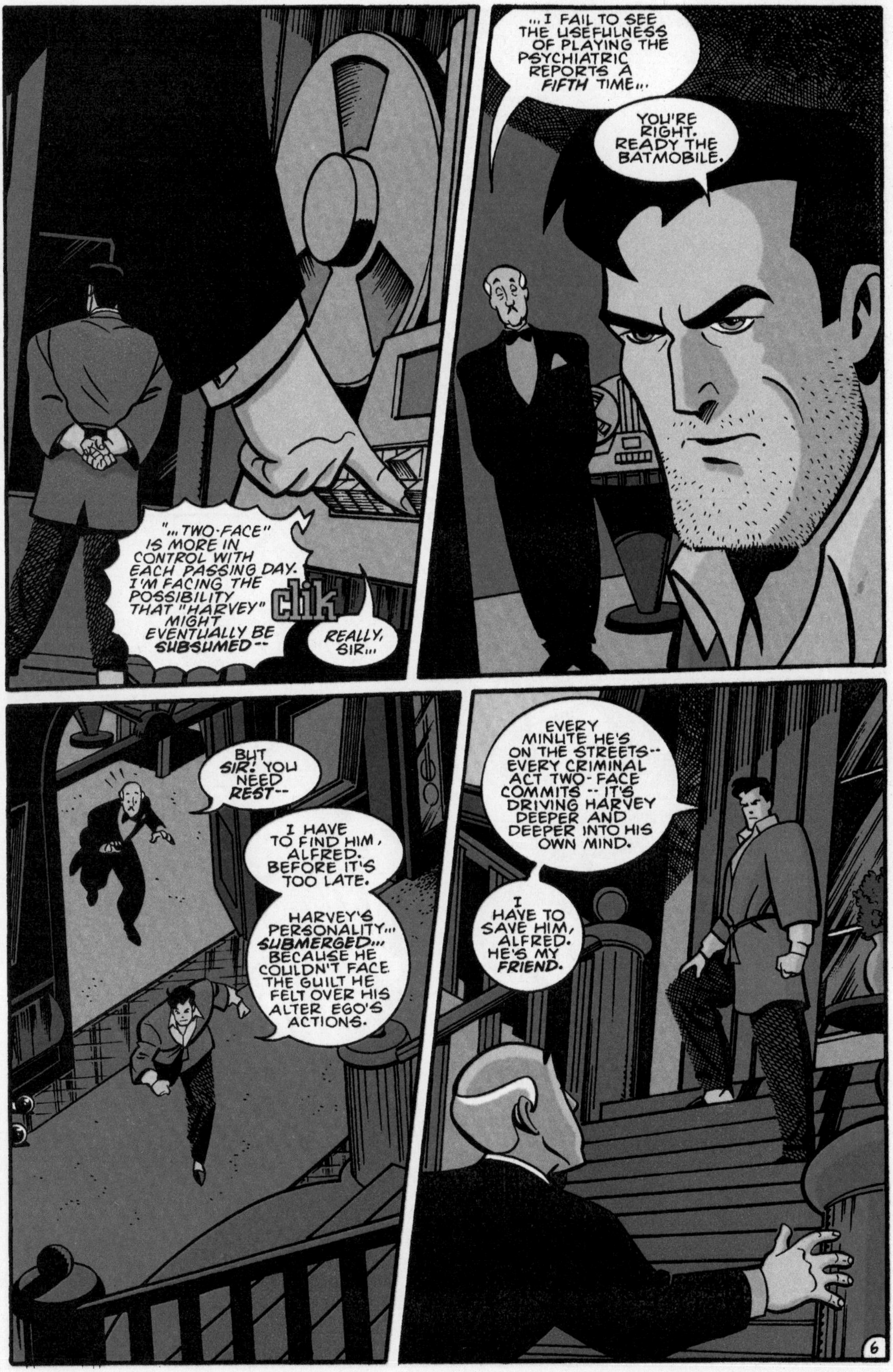
"...TWO-FACE" IS MORE IN CONTROL WITH EACH PASSING DAY. I'M FACING THE POSSIBILITY THAT "HARVEY" MIGHT EVENTUALLY BE SUBSUMED--
CLIK
REALLY, SIR...
...I FAIL TO SEE THE USEFULNESS OF PLAYING THE PSYCHIATRIC REPORTS A FIFTH TIME...
YOU'RE RIGHT. READY THE BATMOBILE.
BUT SIR! YOU NEED REST--
I HAVE TO FIND HIM, ALFRED. BEFORE IT'S TOO LATE.
HARVEY'S PERSONALITY... SUBMERGED... BECAUSE HE COULDN'T FACE THE GUILT HE FELT OVER HIS ALTER EGO'S ACTIONS.
EVERY MINUTE HE'S ON THE STREETS-- EVERY CRIMINAL ACT TWO-FACE COMMITS -- IT'S DRIVING HARVEY DEEPER AND DEEPER INTO HIS OWN MIND.
I HAVE TO SAVE HIM, ALFRED. HE'S MY FRIEND.
6

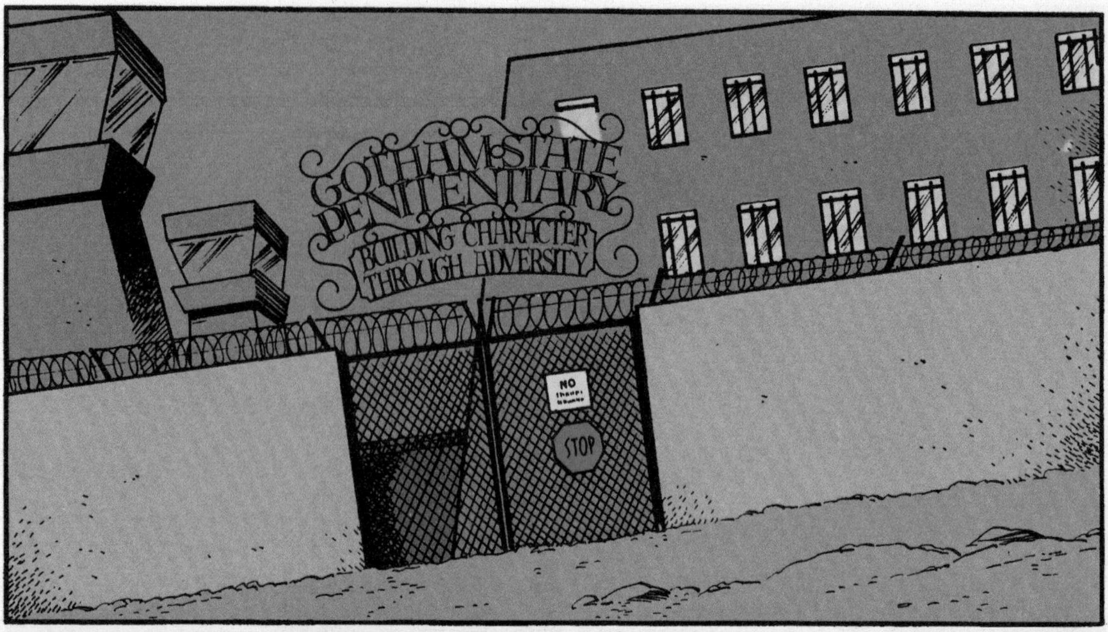
GOTHAM STATE PENITENTIARY
BUILDING CHARACTER THROUGH ADVERSITY
NO
STOP

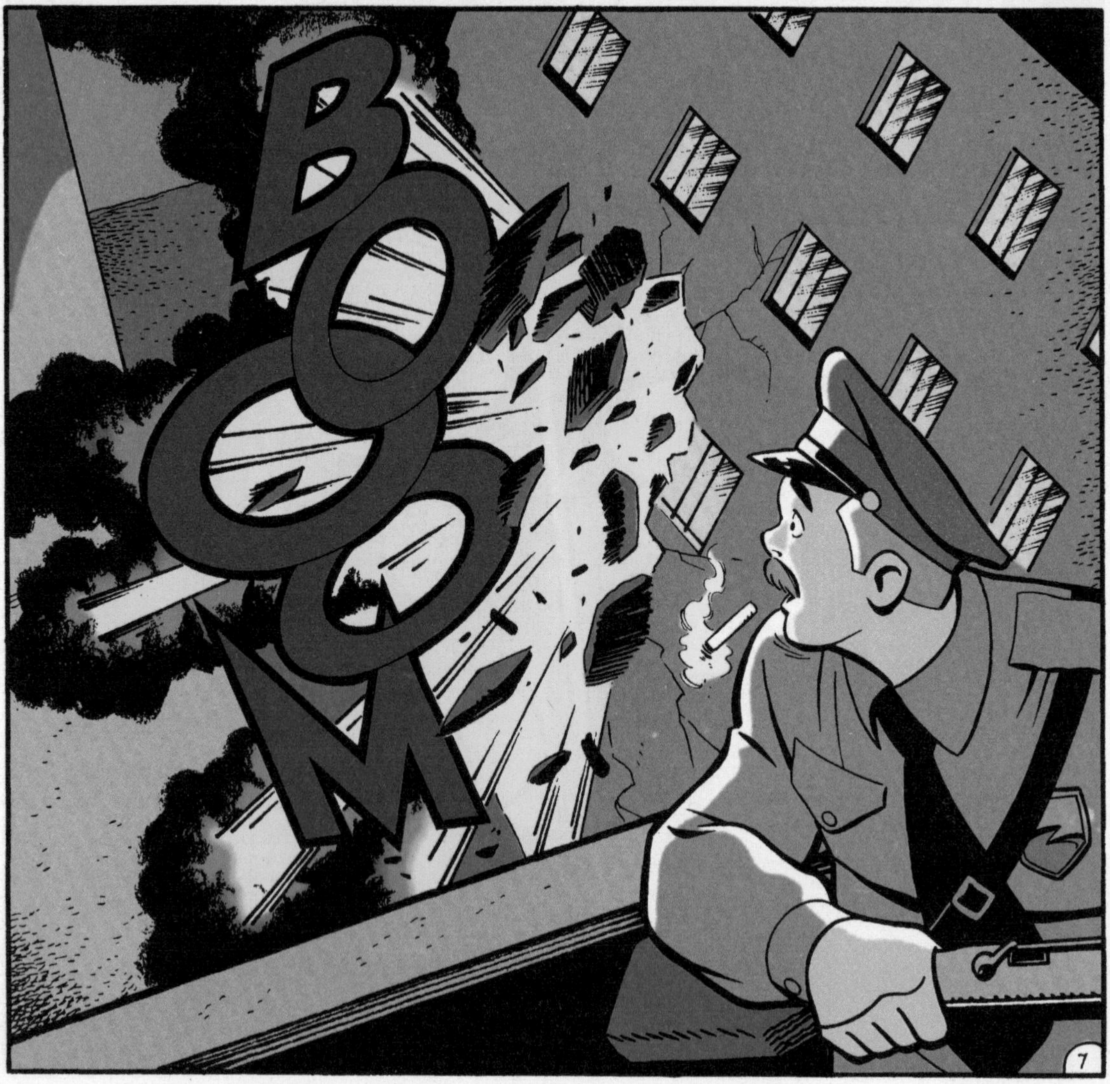
BOOOM

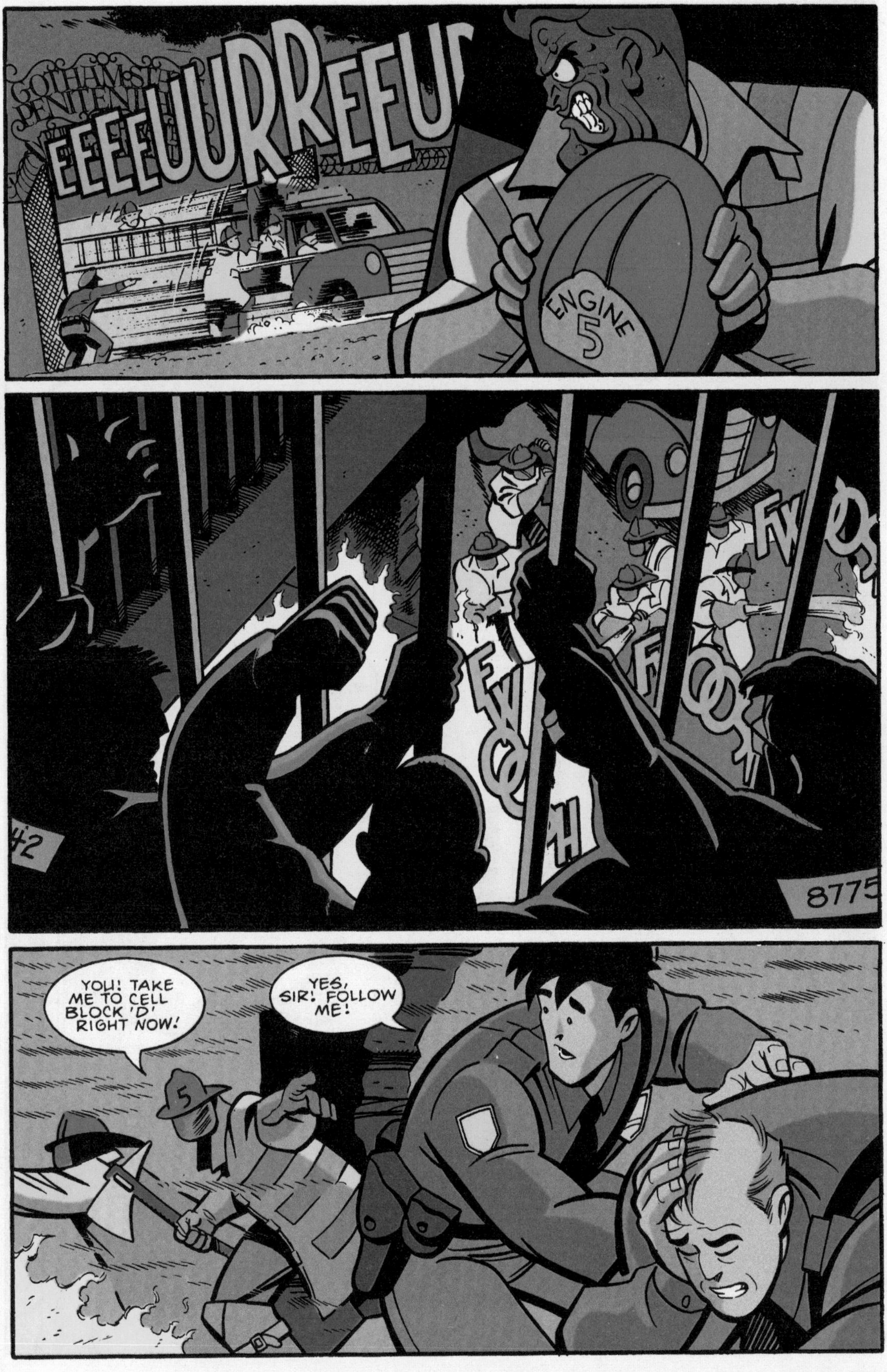
EEEEUURREEEU
ENGINE 5
FWOOSH
FWOOSH
FOOSH
42
8775
YOU! TAKE ME TO CELL BLOCK 'D' RIGHT NOW!
YES, SIR! FOLLOW ME!
5

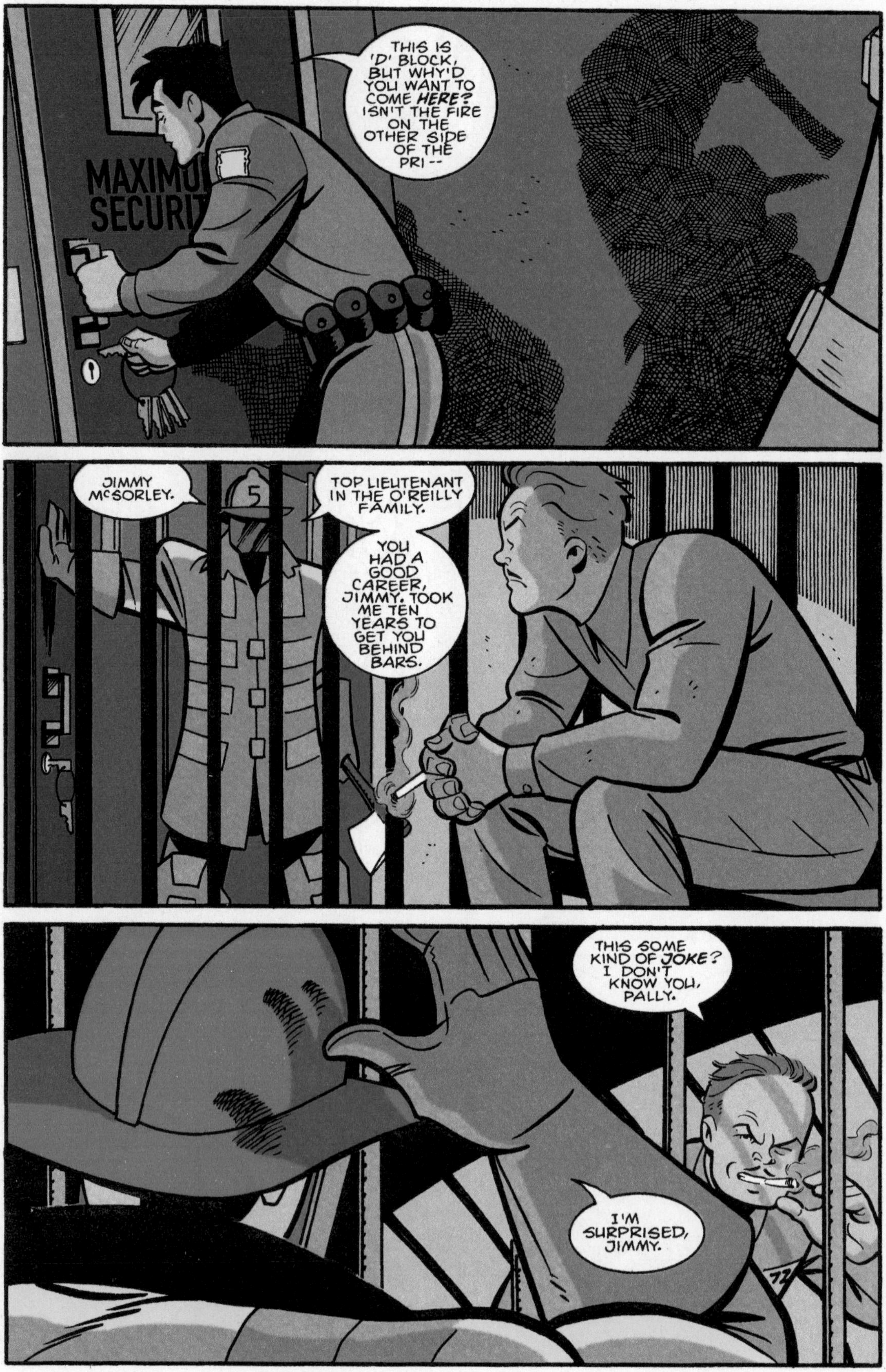
MAXIMUM
SECURITY
THIS IS 'D' BLOCK, BUT WHY'D YOU WANT TO COME HERE? ISN'T THE FIRE ON THE OTHER SIDE OF THE PRI --
5
JIMMY McSORLEY.
TOP LIEUTENANT IN THE O'REILLY FAMILY.
YOU HAD A GOOD CAREER, JIMMY. TOOK ME TEN YEARS TO GET YOU BEHIND BARS.
THIS SOME KIND OF JOKE? I DON'T KNOW YOU, PALLY.
I'M SURPRISED, JIMMY.

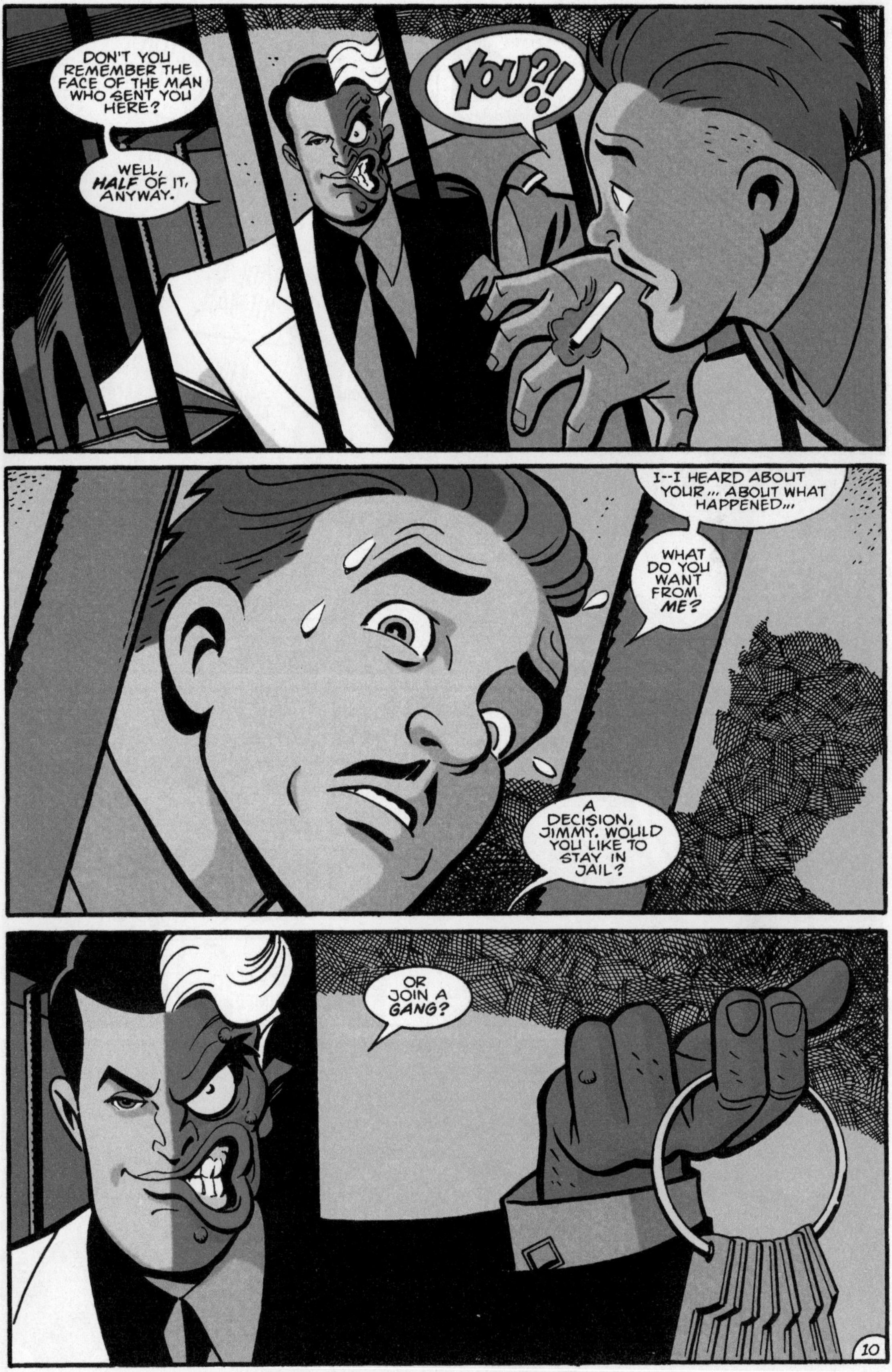
DON'T YOU REMEMBER THE FACE OF THE MAN WHO SENT YOU HERE?
YOU?!
WELL, HALF OF IT, ANYWAY.
I--I HEARD ABOUT YOUR... ABOUT WHAT HAPPENED...
WHAT DO YOU WANT FROM ME?
A DECISION, JIMMY. WOULD YOU LIKE TO STAY IN JAIL?
OR JOIN A GANG?
10

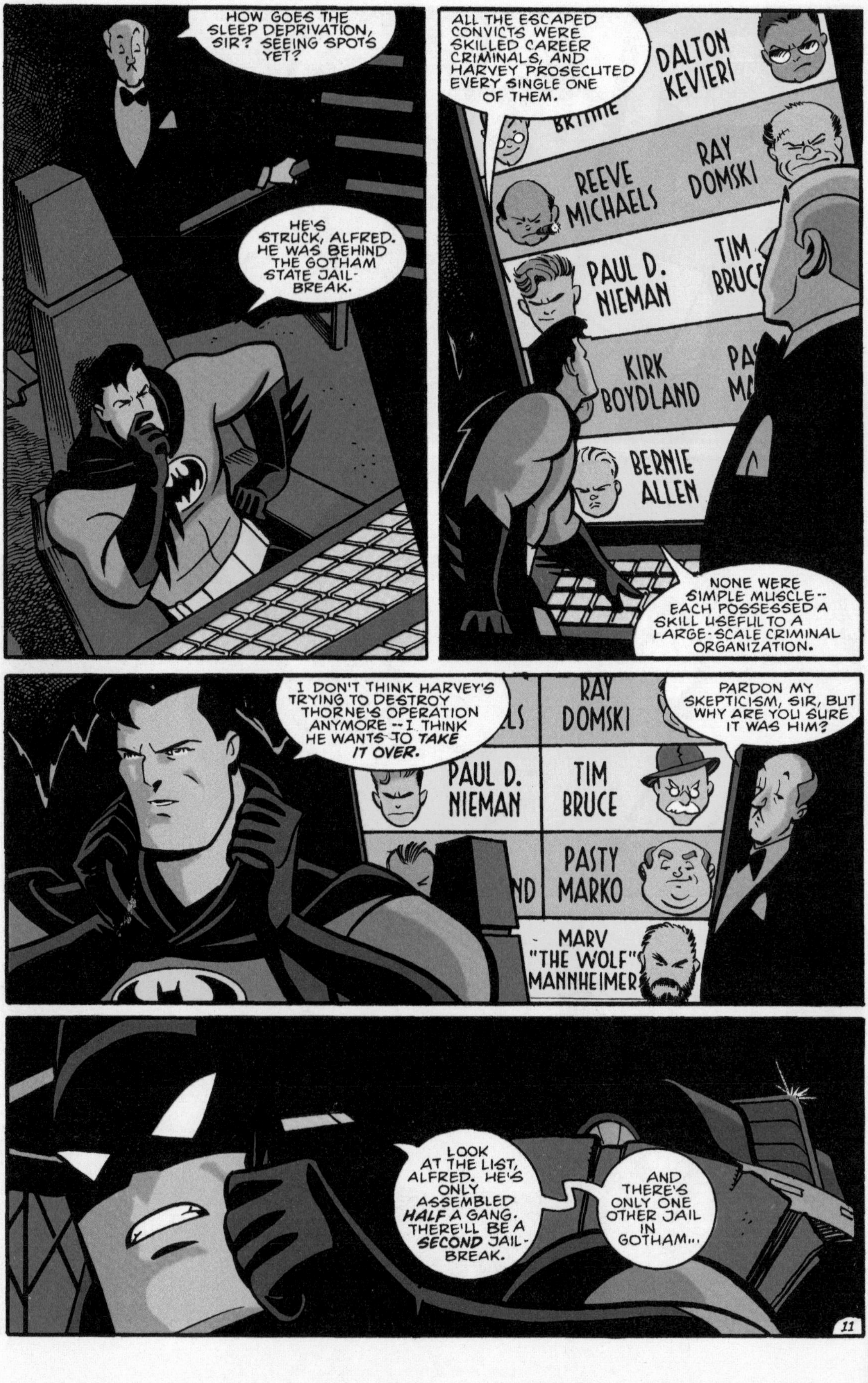
HOW GOES THE SLEEP DEPRIVATION, SIR? SEEING SPOTS YET?
HE'S STRUCK, ALFRED. HE WAS BEHIND THE GOTHAM STATE JAIL-BREAK.
ALL THE ESCAPED CONVICTS WERE SKILLED CAREER CRIMINALS, AND HARVEY PROSECUTED EVERY SINGLE ONE OF THEM.
DALTON KEVIERI
RAY DOMSKI
REEVE MICHAELS
PAUL D. NIEMAN
KIRK BOYDLAND
BERNIE ALLEN
NONE WERE SIMPLE MUSCLE-- EACH POSSESSED A SKILL USEFUL TO A LARGE-SCALE CRIMINAL ORGANIZATION.
I DON'T THINK HARVEY'S TRYING TO DESTROY THORNE'S OPERATION ANYMORE -- I THINK HE WANTS TO *TAKE IT OVER.*
PARDON MY SKEPTICISM, SIR, BUT WHY ARE YOU SURE IT WAS HIM?
RAY DOMSKI
PAUL D. NIEMAN
TIM BRUCE
PASTY MARKO
MARV "THE WOLF" MANNHEIMER
LOOK AT THE LIST, ALFRED. HE'S ONLY ASSEMBLED *HALF* A GANG. THERE'LL BE A *SECOND* JAIL-BREAK.
AND THERE'S ONLY ONE OTHER JAIL IN GOTHAM...

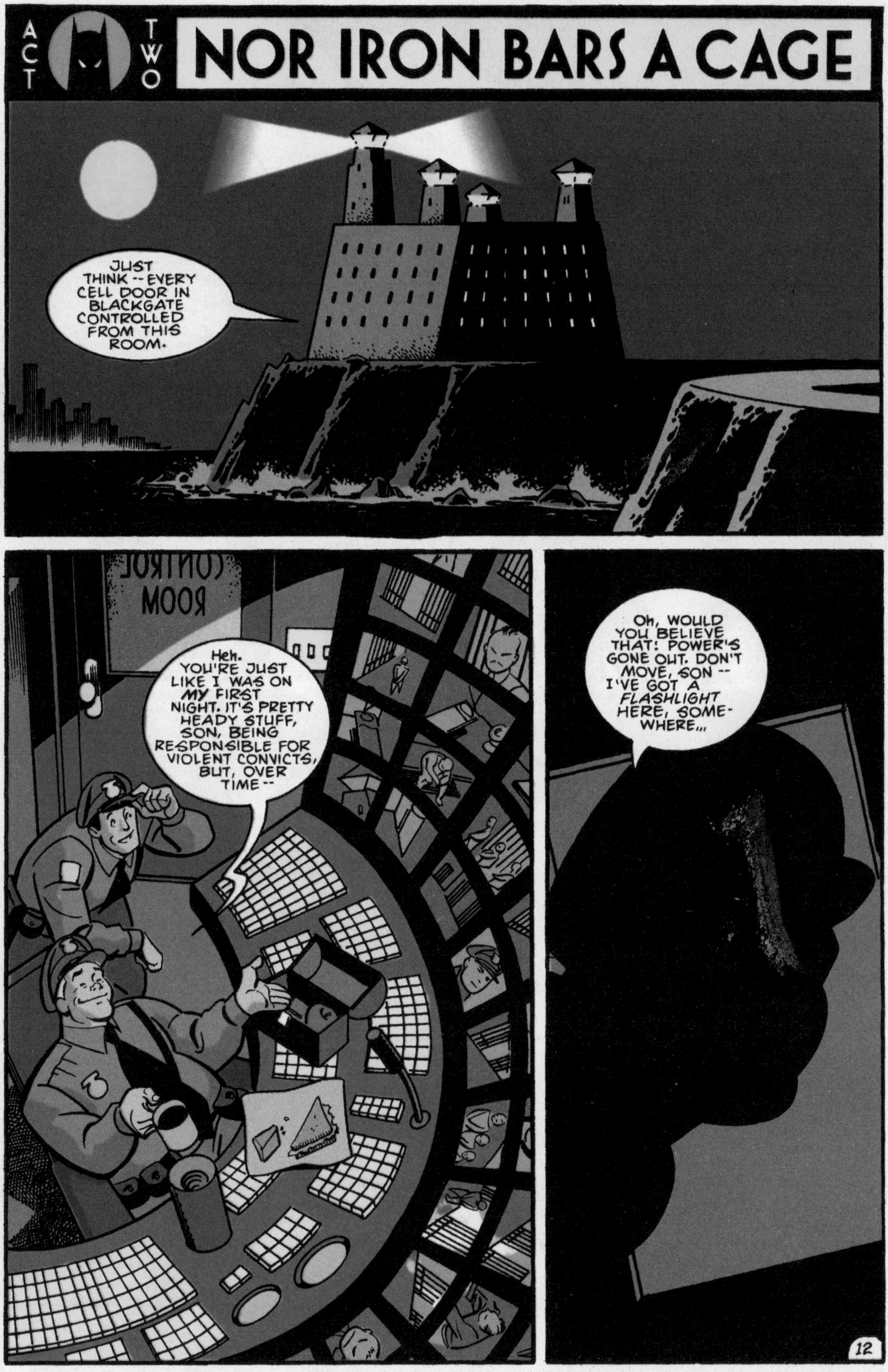

ACT TWO
NOR IRON BARS A CAGE
JUST THINK -- EVERY CELL DOOR IN BLACKGATE CONTROLLED FROM THIS ROOM.
CONTROL ROOM
Heh. YOU'RE JUST LIKE I WAS ON MY FIRST NIGHT. IT'S PRETTY HEADY STUFF, SON, BEING RESPONSIBLE FOR VIOLENT CONVICTS, BUT, OVER TIME --
Oh, WOULD YOU BELIEVE THAT: POWER'S GONE OUT. DON'T MOVE, SON -- I'VE GOT A FLASHLIGHT HERE, SOME-WHERE...

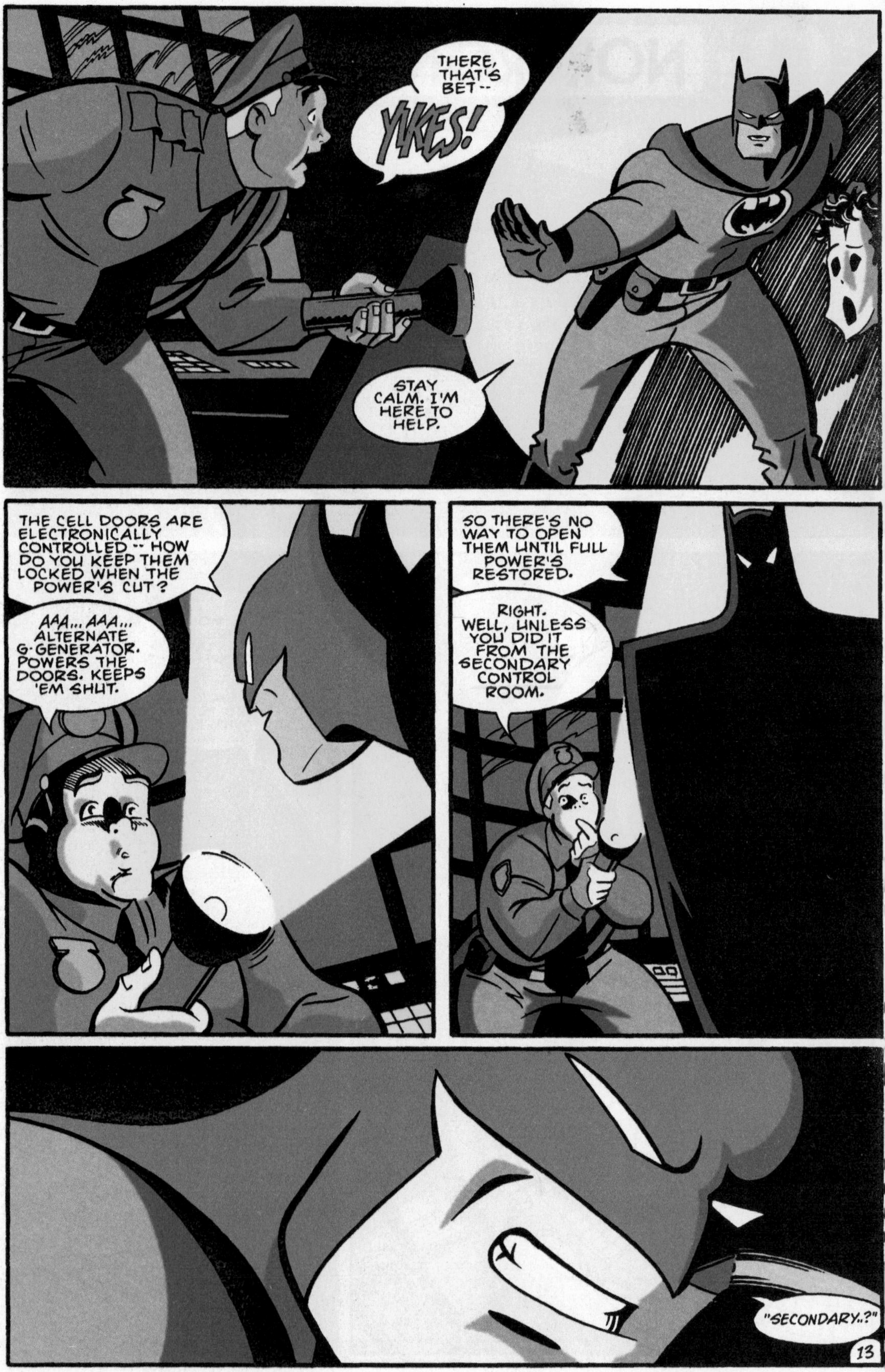
THERE, THAT'S BET--
YIKES!
STAY CALM. I'M HERE TO HELP.
THE CELL DOORS ARE ELECTRONICALLY CONTROLLED -- HOW DO YOU KEEP THEM LOCKED WHEN THE POWER'S CUT?
AAA... AAA... ALTERNATE G-GENERATOR. POWERS THE DOORS. KEEPS 'EM SHUT.
SO THERE'S NO WAY TO OPEN THEM UNTIL FULL POWER'S RESTORED.
RIGHT. WELL, UNLESS YOU DID IT FROM THE SECONDARY CONTROL ROOM.
"SECONDARY..?"

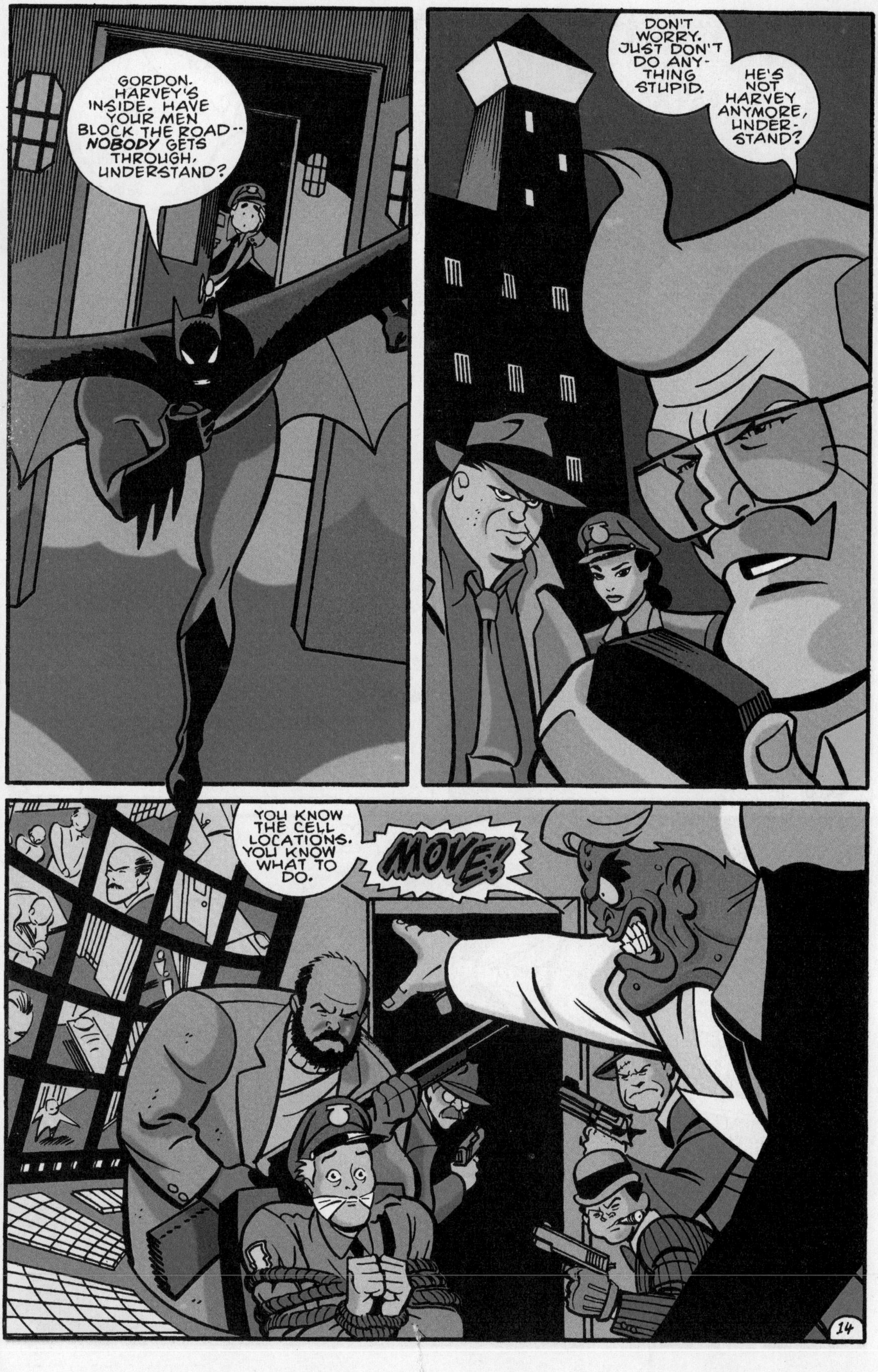
GORDON. HARVEY'S INSIDE. HAVE YOUR MEN BLOCK THE ROAD-- NOBODY GETS THROUGH, UNDERSTAND?
DON'T WORRY. JUST DON'T DO ANY-THING STUPID.
HE'S NOT HARVEY ANYMORE, UNDER-STAND?
YOU KNOW THE CELL LOCATIONS. YOU KNOW WHAT TO DO.
MOVE!
14

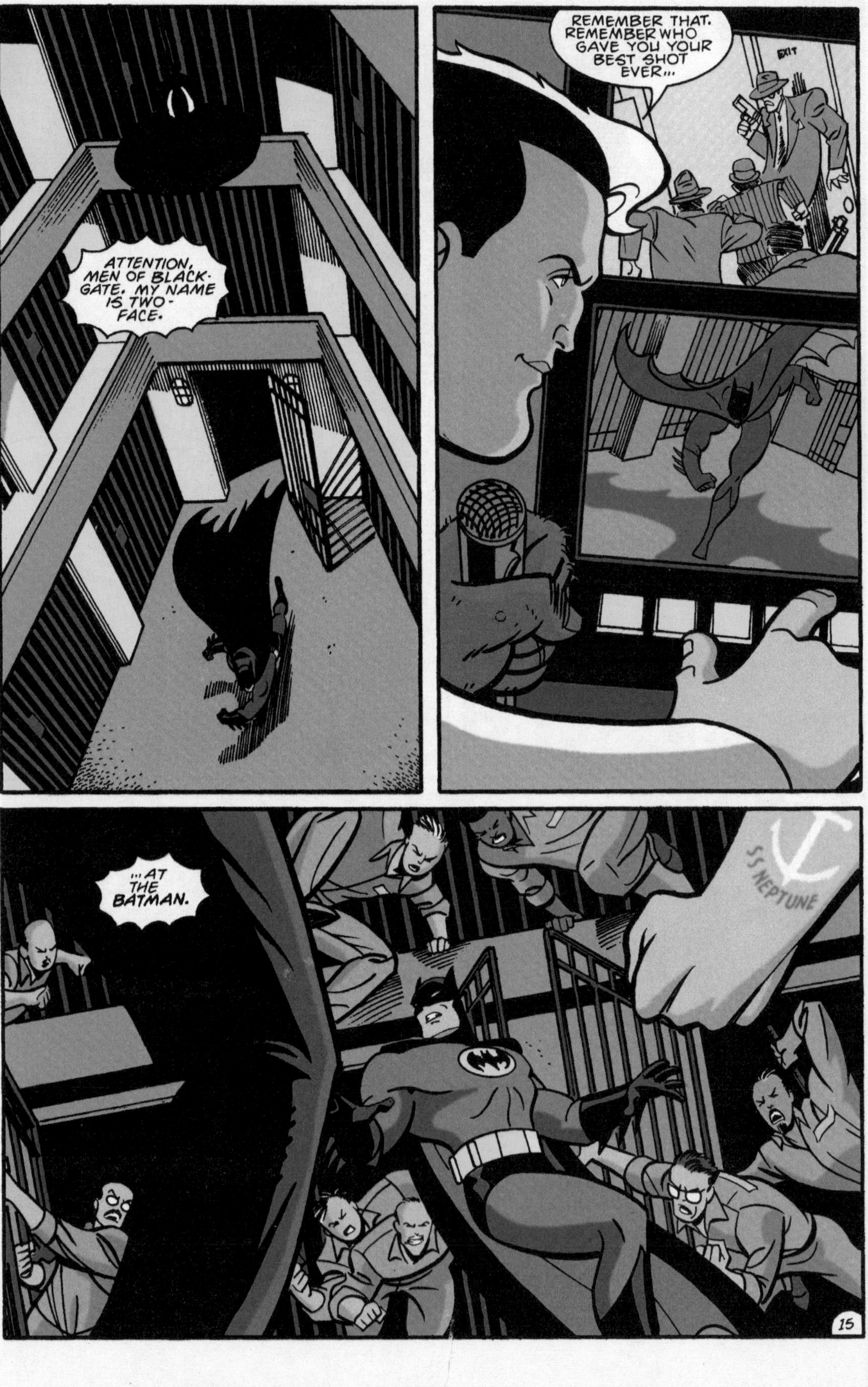

ATTENTION, MEN OF BLACKGATE. MY NAME IS TWO-FACE.
REMEMBER THAT. REMEMBER WHO GAVE YOU YOUR BEST SHOT EVER...
EXIT
...AT THE BATMAN.
SS NEPTUNE

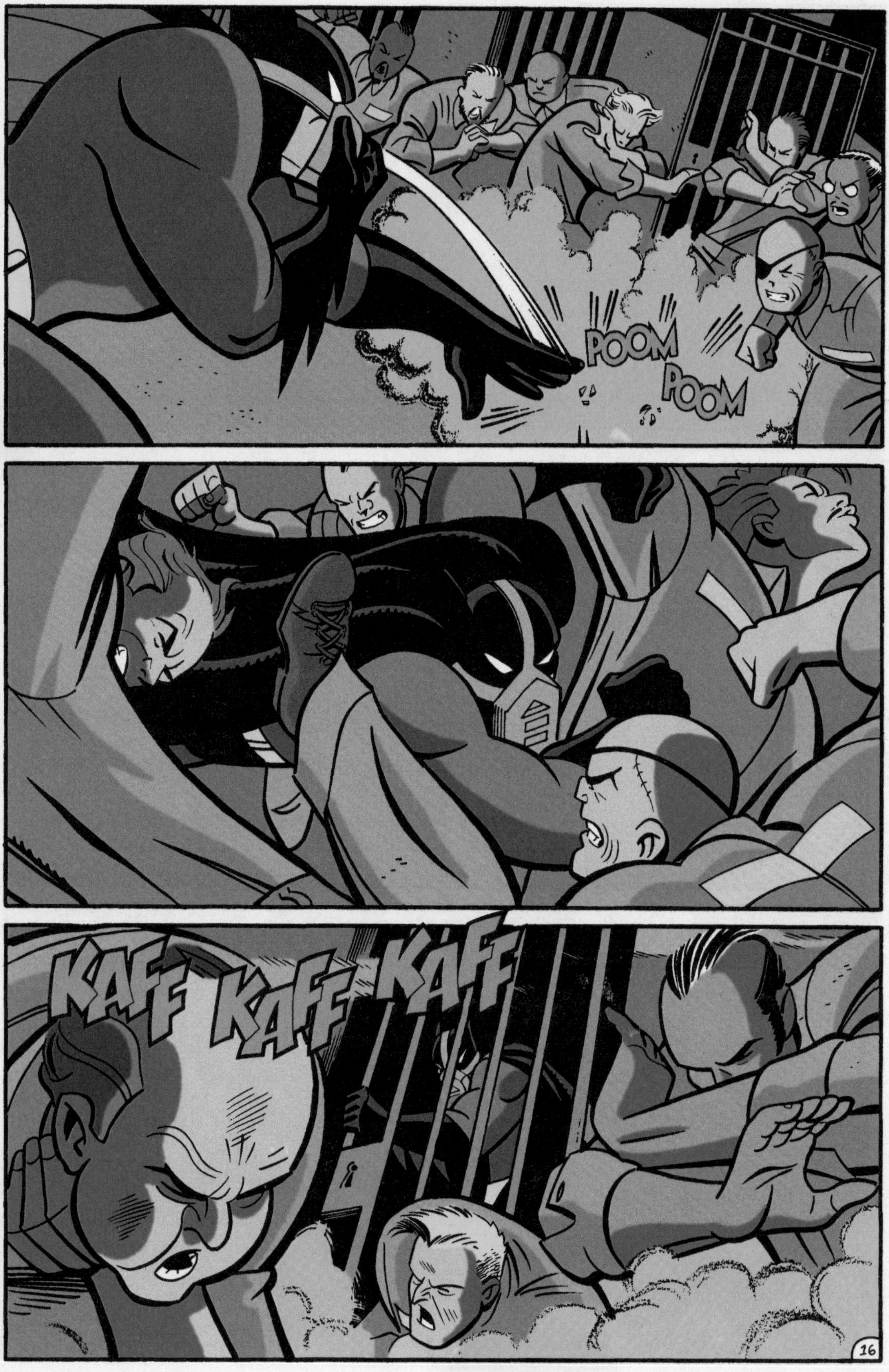
POOM
POOM
KAFF KAFF KAFF

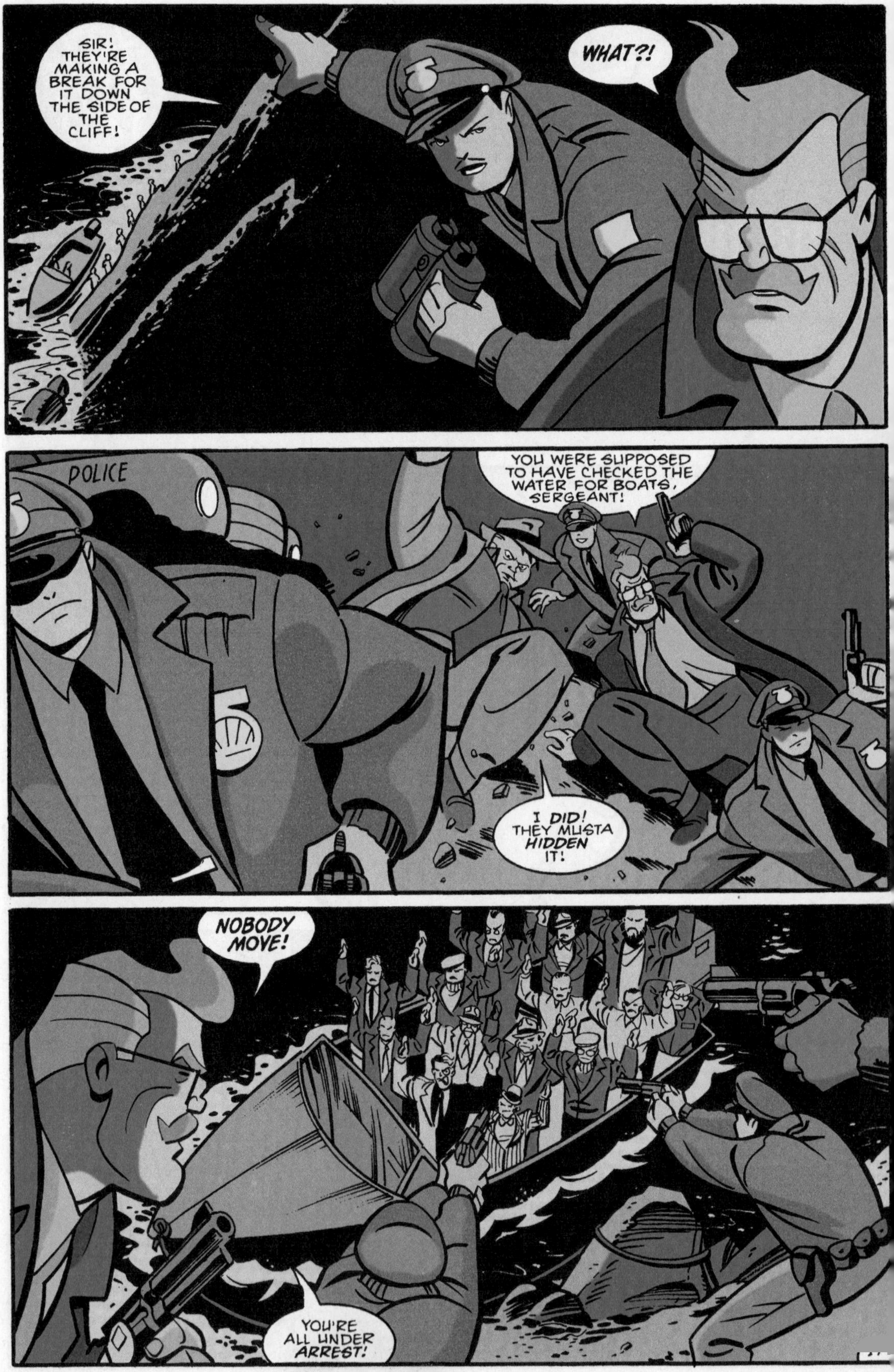
SIR! THEY'RE MAKING A BREAK FOR IT DOWN THE SIDE OF THE CLIFF!
WHAT?!
POLICE
YOU WERE SUPPOSED TO HAVE CHECKED THE WATER FOR BOATS, SERGEANT!
I DID! THEY MUSTA HIDDEN IT!
NOBODY MOVE!
YOU'RE ALL UNDER ARREST!

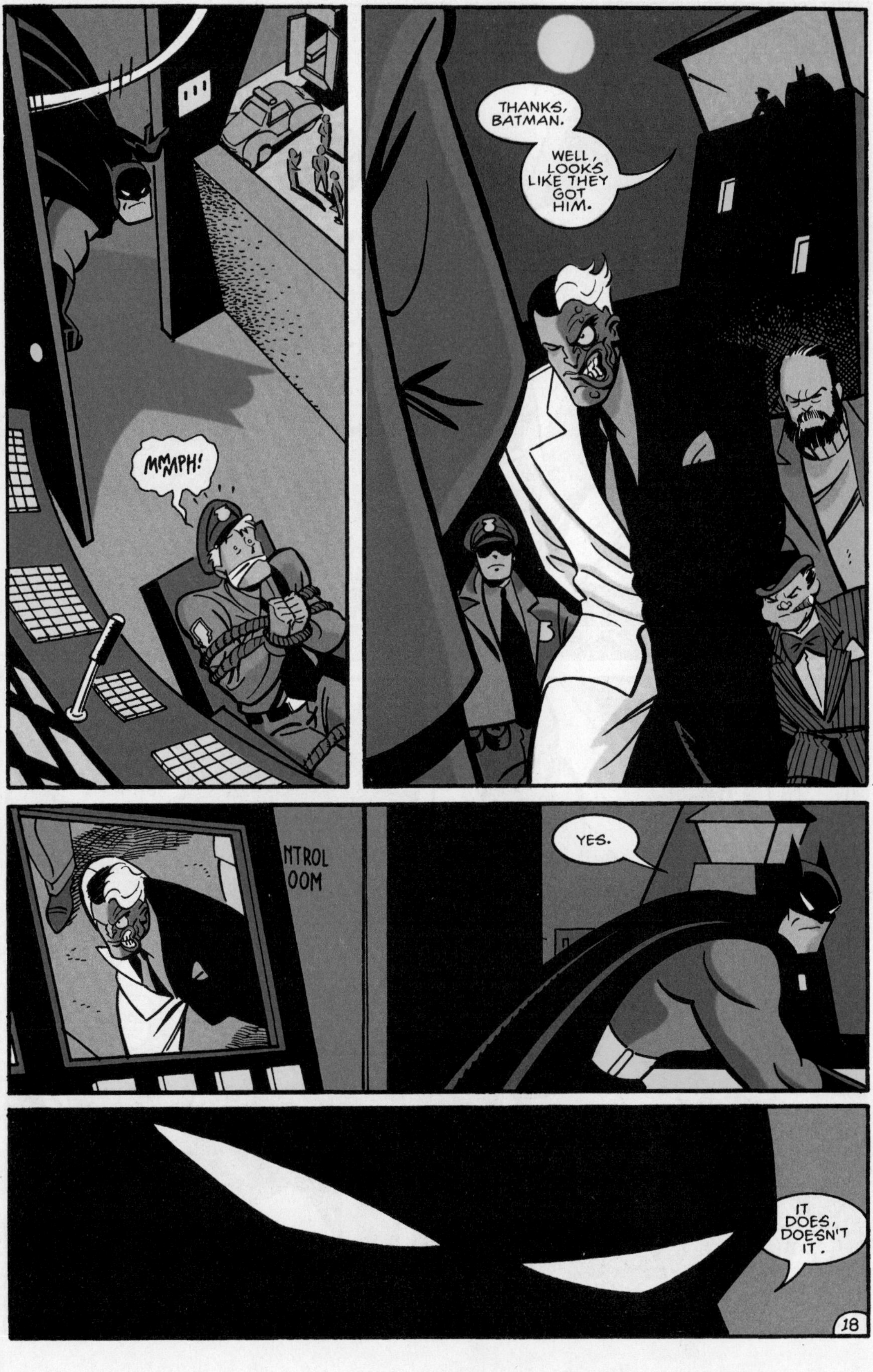
MMMPH!
THANKS, BATMAN.
WELL, LOOKS LIKE THEY GOT HIM.
NTROL
OOM
YES.
IT DOES, DOESN'T IT.

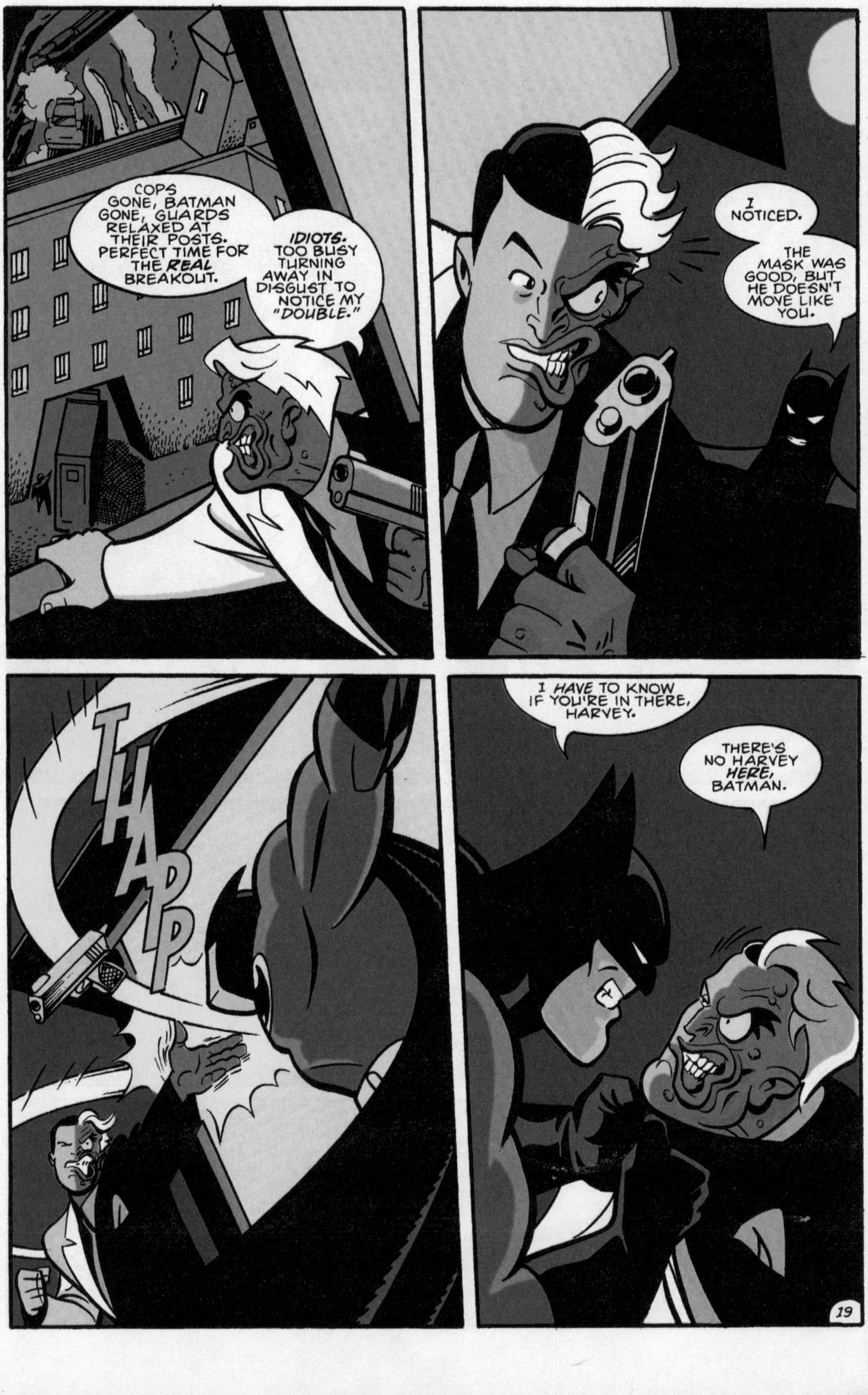
COPS GONE, BATMAN GONE, GUARDS RELAXED AT THEIR POSTS. PERFECT TIME FOR THE REAL BREAKOUT.
IDIOTS. TOO BUSY TURNING AWAY IN DISGUST TO NOTICE MY "DOUBLE."
I NOTICED.
THE MASK WAS GOOD, BUT HE DOESN'T MOVE LIKE YOU.
THAPP
I HAVE TO KNOW IF YOU'RE IN THERE, HARVEY.
THERE'S NO HARVEY HERE, BATMAN.
19

I THINK THERE *IS*. I THINK HARVEY'S THE REASON--

--YOU NEED *THIS*.

I THINK HARVEY'S STILL FIGHTING YOU. YOU TOOK HIS FRIENDS, HIS GOALS, HIS DREAMS, BUT UNTIL YOU CAN *DECIDE* TO COMMIT A CRIME, YOU CAN'T TAKE HIS SOUL.

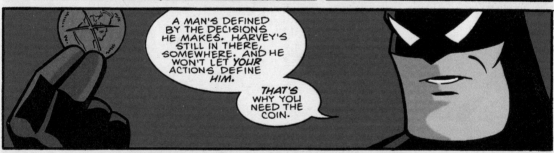

A MAN'S DEFINED BY THE DECISIONS HE MAKES. HARVEY'S STILL IN THERE, SOMEWHERE. AND HE WON'T LET *YOUR* ACTIONS DEFINE *HIM*.

THAT'S WHY YOU NEED THE COIN.

A *THEORY*, BATMAN. JUST A THEORY.

YOU'RE RIGHT. AND AS I SAID, I HAVE TO *KNOW*.

20

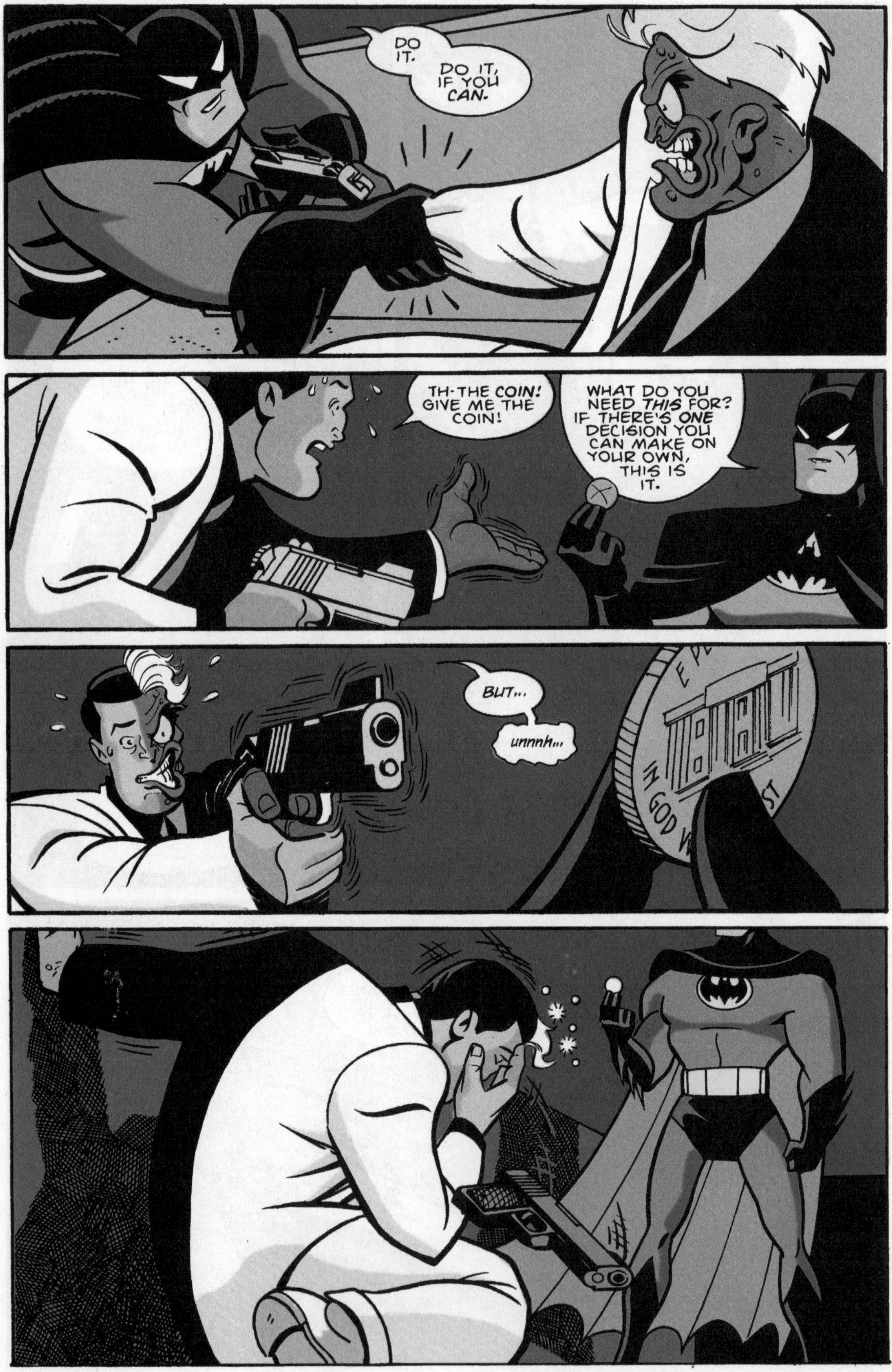

DO IT.
DO IT, IF YOU CAN.
TH-THE COIN! GIVE ME THE COIN!
WHAT DO YOU NEED THIS FOR? IF THERE'S ONE DECISION YOU CAN MAKE ON YOUR OWN, THIS IS IT.
BUT...
unnnh...

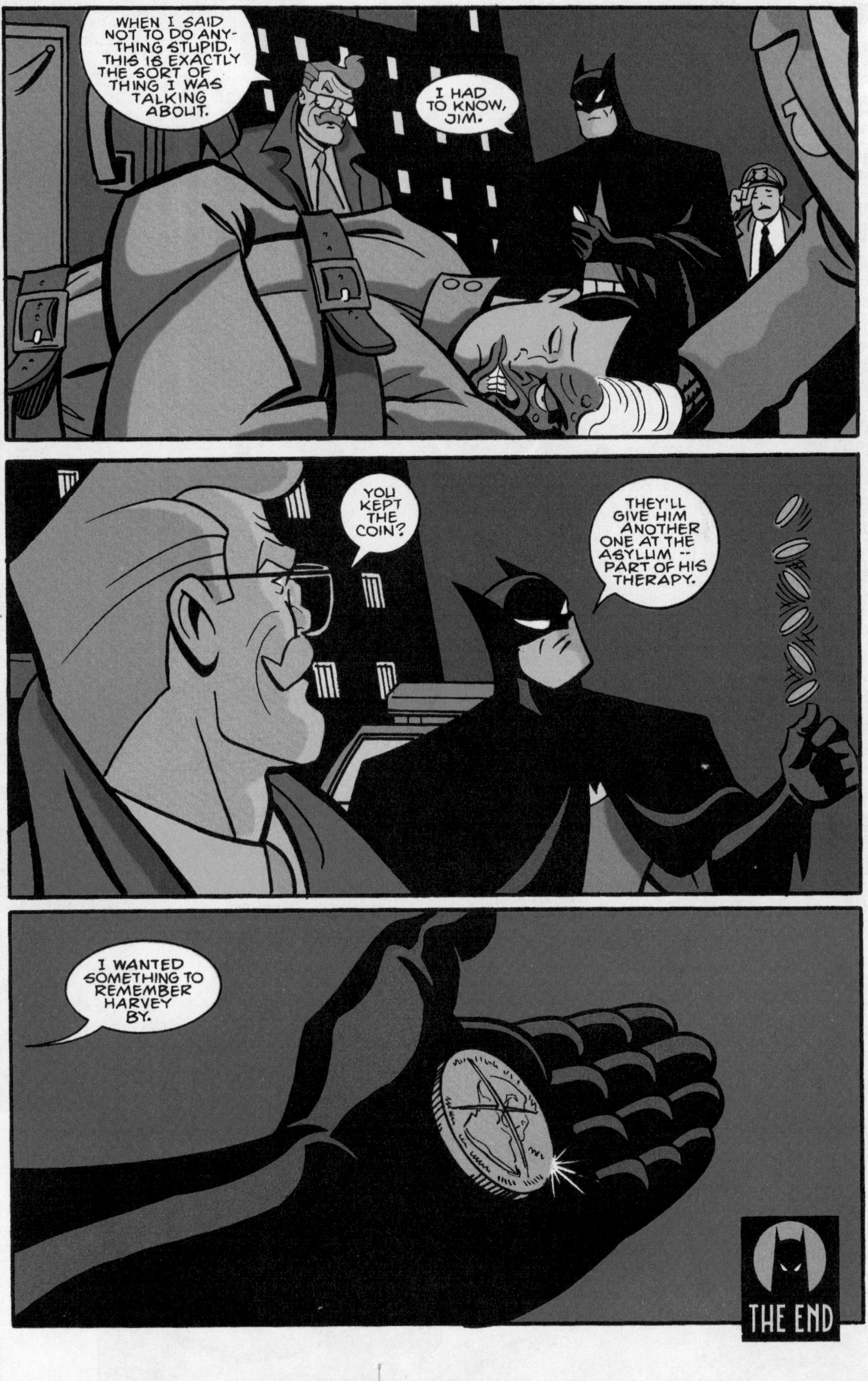
WHEN I SAID NOT TO DO ANYTHING STUPID, THIS IS EXACTLY THE SORT OF THING I WAS TALKING ABOUT.
I HAD TO KNOW, JIM.
YOU KEPT THE COIN?
THEY'LL GIVE HIM ANOTHER ONE AT THE ASYLUM -- PART OF HIS THERAPY.
I WANTED SOMETHING TO REMEMBER HARVEY BY.
THE END

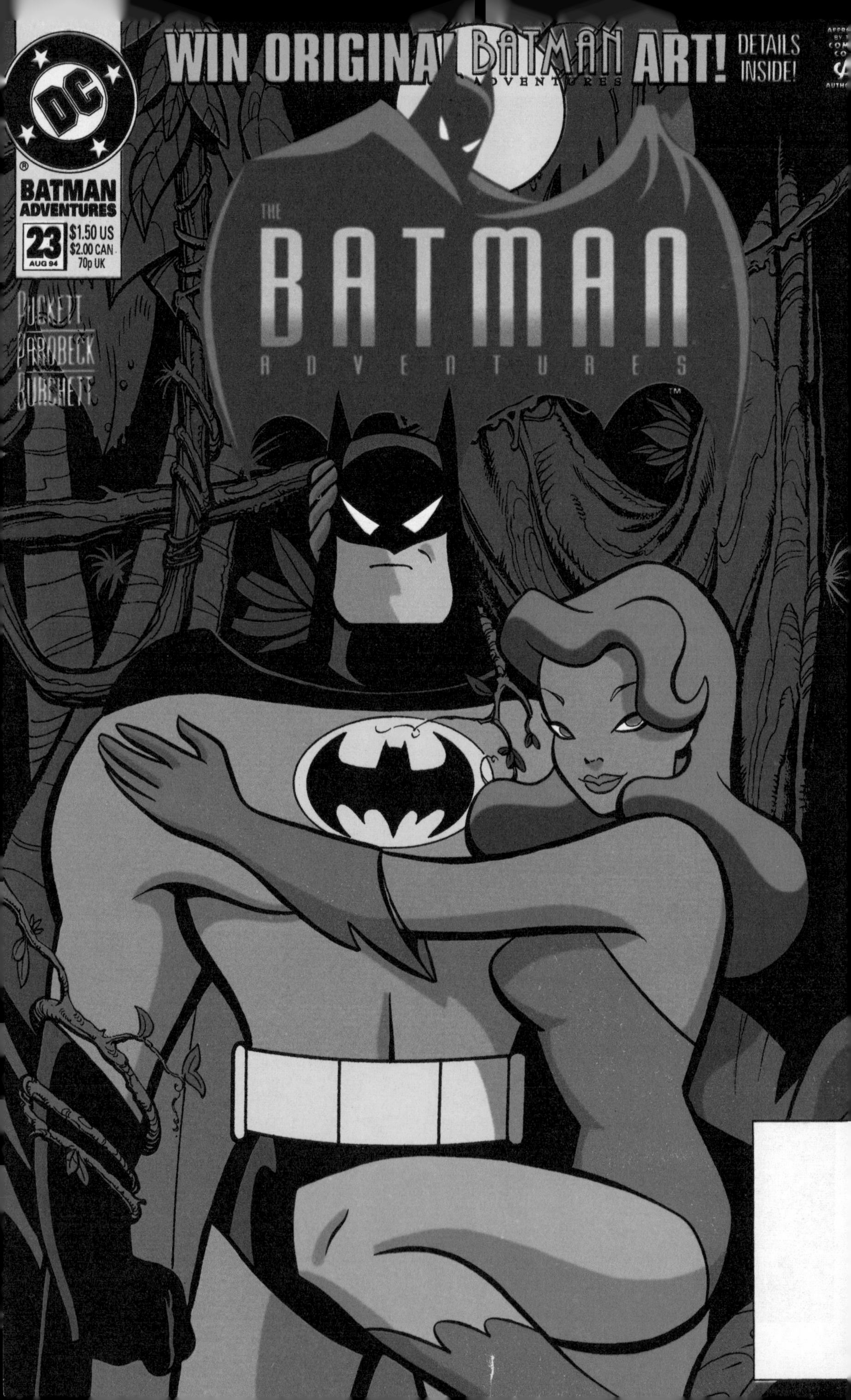

WIN ORIGINAL BATMAN ADVENTURES ART!
DETAILS INSIDE!
DC
BATMAN ADVENTURES
23
AUG 94
$1.50 US
$2.00 CAN
70p UK
PUCKETT
PAROBECK
BURCHETT
THE BATMAN ADVENTURES

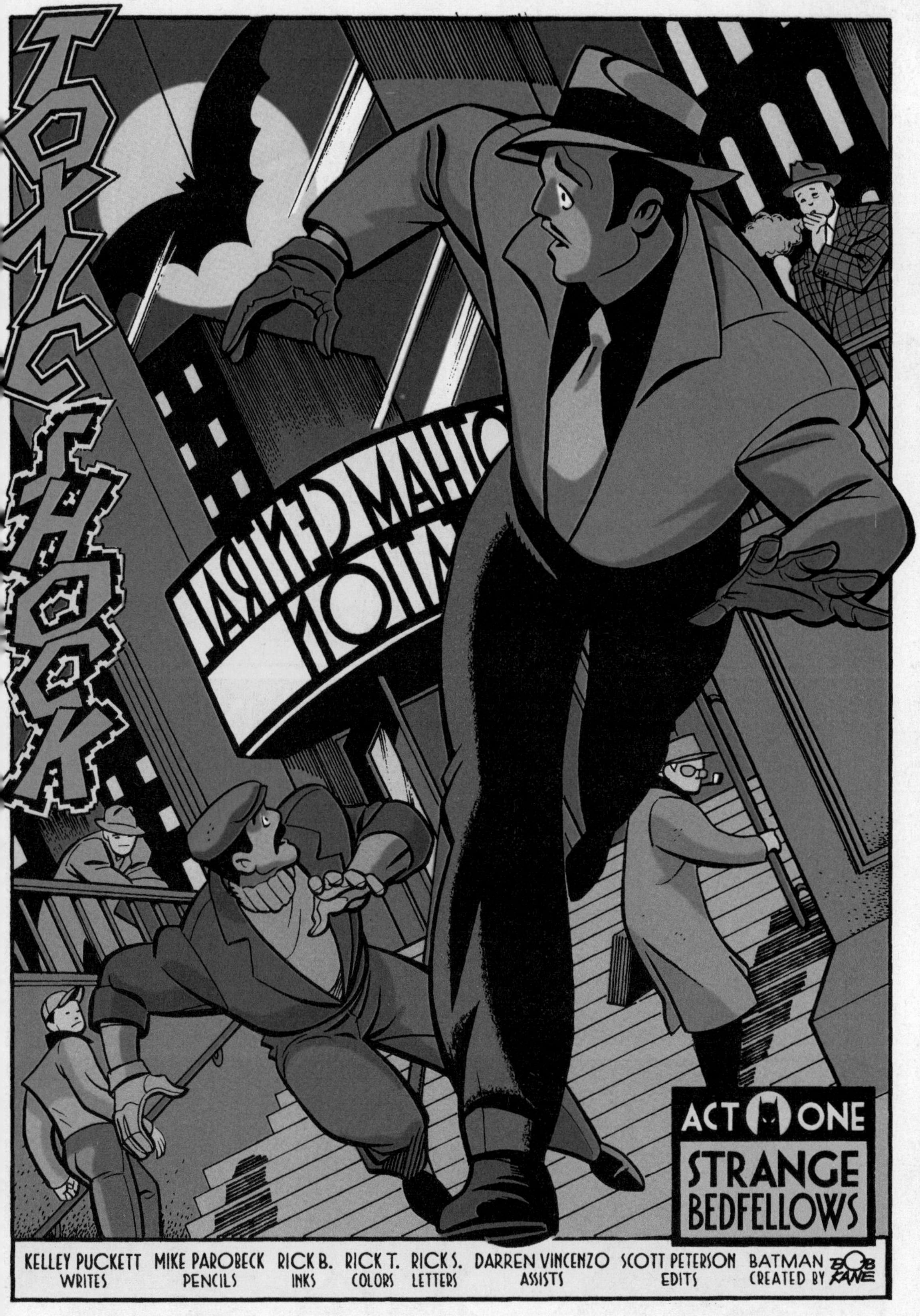
TOXIC SHOCK
ACT ONE
STRANGE BEDFELLOWS
KELLEY PUCKETT WRITES
MIKE PAROBECK PENCILS
RICK B. INKS
RICK T. COLORS
RICK S. LETTERS
DARREN VINCENZO ASSISTS
SCOTT PETERSON EDITS
BATMAN CREATED BY BOB KANE

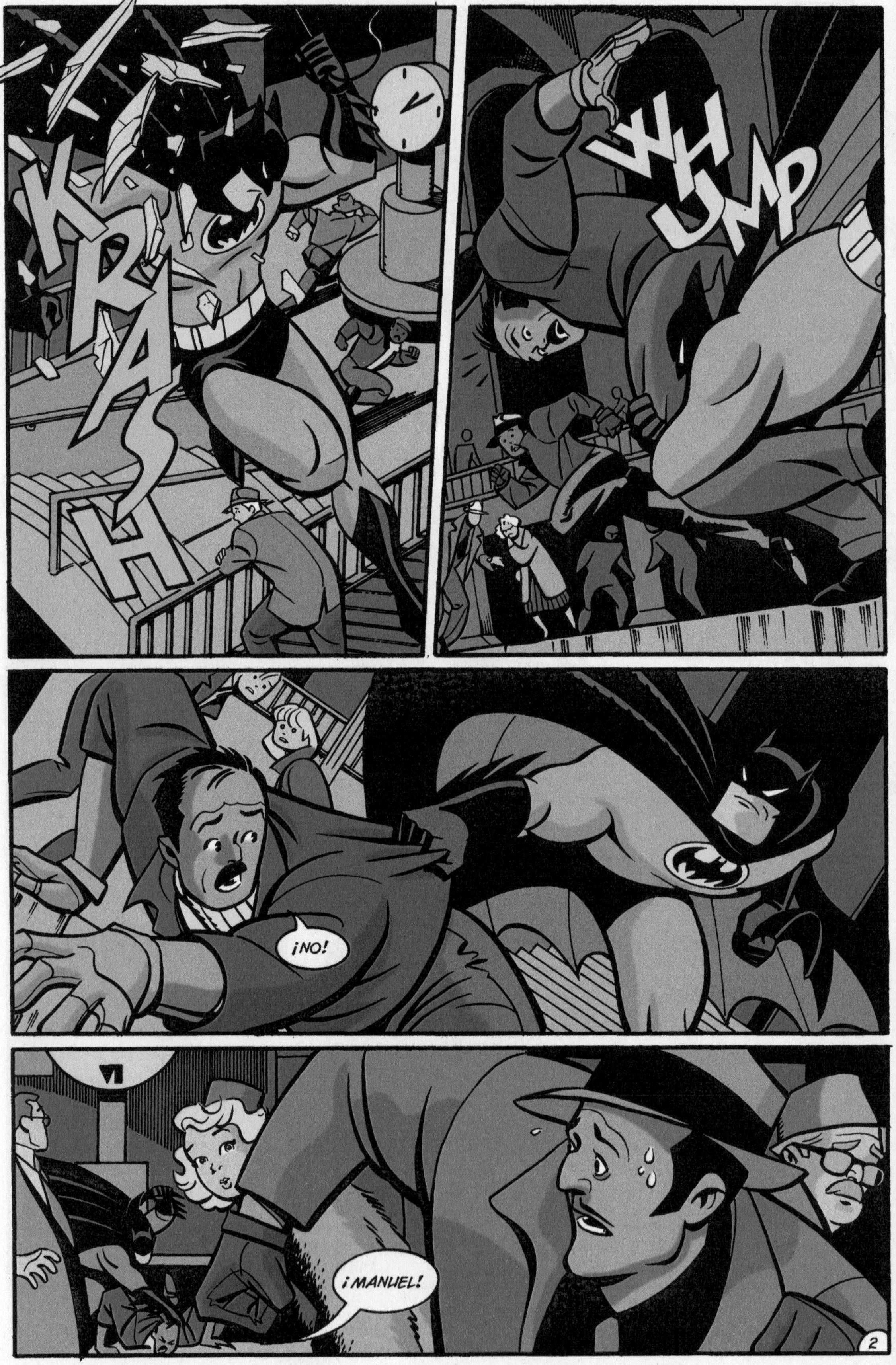
KRAAH
WHUMP
¡NO!
¡MANUEL!

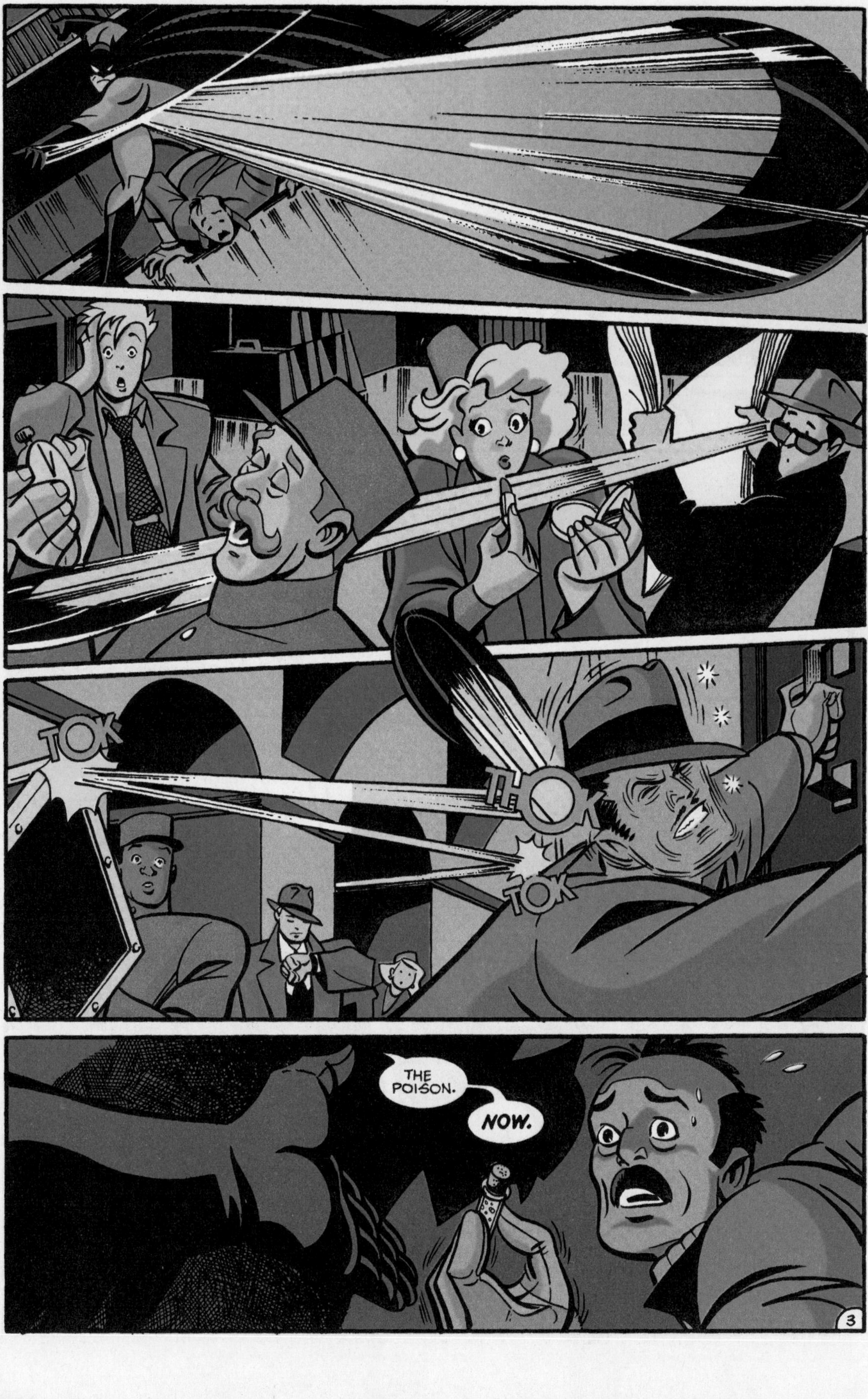
TOK
THOK
TOK
THE POISON.
NOW.

THE DOCTORS ARE DOING ALL THEY CAN, SEÑOR MOLINOS.

FOR YEARS, DIEGO RIVERA HAS CHAMPIONED THE CAUSE OF PRESERVING NATURE. PROTECTING *LIFE*. WHO COULD POISON SUCH A MAN?

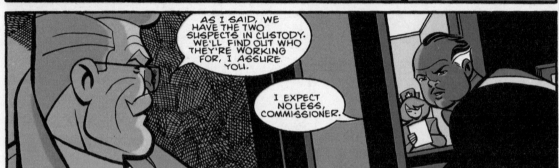

AS I SAID, WE HAVE THE TWO SUSPECTS IN CUSTODY. WE'LL FIND OUT WHO THEY'RE WORKING FOR, I ASSURE YOU.

I EXPECT NO LESS, COMMISSIONER.

THAT WAS GABRIEL MOLINOS --

-- HEAD OF THE SOUTH AMERICAN ECONOMIC COUNCIL AND A COUNTRYMAN OF RIVERA'S.

WHAT DID YOU FIND?

IT'S, IT'S DEADLY, IT'S PLANT- DERIVED, AND THERE'S NO RECORD OF ANYTHING LIKE IT.

THERE *IS* SOMEONE IN GOTHAM WITH THE EXPERTISE TO DEVELOP AN ANTIDOTE. BUT THERE'S A HITCH.

WHAT'S THAT?

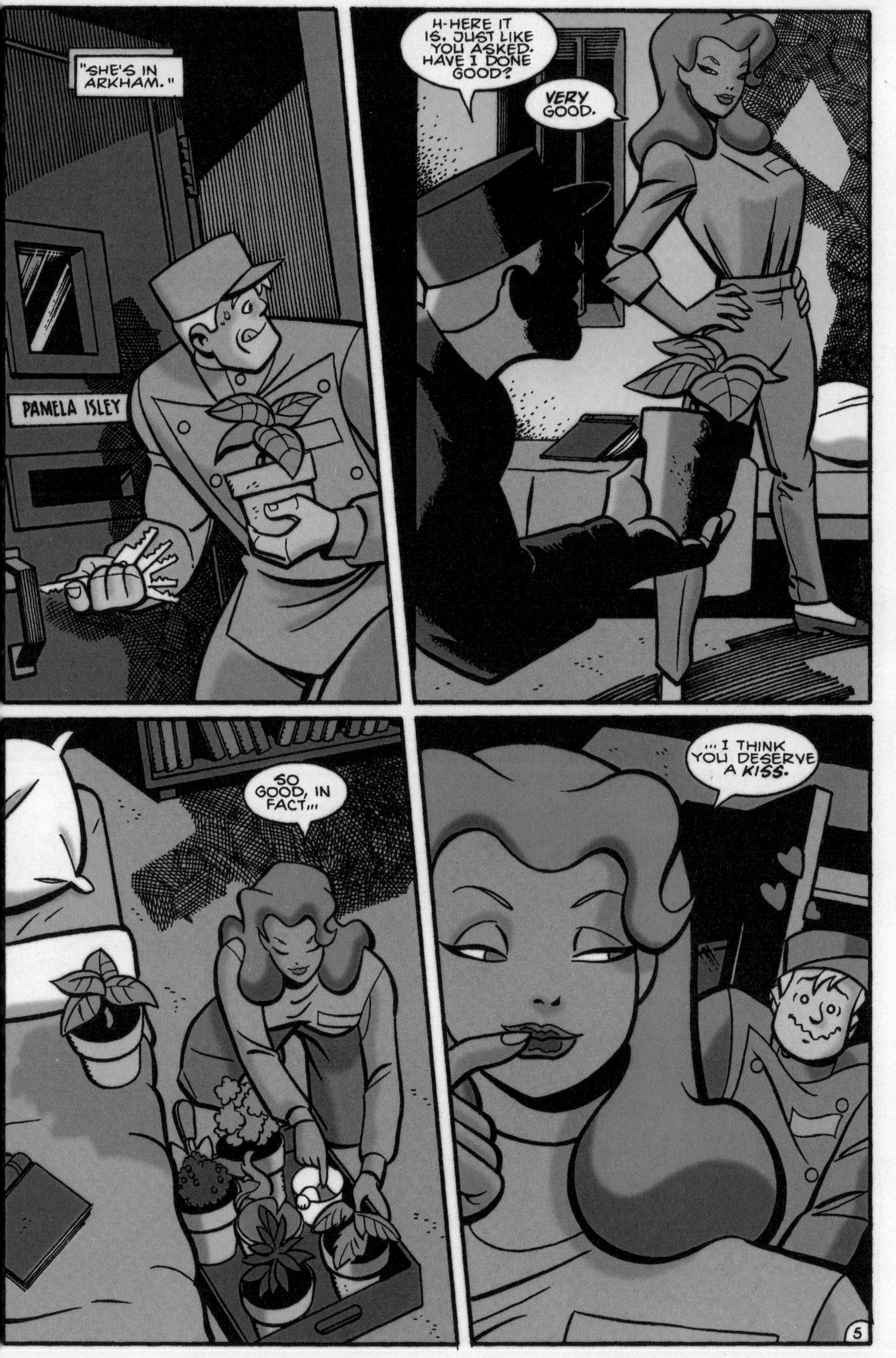

"SHE'S IN ARKHAM."
PAMELA ISLEY
H-HERE IT IS. JUST LIKE YOU ASKED. HAVE I DONE GOOD?
VERY GOOD.
SO GOOD, IN FACT...
...I THINK YOU DESERVE A KISS.

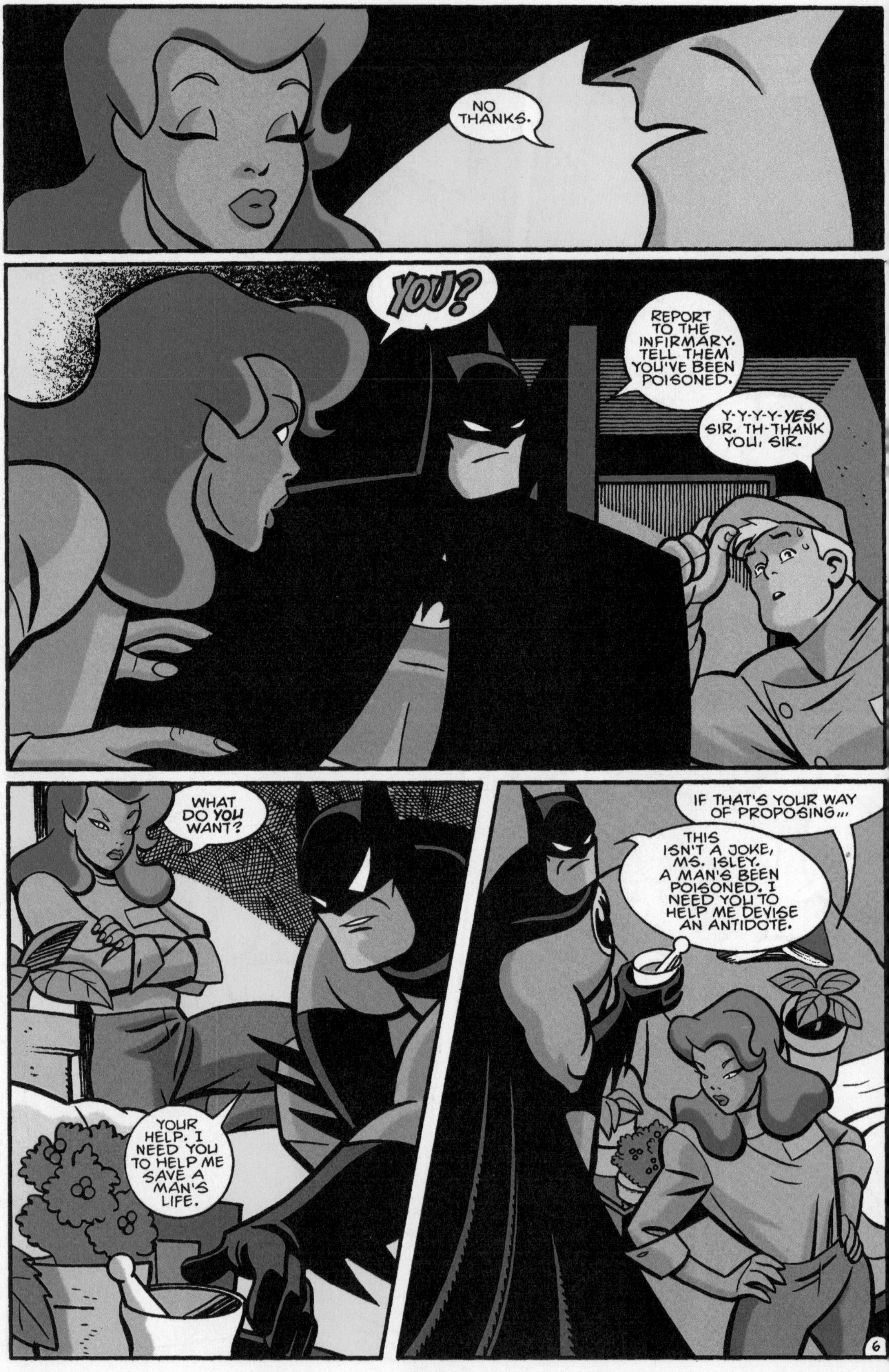
NO THANKS.
YOU?
REPORT TO THE INFIRMARY. TELL THEM YOU'VE BEEN POISONED.
Y-Y-Y-Y-YES SIR. TH-THANK YOU, SIR.
WHAT DO YOU WANT?
YOUR HELP. I NEED YOU TO HELP ME SAVE A MAN'S LIFE.
IF THAT'S YOUR WAY OF PROPOSING...
THIS ISN'T A JOKE, MS. ISLEY. A MAN'S BEEN POISONED. I NEED YOU TO HELP ME DEVISE AN ANTIDOTE.
6

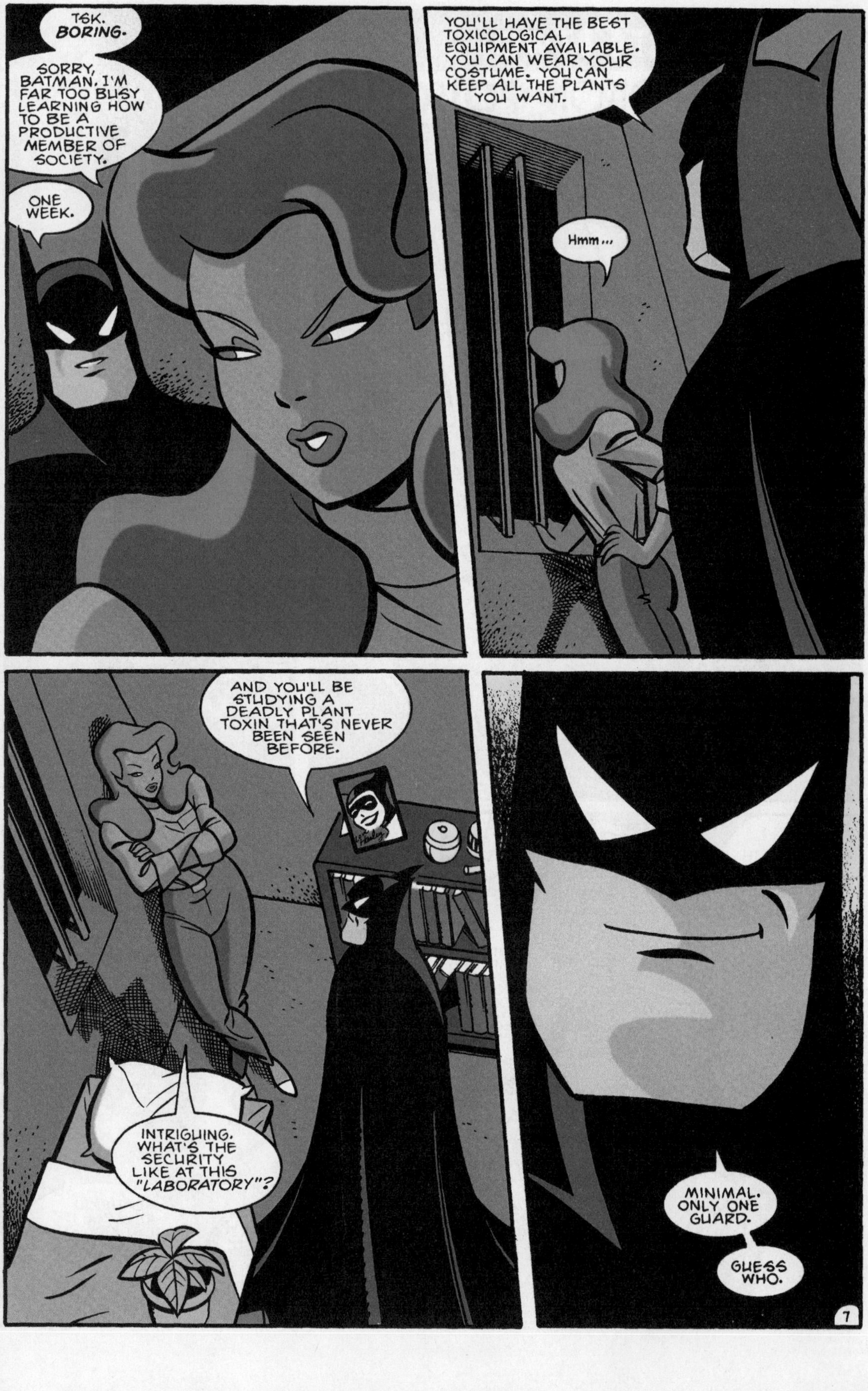
TSK. BORING.
SORRY, BATMAN. I'M FAR TOO BUSY LEARNING HOW TO BE A PRODUCTIVE MEMBER OF SOCIETY.
ONE WEEK.
YOU'LL HAVE THE BEST TOXICOLOGICAL EQUIPMENT AVAILABLE. YOU CAN WEAR YOUR COSTUME. YOU CAN KEEP ALL THE PLANTS YOU WANT.
Hmm...
AND YOU'LL BE STUDYING A DEADLY PLANT TOXIN THAT'S NEVER BEEN SEEN BEFORE.
INTRIGUING. WHAT'S THE SECURITY LIKE AT THIS "LABORATORY"?
MINIMAL. ONLY ONE GUARD.
GUESS WHO.

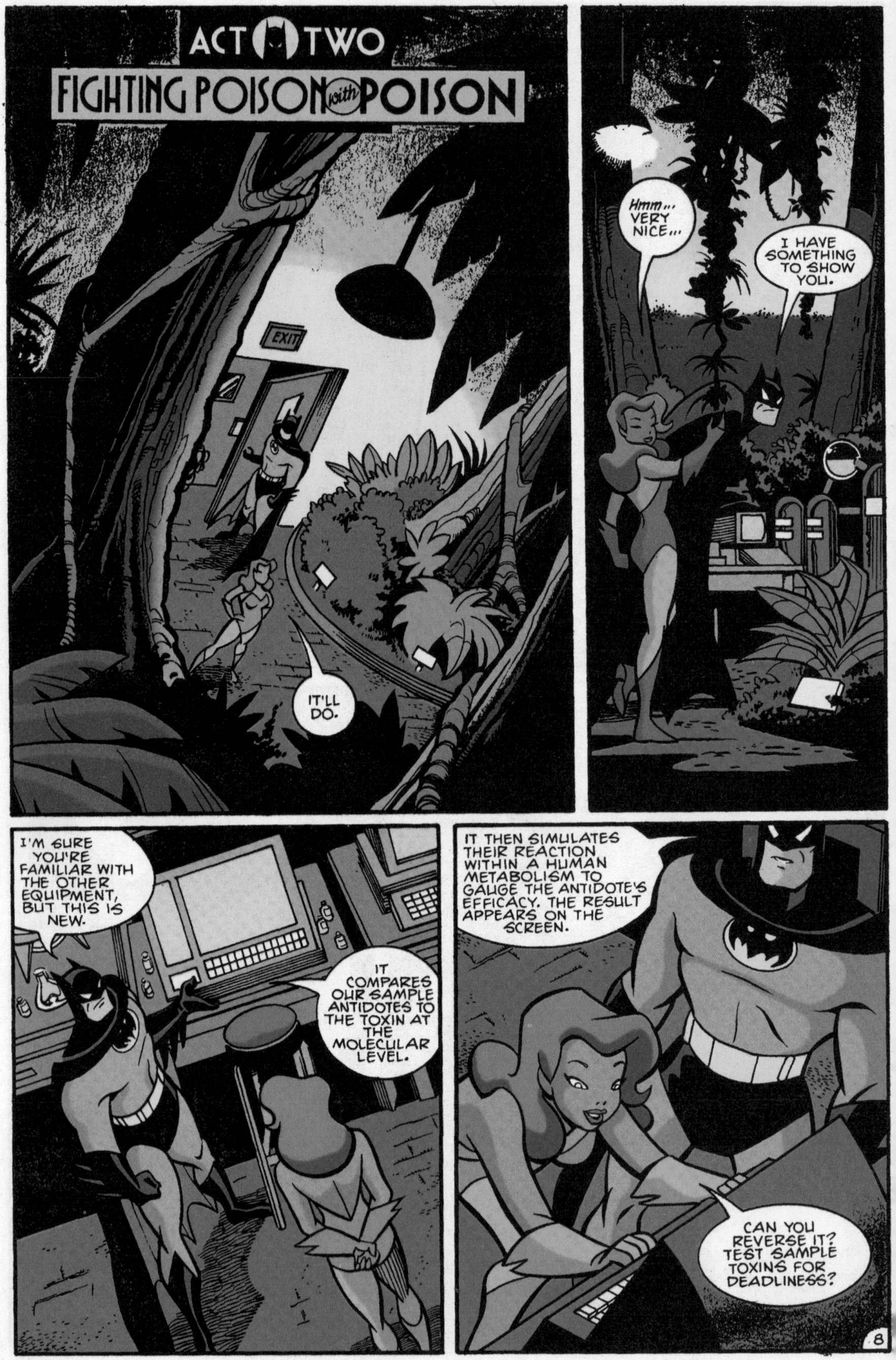
ACT TWO
FIGHTING POISON with POISON
EXIT
IT'LL DO.
Hmm... VERY NICE...
I HAVE SOMETHING TO SHOW YOU.
I'M SURE YOU'RE FAMILIAR WITH THE OTHER EQUIPMENT, BUT THIS IS NEW.
IT COMPARES OUR SAMPLE ANTIDOTES TO THE TOXIN AT THE MOLECULAR LEVEL.
IT THEN SIMULATES THEIR REACTION WITHIN A HUMAN METABOLISM TO GAUGE THE ANTIDOTE'S EFFICACY. THE RESULT APPEARS ON THE SCREEN.
CAN YOU REVERSE IT? TEST SAMPLE TOXINS FOR DEADLINESS?
8

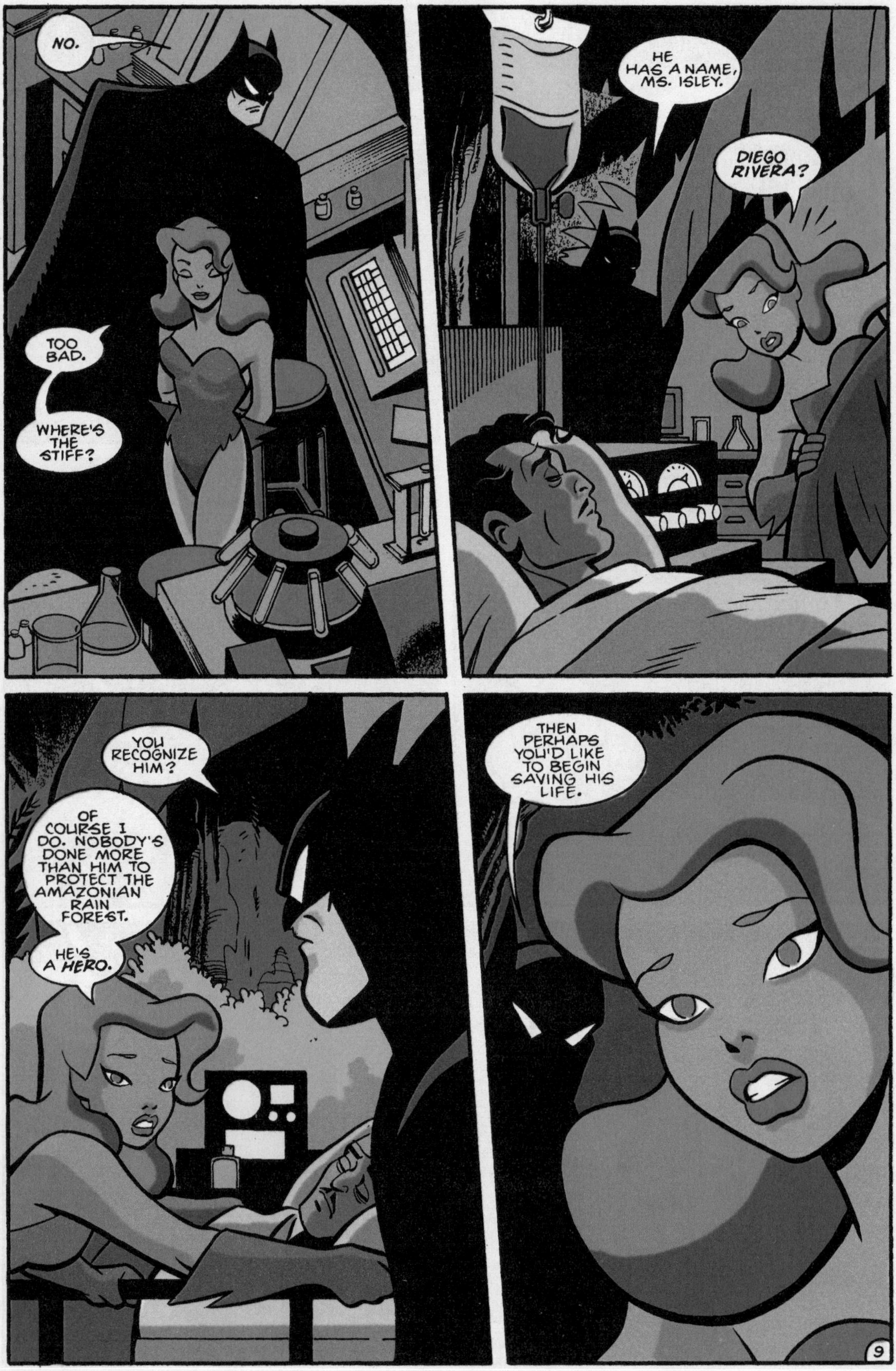
NO.
TOO BAD.
WHERE'S THE STIFF?
HE HAS A NAME, MS. ISLEY.
DIEGO RIVERA?
YOU RECOGNIZE HIM?
OF COURSE I DO. NOBODY'S DONE MORE THAN HIM TO PROTECT THE AMAZONIAN RAIN FOREST.
HE'S A *HERO*.
THEN PERHAPS YOU'D LIKE TO BEGIN SAVING HIS LIFE.

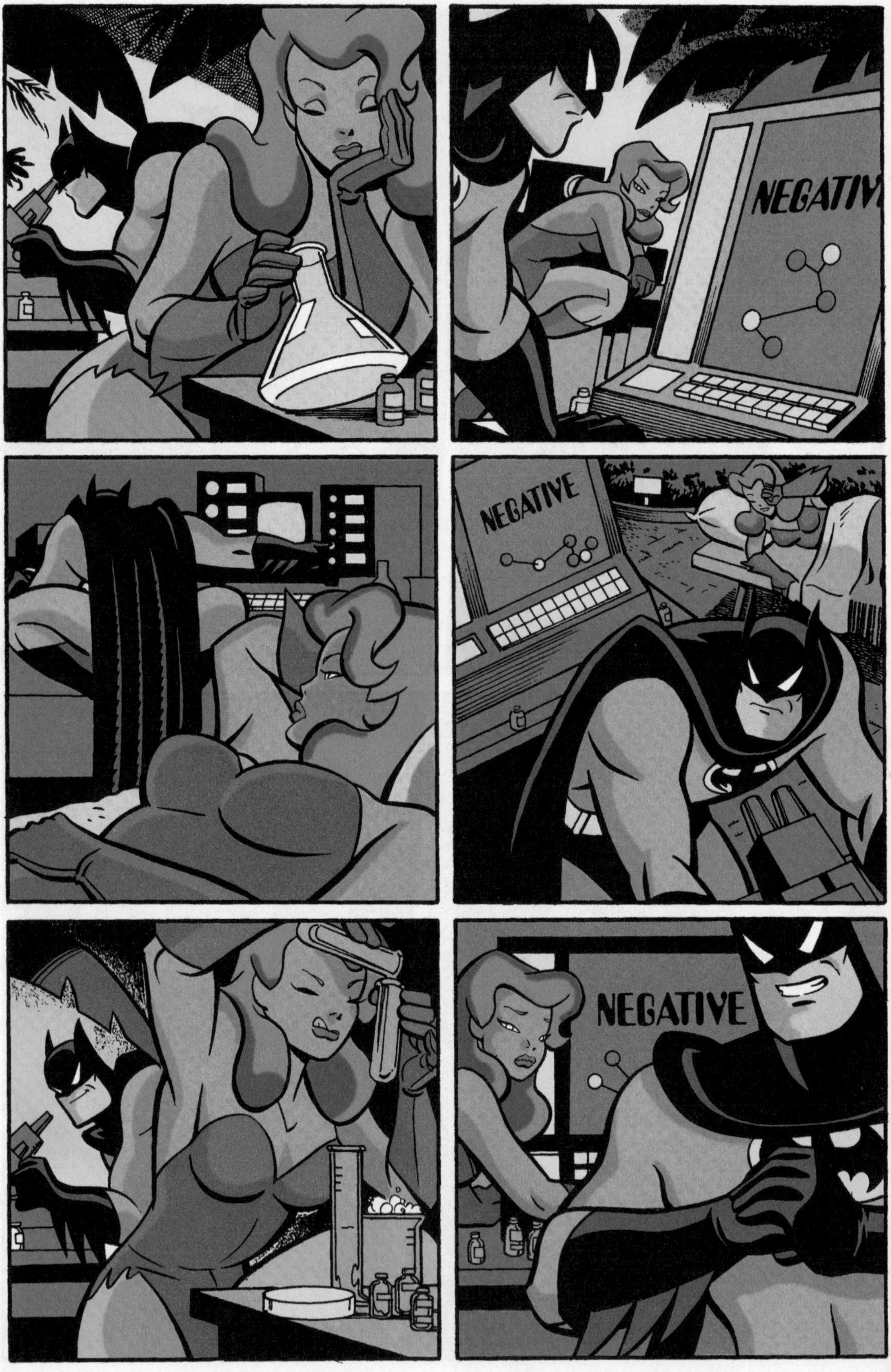
NEGATIVE
NEGATIVE

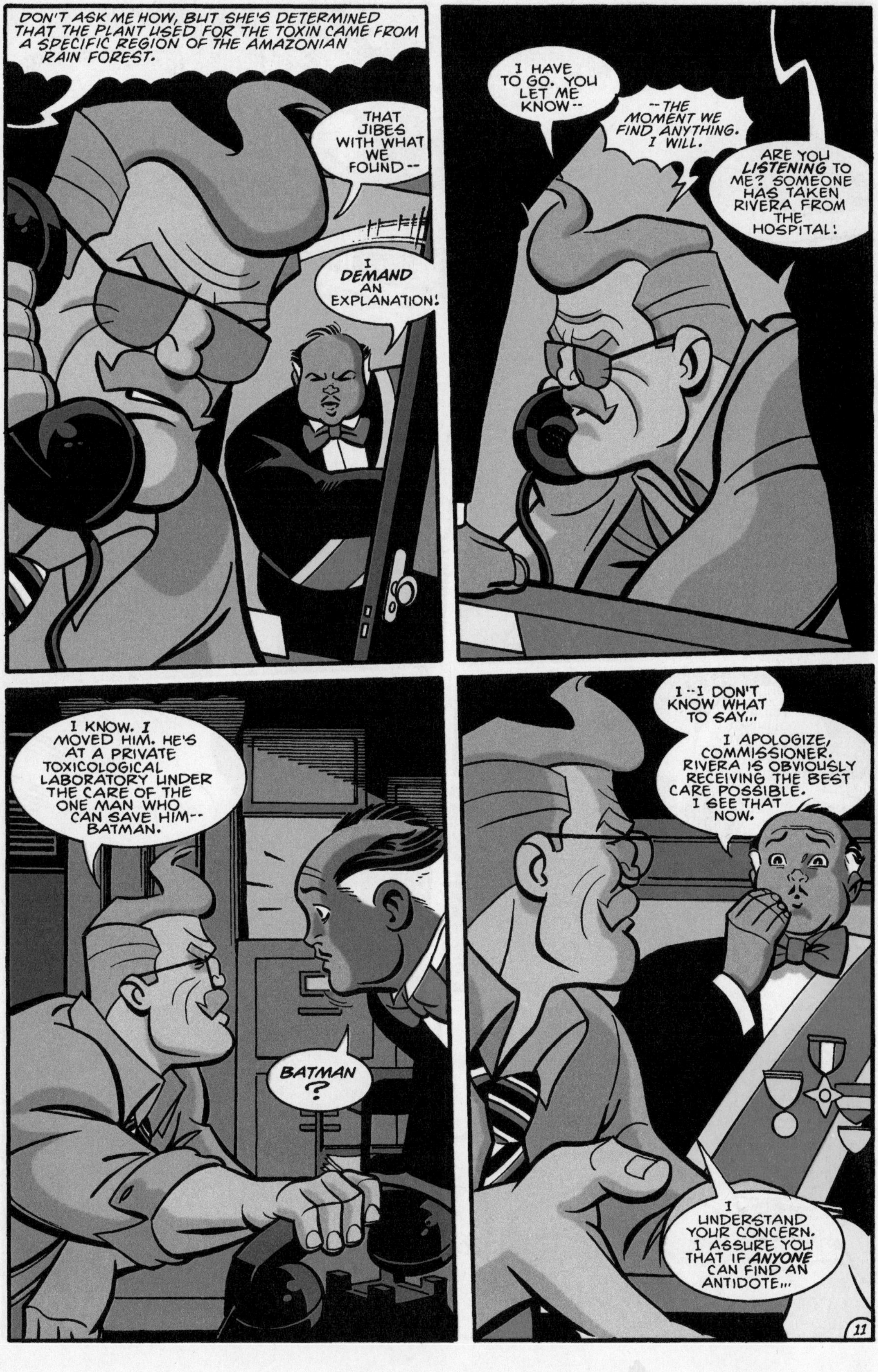

DON'T ASK ME HOW, BUT SHE'S DETERMINED THAT THE PLANT USED FOR THE TOXIN CAME FROM A SPECIFIC REGION OF THE AMAZONIAN RAIN FOREST.
THAT JIBES WITH WHAT WE FOUND--
I DEMAND AN EXPLANATION!
I HAVE TO GO. YOU LET ME KNOW--
--THE MOMENT WE FIND ANYTHING. I WILL.
ARE YOU LISTENING TO ME? SOMEONE HAS TAKEN RIVERA FROM THE HOSPITAL!
I KNOW. I MOVED HIM. HE'S AT A PRIVATE TOXICOLOGICAL LABORATORY UNDER THE CARE OF THE ONE MAN WHO CAN SAVE HIM-- BATMAN.
BATMAN?
I--I DON'T KNOW WHAT TO SAY...
I APOLOGIZE, COMMISSIONER. RIVERA IS OBVIOUSLY RECEIVING THE BEST CARE POSSIBLE. I SEE THAT NOW.
I UNDERSTAND YOUR CONCERN. I ASSURE YOU THAT IF ANYONE CAN FIND AN ANTIDOTE...

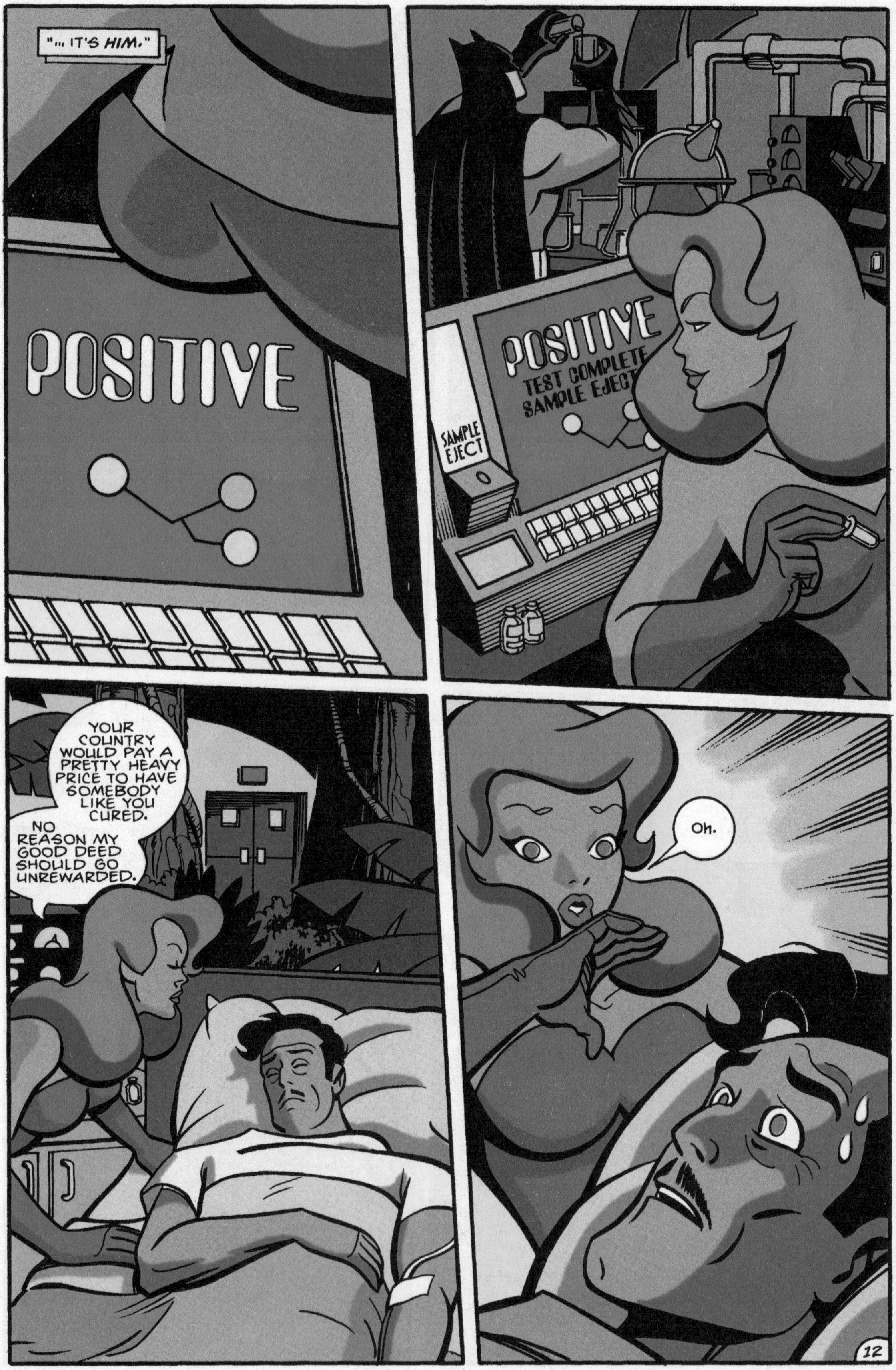
"... IT'S HIM."
POSITIVE
POSITIVE
TEST COMPLETE
SAMPLE EJECT
SAMPLE EJECT
YOUR COUNTRY WOULD PAY A PRETTY HEAVY PRICE TO HAVE SOMEBODY LIKE YOU CURED.
NO REASON MY GOOD DEED SHOULD GO UNREWARDED.
Oh.

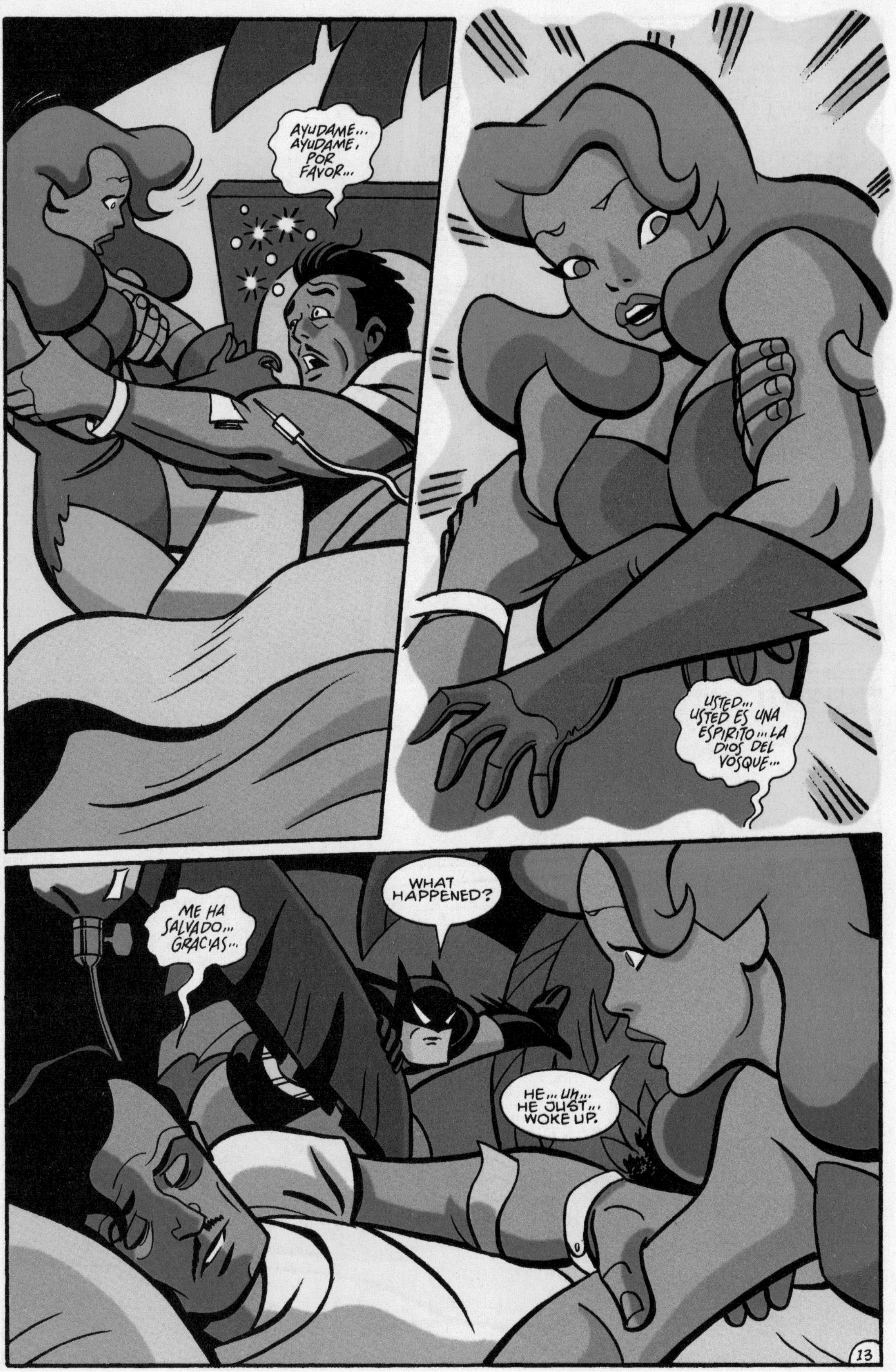
AYUDAME... AYUDAME, POR FAVOR...
USTED... USTED ES UNA ESPIRITO... LA DIOS DEL VOSQUE...
ME HA SALVADO... GRACIAS...
WHAT HAPPENED?
HE... UH... HE JUST... WOKE UP.

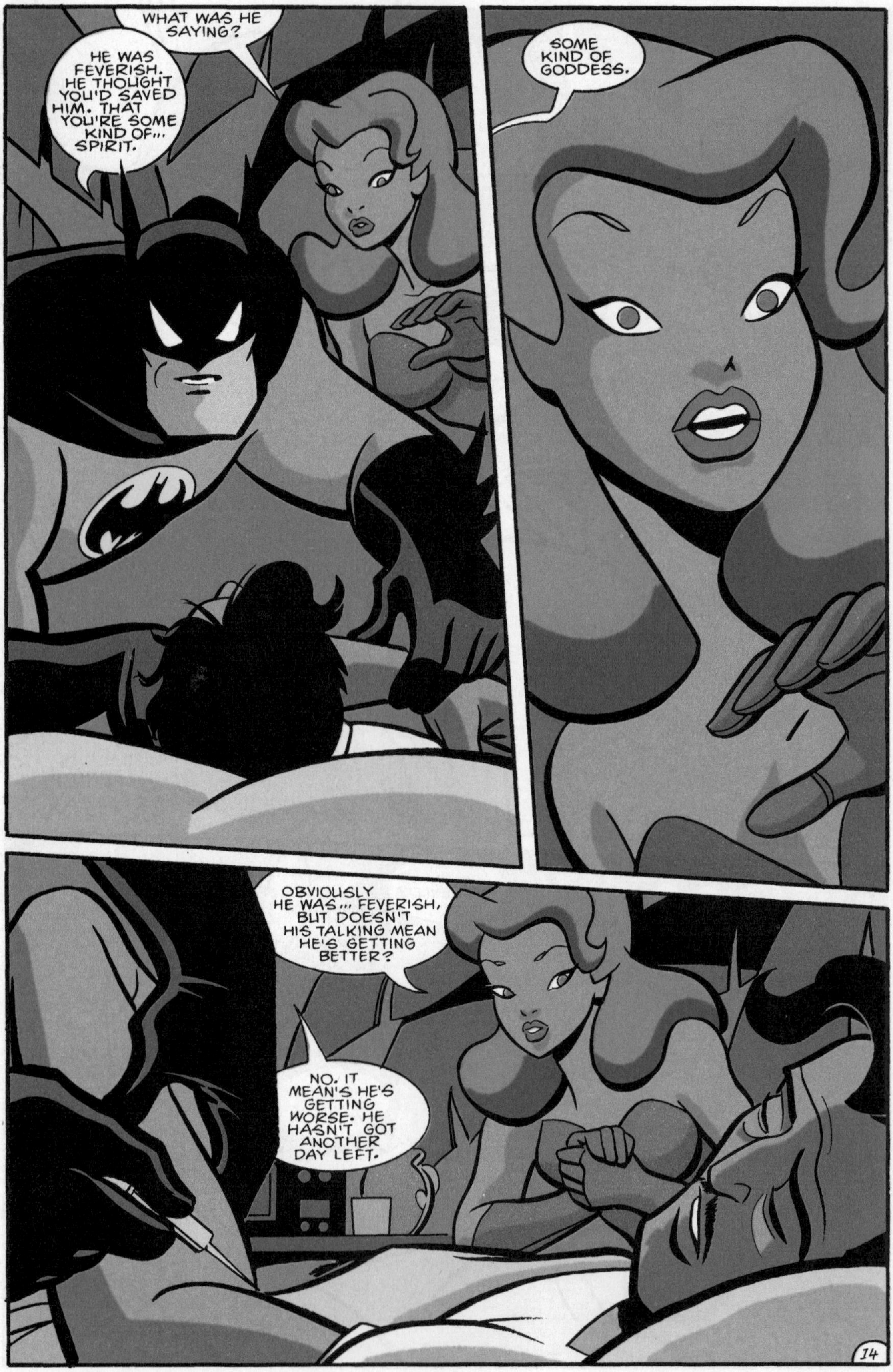
WHAT WAS HE SAYING?
HE WAS FEVERISH. HE THOUGHT YOU'D SAVED HIM. THAT YOU'RE SOME KIND OF... SPIRIT.
SOME KIND OF GODDESS.
OBVIOUSLY HE WAS... FEVERISH, BUT DOESN'T HIS TALKING MEAN HE'S GETTING BETTER?
NO. IT MEAN'S HE'S GETTING WORSE. HE HASN'T GOT ANOTHER DAY LEFT.
14

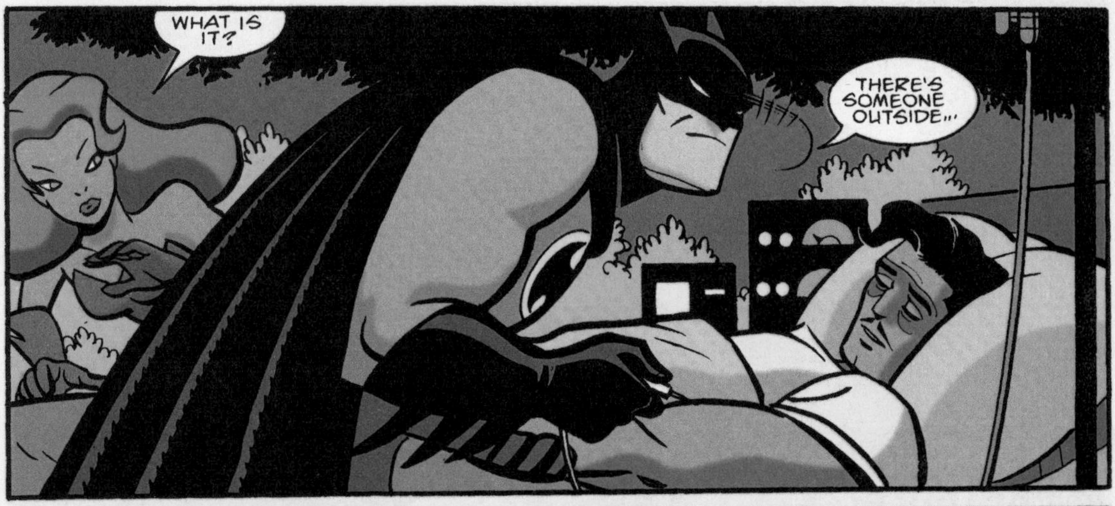
WHAT IS IT?
THERE'S SOMEONE OUTSIDE...

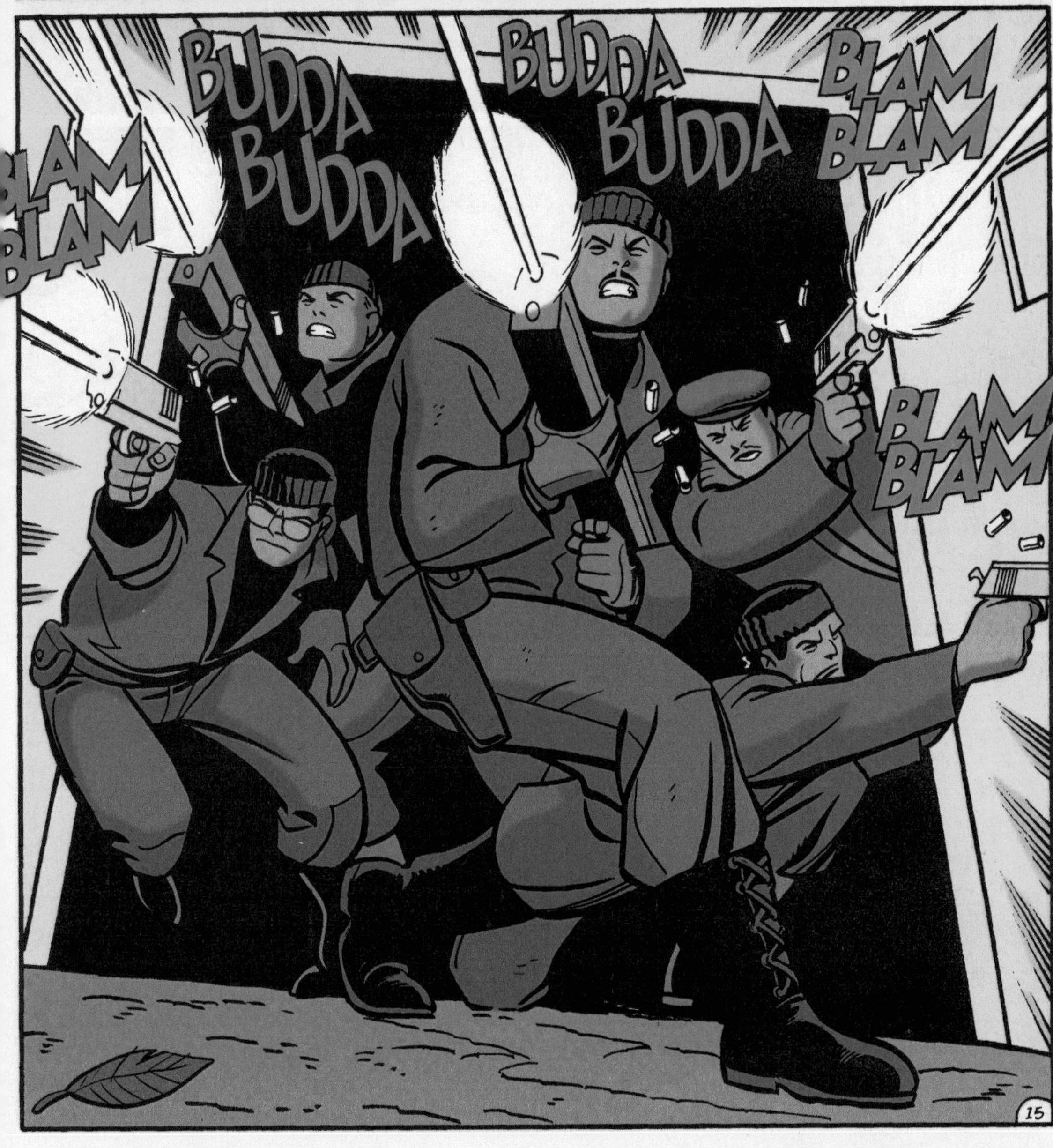
BLAM BLAM
BUDDA BUDDA
BUDDA BUDDA
BLAM BLAM
BLAM BLAM

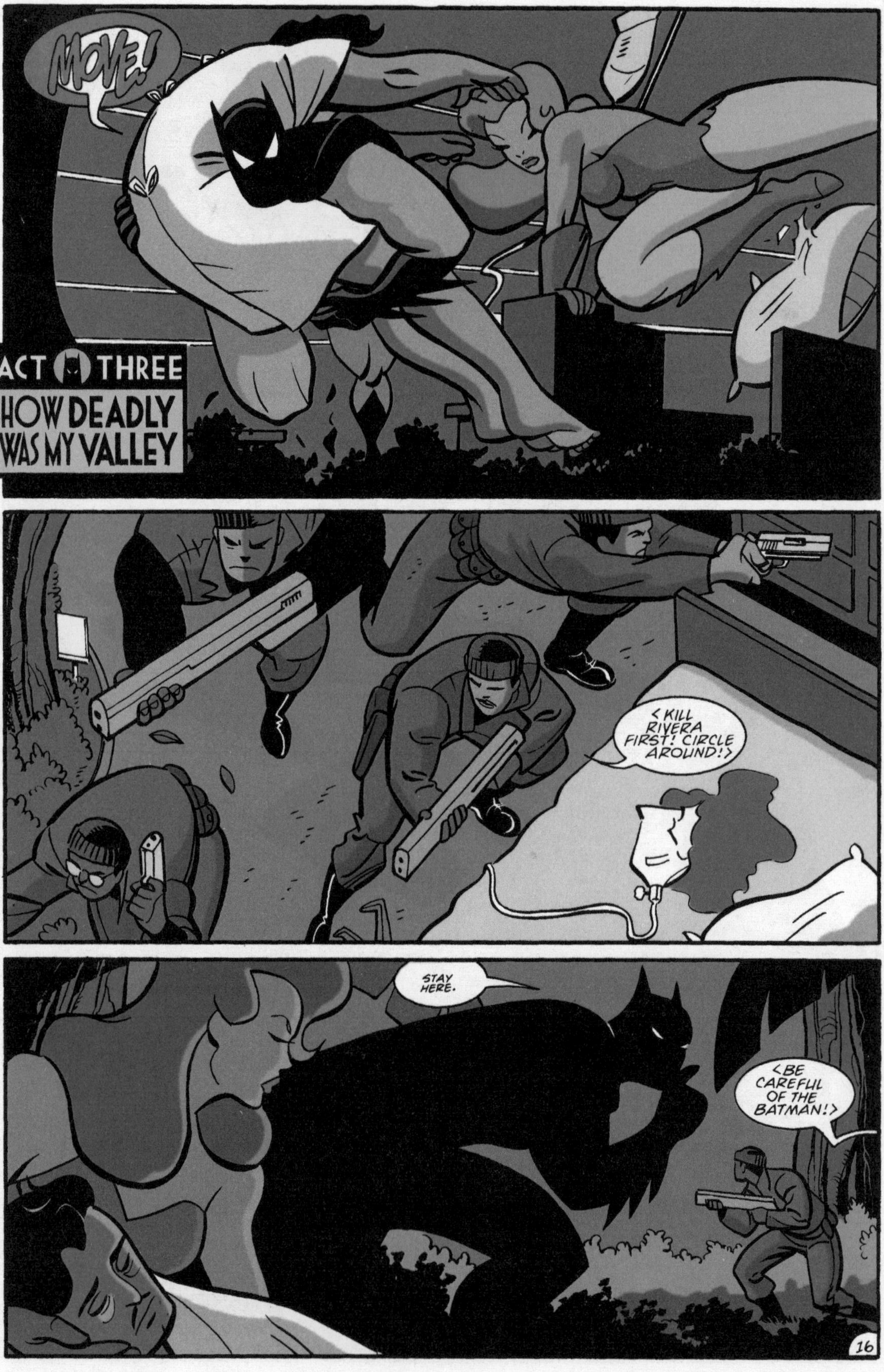
MOVE!
ACT THREE
HOW DEADLY WAS MY VALLEY
< KILL RIVERA FIRST! CIRCLE AROUND! >
STAY HERE.
<BE CAREFUL OF THE BATMAN!>
16

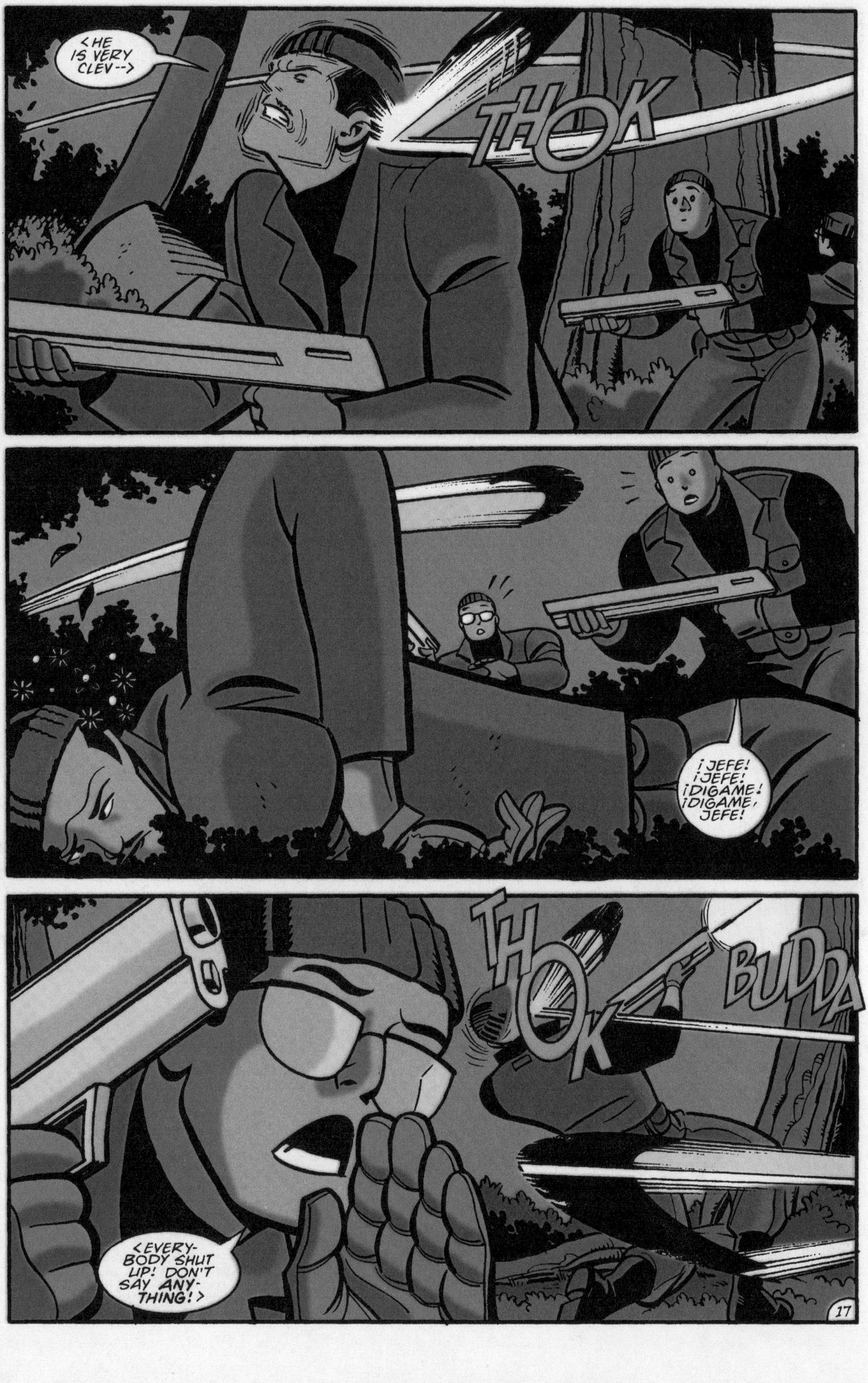
<HE IS VERY CLEV-->
THOK
¡JEFE! ¡JEFE! ¡DIGAME! ¡DIGAME, JEFE!
THOK
BUDDA
<EVERY-BODY SHUT UP! DON'T SAY ANY-THING!>
17

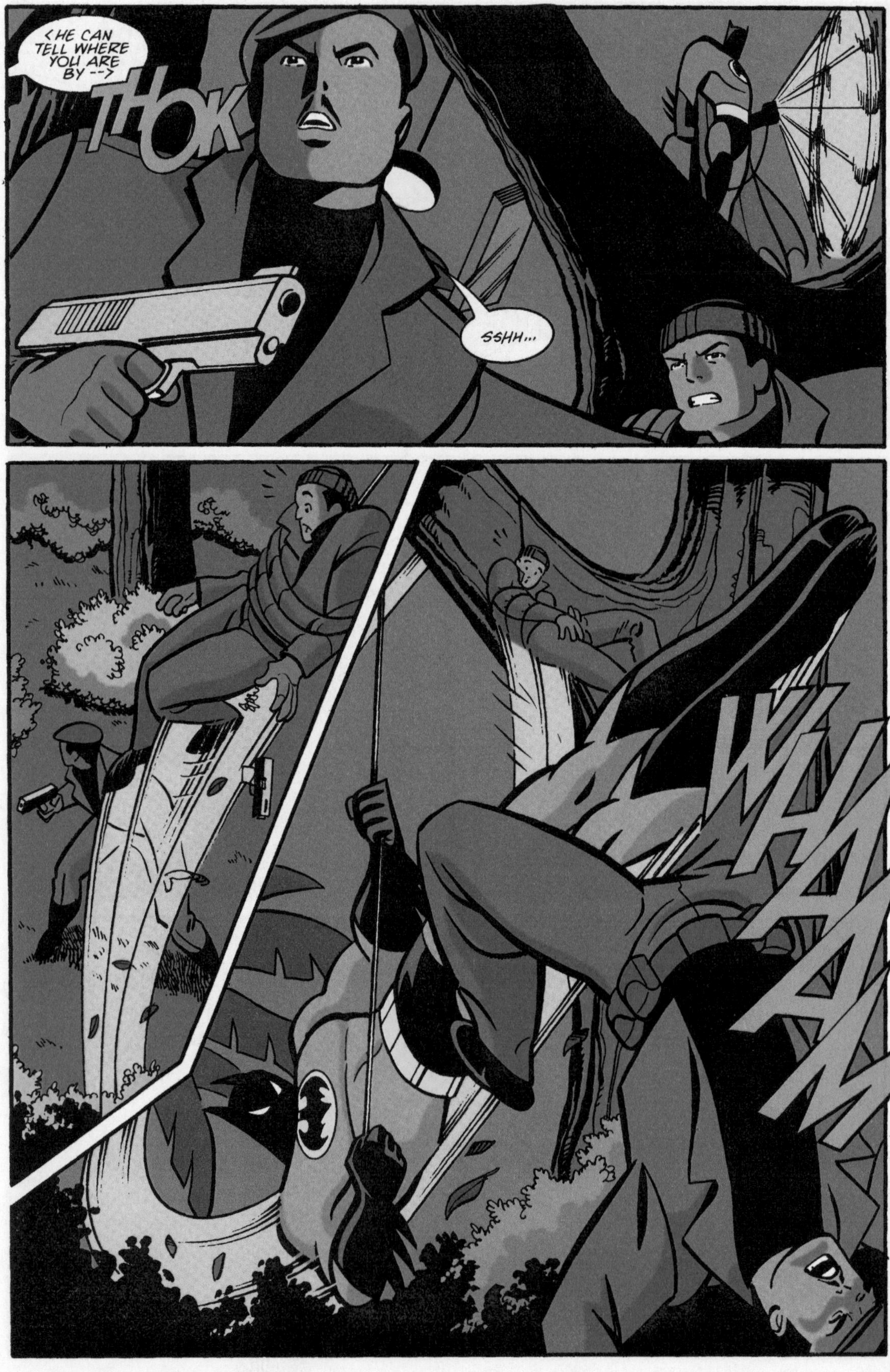
<HE CAN TELL WHERE YOU ARE BY -->
THOK
SSHH...
WHAAM

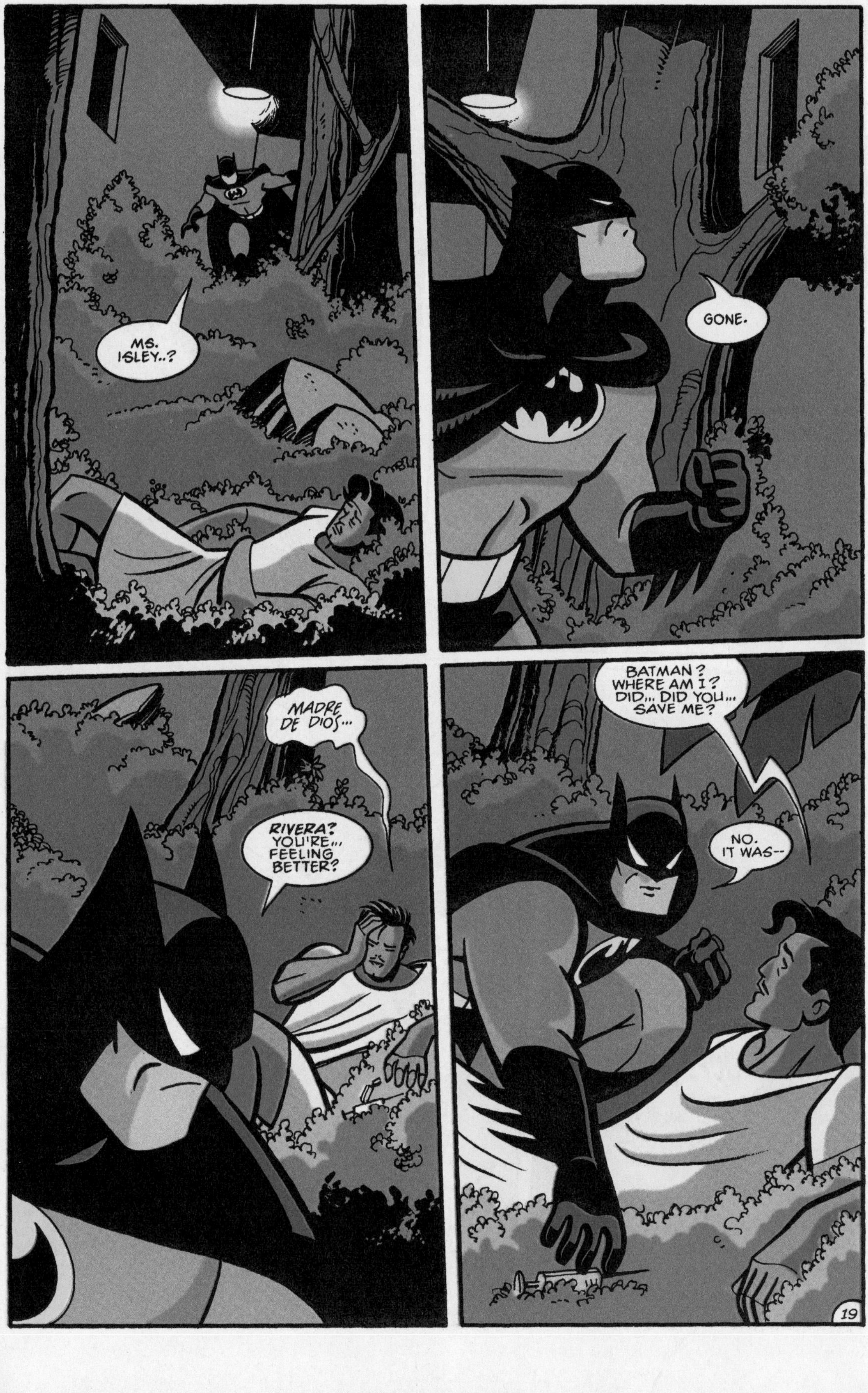
MS. ISLEY..?
GONE.
MADRE DE DIOS...
RIVERA? YOU'RE... FEELING BETTER?
BATMAN? WHERE AM I? DID... DID YOU... SAVE ME?
NO. IT WAS--

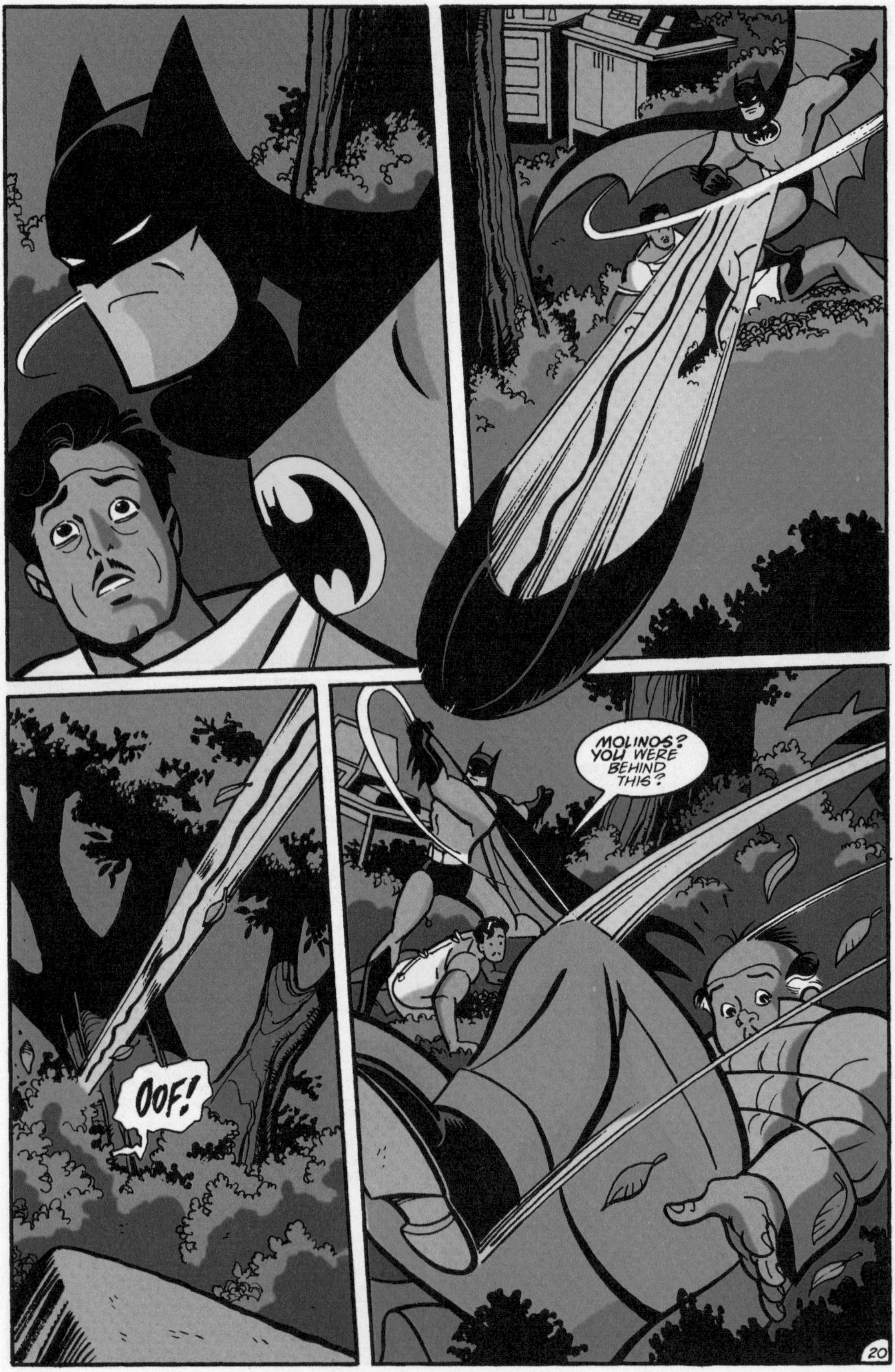
MOLINOS? YOU WERE BEHIND THIS?
OOF!

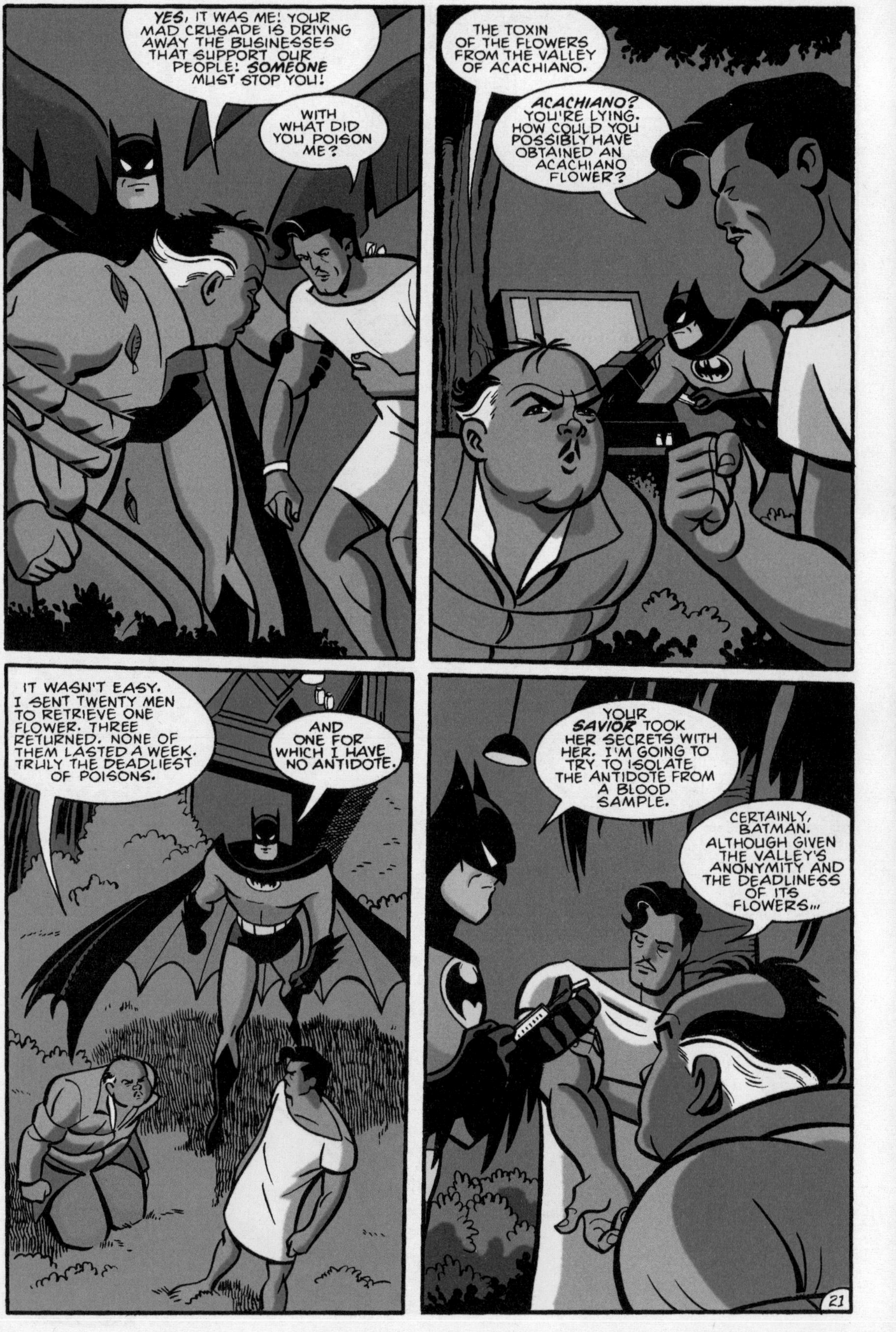
YES, IT WAS ME! YOUR MAD CRUSADE IS DRIVING AWAY THE BUSINESSES THAT SUPPORT OUR PEOPLE: SOMEONE MUST STOP YOU!
WITH WHAT DID YOU POISON ME?
THE TOXIN OF THE FLOWERS FROM THE VALLEY OF ACACHIANO.
ACACHIANO? YOU'RE LYING. HOW COULD YOU POSSIBLY HAVE OBTAINED AN ACACHIANO FLOWER?
IT WASN'T EASY. I SENT TWENTY MEN TO RETRIEVE ONE FLOWER. THREE RETURNED. NONE OF THEM LASTED A WEEK. TRULY THE DEADLIEST OF POISONS.
AND ONE FOR WHICH I HAVE NO ANTIDOTE.
YOUR SAVIOR TOOK HER SECRETS WITH HER. I'M GOING TO TRY TO ISOLATE THE ANTIDOTE FROM A BLOOD SAMPLE.
CERTAINLY, BATMAN. ALTHOUGH GIVEN THE VALLEY'S ANONYMITY AND THE DEADLINESS OF ITS FLOWERS...
21

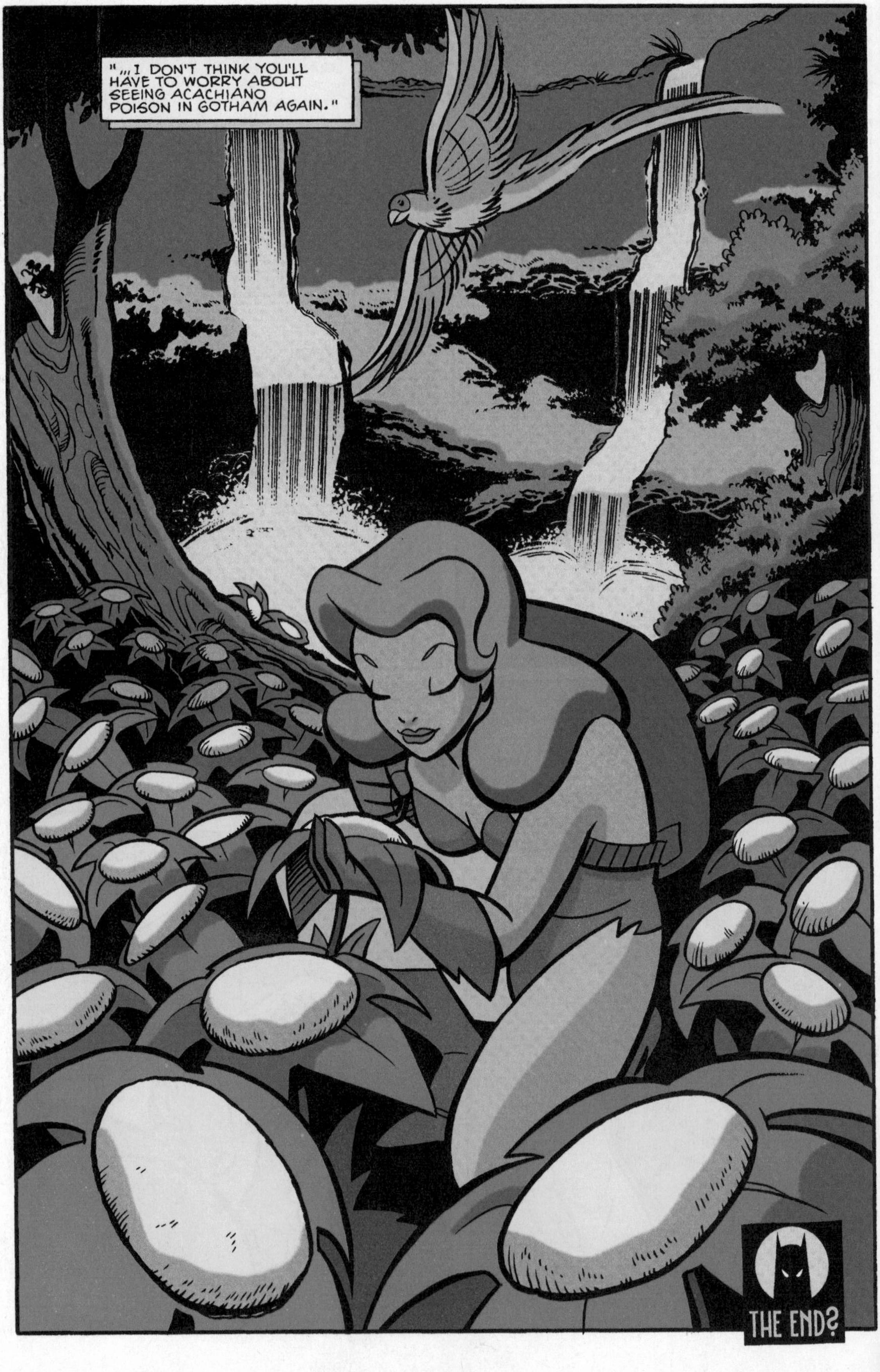
"...I DON'T THINK YOU'LL HAVE TO WORRY ABOUT SEEING ACACHIANO POISON IN GOTHAM AGAIN."
THE END?

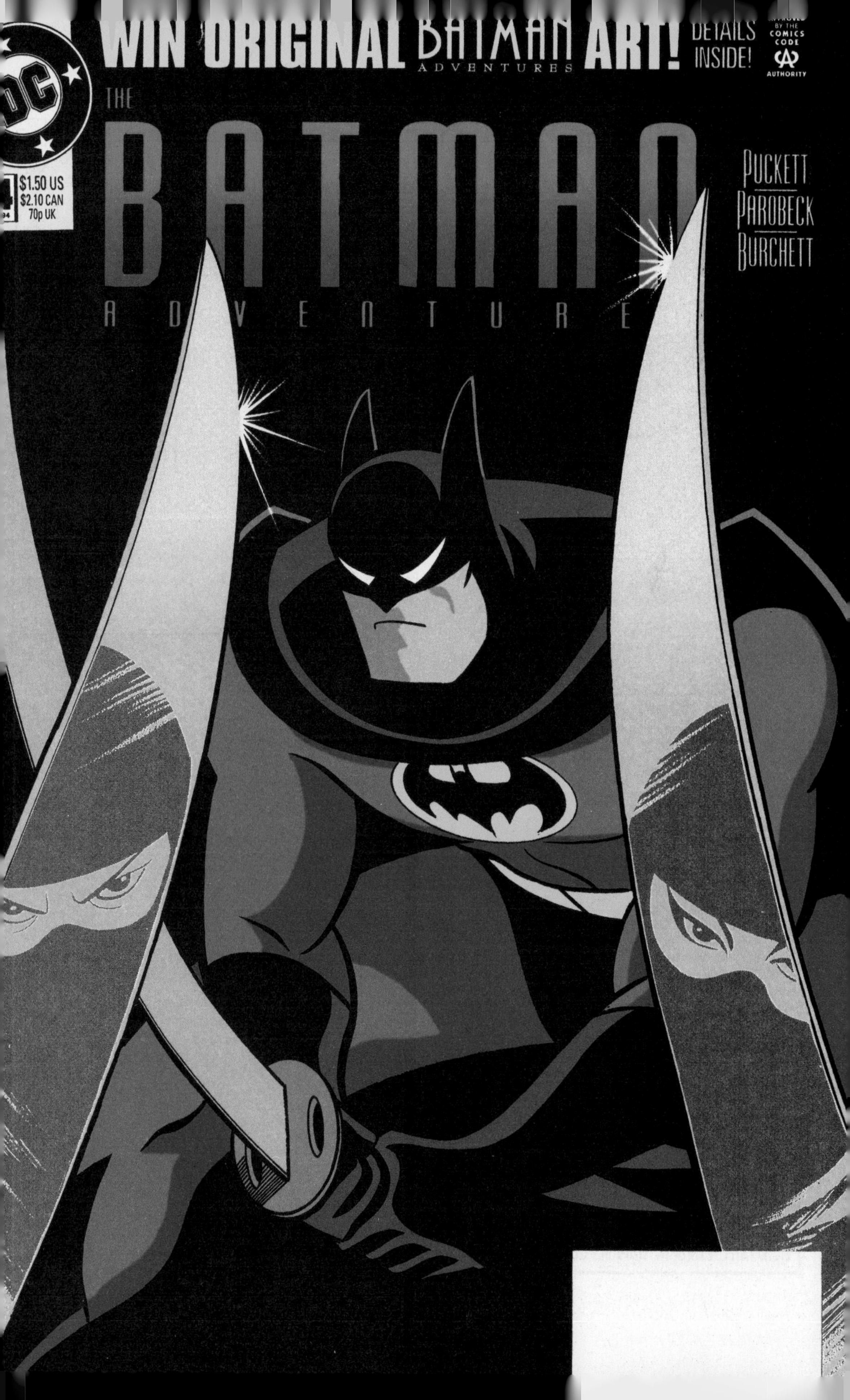

WIN ORIGINAL BATMAN ADVENTURES ART!
DETAILS INSIDE!
BY THE COMICS CODE AUTHORITY
DC
$1.50 US
$2.10 CAN
70p UK
THE BATMAN ADVENTURES
PUCKETT
PAROBECK
BURCHETT

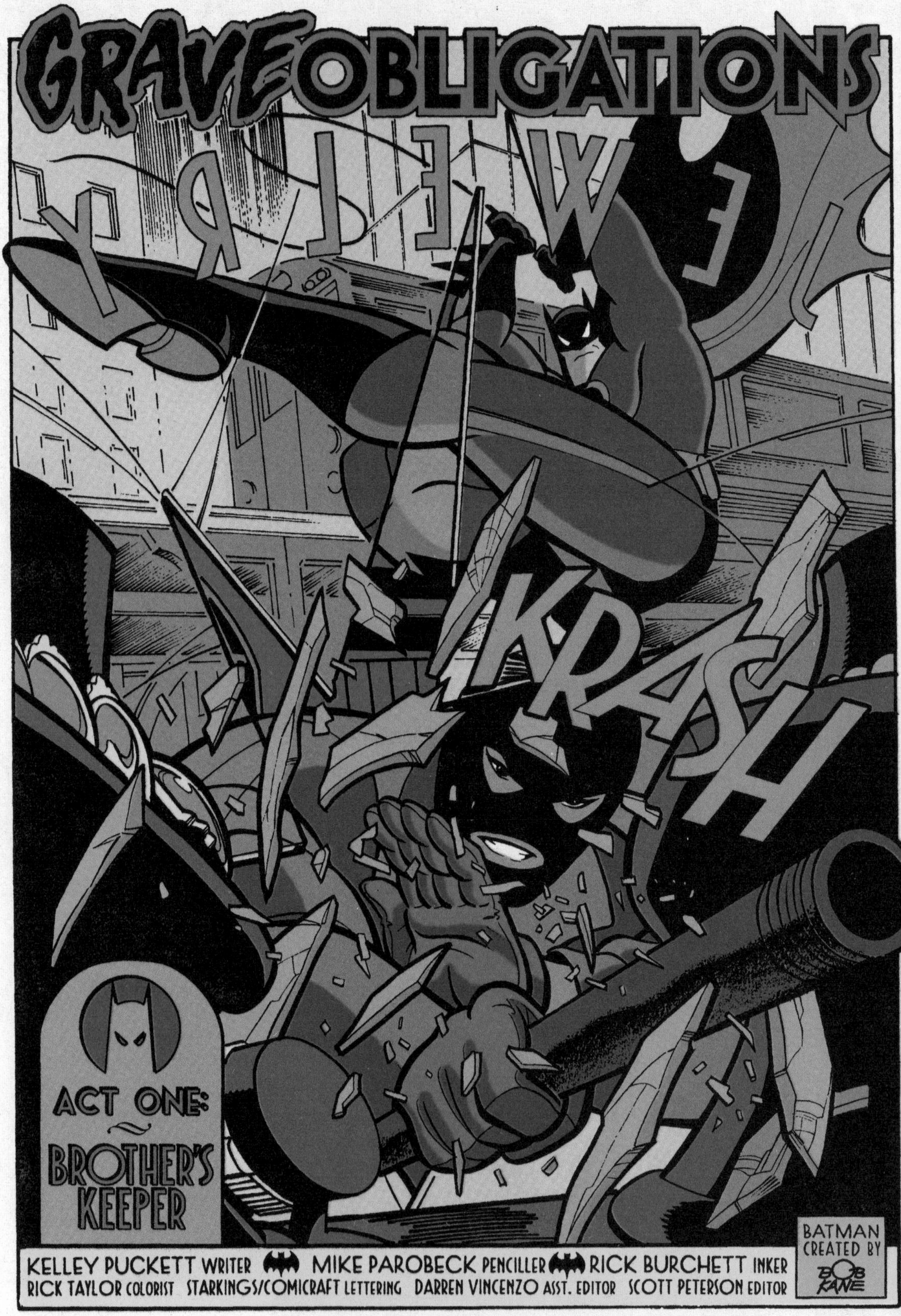
GRAVE OBLIGATIONS
KRASH
ACT ONE:
BROTHER'S KEEPER
KELLEY PUCKETT WRITER MIKE PAROBECK PENCILLER RICK BURCHETT INKER
RICK TAYLOR COLORIST STARKINGS/COMICRAFT LETTERING DARREN VINCENZO ASST. EDITOR SCOTT PETERSON EDITOR
BATMAN CREATED BY BOB KANE

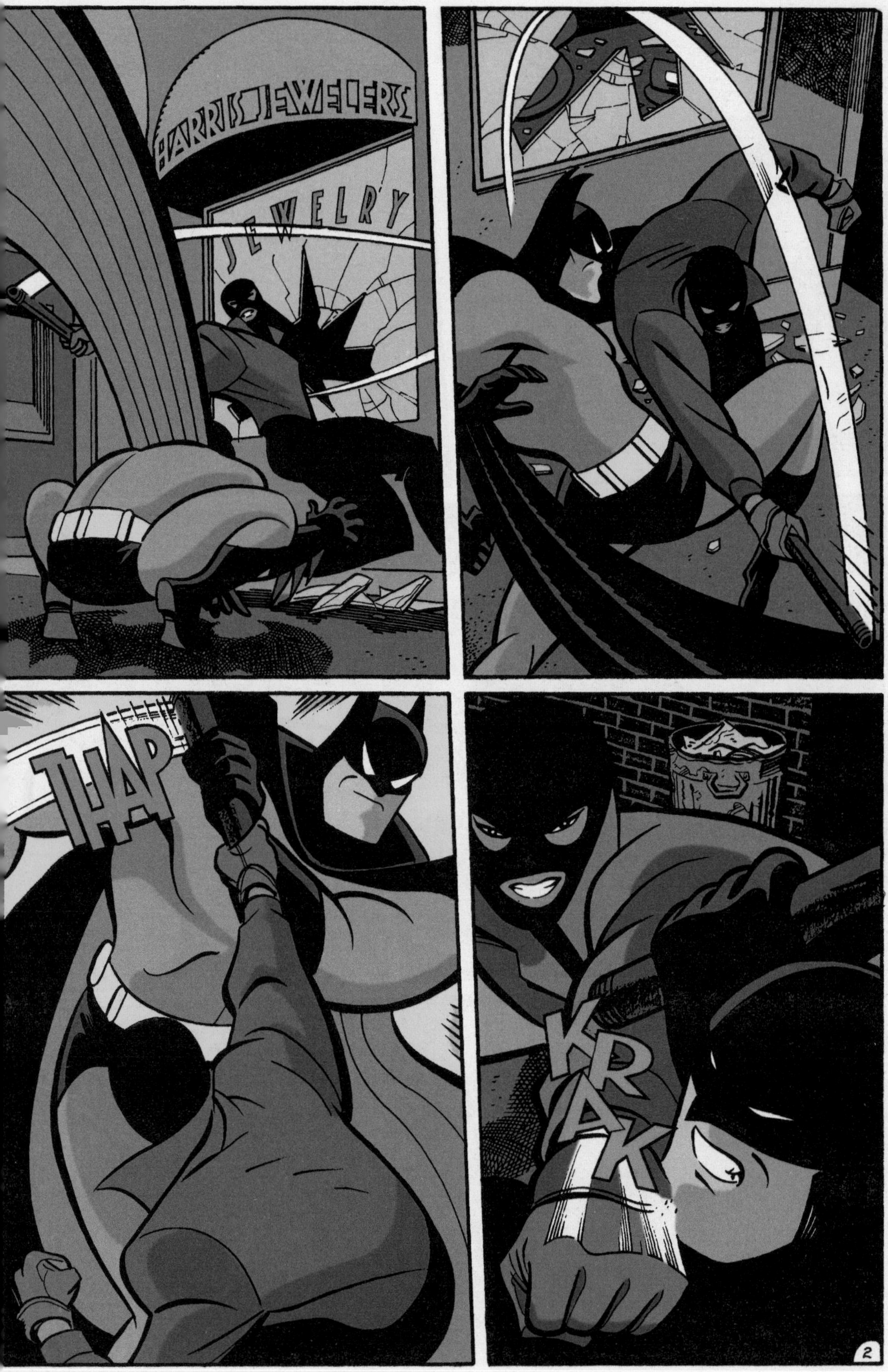
HARRIS JEWELERS
JEWELRY
THAP
KRAK

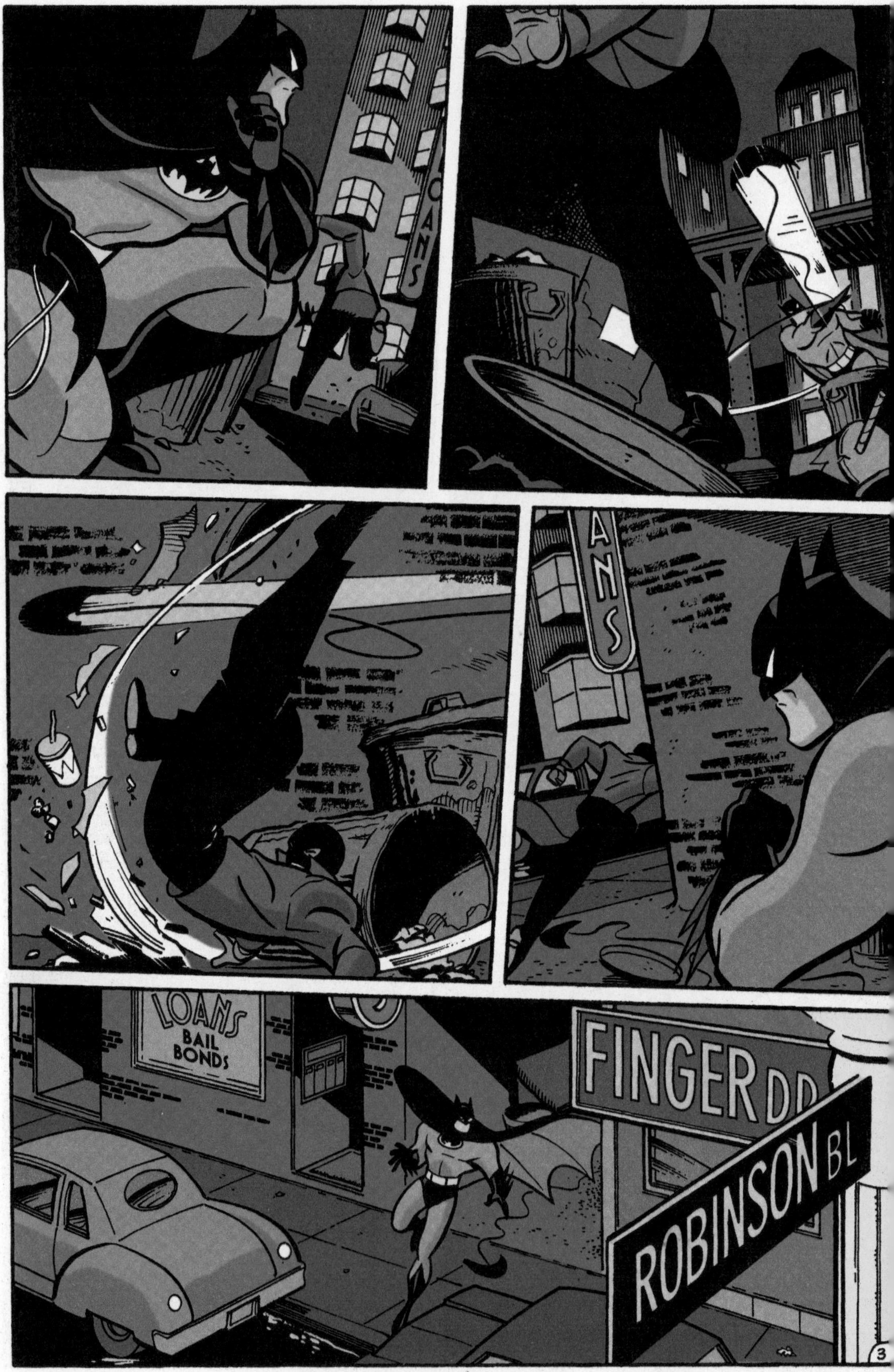
LOANS
BAIL
BONDS
FINGER DR
ROBINSON BL

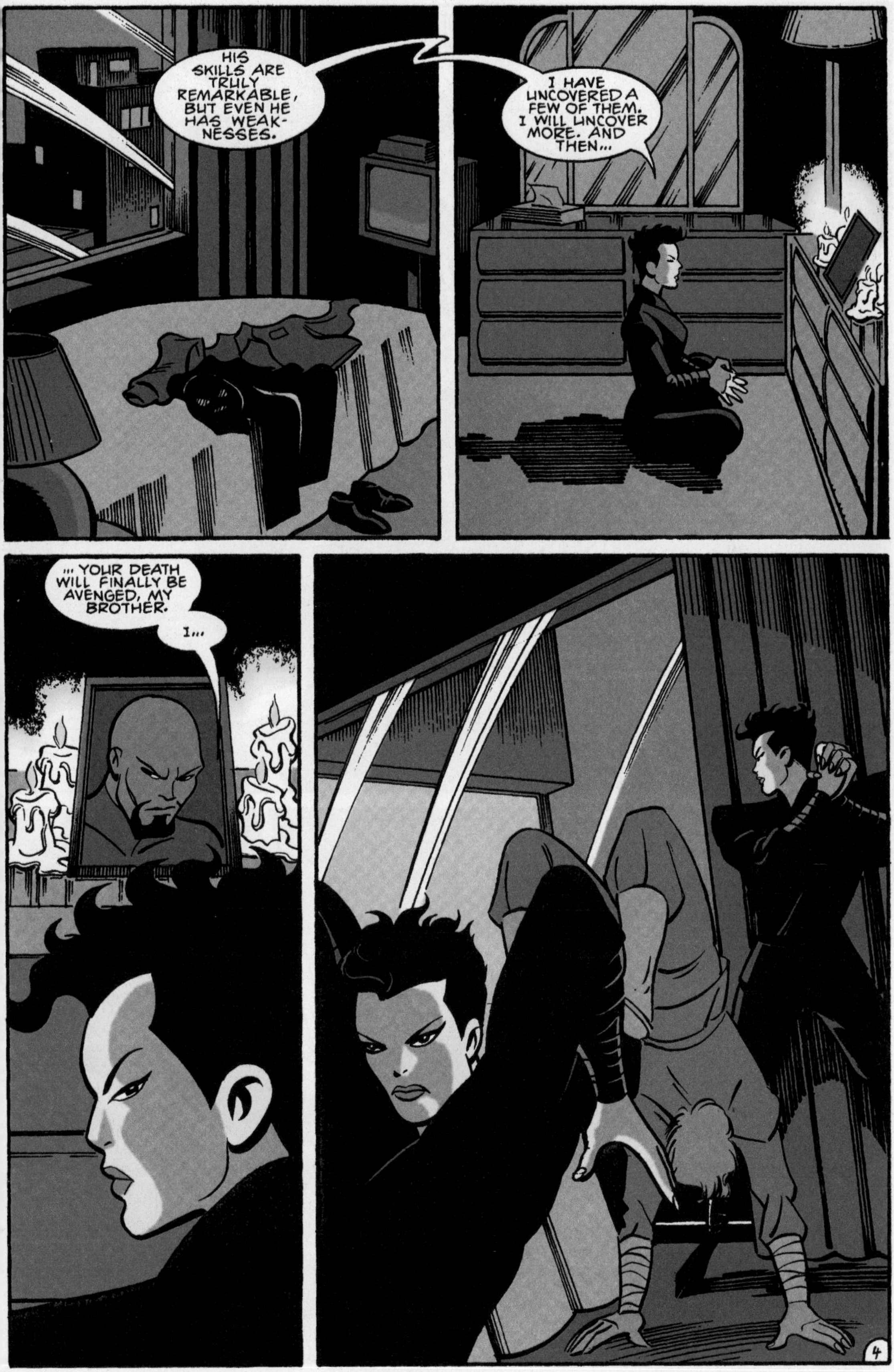
HIS SKILLS ARE TRULY REMARKABLE, BUT EVEN HE HAS WEAK-NESSES.
I HAVE UNCOVERED A FEW OF THEM. I WILL UNCOVER MORE. AND THEN...
...YOUR DEATH WILL FINALLY BE AVENGED, MY BROTHER.
I...

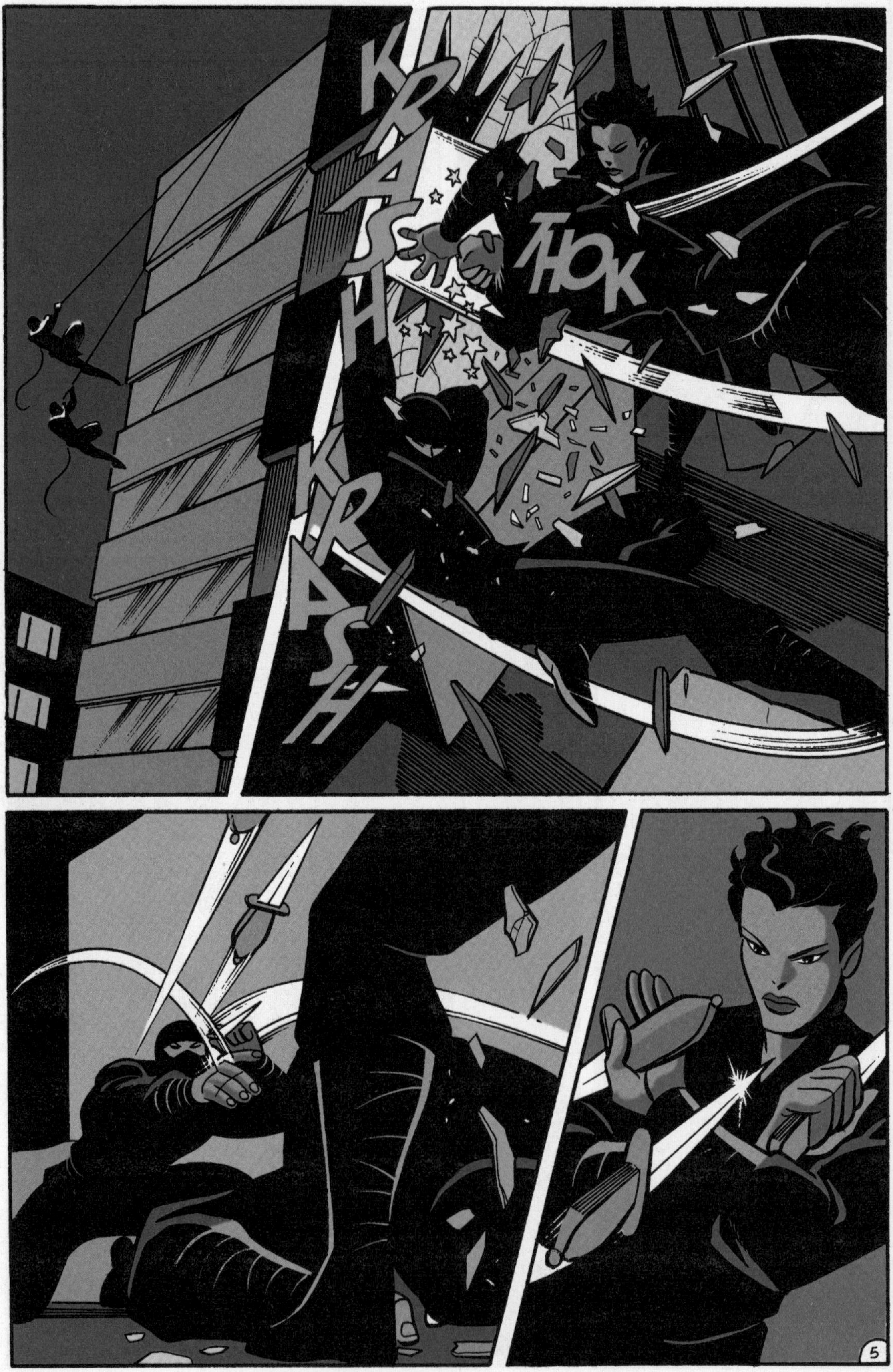
KRASH
THOK
KRASH

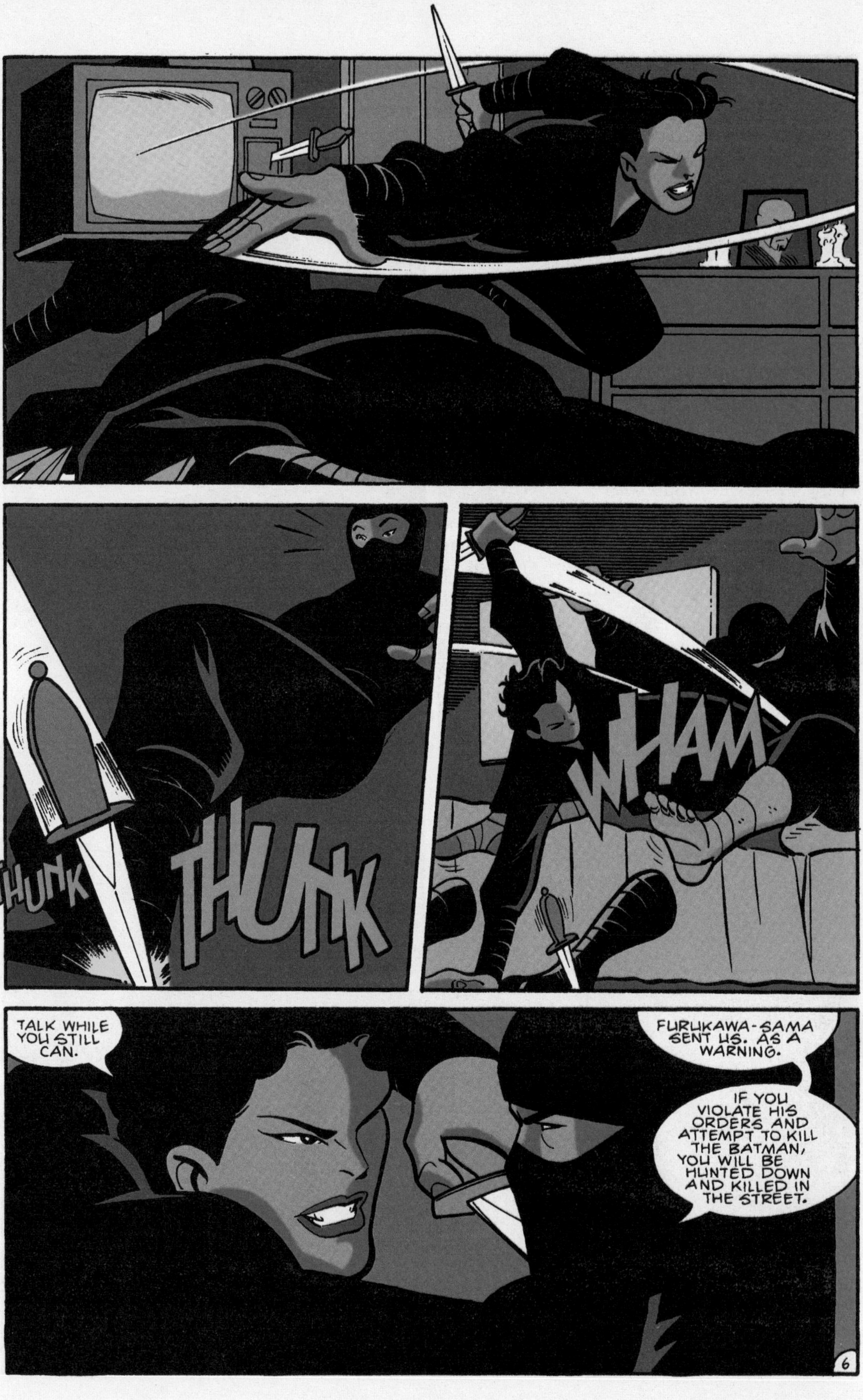
THUNK
THUNK
WHAM
TALK WHILE YOU STILL CAN.
FURUKAWA-SAMA SENT US. AS A WARNING.
IF YOU VIOLATE HIS ORDERS AND ATTEMPT TO KILL THE BATMAN, YOU WILL BE HUNTED DOWN AND KILLED IN THE STREET.

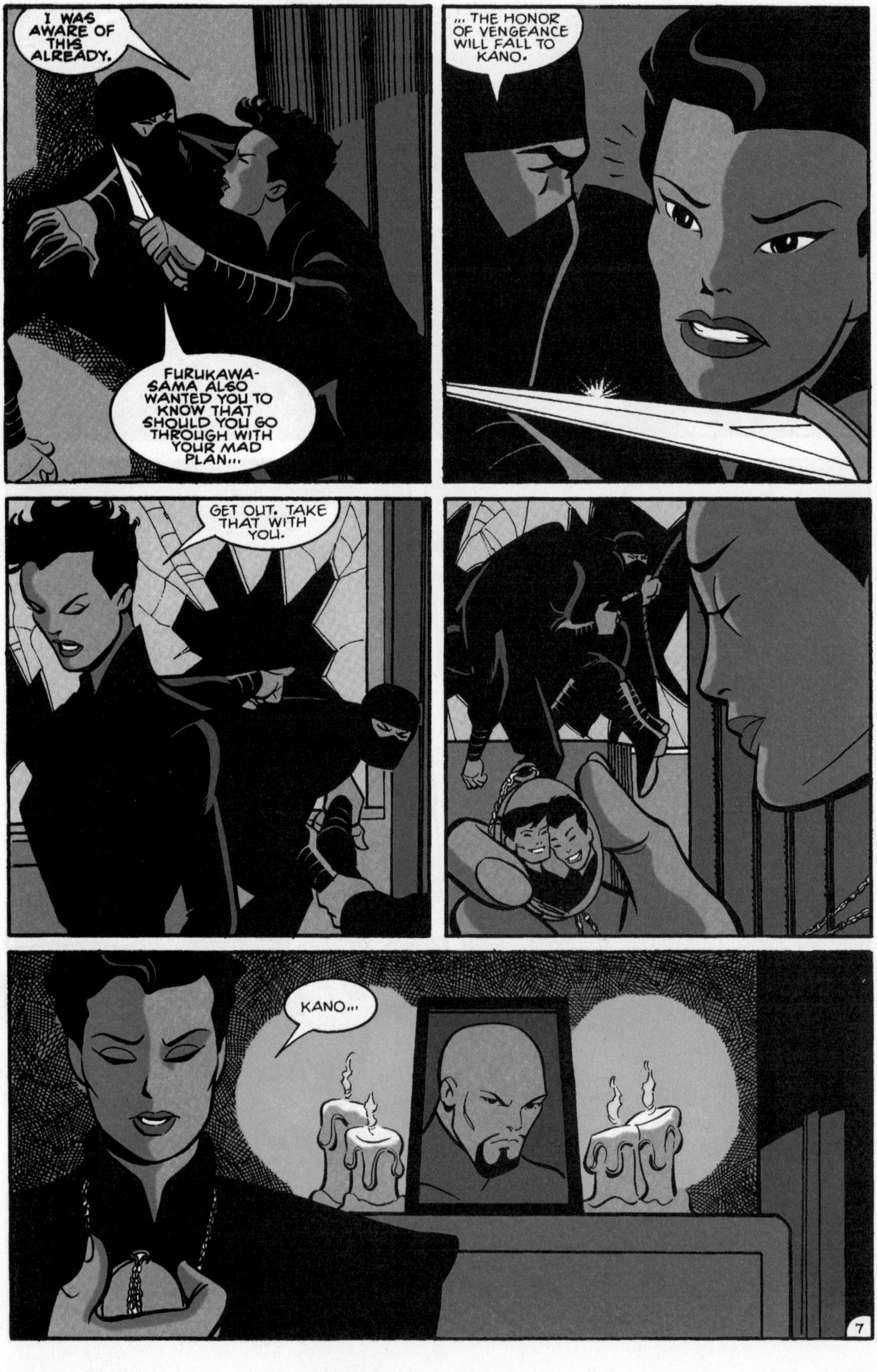

I WAS AWARE OF THIS ALREADY.
FURUKAWA-SAMA ALSO WANTED YOU TO KNOW THAT SHOULD YOU GO THROUGH WITH YOUR MAD PLAN...
... THE HONOR OF VENGEANCE WILL FALL TO KANO.
GET OUT. TAKE THAT WITH YOU.
KANO...

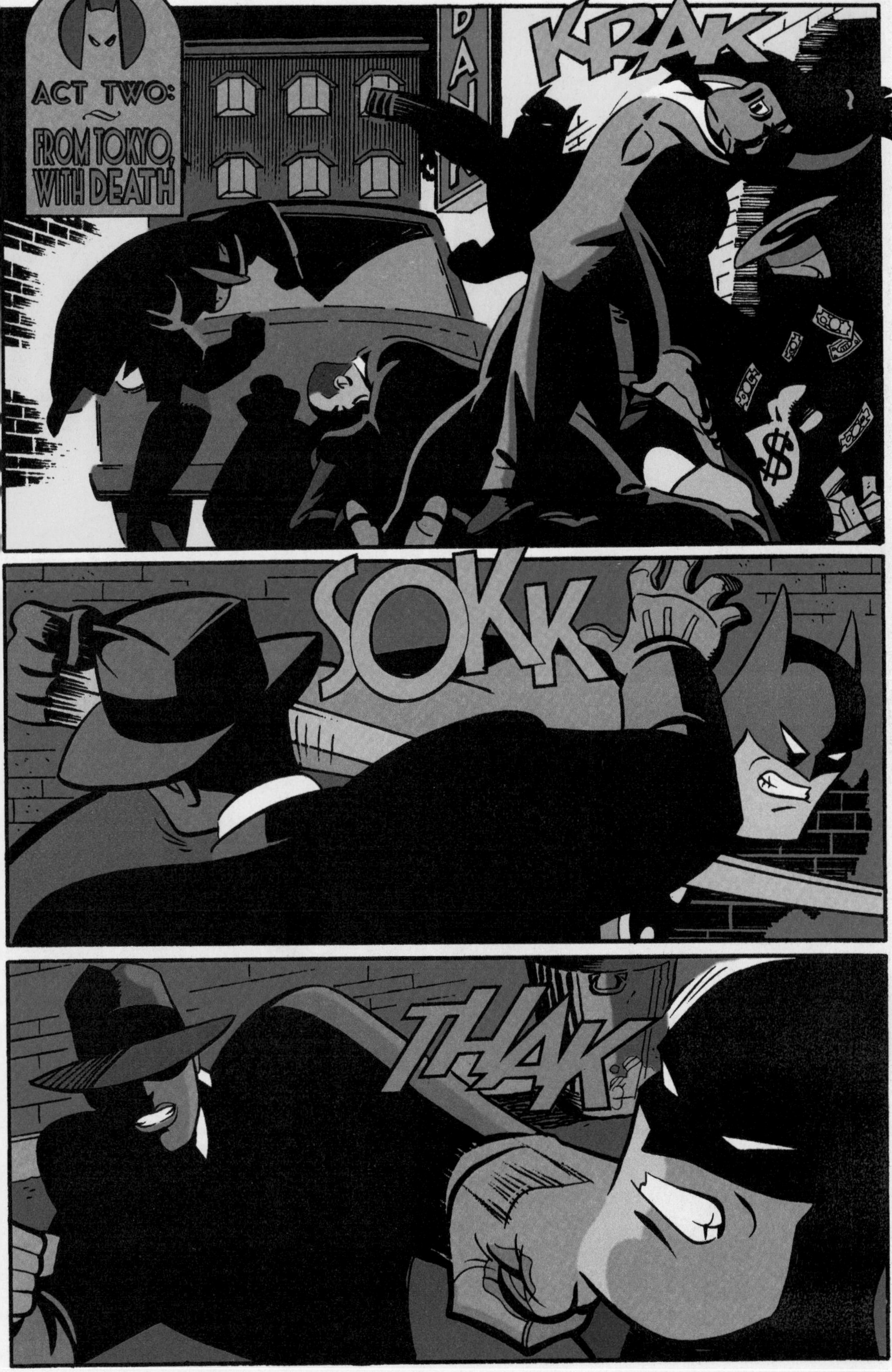
ACT TWO:
FROM TOKYO, WITH DEATH
KRAK
SOKK
THAK

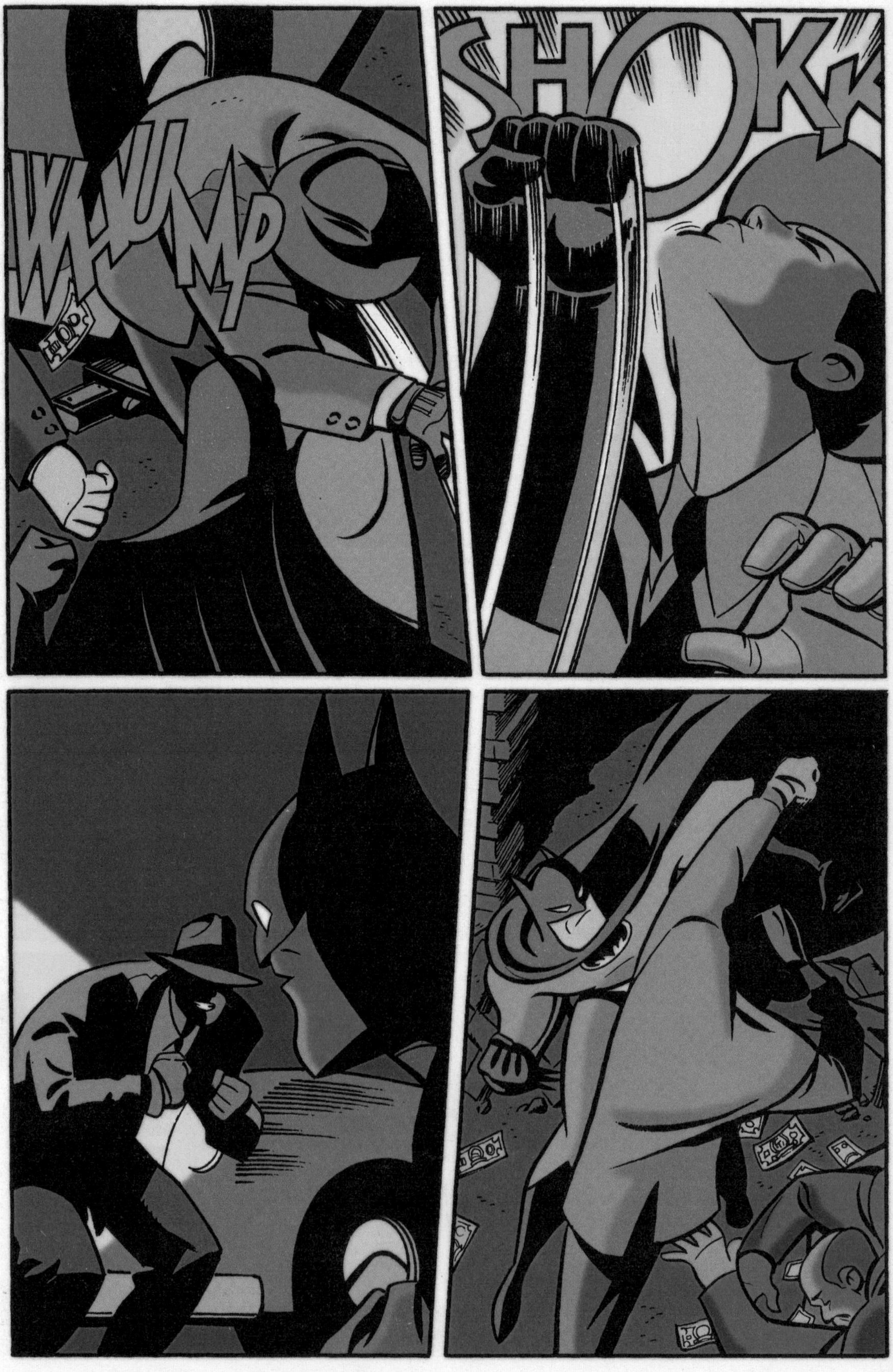
WHUMP
SHOKK

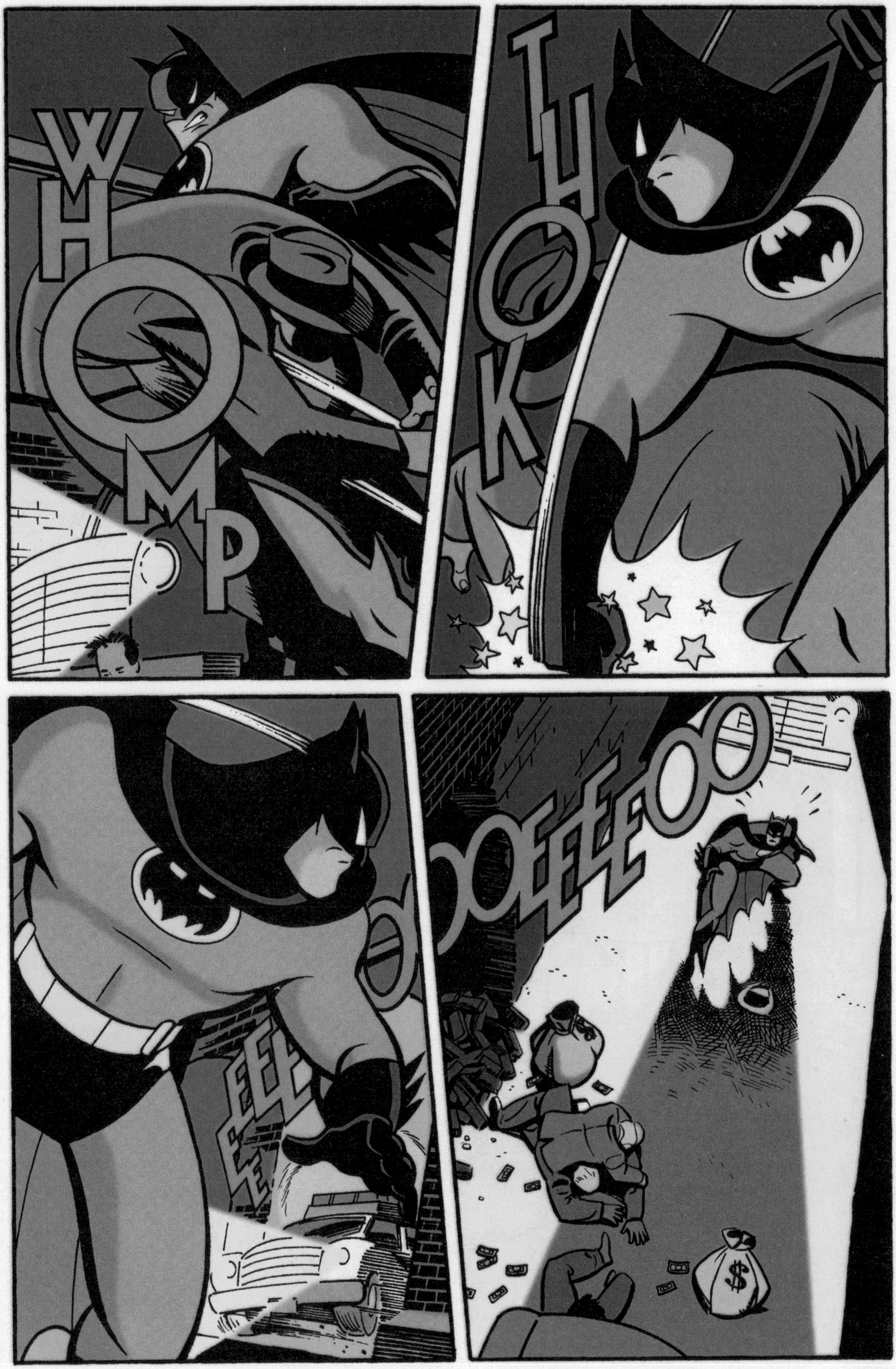
WHOMP
THOK

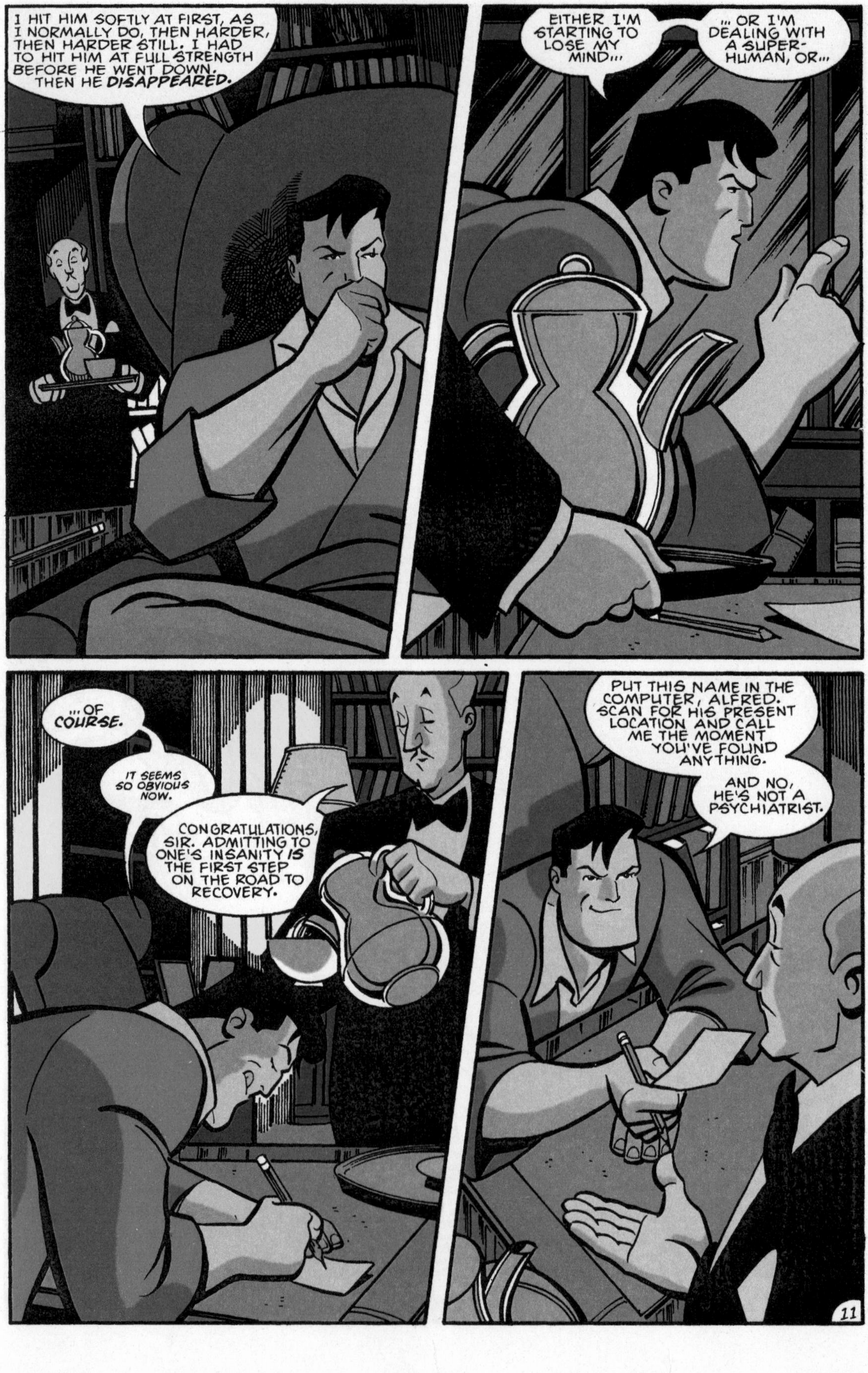
I HIT HIM SOFTLY AT FIRST, AS I NORMALLY DO, THEN HARDER, THEN HARDER STILL. I HAD TO HIT HIM AT FULL STRENGTH BEFORE HE WENT DOWN. THEN HE DISAPPEARED.
EITHER I'M STARTING TO LOSE MY MIND...
...OR I'M DEALING WITH A SUPER-HUMAN, OR...
...OF COURSE.
IT SEEMS SO OBVIOUS NOW.
CONGRATULATIONS, SIR. ADMITTING TO ONE'S INSANITY IS THE FIRST STEP ON THE ROAD TO RECOVERY.
PUT THIS NAME IN THE COMPUTER, ALFRED. SCAN FOR HIS PRESENT LOCATION AND CALL ME THE MOMENT YOU'VE FOUND ANYTHING.
AND NO, HE'S NOT A PSYCHIATRIST.
11

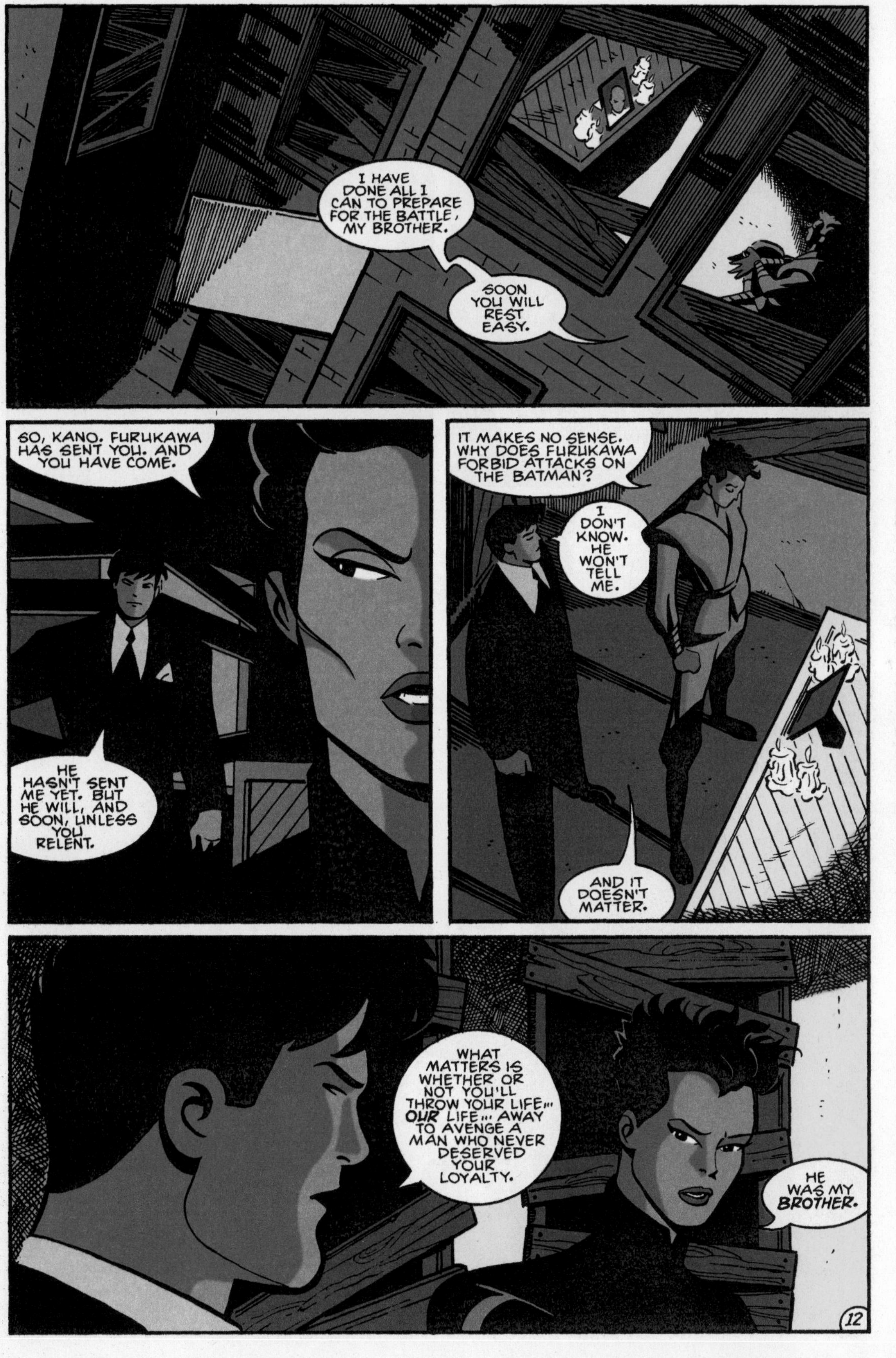
I HAVE DONE ALL I CAN TO PREPARE FOR THE BATTLE, MY BROTHER.
SOON YOU WILL REST EASY.
SO, KANO. FURUKAWA HAS SENT YOU. AND YOU HAVE COME.
HE HASN'T SENT ME YET. BUT HE WILL, AND SOON, UNLESS YOU RELENT.
IT MAKES NO SENSE. WHY DOES FURUKAWA FORBID ATTACKS ON THE BATMAN?
I DON'T KNOW. HE WON'T TELL ME.
AND IT DOESN'T MATTER.
WHAT MATTERS IS WHETHER OR NOT YOU'LL THROW YOUR LIFE... OUR LIFE... AWAY TO AVENGE A MAN WHO NEVER DESERVED YOUR LOYALTY.
HE WAS MY BROTHER.

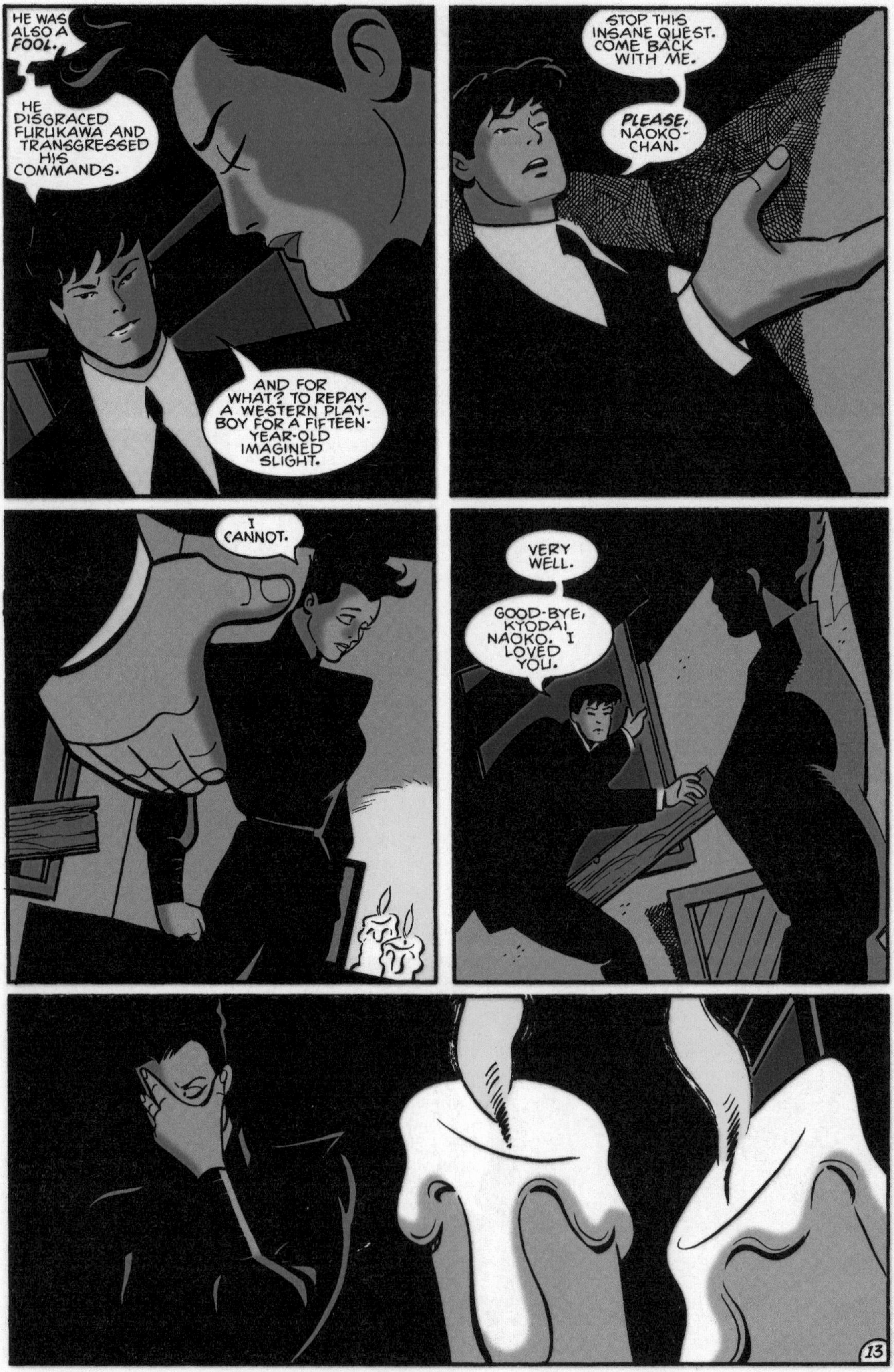
HE WAS ALSO A FOOL.
HE DISGRACED FURUKAWA AND TRANSGRESSED HIS COMMANDS.
AND FOR WHAT? TO REPAY A WESTERN PLAYBOY FOR A FIFTEEN-YEAR-OLD IMAGINED SLIGHT.
STOP THIS INSANE QUEST. COME BACK WITH ME.
PLEASE, NAOKO-CHAN.
I CANNOT.
VERY WELL.
GOOD-BYE, KYODAI NAOKO. I LOVED YOU.

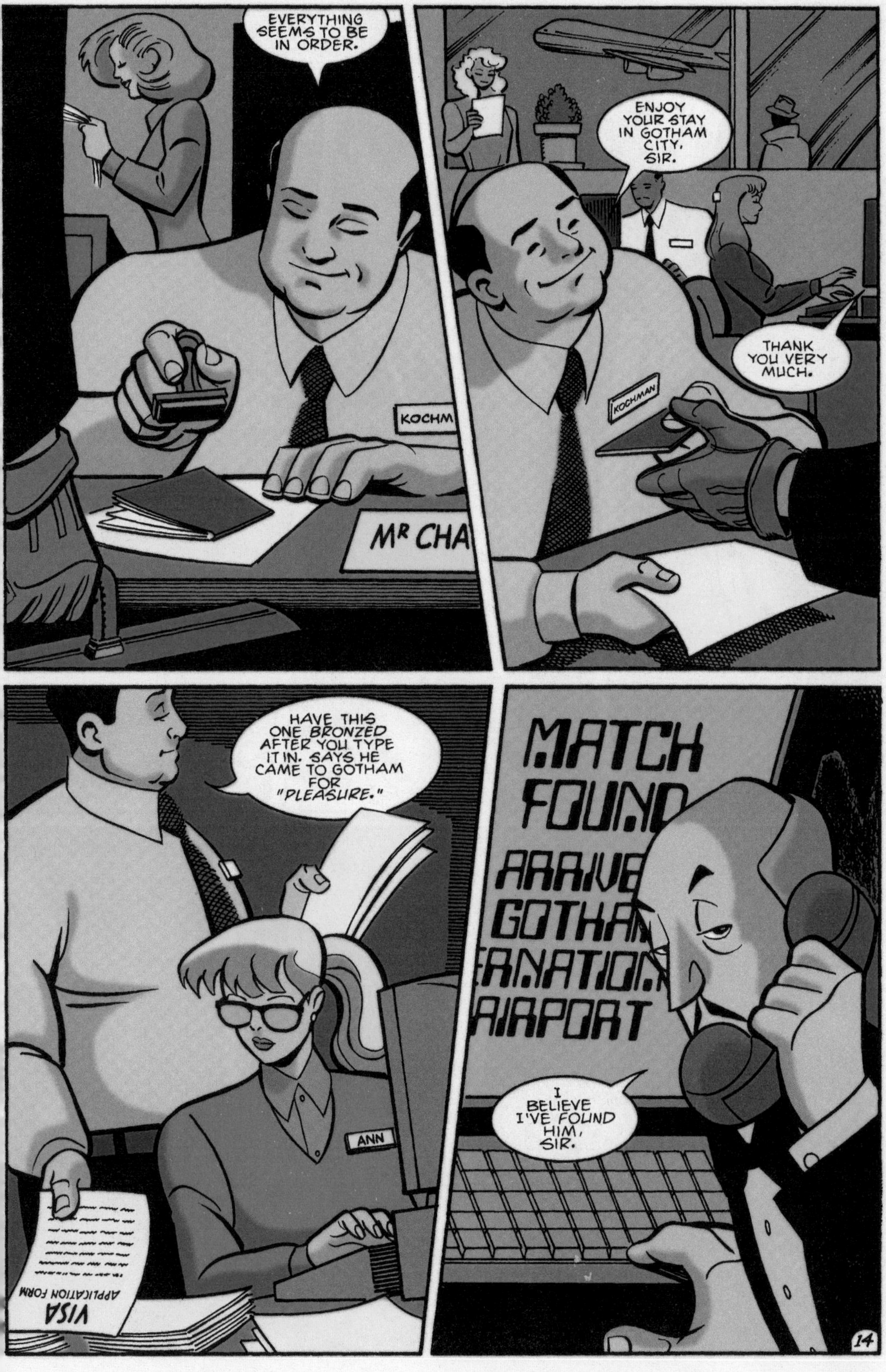
EVERYTHING SEEMS TO BE IN ORDER.
KOCHM
MR CHA
ENJOY YOUR STAY IN GOTHAM CITY, SIR.
KOCHMAN
THANK YOU VERY MUCH.
HAVE THIS ONE BRONZED AFTER YOU TYPE IT IN. SAYS HE CAME TO GOTHAM FOR "PLEASURE."
ANN
VISA
APPLICATION FORM
MATCH FOUND
ARRIVE
GOTHA
ERNATIO
AIRPORT
I BELIEVE I'VE FOUND HIM, SIR.

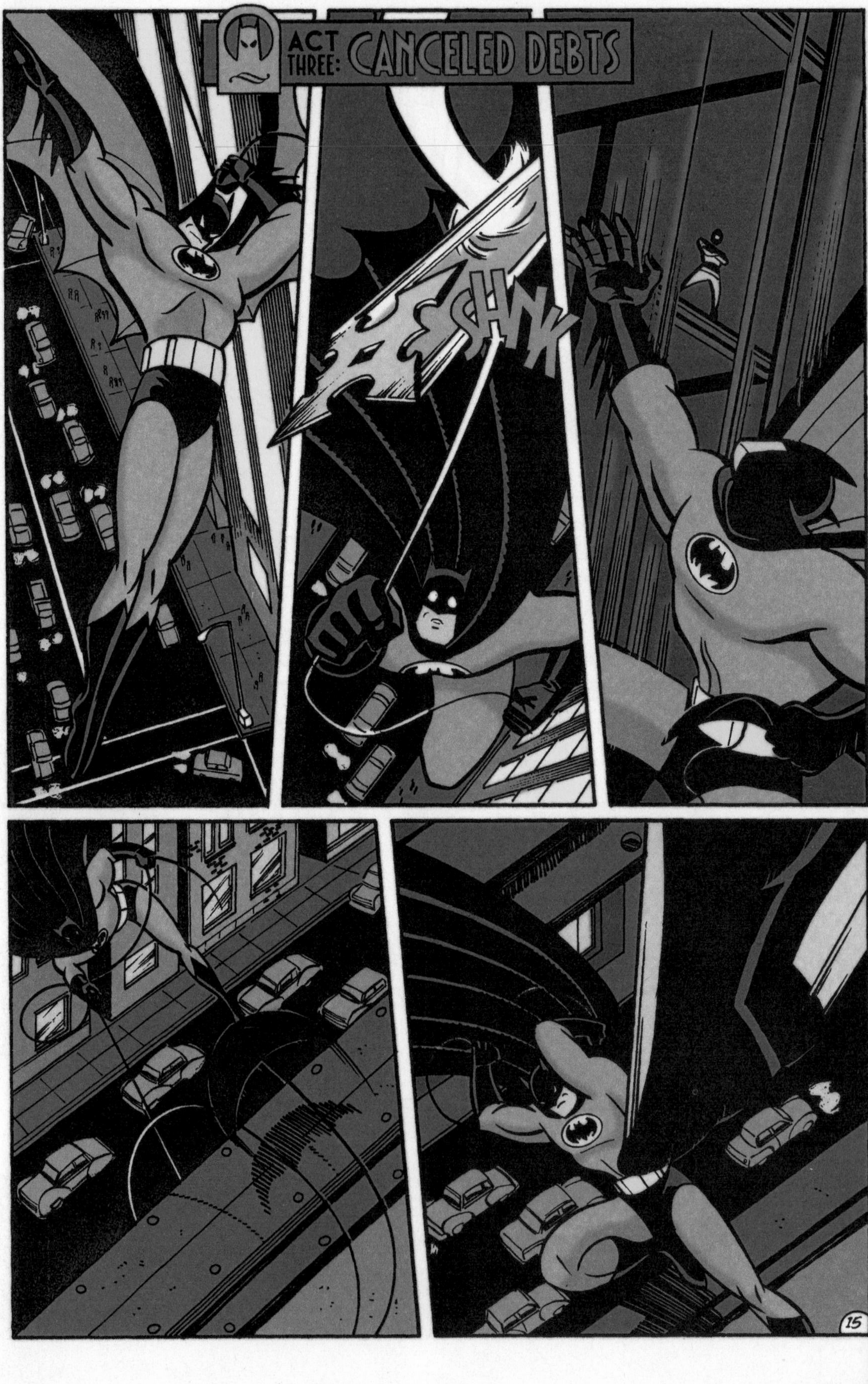
ACT THREE: CANCELED DEBTS
SHNK

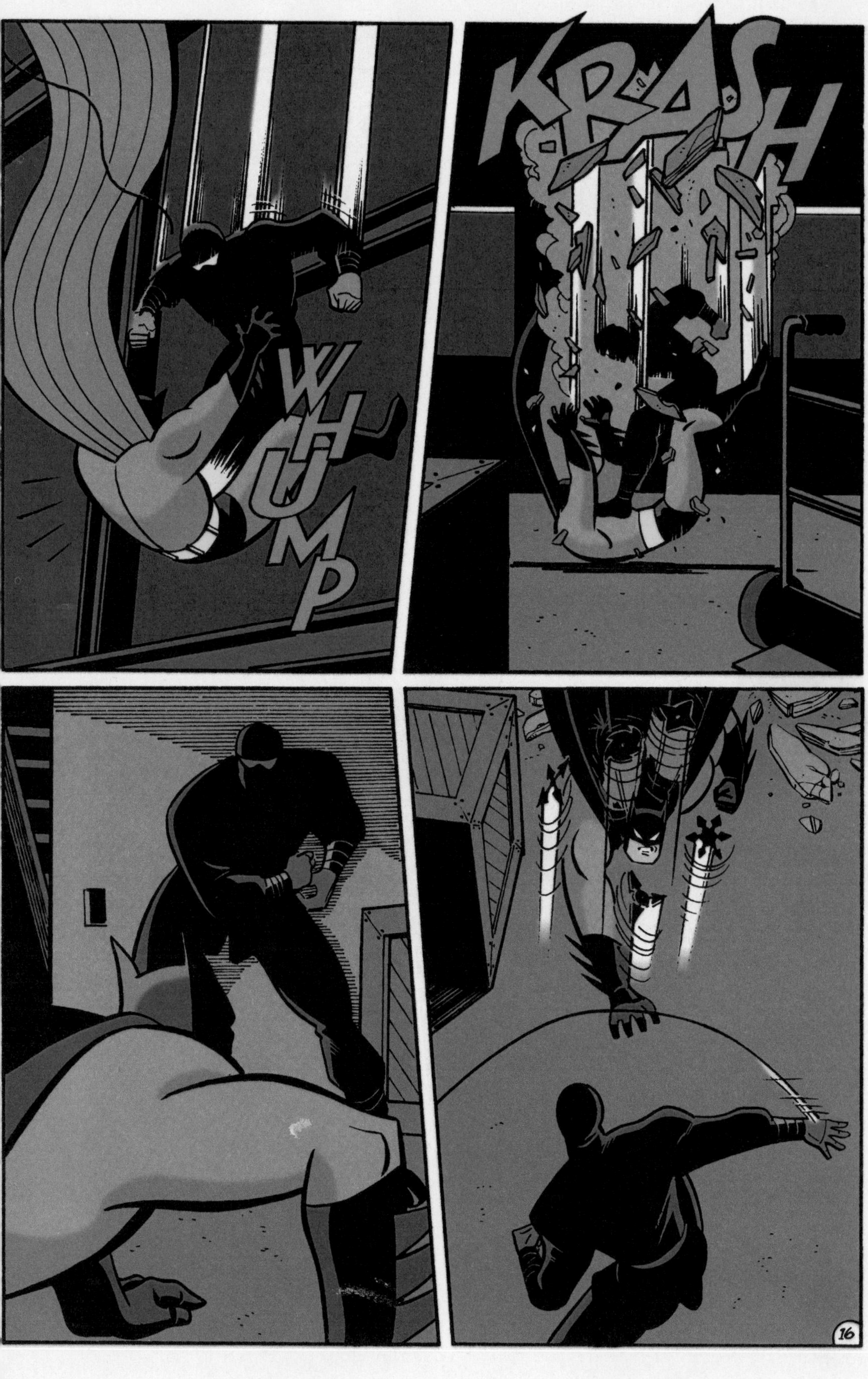
WHUMP
KRASH

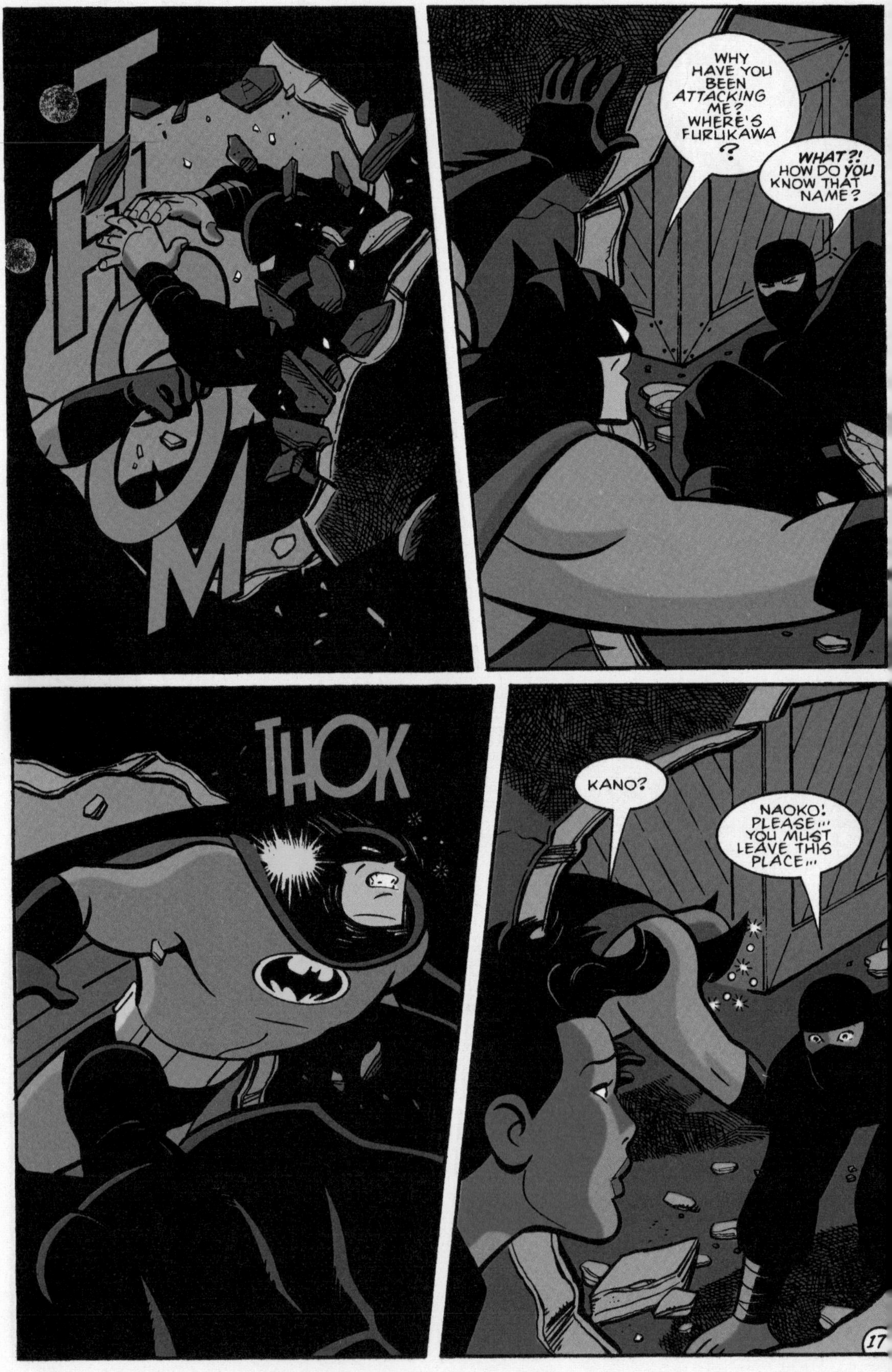
THOOM
WHY HAVE YOU BEEN ATTACKING ME? WHERE'S FURUKAWA?
WHAT?! HOW DO YOU KNOW THAT NAME?
THOK
KANO?
NAOKO! PLEASE... YOU MUST LEAVE THIS PLACE...

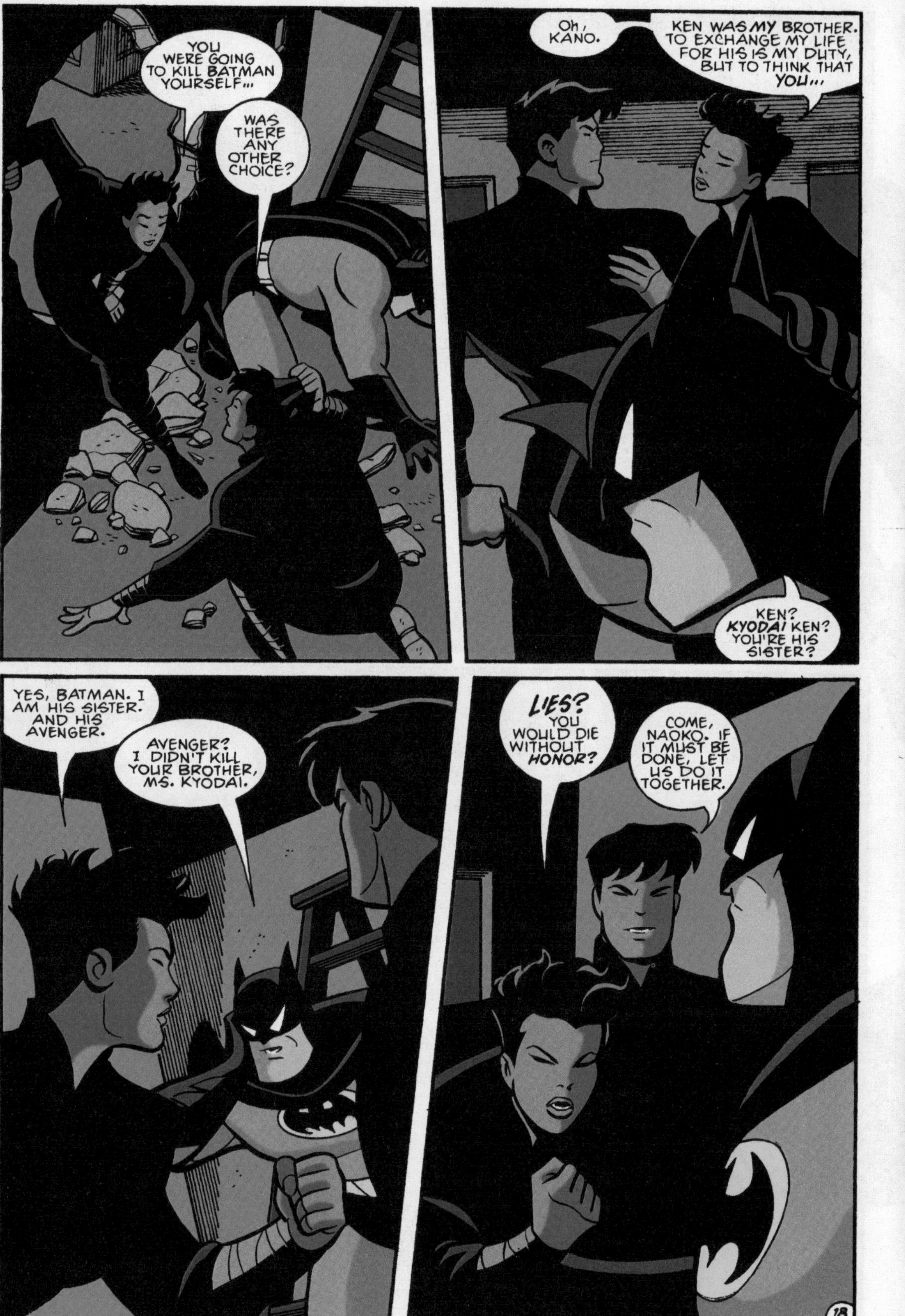
YOU WERE GOING TO KILL BATMAN YOURSELF...
WAS THERE ANY OTHER CHOICE?
OH, KANO.
KEN WAS MY BROTHER. TO EXCHANGE MY LIFE FOR HIS IS MY DUTY, BUT TO THINK THAT YOU...
KEN? KYODAI KEN? YOU'RE HIS SISTER?
YES, BATMAN. I AM HIS SISTER. AND HIS AVENGER.
AVENGER? I DIDN'T KILL YOUR BROTHER, MS. KYODAI.
LIES? YOU WOULD DIE WITHOUT HONOR?
COME, NAOKO. IF IT MUST BE DONE, LET US DO IT TOGETHER.
18

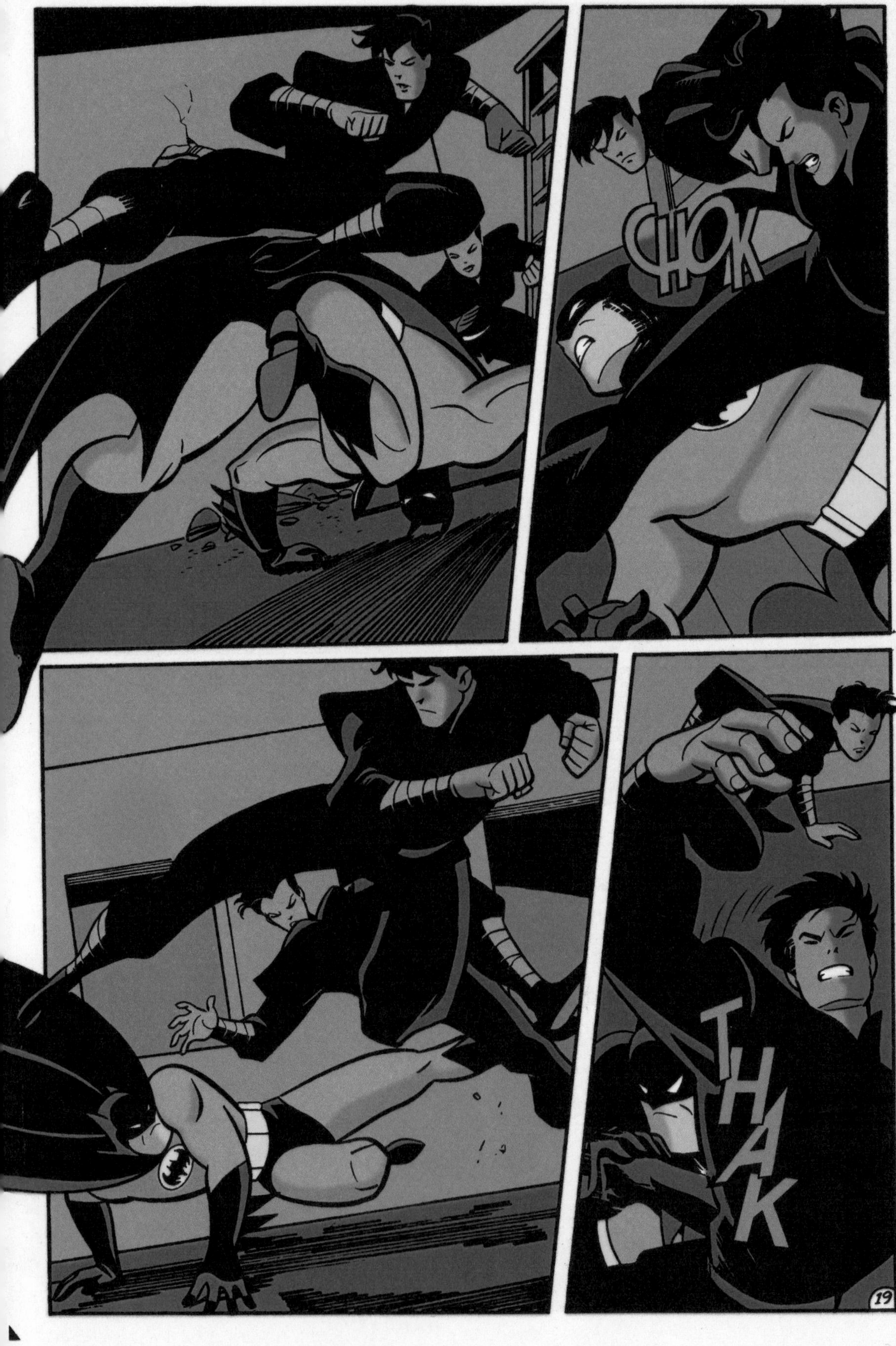
CHOK
THAK

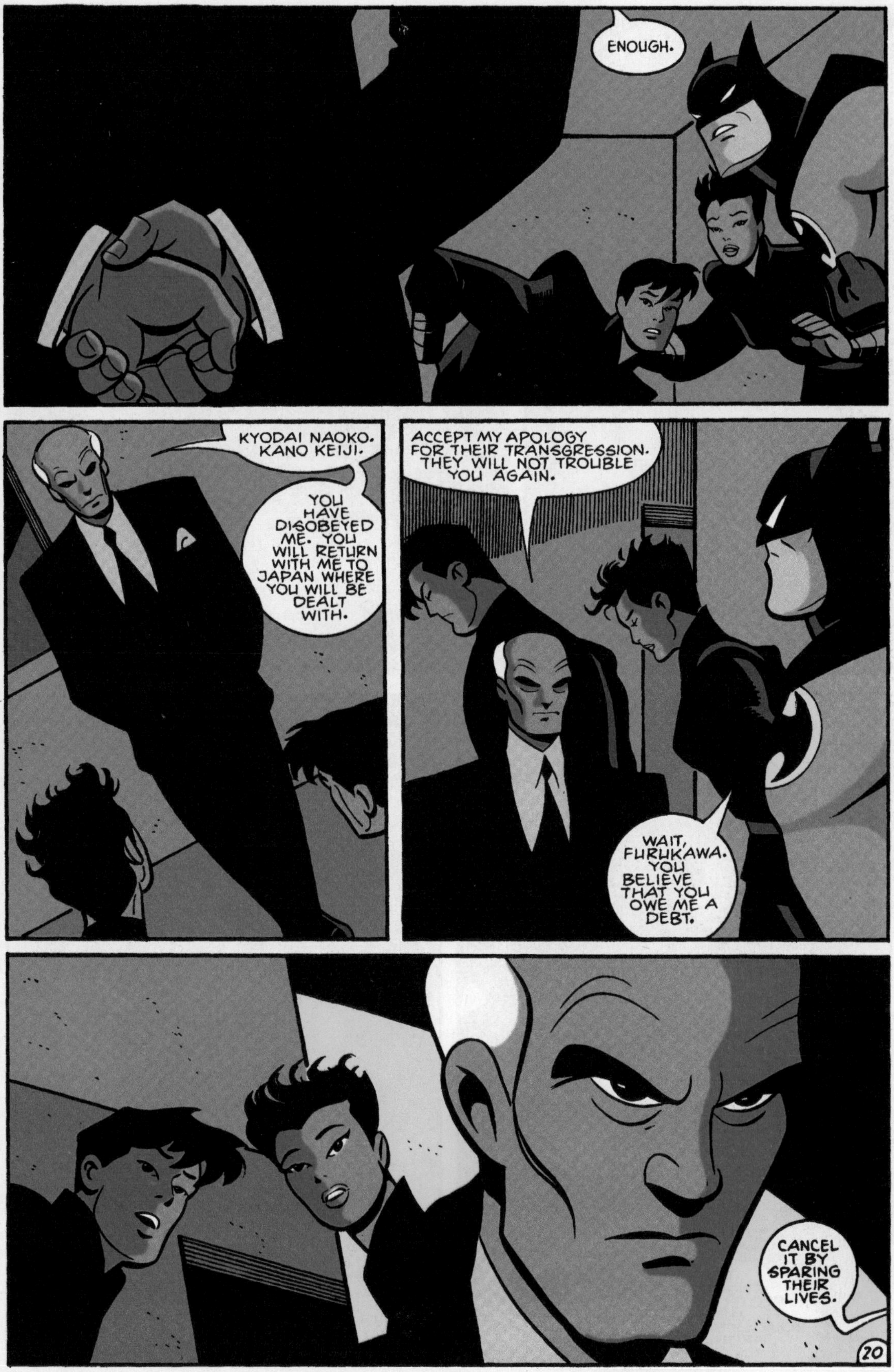

ENOUGH.
KYODAI NAOKO. KANO KEIJI.
YOU HAVE DISOBEYED ME. YOU WILL RETURN WITH ME TO JAPAN WHERE YOU WILL BE DEALT WITH.
ACCEPT MY APOLOGY FOR THEIR TRANSGRESSION. THEY WILL NOT TROUBLE YOU AGAIN.
WAIT, FURUKAWA. YOU BELIEVE THAT YOU OWE ME A DEBT.
CANCEL IT BY SPARING THEIR LIVES.

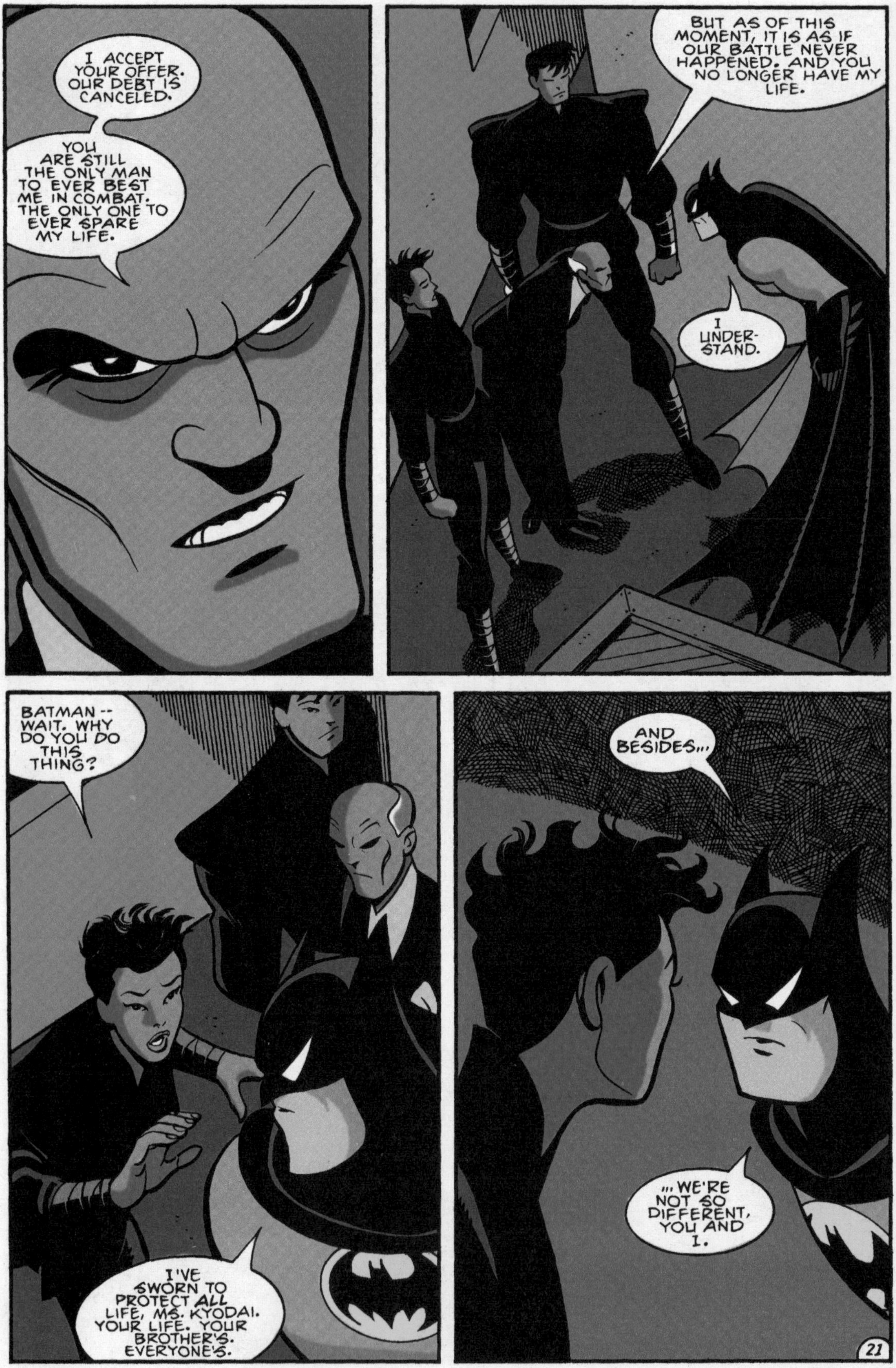

I ACCEPT YOUR OFFER. OUR DEBT IS CANCELED.
YOU ARE STILL THE ONLY MAN TO EVER BEST ME IN COMBAT. THE ONLY ONE TO EVER SPARE MY LIFE.
BUT AS OF THIS MOMENT, IT IS AS IF OUR BATTLE NEVER HAPPENED. AND YOU NO LONGER HAVE MY LIFE.
I UNDER-STAND.
BATMAN -- WAIT. WHY DO YOU DO THIS THING?
I'VE SWORN TO PROTECT ALL LIFE, MS. KYODAI. YOUR LIFE. YOUR BROTHER'S. EVERYONE'S.
AND BESIDES...
...WE'RE NOT SO DIFFERENT, YOU AND I.

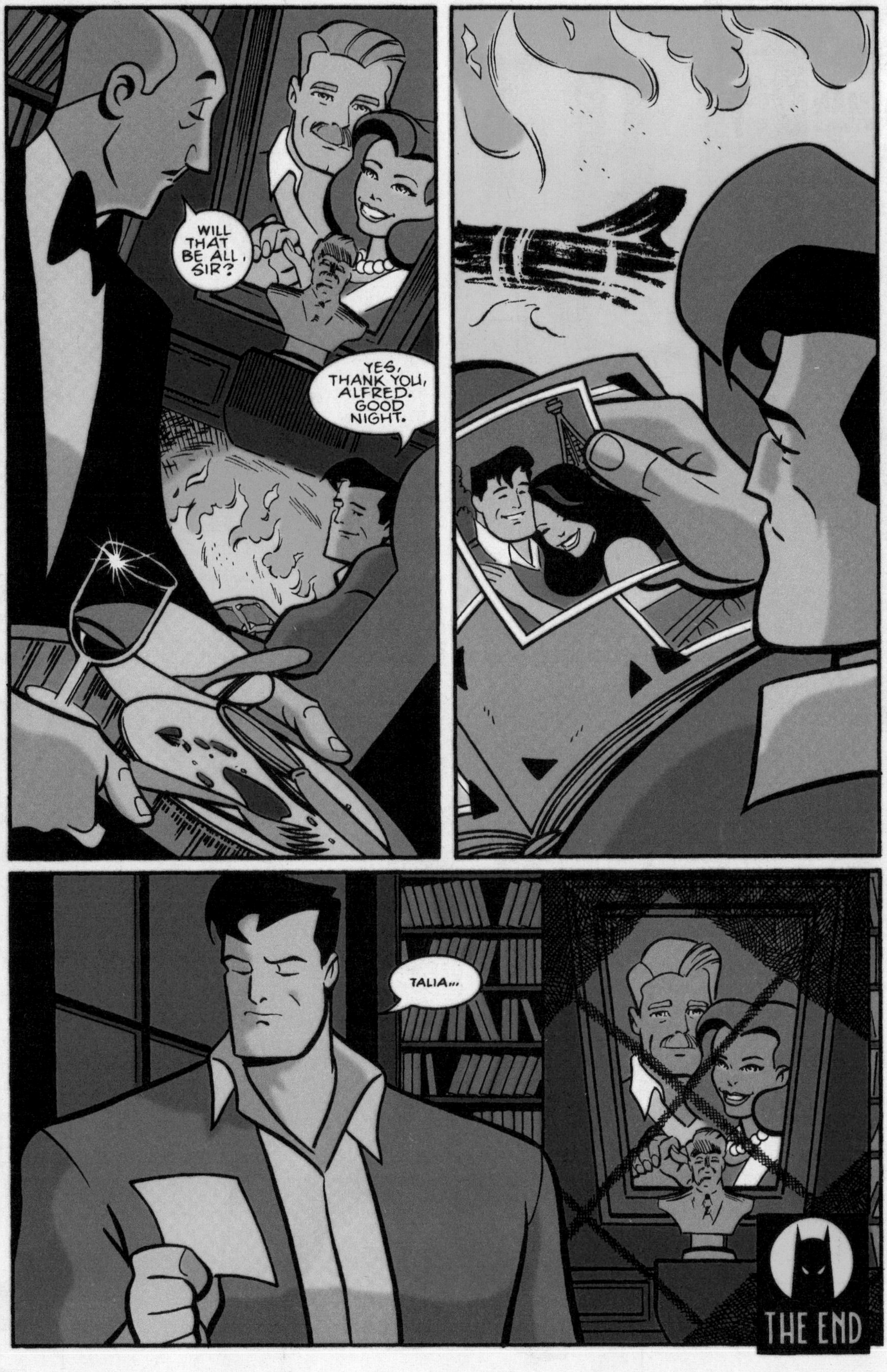
WILL THAT BE ALL, SIR?
YES, THANK YOU, ALFRED. GOOD NIGHT.
TALIA...
THE END

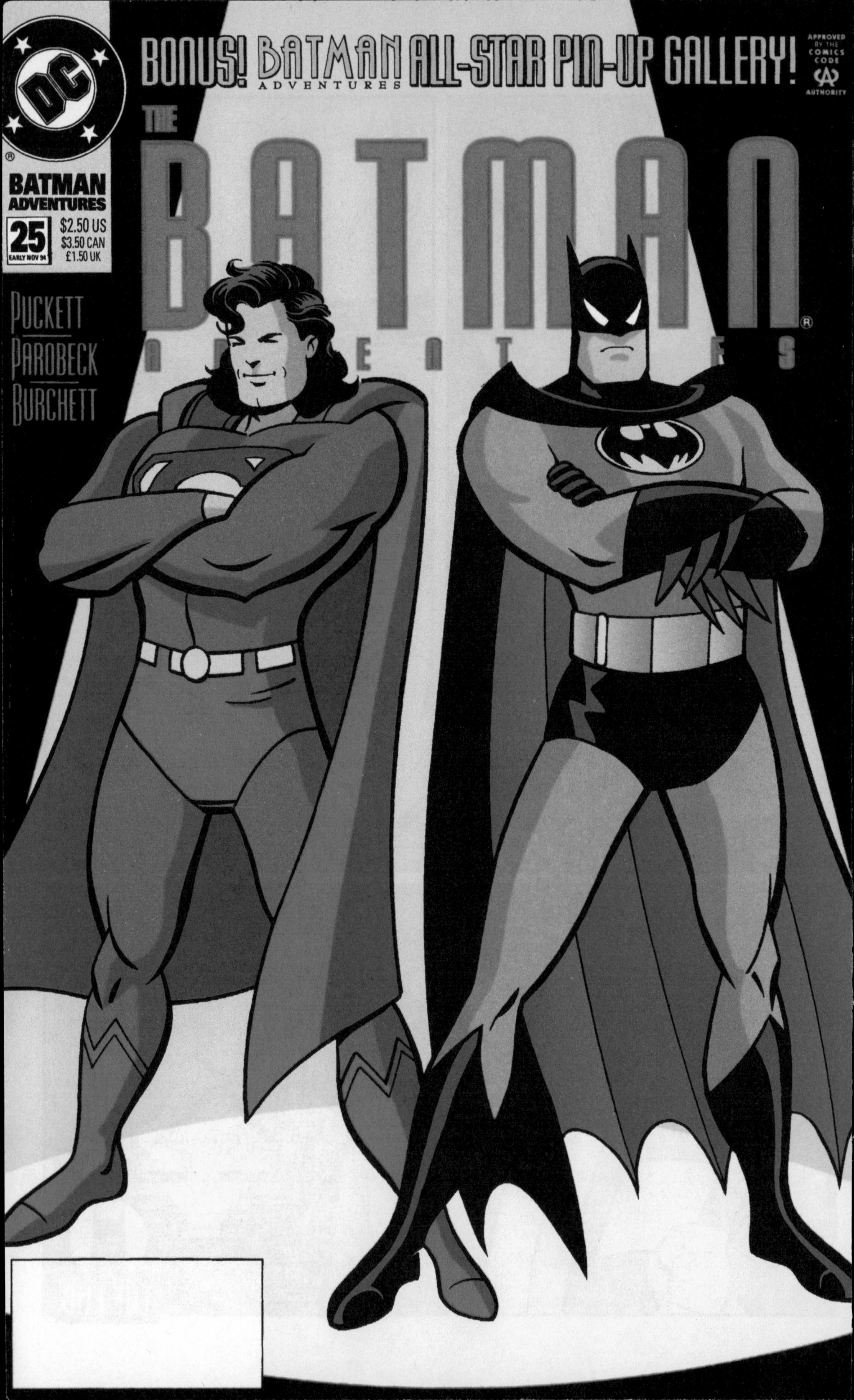

BONUS! BATMAN ADVENTURES ALL-STAR PIN-UP GALLERY!
APPROVED BY THE COMICS CODE AUTHORITY
DC
BATMAN ADVENTURES
25
EARLY NOV 94
$2.50 US
$3.50 CAN
£1.50 UK
THE
BATMAN
PUCKETT
PAROBECK
BURCHETT

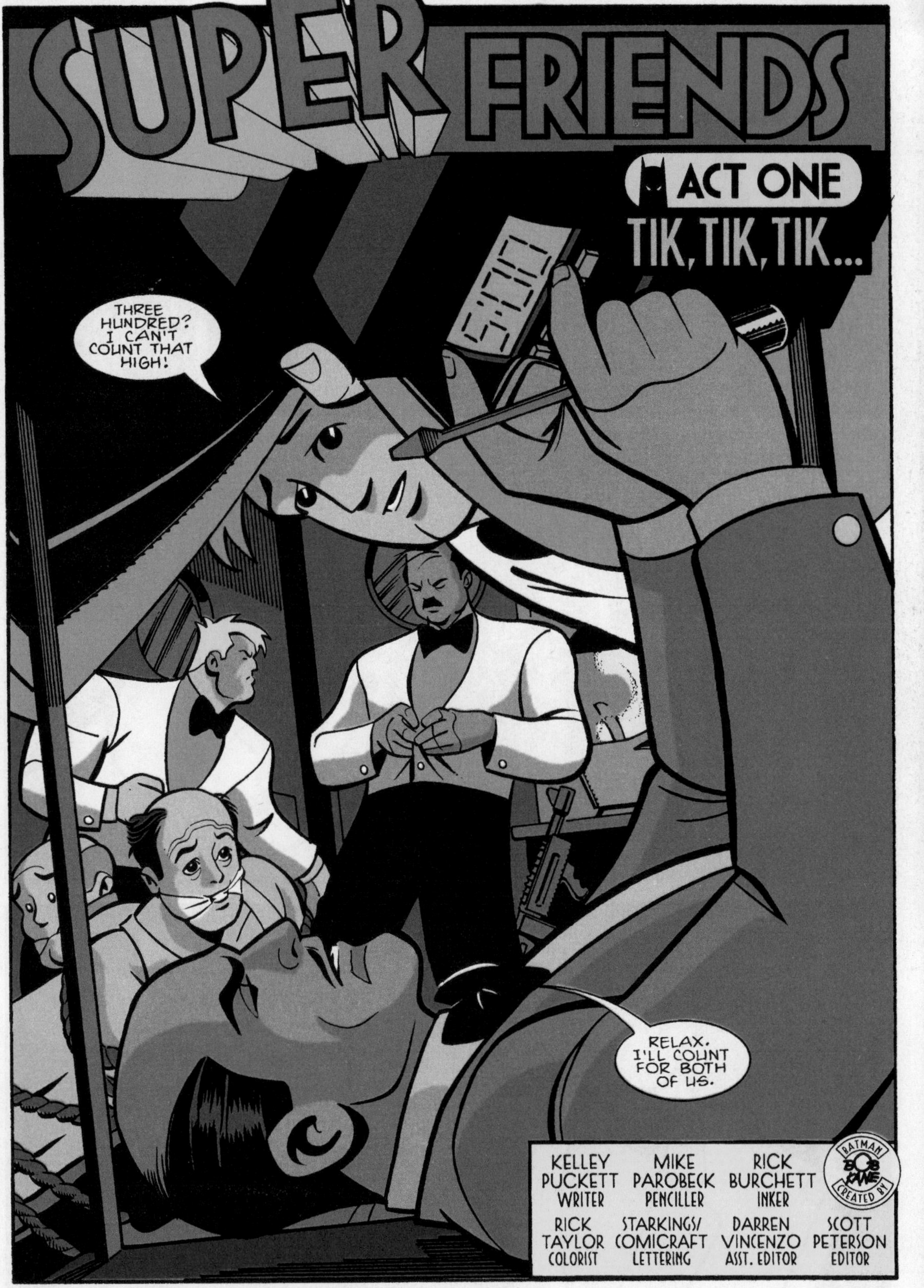
SUPER FRIENDS
ACT ONE
TIK, TIK, TIK...
THREE HUNDRED? I CAN'T COUNT THAT HIGH!
RELAX. I'LL COUNT FOR BOTH OF US.
KELLEY PUCKETT WRITER
MIKE PAROBECK PENCILLER
RICK BURCHETT INKER
BATMAN CREATED BY BOB KANE
RICK TAYLOR COLORIST
STARKINGS/ COMICRAFT LETTERING
DARREN VINCENZO ASST. EDITOR
SCOTT PETERSON EDITOR

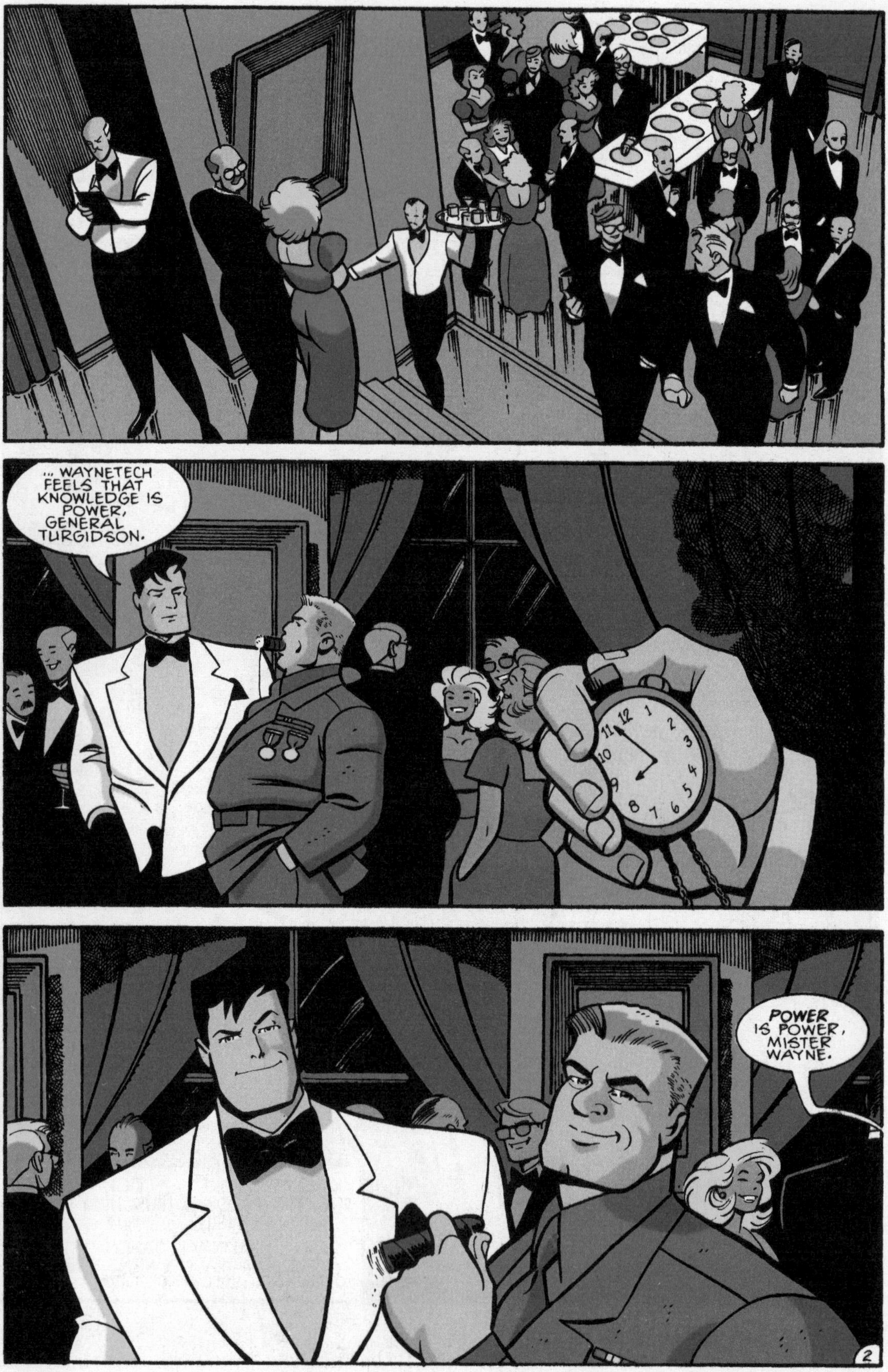
...WAYNETECH FEELS THAT KNOWLEDGE IS POWER, GENERAL TURGIDSON.
POWER IS POWER, MISTER WAYNE.
2

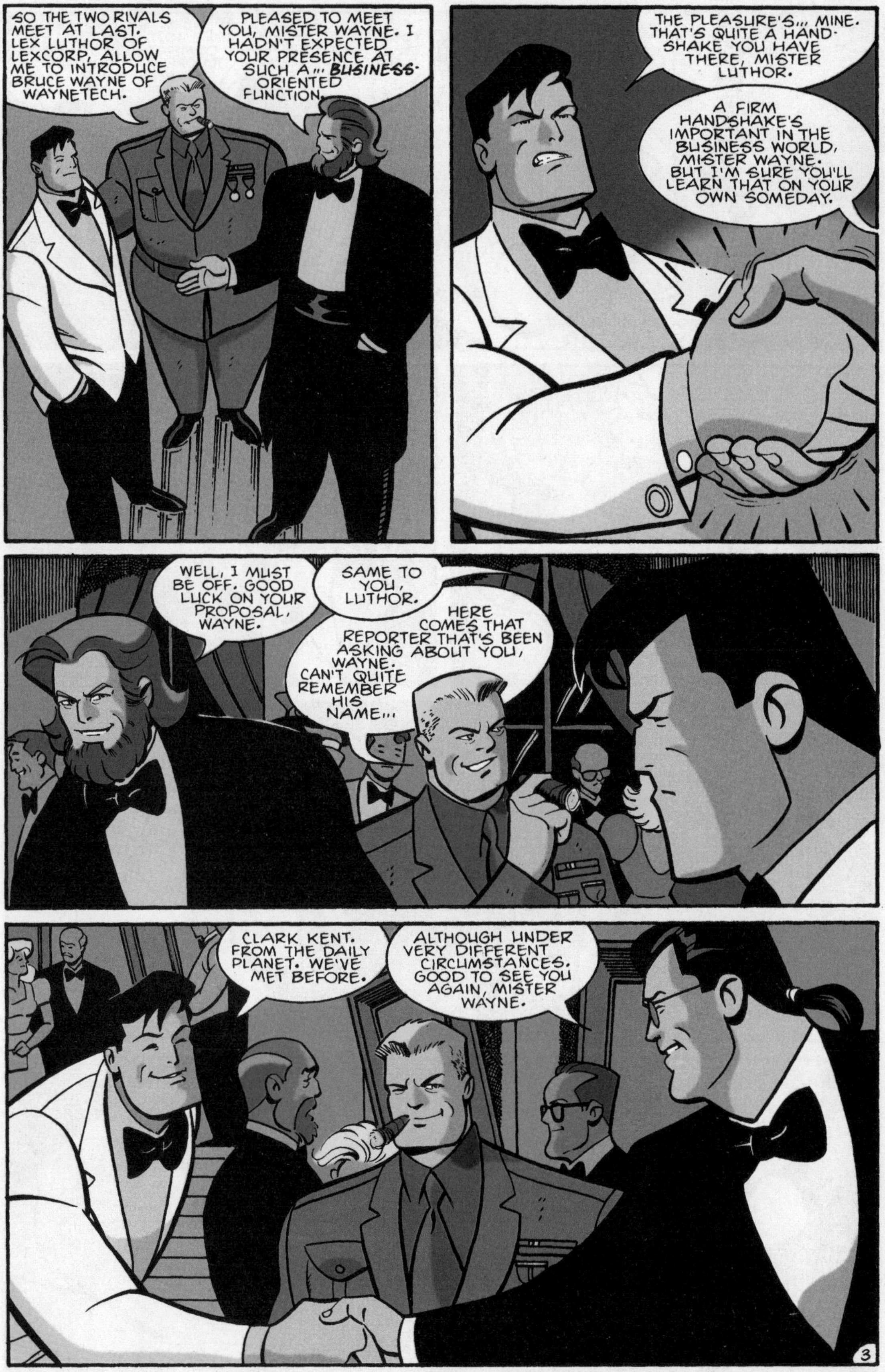
SO THE TWO RIVALS MEET AT LAST. LEX LUTHOR OF LEXCORP, ALLOW ME TO INTRODUCE BRUCE WAYNE OF WAYNETECH.
PLEASED TO MEET YOU, MISTER WAYNE. I HADN'T EXPECTED YOUR PRESENCE AT SUCH A... BUSINESS-ORIENTED FUNCTION.
THE PLEASURE'S... MINE. THAT'S QUITE A HAND-SHAKE YOU HAVE THERE, MISTER LUTHOR.
A FIRM HANDSHAKE'S IMPORTANT IN THE BUSINESS WORLD, MISTER WAYNE. BUT I'M SURE YOU'LL LEARN THAT ON YOUR OWN SOMEDAY.
WELL, I MUST BE OFF. GOOD LUCK ON YOUR PROPOSAL, WAYNE.
SAME TO YOU, LUTHOR.
HERE COMES THAT REPORTER THAT'S BEEN ASKING ABOUT YOU, WAYNE. CAN'T QUITE REMEMBER HIS NAME...
CLARK KENT. FROM THE DAILY PLANET. WE'VE MET BEFORE.
ALTHOUGH UNDER VERY DIFFERENT CIRCUMSTANCES. GOOD TO SEE YOU AGAIN, MISTER WAYNE.

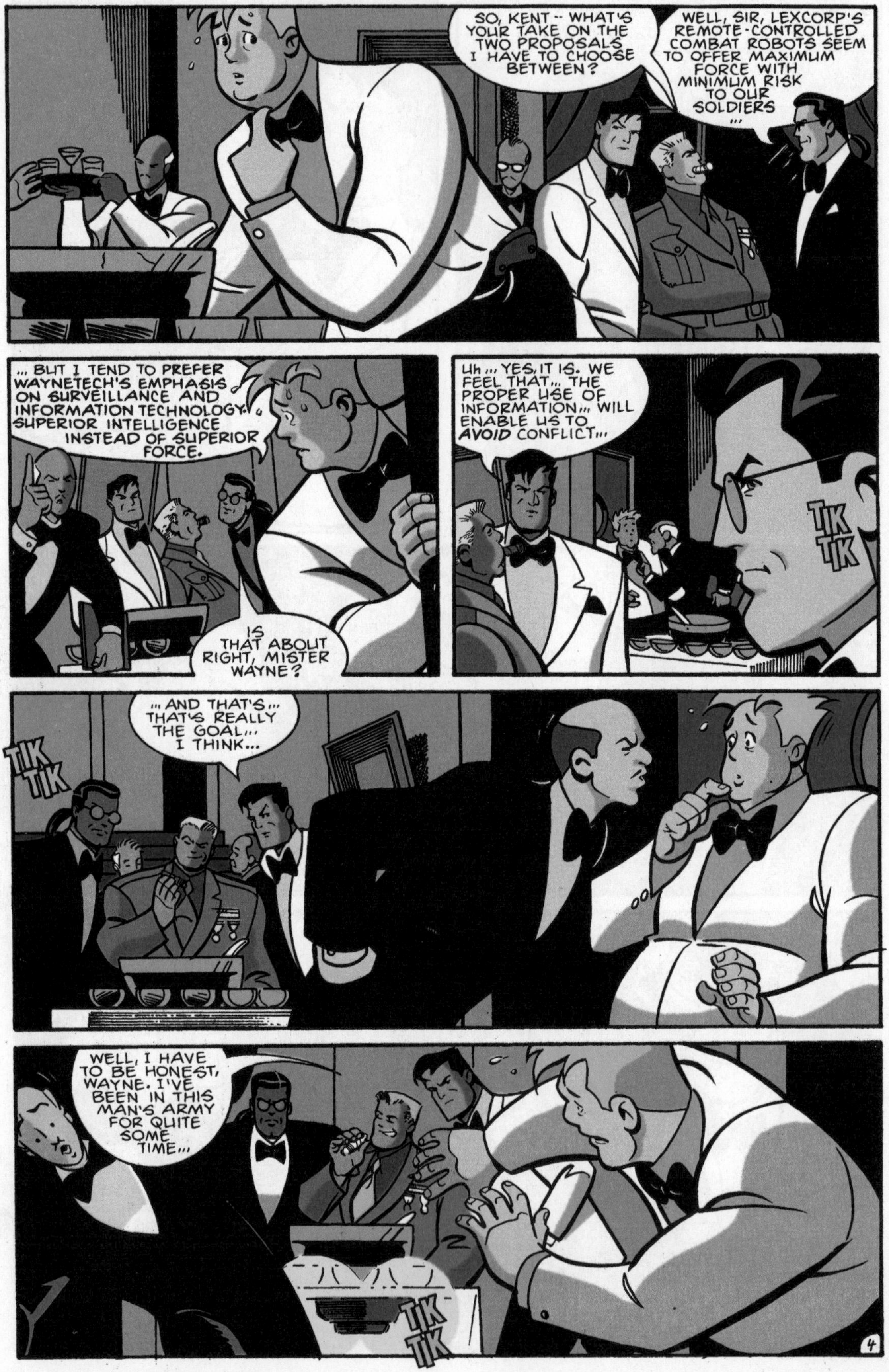
SO, KENT -- WHAT'S YOUR TAKE ON THE TWO PROPOSALS I HAVE TO CHOOSE BETWEEN?
WELL, SIR, LEXCORP'S REMOTE-CONTROLLED COMBAT ROBOTS SEEM TO OFFER MAXIMUM FORCE WITH MINIMUM RISK TO OUR SOLDIERS ...
... BUT I TEND TO PREFER WAYNETECH'S EMPHASIS ON SURVEILLANCE AND INFORMATION TECHNOLOGY. SUPERIOR INTELLIGENCE INSTEAD OF SUPERIOR FORCE.
IS THAT ABOUT RIGHT, MISTER WAYNE?
Uh ... YES, IT IS. WE FEEL THAT ... THE PROPER USE OF INFORMATION ... WILL ENABLE US TO AVOID CONFLICT ...
TIK TIK
... AND THAT'S ... THAT'S REALLY THE GOAL ... I THINK...
TIK TIK
WELL, I HAVE TO BE HONEST, WAYNE. I'VE BEEN IN THIS MAN'S ARMY FOR QUITE SOME TIME ...
TIK TIK
4

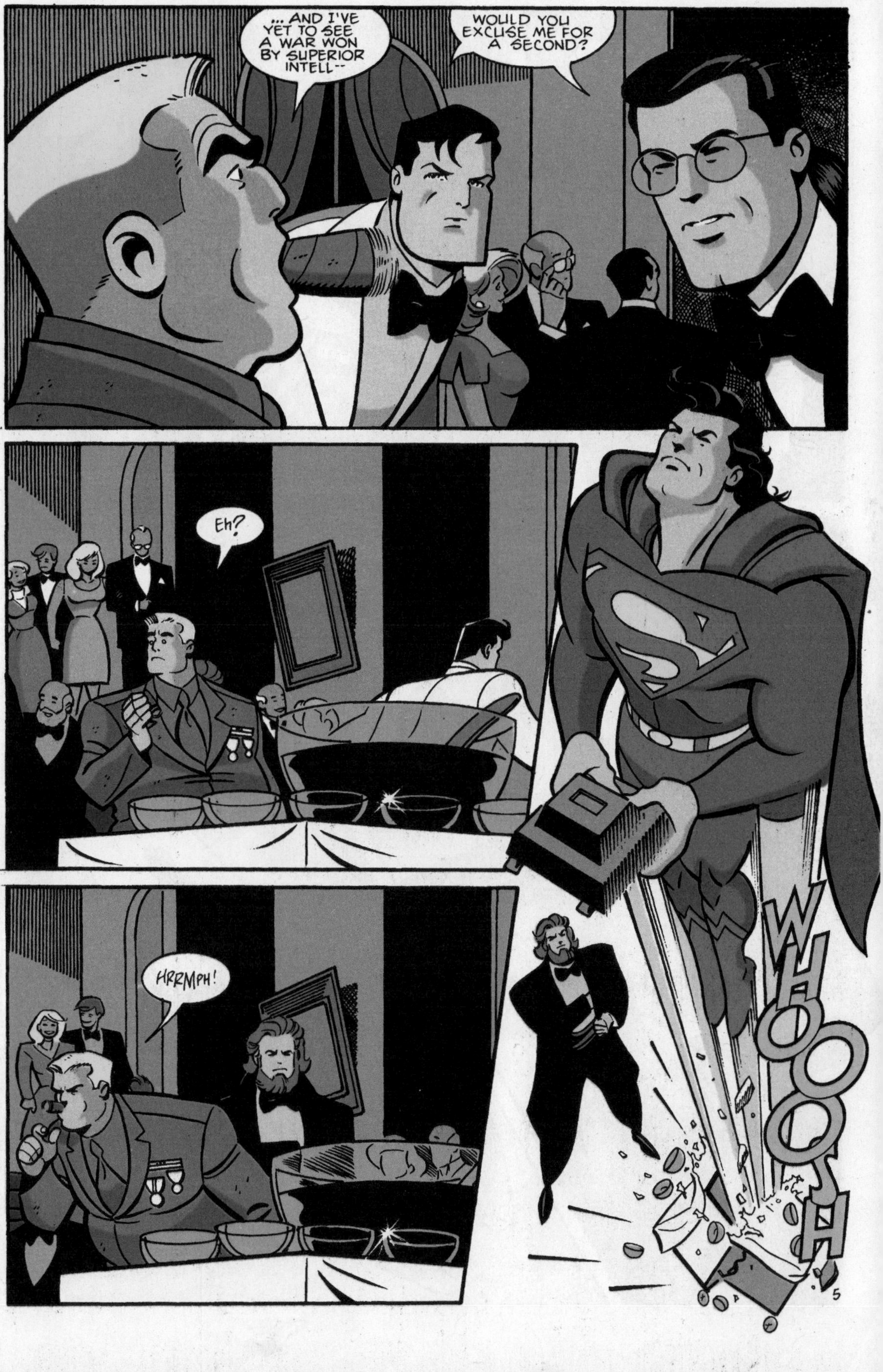

... AND I'VE YET TO SEE A WAR WON BY SUPERIOR INTELL--
WOULD YOU EXCUSE ME FOR A SECOND?
Eh?
HRRMPH!
WHOOOSH

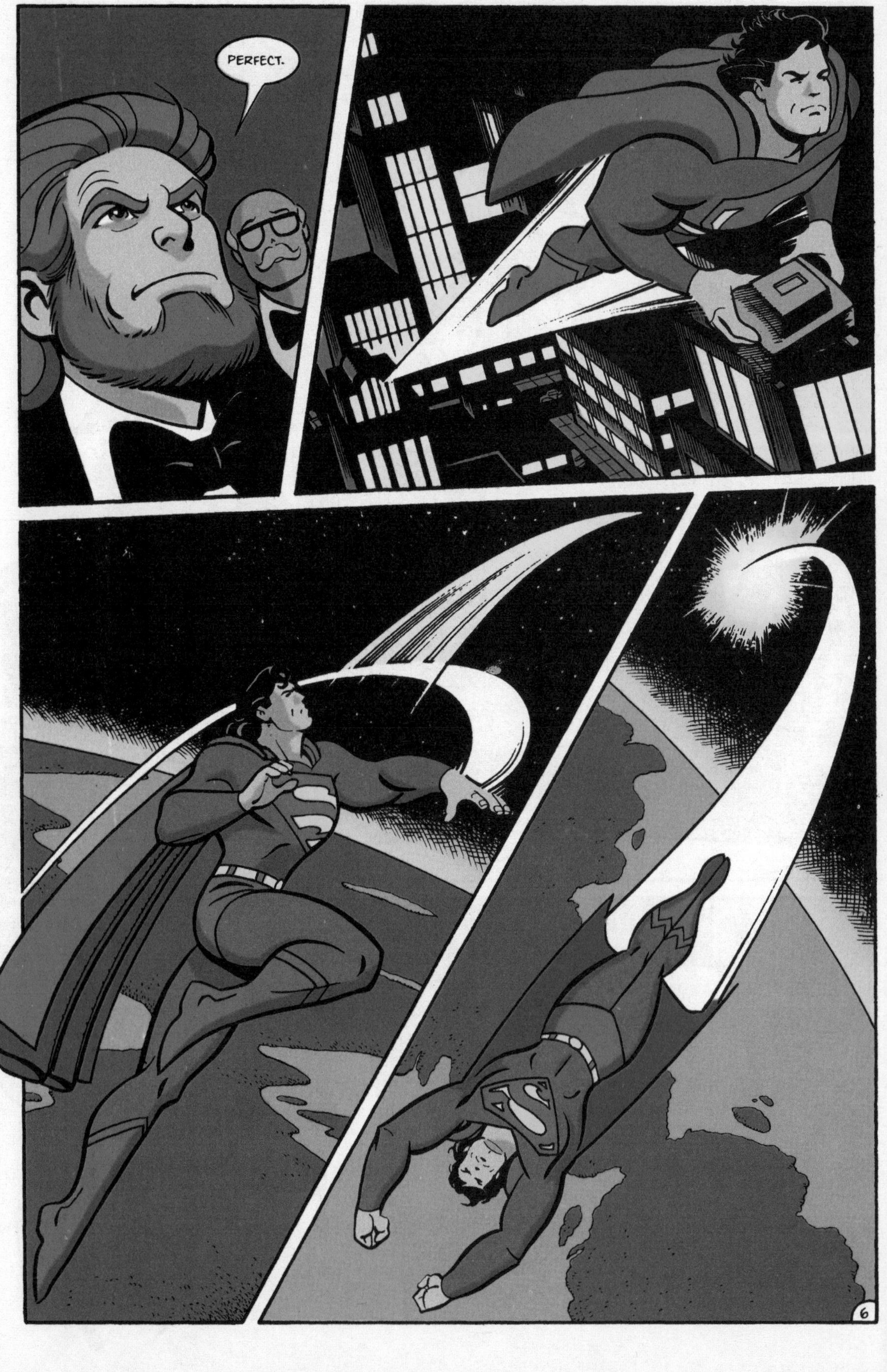
PERFECT.

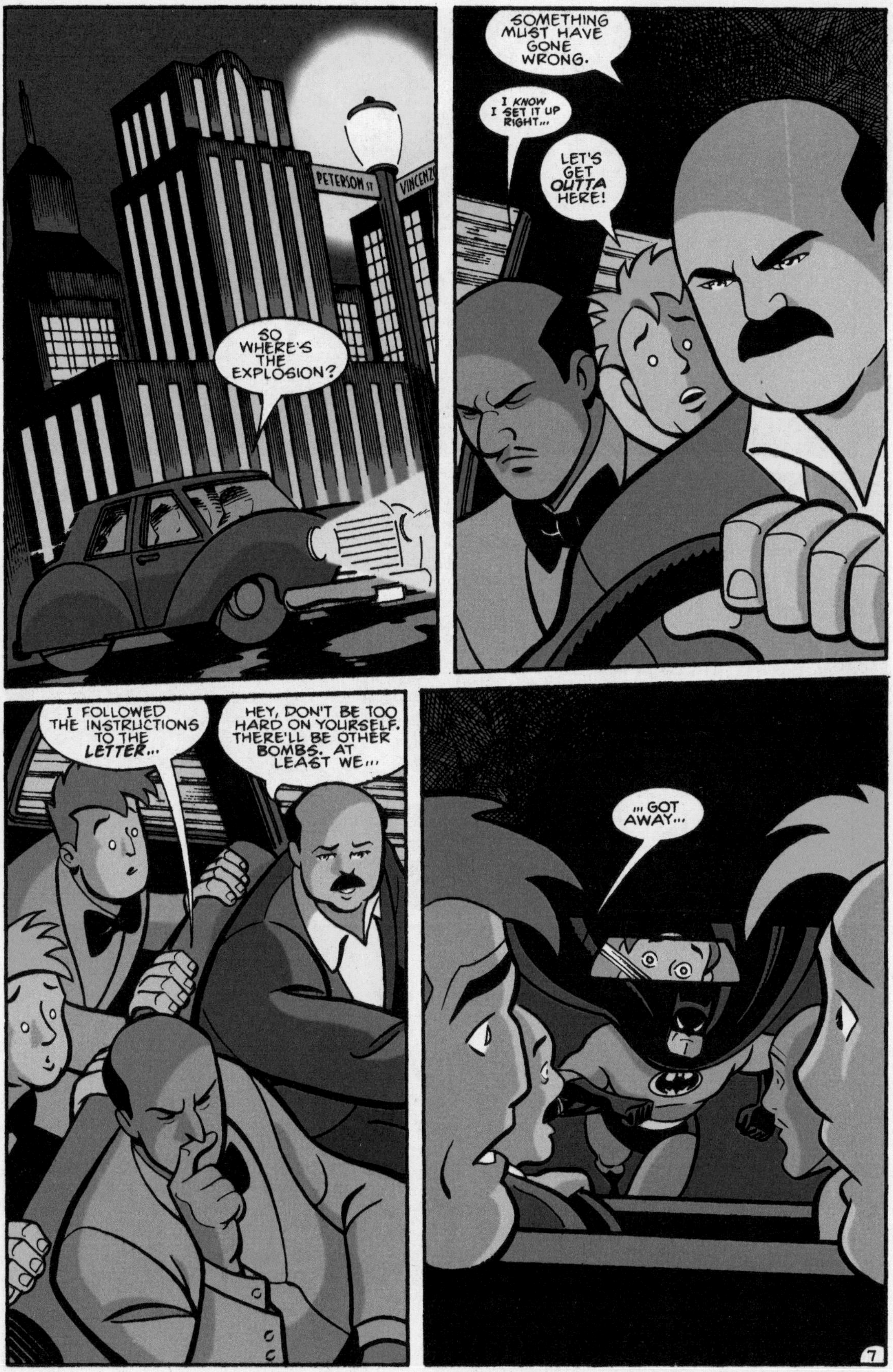
PETERSON ST
VINCENZO
SO WHERE'S THE EXPLOSION?
SOMETHING MUST HAVE GONE WRONG.
I KNOW I SET IT UP RIGHT...
LET'S GET OUTTA HERE!
I FOLLOWED THE INSTRUCTIONS TO THE LETTER...
HEY, DON'T BE TOO HARD ON YOURSELF. THERE'LL BE OTHER BOMBS. AT LEAST WE...
...GOT AWAY...

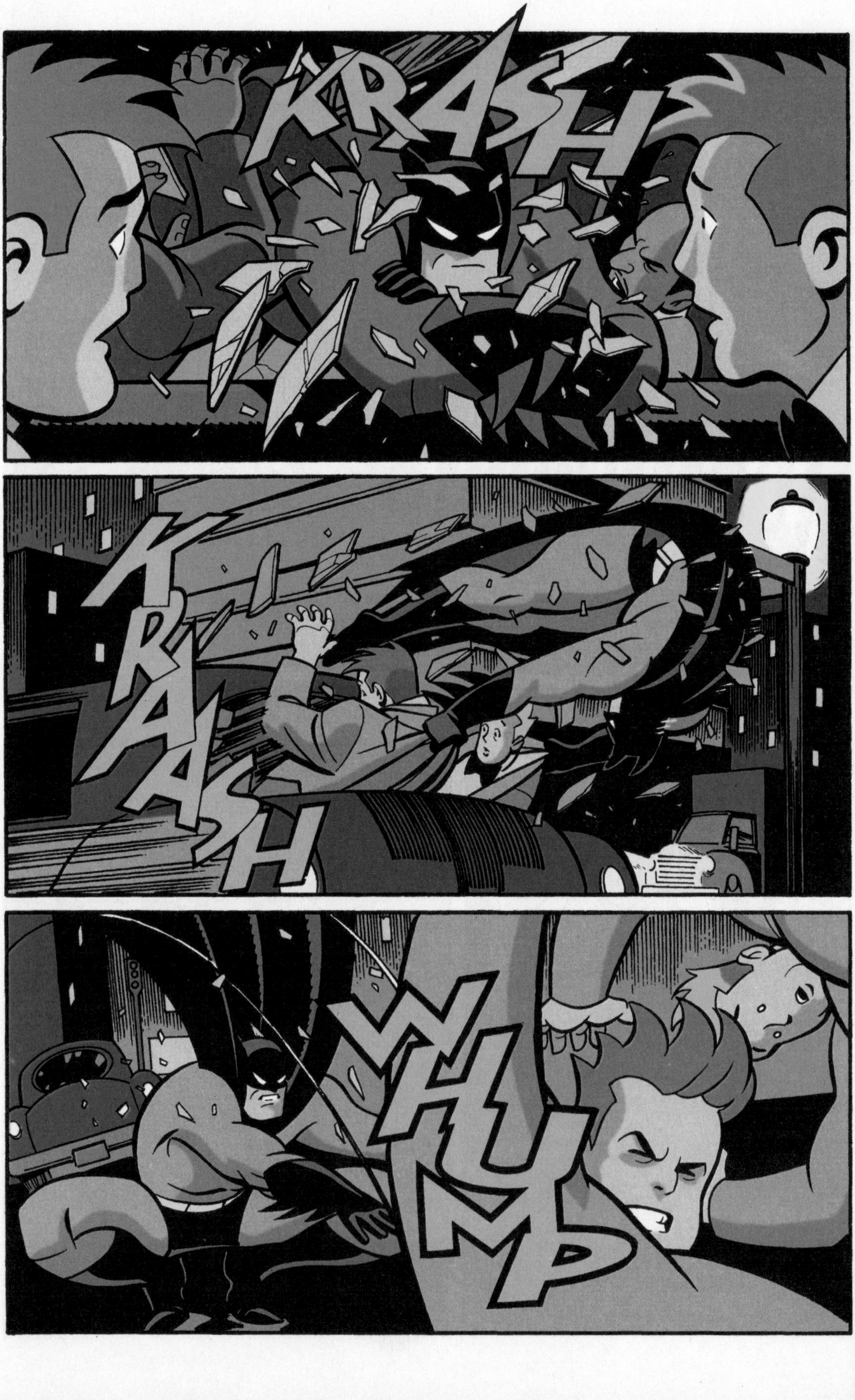
KRASH
KRASH
WHUMP

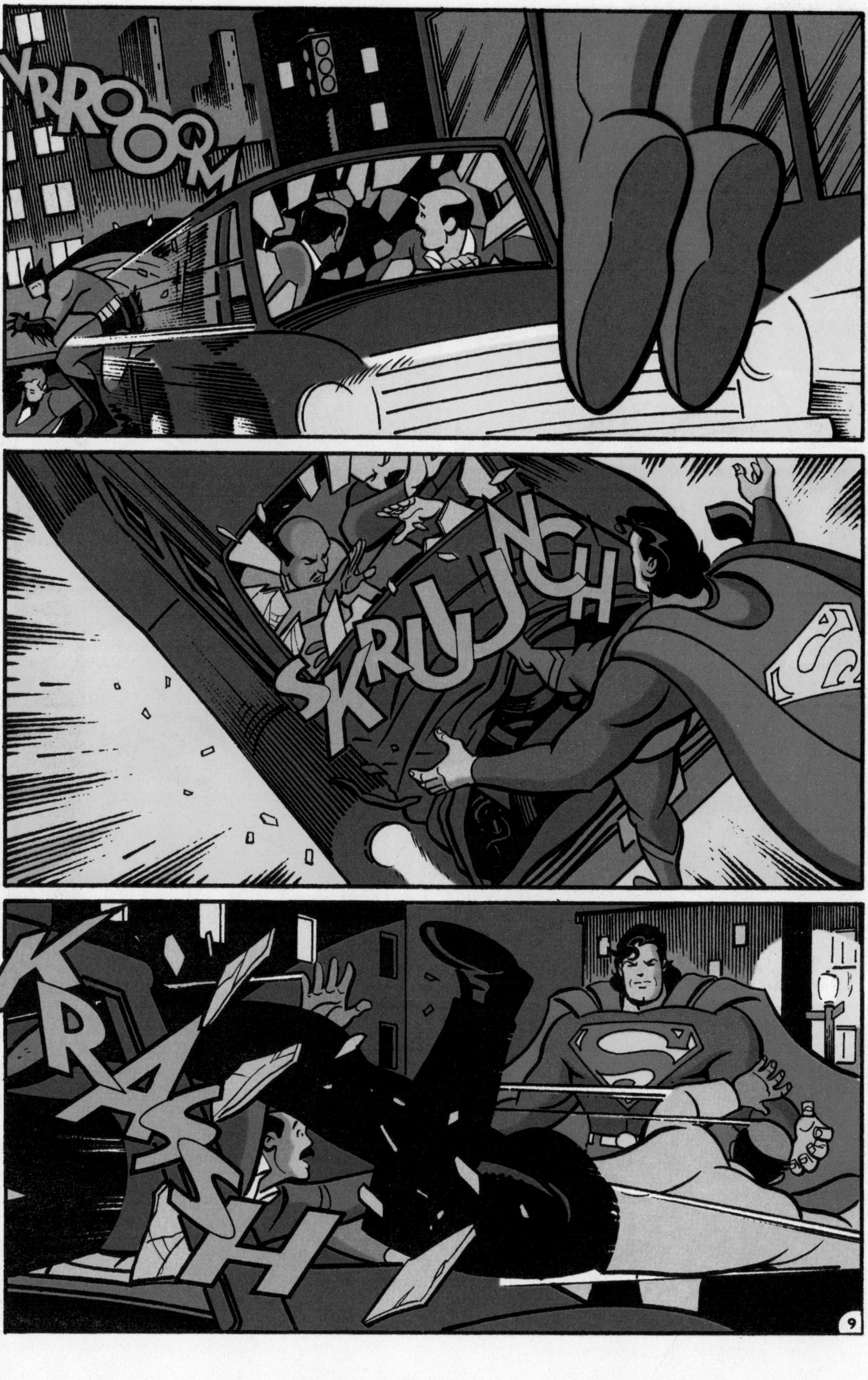
VRROOOM
SKRUUNCH
KRASH

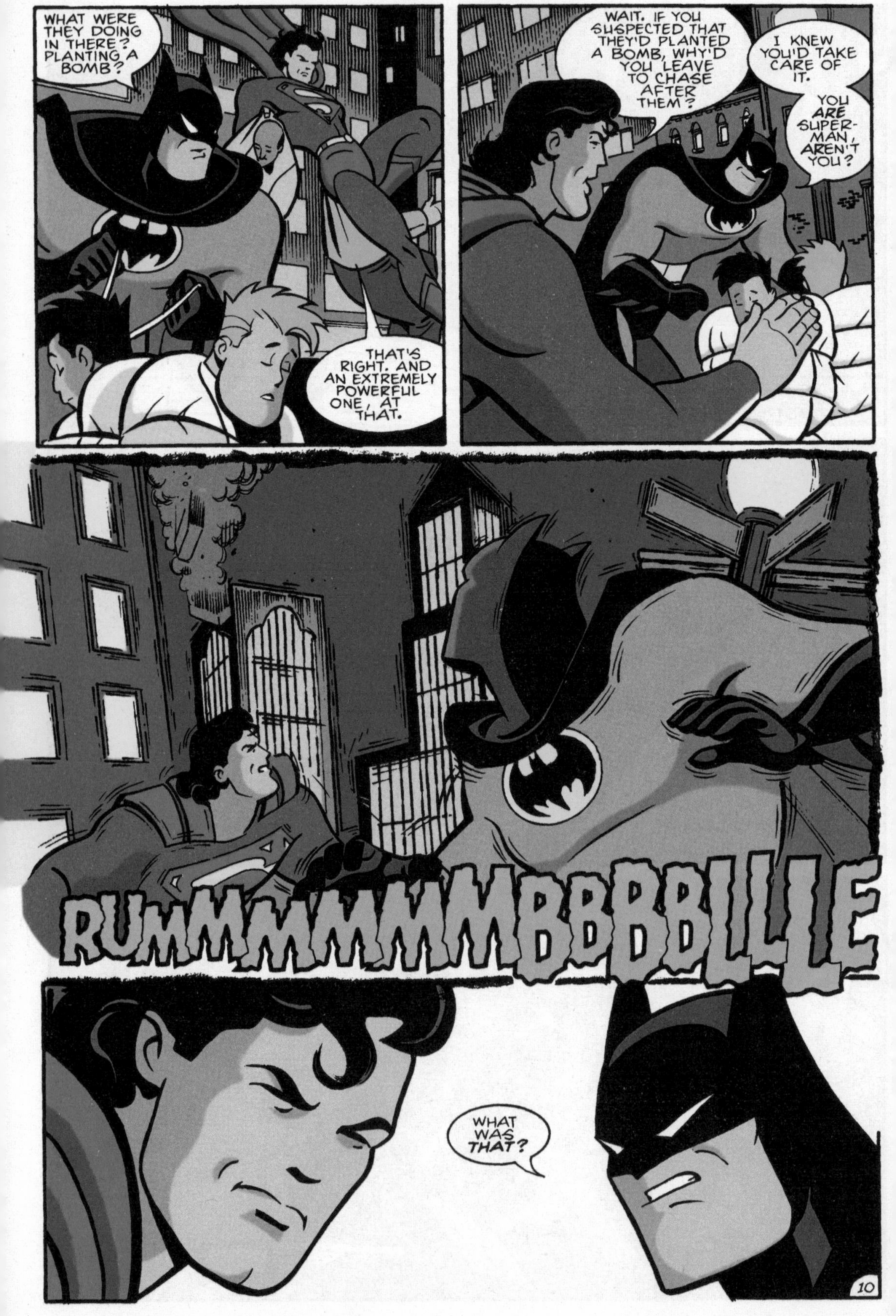
WHAT WERE THEY DOING IN THERE? PLANTING A BOMB?
THAT'S RIGHT. AND AN EXTREMELY POWERFUL ONE, AT THAT.
WAIT. IF YOU SUSPECTED THAT THEY'D PLANTED A BOMB, WHY'D YOU LEAVE TO CHASE AFTER THEM?
I KNEW YOU'D TAKE CARE OF IT.
YOU *ARE* SUPERMAN, AREN'T YOU?
RUMMMMMMMBBBBLLLE
WHAT WAS *THAT*?

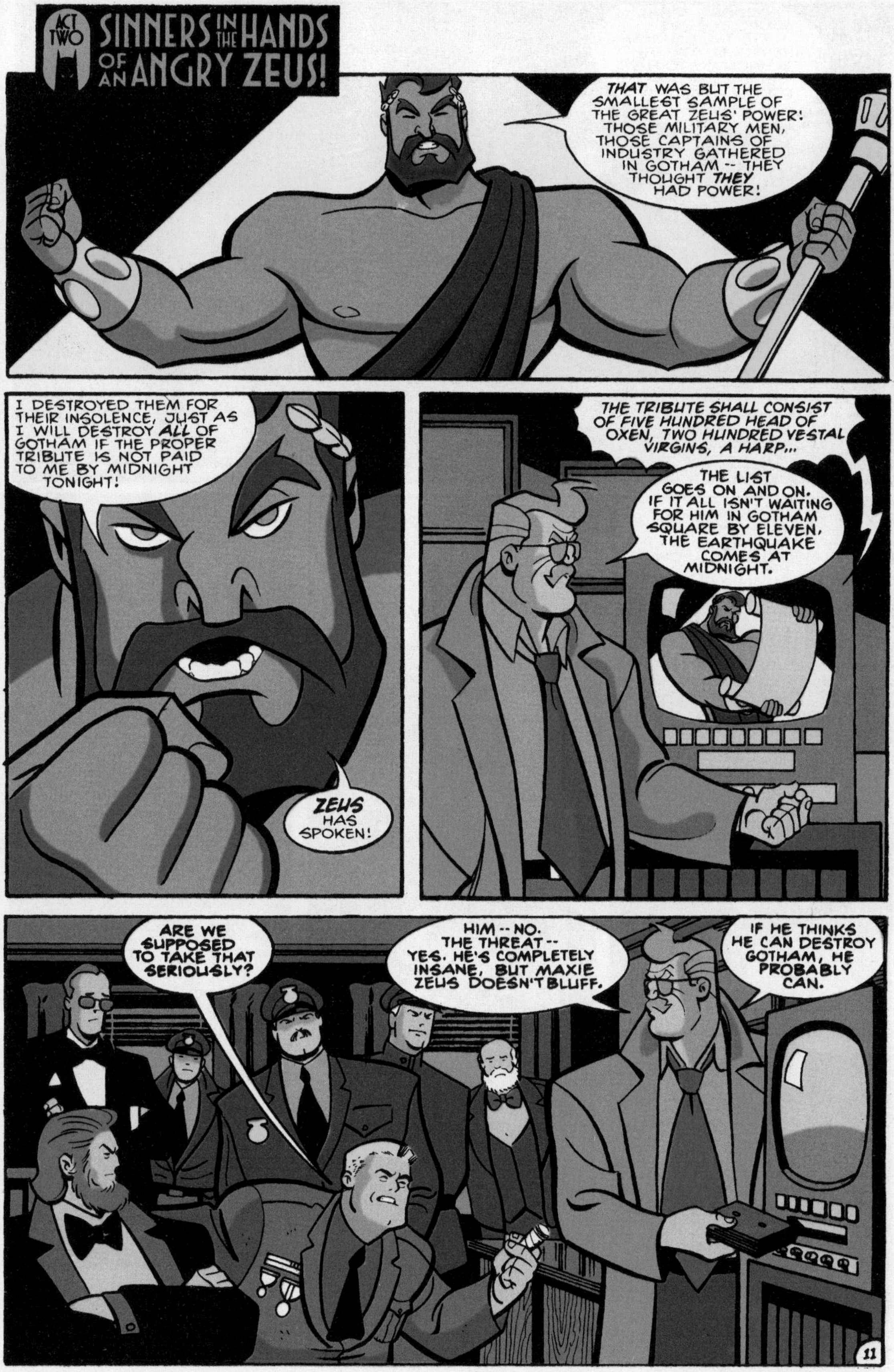
ACT TWO
SINNERS IN THE HANDS OF AN ANGRY ZEUS!
THAT WAS BUT THE SMALLEST SAMPLE OF THE GREAT ZEUS' POWER: THOSE MILITARY MEN, THOSE CAPTAINS OF INDUSTRY GATHERED IN GOTHAM -- THEY THOUGHT THEY HAD POWER!
I DESTROYED THEM FOR THEIR INSOLENCE, JUST AS I WILL DESTROY ALL OF GOTHAM IF THE PROPER TRIBUTE IS NOT PAID TO ME BY MIDNIGHT TONIGHT!
ZEUS HAS SPOKEN!
THE TRIBUTE SHALL CONSIST OF FIVE HUNDRED HEAD OF OXEN, TWO HUNDRED VESTAL VIRGINS, A HARP...
THE LIST GOES ON AND ON. IF IT ALL ISN'T WAITING FOR HIM IN GOTHAM SQUARE BY ELEVEN, THE EARTHQUAKE COMES AT MIDNIGHT.
ARE WE SUPPOSED TO TAKE THAT SERIOUSLY?
HIM -- NO. THE THREAT -- YES. HE'S COMPLETELY INSANE, BUT MAXIE ZEUS DOESN'T BLUFF.
IF HE THINKS HE CAN DESTROY GOTHAM, HE PROBABLY CAN.

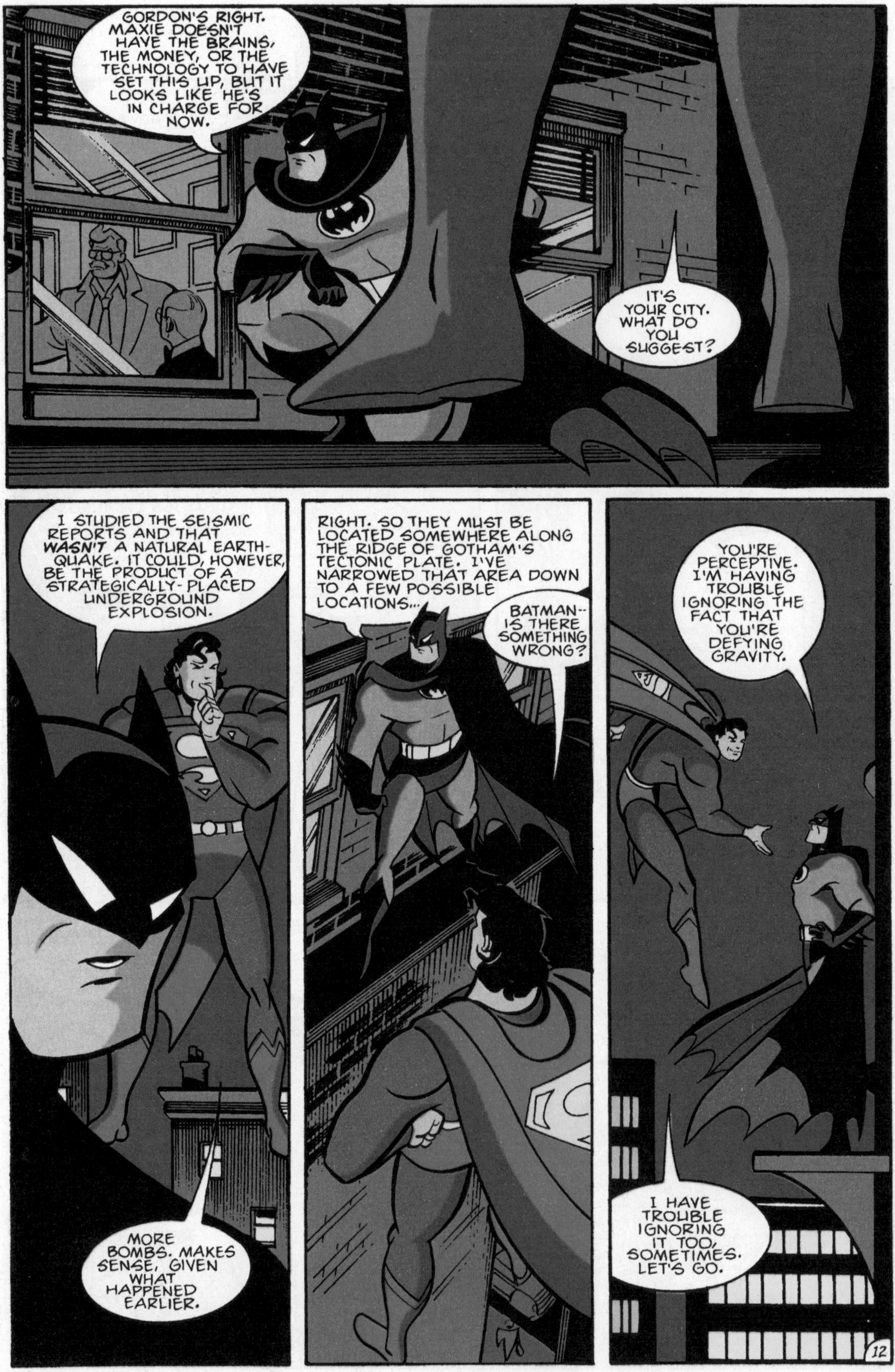

GORDON'S RIGHT. MAXIE DOESN'T HAVE THE BRAINS, THE MONEY, OR THE TECHNOLOGY TO HAVE SET THIS UP, BUT IT LOOKS LIKE HE'S IN CHARGE FOR NOW.
IT'S YOUR CITY. WHAT DO YOU SUGGEST?
I STUDIED THE SEISMIC REPORTS AND THAT WASN'T A NATURAL EARTHQUAKE. IT COULD, HOWEVER, BE THE PRODUCT OF A STRATEGICALLY-PLACED UNDERGROUND EXPLOSION.
MORE BOMBS. MAKES SENSE, GIVEN WHAT HAPPENED EARLIER.
RIGHT. SO THEY MUST BE LOCATED SOMEWHERE ALONG THE RIDGE OF GOTHAM'S TECTONIC PLATE. I'VE NARROWED THAT AREA DOWN TO A FEW POSSIBLE LOCATIONS...
BATMAN-- IS THERE SOMETHING WRONG?
YOU'RE PERCEPTIVE. I'M HAVING TROUBLE IGNORING THE FACT THAT YOU'RE DEFYING GRAVITY.
I HAVE TROUBLE IGNORING IT TOO, SOMETIMES. LET'S GO.

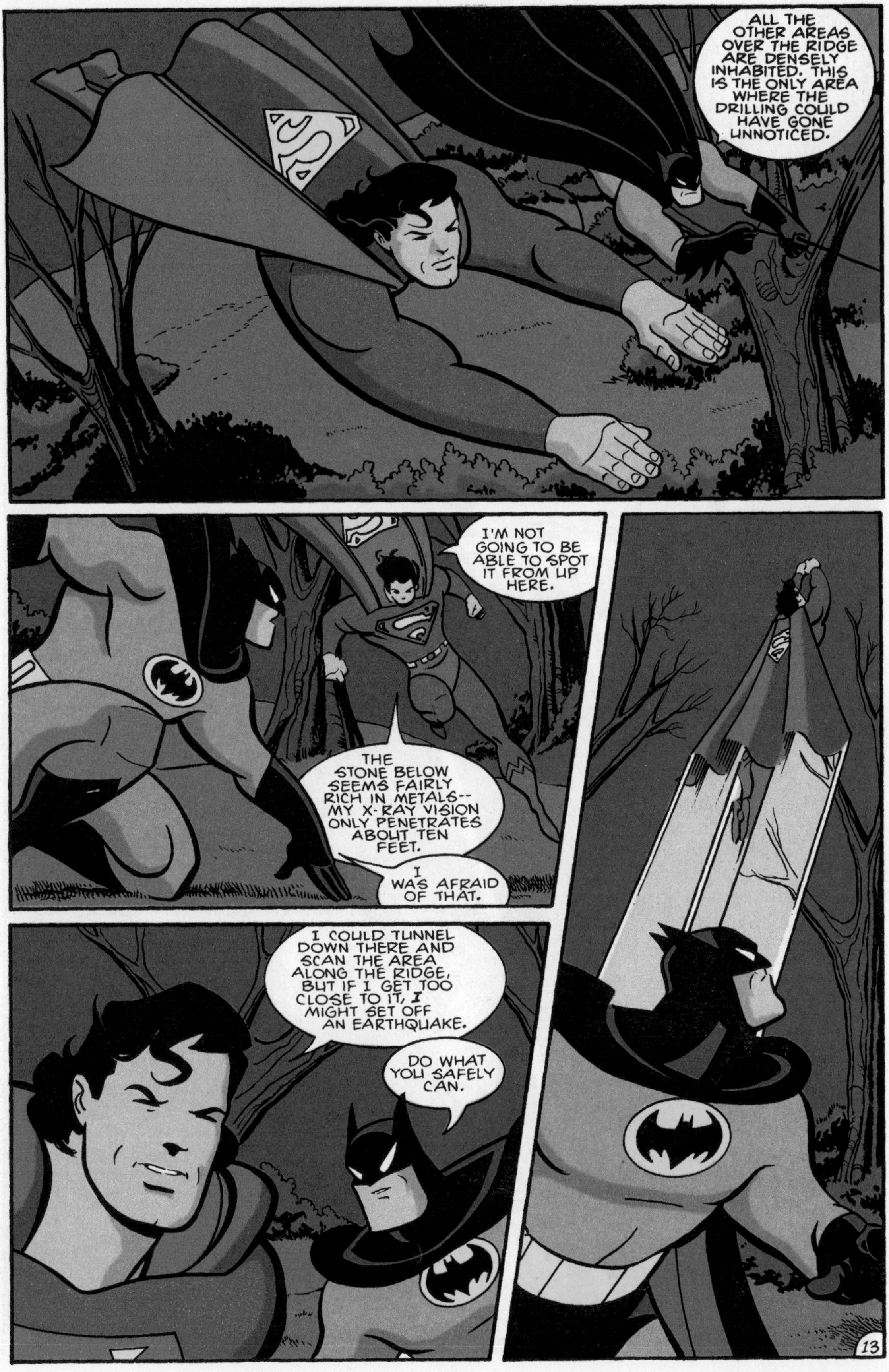
ALL THE OTHER AREAS OVER THE RIDGE ARE DENSELY INHABITED. THIS IS THE ONLY AREA WHERE THE DRILLING COULD HAVE GONE UNNOTICED.
I'M NOT GOING TO BE ABLE TO SPOT IT FROM UP HERE.
THE STONE BELOW SEEMS FAIRLY RICH IN METALS-- MY X-RAY VISION ONLY PENETRATES ABOUT TEN FEET.
I WAS AFRAID OF THAT.
I COULD TUNNEL DOWN THERE AND SCAN THE AREA ALONG THE RIDGE, BUT IF I GET TOO CLOSE TO IT, I MIGHT SET OFF AN EARTHQUAKE.
DO WHAT YOU SAFELY CAN.

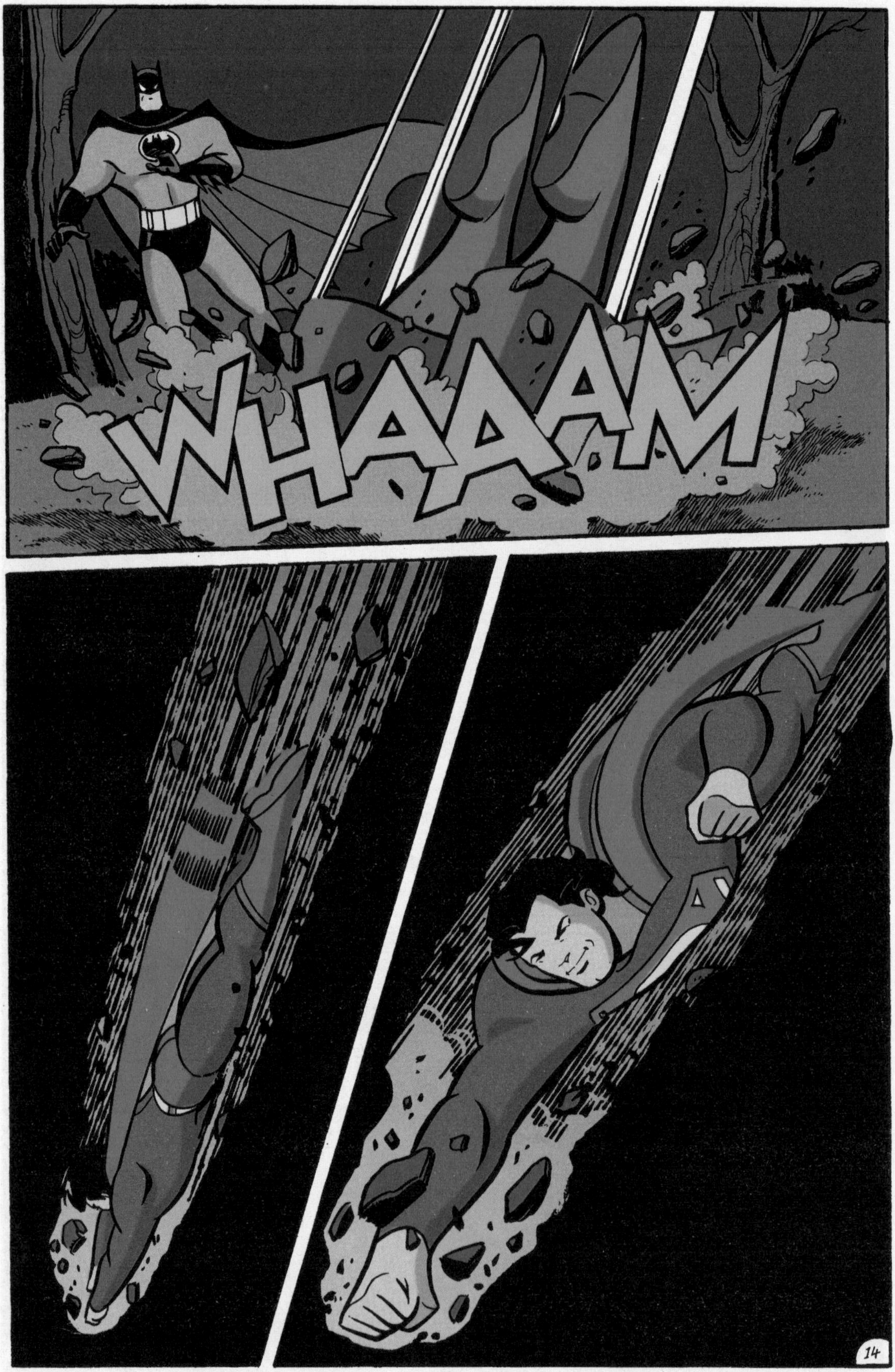
WHAAAM

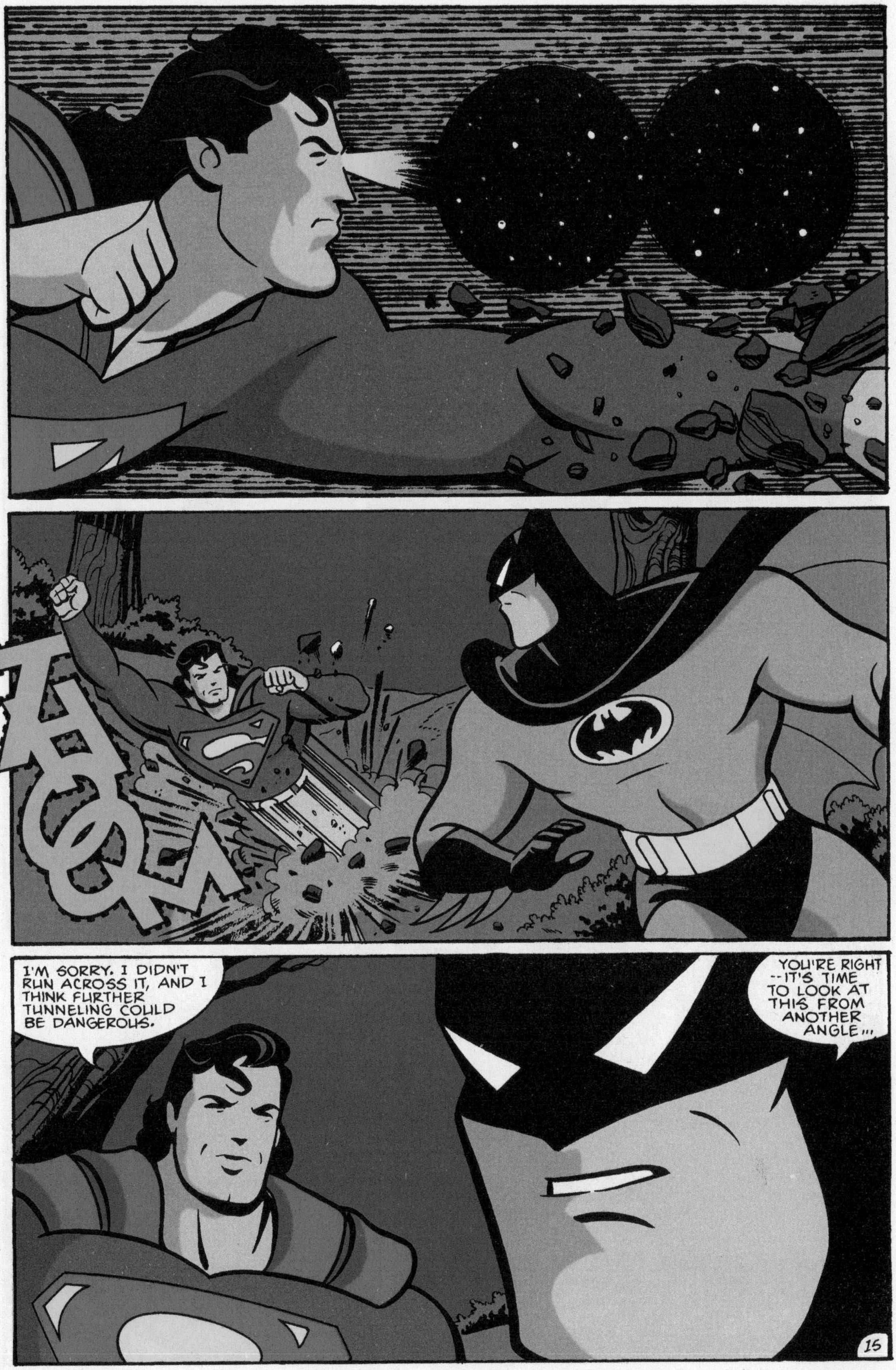
I'M SORRY. I DIDN'T RUN ACROSS IT, AND I THINK FURTHER TUNNELING COULD BE DANGEROUS.
YOU'RE RIGHT --IT'S TIME TO LOOK AT THIS FROM ANOTHER ANGLE...

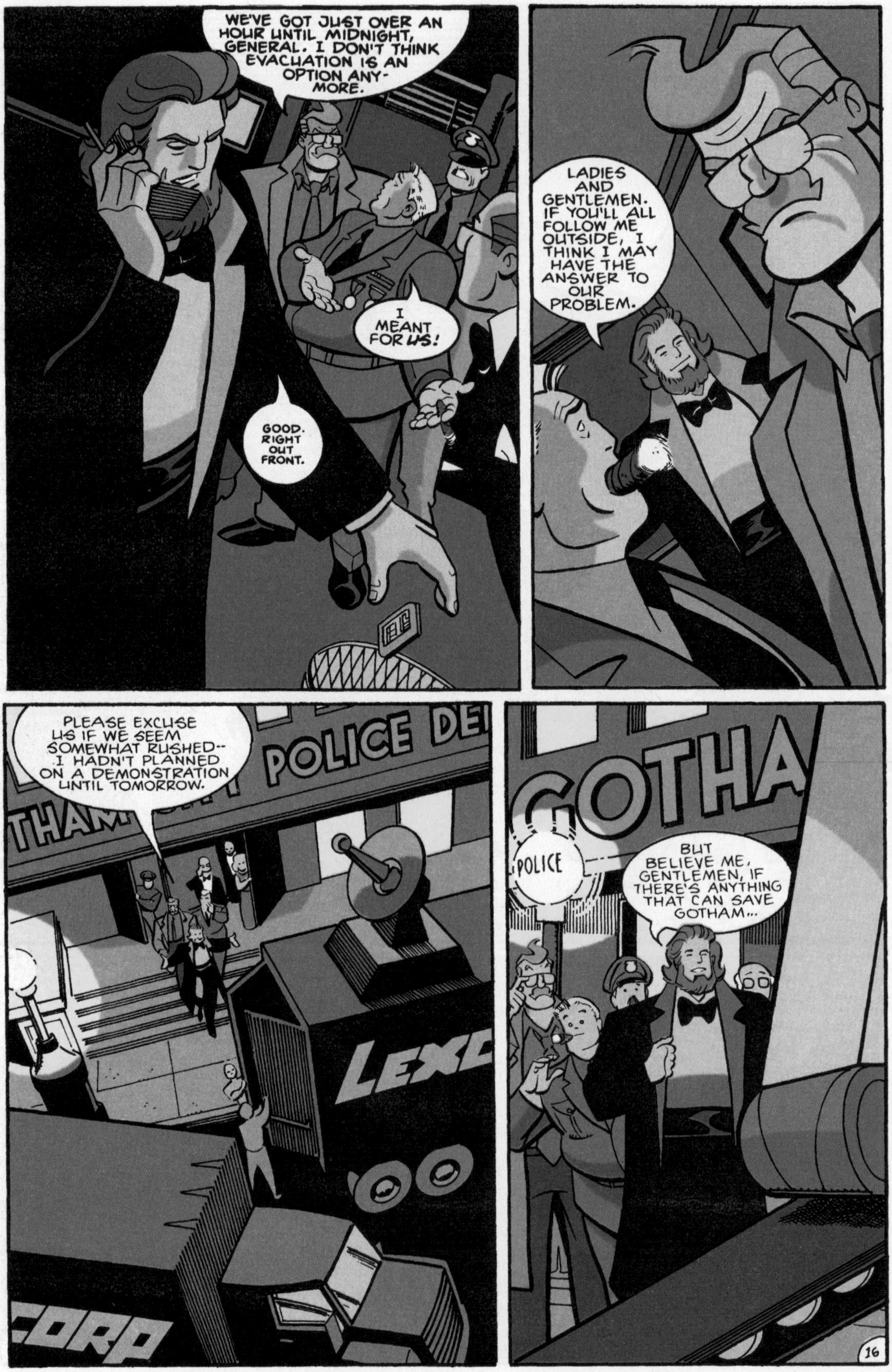
WE'VE GOT JUST OVER AN HOUR UNTIL MIDNIGHT, GENERAL. I DON'T THINK EVACUATION IS AN OPTION ANY-MORE.
I MEANT FOR US!
GOOD. RIGHT OUT FRONT.
LADIES AND GENTLEMEN. IF YOU'LL ALL FOLLOW ME OUTSIDE, I THINK I MAY HAVE THE ANSWER TO OUR PROBLEM.
PLEASE EXCUSE US IF WE SEEM SOMEWHAT RUSHED-- I HADN'T PLANNED ON A DEMONSTRATION UNTIL TOMORROW.
POLICE DE
THAM
LEXC
CORP
GOTHA
POLICE
BUT BELIEVE ME, GENTLEMEN, IF THERE'S ANYTHING THAT CAN SAVE GOTHAM...
16

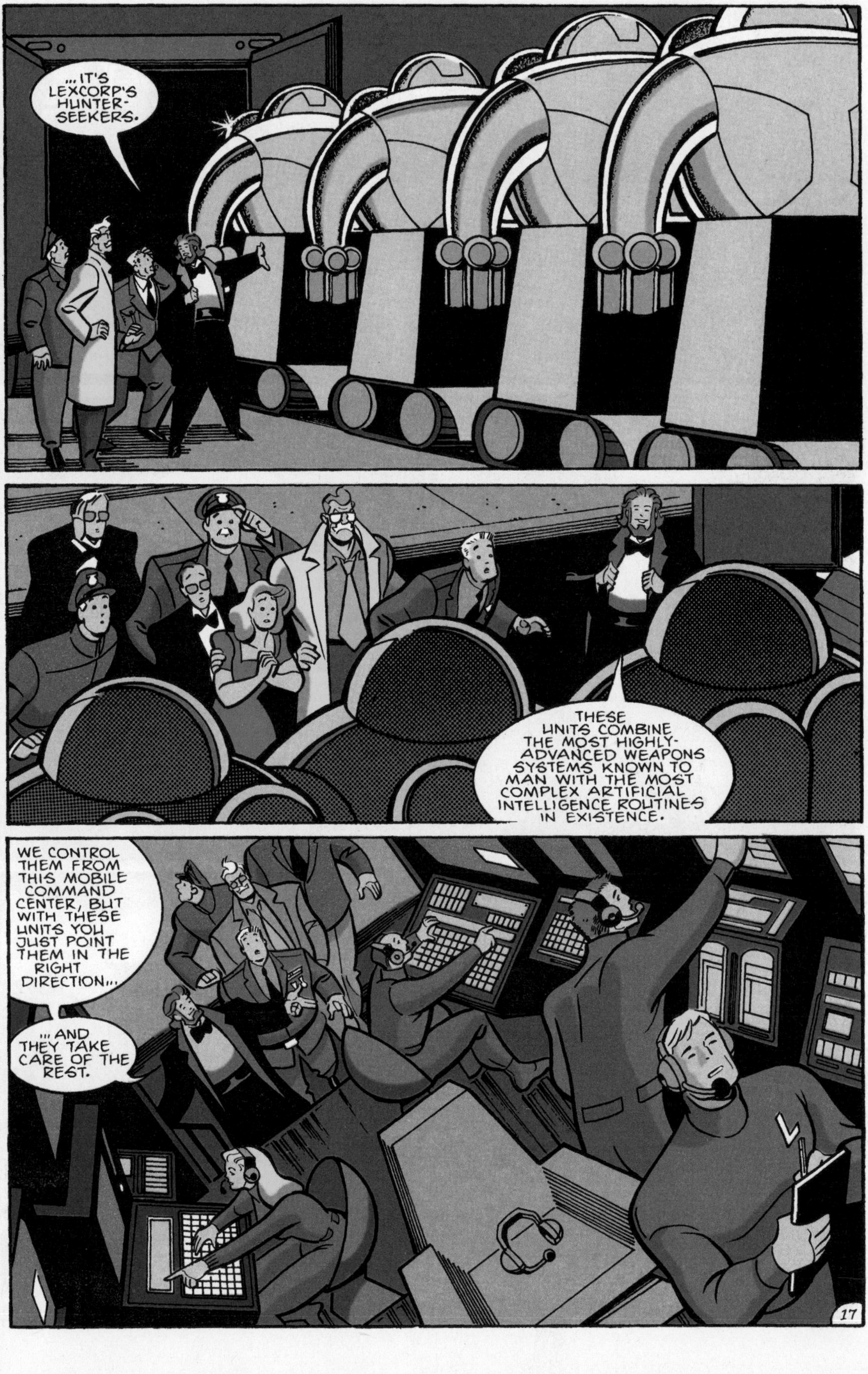
...IT'S LEXCORP'S HUNTER-SEEKERS.
THESE UNITS COMBINE THE MOST HIGHLY-ADVANCED WEAPONS SYSTEMS KNOWN TO MAN WITH THE MOST COMPLEX ARTIFICIAL INTELLIGENCE ROUTINES IN EXISTENCE.
WE CONTROL THEM FROM THIS MOBILE COMMAND CENTER, BUT WITH THESE UNITS YOU JUST POINT THEM IN THE RIGHT DIRECTION...
...AND THEY TAKE CARE OF THE REST.

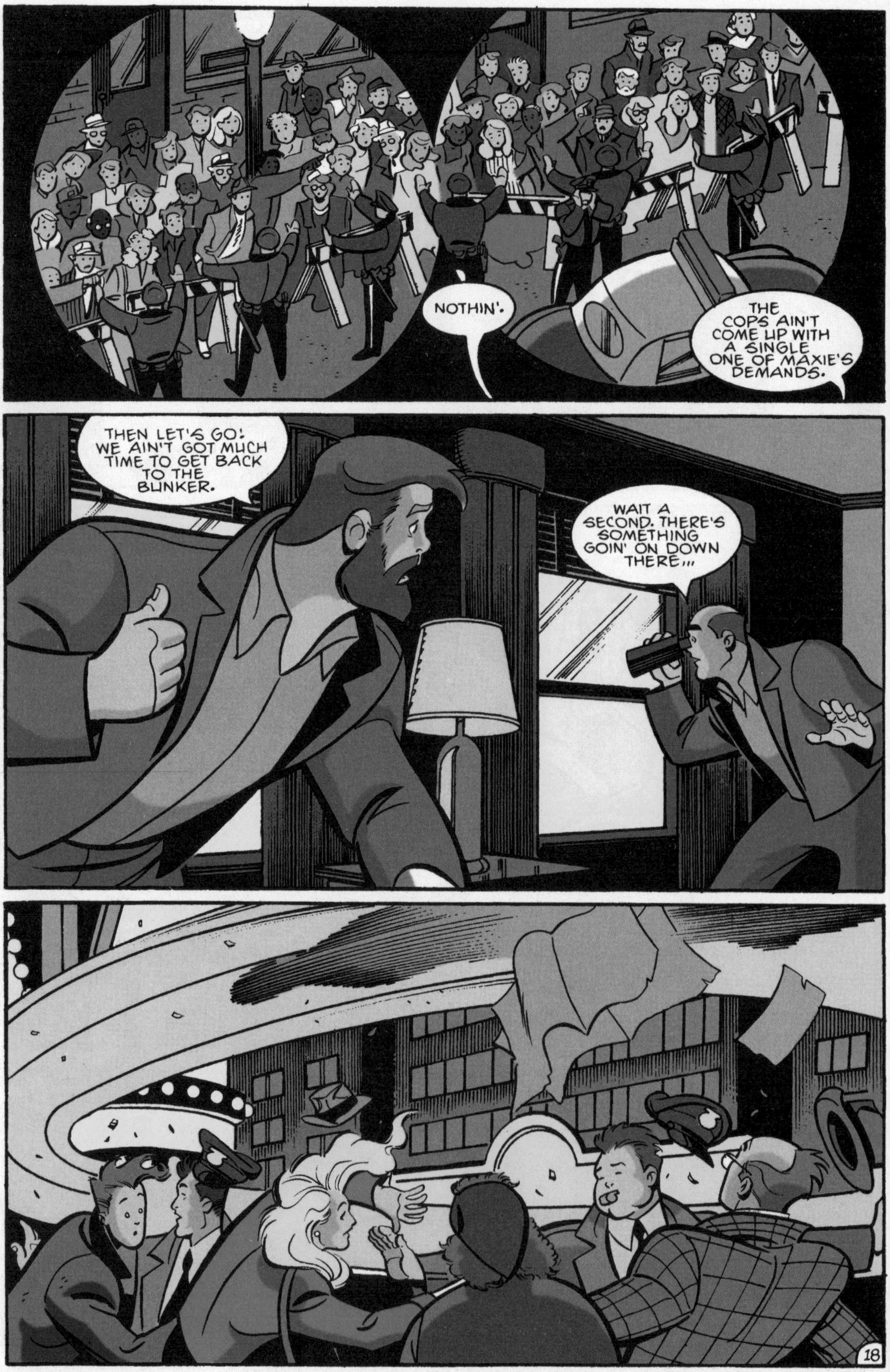
NOTHIN'.
THE COPS AIN'T COME UP WITH A SINGLE ONE OF MAXIE'S DEMANDS.
THEN LET'S GO! WE AIN'T GOT MUCH TIME TO GET BACK TO THE BUNKER.
WAIT A SECOND. THERE'S SOMETHING GOIN' ON DOWN THERE...

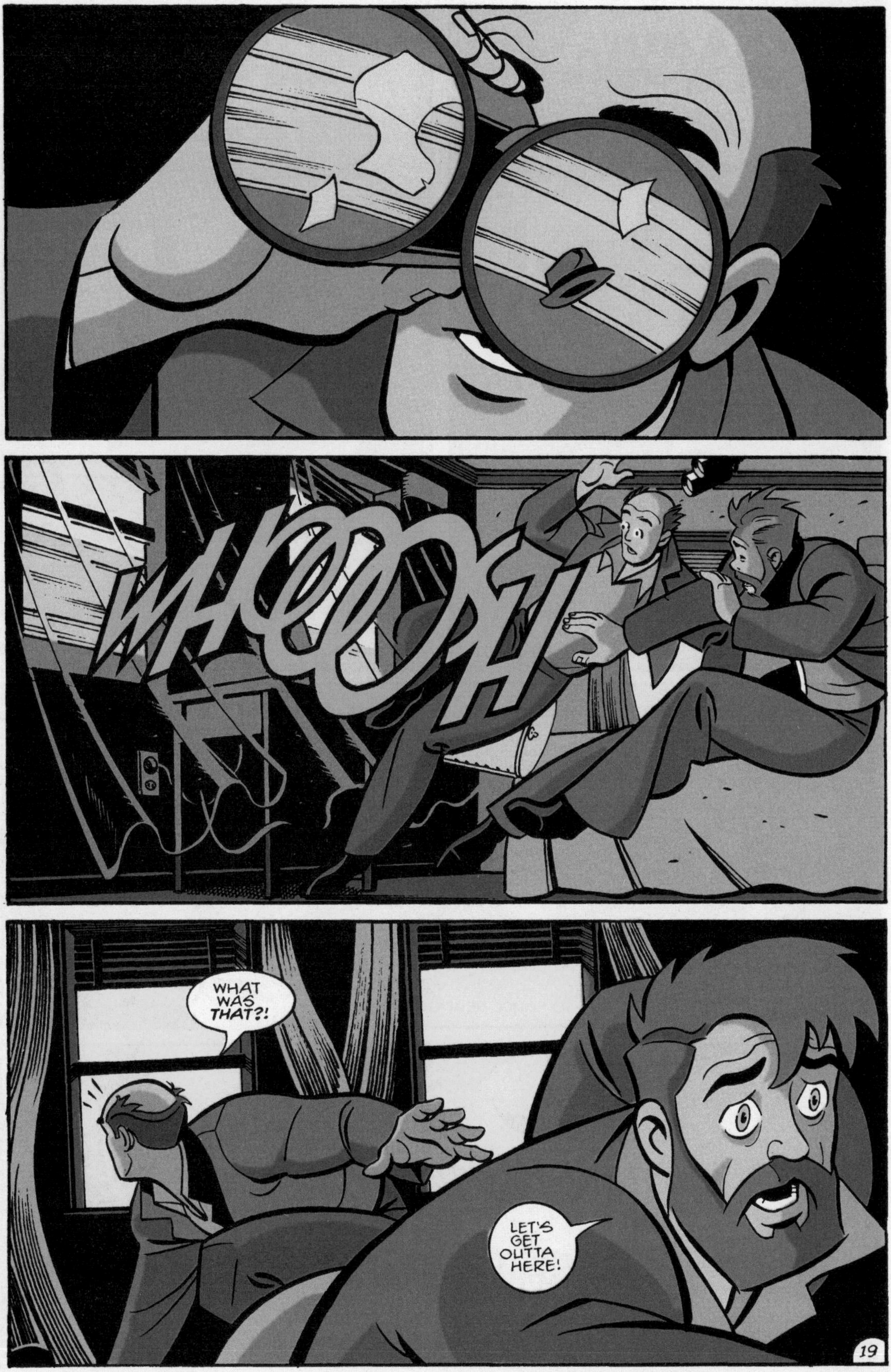
WHOOOSH
WHAT WAS THAT?!
LET'S GET OUTTA HERE!

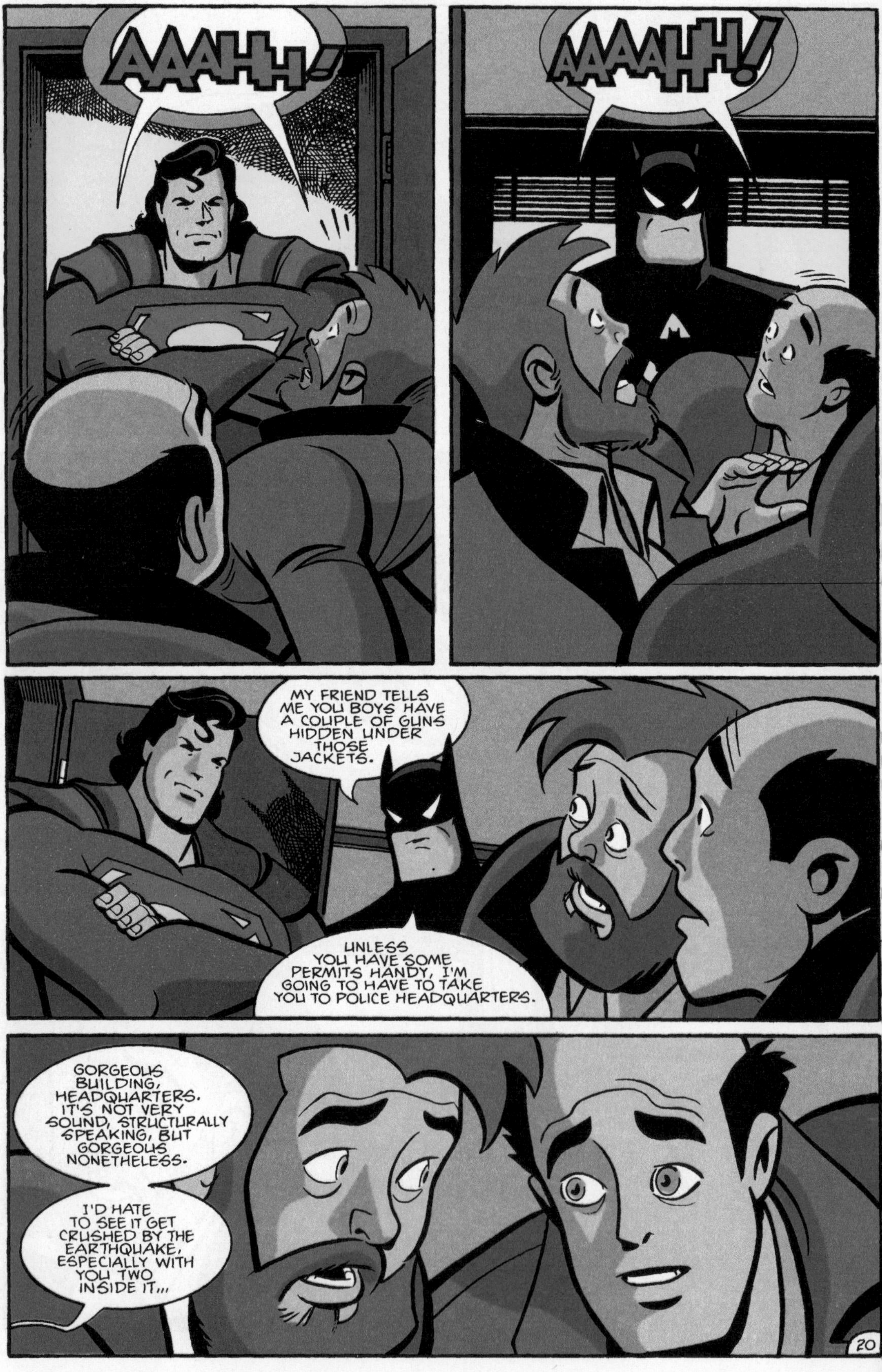
AAAHH!
AAAAHH!
MY FRIEND TELLS ME YOU BOYS HAVE A COUPLE OF GUNS HIDDEN UNDER THOSE JACKETS.
UNLESS YOU HAVE SOME PERMITS HANDY, I'M GOING TO HAVE TO TAKE YOU TO POLICE HEADQUARTERS.
GORGEOUS BUILDING, HEADQUARTERS. IT'S NOT VERY SOUND, STRUCTURALLY SPEAKING, BUT GORGEOUS NONETHELESS.
I'D HATE TO SEE IT GET CRUSHED BY THE EARTHQUAKE, ESPECIALLY WITH YOU TWO INSIDE IT...
20

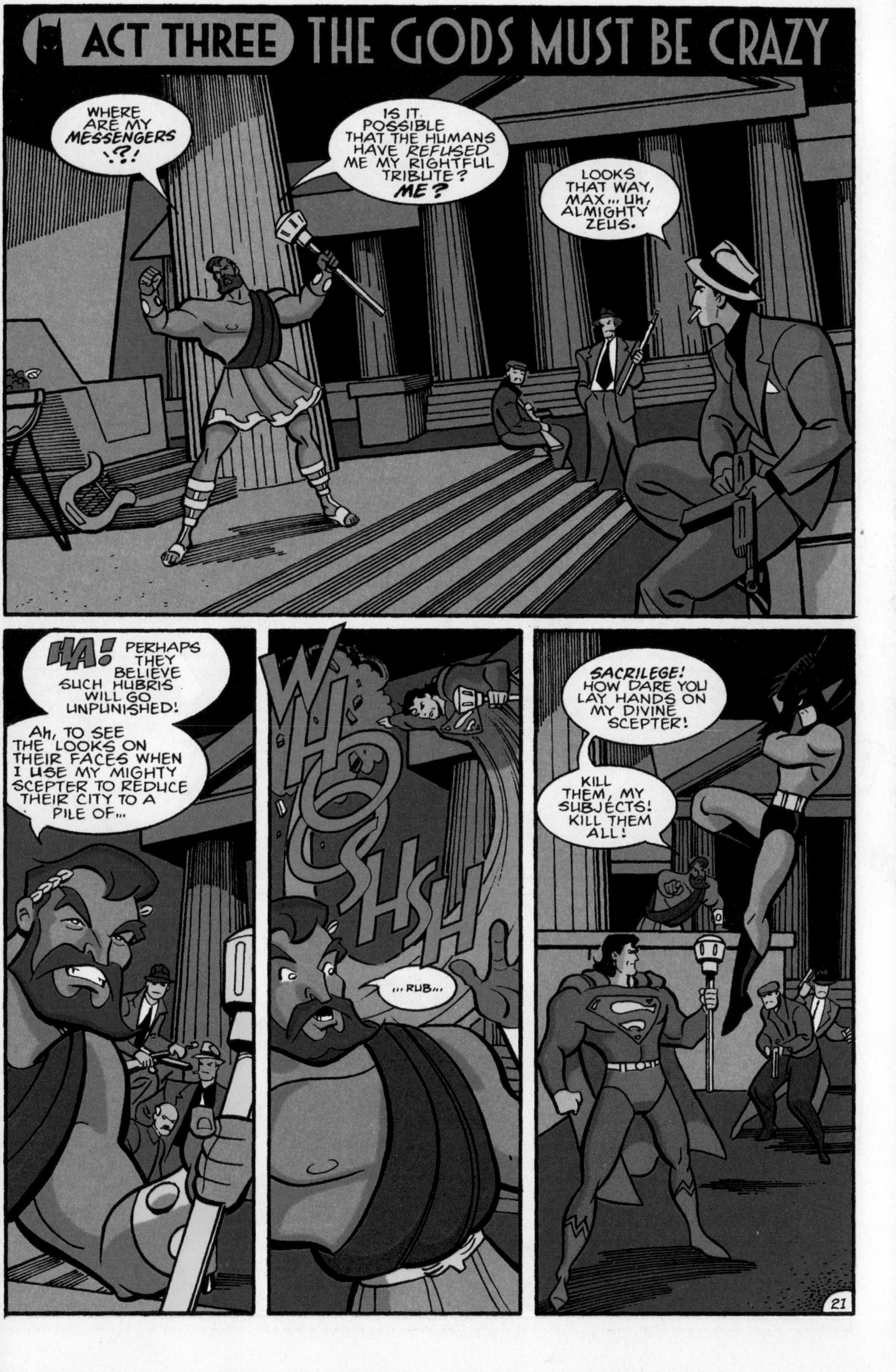

ACT THREE THE GODS MUST BE CRAZY
WHERE ARE MY MESSENGERS !?!
IS IT POSSIBLE THAT THE HUMANS HAVE REFUSED ME MY RIGHTFUL TRIBUTE? ME?
LOOKS THAT WAY, MAX... UH, ALMIGHTY ZEUS.
HA! PERHAPS THEY BELIEVE SUCH HUBRIS WILL GO UNPUNISHED!
AH, TO SEE THE LOOKS ON THEIR FACES WHEN I USE MY MIGHTY SCEPTER TO REDUCE THEIR CITY TO A PILE OF...
WHOOSHSH
...RUB...
SACRILEGE! HOW DARE YOU LAY HANDS ON MY DIVINE SCEPTER!
KILL THEM, MY SUBJECTS! KILL THEM ALL!

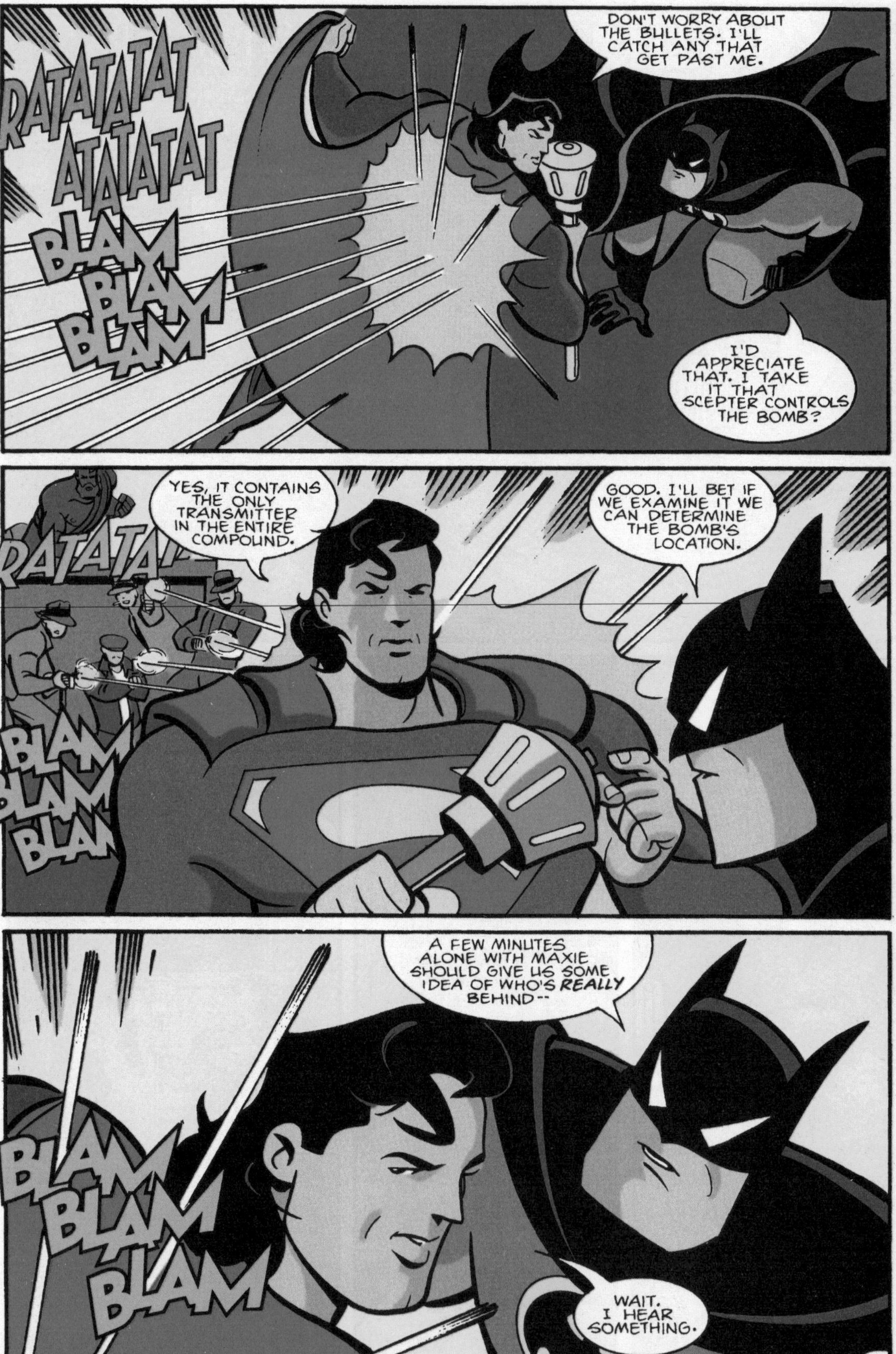
RATATATAT ATATATAT
BLAM BLAM BLAM
DON'T WORRY ABOUT THE BULLETS. I'LL CATCH ANY THAT GET PAST ME.
I'D APPRECIATE THAT. I TAKE IT THAT SCEPTER CONTROLS THE BOMB?
RATATAT
YES, IT CONTAINS THE ONLY TRANSMITTER IN THE ENTIRE COMPOUND.
GOOD. I'LL BET IF WE EXAMINE IT WE CAN DETERMINE THE BOMB'S LOCATION.
BLAM BLAM BLAM
A FEW MINUTES ALONE WITH MAXIE SHOULD GIVE US SOME IDEA OF WHO'S *REALLY* BEHIND--
BLAM BLAM BLAM
WAIT. I HEAR SOMETHING.

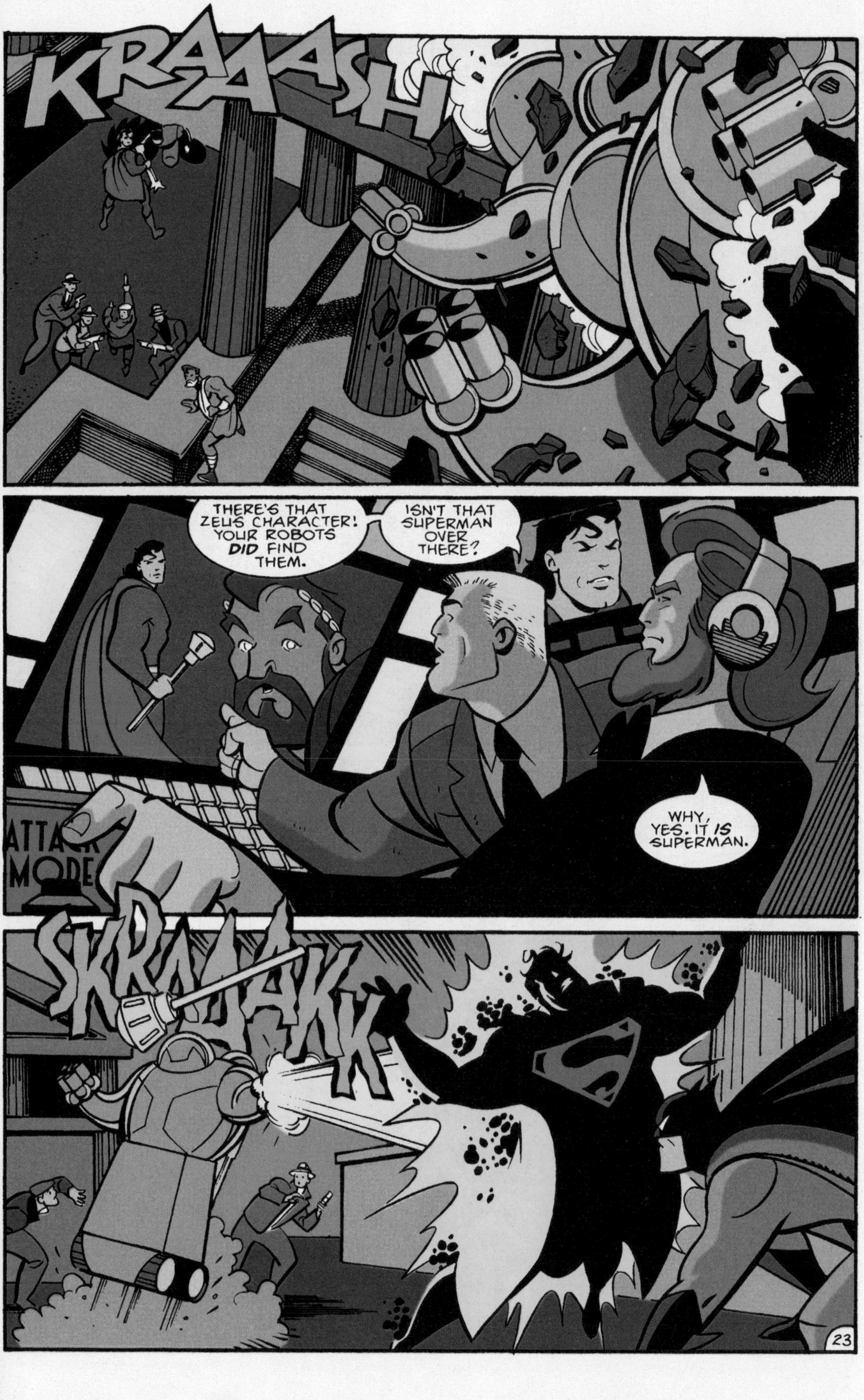
KRAAASH
THERE'S THAT ZEUS CHARACTER! YOUR ROBOTS DID FIND THEM.
ISN'T THAT SUPERMAN OVER THERE?
WHY, YES. IT IS SUPERMAN.
ATTACK MODE
SKRAAKK

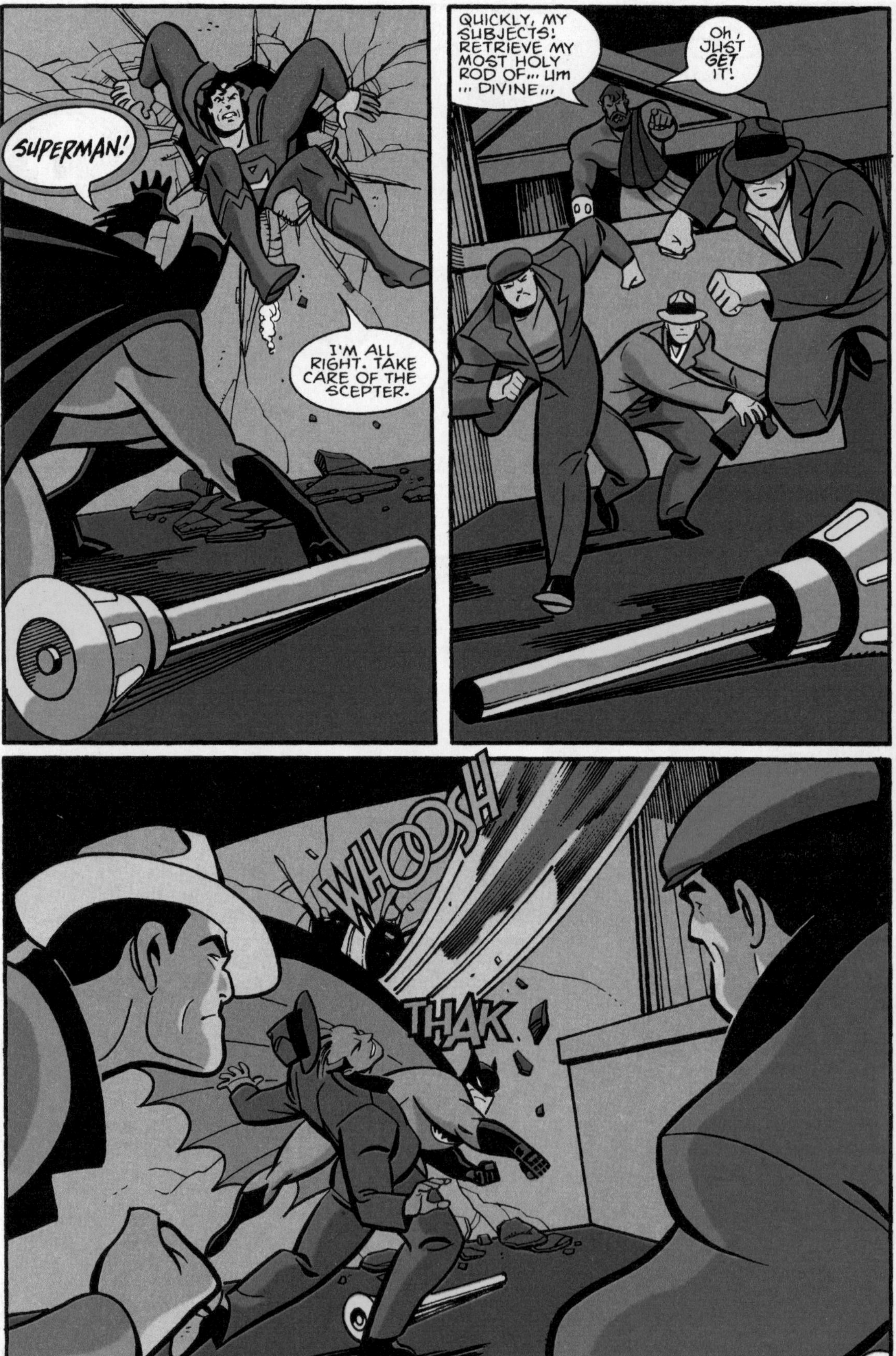
SUPERMAN!
I'M ALL RIGHT. TAKE CARE OF THE SCEPTER.
QUICKLY, MY SUBJECTS! RETRIEVE MY MOST HOLY ROD OF... UM ... DIVINE...
Oh, JUST GET IT!
WHOOSH
THAK
24

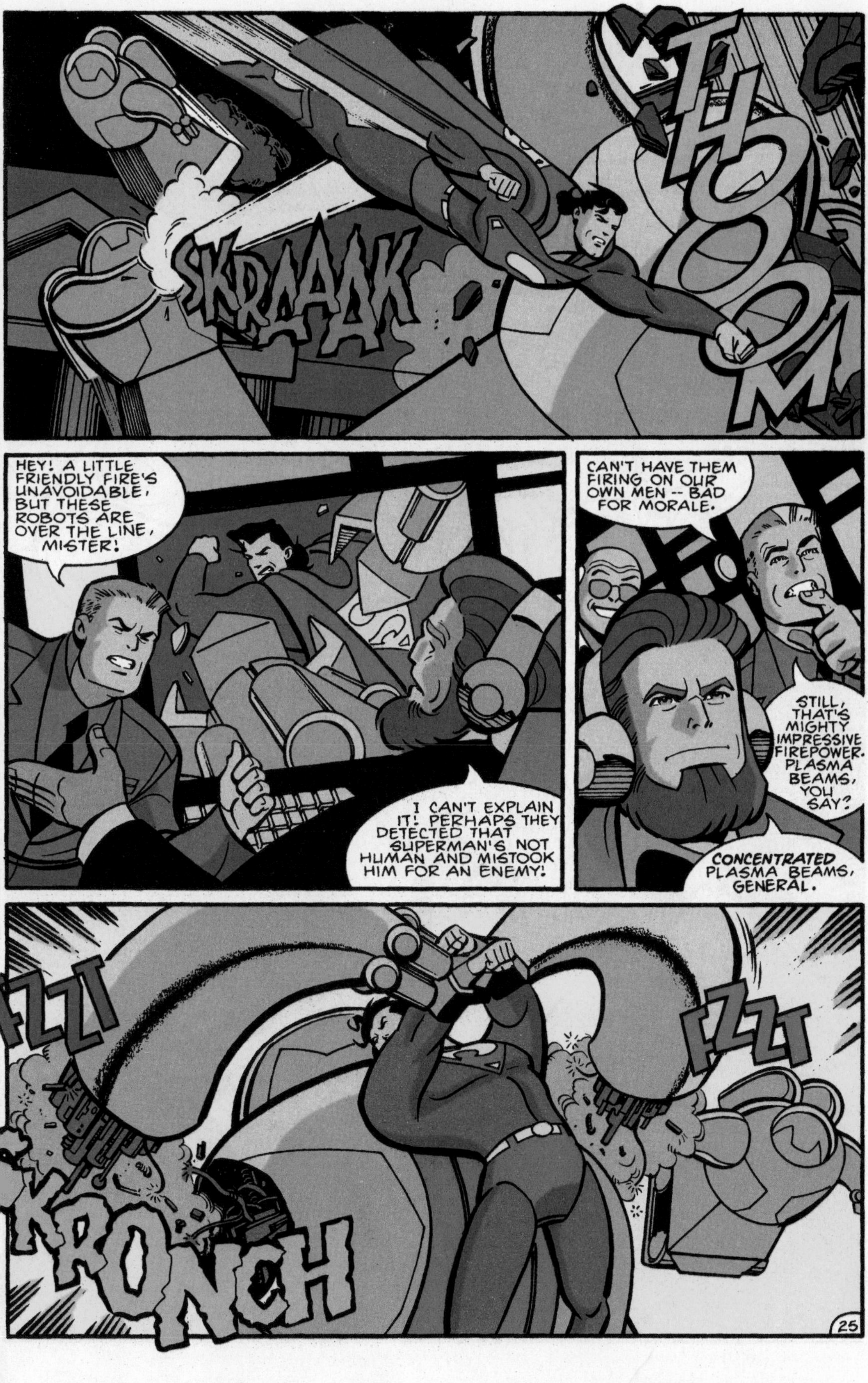
SKRAAAK
THOOOOM
HEY! A LITTLE FRIENDLY FIRE'S UNAVOIDABLE, BUT THESE ROBOTS ARE OVER THE LINE, MISTER!
I CAN'T EXPLAIN IT! PERHAPS THEY DETECTED THAT SUPERMAN'S NOT HUMAN AND MISTOOK HIM FOR AN ENEMY!
CAN'T HAVE THEM FIRING ON OUR OWN MEN -- BAD FOR MORALE.
STILL, THAT'S MIGHTY IMPRESSIVE FIREPOWER. PLASMA BEAMS, YOU SAY?
CONCENTRATED PLASMA BEAMS, GENERAL.
FZZT
FZZT
KRONCH

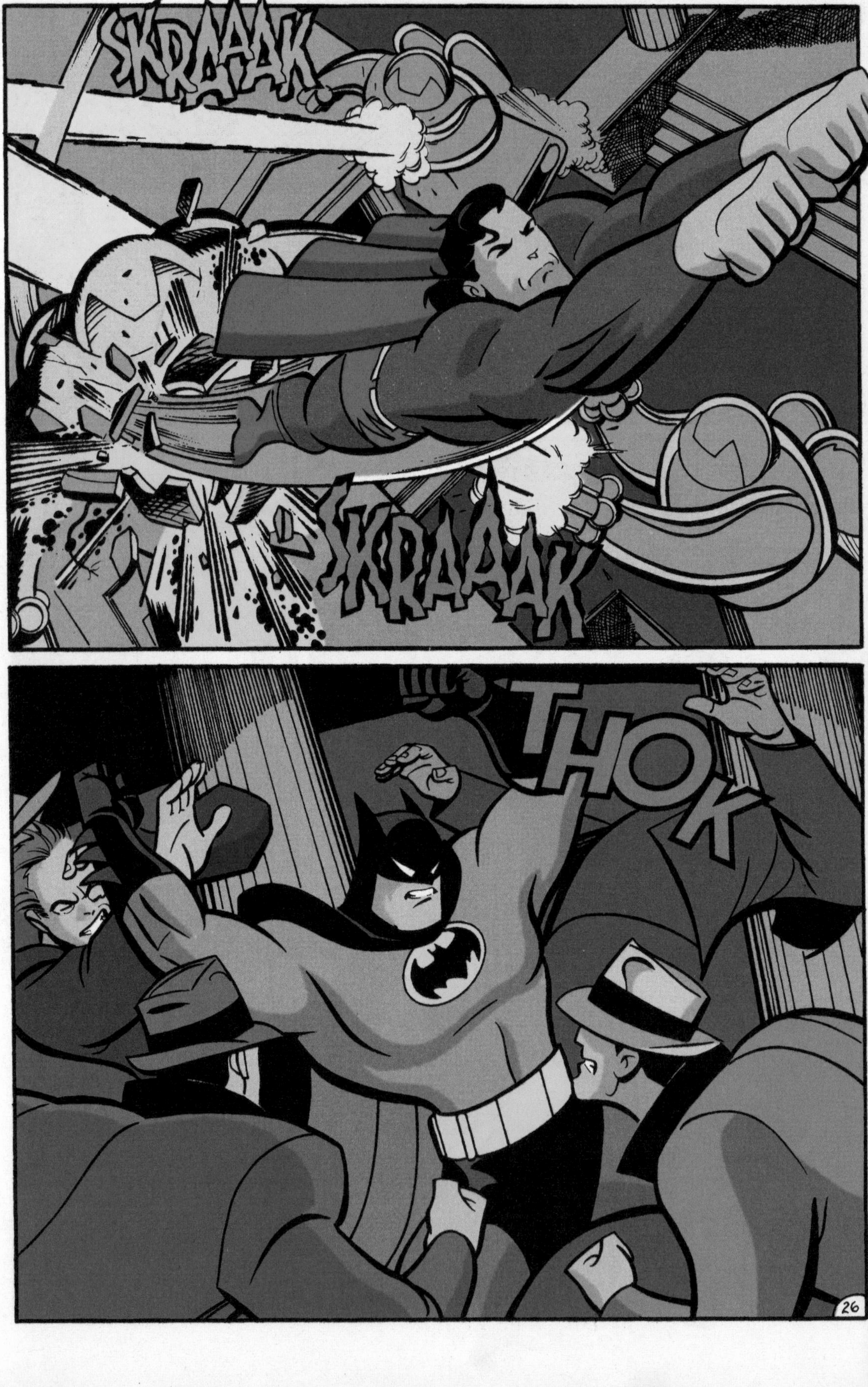
SKRAAAK
SKRAAAK
THOK

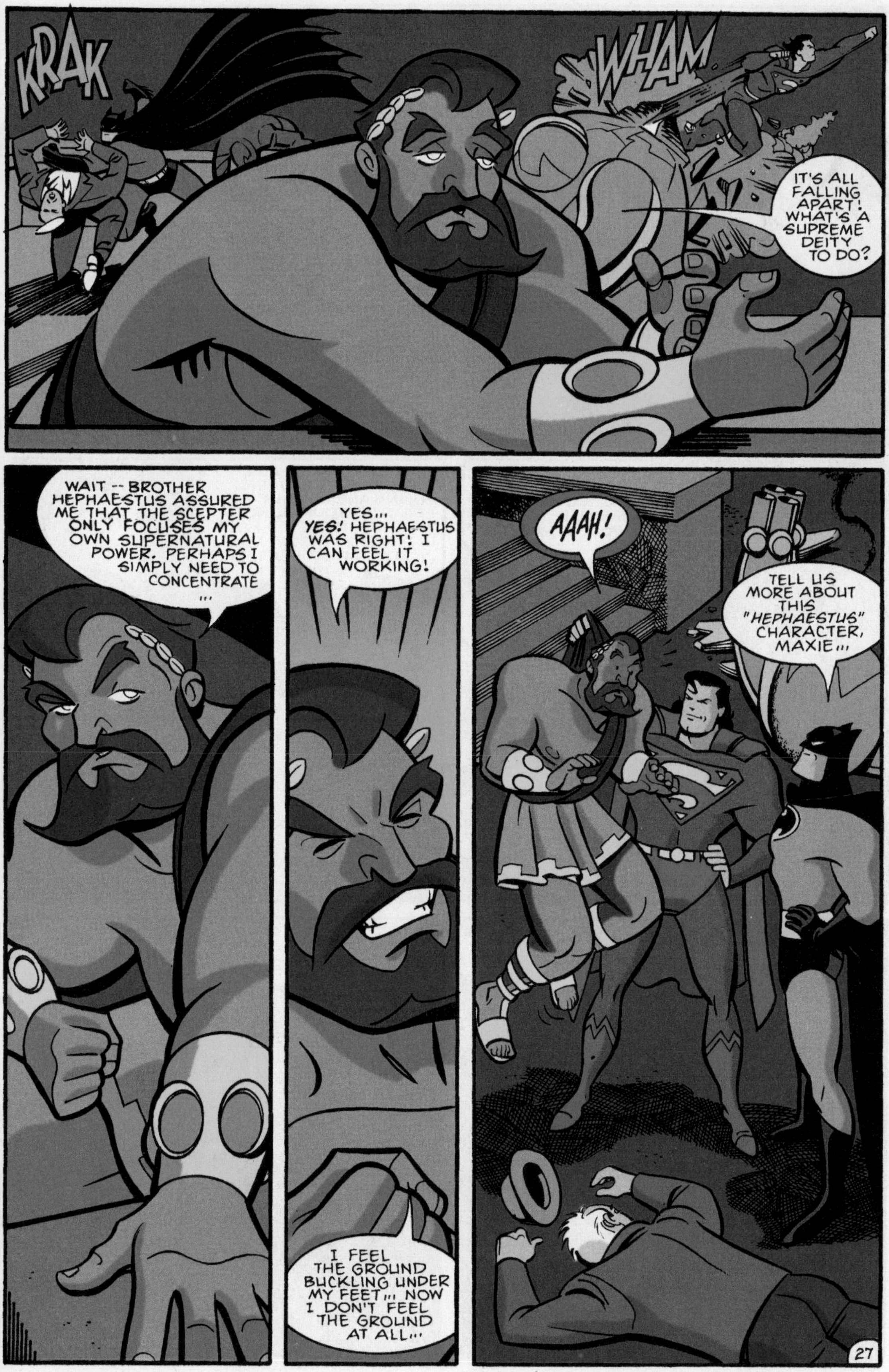
KRAK
WHAM
IT'S ALL FALLING APART! WHAT'S A SUPREME DEITY TO DO?
WAIT -- BROTHER HEPHAESTUS ASSURED ME THAT THE SCEPTER ONLY FOCUSES MY OWN SUPERNATURAL POWER. PERHAPS I SIMPLY NEED TO CONCENTRATE ...
YES... YES! HEPHAESTUS WAS RIGHT! I CAN FEEL IT WORKING!
I FEEL THE GROUND BUCKLING UNDER MY FEET... NOW I DON'T FEEL THE GROUND AT ALL...
AAAH!
TELL US MORE ABOUT THIS "HEPHAESTUS" CHARACTER, MAXIE...

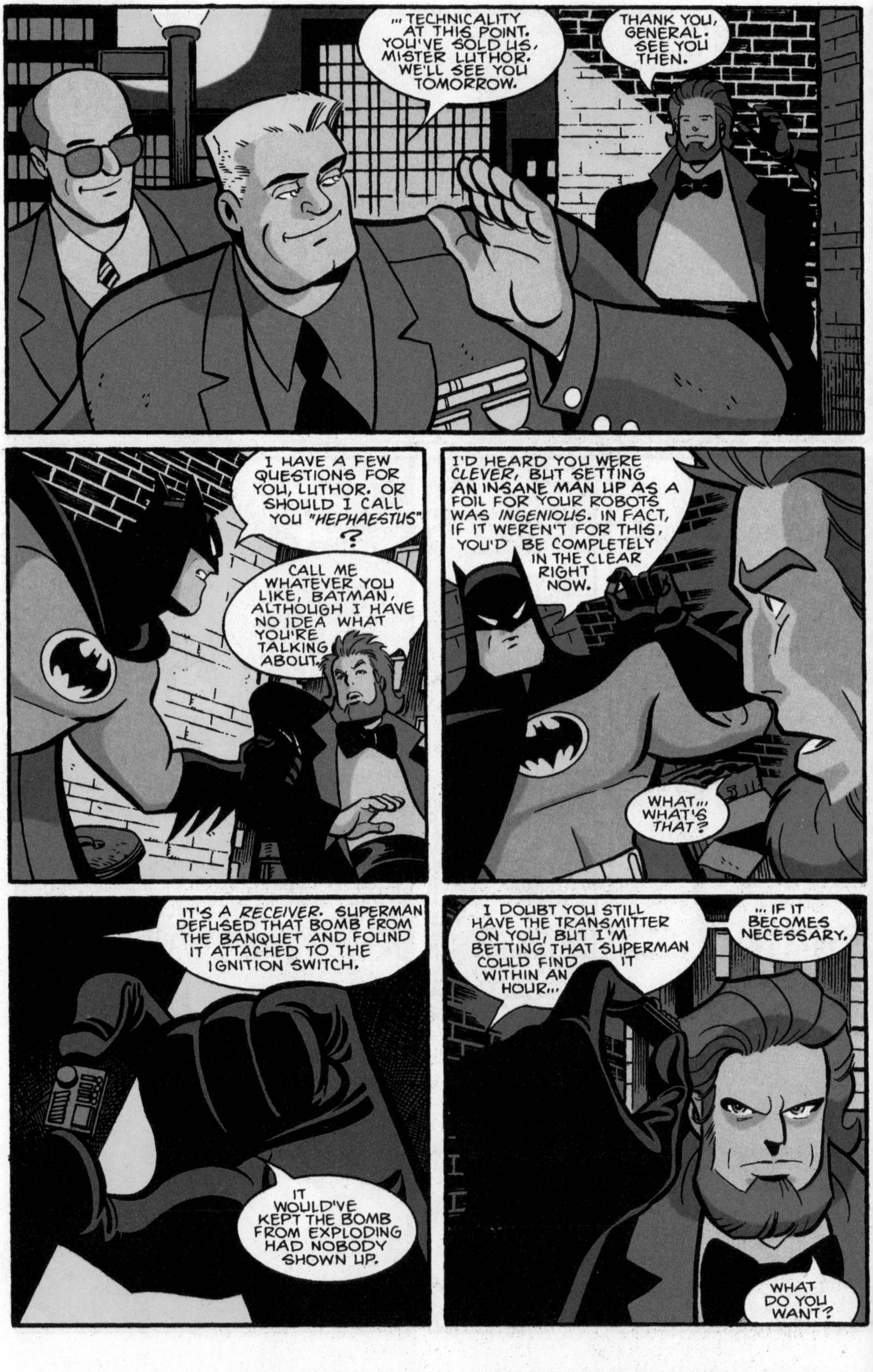
...TECHNICALITY AT THIS POINT. YOU'VE SOLD US, MISTER LUTHOR. WE'LL SEE YOU TOMORROW.
THANK YOU, GENERAL. SEE YOU THEN.
I HAVE A FEW QUESTIONS FOR YOU, LUTHOR. OR SHOULD I CALL YOU "HEPHAESTUS"?
CALL ME WHATEVER YOU LIKE, BATMAN, ALTHOUGH I HAVE NO IDEA WHAT YOU'RE TALKING ABOUT.
I'D HEARD YOU WERE CLEVER, BUT SETTING AN INSANE MAN UP AS A FOIL FOR YOUR ROBOTS WAS INGENIOUS. IN FACT, IF IT WEREN'T FOR THIS, YOU'D BE COMPLETELY IN THE CLEAR RIGHT NOW.
WHAT... WHAT'S THAT?
IT'S A RECEIVER. SUPERMAN DEFUSED THAT BOMB FROM THE BANQUET AND FOUND IT ATTACHED TO THE IGNITION SWITCH.
IT WOULD'VE KEPT THE BOMB FROM EXPLODING HAD NOBODY SHOWN UP.
I DOUBT YOU STILL HAVE THE TRANSMITTER ON YOU, BUT I'M BETTING THAT SUPERMAN COULD FIND IT WITHIN AN HOUR...
...IF IT BECOMES NECESSARY.
WHAT DO YOU WANT?

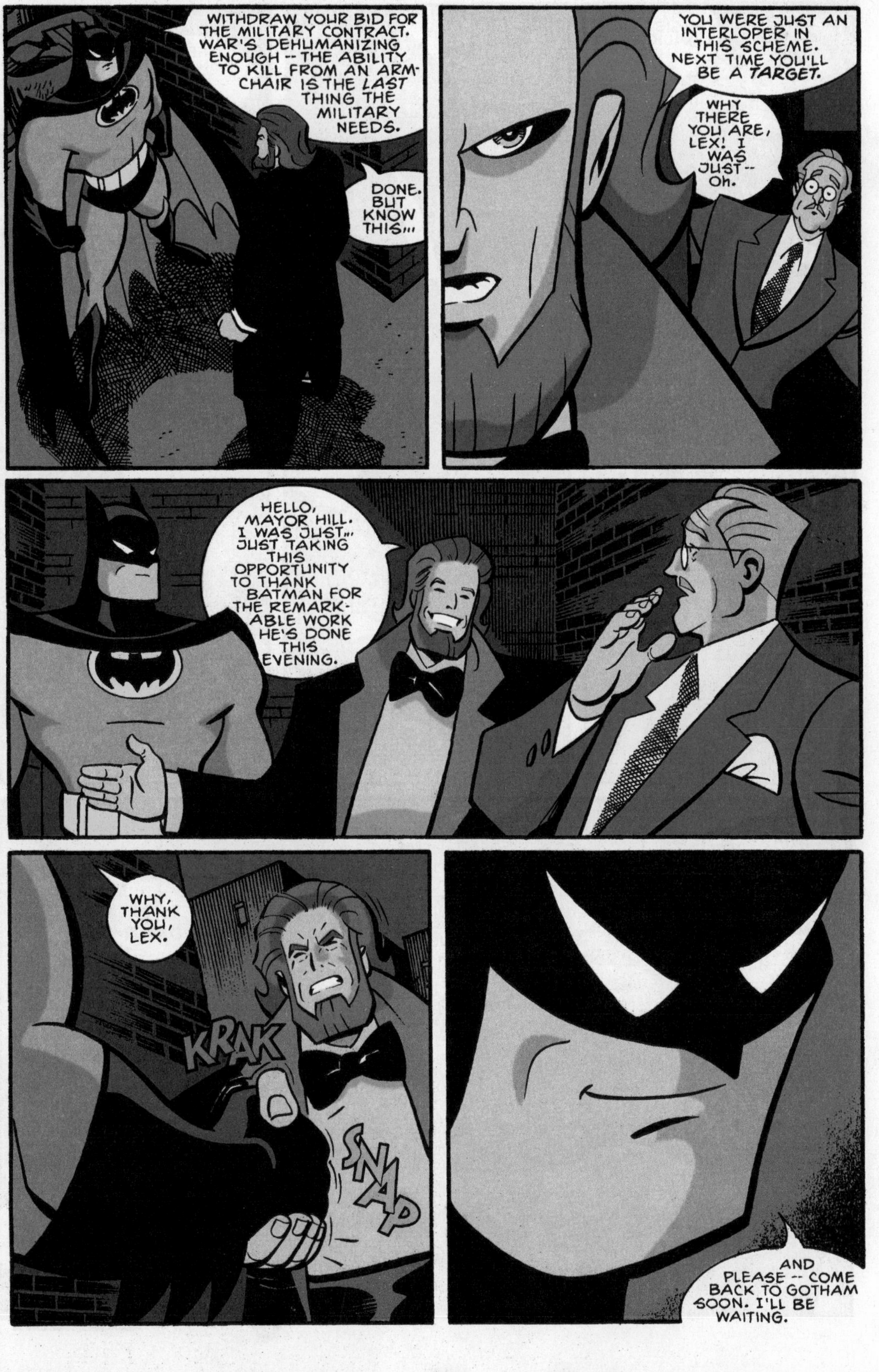
WITHDRAW YOUR BID FOR THE MILITARY CONTRACT. WAR'S DEHUMANIZING ENOUGH -- THE ABILITY TO KILL FROM AN ARM-CHAIR IS THE *LAST* THING THE MILITARY NEEDS.
DONE. BUT KNOW THIS...
YOU WERE JUST AN INTERLOPER IN THIS SCHEME. NEXT TIME YOU'LL BE A *TARGET.*
WHY THERE YOU ARE, LEX! I WAS JUST-- OH.
HELLO, MAYOR HILL. I WAS JUST... JUST TAKING THIS OPPORTUNITY TO THANK BATMAN FOR THE REMARKABLE WORK HE'S DONE THIS EVENING.
WHY, THANK YOU, LEX.
KRAK
SNAP
AND PLEASE -- COME BACK TO GOTHAM SOON. I'LL BE WAITING.

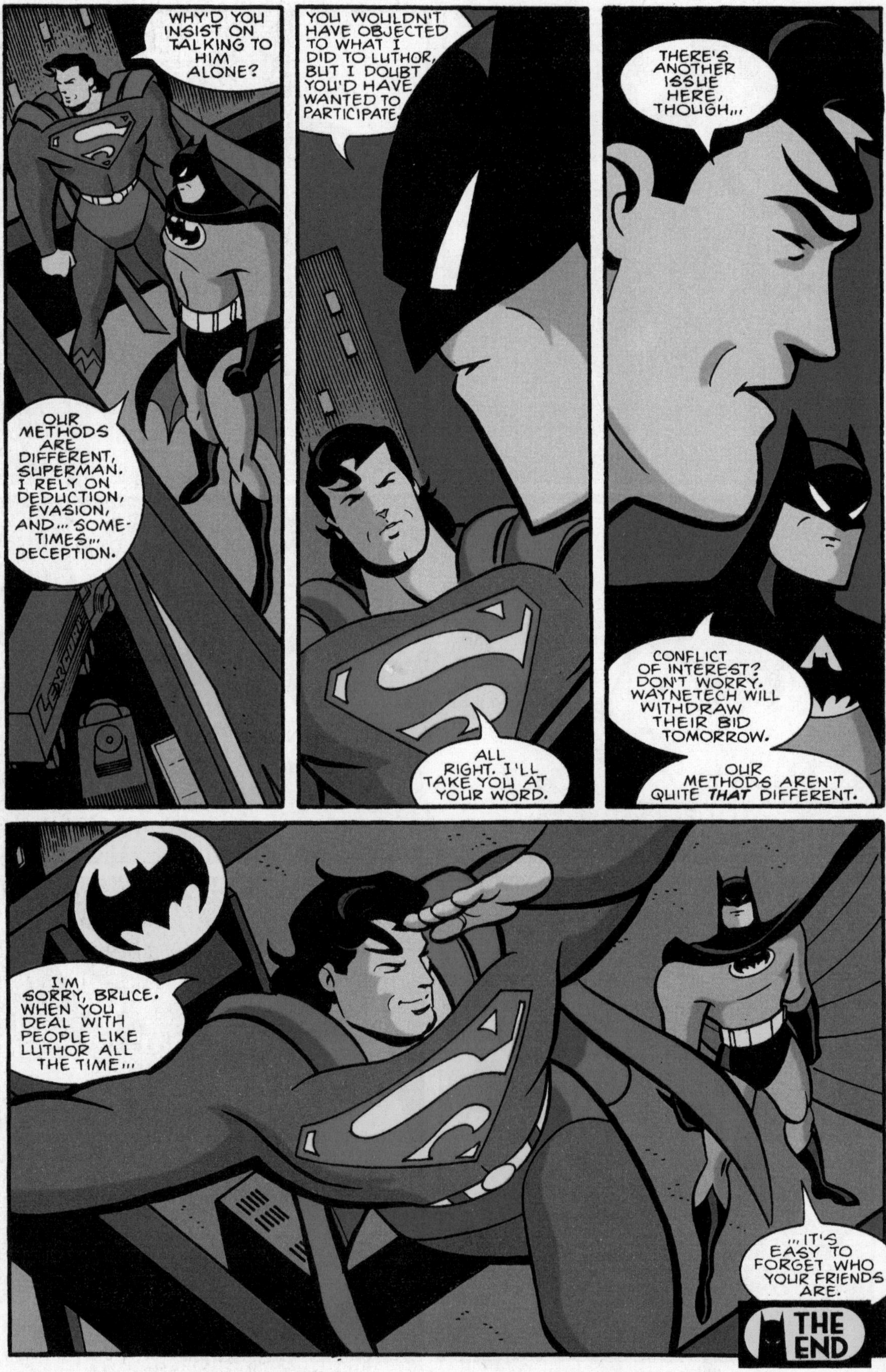
WHY'D YOU INSIST ON TALKING TO HIM ALONE?
OUR METHODS ARE DIFFERENT, SUPERMAN. I RELY ON DEDUCTION, EVASION, AND... SOMETIMES... DECEPTION.
LEXCORP
YOU WOULDN'T HAVE OBJECTED TO WHAT I DID TO LUTHOR, BUT I DOUBT YOU'D HAVE WANTED TO PARTICIPATE.
ALL RIGHT. I'LL TAKE YOU AT YOUR WORD.
THERE'S ANOTHER ISSUE HERE, THOUGH...
CONFLICT OF INTEREST? DON'T WORRY. WAYNETECH WILL WITHDRAW THEIR BID TOMORROW.
OUR METHODS AREN'T QUITE THAT DIFFERENT.
I'M SORRY, BRUCE. WHEN YOU DEAL WITH PEOPLE LIKE LUTHOR ALL THE TIME...
...IT'S EASY TO FORGET WHO YOUR FRIENDS ARE.
THE END

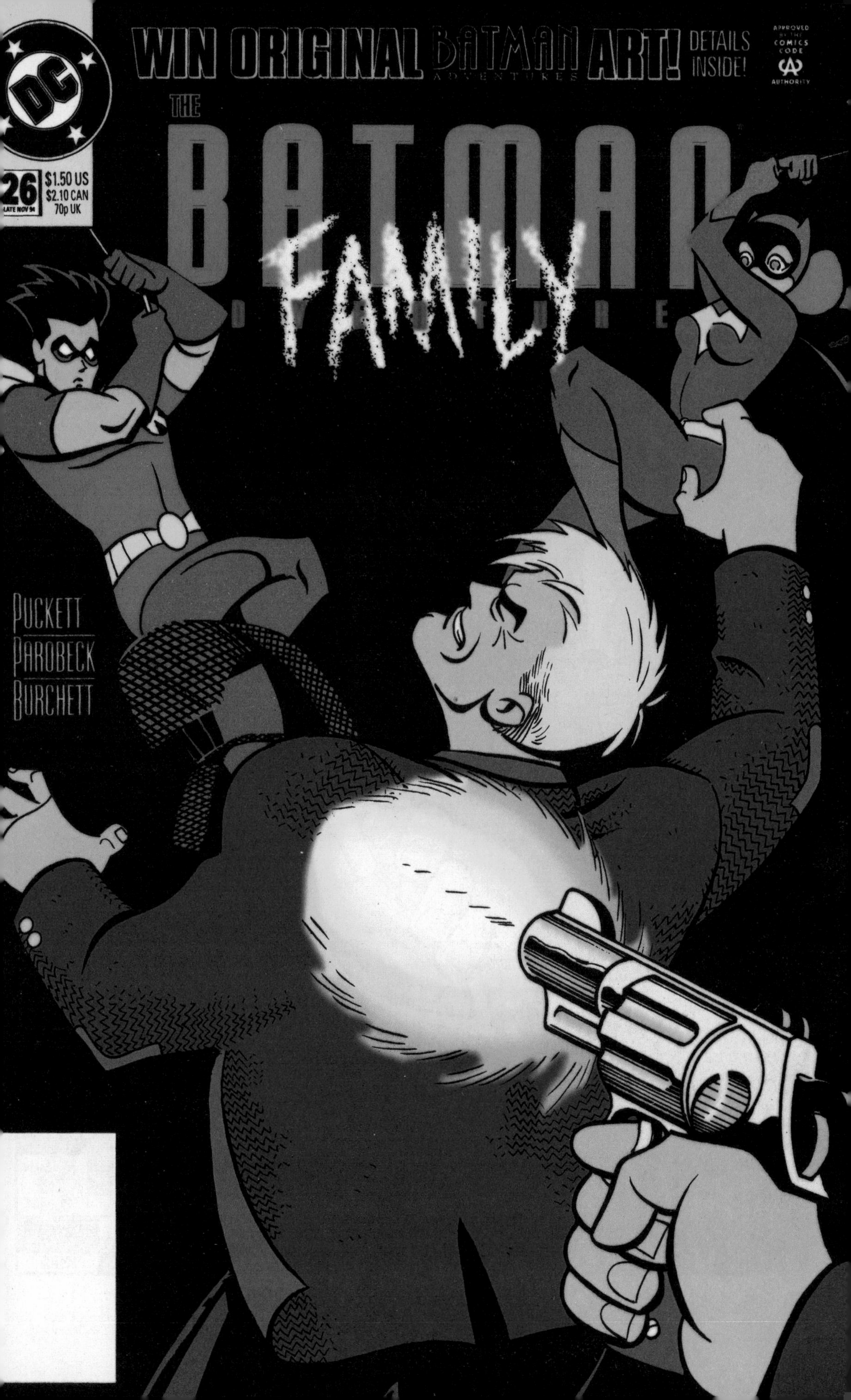
DC
WIN ORIGINAL BATMAN ADVENTURES ART! DETAILS INSIDE!
APPROVED BY THE COMICS CODE AUTHORITY
THE BATMAN ADVENTURES
FAMILY
26 LATE NOV 94
$1.50 US
$2.10 CAN
70p UK
PUCKETT
PAROBECK
BURCHETT

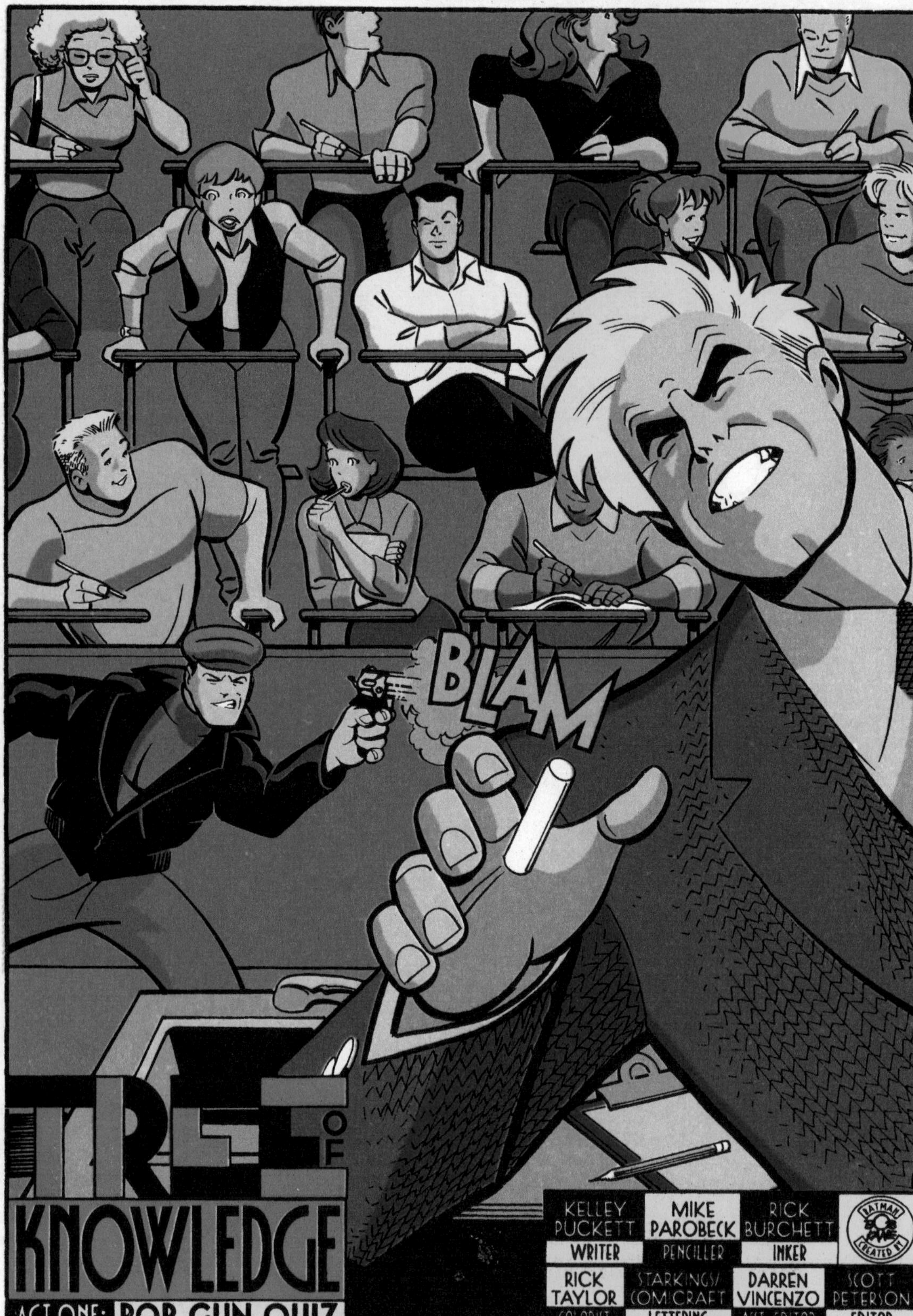
BLAM
TREE OF KNOWLEDGE
ACT ONE: POP GUN QUIZ
KELLEY PUCKETT WRITER
MIKE PAROBECK PENCILLER
RICK BURCHETT INKER
RICK TAYLOR COLORIST
STARKINGS/ COMICRAFT LETTERING
DARREN VINCENZO ASST. EDITOR
SCOTT PETERSON EDITOR
BATMAN CREATED BY BOB KANE

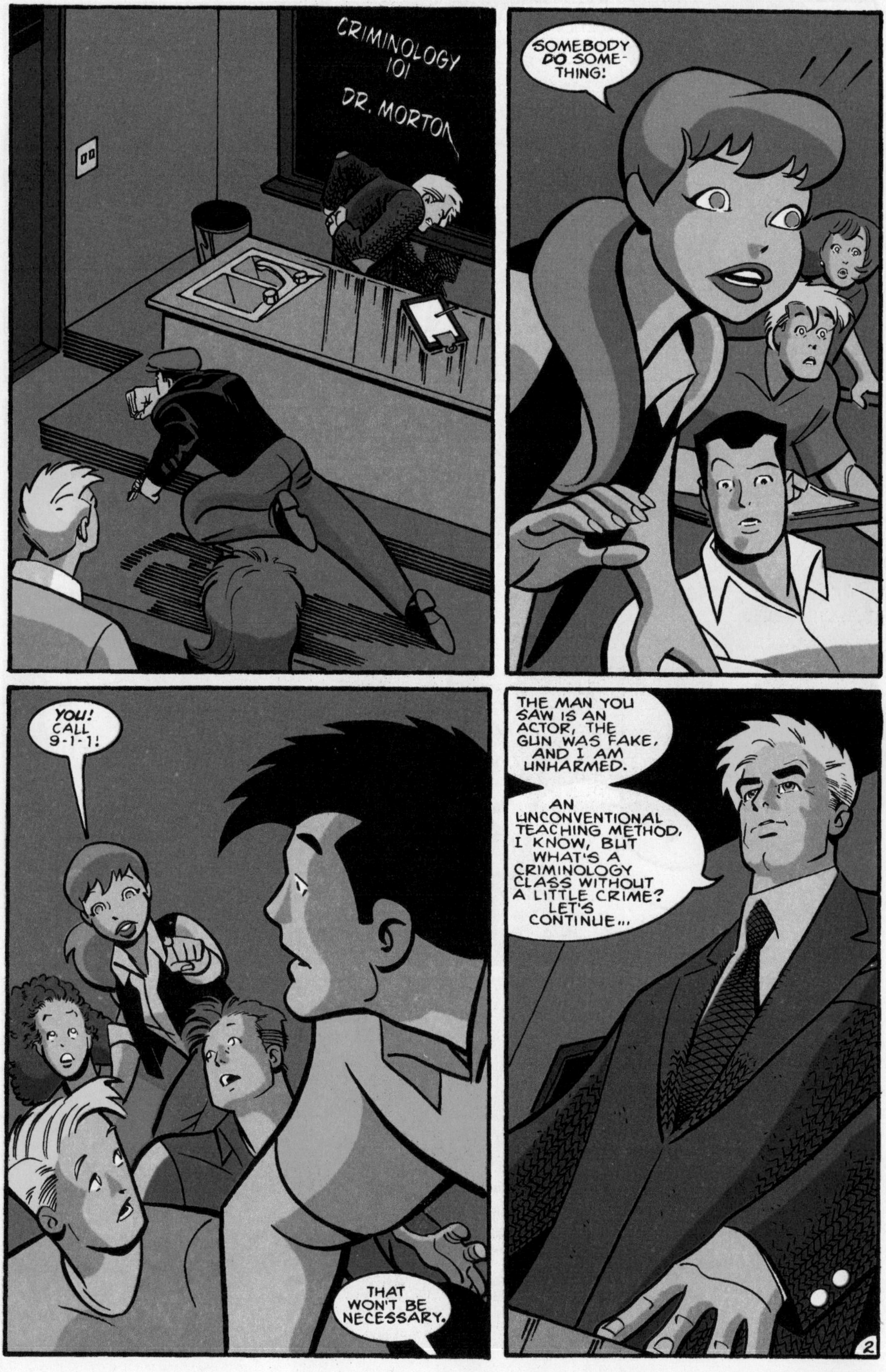
CRIMINOLOGY 101
DR. MORTON
SOMEBODY DO SOMETHING!
YOU! CALL 9-1-1!
THAT WON'T BE NECESSARY.
THE MAN YOU SAW IS AN ACTOR, THE GUN WAS FAKE, AND I AM UNHARMED.
AN UNCONVENTIONAL TEACHING METHOD, I KNOW, BUT WHAT'S A CRIMINOLOGY CLASS WITHOUT A LITTLE CRIME? LET'S CONTINUE...
2

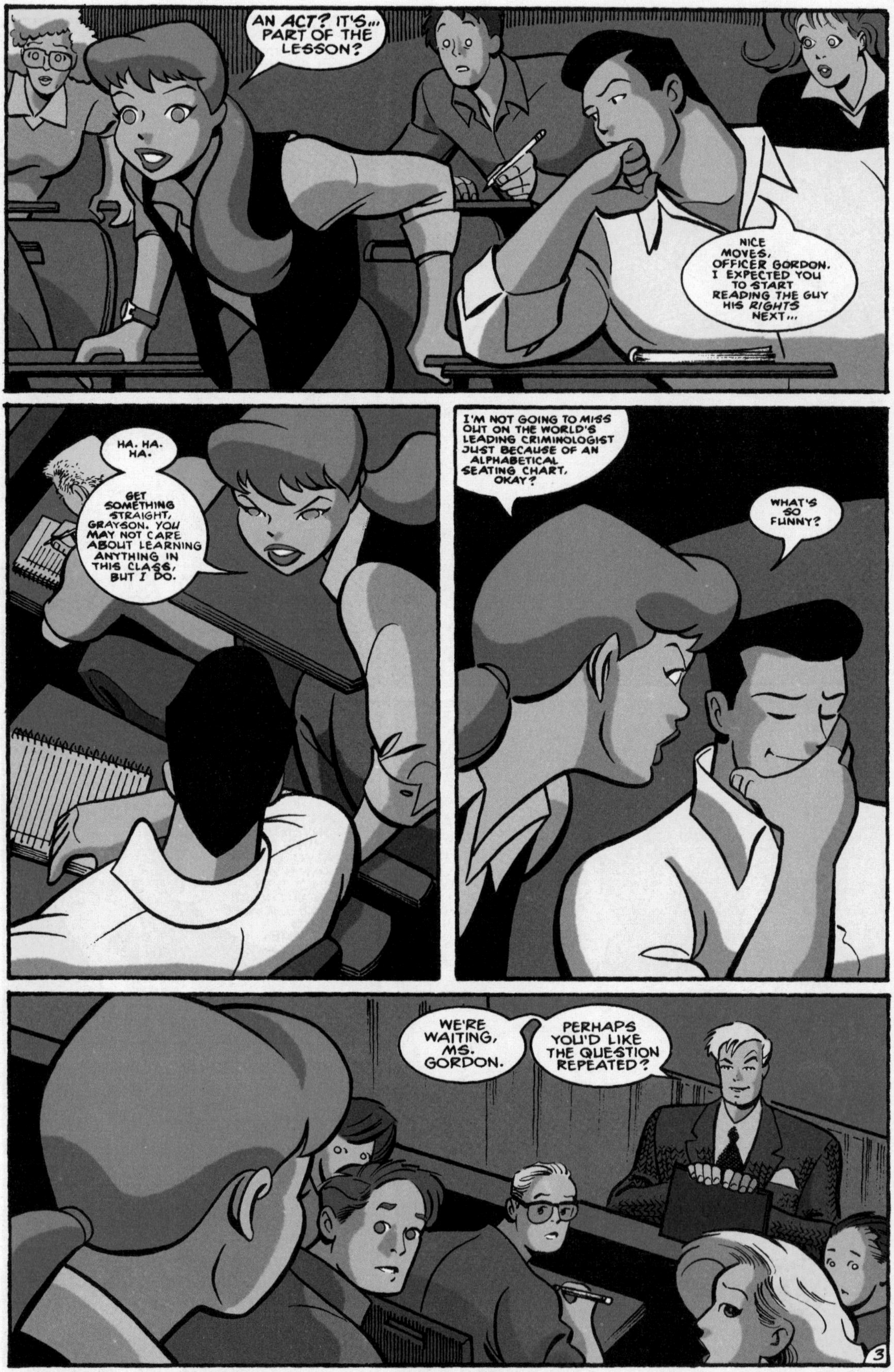
AN ACT? IT'S... PART OF THE LESSON?
NICE MOVES, OFFICER GORDON. I EXPECTED YOU TO START READING THE GUY HIS RIGHTS NEXT...
HA. HA. HA.
GET SOMETHING STRAIGHT, GRAYSON. YOU MAY NOT CARE ABOUT LEARNING ANYTHING IN THIS CLASS, BUT I DO.
I'M NOT GOING TO MISS OUT ON THE WORLD'S LEADING CRIMINOLOGIST JUST BECAUSE OF AN ALPHABETICAL SEATING CHART, OKAY?
WHAT'S SO FUNNY?
WE'RE WAITING, MS. GORDON.
PERHAPS YOU'D LIKE THE QUESTION REPEATED?

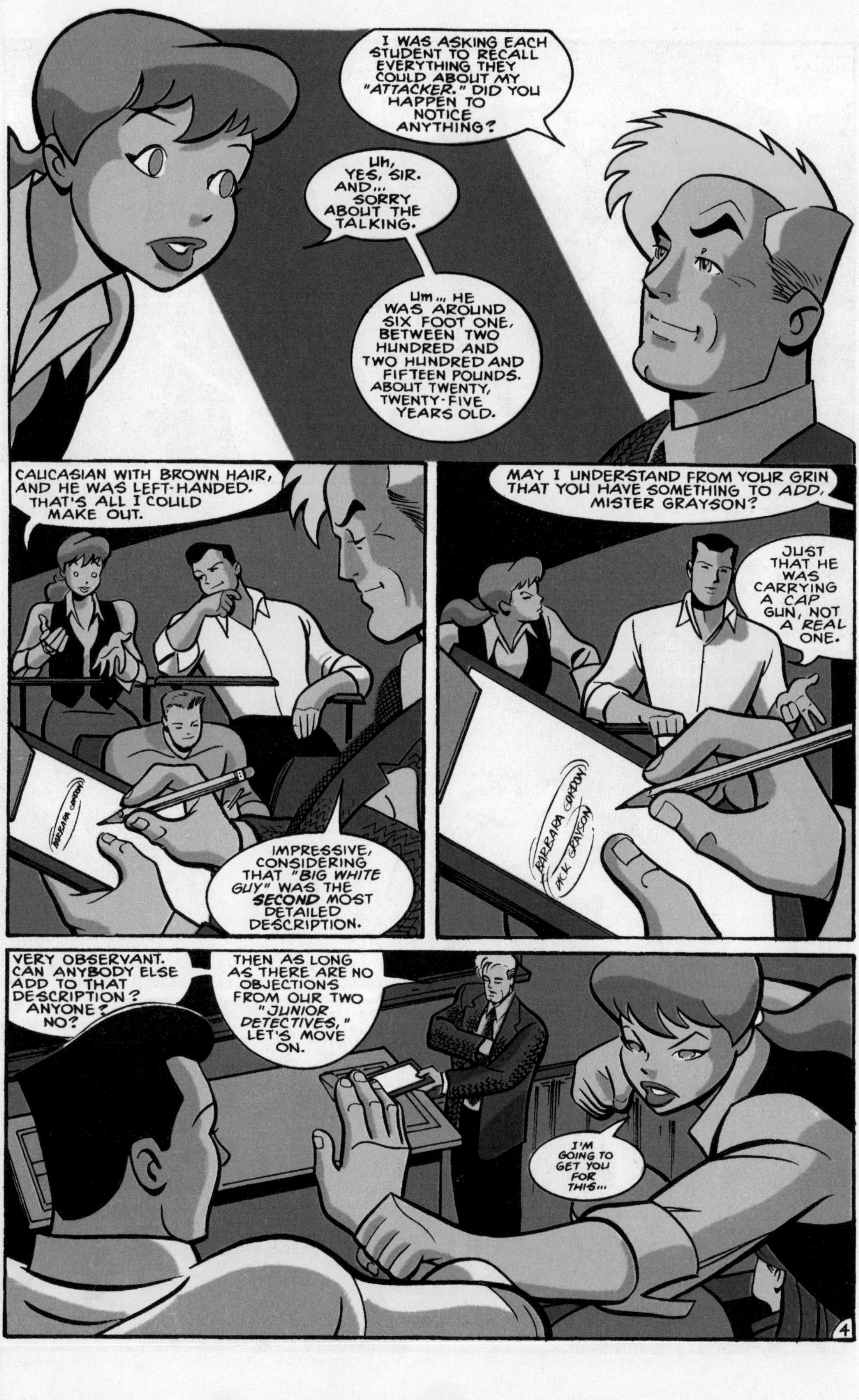
I WAS ASKING EACH STUDENT TO RECALL EVERYTHING THEY COULD ABOUT MY "ATTACKER." DID YOU HAPPEN TO NOTICE ANYTHING?
UH, YES, SIR. AND... SORRY ABOUT THE TALKING.
UM... HE WAS AROUND SIX FOOT ONE, BETWEEN TWO HUNDRED AND TWO HUNDRED AND FIFTEEN POUNDS. ABOUT TWENTY, TWENTY-FIVE YEARS OLD.
CAUCASIAN WITH BROWN HAIR, AND HE WAS LEFT-HANDED. THAT'S ALL I COULD MAKE OUT.
BARBARA GORDON
IMPRESSIVE, CONSIDERING THAT "BIG WHITE GUY" WAS THE SECOND MOST DETAILED DESCRIPTION.
MAY I UNDERSTAND FROM YOUR GRIN THAT YOU HAVE SOMETHING TO ADD, MISTER GRAYSON?
JUST THAT HE WAS CARRYING A CAP GUN, NOT A REAL ONE.
BARBARA GORDON
DICK GRAYSON
VERY OBSERVANT. CAN ANYBODY ELSE ADD TO THAT DESCRIPTION? ANYONE? NO?
THEN AS LONG AS THERE ARE NO OBJECTIONS FROM OUR TWO "JUNIOR DETECTIVES," LET'S MOVE ON.
I'M GOING TO GET YOU FOR THIS...

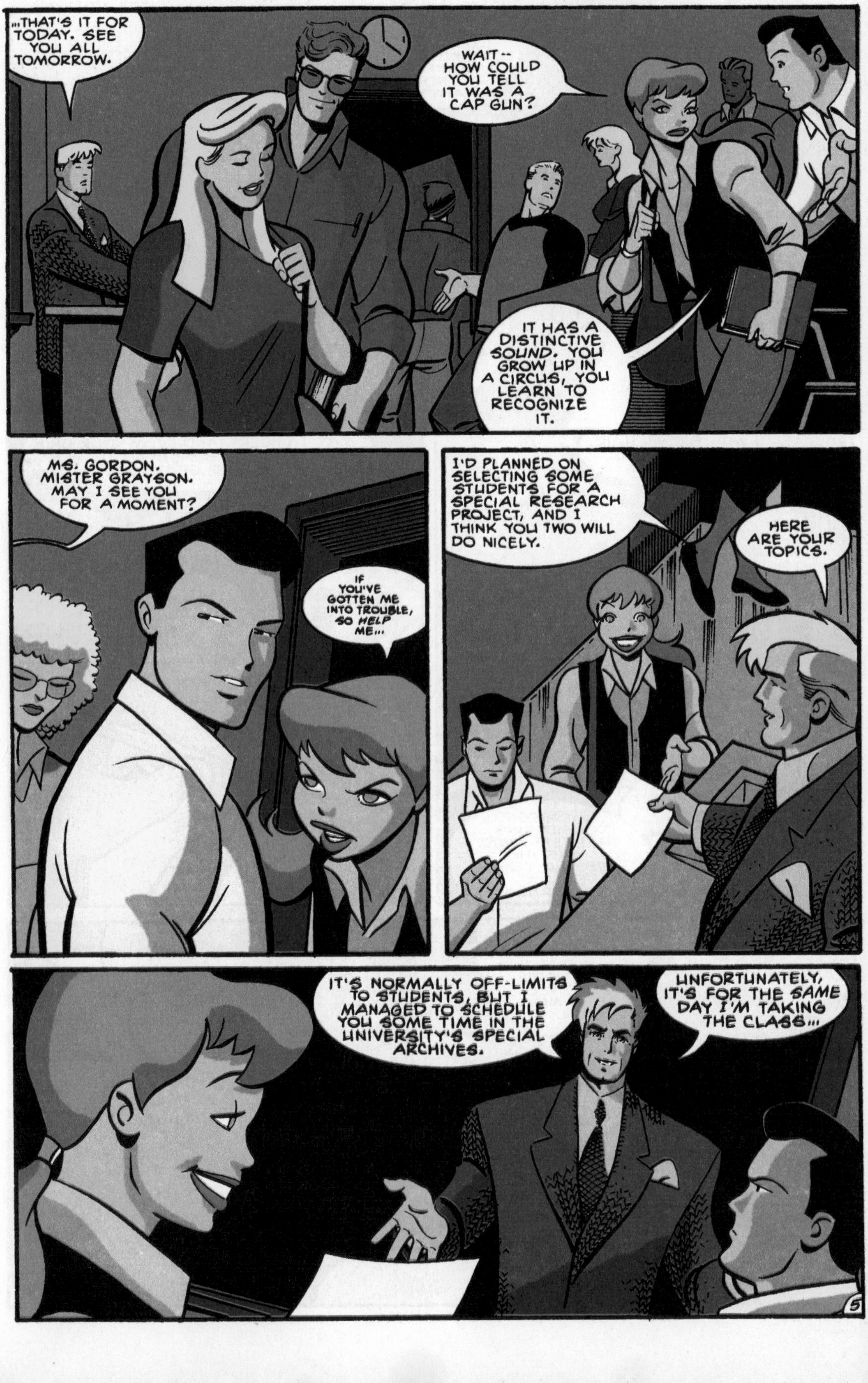
...THAT'S IT FOR TODAY. SEE YOU ALL TOMORROW.
WAIT -- HOW COULD YOU TELL IT WAS A CAP GUN?
IT HAS A DISTINCTIVE SOUND. YOU GROW UP IN A CIRCUS, YOU LEARN TO RECOGNIZE IT.
MS. GORDON. MISTER GRAYSON. MAY I SEE YOU FOR A MOMENT?
IF YOU'VE GOTTEN ME INTO TROUBLE, SO HELP ME...
I'D PLANNED ON SELECTING SOME STUDENTS FOR A SPECIAL RESEARCH PROJECT, AND I THINK YOU TWO WILL DO NICELY.
HERE ARE YOUR TOPICS.
IT'S NORMALLY OFF-LIMITS TO STUDENTS, BUT I MANAGED TO SCHEDULE YOU SOME TIME IN THE UNIVERSITY'S SPECIAL ARCHIVES.
UNFORTUNATELY, IT'S FOR THE SAME DAY I'M TAKING THE CLASS...

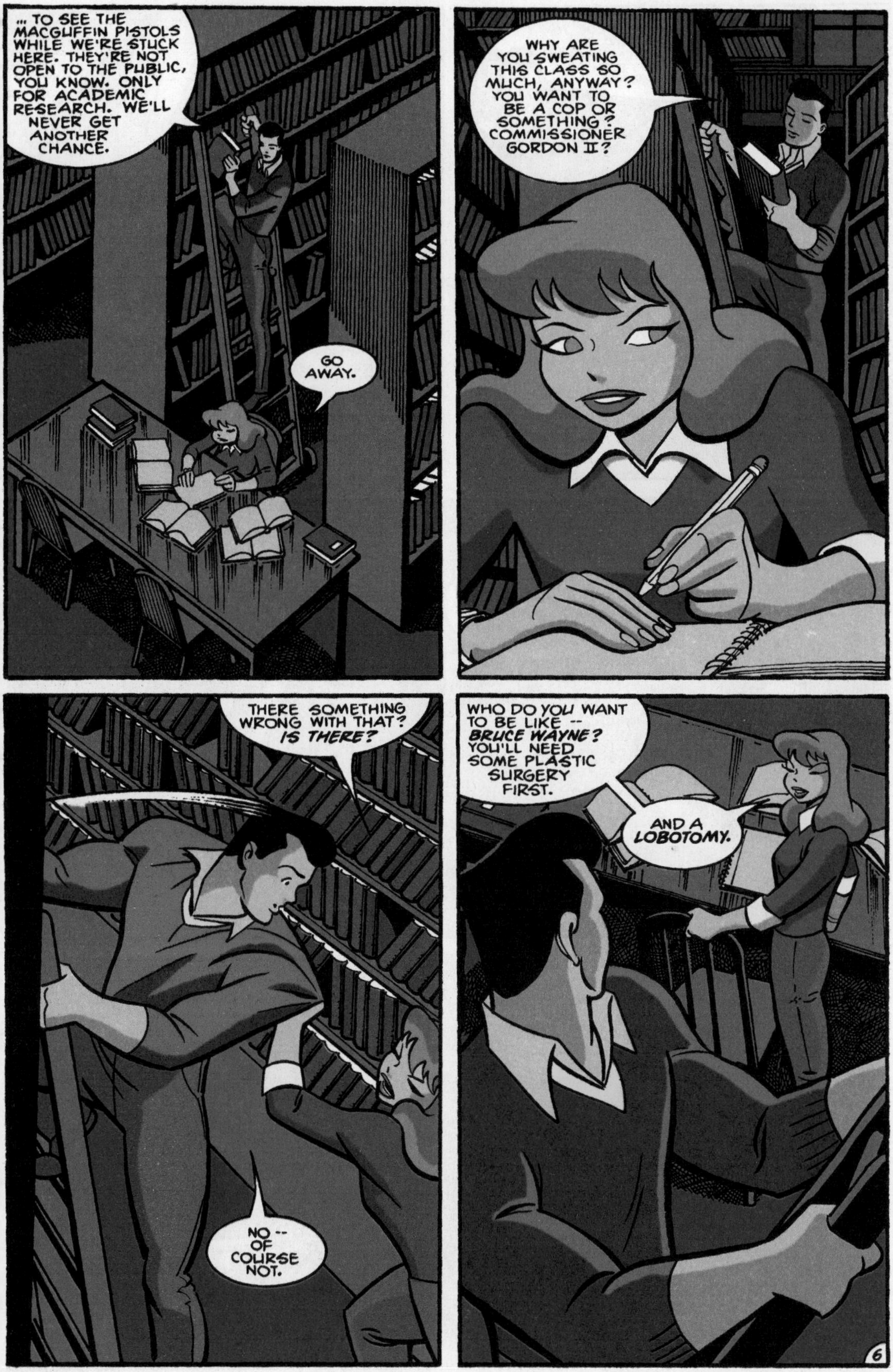
...TO SEE THE MACGUFFIN PISTOLS WHILE WE'RE STUCK HERE. THEY'RE NOT OPEN TO THE PUBLIC, YOU KNOW. ONLY FOR ACADEMIC RESEARCH. WE'LL NEVER GET ANOTHER CHANCE.
GO AWAY.
WHY ARE YOU SWEATING THIS CLASS SO MUCH, ANYWAY? YOU WANT TO BE A COP OR SOMETHING? COMMISSIONER GORDON II?
THERE SOMETHING WRONG WITH THAT? *IS THERE?*
NO -- OF COURSE NOT.
WHO DO YOU WANT TO BE LIKE -- *BRUCE WAYNE?* YOU'LL NEED SOME PLASTIC SURGERY FIRST.
AND A *LOBOTOMY.*

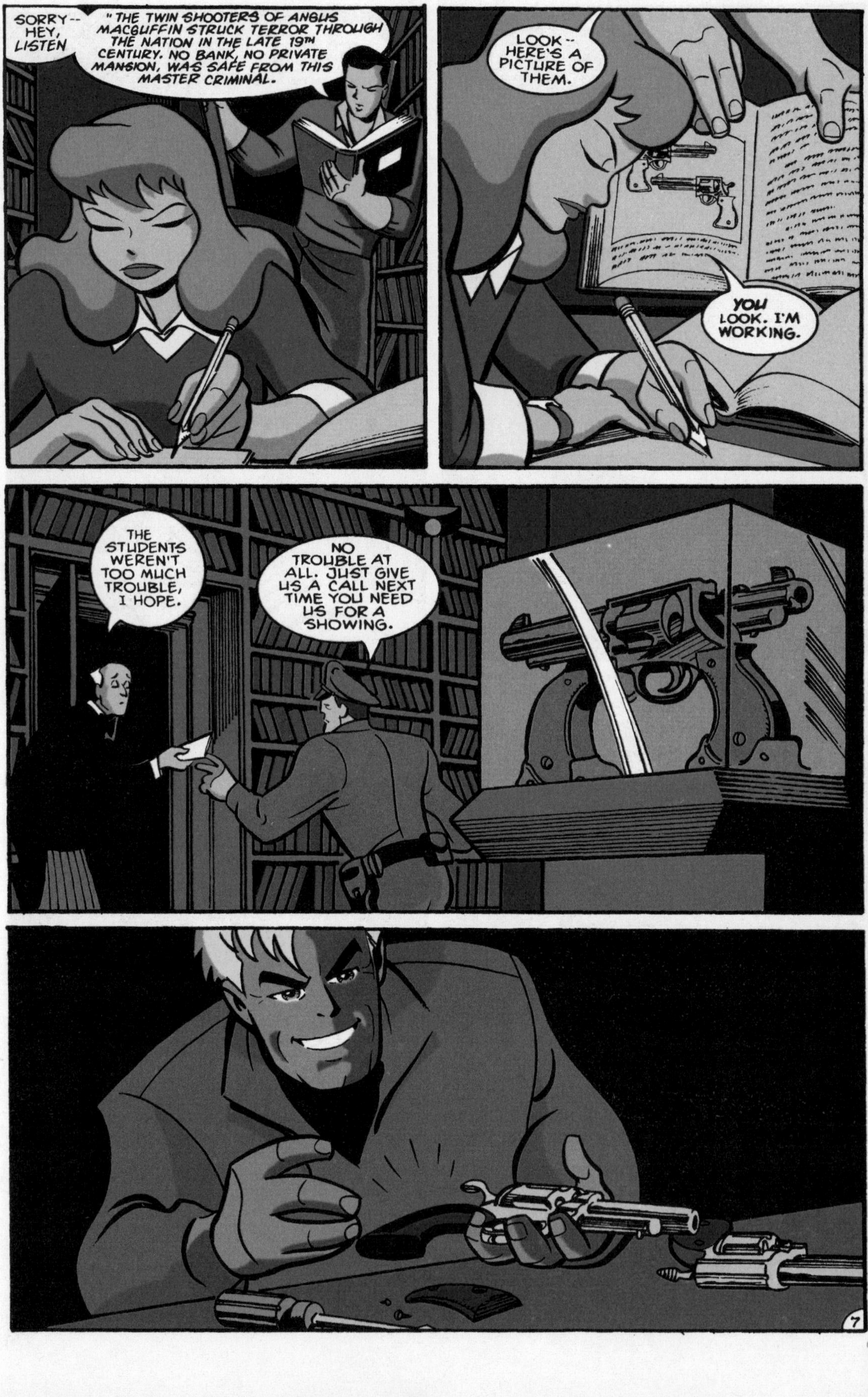
SORRY-- HEY, LISTEN
"THE TWIN SHOOTERS OF ANGUS MACGUFFIN STRUCK TERROR THROUGH THE NATION IN THE LATE 19TH CENTURY. NO BANK, NO PRIVATE MANSION, WAS SAFE FROM THIS MASTER CRIMINAL.
LOOK-- HERE'S A PICTURE OF THEM.
YOU LOOK. I'M WORKING.
THE STUDENTS WEREN'T TOO MUCH TROUBLE, I HOPE.
NO TROUBLE AT ALL. JUST GIVE US A CALL NEXT TIME YOU NEED US FOR A SHOWING.
7

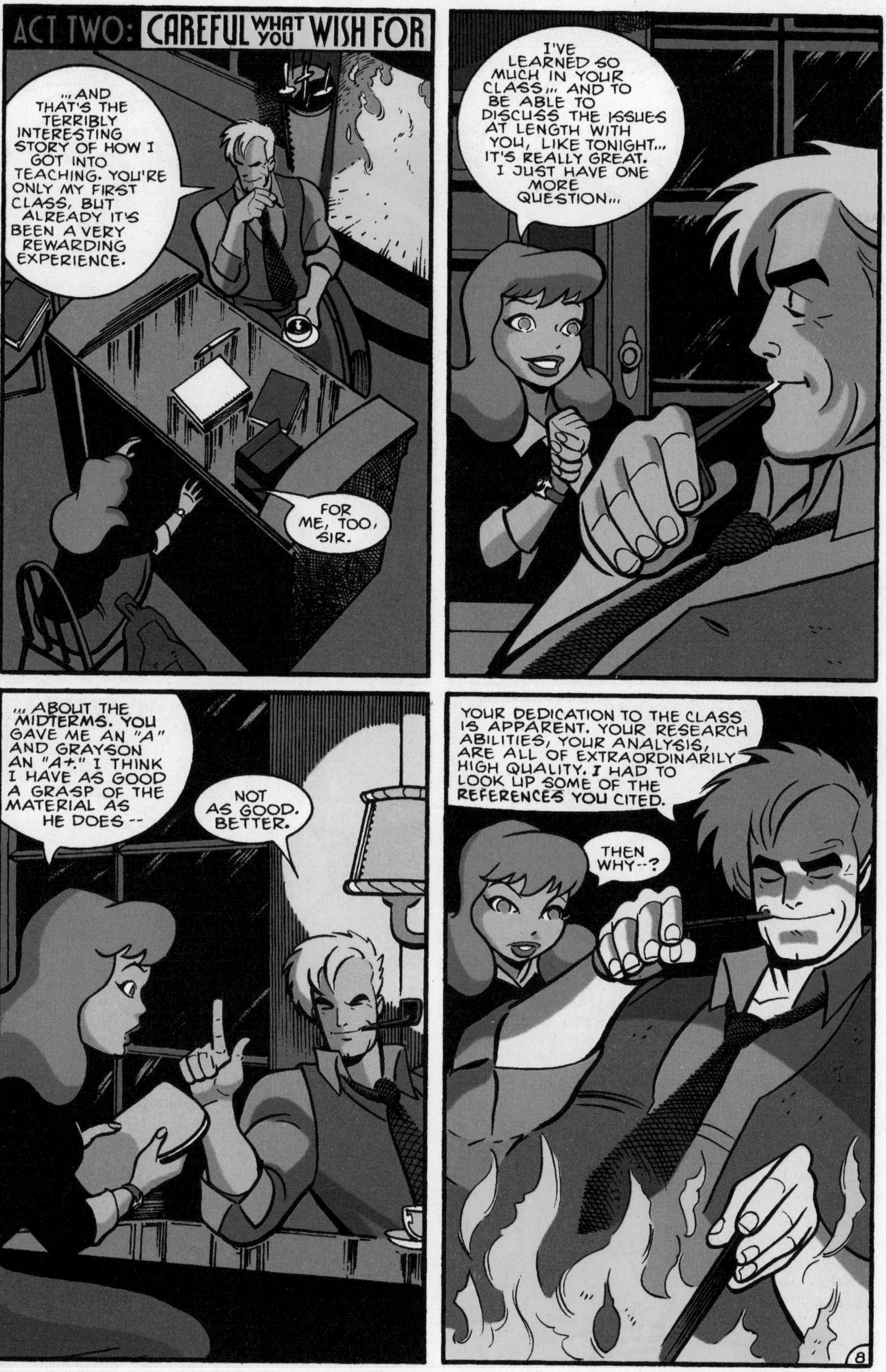
ACT TWO: CAREFUL WHAT YOU WISH FOR
...AND THAT'S THE TERRIBLY INTERESTING STORY OF HOW I GOT INTO TEACHING. YOU'RE ONLY MY FIRST CLASS, BUT ALREADY IT'S BEEN A VERY REWARDING EXPERIENCE.
FOR ME, TOO, SIR.
I'VE LEARNED SO MUCH IN YOUR CLASS... AND TO BE ABLE TO DISCUSS THE ISSUES AT LENGTH WITH YOU, LIKE TONIGHT... IT'S REALLY GREAT. I JUST HAVE ONE MORE QUESTION...
...ABOUT THE MIDTERMS. YOU GAVE ME AN "A" AND GRAYSON AN "A+." I THINK I HAVE AS GOOD A GRASP OF THE MATERIAL AS HE DOES --
NOT AS GOOD. BETTER.
YOUR DEDICATION TO THE CLASS IS APPARENT. YOUR RESEARCH ABILITIES, YOUR ANALYSIS, ARE ALL OF EXTRAORDINARILY HIGH QUALITY. I HAD TO LOOK UP SOME OF THE REFERENCES YOU CITED.
THEN WHY--?
8

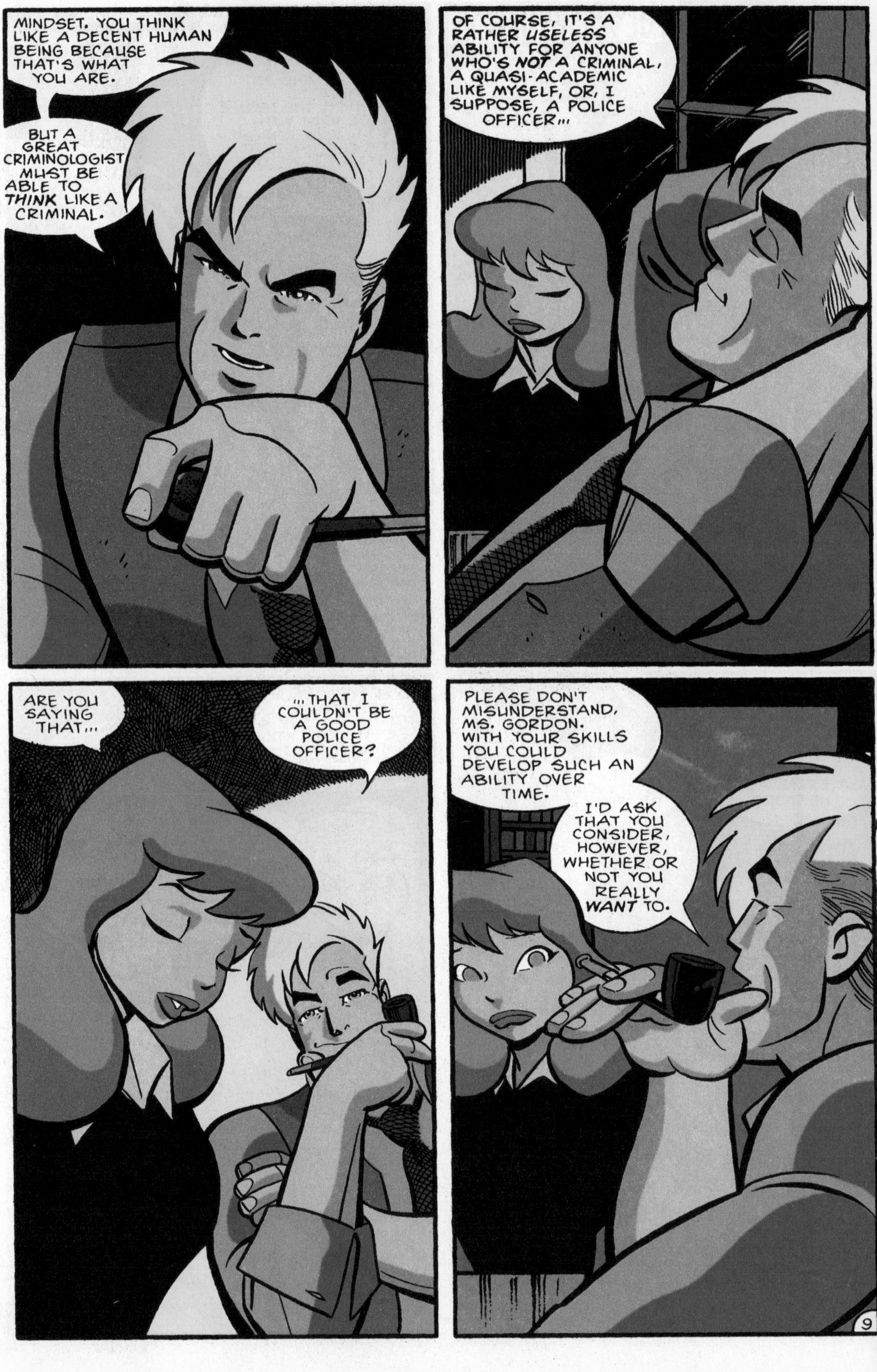
MINDSET. YOU THINK LIKE A DECENT HUMAN BEING BECAUSE THAT'S WHAT YOU ARE.
BUT A GREAT CRIMINOLOGIST MUST BE ABLE TO THINK LIKE A CRIMINAL.
OF COURSE, IT'S A RATHER USELESS ABILITY FOR ANYONE WHO'S NOT A CRIMINAL, A QUASI-ACADEMIC LIKE MYSELF, OR, I SUPPOSE, A POLICE OFFICER...
ARE YOU SAYING THAT...
...THAT I COULDN'T BE A GOOD POLICE OFFICER?
PLEASE DON'T MISUNDERSTAND, MS. GORDON. WITH YOUR SKILLS YOU COULD DEVELOP SUCH AN ABILITY OVER TIME.
I'D ASK THAT YOU CONSIDER, HOWEVER, WHETHER OR NOT YOU REALLY WANT TO.

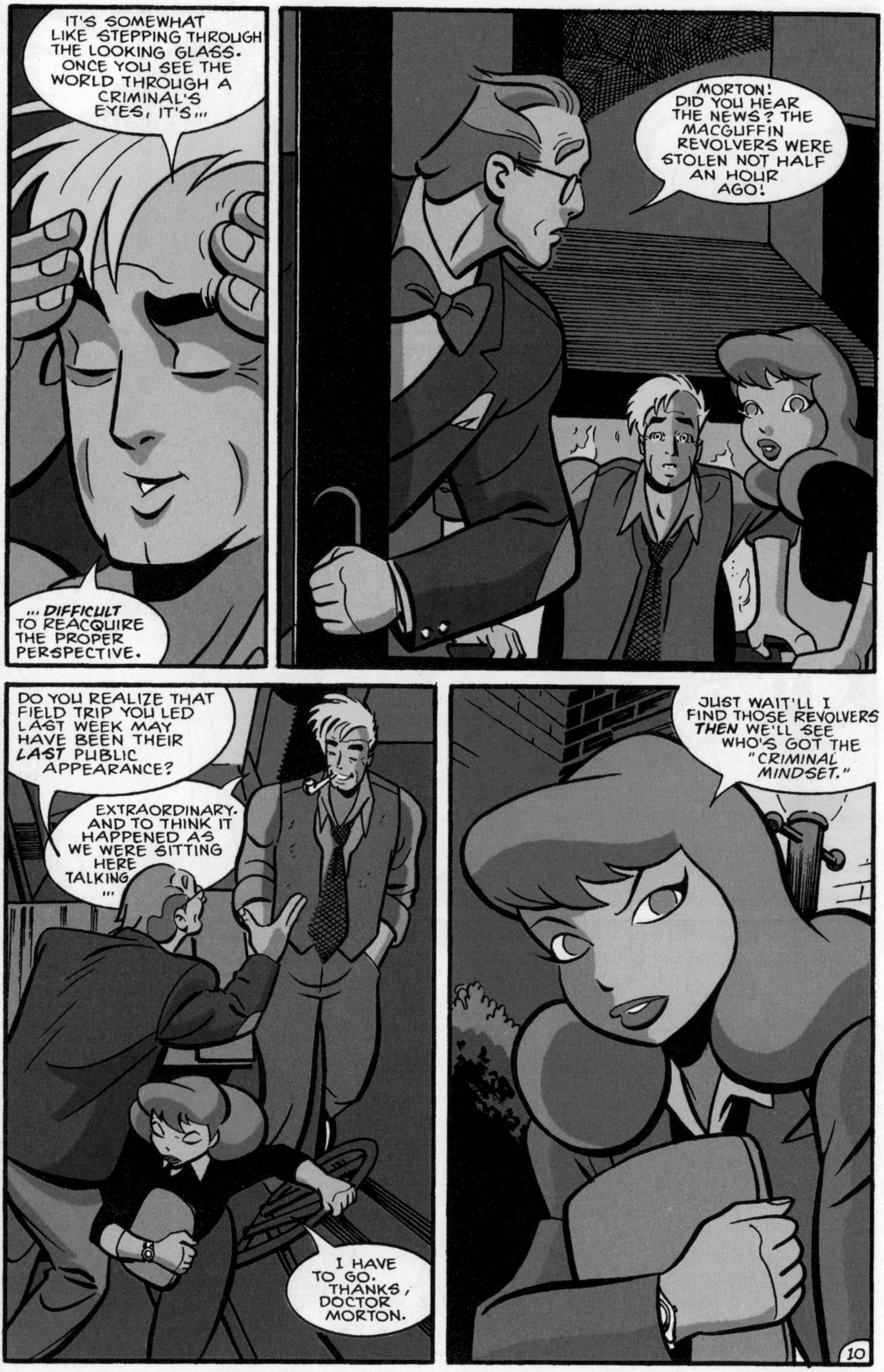

IT'S SOMEWHAT LIKE STEPPING THROUGH THE LOOKING GLASS. ONCE YOU SEE THE WORLD THROUGH A CRIMINAL'S EYES, IT'S...
...DIFFICULT TO REACQUIRE THE PROPER PERSPECTIVE.
MORTON! DID YOU HEAR THE NEWS? THE MACGUFFIN REVOLVERS WERE STOLEN NOT HALF AN HOUR AGO!
DO YOU REALIZE THAT FIELD TRIP YOU LED LAST WEEK MAY HAVE BEEN THEIR LAST PUBLIC APPEARANCE?
EXTRAORDINARY. AND TO THINK IT HAPPENED AS WE WERE SITTING HERE TALKING...
I HAVE TO GO. THANKS, DOCTOR MORTON.
JUST WAIT'LL I FIND THOSE REVOLVERS. THEN WE'LL SEE WHO'S GOT THE "CRIMINAL MINDSET."
10

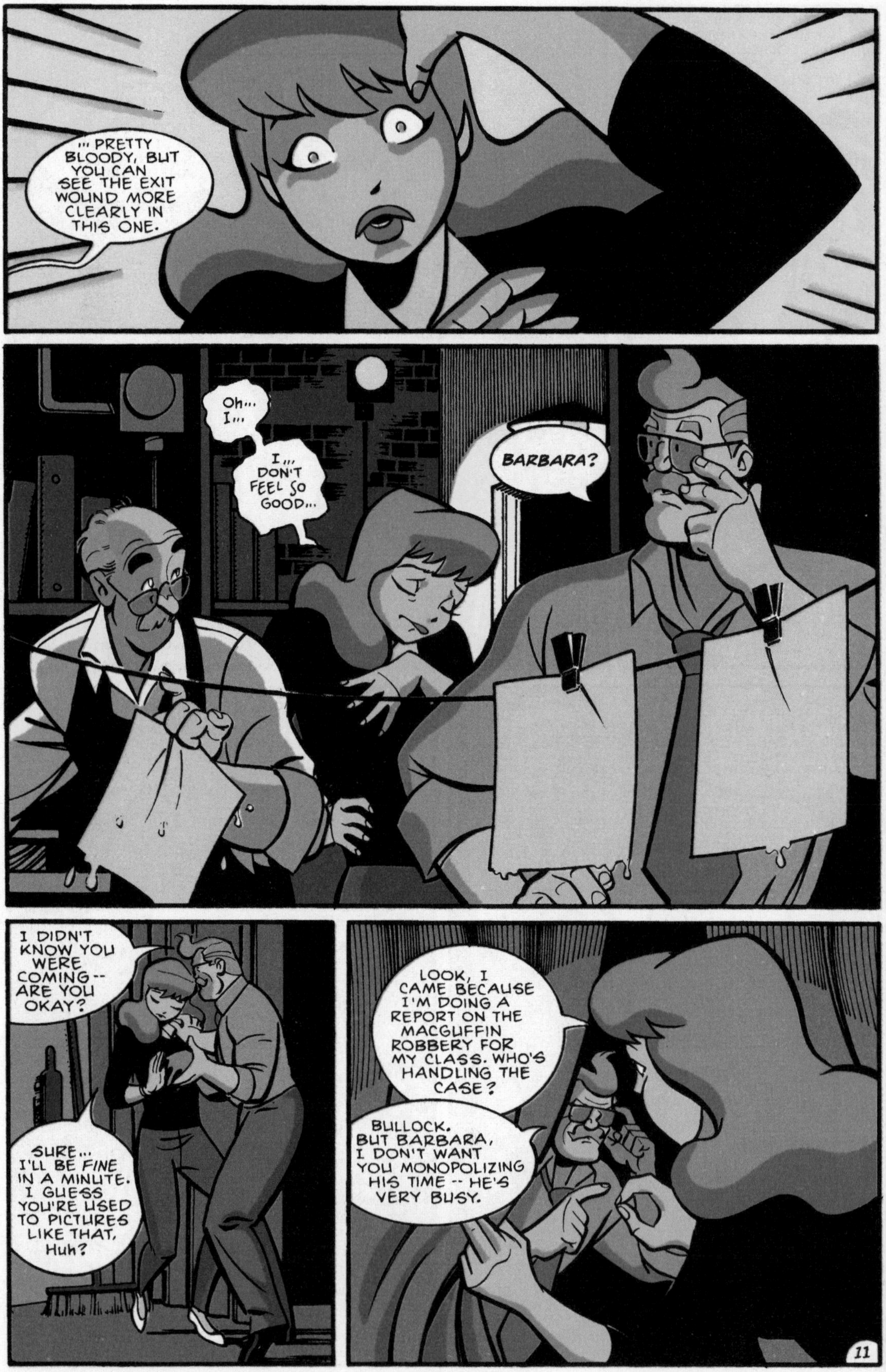
...PRETTY BLOODY, BUT YOU CAN SEE THE EXIT WOUND MORE CLEARLY IN THIS ONE.
Oh... I...
I... DON'T FEEL SO GOOD...
BARBARA?
I DIDN'T KNOW YOU WERE COMING-- ARE YOU OKAY?
SURE... I'LL BE *FINE* IN A MINUTE. I GUESS YOU'RE USED TO PICTURES LIKE THAT, Huh?
LOOK, I CAME BECAUSE I'M DOING A REPORT ON THE MACGUFFIN ROBBERY FOR MY CLASS. WHO'S HANDLING THE CASE?
BULLOCK. BUT BARBARA, I DON'T WANT YOU MONOPOLIZING HIS TIME -- HE'S VERY BUSY.

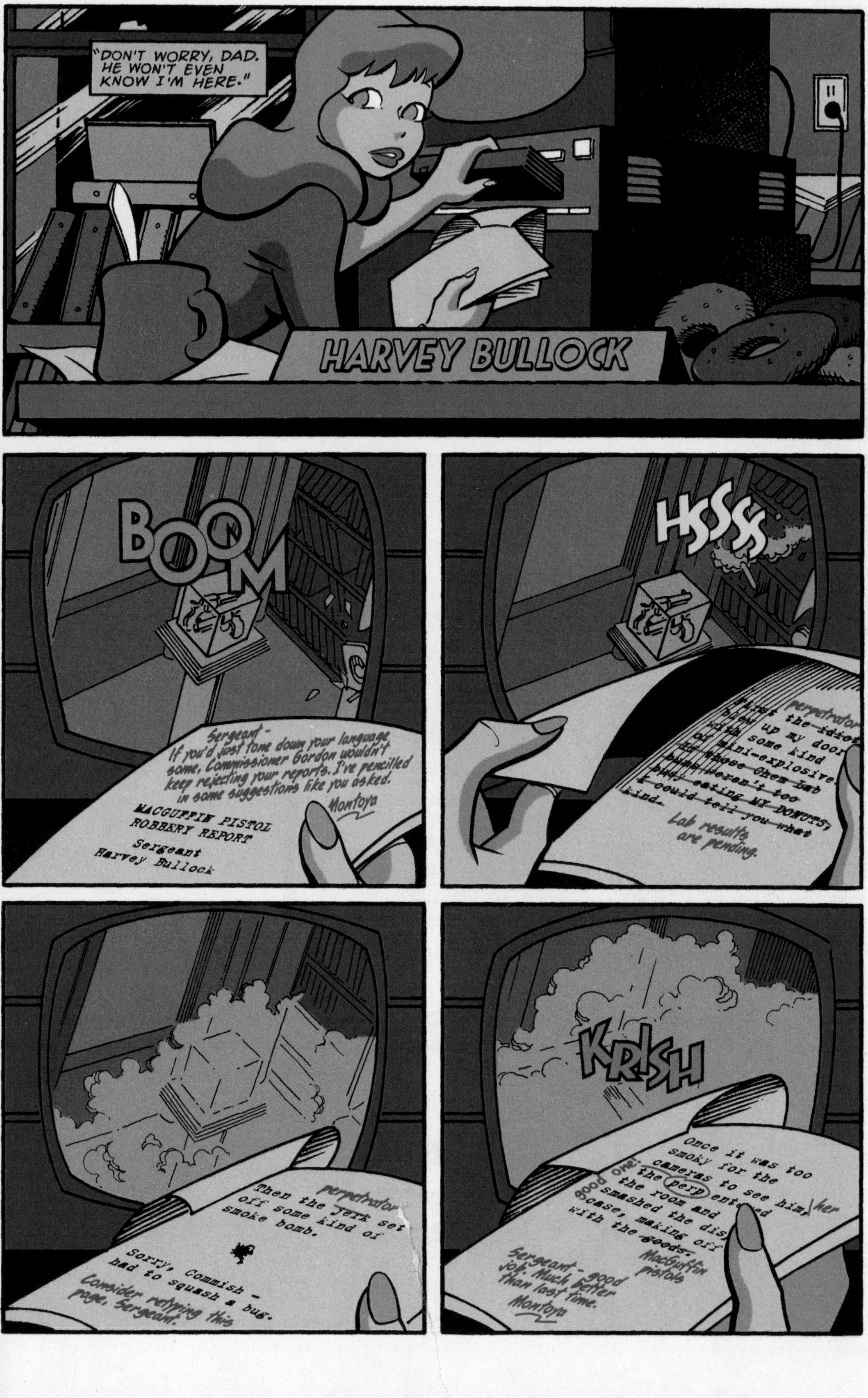
"DON'T WORRY, DAD. HE WON'T EVEN KNOW I'M HERE."
HARVEY BULLOCK
BOOM
Sergeant - If you'd just tone down your language some, Commissioner Gordon wouldn't keep rejecting your reports. I've pencilled in some suggestions like you asked.
Montoya
MACGUFFIN PISTOL ROBBERY REPORT
Sergeant Harvey Bullock
HSSSS
First the idiot perpetrator blew up my door with some kind of mini-explosive. If those Chem Lab bums weren't too busy eating MY DONUTS, I could tell you what kind.
Lab results are pending.
Then the jerk perpetrator set off some kind of smoke bomb.
Sorry, Commish - had to squash a bug.
Consider retyping this page, Sergeant.
KRISH
Once it was too smoky for the cameras to see him, her the perp entered the room and smashed the display case, making off with the goods. MacGuffin pistols
Good one!
Sergeant - good job. Much better than last time.
Montoya

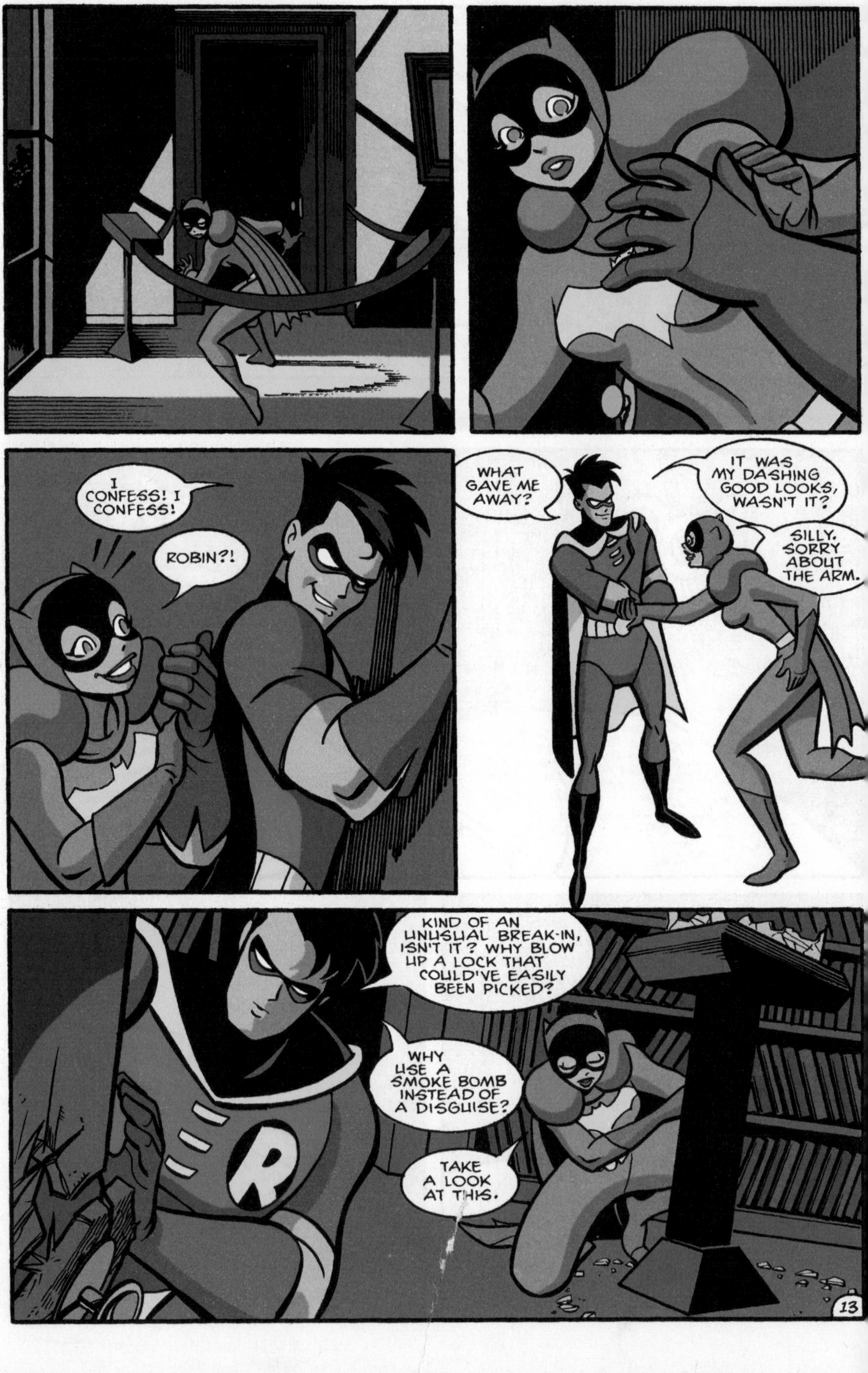
I CONFESS! I CONFESS!
ROBIN?!
WHAT GAVE ME AWAY?
IT WAS MY DASHING GOOD LOOKS, WASN'T IT?
SILLY. SORRY ABOUT THE ARM.
KIND OF AN UNUSUAL BREAK-IN, ISN'T IT? WHY BLOW UP A LOCK THAT COULD'VE EASILY BEEN PICKED?
WHY USE A SMOKE BOMB INSTEAD OF A DISGUISE?
TAKE A LOOK AT THIS.

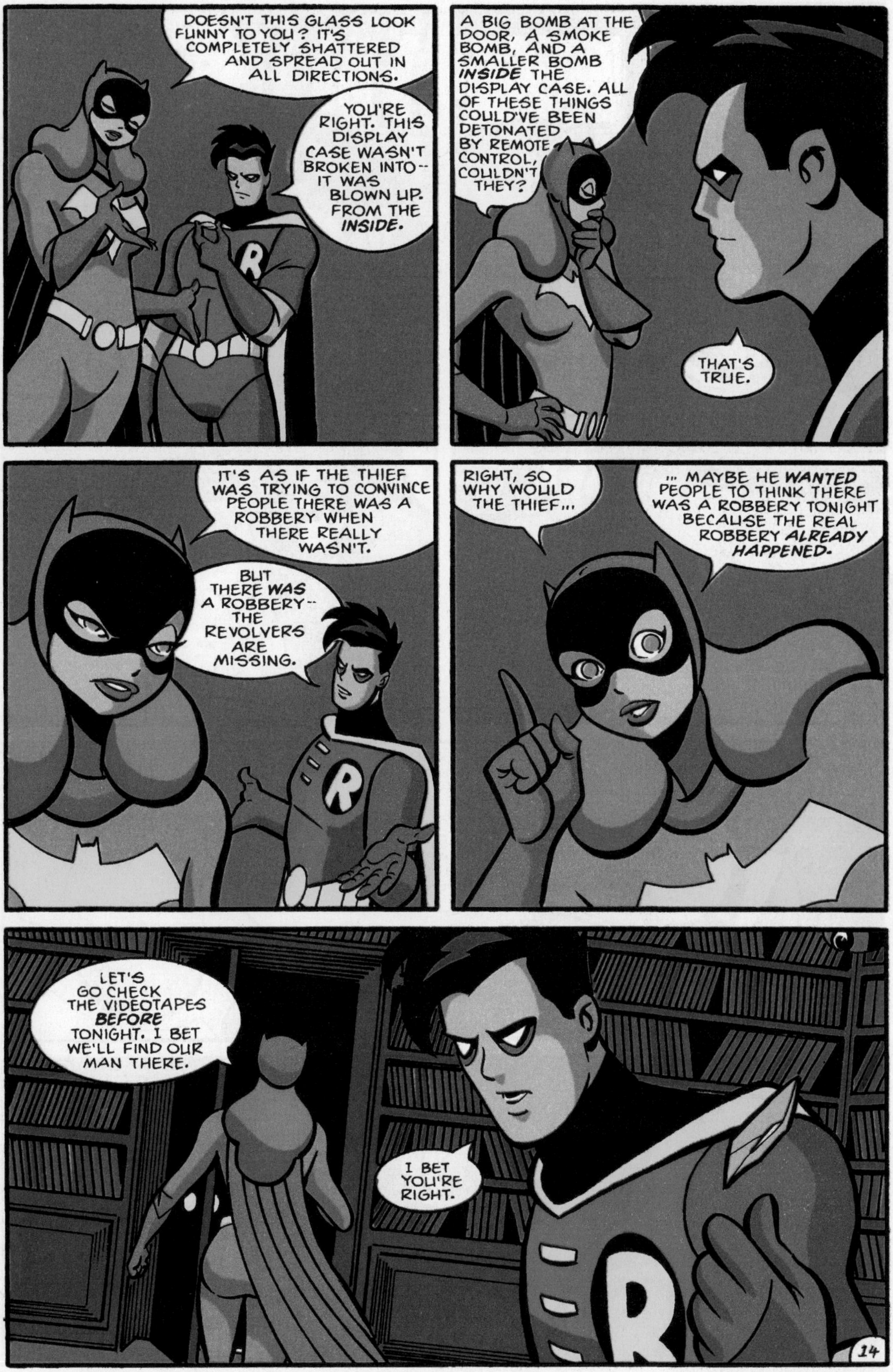
DOESN'T THIS GLASS LOOK FUNNY TO YOU? IT'S COMPLETELY SHATTERED AND SPREAD OUT IN ALL DIRECTIONS.
YOU'RE RIGHT. THIS DISPLAY CASE WASN'T BROKEN INTO-- IT WAS BLOWN UP. FROM THE *INSIDE*.
A BIG BOMB AT THE DOOR, A SMOKE BOMB, AND A SMALLER BOMB *INSIDE* THE DISPLAY CASE. ALL OF THESE THINGS COULD'VE BEEN DETONATED BY REMOTE CONTROL, COULDN'T THEY?
THAT'S TRUE.
IT'S AS IF THE THIEF WAS TRYING TO CONVINCE PEOPLE THERE WAS A ROBBERY WHEN THERE REALLY WASN'T.
BUT THERE *WAS* A ROBBERY-- THE REVOLVERS ARE MISSING.
RIGHT, SO WHY WOULD THE THIEF...
... MAYBE HE *WANTED* PEOPLE TO THINK THERE WAS A ROBBERY TONIGHT BECAUSE THE REAL ROBBERY *ALREADY HAPPENED*.
LET'S GO CHECK THE VIDEOTAPES *BEFORE* TONIGHT. I BET WE'LL FIND OUR MAN THERE.
I BET YOU'RE RIGHT.
14

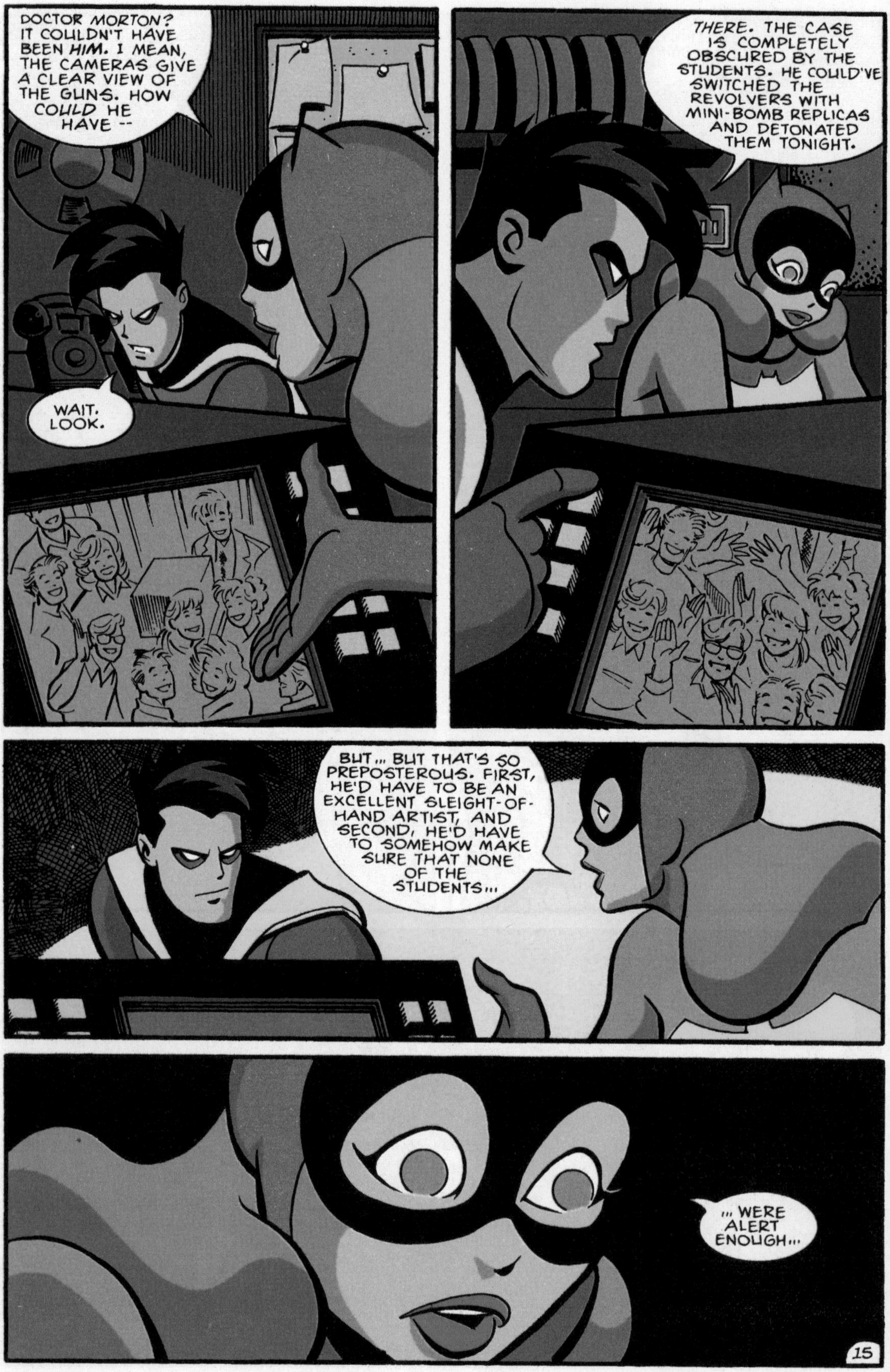
DOCTOR MORTON? IT COULDN'T HAVE BEEN HIM. I MEAN, THE CAMERAS GIVE A CLEAR VIEW OF THE GUNS. HOW COULD HE HAVE --
WAIT. LOOK.
THERE. THE CASE IS COMPLETELY OBSCURED BY THE STUDENTS. HE COULD'VE SWITCHED THE REVOLVERS WITH MINI-BOMB REPLICAS AND DETONATED THEM TONIGHT.
BUT... BUT THAT'S SO PREPOSTEROUS. FIRST, HE'D HAVE TO BE AN EXCELLENT SLEIGHT-OF-HAND ARTIST, AND SECOND, HE'D HAVE TO SOMEHOW MAKE SURE THAT NONE OF THE STUDENTS...
...WERE ALERT ENOUGH...

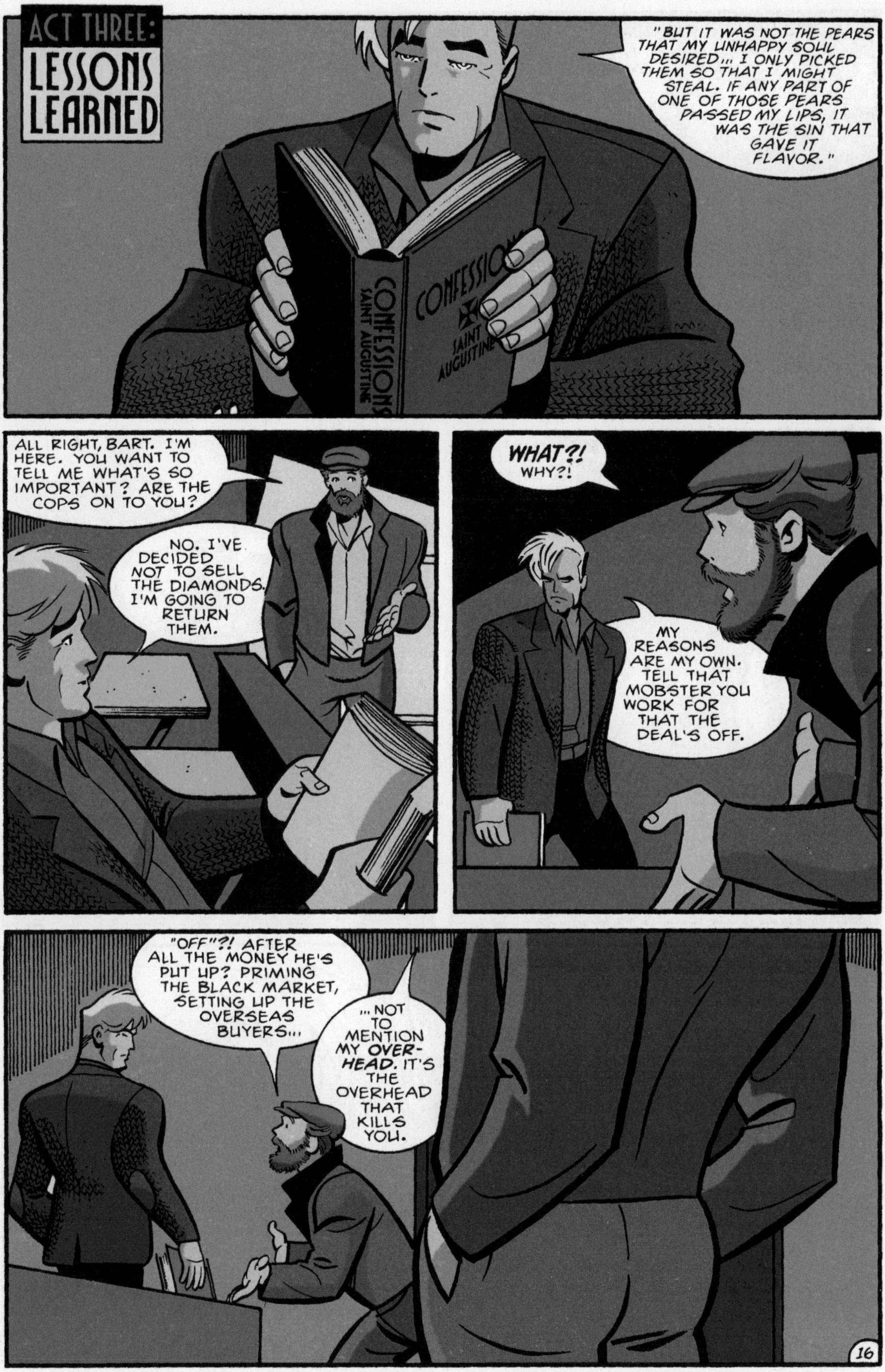
ACT THREE:
LESSONS LEARNED
"BUT IT WAS NOT THE PEARS THAT MY UNHAPPY SOUL DESIRED... I ONLY PICKED THEM SO THAT I MIGHT STEAL. IF ANY PART OF ONE OF THOSE PEARS PASSED MY LIPS, IT WAS THE SIN THAT GAVE IT FLAVOR."
CONFESSIONS SAINT AUGUSTINE
ALL RIGHT, BART. I'M HERE. YOU WANT TO TELL ME WHAT'S SO IMPORTANT? ARE THE COPS ON TO YOU?
NO. I'VE DECIDED NOT TO SELL THE DIAMONDS. I'M GOING TO RETURN THEM.
WHAT?! WHY?!
MY REASONS ARE MY OWN. TELL THAT MOBSTER YOU WORK FOR THAT THE DEAL'S OFF.
"OFF"?! AFTER ALL THE MONEY HE'S PUT UP? PRIMING THE BLACK MARKET, SETTING UP THE OVERSEAS BUYERS...
...NOT TO MENTION MY OVERHEAD. IT'S THE OVERHEAD THAT KILLS YOU.
16

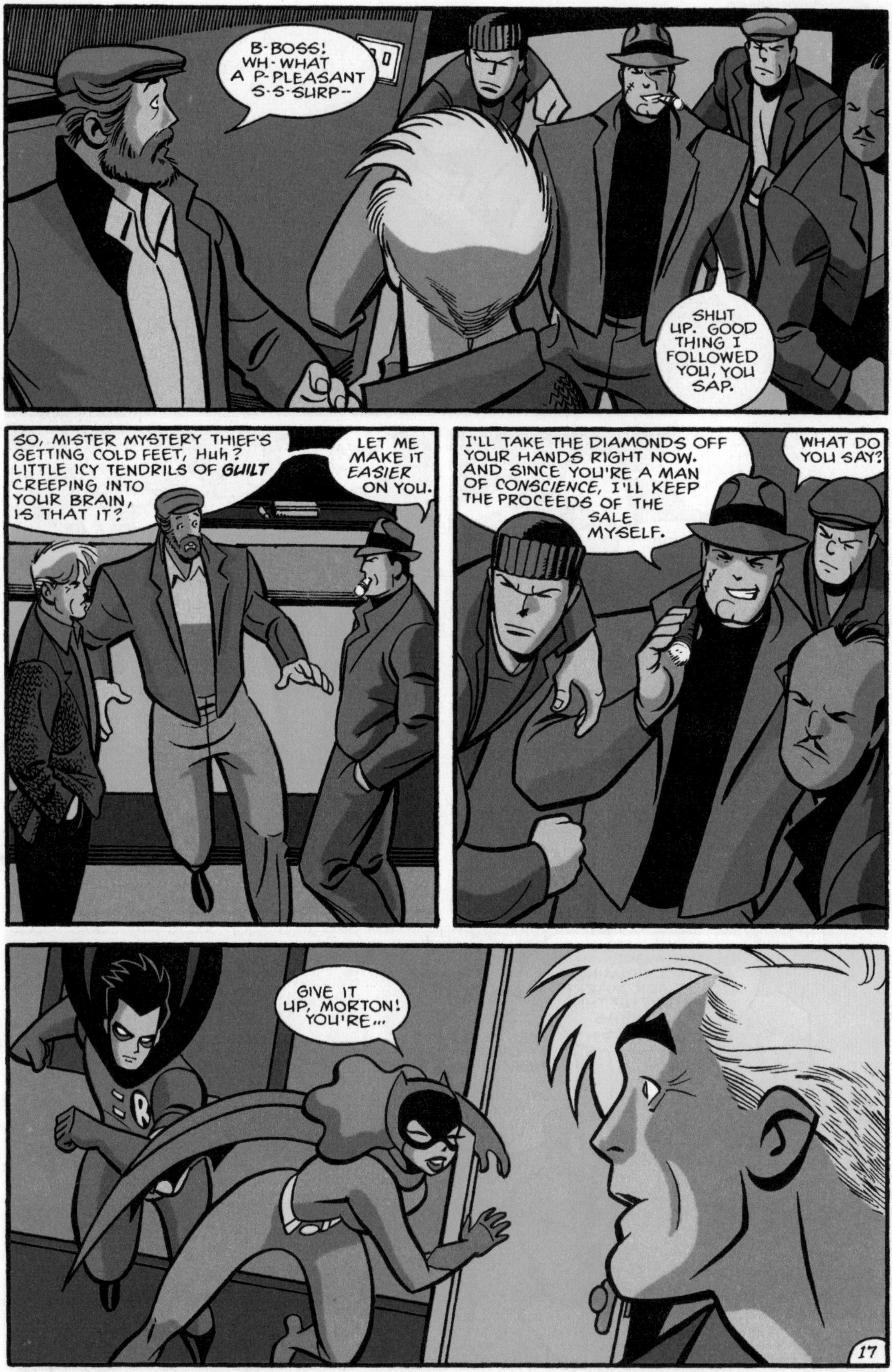
B-BOSS! WH-WHAT A P-PLEASANT S-S-SURP--
SHUT UP. GOOD THING I FOLLOWED YOU, YOU SAP.
SO, MISTER MYSTERY THIEF'S GETTING COLD FEET, Huh? LITTLE ICY TENDRILS OF **GUILT** CREEPING INTO YOUR BRAIN, IS THAT IT?
LET ME MAKE IT *EASIER* ON YOU.
I'LL TAKE THE DIAMONDS OFF YOUR HANDS RIGHT NOW. AND SINCE YOU'RE A MAN OF *CONSCIENCE*, I'LL KEEP THE PROCEEDS OF THE SALE MYSELF.
WHAT DO YOU SAY?
GIVE IT UP, MORTON! YOU'RE...

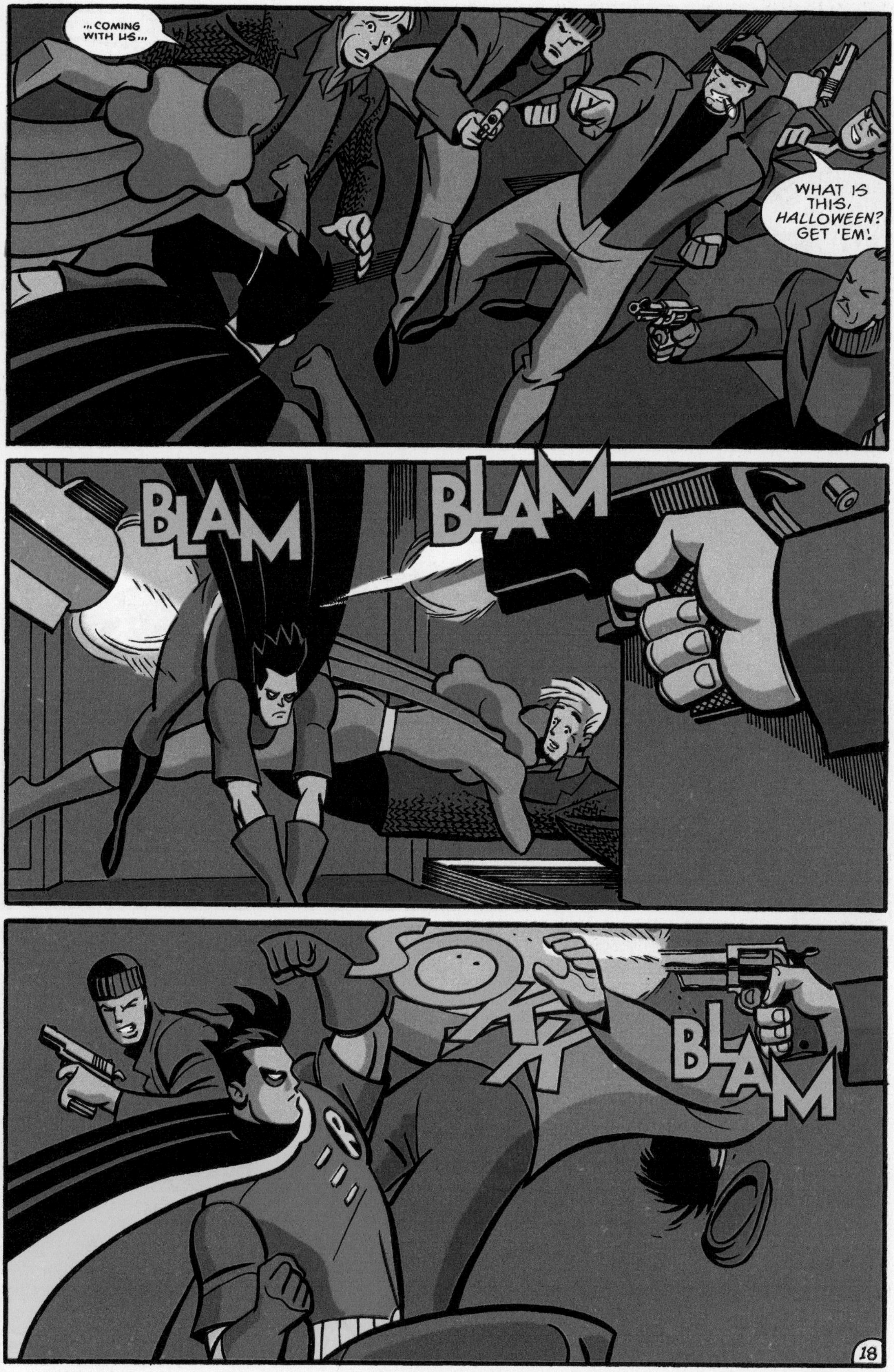
...COMING WITH US...
WHAT IS THIS, HALLOWEEN? GET 'EM!
BLAM
BLAM
SOKK
BLAM
18

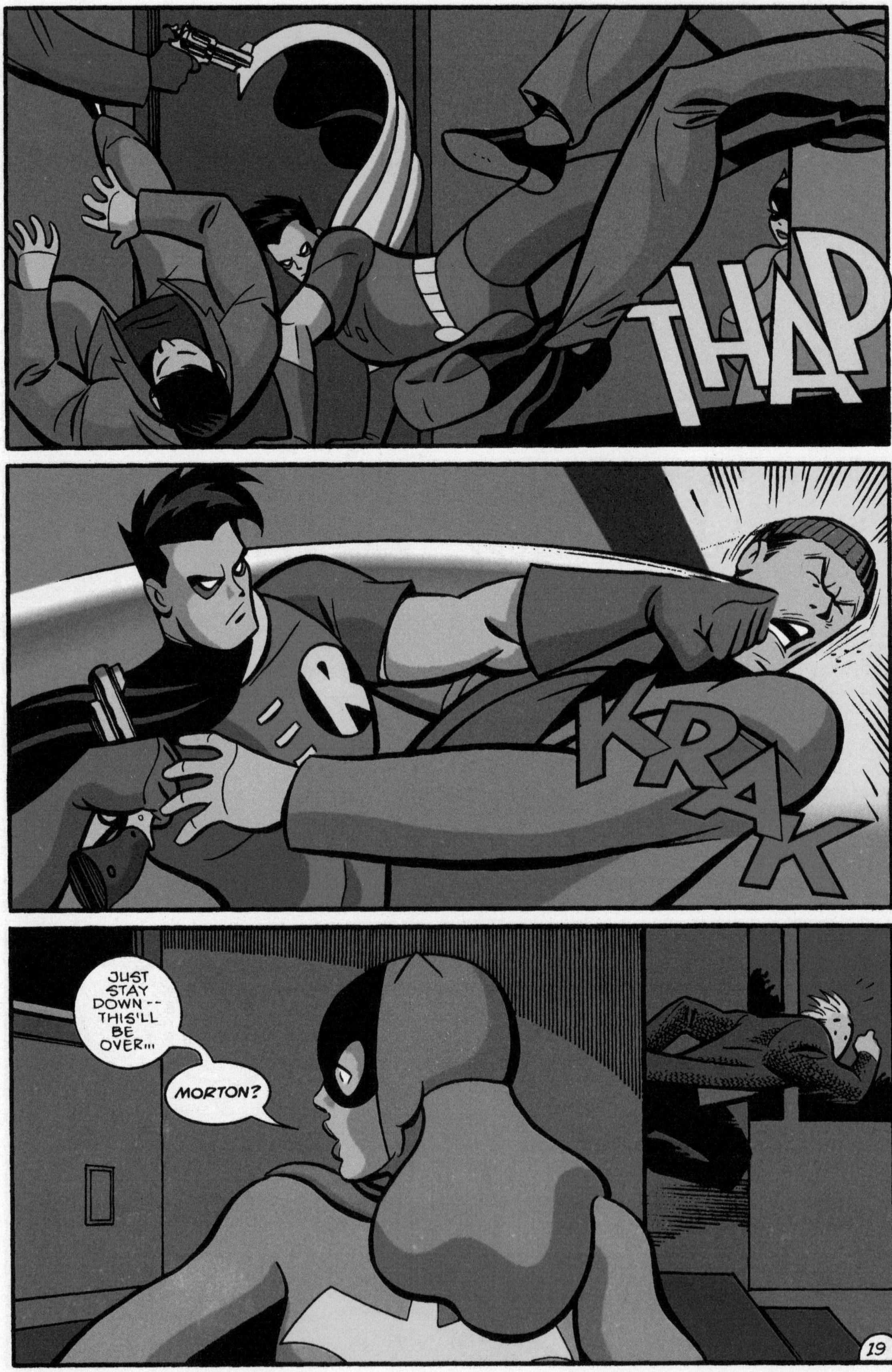
THAP
KRAK
JUST STAY DOWN-- THIS'LL BE OVER...
MORTON?

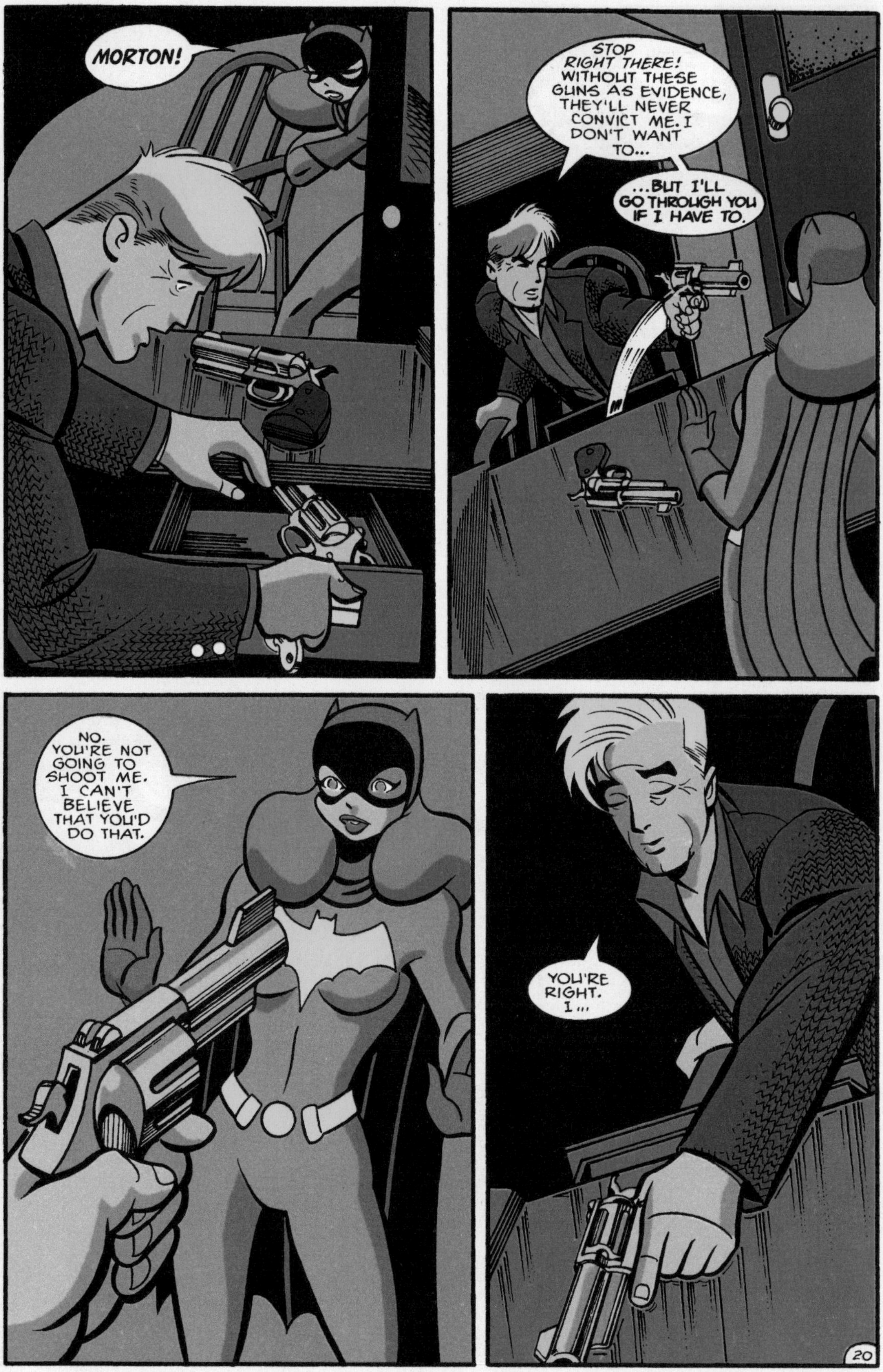
MORTON!
STOP RIGHT THERE! WITHOUT THESE GUNS AS EVIDENCE, THEY'LL NEVER CONVICT ME. I DON'T WANT TO...
...BUT I'LL GO THROUGH YOU IF I HAVE TO.
NO. YOU'RE NOT GOING TO SHOOT ME. I CAN'T BELIEVE THAT YOU'D DO THAT.
YOU'RE RIGHT. I...
20

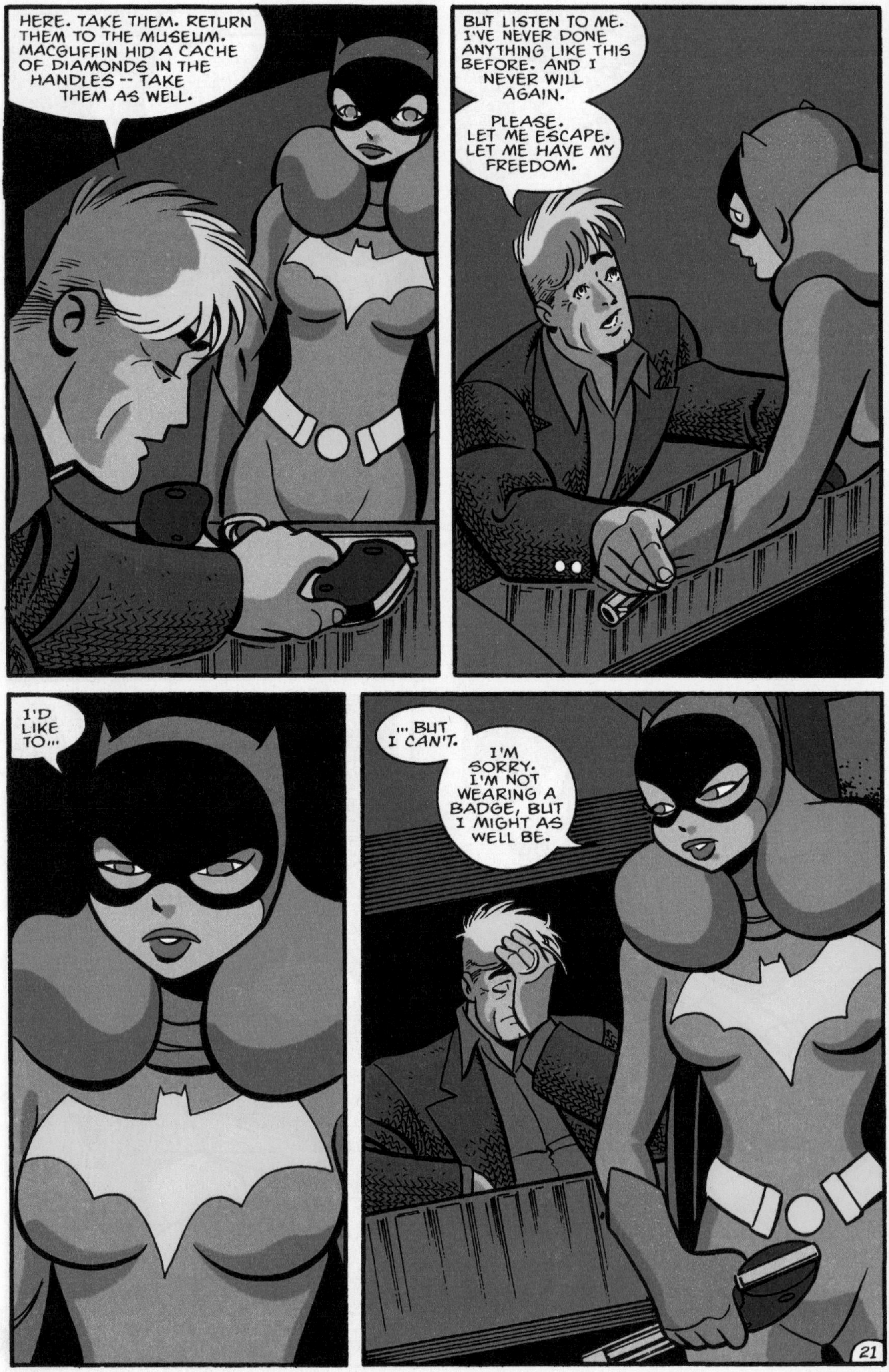
HERE. TAKE THEM. RETURN THEM TO THE MUSEUM. MACGUFFIN HID A CACHE OF DIAMONDS IN THE HANDLES -- TAKE THEM AS WELL.
BUT LISTEN TO ME. I'VE NEVER DONE ANYTHING LIKE THIS BEFORE. AND I NEVER WILL AGAIN.
PLEASE. LET ME ESCAPE. LET ME HAVE MY FREEDOM.
I'D LIKE TO...
...BUT I CAN'T.
I'M SORRY. I'M NOT WEARING A BADGE, BUT I MIGHT AS WELL BE.
21

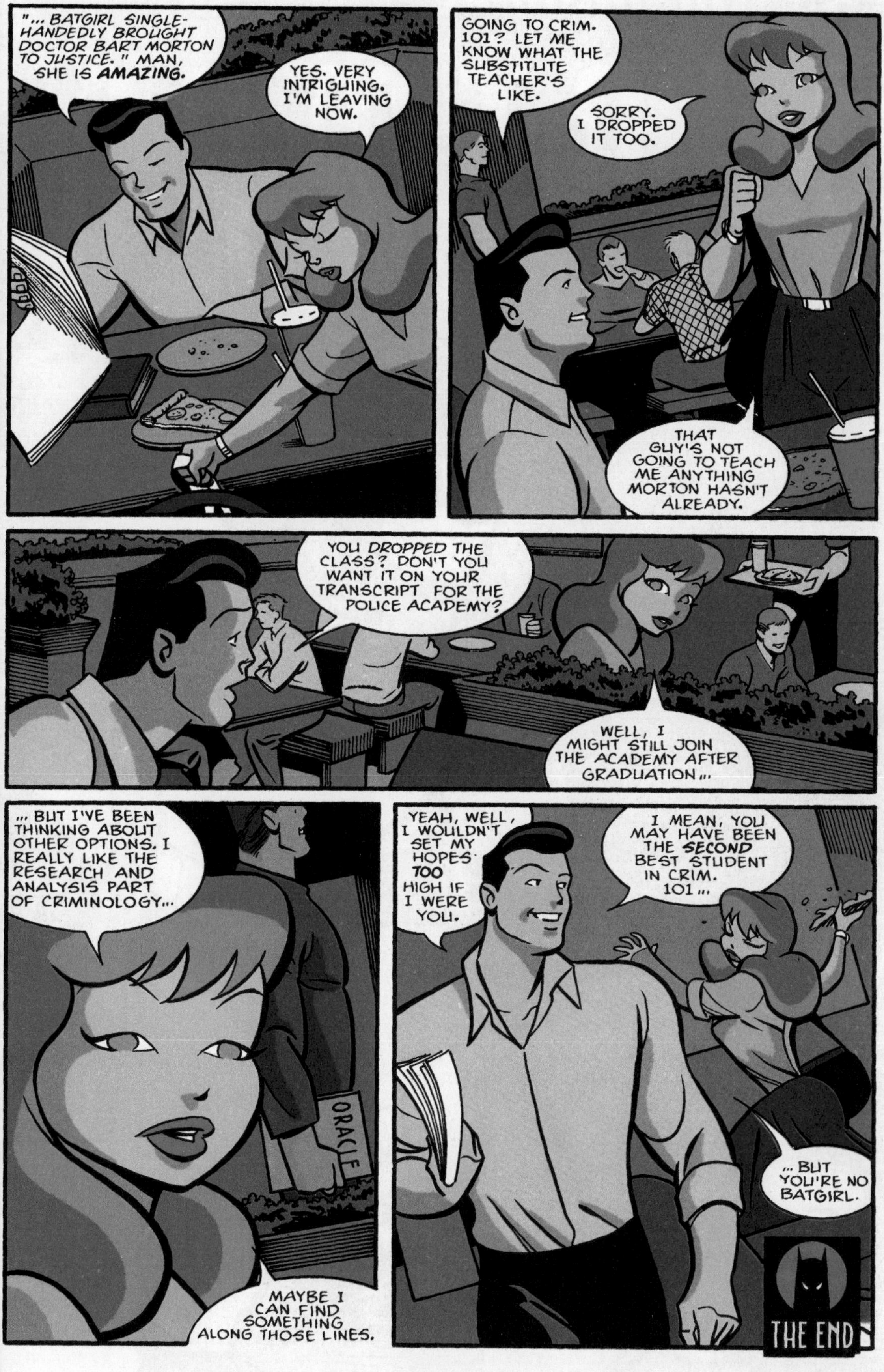
"... BATGIRL SINGLE-HANDEDLY BROUGHT DOCTOR BART MORTON TO JUSTICE." MAN, SHE IS **AMAZING.**
YES. VERY INTRIGUING. I'M LEAVING NOW.
GOING TO CRIM. 101? LET ME KNOW WHAT THE SUBSTITUTE TEACHER'S LIKE.
SORRY. I DROPPED IT TOO.
THAT GUY'S NOT GOING TO TEACH ME ANYTHING MORTON HASN'T ALREADY.
YOU *DROPPED* THE CLASS? DON'T YOU WANT IT ON YOUR TRANSCRIPT FOR THE POLICE ACADEMY?
WELL, I MIGHT STILL JOIN THE ACADEMY AFTER GRADUATION...
... BUT I'VE BEEN THINKING ABOUT OTHER OPTIONS. I REALLY LIKE THE RESEARCH AND ANALYSIS PART OF CRIMINOLOGY...
ORACLE
MAYBE I CAN FIND SOMETHING ALONG THOSE LINES.
YEAH, WELL, I WOULDN'T SET MY HOPES **TOO** HIGH IF I WERE YOU.
I MEAN, YOU MAY HAVE BEEN THE **SECOND** BEST STUDENT IN CRIM. 101...
... BUT YOU'RE NO BATGIRL.
THE END

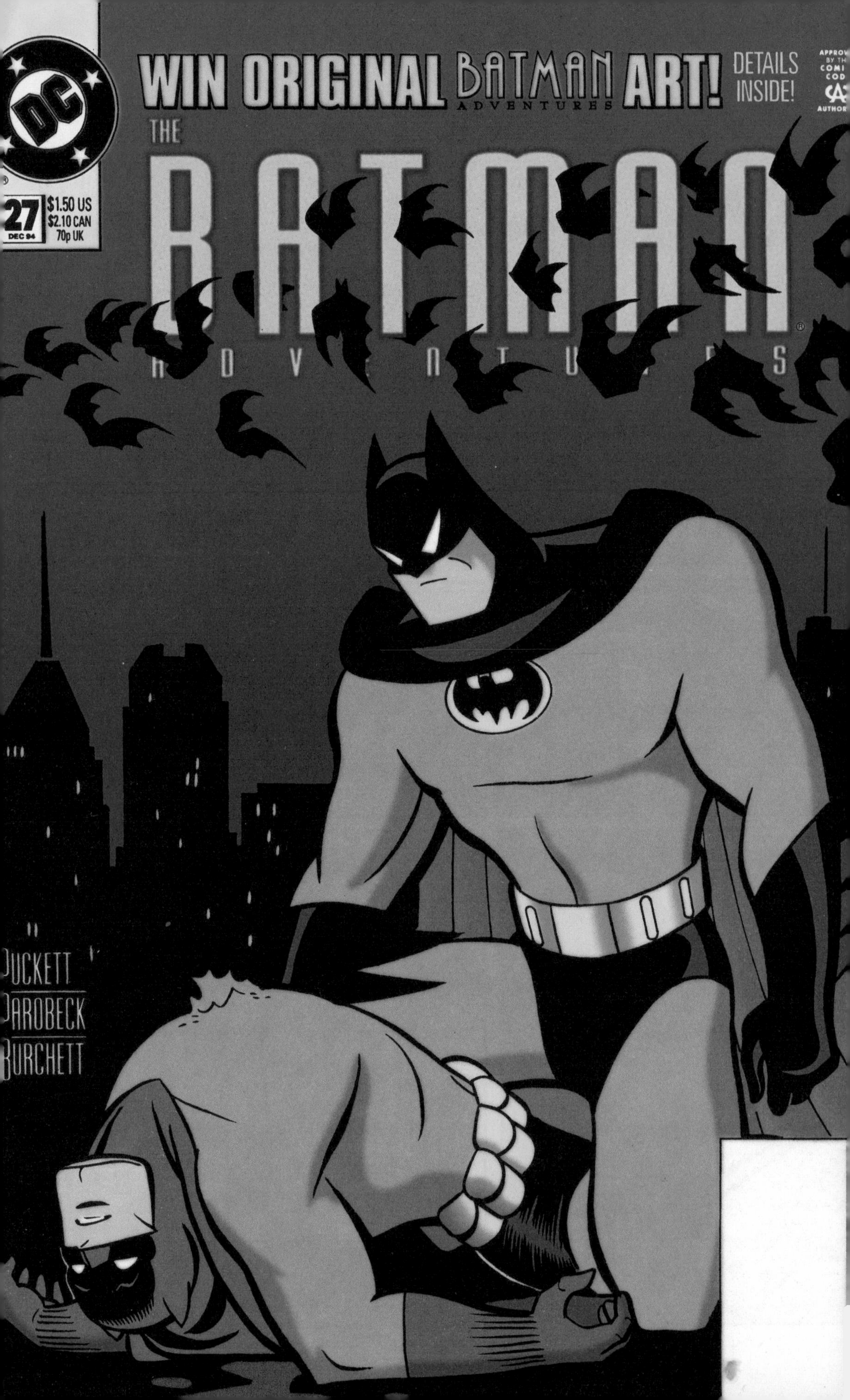
WIN ORIGINAL BATMAN ADVENTURES ART!
DETAILS INSIDE!
THE BATMAN ADVENTURES
27
DEC 94
$1.50 US
$2.10 CAN
70p UK
UCKETT
AROBECK
BURCHETT

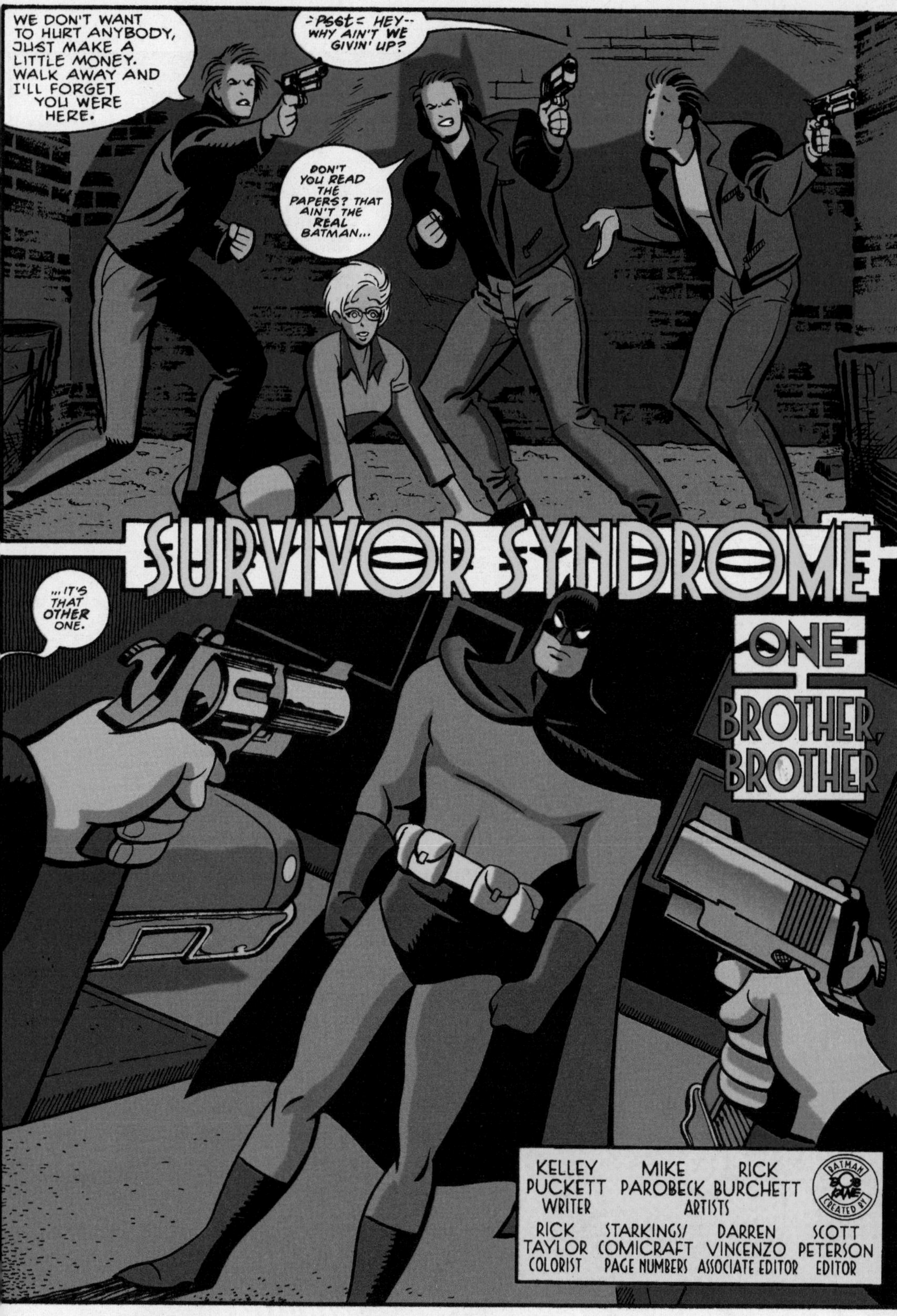

WE DON'T WANT TO HURT ANYBODY, JUST MAKE A LITTLE MONEY. WALK AWAY AND I'LL FORGET YOU WERE HERE.
=PSST= HEY-- WHY AIN'T WE GIVIN' UP?
DON'T YOU READ THE PAPERS? THAT AIN'T THE REAL BATMAN...
SURVIVOR SYNDROME
...IT'S THAT OTHER ONE.
ONE
BROTHER, BROTHER
KELLEY PUCKETT WRITER
MIKE PAROBECK RICK BURCHETT ARTISTS
BATMAN CREATED BY BOB KANE
RICK TAYLOR COLORIST
STARKINGS/ COMICRAFT PAGE NUMBERS
DARREN VINCENZO ASSOCIATE EDITOR
SCOTT PETERSON EDITOR

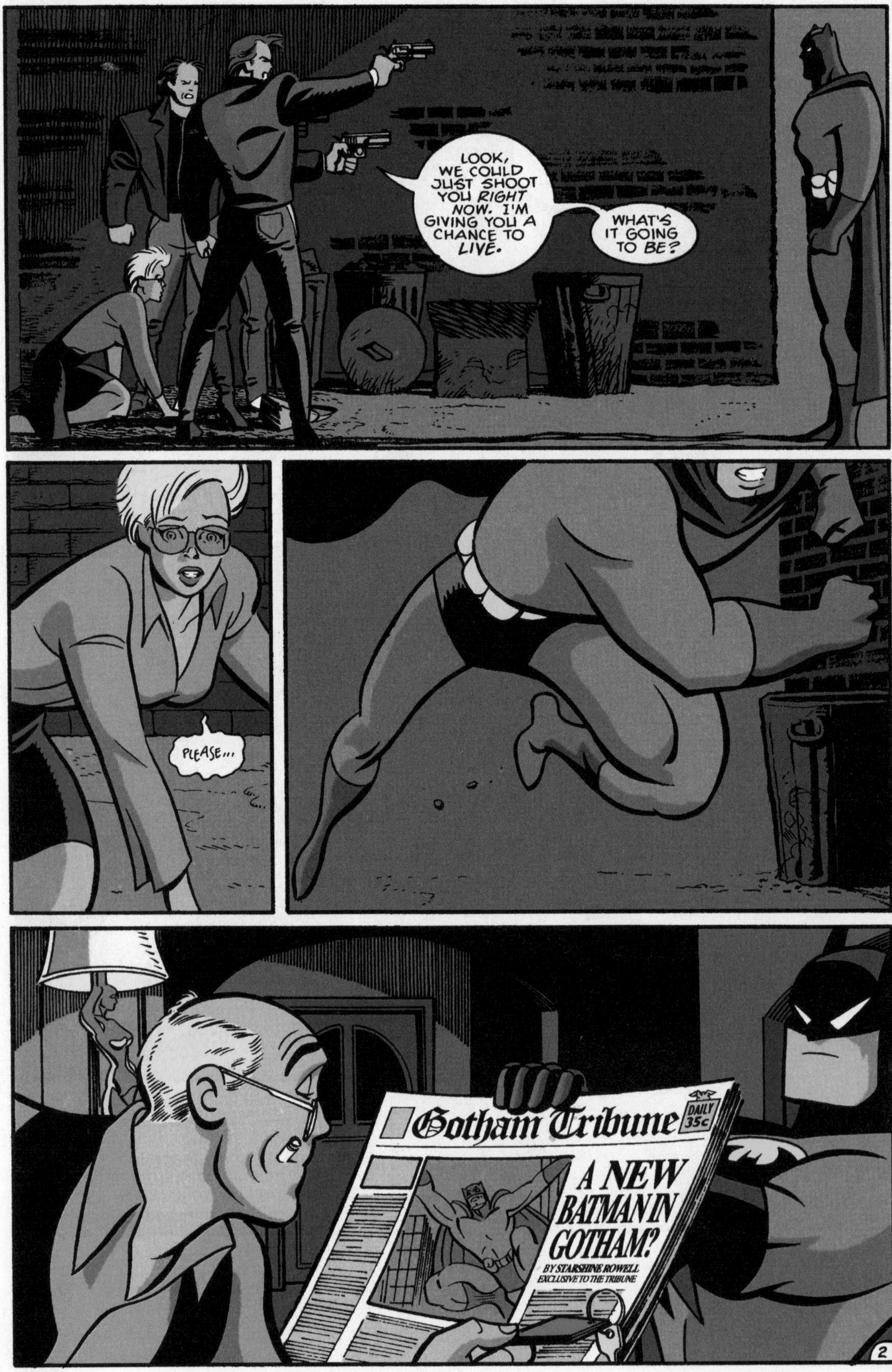
LOOK, WE COULD JUST SHOOT YOU RIGHT NOW. I'M GIVING YOU A CHANCE TO LIVE.
WHAT'S IT GOING TO BE?
PLEASE...
Gotham Tribune
DAILY 35¢
A NEW BATMAN IN GOTHAM?
BY STARSHINE ROWELL
EXCLUSIVE TO THE TRIBUNE
2

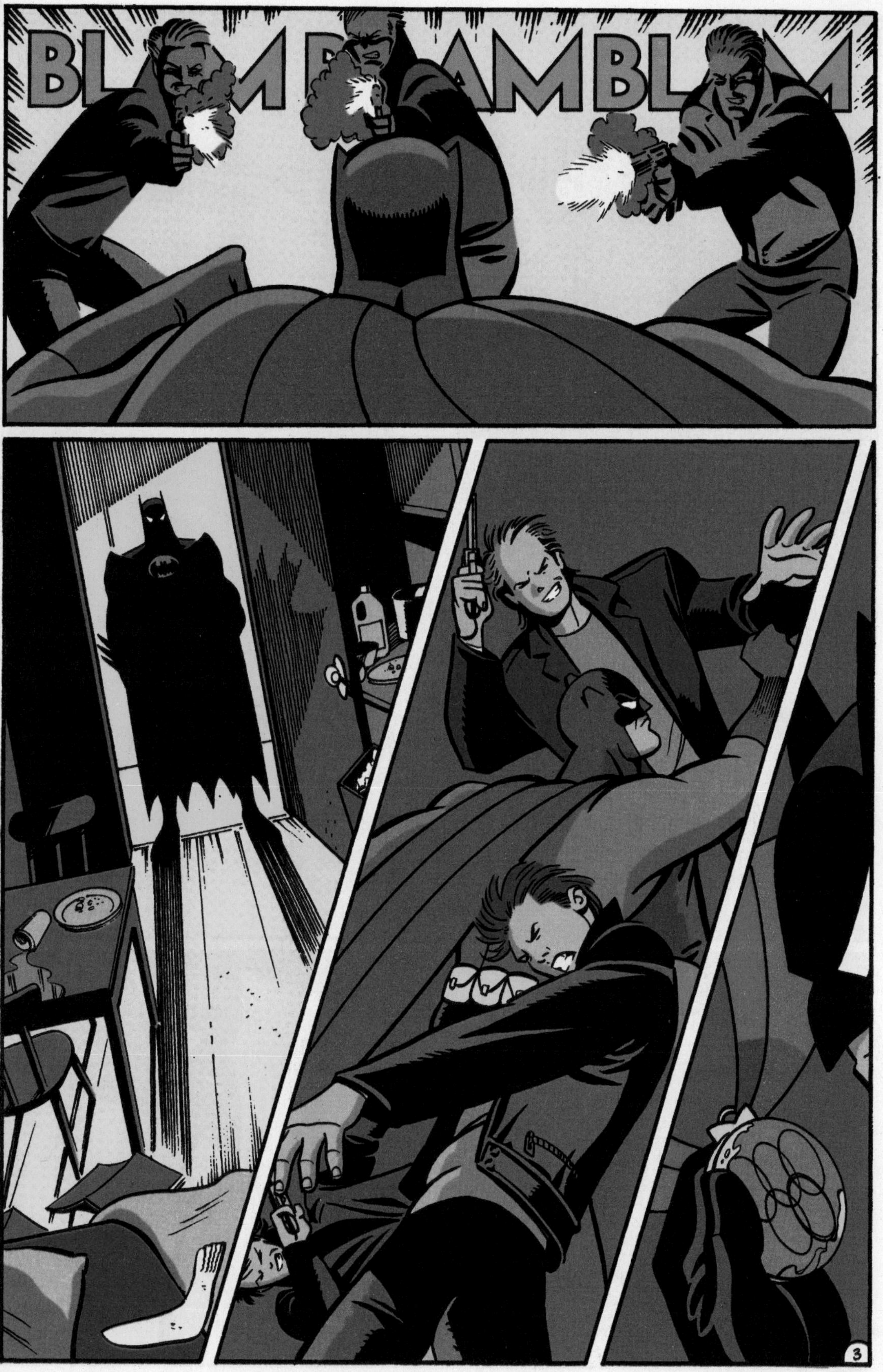

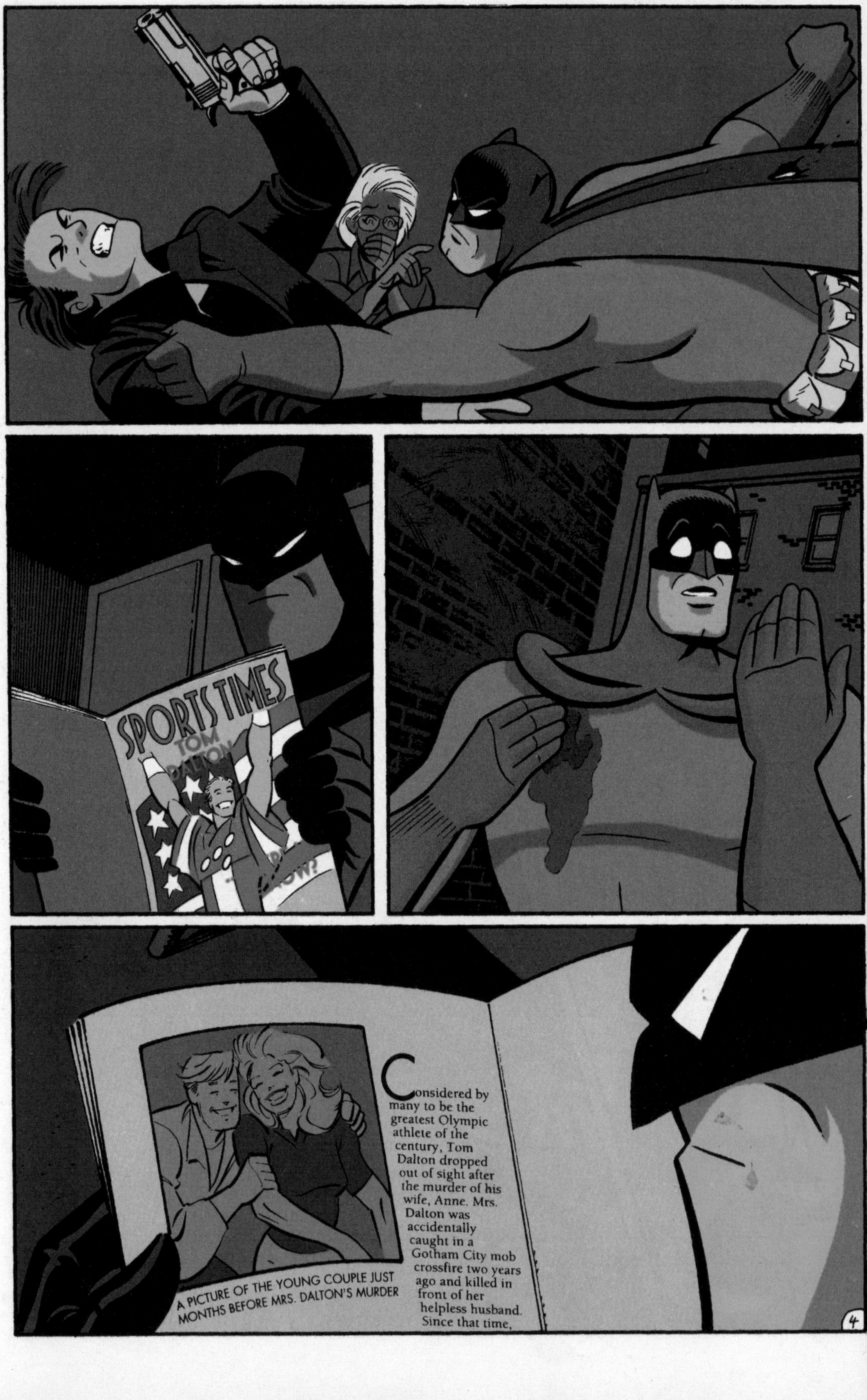
SPORTS TIMES
TOM
DALTON
Considered by many to be the greatest Olympic athlete of the century, Tom Dalton dropped out of sight after the murder of his wife, Anne. Mrs. Dalton was accidentally caught in a Gotham City mob crossfire two years ago and killed in front of her helpless husband. Since that time,
A PICTURE OF THE YOUNG COUPLE JUST MONTHS BEFORE MRS. DALTON'S MURDER

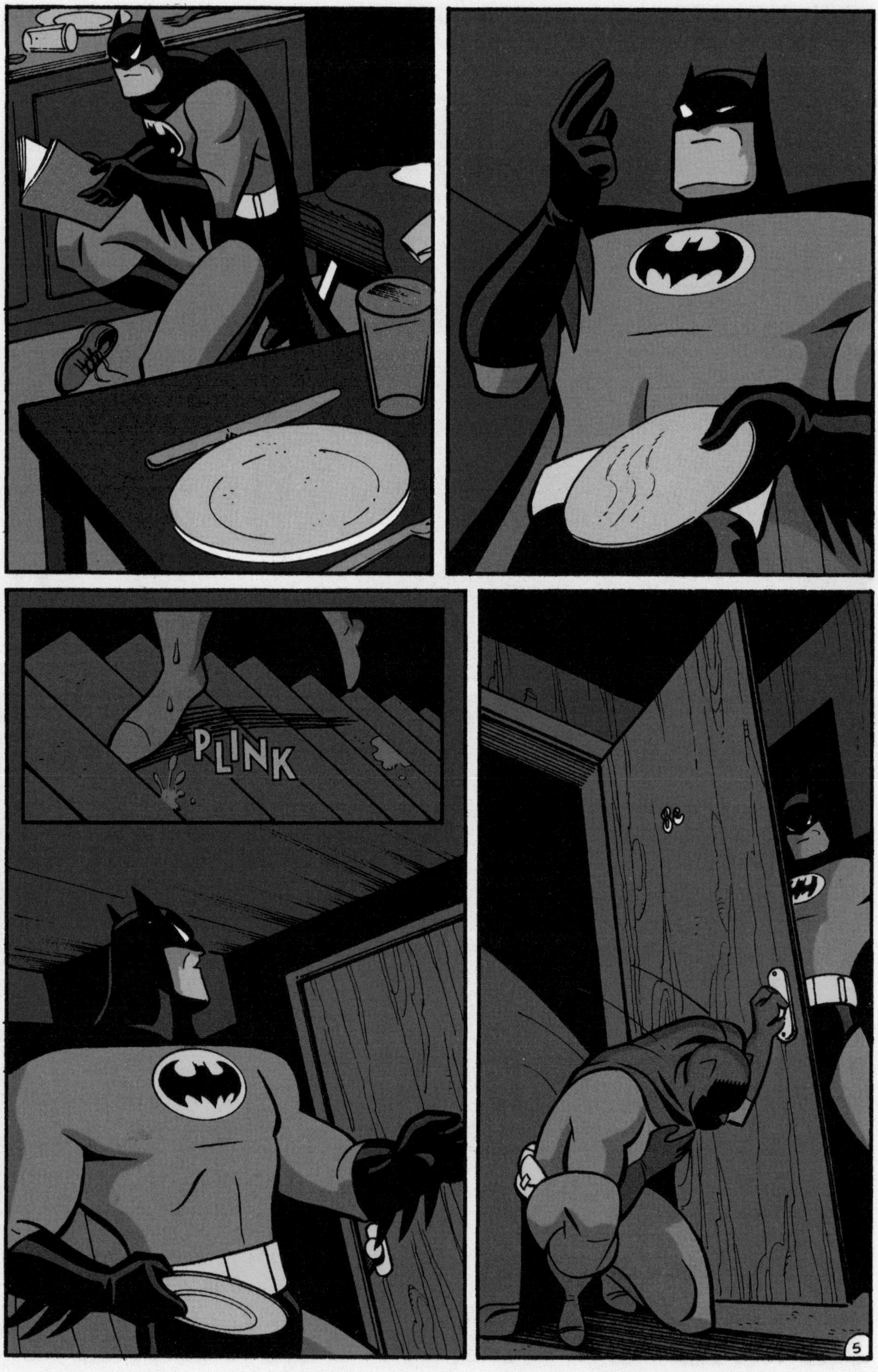
PLINK

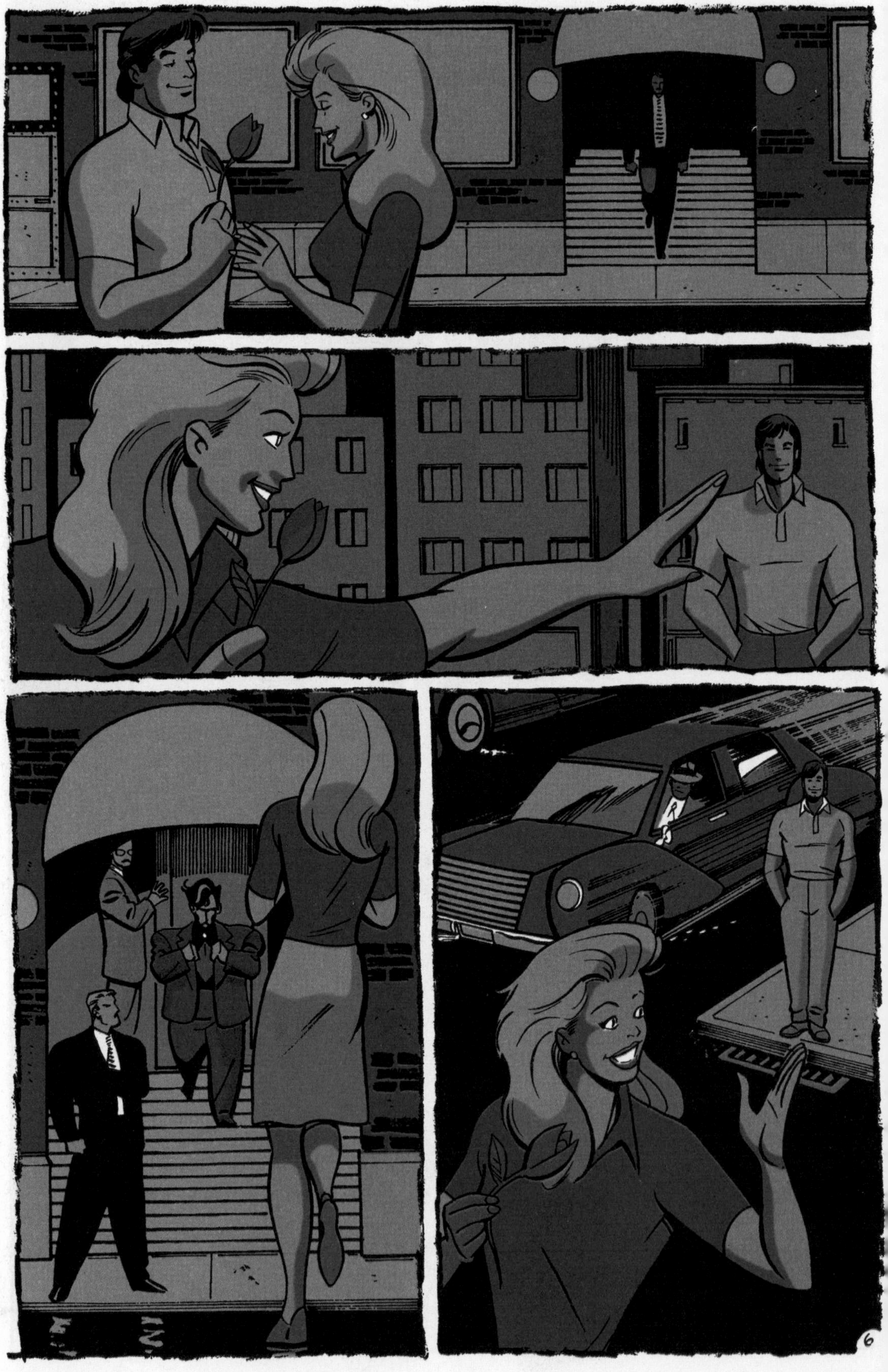

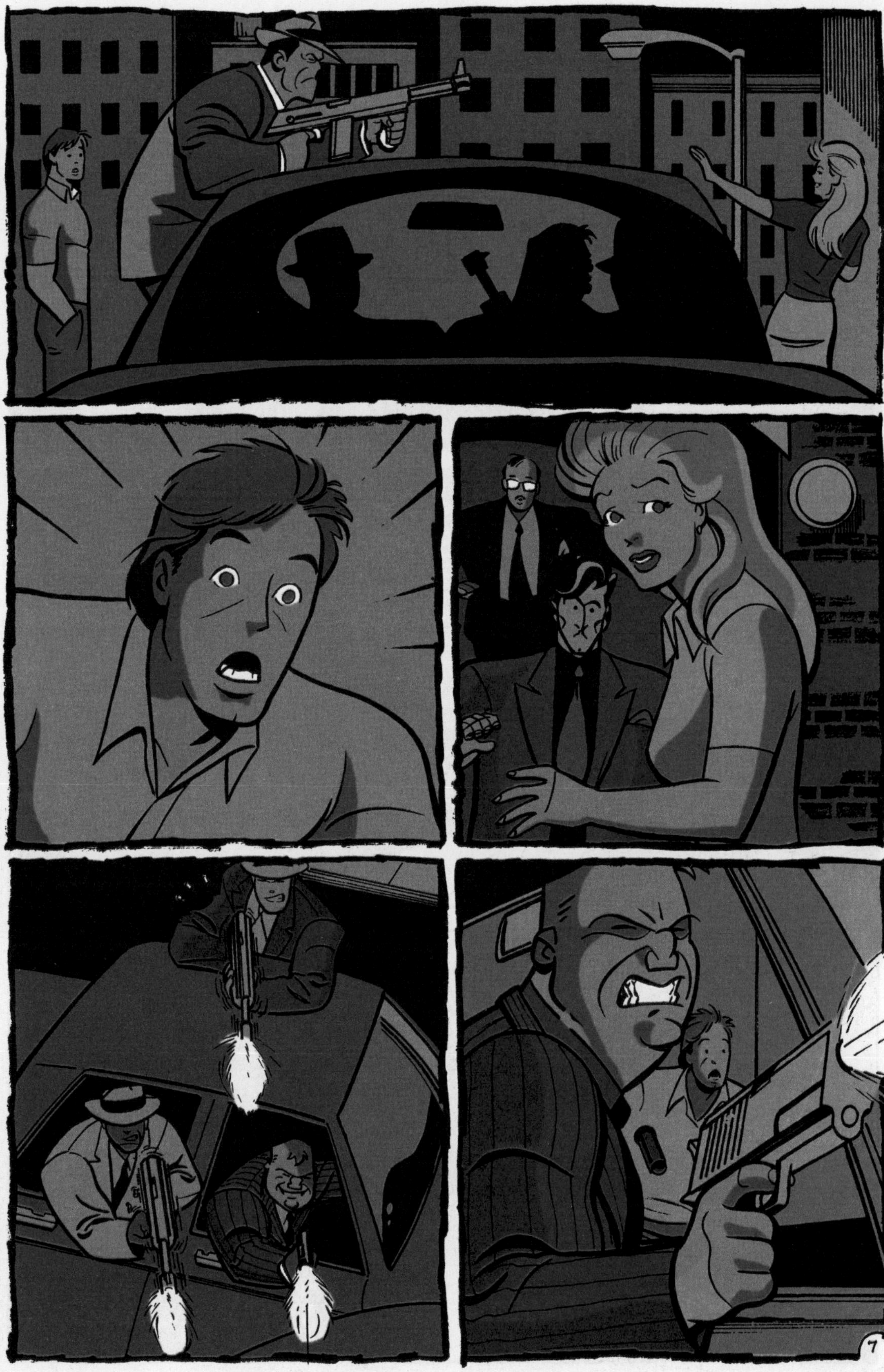

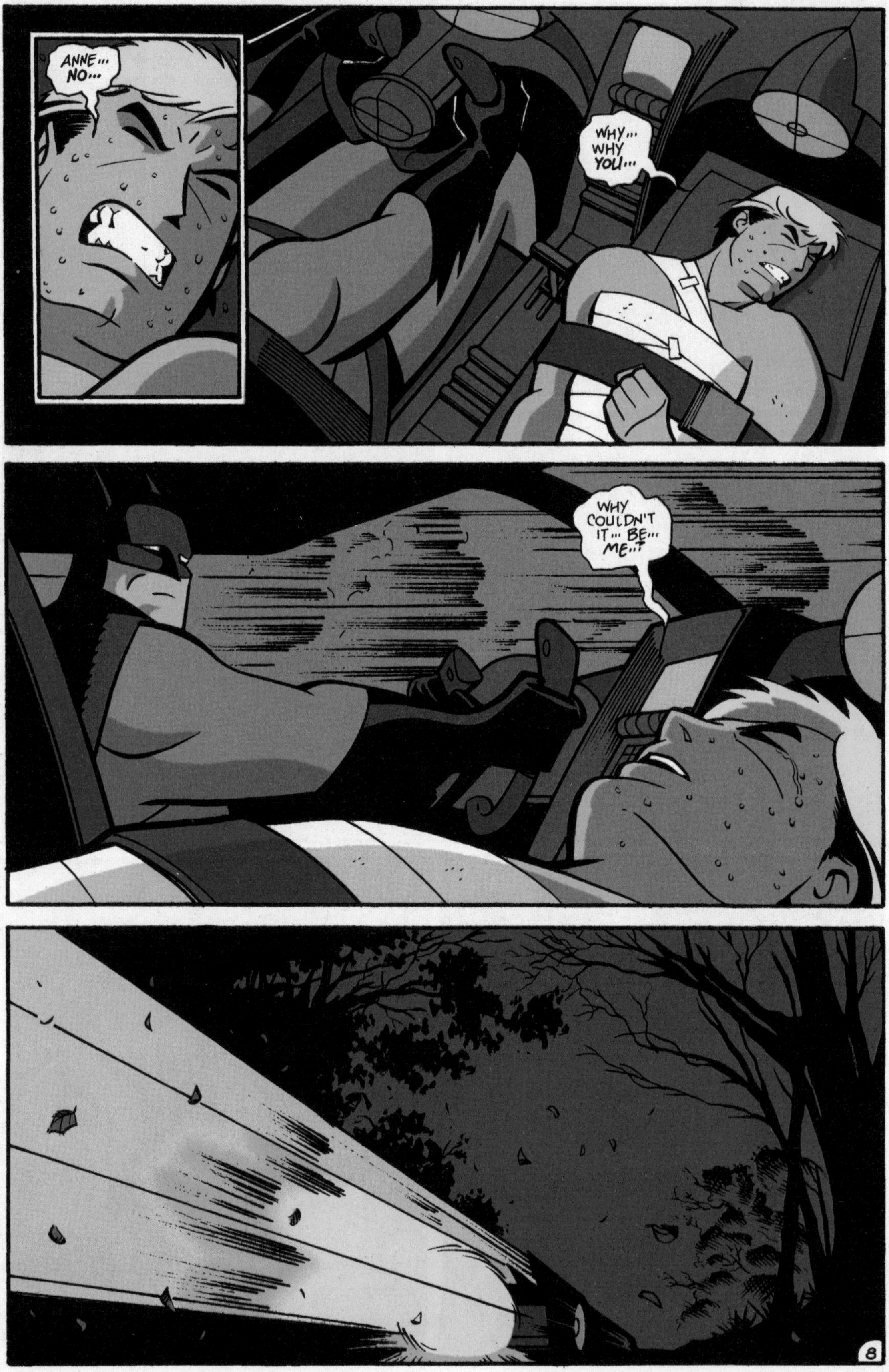
ANNE... NO...
WHY... WHY YOU...
WHY COULDN'T IT... BE... ME...?
8

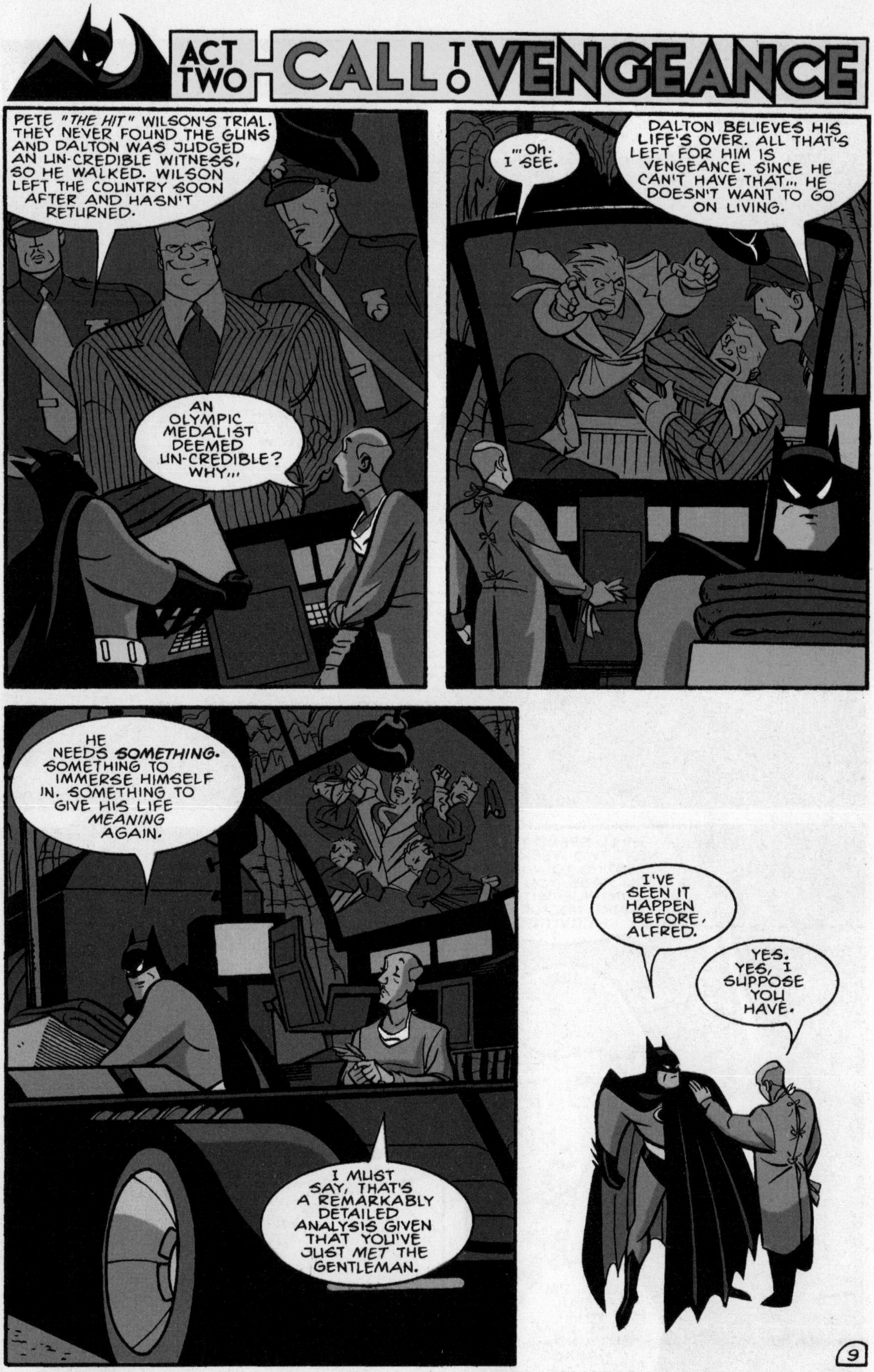
ACT TWO CALL TO VENGEANCE
PETE "THE HIT" WILSON'S TRIAL. THEY NEVER FOUND THE GUNS AND DALTON WAS JUDGED AN UN-CREDIBLE WITNESS, SO HE WALKED. WILSON LEFT THE COUNTRY SOON AFTER AND HASN'T RETURNED.
AN OLYMPIC MEDALIST DEEMED UN-CREDIBLE? WHY...
...Oh. I SEE.
DALTON BELIEVES HIS LIFE'S OVER. ALL THAT'S LEFT FOR HIM IS VENGEANCE. SINCE HE CAN'T HAVE THAT... HE DOESN'T WANT TO GO ON LIVING.
HE NEEDS SOMETHING. SOMETHING TO IMMERSE HIMSELF IN. SOMETHING TO GIVE HIS LIFE MEANING AGAIN.
I MUST SAY, THAT'S A REMARKABLY DETAILED ANALYSIS GIVEN THAT YOU'VE JUST MET THE GENTLEMAN.
I'VE SEEN IT HAPPEN BEFORE, ALFRED.
YES. YES, I SUPPOSE YOU HAVE.

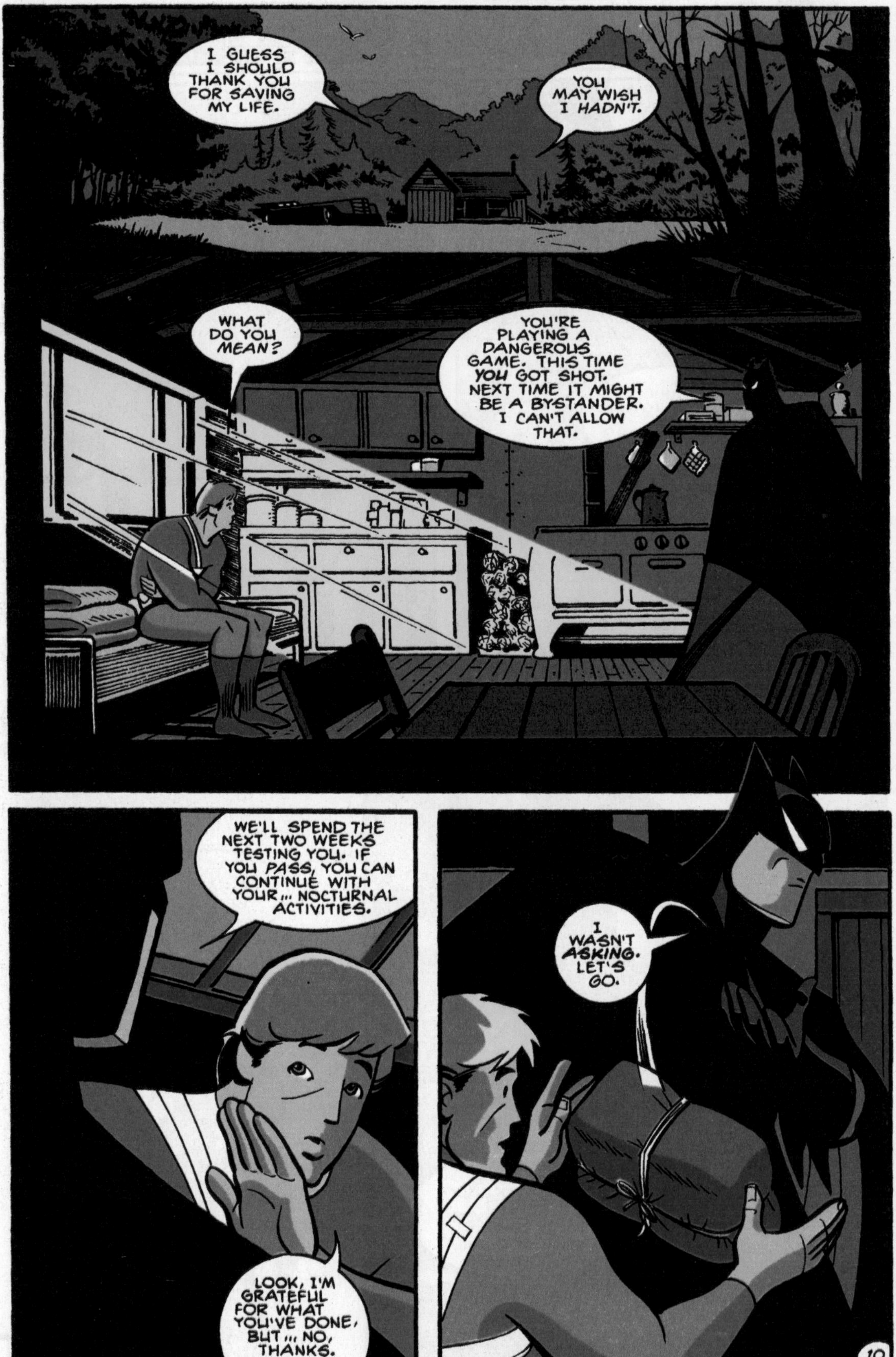

I GUESS I SHOULD THANK YOU FOR SAVING MY LIFE.
YOU MAY WISH I HADN'T.
WHAT DO YOU MEAN?
YOU'RE PLAYING A DANGEROUS GAME. THIS TIME YOU GOT SHOT. NEXT TIME IT MIGHT BE A BYSTANDER. I CAN'T ALLOW THAT.
WE'LL SPEND THE NEXT TWO WEEKS TESTING YOU. IF YOU PASS, YOU CAN CONTINUE WITH YOUR... NOCTURNAL ACTIVITIES.
LOOK, I'M GRATEFUL FOR WHAT YOU'VE DONE, BUT... NO, THANKS.
I WASN'T ASKING. LET'S GO.
10

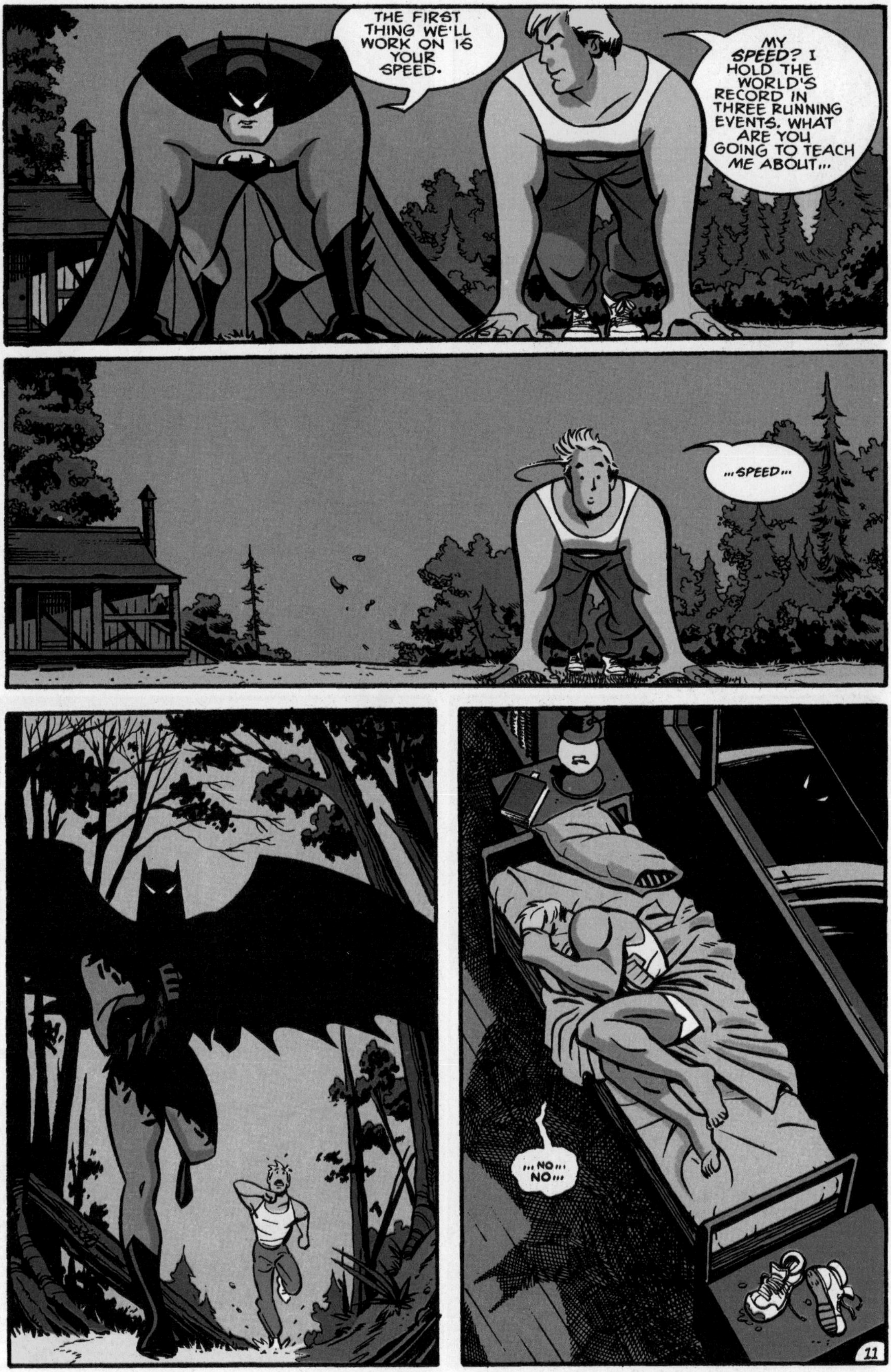
THE FIRST THING WE'LL WORK ON IS YOUR SPEED.
MY SPEED? I HOLD THE WORLD'S RECORD IN THREE RUNNING EVENTS. WHAT ARE YOU GOING TO TEACH ME ABOUT...
...SPEED...
...NO... NO...
11

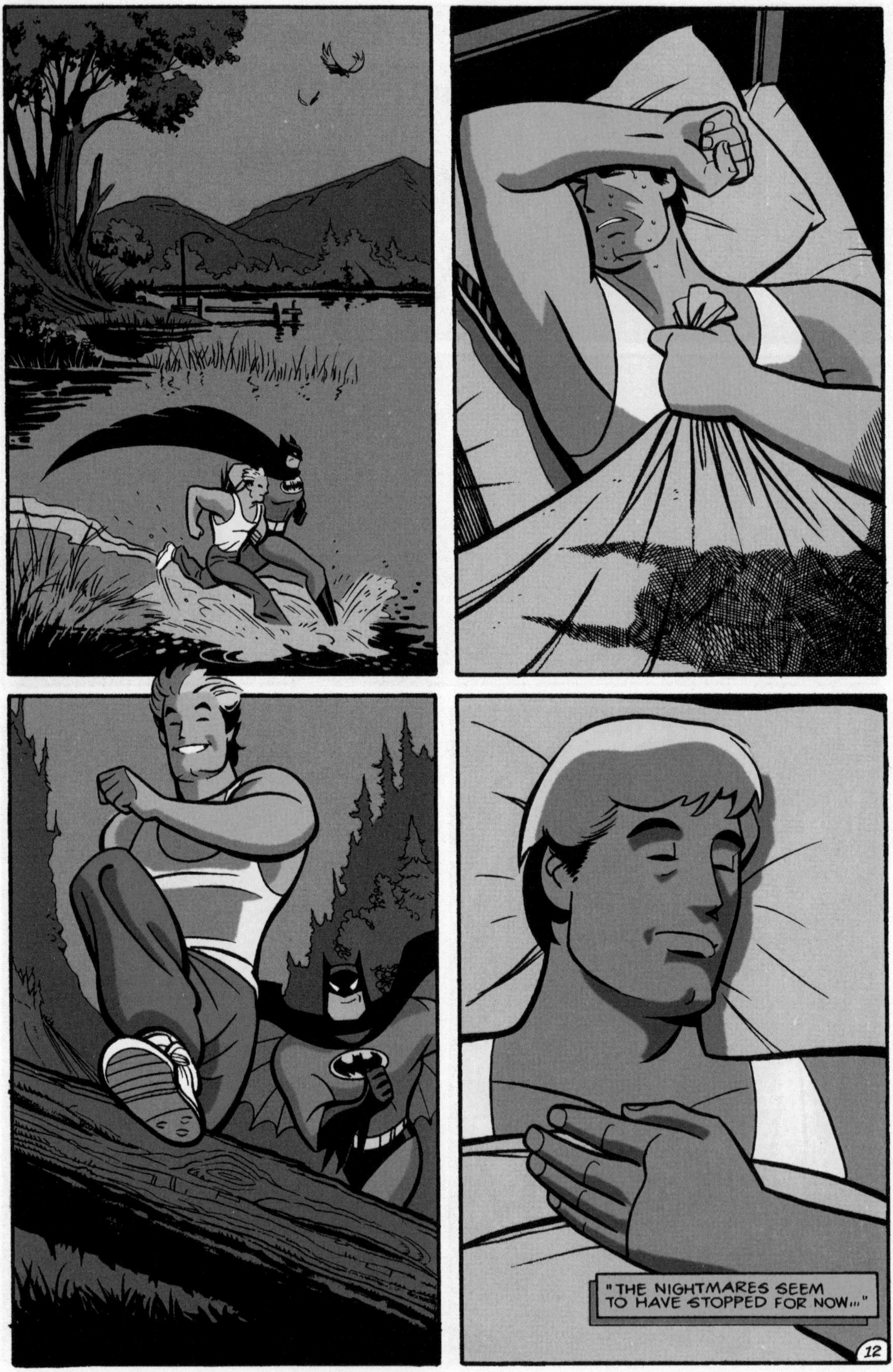
"THE NIGHTMARES SEEM TO HAVE STOPPED FOR NOW..."

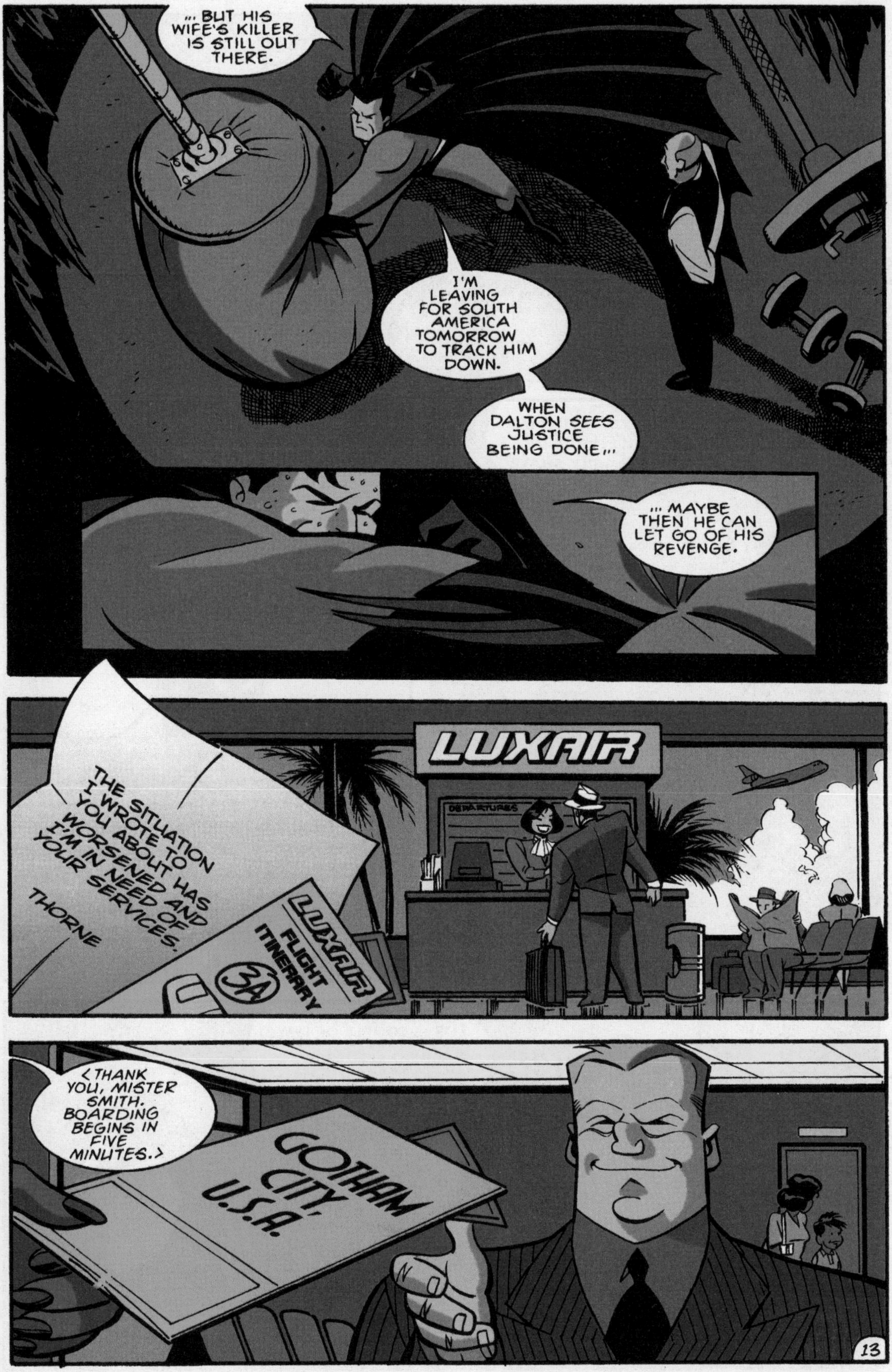

...BUT HIS WIFE'S KILLER IS STILL OUT THERE.
I'M LEAVING FOR SOUTH AMERICA TOMORROW TO TRACK HIM DOWN.
WHEN DALTON SEES JUSTICE BEING DONE...
...MAYBE THEN HE CAN LET GO OF HIS REVENGE.
LUXAIR
DEPARTURES
THE SITUATION I WROTE TO YOU ABOUT HAS WORSENED AND I'M IN NEED OF YOUR SERVICES.
THORNE
LUXAIR
FLIGHT ITINERARY
3A
<THANK YOU, MISTER SMITH. BOARDING BEGINS IN FIVE MINUTES.>
GOTHAM CITY, U.S.A.

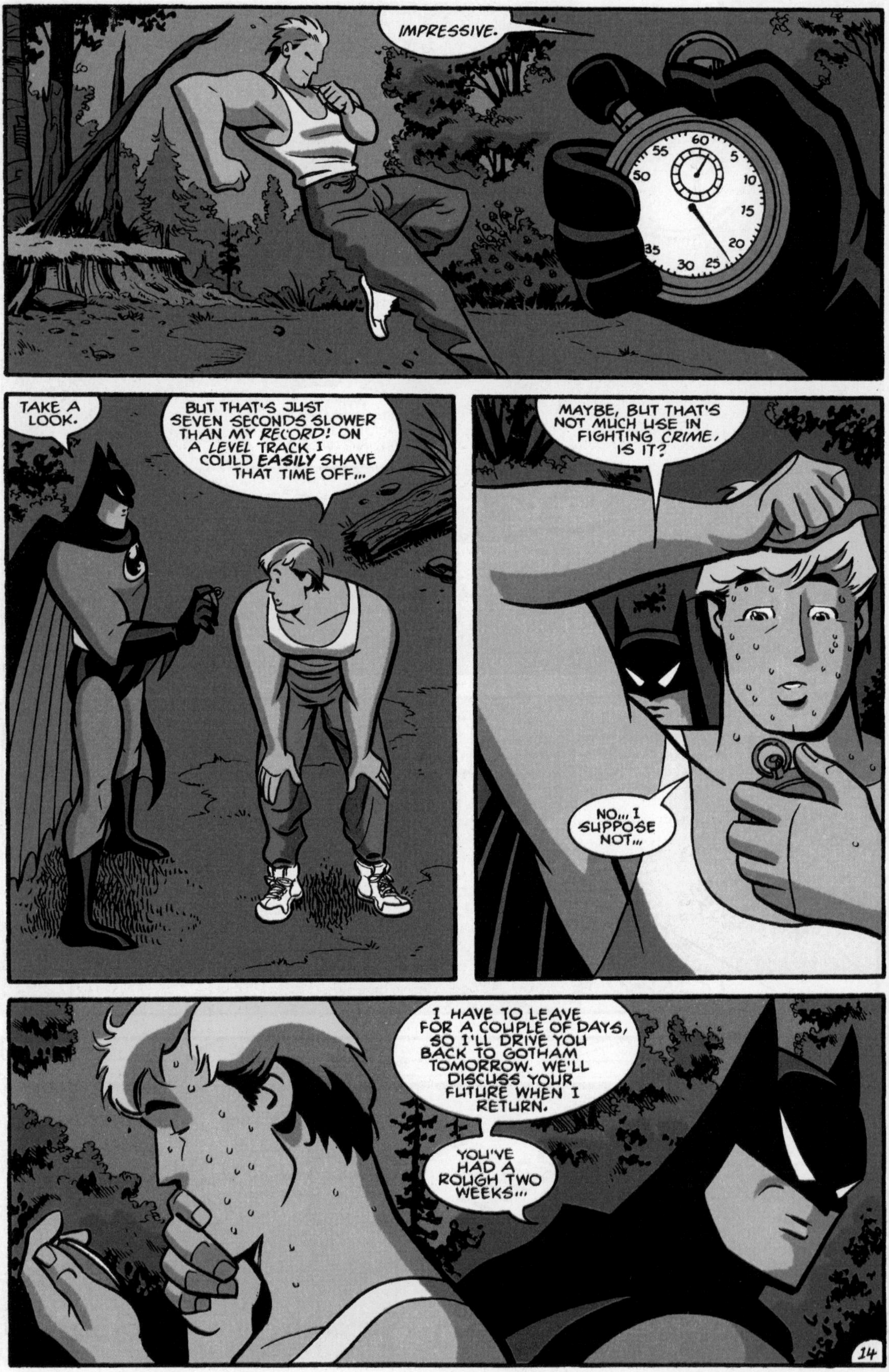
IMPRESSIVE.
TAKE A LOOK.
BUT THAT'S JUST SEVEN SECONDS SLOWER THAN MY RECORD! ON A LEVEL TRACK I COULD EASILY SHAVE THAT TIME OFF...
MAYBE, BUT THAT'S NOT MUCH USE IN FIGHTING CRIME, IS IT?
NO... I SUPPOSE NOT...
I HAVE TO LEAVE FOR A COUPLE OF DAYS, SO I'LL DRIVE YOU BACK TO GOTHAM TOMORROW. WE'LL DISCUSS YOUR FUTURE WHEN I RETURN.
YOU'VE HAD A ROUGH TWO WEEKS...
14

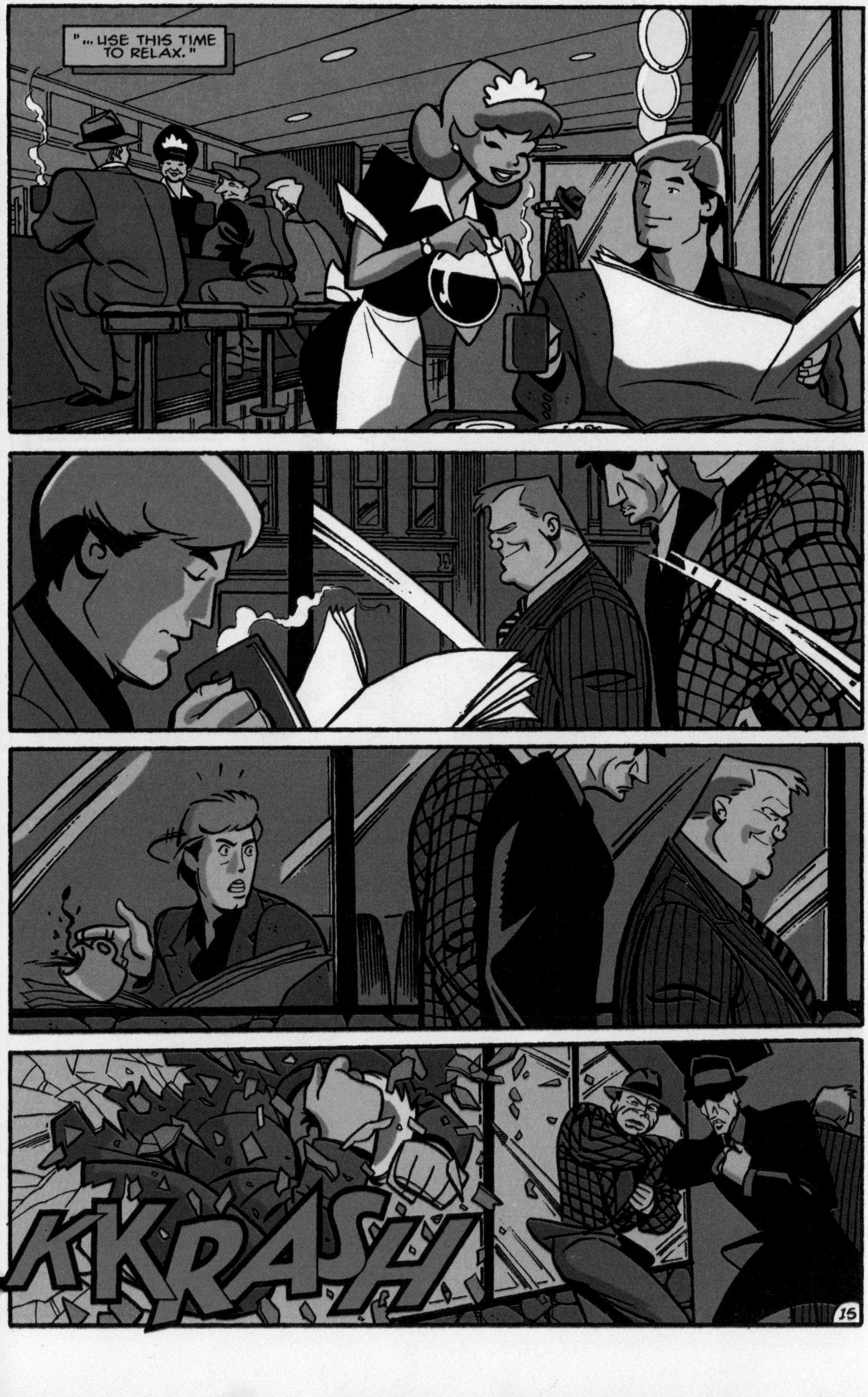
"...USE THIS TIME TO RELAX."
KKRASH

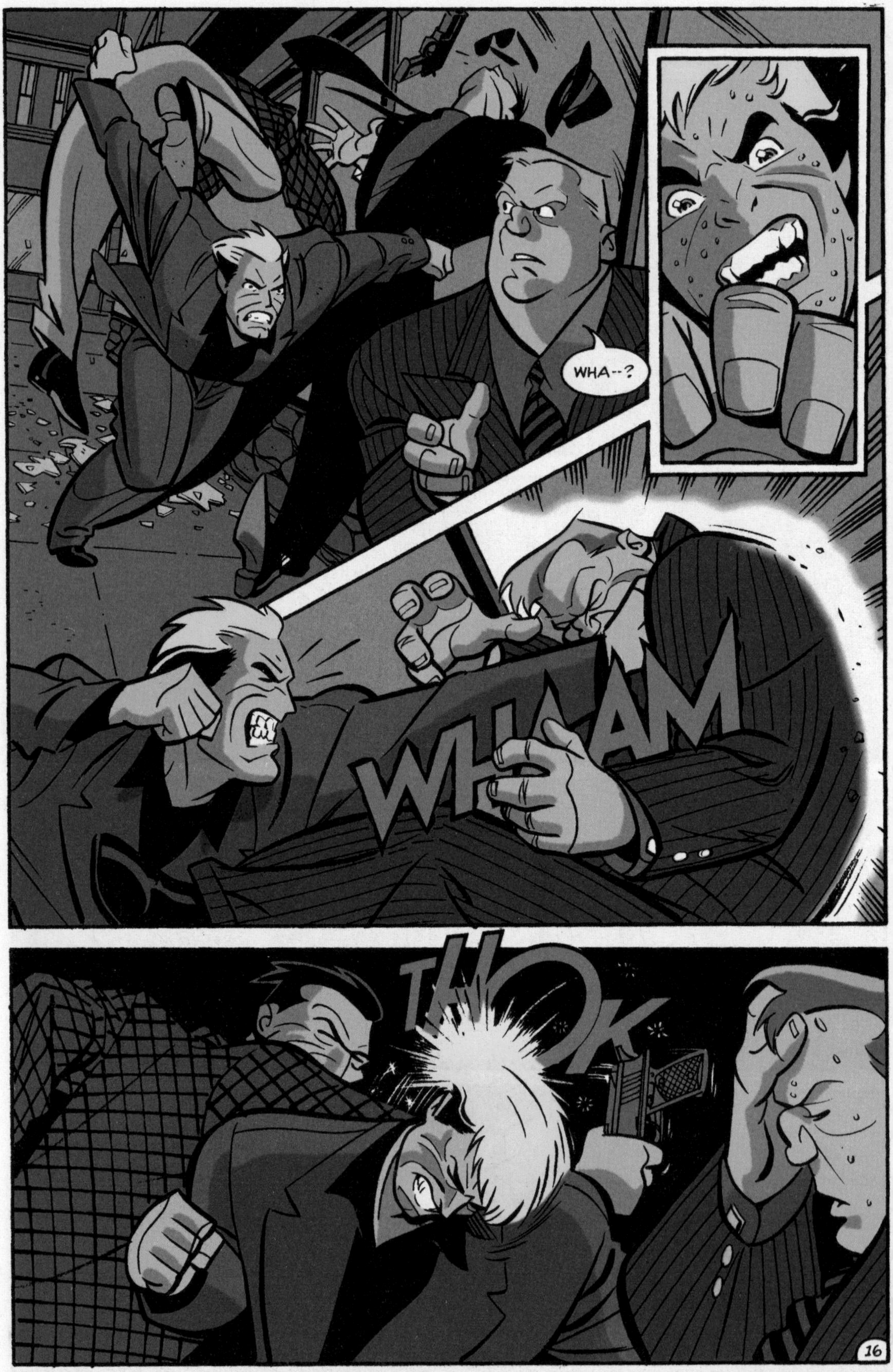
WHA--?
WHAM
THOK

ACT THREE THE UPPER HAND

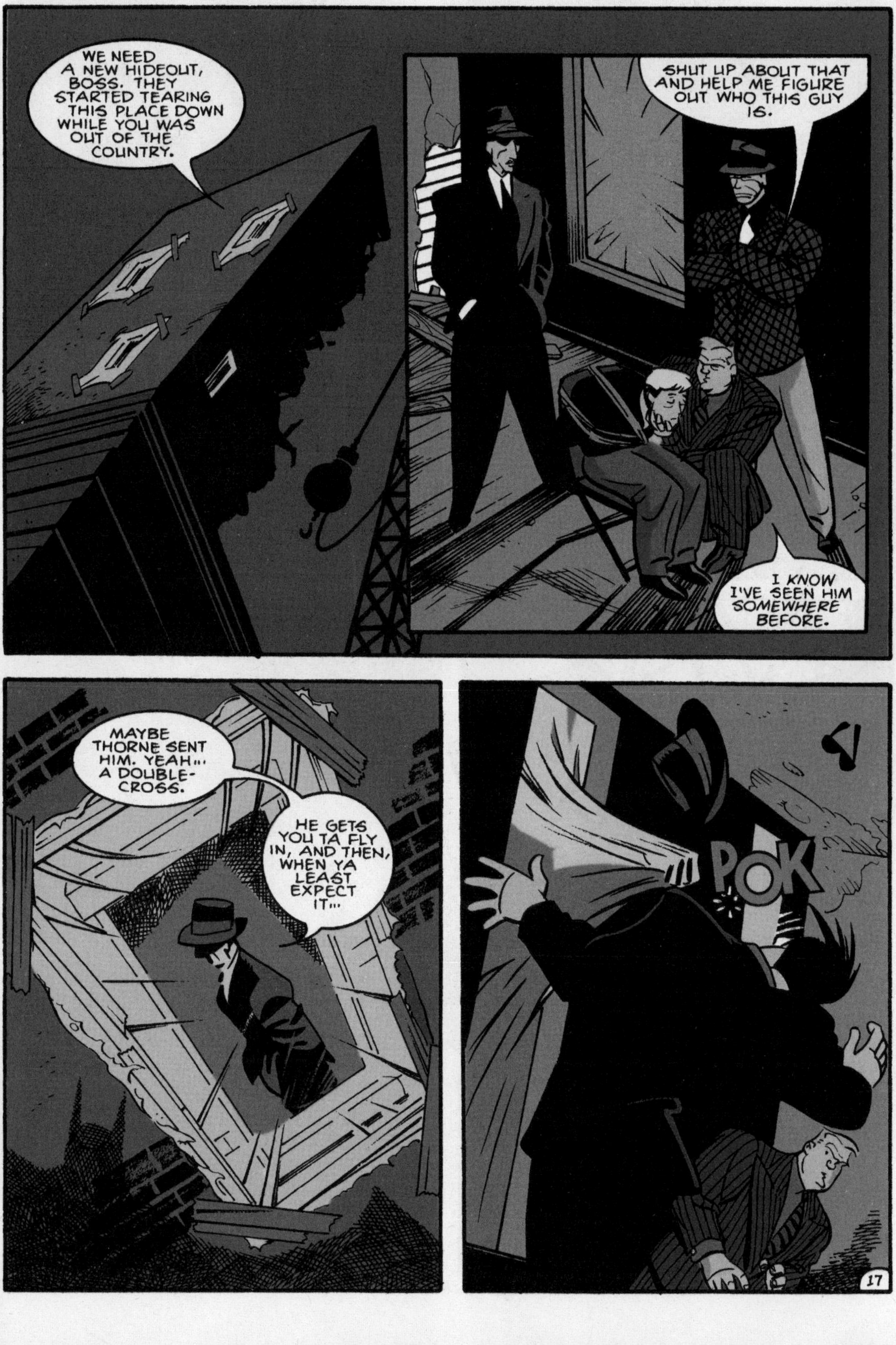

WE NEED A NEW HIDEOUT, BOSS. THEY STARTED TEARING THIS PLACE DOWN WHILE YOU WAS OUT OF THE COUNTRY.
SHUT UP ABOUT THAT AND HELP ME FIGURE OUT WHO THIS GUY IS.
I KNOW I'VE SEEN HIM SOMEWHERE BEFORE.
MAYBE THORNE SENT HIM. YEAH... A DOUBLE-CROSS.
HE GETS YOU TA FLY IN, AND THEN, WHEN YA LEAST EXPECT IT...
POK

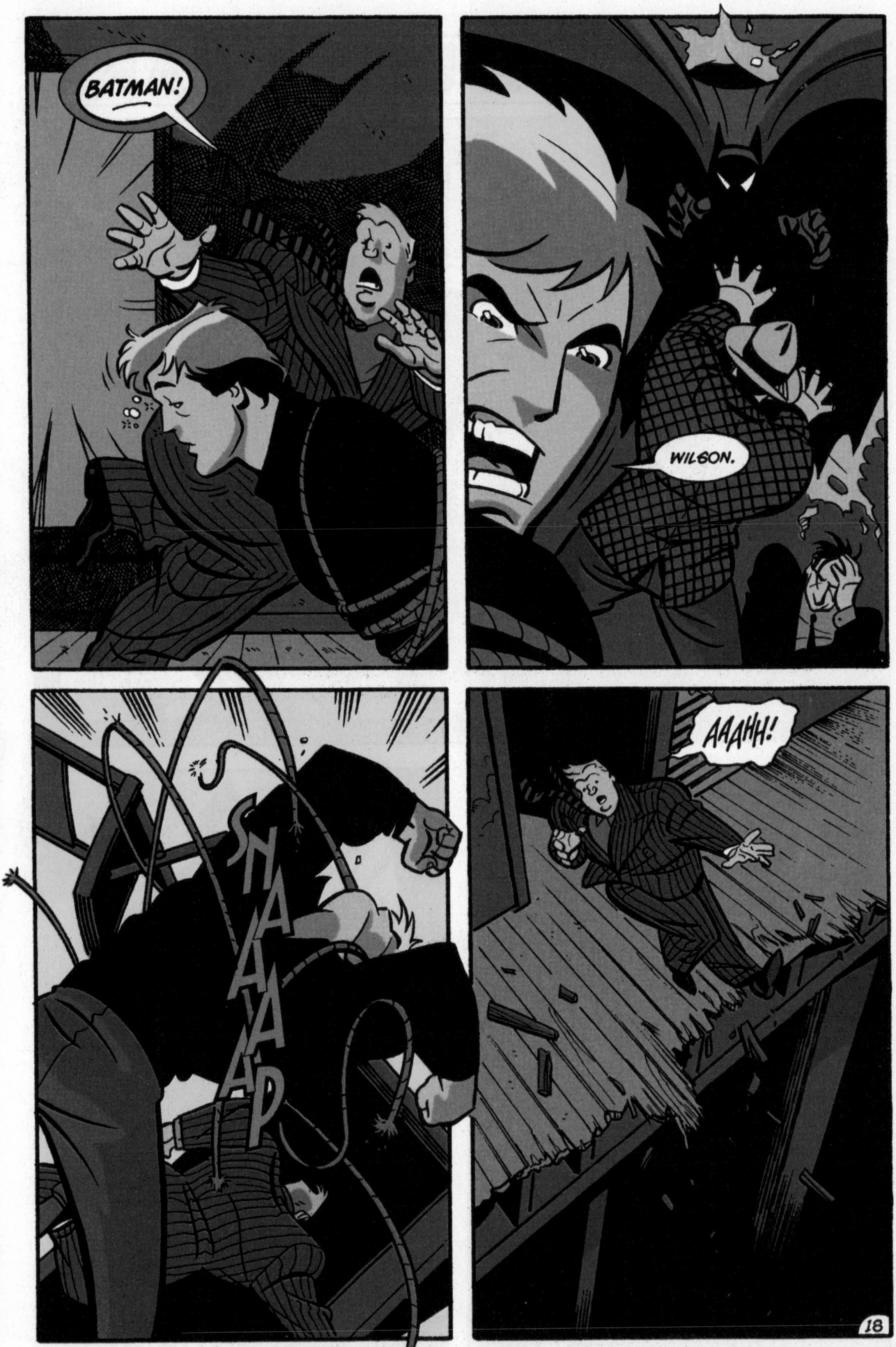
BATMAN!
WILSON.
SHAAAAP
AAAHH!

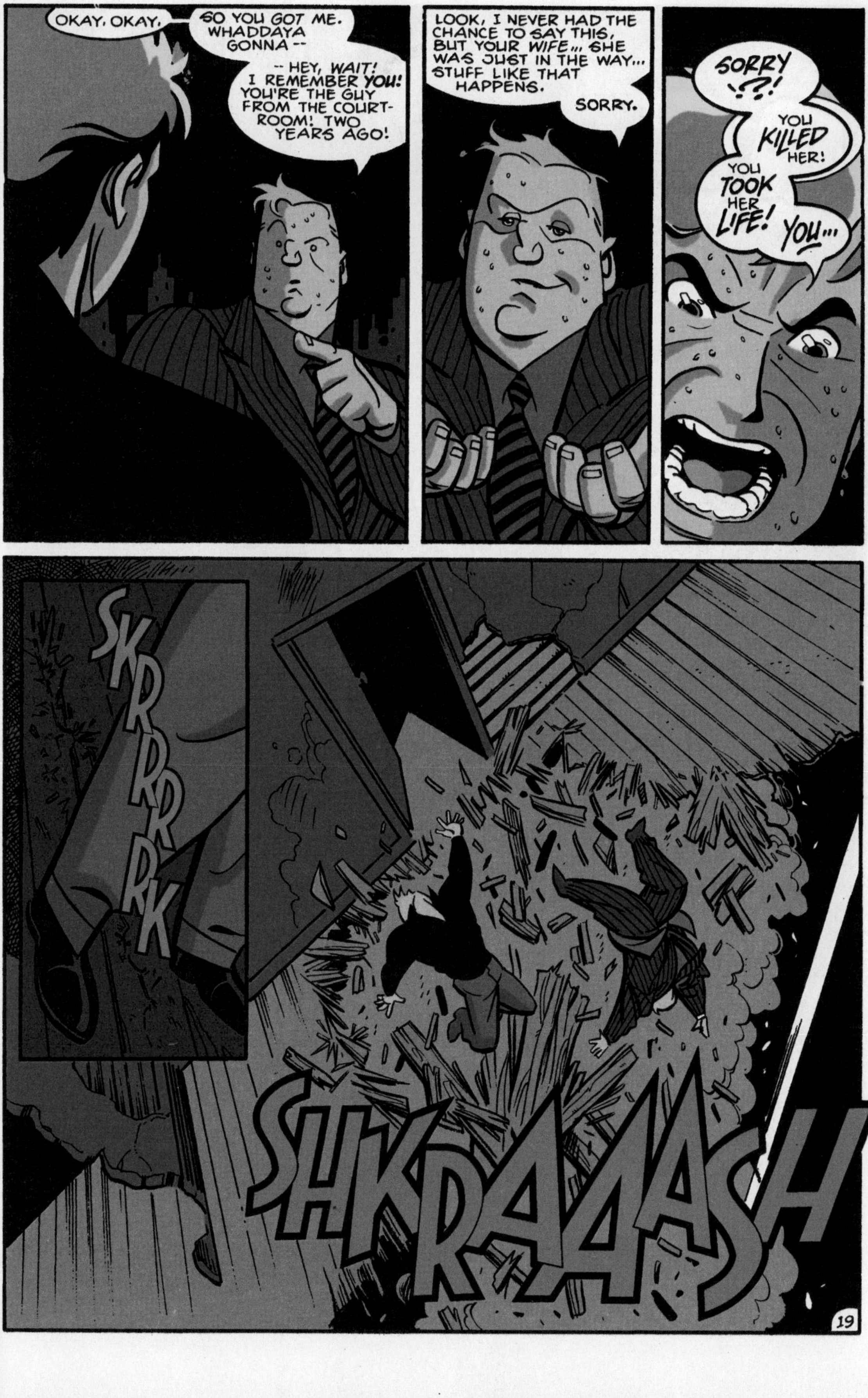
OKAY, OKAY.
SO YOU GOT ME. WHADDAYA GONNA --
-- HEY, WAIT! I REMEMBER YOU! YOU'RE THE GUY FROM THE COURT-ROOM! TWO YEARS AGO!
LOOK, I NEVER HAD THE CHANCE TO SAY THIS, BUT YOUR WIFE... SHE WAS JUST IN THE WAY... STUFF LIKE THAT HAPPENS.
SORRY.
SORRY ?!?!
YOU KILLED HER!
YOU TOOK HER LIFE!
YOU...
SKRRRRK
SHKRAAASH

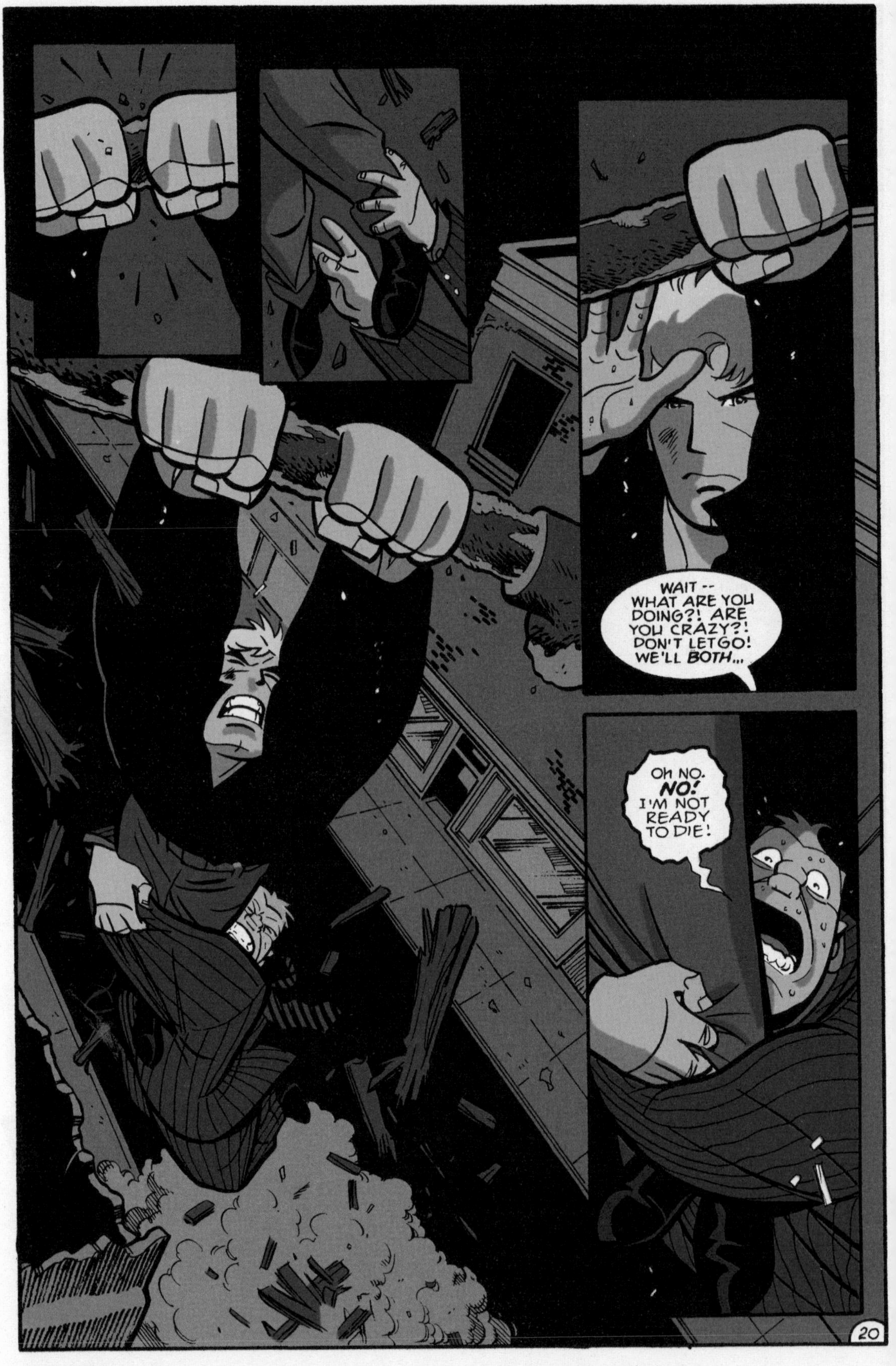
WAIT -- WHAT ARE YOU DOING?! ARE YOU CRAZY?! DON'T LETGO! WE'LL *BOTH*...
OH NO. ***NO!*** I'M NOT READY TO DIE!

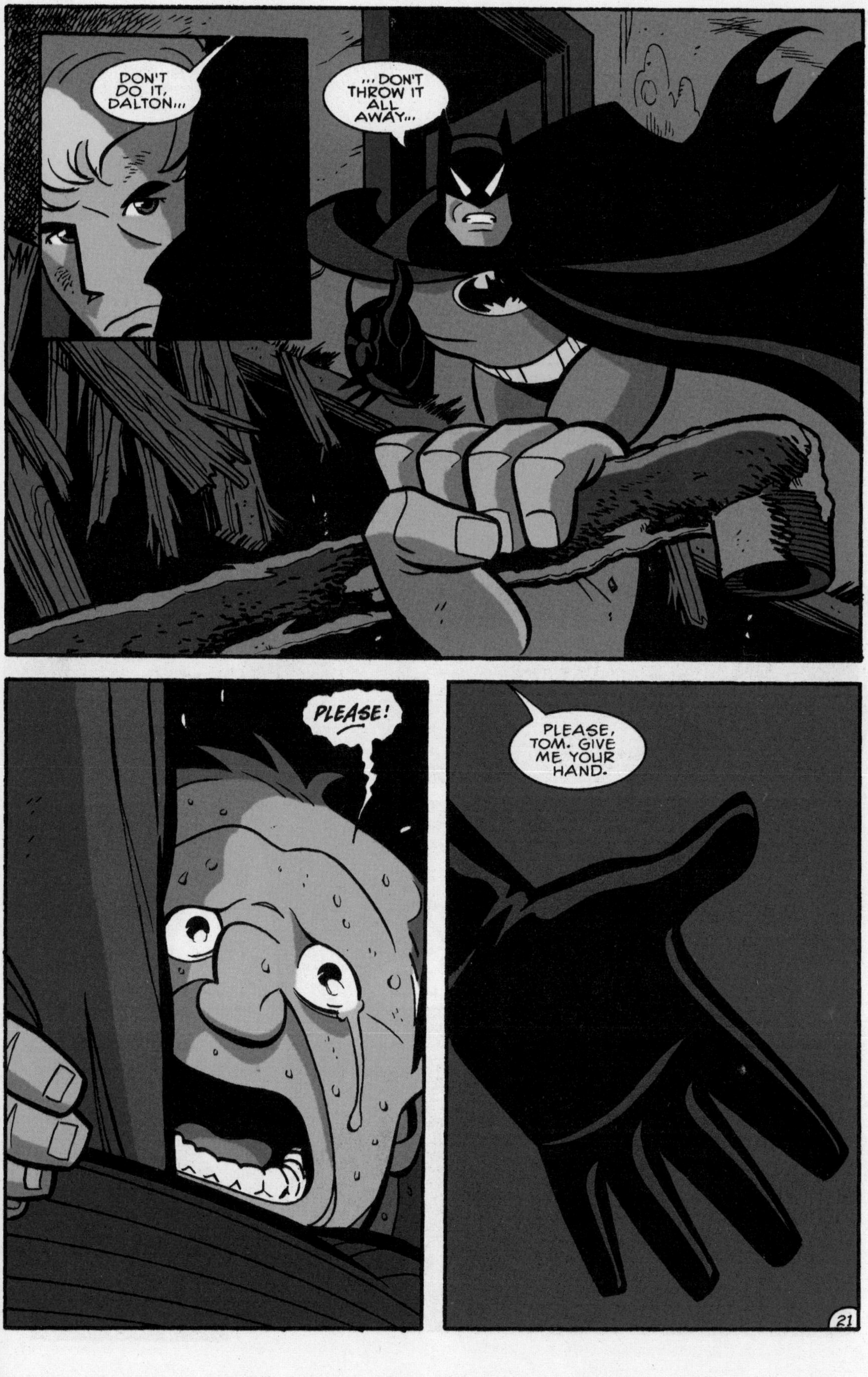
DON'T DO IT, DALTON...
...DON'T THROW IT ALL AWAY...
PLEASE!
PLEASE, TOM. GIVE ME YOUR HAND.

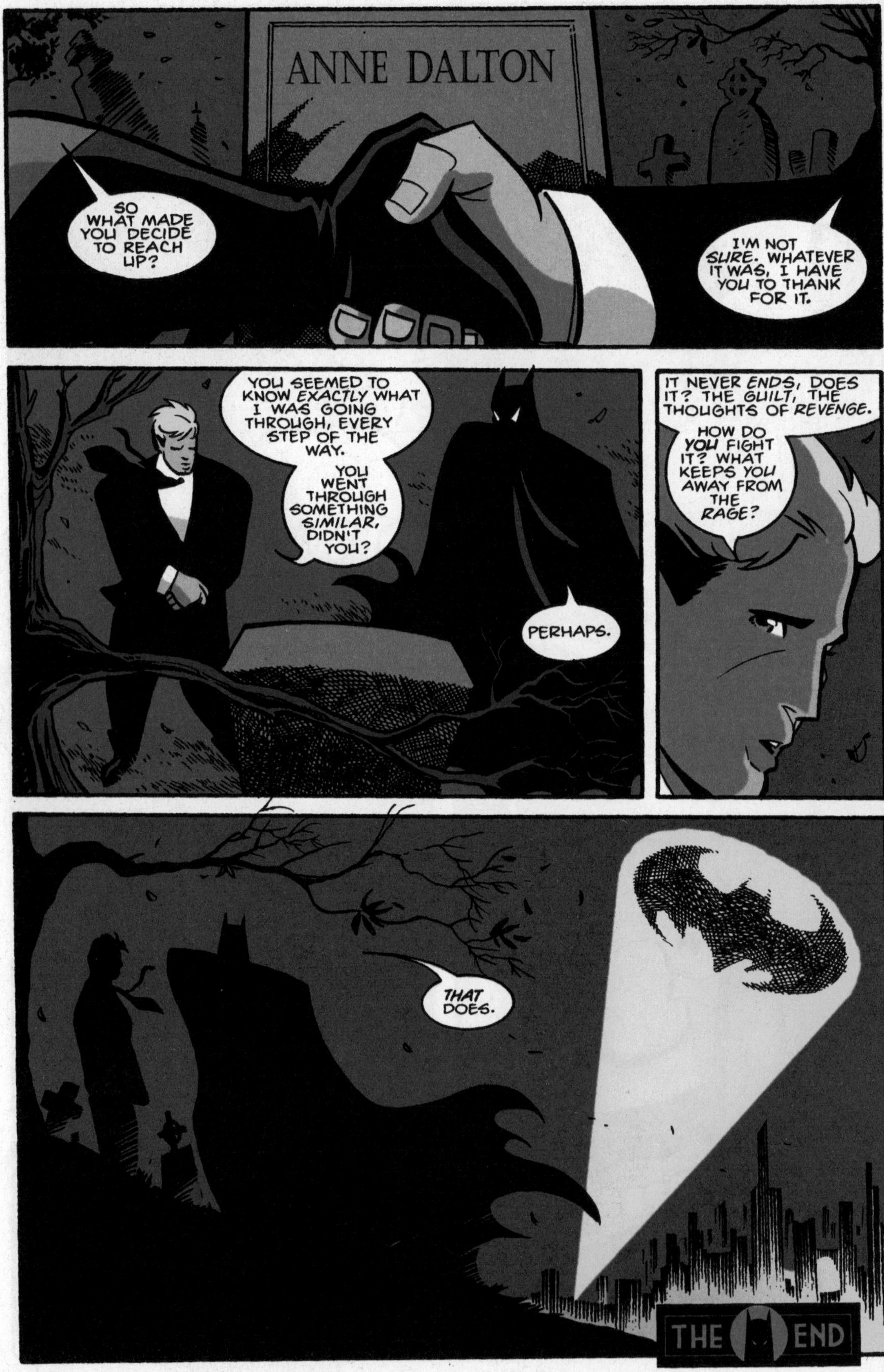
ANNE DALTON
SO WHAT MADE YOU DECIDE TO REACH UP?
I'M NOT SURE. WHATEVER IT WAS, I HAVE YOU TO THANK FOR IT.
YOU SEEMED TO KNOW EXACTLY WHAT I WAS GOING THROUGH, EVERY STEP OF THE WAY.
YOU WENT THROUGH SOMETHING SIMILAR, DIDN'T YOU?
PERHAPS.
IT NEVER ENDS, DOES IT? THE GUILT, THE THOUGHTS OF REVENGE.
HOW DO YOU FIGHT IT? WHAT KEEPS YOU AWAY FROM THE RAGE?
THAT DOES.
THE END

PIN-UP GALLERY

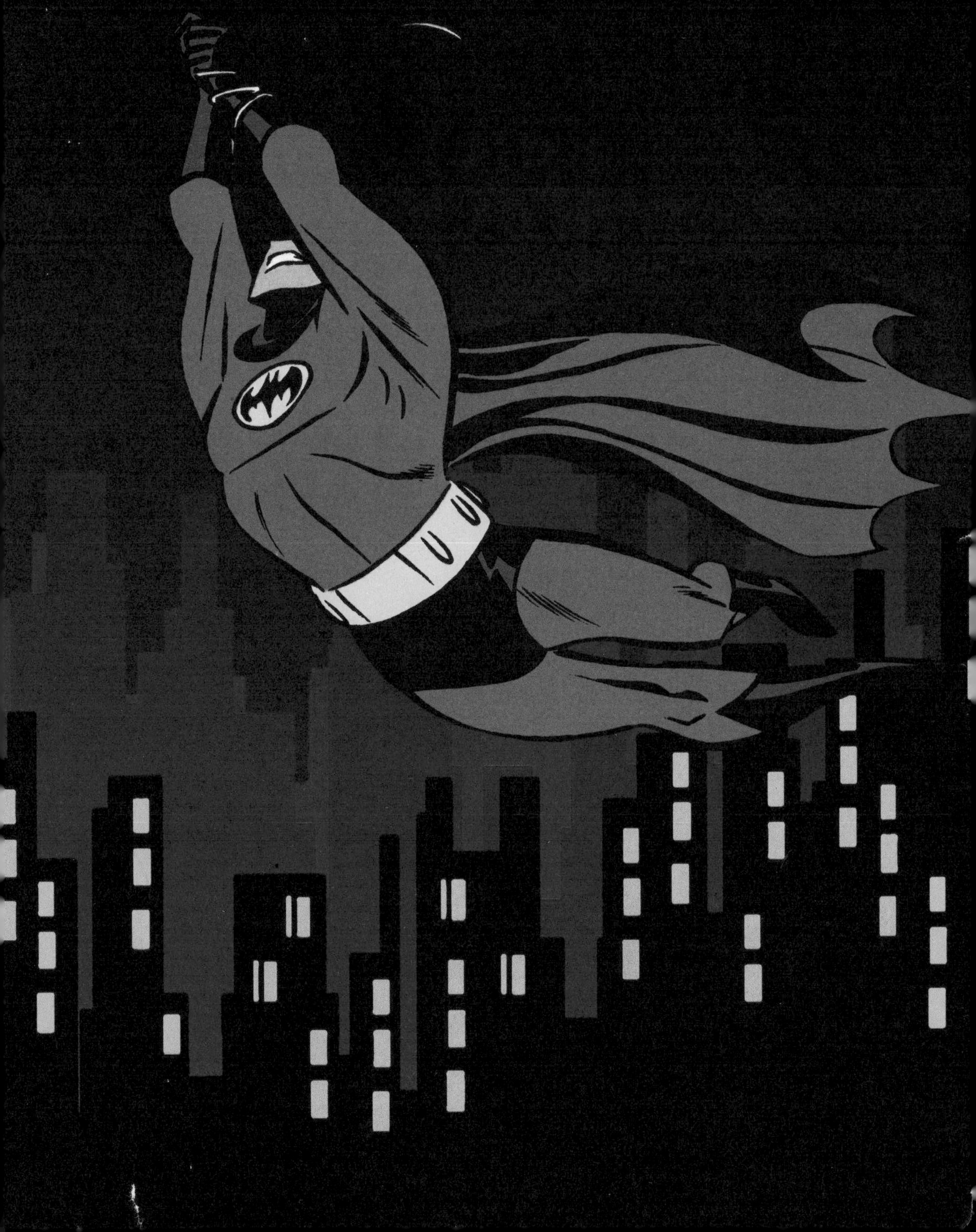

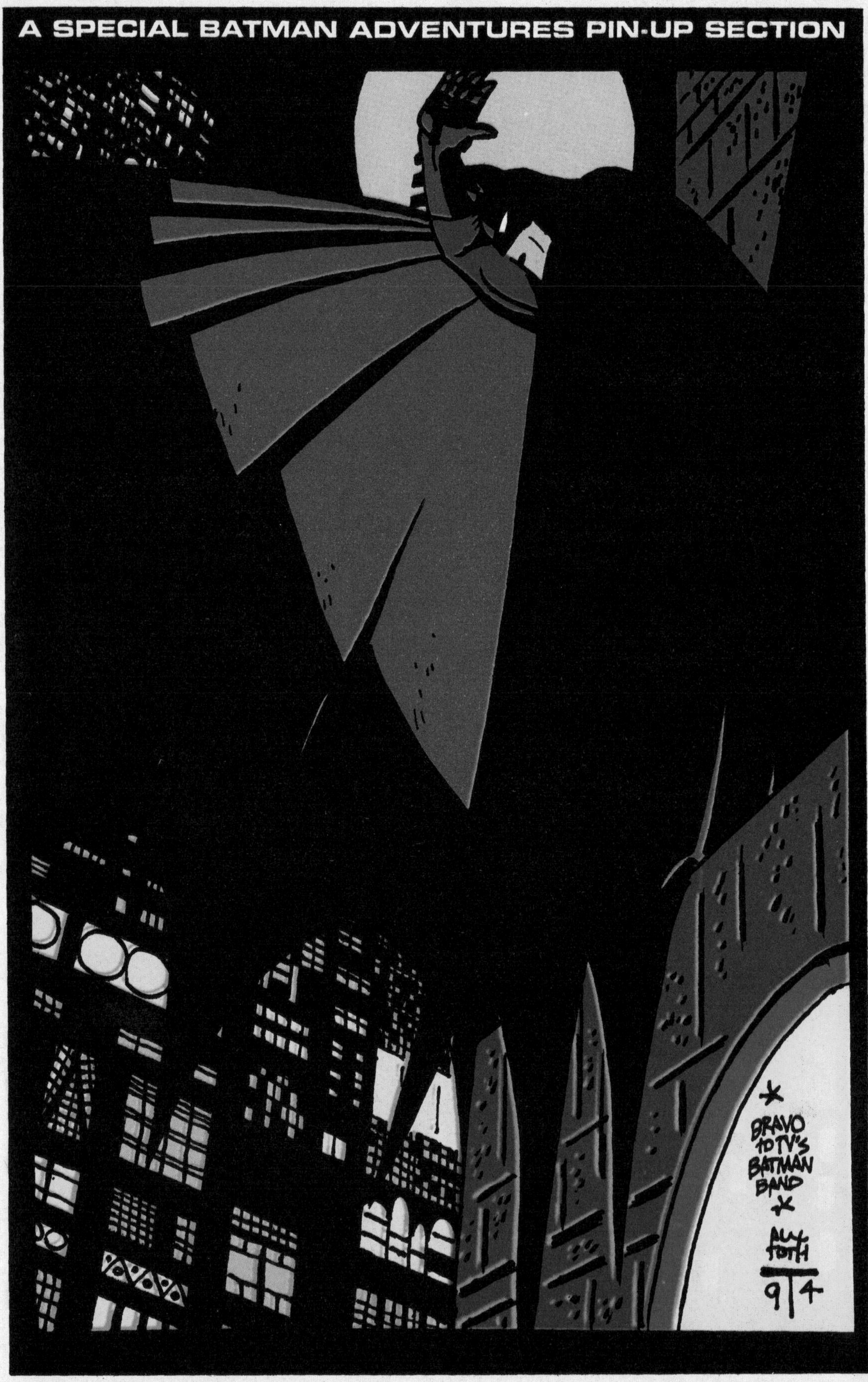
A SPECIAL BATMAN ADVENTURES PIN-UP SECTION
BRAVO TO TV'S BATMAN BAND
ALEX TOTH
9 4

ART **ALEX TOTH** **RICK TAYLOR** COLOR

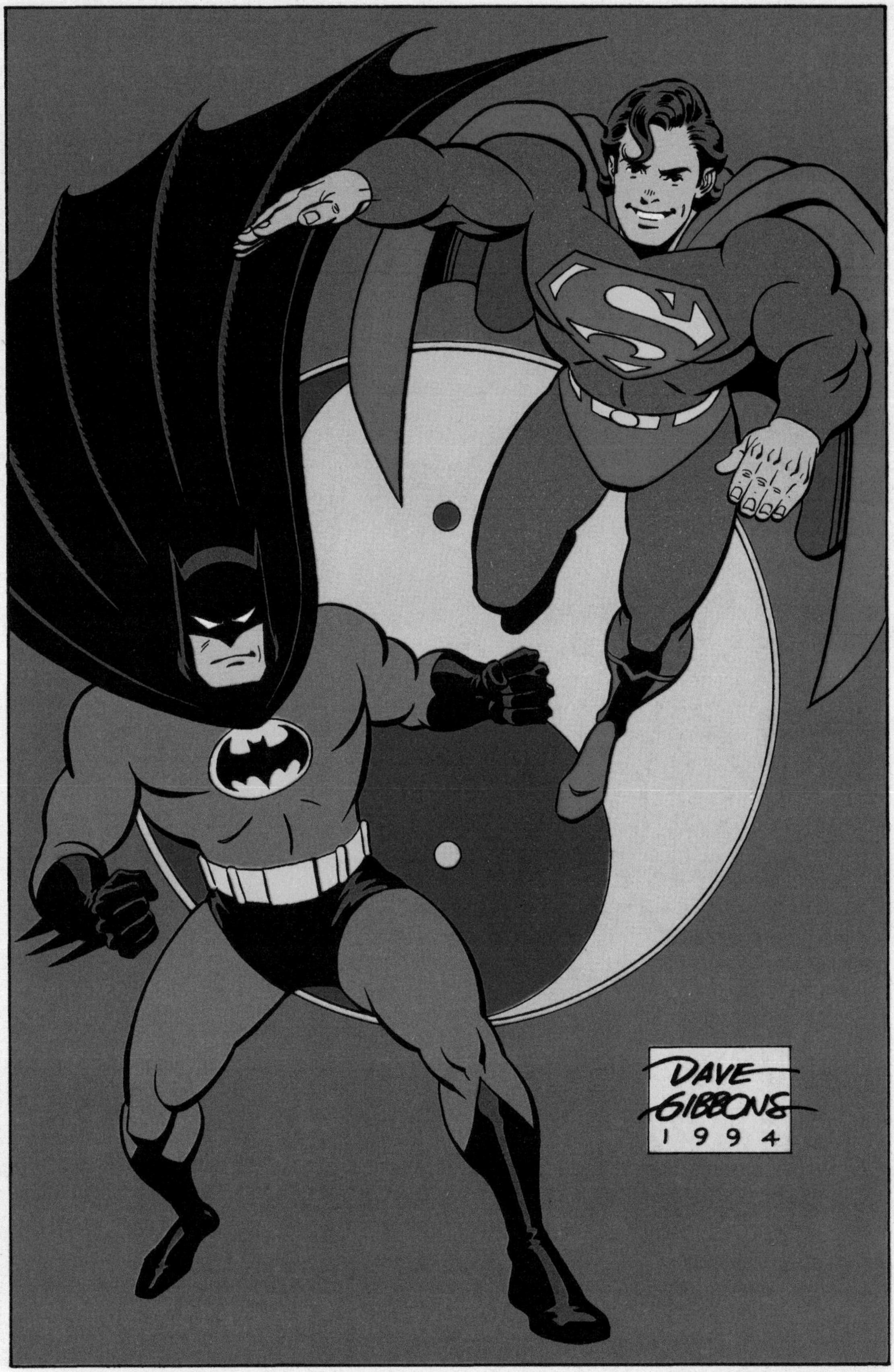
DAVE GIBBONS 1994

ART **DAVE GIBBONS** **RICK TAYLOR** COLOR

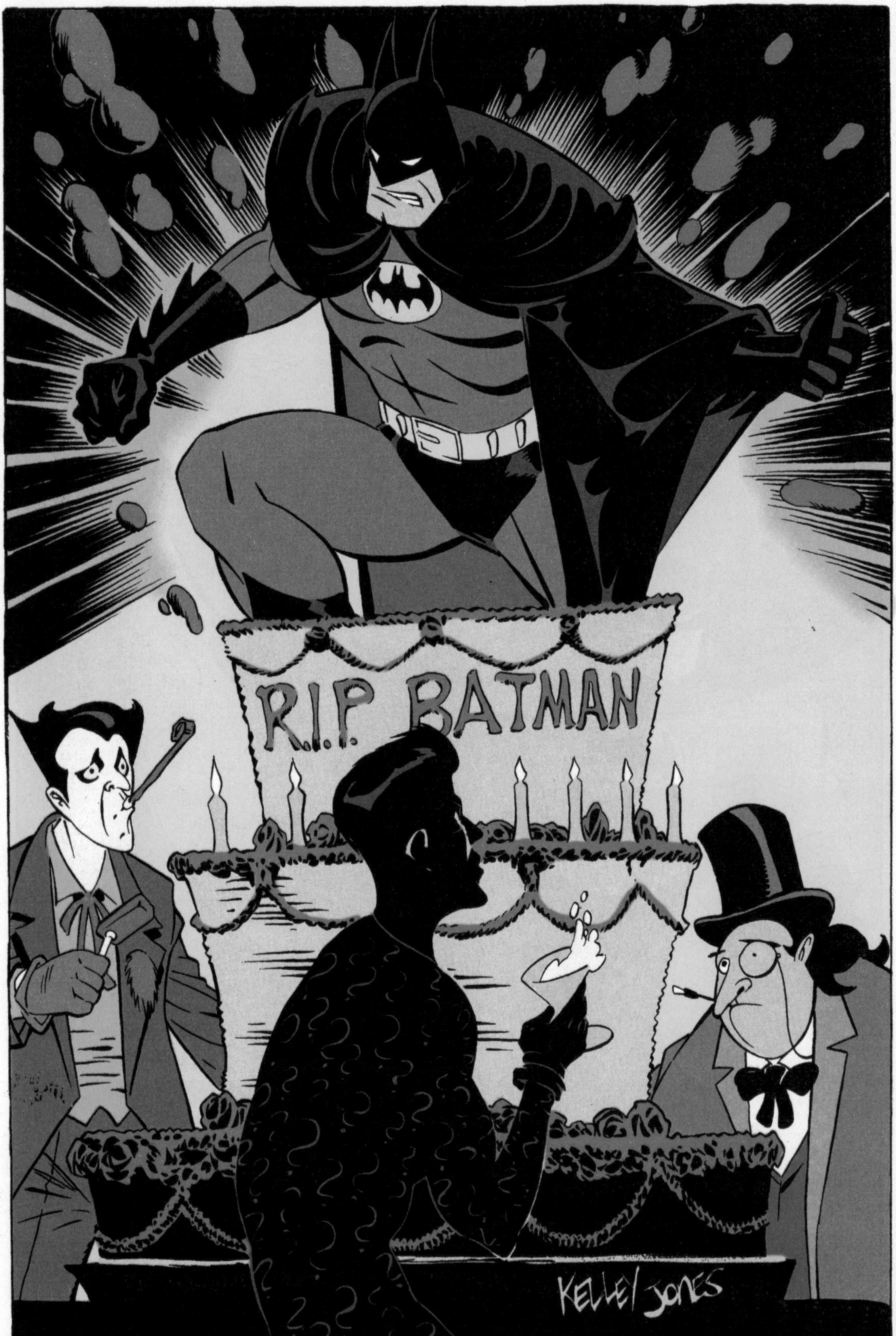
R.I.P. BATMAN
KELLEY JONES

ART **KELLEY JONES** **RICK TAYLOR** COLOR

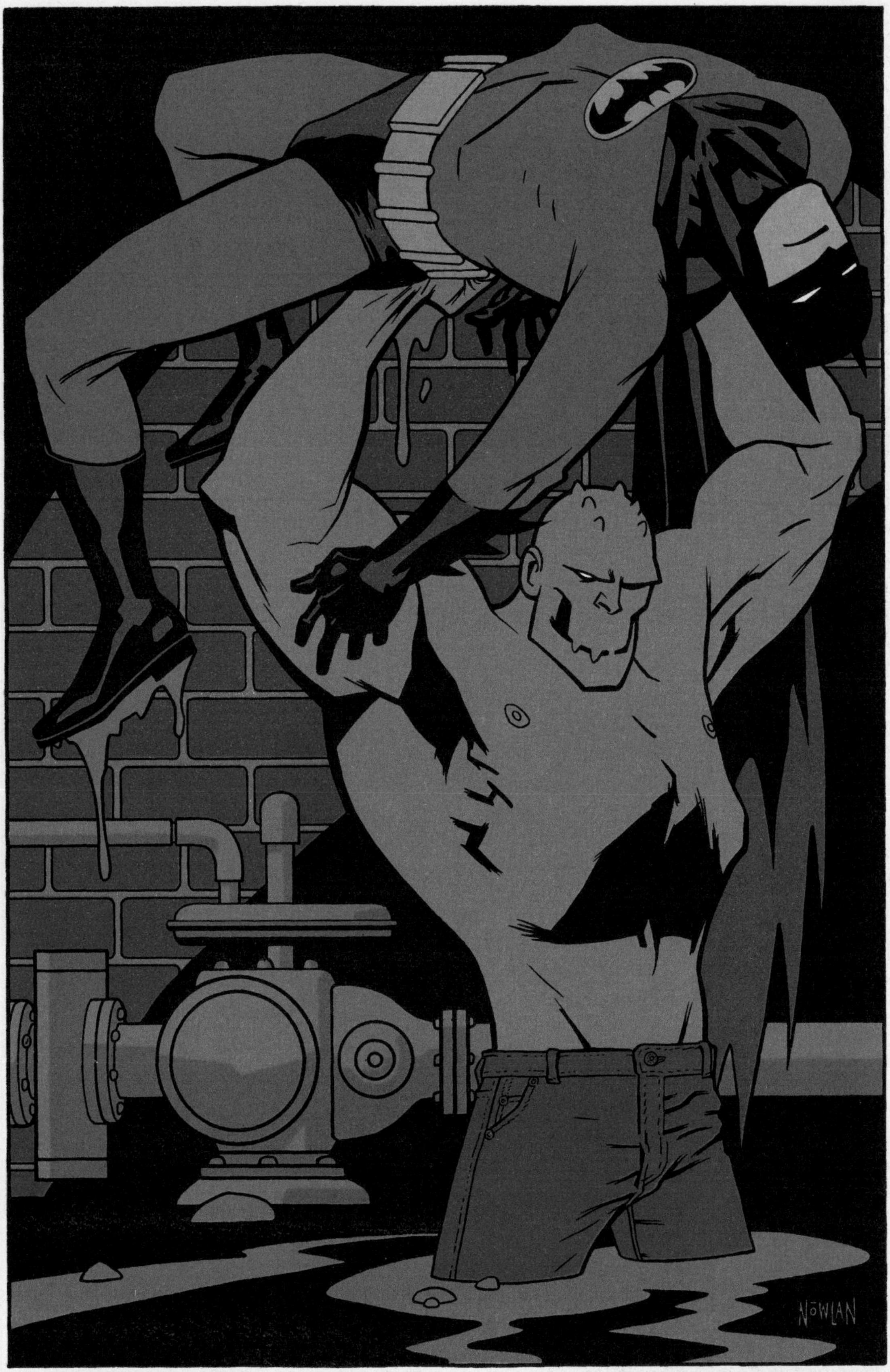
NOWLAN

ART **KEVIN NOWLAN** **RICK TAYLOR** COLOR

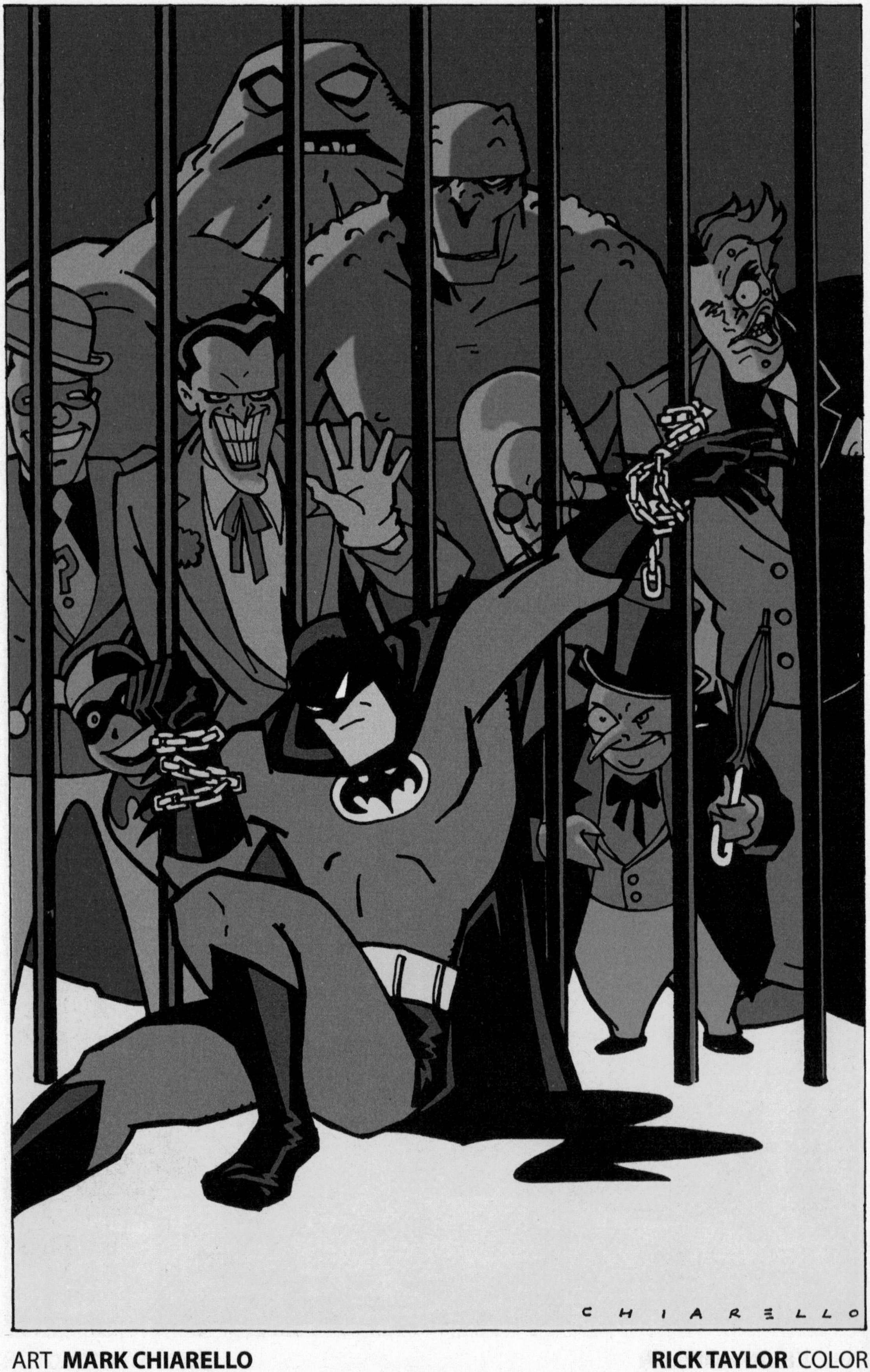
CHIARELLO

ART **MARK CHIARELLO** **RICK TAYLOR** COLOR

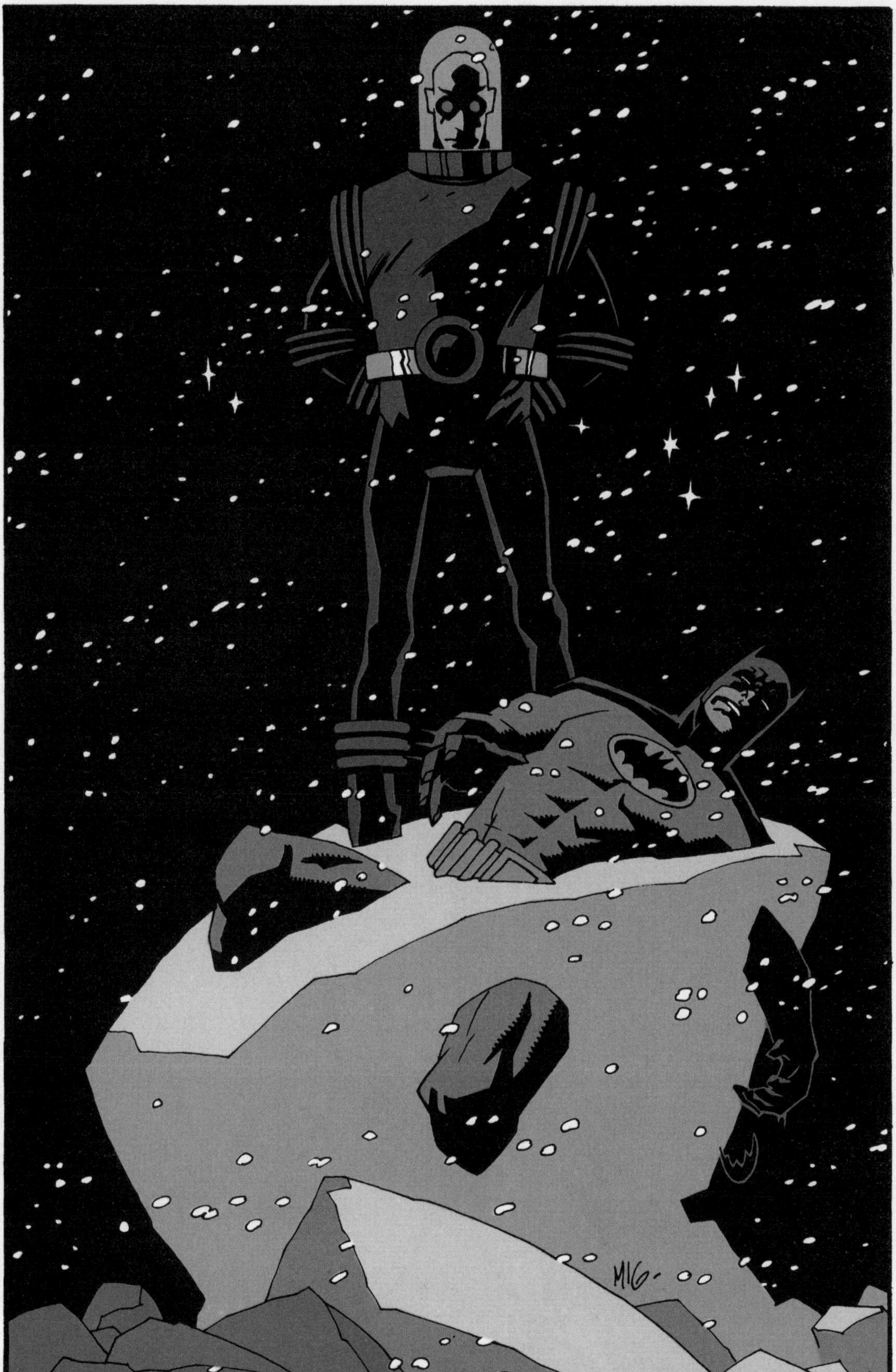
MIG

ART **MIKE MIGNOLA** **RICK TAYLOR** COLOR

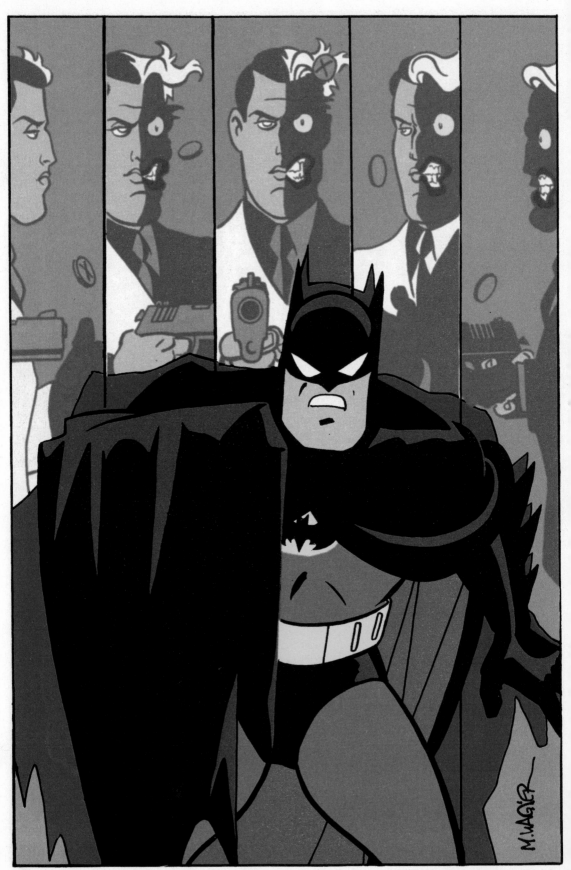

•ART **MATT WAGNER**

RICK TAYLOR COLOR

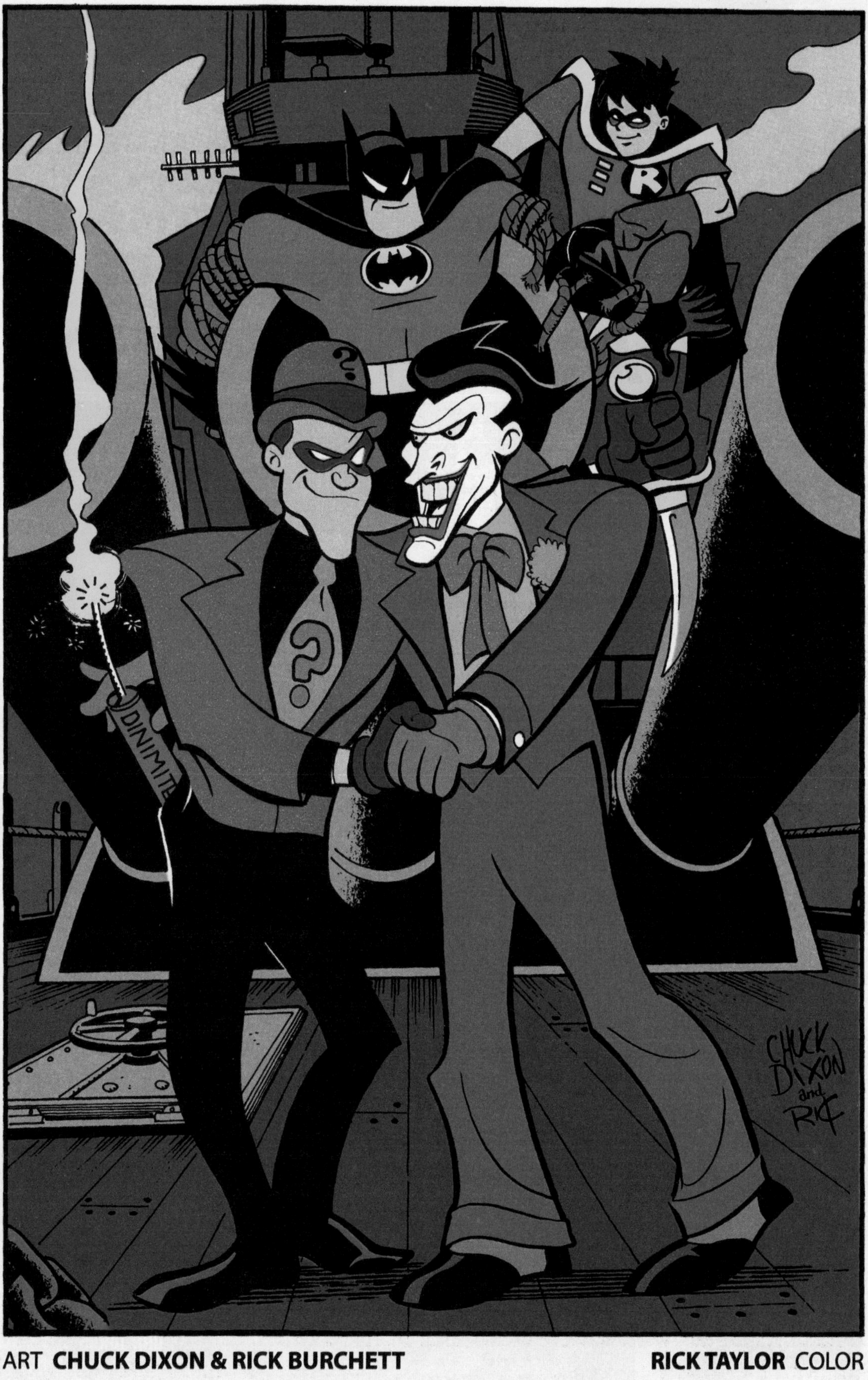
DINIMITE
CHUCK DIXON and RKF

ART **CHUCK DIXON & RICK BURCHETT** **RICK TAYLOR** COLOR

START AT THE BEGINNING!

TEEN TITANS
VOLUME 1: IT'S OUR RIGHT TO FIGHT

TEEN TITANS VOL. 2: THE CULLING

TEEN TITANS VOL. 3: DEATH OF THE FAMILY

THE CULLING: RISE OF THE RAVAGERS

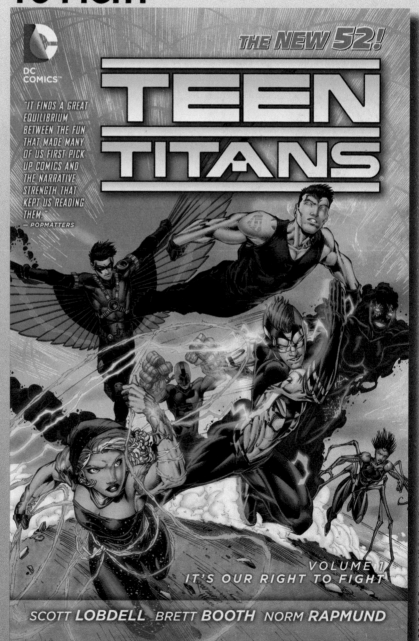

"IT FINDS A GREAT EQUILIBRIUM BETWEEN THE FUN THAT MADE MANY OF US FIRST PICK UP COMICS AND THE NARRATIVE STRENGTH THAT KEPT US READING THEM." — POPMATTERS

SCOTT **LOBDELL** BRETT **BOOTH** NORM **RAPMUND**